A

NORWEGIAN AND LAPLAND TALE.

BAYARD TAYLOR'S

VISIT TO THE AUTHOR OF "AFRAJA."

Bayard Taylor, writing from Berlin to the New York Tribune, gives the following account of his visit to the author of "AFRAJA":

"I was fortunate in having a letter to Theodore Mügge, the author of 'Afraja,' and Eric Randal.' When I called at his residence, according to a previous appointment, a pretty little girl, of seven or eight years old, opened the door. 'Is Herr Dr. Mügge at home?' I asked. She went to an adjacent door, and cried out: 'Father, are you at home?' '*Ja wohl*,' answered a sturdy voice; and presently a tall, broad-shouldered, and rather handsome man of over forty years, made his appearance. He wore a thick, brown beard, spectacles, was a little bald about the temples, and spoke with a decided North-German accent. His manner at first was marked with more reserve than is common among Germans; but I had the pleasure of meeting him more than once, and found that the outer shell covered a kernel of good humor and good feeling.

"Like many other authors, Mügge has received hardly as much honor in his own country as he deserves. His 'Afraja,' *one of the most remarkable romances of this generation*, is just beginning to be read and valued. He was entirely unacquainted with the fact that it had been translated in America, where five or six editions were sold in a very few months. I could give him no better evidence of its success than the experience of a friend of mine, who was carried thirteen miles past his home, on a New Haven railroad train, while absorbed in its pages. He informed me that the idea of the story was suggested to him during his residence at Tromsöe, on the Norwegian coast, where, among some musty official records, he found the minutes of the last trial and execution of a Lapp for witchcraft, about a century ago. This Lapp, who was a sort of chieftain in his clan, had been applied to by some Danish traders to furnish them with good wind during their voyage. He sold them breezes from the right quarter, but the vessel was wrecked, and all hands drowned. When asked, during his trial, whether he had not furnished a bad instead of a good wind, he answered, haughtily: 'Yes, I sold them the bad wind, because I hated them, as I hate you, and all the brood of thieves who have robbed me and my people of our land.' I referred to the character of Niels Helgestad, and spoke of his strong resemblance, in many respects, to one of our Yankee traders of the harder and coarser kind. Mügge assured me that I would find many of the same type still existing, when I should visit the Loffoden Isles. He spent a summer among the scenes described in 'Afraja,' and his descriptions are so remarkably faithful, that Alexander Ziegler used the book as his best guide in going over the same ground this year."

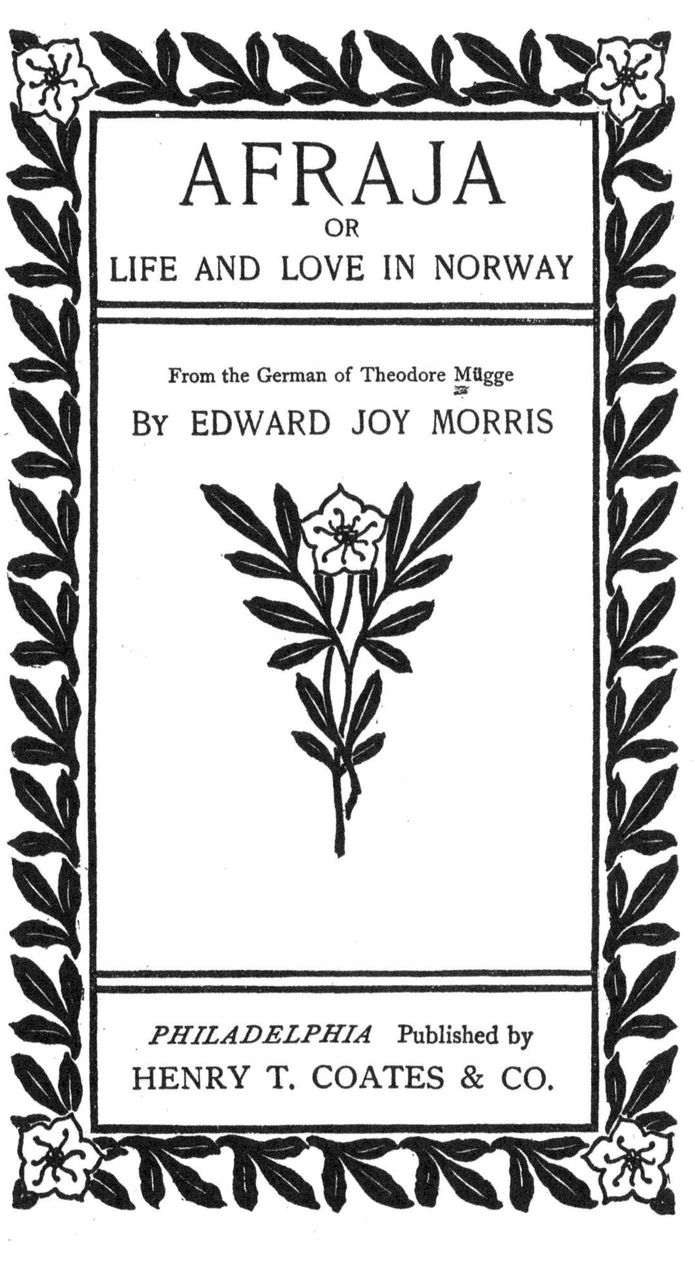

AFRAJA

OR

LIFE AND LOVE IN NORWAY

From the German of Theodore Mügge

By EDWARD JOY MORRIS

PHILADELPHIA Published by

HENRY T. COATES & CO.

PREFACE

BY THE TRANSLATOR.

THE following romance is the production of one of the most distinguished writers of fiction in Germany. It was published in the spring of the present year, and was received with the most cordial approbation by the critical press, as well as by the reading public.

Robert Prutz, a high authority in *belle lettre* criticism, at the conclusion of an extended review of German literature in the *Morgenblatt*, says: "This popular writer has again displayed his genius in a graphic and interesting narration of entirely new and attractive scenes. His romance introduces us to a region with which he is thoroughly acquainted from personal observation, but which is a rare and almost untrodden field of fiction—the remote neighborhood of the North Pole, and those icy, desert steppes, where the Laplander pursues his wandering life of privation and suffering. His life-like descriptions of the manners and customs of this curious people, and the Norwegian settlers on the coasts, are drawn with such power as to awaken the keenest interest in his brilliant story, and to keep the attention of the reader intensely excited from the first to the last page. The characters are portrayed with a rare skill and fidelity to nature, and the whole composition cannot fail to augment the reputation of the author, and to place him in the front rank of German historical novelists."

The reader will discover, in his perusal of this beautiful work of genius, that this praise is fully merited; and he will not fail to remark the high moral tone and pure sentiment which pervades the whole composition—the more striking from its contrast with the depraved taste and corrupting influence of so many of the works of fiction of the present day. It is lamentable to witness the growing depravity of this department of literature, and the unholy zeal with which great talents are prostituted to the inculcation of false views of life and duty, and the diffusion of immoral principles. The success of Afraja, however, in Germany, has demonstrated that the public mind has not lost its partiality for those who seek to refine and elevate the imagination, and to base their hopes of success on an appeal to the higher feelings of our nature.

The aim of the translator has been to faithfully render the original into our own tongue; and if, notwithstanding the inherent difficulties of the undertaking, from the peculiarly idiomatic style of the author, he shall have succeeded, he will have accomplished the grateful task of extending the reputation of a writer of no common order of intellect.

E. J. M.

LIFE AND LOVE

IN

NORWAY.

FIRST PART.

ORIGIN OF NORWAY.

IN the remote north of Europe a legend is current that God, when he had created the world, and was reposing from his labors, was suddenly aroused from his meditation by the fall of a monstrous mass in the abyss of waters. The Creator, as he looked up, perceived the devil, who had seized a prodigious mass of rock, which he had hurled into the deep, so that the axis of the new creation, trembling under the weight, threatened to break, and yet wavers, and will to all eternity. The Lord preserved his work from entire destruction by his mighty power. With one hand he sustained it, and with the other he threatened the base fiend, who, howling with fear, took to flight; but everywhere the fearful pile of rock rose above the waters. High and gloomily it projected out of the swelling flood to the clouds; jagged, wild, and shattered, its naked sides sank into the unfathomable depths, and filled the sea with innumerable cliffs and peaks for many miles. The Maker cast a look of sadness and pity upon this waste, and then took he what remained of fruitful earth, and strewed it over the black rocks. But, alas! it was too sparse to be of much avail. The ground was scarcely covered in the clefts and hollows, and only in a few spots was sufficient deposited to nourish fruit-trees and ripen seeds. The farther to the north, the scantier was the gift, until at last none remained, and the devil's work rested under the curse of eternal barrenness. But God stretched out his omnipotent hand, and blessed the desolate earth. "Although no flower shall here bloom," said the Almighty, "no bird sing, and no blade of grass grow, yet the wicked spirit shall have no share in thee. I will have compassion on thee, and suffer men here to dwell, who, with love and affection shall cling to these rocks, and be happy in their possession." Then the Lord commanded the fish to frequent the sea in vast swarms, and above, on the ice-fields, he placed a wonderful creature, half cow, half deer, which was to nourish man with milk, butter, and flesh, and clothe him with its furry skin.

Thus, according to the saga, originated Norway. For this reason is the sea, on its wild coasts, animated by such multitudes of the finny tribes, and the reindeer found on its deserts of ice and snow, without whose help no human being could live there. What a world of horror and silence there lies concealed! With what awe trembles the heart of the solitary traveller when he wanders among the desert fiords and sounds, where the sea, in labyrinthine folds, loses itself between gloomy, snow-crowned rocks, in inaccessible gulfs and caverns! With what astonishment he beholds his ship gliding through this immensity of cliffs, gigantic rocks, and black granite walls, which wind, as a girdle, for more than three hundred miles around the stony breast of Norway!

Man is but sparsely distributed over the neglected land. Over rocks and swamps must he wander, eternally roving with the reindeer, which nourishes him; in coves and inlets on the sea-shore he lives, solitary and secluded, and, with extreme toil and trouble supplies himself with fish. The land, however, can never become the fixed abode of any one. Deep lies it under swamp and ice, buried in cloud and darkness, without trees or fields, the hut of the peasant, or the lowing of cattle, and the genial blessings which spring from the industry of man, and social intercourse.

Such is the aspect that this region presents when a ship leaves the harbor of Trondheim, and, steering northwardly, pushes through the fiords and sounds. Behind, the coast rises in bold precipices; the fertile spots gradually disappear, and wilder, more naked rocks stretch to the desolate wastes, until the insurmountable glaciers of Helgeland mark the limits of human habitations. Human life withdraws into the bays and inlets. There dwells the merchant and the fisherman of Norman blood, and near them Danes and Laplanders are settled. The Laplander drives his antlered milch-cow over the snowy mountains, and the report of his gun, as he hunts the bear and the wolf, is echoed back from the dark sea-caverns. Wilder and more desolate grows the scene with every new morning. For miles no house is to be seen, and no sail or fishing-boat breaks the dismal monotony. Dolphins sportively gambol around the bows of the ship, and the whale spurts the water into the air; flocks of sea-gulls hover over, and dive upon the moving shoals of herrings; divers and auks spring from the rocks, the eider-duck flutters over the foaming billows, and high in the clear, sharp air, the eagle pair circle around their rocky nest.

At last, winding around a thousand rocky capes, in the midst of this ocean labyrinth, you see the house of a trader upon the declivity of a birch-wooded promontory. There are his warehouses, his vessels, and his boats; there rises the smoke of some ten scattered fishermen's huts among the cliffs, and between them lies a narrow strip of green meadow, through which a brawling brook rushes to the sea. A few minutes more, and all has disappeared. Again the rocky desert meets the eye; again the same sounds surround the ship, and the same deep and unruffled mirror of water reflects the passing sail; and, from the deep ravines the wind rushes out with the fury of a wild beast. Here begins our story.

LIFE AND LOVE
IN
NORWAY.

CHAPTER I.

SOMETHING more than a hundred years ago, on a dark morning in March, a large vessel was steering through these wondrous mazes of rock. She was a Norwegian craft of the stoutest build, such as at this day set out from the northernmost cape for Bergen and intervening ports, twice a summer, to supply the merchants with fish and train oil; and when fully laden with articles of food and merchandise, return to their sea-encompassed havens. A stumped mast rose from the middle of the vessel; forward, the bow shot up to a remarkable height; and near the stern stood an elevated poop-cabin, where the edge of the square sail was made fast to strong posts and iron rings. As the day advanced, the cold, grey fog lifted up, and a faint, quickly-expiring sunbeam flashed over the mountain coasts, and the glaciers which crown their summits. Curiously-scarred ranges of rocks loomed up from the sea, against which the resounding waves broke in sheets of foam. Wind squalls rushed down from the lofty heights, or from the dark mist which enveloped the fiords, lashing the sea into a wild fury, throwing the deeply-laden vessel upon her side, and causing her to tremble, from the force of the replicated blows, in every timber.

A young man stood at the helm of this huge vessel, whose clear blue eyes were anxiously scanning the reefs and rocks, through the devious windings of which the ship urged her way. His nervous hands held the rudder with a firm grasp, against which his strong body gently leaned, and with a steady countenance and observing gaze, he directed the course of the vessel with such masterly skill, that she appeared to obey every nod and word of command. From time to time, the helmsman stretched forward to penetrate with his searching look into the distance; and his sharp-cut features, glowing with fresh color, beamed with excitement. His muscles seemed to expand to their utmost tension; he stroked back his long floating hair under his glazed hat, and gazing joyously upon the reefs and ridges as old acquaintances, he began to hum a song. As he had finished the fifth or sixth verse, the cabin door opened, and another tenant of the vessel stepped out on the deck. A few years older than the helmsman, he was also an entirely different person. Instead of a dark fisherman's jacket, or a rough southwester, he wore a long many-buttoned coat. His hair was combed back, and bound with a ribbon; slender, and tall of stature, he appeared, in his manners and figure, to be a man of the world, and to belong to the privileged class who lay claim to the productions of the earth as their exclusive property. Such he was, in fact. He was the young lord of Marstrand, the scion of a noble house; the estate of which had been sadly impaired by the lavish expense and liberal hospitality of his father and grandfather at the court of Christian the Sixth, in Copenhagen. His father, the chamberlain, died in debt; and here, his son, gentleman of the bed-chamber, and lieutenant of the guards, was voyaging through the wild Polar sea in the yacht of a trader, who lived upon the extreme limits of Finnmark, and whose heir, Björnarne Helgestad, was standing at the helm. The ship had sailed from Trondheim in the spring, to bring salt and provisions to Lofodden, where the great fishery was in full operation; the young Baron was received as a passenger — and in his pocket he carried a donation deed of the King, conferring upon him a broad tract of land, extending into the boundless desert on the northernmost confines of Europe, where there is neither lord nor serf.

It was with no friendly glance that John of Marstrand looked upon the savage coasts, and the foaming sea, as he stepped out of the cabin. The damp fog flew so violently about him, and beat in such heavy drops upon his face and clothes, that he shuddered with cold, and closely buttoned up his coat; then he nodded to the helmsman, who, to the salutations of the morning, added some good-natured remark, which the wind carried away before it could reach the ear.

"What do you think now of this country?" said the helmsman, with a proud, inquiring glance, as the young nobleman approached him. "Is it not magnificent? See, there is the promontory of Kunnen, and directly beyond sweeps the polar circle; farther to the left, in the deep Grimmfiord, you can perceive the gigantic Jökuln islands, which, in ice-pyramids, seemed to run far down into the sea. When the morning sunbeams strike upon them, they glow like molten silver. There is the way to the Salten — you have certainly heard of the salt stream? And here, on this side of those low rocks, you will soon discover the Westfiord. The Westfiord! Do you hear, man? the great fiord with its fishes! Hurrah! What say you? Have you ever seen anything so beautiful?"

"Foolish Björnarne!" exclaimed John, with a jesting smile; "you seem to think we are entering into paradise. You talk as if these gloomy, snow-covered crags bloomed with almond trees; as if this stormy, icy sea was fanned by the softest zephyrs, and its miserable, oil-reeking fish swarms were fragrant with perfume." He turned to the south, and continued, with a suppressed sigh, "No tree, no bush, no flower, no green leaf, no singing-bird, nor blade of grass waving to the breeze. Nothing but horror, darkness, fog, storms, rocks, and the raging sea."

"If the land is so displeasing to you, you had better have remained where you were."

The young Dane looked upon the helmsman, and the expression of his countenance revealed the answer which he gently murmured. "If," whispered he, between his teeth, "I were not obliged to seek my fortune in these wilds, cursed would be the plank which carried me hither."

His melancholy silence, and the manner in which he buried his face in his hands, moved the boasting Björnarne. "You must not," said he, "give yourself up to such sad thoughts—it is not so dreary here as it seems. When the summer comes, the barley ripens even in Tromsöe; flowers bloom in the gardens; currants and blackberries grow luxuriantly in all the clefts and ravines; and upon the fielders the mountain bramble covers the earth for miles with purple and scarlet. You must learn to know and love the land where you have chosen to dwell. I would not change it for any other in the world; for there is none more beautiful or better to be found."

Provoked by the derisive smile of the Dane, he proudly proceeded; "Boast, as you please, of your trees and plains. Have you such rocks, such fiords, and such a prolific sea? Have you bears and reindeers to hunt? Have you a fishery like this, where, with every haul of the seine, millions of creatures are drawn from the deep; where twenty thousand men, for months, lead a joyous life upon the heaving billows."

"No, good Björnarne, we do not, indeed, possess all this," replied John of Marstrand, with a depreciating sneer.

"You shall see it," exclaimed the Norman, joyfully. "The fog is falling, and if you could hear, you would already now in the roar of the waves understand the strange sound which rushes through the Westfiord. There, before us, lies Ostvaagoen; here is the old wife of Salten, and over there the old man with the white head. There, now you catch a glimpse of his hat There rise the peaks of Hindöen, there gleam the glaciers of Tjelloen, and now comes the sun; look up!"

And, as he spoke, the illuminating orb triumphantly broke through the thick veil of cloud, and, as with a magic spell, lit up a countless array of islands, rocks, and gulfs. The Westfiord opened before the astonished vision of the Dane, and exhibited land and sea in all their glory and splendor. Upon one side lay the coast of Norway, with its snowy summits. Salten loomed up behind, with its needle-like peaks, stretching with their inaccessible ice-covered declivities into the heavens, and its ravines and abysses half concealed in gloom. Upon the other side, six miles to the seaward of the Westfiord, extended a chain of dark islands far into the bosom of the ocean—a granite wall against which the ocean, in its most savage fury, for thousands of years had dashed its billows. Innumerable perpendicular pinnacles rose from this insular labyrinth — black, weather-beaten, and torn to their base by the tempests. Their bold summits were veiled by long lines of clouds, and from the gleaming beds of snow, the wondering blue eyes of Jökuln turned to the swelling floods of the fiord, which, with their thousand white teeth, bit the bow of the yacht, shook it like a reed, and drew it into the abyss.

"Look there, now, how beautiful it is!" cried Björnarne with a shout. "There are the Lofodden islands. For twenty miles the view extends over land and sea, and all is grand and glorious. See the grey head of Vaagöen, how it beams in gold. Look how the old woman of Salten nods to him, in her ruddy black mantle. Once they were two giants, children of night, a loving pair, who have here been transformed into rock, and must eternally remain such. Observe how the breakers leap against the rocks, in silvery columns; and see the vast circle of cliffs, whose extent no one has measured, upon which no human foot has ever trod, and where only the eagle, the cormorant, the falcon, and the gull have mounted. See the red-crested *skarfe* there on the crags, and the sea-geese, how they plunge into the green waves, followed by screaming flocks of gulls and falcons Thither the herring shoals are attracted by the scent of prey.

Above, the sky is clear and tranquil; and the fresh, sparkling air awakens all the energies. Is not all this beautiful, and is it not the most sublime spectacle that the human eye can behold?"

"Yes, it is infinitely grand!" said John Marstrand, ravished by the wonderful grandeur and wildness of the scene.

"But the finest of all you do not yet know," continued Björnarne. "Do you see there, those many black dots upon the surface of the water? Those are the fishing-boats. Three thousand boats, with twenty thousand stout-hearted men; and in the gulf of Vaagöen you can already distinguish the flags and masts of the vessels which bring salt for the packing of the fish, and merchandize for the traders. They are filled with all kinds of provisions and stuffs. We shall there find my father, who has twenty boats under his charge. I am sure he will please you, and he will gladly serve you to the best of his ability."

"I have a letter for him," said the passenger, "from the commanding General Münte, in Trondheim."

"You would be welcome, without the recommendatory letter," returned Björnarne, laughing. "At Lyngenfiord, where is our house, but little question is made of your general. You come with me, because you please me, John Marstrand. You are a true fellow, know the value of words, and how to use them, and your arm is ever ready to render aid; these qualities are appreciated with us, and therefore will I be your friend." He lifted his hand from the helm, and seized in earnest grasp that of the nobleman, who responded with an equally friendly pressure. Alone in a strange region, the rough heartiness of his new friend gratified him more than the formal expressions of polite society, which he had so often heard. He knew that Björnarne was incapable of falsehood, that he bore him a true affection; and he was certain that, in the hour of need, he could rely upon him. For his future, this was of great importance.

During the interchange of these confidential expressions, the vessel had crossed the fiord, and rapidly approached Ostvaagen and the fishing-grounds. The small black points floating on the sea gradually enlarged, until finally they came clearly into view, as heavy six-oared boats, in which an incessant activity prevailed. The figures of the fishermen, as they raised their nets and rods, the tremble of the sun's rays upon their leather caps and sea-soaked jackets, the yawls moving about in all directions, and the thousand-voiced tumult, rising above the roar of the waves, united to form an animated picture which yet higher excited the feelings of Marstrand. He felt a longing to mingle in this motley throng; in his enthusiasm he forgot that, in spite of the sunshine, ice-cold gusts, plunging down from the Salten and the Tinden, sweep the sea; and that here, in the Polar zone, within a few minutes, the wildest winter-storm bursts, and with its terrors envelopes land and ocean. At present he thought only of the mirthful fishing uproar, which mocked these horrors. He saw only the fluttering flags on the vessels, and the houses and huts on the rocks and strand, and it seemed to him as if a festival of spring was being celebrated, as he heard the trumpeting and fiddling on the peaks of the grey head of Vaagöen. He shouted for joy, as he saw a genuine Nordlander draw his net, with a ringed cod in every mesh. He waved his hat, as all did, as the vessel urged her way among the fishing smacks, and, surrounded by an hundred boats, whose crews shouted a hearty welcome, steered around the rocks, and to the harbor of the bay, where a number of large and small craft lay at anchor. Some time elapsed before a suitable position could be found in the line of vessels; but at last the cable rolled through the hawser-holes, and the "fair Ilda of Oerenaes" was secured by the long cables, and wearily shook off the drops which hung upon her bows and bulwarks.

Björnarne had his hands full, and it was some time before he could trouble himself about his passenger, who, from the quarter-deck, was attentively regarding the taking of fish, which, in all its details, was passing before his eyes. At the entrance of the bay, around an island of bare rock, called

Skraaven, it was pursued with the most activity. Five or six hundred boats, with three or four thousand fishermen, were there engaged in fishing. The nets were incessantly cast and drawn, with song and shout; for all were overladen with fish, and great care was observed in extricating them from the meshes, to prevent the laceration of the threads. At many other spots there were immense cables, to which more than a thousand angling rods were fastened; for the angle was more in use then than at present. The fishermen next hurried with their full boats into the bay, where, upon the rocks, scaffolds of poles, and tables for the disembowelling of the fish, and huts for shelter and rest were erected. The fish were brought hither from the boats, seized by blood-red hands, and thrown upon the tables. Sharp knives opened the body, with a grip of the finger the entrails were extracted, and, with a second cut, the head flew off into one tub, and the oily liver into another. The other parts were cast upon a nauseous heap of blood and viscera, and what a moment before was a living creature, hung, severed, and shaking in the wind, upon the drying-stand. The men pursued their murderous occupation with incredible dexterity and quickness. The lust of slaughter glowed in their eyes. They held the bloody knife between the teeth, whilst their hands were plunged in the belly of the dying creature, and, in their enthusiasm, they bit the unctuously fat livers, when they appeared unusually white and dainty. With naked arms, and broad, open bosoms, spattered with blood, they looked like cannibals celebrating a horrid feast of triumph. They greedily sought for the largest and stoutest victims, exercised upon them their executioner's office with double zest, and made merry with the sufferings and violent struggles of the unfortunate wretches. Marstrand soon felt a disgust for this monotonous slaughter. He turned away, saying to himself, "It is a cruel, cowardly torture — I will see no more of it. For this, twenty thousand men are attracted to these naked rocks; for this, they shout and yell like persons possessed, despite the storms of the polar sea. What a rude, coarse people—what an absence of humane sensations! No," continued he, "most of them would remain at home, were they not driven by necessity to these latitudes. And does not want also drive me into this land of ice and mountain?" said he, musingly. "But fish I cannot catch—accursed be this filthy, bloody business! A pestilential smell is wafted hither from the fishing-banks; and these heaps of entrails, these tubs of train-oil and livers, these bloody heads, these wild, screaming flocks of birds, seeking their share of the prey, those dirty, oil-reeking men there; the one is as disgusting and horrible as the other——"

Björnarne clapped him on the shoulder, and exclaimed in his loud tones, "You must not meditate so much, friend John; you must be brisk and gay, for here every one is in good-humor. The whole year through, young and old, rejoice for the fishing at Lofodden; and no man in all Nordland hires himself out, without making it a condition that he shall join the expedition to the islands. How do you like it?"

"Better at a distance, than near at hand," replied Marstrand, with a smile.

"You are no Norman," said Björnarne, "otherwise you would not speak so; but wait, you will soon change your opinion. I am as glad as if all the fish in Westfiord belonged to me. My sister has come with my father. See you yonder boat. There they are." He drew Marstrand away with him, and at that moment the boat touched the vessel, from which a rope-ladder was thrown over, which the sea swayed about as it rose and fell. A robust man, in a blue fisherman's coat, with a leather cape thrown over his shoulders, lifted up a young girl on the seat before him, whose dark blonde hair escaped in flowing tresses from beneath a gaily-striped fishing-hat.

"Take firm hold of the ladder, Ilda," said the old man.

In the next moment the young girl stood upon the steps, and carefully climbing upward, as soon as she set foot on the deck, grasped her brother with both hands.

"Are you not surprised to see me, Björnarne?" said she, in a friendly tone.

"God's joy be with you, Ilda!" he tenderly replied. "Have you had a good voyage?"

"A fortunate voyage, Björnarne; I hope yours has been as happy?"

"Perfectly so; and how goes the fishing?"

"Wonderfully well, Björnarne. All the scaffolds are full. Yesterday was such a day as rarely happens, old people say. Fat, huge fish that tore the nets. It is a rare pleasure, Björnarne; I am never tired of seeing and hearing. Father's vessels are filled, all the casks are full of liver oil, and the fish are extraordinarily fat. It will be a good year, Björnarne; a good voyage to Bergen; full vessels."

Here she looked around, and her laughing face suddenly assumed a graver aspect, as her glance lighted on the stranger. She was a tall, stout damsel, firmly set, of the true Norman stock, with a strong resemblance to her brother. The same strongly-marked features, the same broad brow, and clear, beaming eyes; but all was so firmly stamped, and so fully formed, that the absence of soft, feminine traits could easily offend a spoiled eye. So it was with John Marstrand. He could hardly suppress a laugh of derision, as he looked upon her, and remembered with what eloquent boasting Björnarne had praised this sister, in honor of whose charms the yacht had been christened with the name of "the fair Ilda of Oerenäes."

"A beauty born under the sixty-ninth degree of north latitude, among whales, cod-fish, and reindeer, can indeed vary a little from our standard," said he, in an undertone, "but this one here, in her neats'-leather shoes, her green, red-trimmed frieze gown, her fur-jacket, and leather apron, with white woollen gloves upon her coarse hands, appears too bear-like, and polar-proportioned."

While he made this observation to himself, Björnarne whispered something to his sister, and then said aloud: "I have brought a friend with me, Ilda, who will dwell with us. John Marstrand is his name, and this is he. Give him your hand, sister."

The young girl mistrustfully examined the stranger with her bright eyes, and then, in obedience to the request of her brother, extended him her hand; in her strong-toned voice, saying, "You are welcome, sir, to the country. God's peace be with you!"

"Many thanks, Miss Ilda," replied Marstrand, courteously; "your wish is the kindest that can be made."

She turned to her father, whom Björnarne was helping on deck.

"Are you again here, youngster?" said the trader of the fiord, heartily shaking him by the hands. "You are welcome! You come at the right time, if all is safe on board."

"All's right, father," responded the son. "Nothing is missing; not even a nail, or a handful of salt."

The old man nodded approvingly, and uttered a peculiar guttural tone, a sort of grunt, which frequently, in Norway, is reckoned a sign of satisfaction, and sounds like a prolonged nuh!

"Nuh!" resumed he; "you are a brave boy, Björnarne; you have a good hand, in which business prospers. Is it not so?"

"I think so, father," said Björnarne, laughing; "and I guess I come at the right moment with my salt and bacon."

The trader turned half around to Marstrand, and regarded him with a measuring, sly look. The leather color of his long, hard countenance seemed to take a browner hue, and the deep wrinkles on his brow drew closer together over his broad nose. "We will see, Björnarne," said he; "but you have brought a passenger with you; one, I suppose, who desires to see matters close at hand. Is it not so?"

"I believe so, father."

"Nuh!" grunted the old man again; and around his mouth

played a smile, which quickly disappeared. He went up to Marstrand, and gave him his hand. "You are welcome, sir, to Lofodden," said he; "you bring fine weather with you. Would we had had it earlier; it is, however, good enough as it is. You have come at a good time to see a wonderfully lucky fishing."

"My best luck is to find you here," answered Marstrand, "as I have need of your counsel and assistance. I have come to an entirely strange country, to seek my fortune."

"I have often heard the birds pipe the same tune. They all sing the same song, when they fly hither from Denmark; and seem to think gold grows on the Lapland Tjellen, and it needs only to stoop and pick it up, to line the pockets. Soft hands and small feet are as little adapted to this region, as the lisping speech of Copenhagen. Is it not so?" he said, with a good-humored nod to the stranger.

"I have brought a letter from Trondheim, which will give you better information concerning myself."

"Nuh!" exclaimed the old man, "let every one enjoy his luck. It is a frank-spoken word of Niels Helgestad, sir. Learn how it goes with a fortune-hunter in this country. Voluntarily no one comes hither; it is the last resource. Many, however, fail, because they cannot suffer."

The look which, with his last words, he cast upon the young Dane, was a mixture of warning and sympathy, that Marstrand thoroughly understood. Niels Helgestad took the letter, opened it, and read it, leaning against the bulwark; whilst, from time to time, he observed his guest and the fishing-grounds, and seemed to count the full boats as they came in. At last he crumpled up the paper, and thrust it in his coat pocket.

"What a man can do," he suddenly ejaculated, "to help his fellow-man, shall honestly be done. How do you propose to begin, Herr Marstrand?"

"I think," replied the latter, "of presenting my donation letter to the farmer of the crown domains in Tromsöe, and tc seek the land which our gracious sovereign has bestowed upon me."

"He has kindly acted, our lord in Copenhagen," said the old man. "But what do you intend to do further, when the Amtmann has said—'There, above, lie the Tjellen; go thither and seek your lands.'"

"Then," said Marstrand, confused, "then I will choose the richest lands."

"Fertile land!" screamed the trader, in a roar of laughter. "The holy Olaf enlighten you, Herr! Who has informed you that you will find fertility here? Go home, if you wish to plant grain. But, no matter," said he, in a subdued tone, as he remarked Marstrand's embarrassment, "you did not know the wilderness which lies behind these rocks. Yet the eye of a prudent man can well discern the point where the royal patent can force wheat with golden ears out of the rock."

For a moment he scrutinizingly scanned his guest, and then addressed him, "Do you bring any money with you?"

"I am not entirely without means," he replied.

"Much it cannot be," said Helgestad: "for had you money, you would have remained quietly at home, and gambled, danced, and rioted in feasts and frolics. This is the life of the great lords, who know no work, but despise and deride the laboring man."

"Herr Helgestad," exclaimed Marstrand, reddening, "I am not here to be thus spoken to by you."

"Nuh!" said the trader, quietly; "if I had not hit the nail on the head, you would not snap at the remark. But to the point. How much money have you?"

"A thousand *species*, and something over," replied the young nobleman, hesitatingly.

"It is enough for a beginning," continued Helgestad, with deliberation, "if it be truly so."

He regarded Marstrand with such a distrustful, cunning smile, that the latter vexedly replied, "I hope you do not think that

3*

I lie, and make a pretence to the possession of money which I have not."

"I believe you," said Helgestad. "There are many instances, however, of young lords who come here to get rich. They speak to the people of their estates at home, and their noble relatives; swear by their honor and conscience, and contract great debts. There have been such here, who would have run a man through the body who doubted their word, but at last ran off like scoundrels and villains; and all that they asserted turned out to be falsehood and deception. Will you listen to my advice, Herr Marstrand?"

"Most cheerfully," said he.

"He who would live here, and make money," said the trader, as he propped himself up against the bulwark, "must engage in trade; otherwise, he can do nothing. Trade, sir, that is the thing. We will speak hereafter of your land patent, at a proper time; it is now necessary to make a great venture, and this is the very moment. Who would live here, if the sea were not full of fish? The fish, Herr Marstrand, that is the attraction. Lofodden is a treasure for us all, and one that is inexhaustible. Every year, in March, those dumb creatures, the cod, resort in immense swarms to the Westfiord to spawn, and notwithstanding the millions that are caught, the number never diminishes. Hither we come also. From the North Cape to Trondheim, all who can, twenty thousand men and more, gather here on account of the fishery. Do you know how many we have taken within the last four weeks? More than fifteen millions. The scaffolds are all full to breaking; the yachts are all crammed with salted fish and livers Train oil will be cheap, Herr Marstrand; fish is to be obtained for a half *species* the *vaage*, and that is forty-eight good pounds. It is a real luck for us," said he, with a grin, "that there are Catholic Christians in the world—in Portugal, Italy, Spain, Germany, and other countries, by whatever names you call them. We rarely eat the dried stuff, which tastes like wood, and looks like petrified shingle;

in the south, however, among Catholic people, it is the fasting food for poor and rich, and the cheaper it is, the more is bought."

"I understand nothing of such business," said Marstrand, "and cannot engage in a fish speculation. Who will sell to me, if the profit is so considerable," said he, as he saw the frown of the trader.

"One must understand how to take advantage of opportunities. The fish are now to be bought cheap. Every one willingly parts with some of his abundant stock for ready money. If you were acquainted with the country, you would understand its customs. It is all barter here, and money is a rarity. The fisherman, the Northman, and Quane, as well as the Laplander, all borrow from the trader, who provides them with what they need for the whole year. They give him in return the product of their nets. The trader borrows also of the great merchants in Bergen, and sends to them ship-loads of cod-fish, salted fish, and train-oil. All whom you here see fishing are in the service of merchants and proprietors on the coast, and have their accounts in the credit-book. Each fish is numbered and reckoned for, as it is hung on the drying-stand; when it reaches Bergen, it is worth from three to six times as much as at first — do you understand, Herr? In a year like this, when there is a superabundance, sales are made on the spot, and others have a chance in the speculation. It may be that you can make a good hit."

Marstrand stood musing and in doubt. "Nuh!" said the old man, "every one must act as he has the heart. Trade is uncertain; he who has no confidence must not embark in it."

"As the catch is so abundant," replied Marstrand, "large profit, it seems to me, cannot be expected this year. All commissions can be easily executed, the storehouses are full to repletion, and the prices must fall."

Helgestad, for the first time, suffered his eye to rest with gratification upon the young adventurer. "You have an eye to trade, Herr," he said, "such as is rarely met with among your like: the thing will turn out differently from what you suppose. To-day is Saint Gertrude's day; and it is not a good sign if the sun shines. Stormy weather is certain to follow, according to an old saying in these parts. The fish there upon the rocks and the scaffolds continue to hang until June, whilst we all go home, press out the oil, and then deliver it at Bergen That is the first voyage in every year. In the month of June the yachts return to load the catch; and then many have reason to repent that they did not build their drying-stands higher. Fishermen are a reckless, giddy race, forgetful of the future, and avoiding labor and trouble as much as they can. There are heavy snows down to April and May, which often bury up the scaffolds and fish. When the crews land and seek the fish, they find only stinking flesh and worms. What ought to have brought money, must be cast into the sea; and so the whole of a rich fishery is often lost. It may happen so again, Herr Marstrand."

A crafty smile illuminated his features, and Marstrand began to feel a desire for, and confidence in, the fish speculation. He looked upon both the children of his counsellor, who heard all in silence. The tall maiden stood next to him, and fixed her eyes inquiringly, though with rather an indifferent regard, upon his countenance; Björnarne, however, nodded assent, and seemed surprised at his father's frankness.

"Good!" said the young man, "I am willing. I do not understand trade, but I rely upon your sympathy to make a purchase for me."

"I will do it," said Helgestad, cordially grasping his hand. "It is agreed between us, and I give you the word of a Norwegian. To-day, a fine number from Vaage was offered me, which I declined, as I have enough, with what God has bestowed upon me. I shall now look out, and see if I cannot drive a good bargain. Ho, boat!" he cried out over the bulwark of the yacht. "Be ready, Ole, my boy. You, Herr, remain on board with the children, until I return. Bring out the best you have, Björnarne; set the table, Ilda. I shall send or bring a fresh dish of fish."

With these words he descended the ladder, and he was surely in his best humor, for he twice looked up with a broad grin, and called to his daughter to take care to hunt up the fine things Björnarne had brought for her from Trondheim.

CHAPTER II.

BJÖRNARNE was heartily glad at the drift the affair of his friend had taken, whom he repeatedly assured it could not have resulted better, and that the advice of his father was excellent. "He is a man who knows how to make his way, and troubles himself but little about the business of others; he must, therefore, hold you in high esteem. Now he has taken your business upon his own shoulders, and he will take care that he dees not fail in it, Dismiss all care, John Marstrand; let us eat and be merry; my sister Ilda loves a friendly face. She is a girl," said he, "who stands firm upon her legs, and holds her head proudly on her neck. You shall see her dance to-day there in Ostvaagen, for there is a ball to-night at the Gaard. She will astonish you with her agility of foot."

In the meanwhile, Ilda was engaged in removing from the chests whatever was necessary to furnish the table with. She was quick of hand, and yet all her movements appeared to be measured and slow. A cold seriousness characterized her countenance, which only now and then lighted up at the gay rattle of her brother, to again settle back into its natural quietude. She moved up and down the shaking ship with a secure step, without ever losing her balance. She went to and fro, bringing meal and provisions to the cooking caboose, within whose narrow limits she soon established order. She answered Marstrand's questions and polite speeches in an indifferent manner; for the most part without looking at him, which excited no little mortification on his part; and he repeated scornfully to himself Björnarne's words, "she stands firmly on her legs; but as to her nimble-footedness I have some doubt."

The table was at last ready, upon which one of the national dishes, groat soup, with dried plums and herrings, was served up. Björnarne's face kindled with gratification. "Bravo, sister! you are a famous cook. I have long been deprived of the finest dish, dear girl, which a man can find. Let us set to, John Marstrand; you must be hungry."

That was true, indeed, of the young nobleman; but he had no liking for the precious dish. He felt an inward horror of it; yet he seized a spoon, and was dipping it into the plate, as Ilda laid her hand upon his arm, saying to him, in an earnest manner, "First let us pray, as is proper."

"I really forgot it," said Björnarne, smiling, "I have been so long away from home. On ship-board, amid the rocking of winds and waves, and where time is scant, it cannot always be observed. You are right, sister; let us pray."

He folded his hands, and smilingly turned to his friend, who followed his example. Ilda pronounced the table prayer, and her face expressed a reproving displeasure at the levity of her companions, which was not unobserved by them.

"You must know," said Björnarne, as the plates were filled, "that Ilda is a religious maiden, who is thoroughly versed in the Bible, and never misses going to church, be the weather bad as it may. And it is no joke," continued he, "in the winter season to cross the fiord for two miles, in open boat, when the tempest rages, and the ice drifts. The church lies deep within the inner bay, on account of the Finns, who live on the mountains. Many a one bolts his door to, piles up the logs upon his hearth, and lets the parson preach to suit himself.

The Laplanders come down thither from the Tjellen, and listen, without understanding a word, and return as stupid as they came."

"You are an unrighteous man, Björnarne," said Ilda, angrily.

"Nuh!" said the brother, with a laugh, "I know what you mean. I will explain to you, John, what Ilda means. She is a Christian at heart, and she wishes to make others such. We have a pastor in the country, Klaus Hornemann by name, who has taken it into his head to convert and baptise the heathen Finns, reindeer shepherds, and Laplanders, who wander about through the boundless wilderness. My sister faithfully aids him in his labors, and she so long implored her father, that he has consented to take into our house the daughter of an old churl who has some fame among his people as a sorcerer. The old Afraja unwillingly enough consented, for they have as great a dislike to us as fire to water; it cost a good quantity of tobacco, brandy, and hard threats, before he would let the girl come down among us. Now we have her at home, and Ilda has tamed her so, that she can sew; and has taught her reading, and all kinds of arts. You will see, John Marstrand, how ready she is, and how quick she is at comprehension; for God has not sent them into the world without understanding. But because this one is an exception to her race, and is neither dirty, thievish, nor corrupt, but good and friendly, so that she has won the good-will of all, Ilda thinks I unjustly despise a people whom no Norman touches, but kicks out of the way."

"Whoever bears a Christian name," said Ilda, and her eyes flashed while she spoke, "should esteem a man, wherever he is found, as his brother, and give him his hand."

"The Lapps are not men!" exclaimed Björnarne. "They are beasts, worse than swine and rooks!"

"For shame, for shame, brother!" responded the brave girl. "What you say is spoken without reflection, and that most do, who think like you. And yet, I am sure, you have not such a bad opinion of them," she said, with a significant smile. "Have you not been with Gula in the Tjellen? have you not sat in the *gamme* of her father, eaten his meat, drank his milk, and held friendly conversation with him?"

A cloud of confusion swept across Björnarne's face, over which he passed his hand, and laughingly replied; "You do not know what you are talking about, sister Ilda. As if one could not for once sit in a gamme, and partake of reindeer's-meat and milk with a Lapp, who counts thousands of herds for his own, and, besides, is a kind of prince and patriarch, a wiseacre and magician, among his people. Yet, while we are sitting here, time is passing, and our guest appears to have lost his appetite; his soup is growing cold."

The young nobleman had laid the spoon aside, for the sweet soup and the salted fish was in no wise agreeable to his taste Björnarne laughed aloud, as he observed the expression of aversion which appeared on Marstrand's countenance. "You Danes do not know how good it tastes," said he. "It is a famous old Nordland dish, in quest of which every one of us would travel miles."

"I do not envy you it, and I wish you a perfect appetite," replied the younker. "As a Dane, however, you must excuse me for declining it."

"He who leaves his native country, and goes to dwell among a strange people, must take their manners and customs, meats and drinks, as he finds them," answered Ilda. "You are wrong, Herr, if you wish to be among us different from ourselves."

The smile which accompanied her reproof was so gracious, that Marstrand, he hardly knew why, took up the spoon again, and with such heartiness fell upon the dish, that the plate was soon emptied.

The loud laughter of the brother and sister, as he raised himself up from his effort, like a hero who has performed a great feat, aroused his mirth. He responded gaily to the jesting applause, and found that the daughter of the trader of the fiords showed him much more confidence than before.

"You have demonstrated that you are not wanting in good-will; therefore take also now fish and meat, such as we have to offer, that you may grow familiar with our fare."

The repast finished much more harmoniously than it had began. Björnarne brought glasses out of the chest, and a flask of old Madeira. A toast was then given, to a hearty welcome in the land, to good luck and prosperity, to steady friendship, and, at last, also, that John Marstrand might build himself a nouse in the neighborhood of Lyngenfiord, and there pass his life in blessed happiness and joy.

"Take care," said Björnarne, "you will be pleased sooner than you think; and when once these wild rocks and waters have won your affection, you will never more be able to tear yourself away from them. I have often heard of, and seen people come among us, who, for the first year, were almost driven to take their own lives, from the antipathy they felt for the land. They were soon again in good spirits; and they finally found it so attractive, that nothing could induce them to return to their native country, although they had sufficiency of money and goods there."

Marstrand looked around. He could not believe that a man who had made his fortune would not immediately flee from these wilds. "That is curious," said he; "wonderfully strange!"

"It is easy to explain, and quite natural," answered Ilda. "The men who came were strange and forlorn. Solitude and privation oppressed their spirits. By degrees, they acquired friends, their prosperity increased, they labored, and found hap piness and tranquillity in the bosom of their family. In th world from which you come, John Marstrand, people live amidst all kinds of amusements and distractions; with us, you have nothing but your own house. Therein you must seek all the happiness that is given to you on earth."

The young man was convinced of the truth of her remark Nothing but the narrow circle of the house, a retired, tranquil life in a wilderness, where weeks and months pass by without ever seeing your threshold crossed by a strange foot, that it was which, in the best case, he could obtain; and Ilda pronounced it with the assurance of a prophet, yet in a tone which seemed to indicate that it was the highest and best aim of man."

"My sister is indeed right," said Björnarne, "it is so with us. Whoever comes here must learn to endure solitude, and to eradicate all anxious longings from his heart. Did you not leave a wife at home, John Marstrand; a bride, perhaps?"

"No," replied the younker, laughing.

"Or a maiden whom you love as your eyes?" inquired the indefatigable Norman, further.

"Also no, Björnarne. Our maidens," he good-naturedly shook his head, "would not so easily follow a husband into these wastes of snow and fish."

As he looked up, he met the eyes of Ilda. They were fixed upon him with an expression of astonishment, but they glowed with a tender and friendly feeling, as if to inspire him with consolation, and she said, in her deep-toned voice, "I think you are in error, Herr. Maidens everywhere have God's voice in their hearts, which says to them: 'Follow him whom you love wherever he may be upon the earth,' as it is written in the Holy Scriptures."

"Then," he replied, "no one, at least, has manifested such love to me, as that of which you speak; especially—but it may also in time fall to my lot. With the King's letter in pocket, I have come hither in quest of fortune. Let it present itself to me as it may—as whale, reindeer, or peasant who tills his little field, or as a trader in the darkest depths of the fiord, I will embrace and hold fast to it; and perhaps it may be my destiny there to find my house and happiness."

As he ceased, Björnarne exclaimed, "You are a valiant man,

and you will prosper. You will build your house as soon as you choose. Do you not think so, Ilda?"

"He who will establish the happiness of his house, must bring peace and contentment into it; the giddy in thought and action are fickle, and to-day that appears right, which to-morrow is wrong. Thy friend, Björnarne, must first be at peace with himself, and learn to know us, before we can further judge." Then she stood up and exclaimed, "Here comes father back. His boat is already at the foot of the ladder."

In a few moments more, the heavy tread of the trader resounded on the deck, and with some haste he labored along between the bales and barrels down to the cabin steps.

"Nuh!" he said, as he entered, "you have cleared the table during my absence; but serve up again, Ilda, I shall be satisfied with what remains; and bring me another flask, Björnarne, I am hungry and thirsty from business and talking. Nothing in this world, Herr Marstrand, without trouble." He took off his cap, drew a stool to the table, and stroked his yellow, gray, long-falling hair with both hands from his wrinkled brow. For a few minutes he sat perfectly silent, as if he wished to think over exactly what he was about to say; then he raised up his head, and said to Marstrand, "The bargain is made. Two thousand vaage of good fish have been selected for you, and hung up to dry, that makes a thousand *species* to-day, at six o'clock this evening, in Ostvaagöen there."

"Good," said Marstrand, "the money shall be forthcoming."

"Pour on!" said Helgestad, good-naturedly, "you will not repent of your purchase. You can gain five and six-fold, if you have luck; as the first venture of a trader turns out, so goes it with the next one. Luck gives courage, and courage luck. A faint heart gains nothing, a man must confide in himself: and here, in this country, it is necessary, above all things, to have the eyes before or behind, according to circumstances." He next began a long examination of his protegé, from whom, through a thousand cross-questions, he extracted all he desired to know He looked at the royal patent, read it syllable by syllable, and appeared to study it in detail; while he talked of trade, of Denmark, and its relation with the German provinces, which then, through Flensburg, possessed a considerable part of the commerce with Nordland and Finnmark. All his observations were keen and to the point, and showed a perfect acquaintance with the actual condition and relations of both the United Provinces. The wretched finances, and the anarchical disorder of the governmeut in Copenhagen, the prodigality of the court, and the idle, arrogant swarms of officials were likewise criticised with unsparing truth by the trader of the fiords, beyond the polar circle. His guest, with whom he emptied glass after glass, was in no degree spared, and he seemed to take particular pleasure in showing him what he was, and what he must be.

"You have brought smooth hands with you," said he, laughing, while he opened his own coarse, thick fist, "but you will soon lose the white fingers, if you wish to push your way. Nuh! you will succeed. You are a man who must know that no royal palace, with marble halls and music bands, exists here. The old Tjellen there are our palaces and castles, and there they will stand as long as the world lasts. They have halls and columns enough, and there is no king nor sultan so grand, and the tempest fills them with glorious music."

"I know," said Marstrand, "that I must expect to work hard. You can depend upon me, Herr Helgestad, I am prepared to do my duty."

"I will tell you what I have calculated," replied the trader, confidentially. "I have a house in Lyngenfiord, you know. It is a fine situation, frequented on all sides. Three markets in the year are close at hand, to which the Quanes and Tjeld-lapps resort from the mountains; and there is, besides, abundant trade with the fishing people of the neighborhood. A perfect labyrinth of sounds converge at that point, and there is many a blessed little spot yet waste and unoccupied. I know of one where a skilful man can put up a house, and make himself a handsome living."

"And shall I settle myself there?" asked Marstrand.

"That is my opinion," said the old man. "*Seyfish* and *syld* come up to your door. There are also serviceable people at hand, whom you can avail yourself of. In half a day, with wind and tide, you can reach Tromsöe; it is a sheltered, happy paradise. Rocks and islands full of gulls, Skarve and Alken; also eider-down ducks, and their breeding-places on the rocks. There is a feather trade, which brings money. Thereby, in the ravines, wood enough, more than enough—great, mighty trees." He nodded to the guest, and, with a shrewd contraction of the brow, whispered to him, "I think you understand it; is it not so? Wood enough, Herr!"

Marstrand looked at him steadily, without exactly appreciating the excellence of the locality, but Helgestad gave him a wink, and continued, "You must settle the affair soon in Tromsöe. *Voigt* Paulsen is a man whom you can gain if you choose. You must hold your patent under his nose, that he may read its contents. The sooner you begin the better."

"Will he also grant me the land of which you speak?"

"I think so," replied Helgestad, impatiently. "In the meantime, you can reside with me until you see your way clear, and are established. Build a dwelling and a store-house near at hand; buy boats and fishing-tackle, with a yacht for the Bergen voyages. You must yourself provide the stock of a shop."

A deep blush suffused Marstrand's face. "Must I keep a shop," shouted he, horrified at the idea, "a shop for Lapps and Quanes?"

"A shop," answered Helgestad, cooly; "or do you think to live here as a gentleman of the bed-chamber? You should have remained at home in silk robes and red hose, if it pleases you so much better."

"It is impossible," said the young nobleman, clasping his

hands. "I cannot think of it — the shop must be dispensed with."

"It is absolutely necessary that you keep one, as all do who desire success. There are many persons here who can count out upon the table their fifty or hundred thousand *species*, who yet keep a shop."

"But if I also," said Marstrand, "should wish to buy, to build, and establish myself, it requires money, and I have none."

"You have a friend in Lyngenfiord," replied the trader, emphatically, "who will see to it that you want nothing. I have money and goods enough to set you up properly."

"In heaven's name, then," said Marstrand, with desperate resolution, "I will do as you advise, because I think you understand it best. No one knows what he is capable of, and what necessity can make of him."

"You are right," said Helgestad; "it is a good instructor, and it gives prudence, and sharpens the vision and the wit. It will be your fault, if others eat the apple that was baked for you."

He stood up, and drew a huge, thick watch from his pocket, which hung from his vest by a long silver chain. It is time that we set out; we shall just have time to reach Ostvaagen and transact the business, before the ball at the Gaard begins. Bring out your money; and hurry, Herr Marstrand, or Björnarne and Ilda will be there before us. They would not, for all the world, miss a fandango or hop."

Marstrand opened his trunk, and took out the purse filled with gold coin, the whole of his riches. He counted the pieces, whose clear ring greatly gratified the avaricious Helgestad, as he stood overlooking the reckoning, and reducing them into louis-d'ors.

"Now away!" said he, "do not carry the purse in your hand, but secure it in the bottom of your pocket, before we descend to the boat. Misfortune is cheap; and the sea returns nothing that has fallen into it. Many a thing lies buried there till the last day."

The cautious trader pushed his anxiety for his young friend almost too far; for on the deck, he also warned him not to be in too great a hurry to get into the boat, because he might easily fall into the water, and as he sat alongside of him in the yawl, he related terrible stories of fisherman and sailors who had fallen from vessels, and had been drawn under the keel, or been seized by sharks; for the voracious monsters of the Atlantic often penetrate into the innermost recesses of the sounds and fiords. Marstrand smiled, but it gratified him to see the active interest taken in his welfare by so worthy a man. He no longer felt alone in that strange land; he had found people who sympathized with him. This old trader, with his rough, hard manners, showed him a rare affection, and there, upon the taffrail of the yacht, leaned his two children, upon whose good-will he could firmly rely.

While the boat, rapidly rowed by two stout fishermen towards the land, glided between rocks and shoals, and by numerous fishing-stations, Helgestad named the merchants to whom the catch belonged, and spoke of their dwellings, their fortunes, their families, their careers, and adventures; so that it was evident, he was thoroughly posted up in all that had happened for many a year, a hundred miles up and down the coast. He knew not only the rich, but also the fishing folk, many of whom he called by name, addressing them amusing inquiries, and responding to their greetings in such a manner as to awaken the most riotous mirth.

Helgestad laughed, and said to Marstrand, "There is great fun here, is there not? I think you will long remember this year, and forget its hard hours. The recollection of happy days is a delightful thing, Herr Marstrand; it consoles man in distress, inspires him with hope, and, in this respect, we are all alike. One thinks of this, another of that. You think of your banquets in Copenhagen, of the gaily-dressed dames, and the princes; the fisherman there, of the largest cod and the fullest net; I, upon the profit of train-oil in Bergen. The pleasures of memory are to all the same."

Marstrand laughed aloud at the complacency of Helgestad, who, as he closed his philosophical observations, exclaimed, with redoubled emphasis, "It is a fine thing that, but every one must see to it that his reminiscences are agreeable. Is it not so, Ole Gormson? I think so. Take care of the stones, Ole."

The boat flew on the rocky beach, and, as Marstrand looked around, three Normans stood there in their long, dark coats, and huge caps, who took hold of the yawl and drew it on the strand.

An old wooden ladder, with broken rounds, conducted to the rocks, where stood the Gaard of Ostvaagen. It was a log house, painted red, with small windows, a roof of earth, and heavy limbs of trees, upon which, for security against the storms, large stones had been laid. From the dirty front room, a small, dark passage between casks, nets, angling-rods, and fishing-tackle, led to a hall, which took up almost the whole interior of the house, and served the double purpose of a sitting and reception-room to the occupant of the Gaard of Ostvaagen.

Upon one side was a brown cupboard, set out with bottles, pitchers, and glasses; tables and benches were arranged against the opposite wall, and some men sat there, leaning on their elbows—sinewy, heavy figures, in leathern jerkins, over which their long hair fell in tangled disorder. The gravity of their demeanor was in no degree disturbed by the entrance of Helgestad and his companion. A glance or two at the stranger, who appeared in their midst in such unwonted garb, was sufficient to satisfy their curiosity; they appeared to trouble themselves scarcely more about the trade, which was begun and closed at their elbows, although they certainly lost not a word, and seriously pondered the transaction, to judge by the movements of their eyes and lips.

"You have here three of the best men, whose word is as firm as the mountains," said Helgestad, after he had made Marstrand acquainted with the venders. "But to business. Bought of Olaf Gödvad, eight hundred fish; from Henrik Neilson, six hundred; from Gulick Stevenson, six hundred; in all two thousand, selected according to my choice, and consigned to me on your account. Shake hands, Herr Marstrand; and now count out the *species* on the table, where many a one has lain before. Mary," shouted he, joyously, to the old woman who was seated on a stool by the fire on the hearth, "bring us punch, hot punch! we must drink to prosperous trade. It is a cold night, storm streaks lie athwart the sky, and on Salten's needles. Or would you prefer Madeira toddy? Bring Madeira toddy, Mary; it is better for you, Herr Marstrand. You have brought with you a fine face, and it would be a pity if it were to turn brown or red."

Marstrand emptied his pocket of the money, which was carefully counted over, and examined with sharp inspection, before it was gathered up by the hard hands of the fish traders, and deposited in their purses. As Marstrand pocketed the empty purse, an anxious thought came over him, which almost led him to repent of what he had done. "What if these unknown men were in combination to defraud him of what he possessed!" He had remarked how closely they regarded each other, and how cunningly they seemed to interchange glances, and how piteously the spectators looked upon him. Old Helgestad himself appeared pretty much like a sharper who has made a lucky throw of the dice. There was no time, however, for the Danish younker to surrender himself to these sad thoughts; his money was gone, and he was surrounded by men who, evidently, were not to be trifled with. Now came the punch and toddy. Short Holland pipes and tobacco were laid upon the table; his health was drunk, he was shaken by the hands, and all kinds of questions asked him, and, as the ice of the first introduction was broken, the traders and fishermen gathered around the new comer, to hear what he had to relate that was interesting of the Danish capital.

Time passed away quickly enough for Marstrand, who, for his part, learnt much that was new and instructive to him. The trading operations of this remote coast-land were on the increase, the fishing business had never been so active; and for this reason the Danish government directed a closer attention to Finnmark, and sought, through the sale of privileges, trading-posts, and useful land, to increase its sources of revenue.

A greater number of guests gradually came in, all full of joy at the excellent catch, and bent on giving full vent to their gratification. The host of Ostvaagen and his traders had enough to do, to fill and refill the glasses with punch and toddy, which were incessantly drained; uproar, and laughter, and tobacco smoke filled the large room, and mingled with the odor of fish and fat, which all exhaled from the crown of the head to the sole of the feet. The evening grew darker, and a dozen rude lights were brought in and stuck in empty bottles, but their feeble glimmer was not sufficient to overcome the gloom. Many voigts, sorenskriver, and other officials had come from the islands and the coast, to meet their friends and transact business. All drank the strong liquors like water, all shouted and screamed, and between the clouds of smoke there opened, from time to time, rifts, through which could be seen in a row against the wall, the hard-featured visages of the traders, who slowly drained their glasses, and secretly pondered upon the advantage they could gain of one or the other of the bystanders.

After some time, there was a cessation in this din. A six foot tall Nordlander sprang into the room, and while he pushed those next to him to the right and left, he cried out in a bold voice, "Place for the music! Here comes the music! Give place, you there in the green coat, to the musicians.

The young Herr of Nordland appeared to belong to the *elite*, for he wore a new blue jacket, and a large and gay cravat; but he took hold of Marstrand so roughly that the latter angrily extricated himself from his grasp. The Nordlander did not, however, desist; but coolly looking in the flushed face of the Danish younker, exclaimed; "Can't you hear or see? Sheer off! the dance is to begin; or are your legs made fast to the earth, like the roots of a birch tree"

"Neither my leg nor my arm," said Marstrand.

The Nordlander appeared to consider if he had rightly understood, then doubling up his fists, he said to his antagonist, with an air of defiance; "If you wish to fight, come on; but first get away from there, if you have brains enough to understand."

At this moment Björnarne entered with Ilda and a young man.

"Holla, Olaf, my dear fellow!" exclaimed Björnarne: "peace be with you. It is a year and more since we have met. Here is my sister Ilda, who has promised herself to you for the first dance; for the second, she is engaged to Paul Petersen; and for the third, I have the preference."

"Right glad am I to see you here again," said he, shaking Björnarne by the hand, "but"—looking to Marstrand, who had, in the meanwhile, stepped back—"I have a dispute to settle here."

"Do you refer to yonder person?" asked Björnarne. "Let him alone, Olaf. He is a Dane, a stranger, who is unacquainted with our customs."

"Good, let the Danish ape run, then," said the Nordlander. "There is the music; give me your hand, Miss Ilda; it must not be said, that the ball in Gaard von Ostvaagoen was opened by any other than Ilda Helgestad and Olaf Veigand."

With one arm he clasped Ilda's waist, and with the other he pitched the packs of the fishermen in a pile, and thus opened a clear space, in which three or four couple whirled about to the clang of the music, whose shrill tones were accompanied by the shouts of the noisy, half-intoxicated spectators.

Two violins, a trumpet, and a kind of flageolet, formed a dancing music of the drollest species. The two men who played the stringed instruments upon their knees, were, doubtless, artists from the Hardanger mountains, where the peasants themselves make these violins, and perform upon them with their fingers and a small bow. The trumpeter, who pealed in long blasts between the tinkling, appeared to be a disbanded soldier from a coast town; the flutist was evidently a son of the outcast people of the wilderness, a Lapp, whose oblique eyes, and high, protruding cheek-bones, gave clear proof of his Mongolian descent. The shrill tones of his pipe kept good time, and led the music of the dance; a crowd gathered around him, who were highly delighted with his wonderful display of artistic skill, which they manifested by loud acclamations, and by offerings of flowing glasses of hot drinks.

Such was the ball in Gaard von Ostvaagoen; and it extended late into the night, with universal satisfaction. The daughters and wives of the traders and *voigts*, with the young girls and old women from the vicinity, were indefatigable dancers. They whirled through the double quick-step and reel with unheard of agility, while the young men, to the peril of their necks, leaped to the ceiling, and shook the building with their powerful stamping on the floor. By degrees, old and young alike were fascinated by the sport, and all joined in the giddy whirl. Even the old traders sprang from their seats to seek a partner, though it were the old hostess herself. Marstrand seemed to be the only one who did not find pleasure in the wild uproar. He leaned up against a corner, and quietly surveyed the scene; for none seemed to trouble themselves about him. Björnarne danced like one possessed, and Ilda was constantly on the floor with one partner or another. Suddenly, however, the old Helgestad took the younker by the arm, and drew him out of the corner. "Nuh!" said he, "you stand there like a statue of stone. Do you not like the dance? It seems to me so, and I will show you one also whom it does not please. There is the nephew of *voigt* Peter Paulsen in Tromsöe, his secretary and assistant; he is a man of your pattern, but one who does not please everybody. I must tell you something, Herr, before we go further. He is a creature that one must not approach with an open hand. It would be well for you if your letter were laid before him in Tromsöe. You must, therefore, make his acquaintance; you will, at best, know how to use your net."

With these words, leading Marstrand by the hand, he strode directly across the room to a spot where, upon the corner bench near the door, with other persons, sat the young man who had come with Ilda and Björnarne. He was earnestly engaged in conversation with his neighbor, and Helgestad was obliged to shake him before he turned round, and directed his pale, yellowish, pock-marked face towards the trader. A forest of dark red hair covered his head, and his large, protruding eyes glittered under long red lashes. He arose in a friendly manner, and extended his hand to Marstrand, as Helgestad pointing to him, said: "Here, Paul Petersen, here is a friend who desires to know you. He is from the south, from Copenhagen, where you were so much pleased. I think you will suit each other, and will become friends. Is it not so?"

"Herr Marstrand," said the young man, politely, "I heard of your arrival, and would have already called upon you, if I had not been detained by friends. You are welcome to the country, whose greatest glory, the fishery at Lofodden, you have just seen. I need not ask you what you think of it," continued he, with a broad laugh; "one must have strong nerves for such enjoyments: if it is true that you propose to take up your abode among us, you will soon get accustomed to it, and, perhaps, in a few years, like these good people here, you will be involved in the same pleasures; who talk of them the whole year through, and eagerly look forward to their renewal in the next season."

He cast a scrutinising glance upon the circle of dancers, and then invited the younker to take a seat upon the bench, where a couple of *voigts* and *sorenskriver* were sitting, whose acquaintance led to a long conversation about Copenhagen, and the life and manners of the capital, of which Paul Petersen had much to relate himself. He had resided there several years, studying law, and had practised in Christiana, and, by the influence of his uncle, had been placed in a desirable position in Tromsöe. His amusing anecdotes, and his friendly tone, did not fail to favorably impress Marstrand. Here, at length, was a person who spoke like an educated man, who had seen the world, and whose superior intellect manifested itself in everything he said and did. While Marstrand was obliged to drink punch and toddy with all the voigts and writers, he felt a growing partiality for the nephew of the voigt of Tromsöe, and at last he could not refrain from cordially shaking him by the hand, and expressing his gratification at the acquisition of so valuable an acquaintance.

"It cannot be more so to you than to me, Herr Marstrand," replied Petersen. "When you have been here a little longer, you will see what it is to have a friend with whom you can talk of men and the world."

"And how have you endured," said the younker, "for so many long years, to talk of nothing but codfish, train-oil, herrings, and eider-geese?"

Paul Petersen smilingly looked at his neighbor, who had not heard the strange remark, and said, "I think we had better leave this tobacco, brandy, and fat-smelling ball-room, and take a little fresh air. The moon shines clear over the Westfiord, and lights up Salten, the islands, and the whole coast. It is a magnificent sight. I will conduct you to an eminence, and I think the walk will do us both good."

As they passed out, it was exactly as the secretary had said. Not ten steps before the door, the sea sported with its tranquil waters, and softly murmured against the moonlit rocks. The fishing-grounds, so animated by day, lay perfectly still in the glowing flood. Peace was in nature, peace in the heavens and on earth, peace even in the great kingdom of the deep. A sublime, holy tranquillity everywhere prevailed, except in the little inn, where the noise of the trumpet and flute, and the tread of the dancers, yet resounded. Upon the threshold, Paul Petersen stopped his new friend, and drew him to one of the illuminated windows. "You asked me, what induced me to live among these people? I will tell you. The same longing for this wild, rocky land, which seizes every one who has ever set foot upon it. Do you see the man there in the corner? He is the sorenskriver of Steilve, a rock on the end of the Lofodden group, where he has lived for ten years. It is a savage spot, a wilder and more dreary one does not exist; and yet he formerly lived in Christiana, and belongs to a distinguished family. But his post brings him fully five thousand *species* annually; therefore he remains there, and hoards up his money. Observe the voigts of Salten and Hindoen; they have double the income of the best voigt stations in all Norway; and now, reflect upon this, Herr Marstrand — whoever comes here will make money and grow rich. Even the miserable Lapp, who drives his reindeer in the wilderness, gathers his silver *species*, and buries them. You also, Herr Marstrand, will catch this wonderful love of traffic; and you are already under its influence."

"Thus far, I feel but little of it," said Marstrand, laughing.

"Ha, ha!" exclaimed the secretary, "I deny it. You set foot for the first time to-day in Lofodden, and your whole cash has been invested in a bold speculation. You, a man of noble descent, who look with contempt upon fish traders, you have caught the fever of speculation which prevails in this trafficking community. Once more, Herr Marstrand, I say there is no one here who does not seek, by some process or other, to get rich; and I forewarn you that you will be seized by the same avaricious passion, and that you will cling to these rocks, if you succeed in your present venture."

"And why shall I not succeed, Herr Petersen?" replied Marstrand. "I came here to settle, and I think the counsel of the friend who encouraged me to my first speculation was a good one."

"It may be," said the secretary; "no one knows. Luck or accident decides in all such affairs. You may rest assured, however, that Niels Helgestad does nothing to his own disadvantage."

"What benefit can he expect to derive from this affair?"

Paul Petersen ceased speaking, and both proceeded to a narrow, steep path between the rocks, which lay concealed in the darkness. The secretary suddenly stood still, and said, "If, for example, Niels Helgestad had received a cargo of salt in his yacht from Trondheim, which he could sell at a profit to the people here, who indeed have fish, but no ready money, and if he could procure them a purchaser of two thousand vaagen of fish, at a good price in *species*, and pocket the same for his salt, it is evident, Herr Marstrand, that he knows how to advance his own interests."

"Is your illustration drawn from the reality?" inquired Marstrand.

"I will not assert it—God defend me! But among the many crafty heads here, Niels Helgestad is the craftiest. 'He hears,' as his neighbors say, 'the grass grow;' and no one ever reaped where he sowed. You came with Björnarne from Trondheim. He is a good, honest fellow, yet entirely subservient to the will of his father. The maiden Ilda, on the contrary, has more of her father's mind. She knows how to promote her own interests; and she is, withal, so demure and modest, that she is regarded as a model for all the young girls in the land."

A feeling of aversion against the secretary was excited in Marstrand. "It seems," said he, "as if you did not participate in this opinion."

"I?" replied his companion, smiling. "It may be that I, as others, think differently, and have my own view of things. But she is a discreet and intelligent girl — cold, prudent, and proud. No one," rejoined Petersen, "can boast of her favor, although many have sought for it. Miss Ilda is indeed a precious prize, for Niels Helgestad is rated to be worth much more than a hundred thousand *species*. Position, rank, and title are laughed at here, Herr Marstrand; smooth thalers, yachts, and trading-posts are alone held in esteem. I have heard that you are going to Lyngenfiord with Helgestad."

"I have been invited to go there," said the younker.

"Have you traced out a plan for your future career?" asked his friend.

Marstrand thought of Helgestad's admonition. "I have not yet decided upon anything."

"Come to Tromsöe, then," said Petersen. "It will give me pleasure to be useful to you. I have some influence with my uncle, who perhaps will be able to provide for you. It would be best to buy a trading-post, but they are dear, and new ones are not to be obtained but by the express concession of government. The shop-dealing in the fiords, the fish and feather trade, all yield money, if speculations are successful; but one must have considerable skill and experience, and years often elapse before a lucky hit is made. Settle yourself in Tromsöe; the government will make it a place of trade. Establish an oil-factory there, or set up a commission business; perhaps you will grow rich in time, and then you can flee from this land of cod-fish and herring, and return to fair Copenhagen, which you, no doubt, would be glad to do as soon as possible."

Marstrand said nothing, for, at that moment, they passed between the rocks, and stood now on the edge of the bay, close to the Westfiord. Before them, the trading vessels swayed to and fro on the gently-heaving sea. The moon hung over the needle-like peaks of Salten, and revealed with its rays the whole chain of these wild mountains, with their gleaming ice-slopes and snow-fields. This vast panorama of land and sea, overhung by night and shadow, lay immovable and impenetrable before them. A death-like silence had settled upon the scene, and only from time to time a wave leaped against a sea-encompassed rock, and broke in foam and yest — or a stone, loosened from the steep sides of the mountain, bounded downwards—or a puff of wind, with a sullen moan, escaped from the cragged summits of the Old Man of Vaagoen, and softly whimpered through the rigging of the yachts and brigs.

After a long silence, Paul Petersen resumed; "There can be nothing wilder, in the whole world, than this Westfiord and the Lofodden—this fearful array of cliffs, glaciers, black rocks, and sea. But I have often gazed upon it, and you will probably look upon the view oftener than will be agreeable. Let us return."

The Danish younker did not heed the suggestion. He sat down upon a block of rock, and folded his arms upon his breast.

"Do you intend to remain here?" asked the secretary.

"Yes; leave me alone."

"Very well; but take care not to slide off, and forget not the reality in your philosophising. Close to these rocks the sea is four hundred feet deep. And now, one more word of advice, Herr Marstrand. Beware of subtilities. Here, on land, every one must keep his eyes open, and not indulge in poetical dreams. The jagged rock there is a stone; the glacier above, cold ice; and the sea, salt water, in which the useful cod swims." He regarded the Dane, upon whose face the moon was shining, and continued, with a smile; "Return soon, take a glass of hot toddy, and dance a Nordland fandango with Miss Ilda — her consent will not be withheld."

"By heavens! I believe he is right," exclaimed Marstrand, as he was left alone. "Here every one stands upon his own legs, and only a fool could suppose he would lend them to another. There is no doubt that the old Helgestad pirated off my money to get rid of his salt, and that he would not feel the slightest compunction of conscience if I were stripped of my last farthing. Henceforward I will keep my eyes open, and it will be difficult for them to deceive me; and this fool of a secretary, who regards me as his rival, as if I were in a condition to soften the iron heart of the maiden Ilda"—he broke off, and fixed his eyes upon the flitting clouds, which, loosened from the rocks of Salten, sailed away in vapory forms to the southward. "I wish I could accompany you, and yet I must remain here. The sagacious *bursche* was again right; I cannot already leave this bewitched land, where one lives and loves, with an insatiable thirst for money and riches, to heap up between these naked rocks."

At this moment he heard a rustling behind him, and, as he looked up, Miss Ilda stood alongside of him. "I have come to seek you, John Marstrand," said she, "because Paul Petersen told me you were sitting here on the cliff, talking to the moon, and were invoking the old Nornes, with their enchanted songs, to chase sorrow from your heart."

"Paul Petersen is a fool," replied Marstrand, and his countenance glowed with a deep red flush.

"He is no fool," continued Ilda, "he knows well what he does; but you must not give him occasion to ridicule you."

"Well and good, let him jest — I jest also upon myself."

She approached nearer to him, and looked him earnestly in the eye. The moon lighted up her open, firm-set features, and she gently shook her head, as, in a reproving tone, she replied, "You must not. He who makes a jest of himself must either be very foolish or very unhappy. You are neither."

"And if I were, Miss Ilda?"

"The men of the south must be very giddy-minded," responded she, smiling; "yet you have something in your eye that speaks to the contrary. Unhappy you are not, if you are a man who knows how to support the heavy burden of life. You seek to win a new home, and you must have courage. To-morrow we leave for Lyngenfiord—you will see how beautiful it is with us. We shall also exert ourselves to make it agreeable to you."

"Will you also have a care for me?" inquired Marstrand, extending her his hand.

"Will I?" replied she, kindly; "to be sure I will."

They stood opposite to each other. Thankfully he gazed in her face, upon which the moon shed a flood of light.

"You must now accompany me," said Ilda. "I ask you to dance — you will not refuse me?"

"Certainly not."

"So, come, you have already been missed."

He went with her, and the ball in Ostvaagoen soon had one dancer more.

CHAPTER III.

On the second morning after this *fête*, the Fair Ilda of Orenaes weighed anchor, and sailed through the sound of Hindoen to the north. Niels Helgestad had been engaged the whole day through in his business, and had finished it too late to avail himself of the flood tide. He had disposed of his salt, crammed his yacht with large barrels of train-oil and fish-heads, inspected his fish-scaffolds, and had delivered Marstrand's stores to their proprietors, upon whom he disinterestedly bestowed some sound advice, and the benefits of his experience, until at last, late in the evening, all was ready; with the earliest dawn, the great sail of the yacht was loosened to the breeze. Björnarne remained behind with the boats and the fishing-tackle, which he was to bring home, with his father's second yacht.

When Marstrand came on deck, the Lofodden already lay far in the distance, behind a screen of dark cloud, above which the peaks of Ostvaagen rose preëminent. It all seemed to him as a dream. He could scarcely conceive that there, behind the cliffs, his codfish were swinging on the scaffolds; as a wild snow-blast broke loose, and enveloped land and sea, he felt all the cares of a proprietor, and his anxiety about his property drove him, in a meditative mood, up and down the deck.

"Nuh!" exclaimed old Helgestad, pleasantly, as he came up from below, and observed Marstrand, dressed in a leathern coat, lined with green frieze, and wearing a heavy cap of reindeer's-skin, after the manner of the traders, all of which he had bought, at the suggestion of Ilda, in Ostvaagen. "Now you look like a respectable man. You acted wisely in throwing off a dress unsuitable to the country; you may lay it up in your trunk as a reminiscence for your children."

"Snow and storm are gathering over the Lofodden, Herr Helgestad," said Marstrand.

"You are already anxious?" rejoined the old trader, laughing. "It is a good sign, when you have your goods in eye; there is no occasion for alarm. Snow-storms and bad weather prevail down to June; your fish, however, hang as securely as in the bosom of Abraham."

"And have you no fear lest strange hands may carry them off, or change them?"

"Who will take them?" replied Helgestad, impatiently. "Every one here knows his own—we have no fear in Nordland of thieves; such robbery would be the greatest disgrace a man could bring upon himself."

Thus assured, Marstrand was able the more contentedly to get through that and the three following days, which he passed on board the yacht, as she glided through the sounds and fiords. The heavy craft, at last, with stream and wind, shot through the channel of Tromsöe, where the church, surrounded by a few red-painted log and frame houses, rose before the sight of the voyagers.

"We will not pass by our chief town without exhibiting your

land patent to Voigt Peter Paulsen," said Helgestad; "for, between ourselves, it would be better if we could secure its registration on the spot, before the return of Paul Petersen to his uncle's house." He slily winked his eyes, and continued; "This is a fine visit, Herr: and Voigt Paulsen is a man who esteems a handsome dress. Put on your best coat, and hang that thing by your side, which you have down in the cabin. Some day, hereafter, you can make a capital harpoon out of it. Hold there! to land, Niels," he shouted to the man at the helm, "and hurry, for we have no time to lose."

As Marstrand put on his gold-embroidered coat, and with his sword by his side, and his plumed hat in hand, re-entered the cabin, Miss Ilda sat near the stove, watching the cooking meal, and mending the fur cloak of her father. Her head was closely bent over her work, and her large fingers diligently plied the needle.

He had often, of late, seen and spoken with Ilda, without, in the least, becoming more intimate than on the first acquaintance. The earnestness of her disposition, and her retiring nature, remained the same, and prevented any familiar intercourse. Monosyllabic answers were given to all his inquiries; she quietly listened to his narrations, with but little comment, and only, sometimes, when Marstrand expressed an opinion, could he observe any particular interest on her part.

"By heavens!" said he, as he for hours paced the deck, "it is uncomfortable to be in the society of this iron-hearted maiden. If 'silence is the charm of women,' as the old Greeks insisted, she would fill up their *beau ideal*. Her eye is motionless, and not a feature of her countenance changes, and yet she is intelligent. There is always something in her remarks which excites attention, but in the next moment, my dislike to her increases."

As he now, in his dazzling red coat, stood before her, he flattered himself that his stately figure and costume could not fail to make an impression upon her. He did not exactly know why he should seek to please her; and he felt vexed, when he saw her so complacently look at him, from her seat, and then resume her work.

Marstrand passed by her in dumb silence to the door, from which, as he opened it, he turned and said: "Adieu, Miss Ilda."

"Are you going to Tromsöe?" said she.

"I am to present my land patent to the voigt. It may be that I shall remain there."

"Farewell, Herr! God's peace accompany you!"

Marstrand, nettled at this cool salutation, bounded up the steps, with the firm intention of remaining at Tromsöe. Helgestad, who was on deck awaiting him, wrapped up in his leather coat, laughed outright as he espied the Dane. "Nuh!" he exclaimed, "St. Olaf protect us. You look like a boiled lobster. You will, no doubt, be glad when you can again lay aside this foolish embroidered coat; and we shall, therefore, settle our business with Voigt Paulsen as soon as possible. You must, however, throw something over it; otherwise, we shall have all the boys at our heels, who will think that Niels Helgestad has caught a wild man in the woods, for exhibition."

With a hearty burst of laughter, he descended to the boat, whilst the yacht lazily furled her sail, and came to anchor close under the land. Marstrand followed him, and the boat was soon rowed to the landing, where a crowd of laborers, fishermen, and custom-house officers had gathered.

Helgestad was well known in this, then the northernmost emporium of trade in Europe. His yacht was the first to return from the fishing-grounds, and she was hailed with shouts of joy. Everybody pressed upon him with inquiries, and expressed their gratification at the news with a triple hurrah, in which Lapps, Quanes, and Normen all joined. The whole throng then accompanied the trader, who took his companion by the arm, to where a semi-circle of houses of better appearance, of which one was the voigt's, stood.

Tromsöe at that period did not, as now, possess municipal privileges; but it was the first mart and lading-place of Finnmark, although it contained a population of only 600 persons. Finnmark, also, had no Amtmann; but the Voigt of Tromsöe was the highest magistrate, and his authority extended from Lofodden to the North Cape, a coast-land of one hundred miles; he received tribute from the Lapland tribes, and granted permits of settlement to the Quanes or Finlanders, who wandered over from the shores of the Gulf of Bothnia; throughout this whole region, he exercised police functions, and administered justice. The Voigt of Tromsöe was, consequently, a royal governor, stadtholder, and supreme judge — an important, influential person, whose services were compensated, not so much by a large salary, as by extraordinary sources of income: his favor was, also, rarely to be gained but by large gifts.

"Now, let me look to it," said Helgestad, with a sly wink, as he pushed Marstrand up the steps which led to the wooden palace of the voigt. He opened the door, and entered through the vestibule into the sitting-room, leaving his companion to follow him. Marstrand remained standing on the threshold, and surveying the dreary-looking room, whose walls were painted in dark red oil colors. A number of huge chairs, of Norwegian birch, stood around a table full of glasses and bottles, and behind them sat two men, of whom one, in a dark garment, with a care-worn and reverend aspect, and silvery white hair, appeared to be a clergyman. The other, who wore a fur robe of wolf's-skin, was, beyond doubt, the high officer who ruled over Finnmark. His sharp grey eyes glimmered from beneath a low brow, and, from the coppery red of his nose and cheeks, it was evident that the punch-glass before him had, in the course of the year, been plied with persevering assiduity.

As Helgestad opened the door, the voigt looked up. "Is it you?" exclaimed he, with a loud, hard voice. "You are welcome, Niels! You come from Lofodden. It is a lucky year, which will fill your pockets with gold."

"God grant it!" said the trader, shaking hands with the voigt.

"Have you seen my nephew, Niels?" he continued.

"Certainly, Voigt; and my Ilda danced with him until day-break. He is an active, good-humored fellow. I like him much."

"Sit down, friend Niels. Take a glass of punch, and try my Holland canaster.

"I think you and the parson have already given it a thorough trial," said Helgestad; "the house is so full of smoke, that I can hardly recognise his reverence."

"No, no!" said the voigt, smiling. "Klaus Hornemann will not touch the smoking weed. He differs from all other parsons, who never let a full glass stand before them. You know him, Niels. But," observing Marstrand, "whom have you brought with you."

"It is a Danish Herr," replied the merchant, "who has business in the land. He came with me from Lofodden, where he contracted a friendship with your nephew, and is here to pay his uncle a visit."

"You are welcome in my house," said the voigt, who, when in his visitor he recognized an officer, and, in the further course of conversation, learned that he was a gentleman of the bed-chamber, and of ancient, noble stock, felt himself greatly complimented. With Norman hospitality, he insisted on his eating and drinking with him; but his cordiality evidently cooled off, as Helgestad said; "I think you will often see the gentleman, and drink many a hot glass with him. He will remain in the country, and has brought a royal letter with him. Nuh! you wish him good-luck in the affair; is it not so?"

The voigt measured the young lord with mistrustful eye. "By heavens! I would not have believed such to be his intention. It is a hard undertaking for white hands. Have you devised a plan, Herr Marstrand, to begin with?"

The younker looked at his friend, who made a slight sign of negation.

"I have no plan, Herr Voigt," he replied; "and I am entirely unacquainted with the state of things."

The voigt regarded him with a greedy, searching look, "Where is your donation letter?" he inquired.

"Here is the original," responded Marstrand, as he drew it from his pocket.

"Shall select such land as suits him," muttered the voigt, reading; "also trading-posts establish, and carry on trade and fishing. It is a wonder our masters in Copenhagen do not give all the land away," he rejoined, smiling; "they are very common, these donation letters." He scrutinised Marstrand, and said, "Has my nephew, Paul, also read it?"

"Certainly he has," replied Helgestad, in Marstrand's place, "he read it twice."

"And what did he say?"

"He desired me to visit him in Tromsöe, and to ask your advice," replied Marstrand, impatiently.

"With all my heart, Herr Marstrand," said the voigt; "we will consider it maturely—I will give it all my study. There are, however, many kinds of donation letters, and we have also laws and prescriptions, which must be observed. At present, every one insists upon his pretensions, and even the Lapps have their claims. About this very matter, Helgestad, pastor Hornemann comes to Tromsöe. He complains that the people are maltreated by traders and law-officers, who take their old pasture-grounds, and, moreover, rob, exact illegal taxes, plunder, despoil, vex, and trample their rights under foot. I have too much trouble with other people, to annoy myself with such scoundrels, who set all law and order at defiance."

"You do the poor, harassed people injustice," replied the pastor, in a mild tone. "God created them as well as us; and if we are superior to them in education and manners, we have a double duty to help them. Our holy religion commands me, in the name of humanity and justice, to intercede for them."

"For Christians, do what you please, Herr," exclaimed the voigt; "convert also on my account these reindeer-drivers from the worship of Jubinal and Pekel, but do not make yourself the ambassador of the old villain Afraja, who is one of the veriest scamps that ever trod on reindeer-leather. There is no greater plague in all Finnmark, than this vicious and depraved race."

These last words Herr Paulsen directed to Marstrand, who, unmoved by his rude remarks to the pastor, for whom he had conceived a high regard, responded, in a decided tone; "They are subjects of the king, Herr Voigt, and it certainly is the intention of his Majesty, that no injustice should be committed, even against the most humble, be he Christian or heathen, Dane, Norman, or Lapp."

The voigt was evidently astonished at the tone of the speaker, and his eyes glowed with a vindictive and malicious expression. "I have a word to say to you, voigt," said Helgestad, interrupting.

He took the letter from the table, and led Paulsen to the farthest corner, by a window, where he began a whispering conversation with him. From the few disjointed words that reached him, Marstrand could not doubt but that Helgestad was endeavoring to persuade the voigt to a recognition of the patent, to its registration, and to the granting of permission for the selection of the land he desired.

What arguments he advanced were, of course, unknown to him; but that his protector spared no kind of inducement which could influence the voigt, was evident from the zeal with which he sought to overcome the apparent reluctance of the latter to accede to his request. At last, Helgestad seemed to have prevailed, for he took the voigt by the hand, and said, half aloud; "I think you know me, voigt—you may rely upon me—I will be responsible."

"Good, Niels," said the voigt; "I will do the Herr the favor —but it is also a duty to act with circumspection. I should, above all things, wait for my nephew Paul, who understands the question. Come in my office, and we will settle the affair on the spot."

Both withdrew, and when they had gone, the pastor pressed the hand of Marstrand. "Receive my thanks for your kind word; it does my heart good to know a man who raises his voice in behalf of the oppressed."

"It requires more than a word," replied the Dane; "and I fear no one here has the disposition to sustain your noble zeal."

"You are right, my young friend," said the pastor, with a sigh. "Alas! there are but few men in this country who do not curse and despise the unfortunate races of people who live among us, in a wild and savage state; but there are some good souls, into whose hearts heaven has infused love and compassion. You are to live among us; promise me always to be a protector and intercessor between the oppressed and their oppressors."

"I cheerfully promise it," said Marstrand, "for I abominate injustice."

"And I," continued the pastor, smiling, "for forty years have labored to awaken a feeling of justice and Christian love among these hard rocky wastes."

"As the Voigt of Tromsöe, himself, has so little sense of right, there can be but little reliance placed upon his protection of those subjected to his rule," responded the young man.

"Hush! hush!" whispered Klaus Hornemann, "we will not complain of the weaknesses of mankind. Nothing is more difficult than a contest with the prejudices of the age: and are there not many outcasts on earth? Do not millions suffer on account of bitter wrong? Did not the purest and best of mortals expire upon the cross? The time will come, when men will grow better — when they will earnestly seek for truth and light. We must strive to lead them thither; that is our task."

Here the conversation was interrupted by the entrance of the voigt and Helgestad; and, with as much courtesy as he was master of, Herr Paulsen went up to Marstrand, and delivered him a sealed paper.

"I have recognised the justice of your request, Herr Marstrand, and the letter of his Majesty has been entered in the Register. Permission is granted you to choose at will the land assigned to you; as soon as you have made a selection, a deed of possession shall be made out. And now, as much luck, Herr Baron, as you can desire. Should you need counsel, come to Tromsöe. You are, however, in the best hands. Niels Helgestad will supply my place; you could not find a more prudent man."

His eye turned from Marstrand to the old trader, who silently took his hat, and, at the same time, swung off a full glass. "Pour on, voigt!" he exclaimed. "A ship in a storm knows not whether she will ever reach port again; let every one keep his eyes open against rocks and shoals; and now let us drink to the fulfilment of all our wishes."

"Right, Niels," shouted Paulsen, heartily; "may all our wishes be fulfilled. Will you not stay with me?"

"No, voigt, it is impossible."

"Go, then, with God's blessing! Remember me to Miss Ilda; I will bet that Paul is not absent long. The beautiful girl! she turns the heads of all the young men. You are particularly fortunate, Herr Marstrand, to travel in such society; but take care of your heart, Herr, it is a ticklish thing to manage. Another glass, Niels, to the health of Miss Ilda. Ten thousand devils! yet another; Paul would not forgive us, if we forgot to toast Ilda."

The voigt would receive no refusals of compliance with his request; but, at last, his guests rising to depart, he accompanied them to the head of the steps, and stood shouting after them, in the darkness of the night, greetings to Ilda.

Helgestad, in the meantime, reviewed the store-houses and buildings, and appeared to be buried in thought; finally he said, "Nothing more stands in your way, Herr Marstrand; you could dispose of your affair as you pleased, but it was not your merit that secured the validity of your letter."

"I know how much I am indebted to you," replied Marstrand.

"Nuh!" rejoined the trader, "it was no witchcraft—but you could have obtained it more easily, if you had been more prudent. Who asked you to be an advocate for the Lapps? I think, however, you were excited by the pious Klaus Hornemann, who has had the folly, from youth upward, to lie in the *gamme* with the rabble, to endeavor to make decent, respectable men of them. When you know them, you will see the folly of wasting words with such a clan of thieves and sharpers."

The boat was again alongside of the yacht, and now, as he again mounted the ladder, a thought of Ilda came over the Dane. He did not wait for old Helgestad, but he bounded forward to the poop cabin, and lightly descended the steps, and looked through the half-opened door. The young girl sat at her work, but the needle rested in her hand. Her fingers were closed; silently, in deep meditation, she communed with her thoughts, and this melancholy earnestness gave her countenance a noble and more beautiful expression. The noise at the door aroused her, and, as she looked up, she saw him standing there.

A semblance of joy illumined her features, and, as he extended her his hand, he felt, as he thought, a slight tremor. "Here am I again," he exclaimed, "and right glad am I to see you."

She looked at him with a smile, as if she wished to discover the truth. "I am as glad as you," she answered.

"And, as I think, I shall not soon again leave you," he continued. "My land patent is admitted—your father has procured its registration. I am at liberty to select my land, and to build my house where I please. It will be in your neighborhood, if you do not object."

"You know we all bear you good-will," she rejoined

"How strange I find myself in this red and golden dress," continued he. "Your father is right—it is hot and uncomfortable The fur coat and the leathern cape, that is the costume which becomes me; and I impatiently await the time when I can convert this useless sword into a harpoon."

The regard of the maiden grew more friendly as he spoke. A soft glow animated her dark blue eyes, and, with evident sympathy, she replied, "I am glad to hear that, John Marstrand. You will soon accustom yourself to your new country."

"As it seems, I please you more in this leathern jacket than in my embroidered coat."

The cold tranquillity of her disposition immediately took the place of friendship, and, as she resumed her needle, she said; "There comes my father, and he will be surprised to find you in the dazzling coat which, as you say, is annoying to you."

With no little vexation at himself and Ilda, Marstrand withdrew; but as he entered again, clad in his Norwegian jacket, he was heartily received by Helgestad. Ilda had, in the meantime, arranged the table, and while the yacht, with a fresh breeze, was driven along in the moonlit night, the voyagers sat up late together; for Helgestad constantly kept alive the attention of Marstrand with his many and curious anecdotes.

It was not merely accidental, also, that he fell into conversation about his domestic affairs, and it in some degree confirmed what Paul Petersen had said of him. "It is a rare thing to find sound sense and talent among men, and there are few who seriously ponder upon their conduct — many thoughtlessly run to ruin. Nuh! every man has his peculiarities; it would be to me the greatest earthly sorrow, to live to see my children frivolous and wasteful."

Ilda raised her head, and gazed at her father inquiringly.

"Nuh!" he continued, "I am sure nothing of the kind will occur. I have trained them up to good morals and obedience; I will never permit anything to the contrary. I have frankly declared my principles. Last year, a man came to me—he was a gallant fellow, I must confess, knew how to drive a speculation, and had some bottom. 'Look at me, Niels Helgestad,' said he; 'am I not a proper man for your daughter?' 'Do you think so?' I asked, 'I do,' said he. 'And I do not,' I replied. 'Wherefore?' he responded. 'I will tell you,' I rejoined; and I conducted him to the window, showed him, in silence, my yachts in the fiord, my store-houses there, opened my credit-book, and exhibited its contents, and, unlocking my closets, gave him a glance therein. 'Now you know it,' said I; 'I think you understand.' 'I understand your meaning,' he replied; 'but what says Miss Ilda?' Thereupon the maiden laughed out, and said; 'My father has calculated well; he knows me, and what is suitable for me.' Is it not so, Ilda?"

"Precisely so, father," responded Ilda; "and I think it will always be so."

As the moon had set, the yacht anchored in a sound; for it is impossible, even for the most experienced pilots, to steer a foot in the darkness in these rocky mazes.

Marstrand lay a long time in a sleepless state upon his bed, reflecting upon what he had heard. "If, indeed," thought he, "that was intended as a hint to me, it has not fallen upon stony ground. I will, henceforward, relieve this calculating beauty from her scruples. It would, surely, be madness for me to deprive myself of the confidence of the only friends that I possess."

He awoke late in the morning: it was bright day, and over his head the bustle had already begun. He jumped up, hurried on his clothes, and entered the cabin, without finding any one there. He then repaired to the deck, where he arrived just in time to see the vessel enter a broad bay, at the end of which, between some low rocks, a yacht and several boats lay at anchor; before them was a large store-house, built on piles over the water.

Ilda stood on the bow, and gave him a friendly nod as he approached. "You have slept too long, or you would have seen the Lyngenfiord. Far in the distance there, you can yet see the church of Lyngen; and yonder tumbles the Snibotsjok, with its feathery foam of water, from the Lapland mountains."

"And there, behind the rocky point, no doubt, lies your father's house?"

"You have guessed aright," said she; "it is the Gaard von Ostvaagoen. Does it please you?"

The Dane regarded the jagged walls of rock, which heaved up their splintered, and ice and snow-covered precipices. Above lay the snow, and higher rose the lofty peaks, shooting up in dazzling lines, and breaking away into vast plains of ice. He gave no answer.

"You will find it beautiful in summer," said Ilda, "when the birches everywhere put on their green livery, when grass and flowers surround our little brook, and the brown Ptarmigen come down from the mountains."

At this moment the yacht doubled the promontory, and revealed the house of the trader, close at hand. It lay behind some store-houses, upon rising ground, between a birch wood and the mountain which formed a crescent around it. Painted red, with white windows, a dozen small birchen and clay huts alongside, and in front a great warehouse, it made quite an imposing appearance. From its birch-wood roof, a large flag waved in welcome of the lord of the house; and, as the yacht drew near to the pile wharf, a loud hurrah arose from the ships and boats. All the inhabitants and dependents of the Gaard threw themselves into boats, and rowed to meet the long-wished-for, home-returning vessel. In a few minutes more, a dozen women and children clambered up the sides on deck; and Marstrand thought he had never seen such extraordinary human figures as these, which, like so many demons, overran the ship.

They were the families of the fishermen who had gone to Lofodden, and who now, with riotous shouts, hailed the return of their fathers and husbands. Long, yellow, and shaggy hair almost covered over their strong, bony faces; fur jackets and coats enveloped their bodies. The men of Gaard, in their leathern capes and fur caps, and the sailors, in their huge caps and brown jackets, made up a variegated maze of figures, which did not settle into order until the yacht was brought to at the pile-work, and all had time tranquilly to recount their adventures. Helgestad had enough to do in giving the necessary orders, and in listening to the reports of his steward, who was the most important person in the crowd. Miss Ilda was greeted and occupied by others, and Marstrand followed their steps in silence. Inquiring, curious glances fastened upon the stranger, but no one troubled himself further about him — and the deep guttural tones of this wild population, almost incomprehensible by him, completed the sense of abandonment which he felt. Near to the house, his roving eyes directed themselves upon an object which aroused his interest. Ilda's loud voice was heard above the din, calling to a young girl, who hurriedly ran down the steep ground, threw her arms about Ilda's neck, and covered her with kisses and embraces.

"God's peace be with you, Gula!" said the daughter of the trader, as the first storm of caresses was over. "How have you been?"

"Very well, my beloved sister," she responded, with renewed tenderness; "and are you all well — and Björnarne?"

"All well, Gula! Björnarne comes with the yacht. There was a great catch, Gula, and we have had much pleasure. No cask is empty. I do not come alone, also," she continued, as she turned her regards to Marstrand, by her side. "We bring a guest, a Danish gentleman, who has come to take up his abode among us."

Gula observed the stranger with a scrutinising stare. Her large black eyes glowed with surprise, until she modestly withdrew them, and her face became suffused with a deep blush. Marstrand himself was also not a little astounded; he had formed an entirely different idea of the Lapland maiden, from the reports of others. The Normans gave such frightful accounts of all that bore the name of Lapps, that it was almost impossible to conceive a member of this unhappy race to be anything else than a forlorn, monkey-like creature, whose ugliness was calculated to excite the most profound disgust; Gula gave the lie to all these prejudicial accounts. She was small, yet uncommonly elegant in shape, and of perfect proportions. Her dark robe fitted tightly around the waist, where it joined the boddice, which, in plaits, rose up high on the neck. Over it she wore a jacket of fine otter-skin, which was trimmed with the white feathery skin of Norwegian strand-birds. A chain of medals encircled her neck, and her shining black tresses, bound round with dark red ribbon, floated loosely over her shoulders. Such was the pleasing picture of a beautiful young girl, upon whom one gazed with delight, and whose small, fine face, with sparkling eyes, was, in spite of a yellowish skin, so well formed, and so admirably proportioned in all its features, that no one could refrain from regarding her as a most lovely and fascinating person.

"Ha!" said Ilda, laughingly, as she accompanied her friend to the house, "you have put on your Sunday attire to-day."

"In your honor, Ilda," she answered, "and because I thought Björnarne would come with you; Björnarne and your father, in short, all, all."

"Father is here," said Helgestad, catching the remark. "God bless you, my little maiden; you are dressed out like a swallow. It's a pity that Paul Petersen cannot see you now—he would no more jest about you. Nuh!" he continued, as he shook Marstrand by the hand, "you are welcome to Gaard von

Orenaes, Herr; and now let us enter, and see what Gula has upon the table. You must be hungry and thirsty—a fresh wind is blowing from the Horfjeld cliffs."

He pushed his guest before him into the house, and they entered a large, low room, where a spread table was standing. Gula ran into the kitchen, and brought in a smoking dish, in which a great piece of meat swam in a vegetable soup. Next were introduced salmon and haddock; also German potatoes, such as were brought by the yachts from Bergen. In a large basket lay thin, hard slices of oat-bread, and on the corner of the table were full bottles of gin, which the distilleries in Flensburg prepared for the traders of Finnmark.

Helgestad and his companions devoted themselves so zealously to all these good things, that but few words were spoken during the repast. As the landlord, however, after rendering thanks to God for restoring him in health and plenty to Lyngenfiord, raised his glass, the conversation grew more animated, and it naturally soon turned upon Marstrand's future prospects.

"You will learn here," said Helgestad, "the domestic life of a Norwegian merchant — you are in a good school. It will be well, also, until Björnarne returns, for you to assist me in all kinds of affairs—in pressing oil, in the ware-house, and also in selling and trading with the fishermen and the neighbors. You will, in this manner, learn to calculate, and it will be of service to you."

"I am willing to learn, and you cannot give me too much to do," said Marstrand.

"Nuh!" rejoined Helgestad, "you are a capital fellow, and it will go better than you imagine. When Björnarne returns, we will speak further. We must now see after the yacht, unload the barrels, and bring the livers under the presses. It is hard work, but it must be done; nothing is effected in this world without an effort."

Marstrand declared that he was ready, and he was soon hard at work, with Helgestad, in the ware-house. Some dozen and more of women and children turned the barrels out of the hold of the vessel, brought their contents under the oil-presses, and carried what was not immediately necessary into the store-house. Marstrand did not want in zeal or courage to prosecute the detested employment. But it was, as Helgestad had said, much easier than he had conceived. The old trader initiated him into the mysteries of his business, and instructed him how the clear white liver oil must be first drained off, then how the first pressing must be separated from the second, and how much higher price could be commanded in the sale, if proper discretion and care was exercised. After such a long spell of inactivity, labor was a real enjoyment for the young man, and he felt much stronger and more cheerful for it. The heavens hung clear and blue over the dusky fiord, which lost itself, in mysterious indistinctness, among its precipitous crags. Fresh breezes blew from the snowy summits, the fish leaped from the sea, and the shrieking grey gulls swarmed around the vessels.

As long as it was day, the work was vigorously prosecuted, and terminated only when the lights of Gaard shone through the twilight. The yacht was unladen, and Helgestad good-naturedly shook his fellow-laborer by the hand.

"Nuh!" he exclaimed, "enough for to-day. It is more comfortable now by the stove, glass in hand."

They proceeded to the house, and entered the hall which divided the rooms on either side. The one side was the shop of the trader, which was filled with a great variety of stores. Helgestad introduced Marstrand within it, and showed him the angling-rods and fishing-tackle, together with the clothing and utensils used by fishermen and hunters. The large chests were filled with flour and vegetables; iron-ware, cups, pots, and the most diverse kinds of things were huddled together on the shelves — hemp-lines, table and bed linen, thread, ribbon, and female finery were heaped up with fur-skins, scissors, hatchets, and arms; and, in short, there was nothing of utility in the country that was not to be found in this motley collection.

"It is such a shop as ought to be," said the trader, "and you can take a lesson from it. We will take care that you have such an assortment in your house."

Marstrand smiled doubtingly. He could not yet conceive that he would wait on Lapps and fishermen, but he suppressed all scruples. Helgestad carried him further through the side-rooms, and showed him even the great brown-stained walnut bureau which he had brought with him, two years previously, from Bergen, and gave an insight into the drawers, where a large quantity of money was kept. At last, after making the round of the building, in which Helgestad led the way without a light, and steering through a maze of chests, sacks, and barrels, they returned to the sitting-room. This was exceedingly snug and comfortable. The beams were covered over with laths, painted in blue and white stripes; the floor of Norwegian pine-wood, was perfectly white and clean. A sort of carpet of reindeer-skin lay near the fire-place, where stood chairs and tables. Around the walls ran ledges, upon which an array of tin vessels, burnished bright as silver, were arranged in long rows, and under this border, verses and extracts from Scripture were painted by an artistical hand. A pair of party-colored bureaus, and large chests, bound with brass, in which the women bring their dowry in marriage, a Holland looking-glass, in gilt frame, and an old English clock, together with a huge brick stove, made up the furniture of the side-wall.

Helgestad stretched himself out at full length in his grandfather's chair, and insisted upon Marstrand's sitting opposite to him. "Push the table here, girls," said he to Ilda and Gula, "we are tired men, who have need of food and drink, and warmth."

The table was soon placed alongside of the stove, meat was served up, and Gula brought the tea-kettle, and prepared tumblers full of toddy. She perfectly understood her duty; she performed her functions of cup-bearer, moreover, in such a taking, friendly manner, ran hither and thither with such light-footed readiness and good-nature, that Marstrand was equally gratified and surprised. Her dark eyes twinkled roguishly, as Helgestad, from time to time, extended her his empty glass; and whilst Ilda sat spinning wool, she whispered remarks in her ear, which were certainly very amusing, for the serious maiden turned away her face from irrepressible laughter, and would hear no more.

"Nuh!" said the old merchant, when hunger and thirst seemed to be appeased, "you have come to a pause, Herr Marstrand—you might as well fill up your time in another manner." He beckoned to Gula, who perfectly understood what he meant, for she flew to a cupboard, and immediately returned with a small porcelain box, and two Holland clay-pipes.

"Voigt Paulsen will find himself mistaken, in supposing that he alone possesses the genuine weed. This is pure Virginia; fill your pipe and empty your glass. Gula, the poor child, has been on the run for a quarter of an hour."

Marstrand reached his tumbler to the ready maiden, saying, "You are altogether too attentive, dear Gula; no king was ever so elegantly and perfectly served by his best page."

"That is merited praise to Gula," continued Helgestad. "It must be confessed that she is an excellent girl; she has managed my house with judgment and sound sense, while we were at the Lofodden." Here he stopped, for what he was on the point of saying, notwithstanding his want of refinement, appeared to him not to be exactly proper; but he continued, in a more moderate tone; "Would it were in my power to prove to you how highly I esteem you—but, I imagine, you know it already. Is it not so?"

"Yes, Herr," answered Gula, softly; and her smiling face shone with a charming expression. "I know that you, and all, love me, and I am sensible of the great gratitude I owe you."

"Nuh!" said Helgestad, "she is a rarity, such as will not again be found in Lapland. The Lapps are the most ungrateful beings God ever created."

"It seems to me," replied Marstrand, "that no particular pains are taken, by rendering them services, to excite their gratitude."

"Oh, ho!" exclaimed the trader, "you have also taken it into your head to praise the people."

"I do not praise them," responded Marstrand; "but why should I scorn and condemn them? As Gula is a daughter of this neglected race, and as she is good and intelligent, why should not many more become such, if good people would take pity on them? God has bestowed the seed of his spirit upon all who bear the name of man; and those who, by cultivation and education, are wiser and better, have a double duty to assist their fellow-men."

An inexpressible gratitude beamed in Gula's eyes. Ilda looked up from her spindle, and attentively regarded the young man; Helgestad, however, sipped at his glass, and observed, with his usual sarcasm; "Nuh! You speak like a preacher, or a man who has the matter at heart; but you will soon change your mind when you know them, and you will not want opportunities. 'Let good enough alone,'" he continued, "we must not lose time. We have here wine and women, but music is wanting, and that we must have also. Bring your guitar, Gula, and show the Herr that all the good voices are not confined to Copenhagen."

Gula ran to the next room, and quickly returned with a guitar of the simplest kind. Five cords were stretched over the curved neck of the instrument, whose threads were fastened, in an imperfect manner, around the music-hole. It was beaten with a wooden wand, and the tones elicited, by their softness, produced quite a pleasing effect.

"Sing us The Praise of the North," said Helgestad, as Gula laid the guitar in the lap of her friend.

Ilda, with ready compliance, put aside her spindle, and then began one of those deep-toned, long-resounding, popular melodies, which celebrate the beauty, grandeur, and wild majesty of Norway. The sea, the rocks, the forests, the water-falls, and the free life of the shepherds, hunters, and fishermen filled up the strophes, each of which terminated with a passionate laud of the glorious old Norman land. Helgestad beat time with his glass, and, with the last strophe, all joined in the song, and closed it with a loud hurrah for Norway.

"That is a song," exclaimed Helgestad, "the like of which no people on earth possess; for none possess such a country as Norway. Nuh! Ilda sings like a genuine Norman maiden, for she has a sympathetic heart in her breast. Is it not so?"

Marstrand expressed his assent, which Helgestad received with paternal pride. "You are a judge," said he, "but you might travel all Finnmark through without hearing such singing."

"Has not Gula, also, learned to sing, from such an instructress?" inquired Marstrand.

"You shall hear what a maiden knows, who springs from a people without three tones in their throat. Let us hear one of your songs, Gula; a true Lapland song, such as is heard in the Kilpisjaure, when the reindeer are driven home at evening."

Gula whizzed the wand over the chords, and her soft voice hurriedly hummed a chant of unknown words. By degrees, her features grew more animated, her dark eyes wandered inquiringly around, her breast heaved with emotion, and her sharp-sounding tones trembled and wavered, and, at last, she suddenly ceased, the wand fell from her hand, and, with sunken head she glared wildly about her.

"What ails you?" sympathisingly asked the guest.

"It is nothing," said Helgestad, complacently draining his glass. "She has sung to you of the brown herds, how they lie reclining under the birch trees, and the springs, where the wild-fowl scream, and the wind rushes through the branches, how the calves leap and lick the hands, and how the grandmother sits by the fire, stirring the broth. It is a kind of poetry which prevails all over the wilderness, Herr Marstrand, where the reindeer wanders, and the hut of the Lapp is found; were he a thousand miles away, and in a king's palace, its sounds would arouse a Laplander to his inmost core, and excite a longing for the free and roving life of his native mountains."

"Where is the man," exclaimed Marstrand, with excitement, "who does not cling, with mysterious affection, to the land of his birth?"

"But enough for to-day," said Helgestad, "you must be tired, and I will conduct you to your chamber." Thereupon he led his guest to the upper story, where, in a small, neat room, a bed stood against the farther wall. "Sleep in peace," said the trader; "I think you will find it soft enough. Look, the girls have given you a bed stuffed with the feathers of a thousand pair of eider-down ducks, such as a prince could scarcely procure."

Marstrand sank deep in the elastic down, which closed up around him, and he soon fell into a deep sleep, from which he awoke only when the clear sun-light broke through the little windows, and lighted up the browned rafters of the chamber.

CHAPTER IV.

As this first day was passed in Orenaes, so followed many others, with the same interchange of labor and rest. From morning till eve, active industry prevailed in the ware-houses and yachts, but, at night, the family re-assembled around the great stove, where all kinds of tales and anecdotes were related, many of which interested Marstrand much.

The Gaard or court of the old Helgestad was surrounded by a dozen clay huts, occupied, in part, by the families of the Norman fishermen, and Quanes or Finnland emigrants, all of whom were dependent upon the trader, and constituted his immediate vassals. They, as well as all the dwellers on this deep arm of the Lyngenfiord, gave to Helgestad what they took in the fishery and chase, and received from him, in exchange, clothing, flour, brandy, angling-rods, and whatever else they had need of. Every one had his account in the huge debtors'-book, down to the close of the fishery at Lofodden, when the yearly settlement was regularly made. This time had now arrived, and Marstrand, who, for his rank, was unusually ready in writing and reckoning, under Helgestad's supervision, prepared the accounts of the fishermen, and was thus introduced to a knowledge of the details of the trade. What each one received from the shop stood upon one side, and upon the other was inscribed the credit for the articles delivered. A high price was exacted for all wares, and the profit was, of course, large; the price for the fish, fixed by a commission of fishermen and merchants at Lofodden, was so low, that the most could scarcely keep out of debt, many remained in arrears, and not a few were obliged to borrow, which, however, was not paid in money, but carried to their account.

"I see," said Helgestad, "that you are surprised at this mode of dealing; but there would be no traffic in Finnmark, were it not so. The fishing folk should never have money in hand, because they would cease to labor. I warn you also, Herr Marstrand, to look to it, that whoever is once in your debt, does not get out of it, unless you will trust him no more, because he is growing old and infirm, and cannot, therefore, buffet the storms and catch fish."

"But I observe some on your book," replied Marstrand, "who are free from debt, and have something to their credit."

"Nuh!" responded the trader, slyly; "a week will not elapse, before they are again in my hands. Upon their return from the Lofodden, they are reckless, and lead a rollicking life. There is, moreover, a rule and custom among us, that no trader must lend to a fisherman who deals with another. No one can take him up, unless his previous creditor permits it; look around upon the sounds and fiords, and little fishing-stations, with their huts, and a pair of acres of land and meadow; they are all in our hands. We have either bought them, and leased them to the people who reside there, or we have lent money on them, and could eject the tenants at any time we chose. We could sell their cow, take their boat, and reduce them to such absolute misery and poverty, that no alternative would be left them but a leap into the sea."

"And this, probably, is no rare occurrence," said the young nobleman.

"Nuh!" grunted Helgestad, "as long as a man can work, there is a possibility of discharging his debts; and while there is such a prospect, no trader would rashly put a rope about the neck of a good customer. Every one who is wise will look after his property, and, where he perceives danger, lend no further, and, when the proper time has arrived, will invoke the interposition of the sorenskriver."

"In this manner," said Marstrand, whose sense of justice was excited, "the fishermen and laboring people must be perfectly drained, and without ever being able to escape from their wretchedness."

Helgestad regarded him with a sullen stare. "You speak like a fool," said he; "in saying that the traders are the scourge of the country. Were you a merchant, you would open your eyes, and confess that it cannot be otherwise. The fishermen and coast-people, Normans, Quanes, and Danes, must all be our servants; they must all be kept in a state of dependence and poverty, otherwise we could not exist. It is a fact, Herr. He who does not understand the art of so reckoning, that nothing remains to these lazy, improvident people, and of unsparingly dealing with them, when nothing more is to be had from them, had better not engage in the trade."

It was evident to Marstrand that he must remain silent—and what objections had he, indeed, to urge? Helgestad was neither better nor worse than the other merchants. All had the same aim, and defrauded alike; but these fishermen, hunters, and shepherds also formed a savage, idle, and rude mass, who were only impelled to labor by hunger, from the cradle to the grave.

Amid this continual activity, Sunday arrived, and Marstrand was rejoiced to be able to pass this day of rest free from the cares of traffic and the account-books. On the previous evening, as he came up from the fiord, he met Gula at the door, who gave him a friendly greeting.

"You have toiled late," said she; "but to-morrow you will have, in recompense, a glad Sunday."

"Is there a dance?" asked he, in jest.

"A dance! Heaven defend us, Herr!" was the answer. "We do not often dance in Orenaes Gaard. You must go to church."

Marstrand turned to observe the arm of the sea, over whose misty veil the high summits of the little church of Lyngen were visible in the distance. "Heavy ice-flakes are drifting in the fiord, and we shall have a storm. I prefer to remain at home by the fire."

"You are a pious man, with a truth," replied Gula, jocularly. "Miss Ilda will teach you better. There is to be a thanksgiving at church, at which all must be present."

"Do you accompany us, also?"

"I? No," was her laughing reply. "I am not the child of one who possesses yachts and trading-posts. I stay at home; yet, if you will pray for me, I will keep the fire bright for your sake."

"You are a little heathen, as I observe," said Marstrand; "who leaves the church to take care of itself, and rather sits by the hearth at home."

"When you come back at noon," said she, "and if the day is favorable, I will lead you to a beautiful little spot, whence there is an extensive view over land and sea, in clear weather."

"I shall hold you to your word," he cried after her, as Gula sprang into the house, upon seeing Helgestad open the door and look out.

Miss Ilda sat by the table sewing her father's silk vest, but Helgestad held in his hand the new broad-brimmed hat which Björnarne had brought him from Trondheim.

"I am thinking of you," he said to the young man, "and our visit to church. Pastor Sture will preach us a famous thanksgiving sermon for the rich fishery at Lofodden, and you must accompany us, Herr Marstrand. You see that the people are all gathering from near and far. It is necessary that you get acquainted with them as much as possible."

The invitation was not to be refused, and, the whole evening through, the church festivity formed the topic of conversation. The next morning, while it was yet dark, the wooden building echoed again with the voices and tread of the joyous people; and Marstrand had scarcely dressed himself, before he was summoned to breakfast, and urged to make haste.

He had put on his best attire. A green frock-coat, with gold lace, such as was then worn by gentlemen in society in Copenhagen, fitted tightly around his slender waist, and over it he had thrown the short jacket of blue fox-skin which Helgestad had bought for him. His dark blond hair, loosely bound by a ribbon, fell in rich ringlets over his shoulders; and his appearance, even to the boots, was so pleasing, that Helgestad himself regarded him with admiration.

"Nuh!" he exclaimed, "you understand how to put on your things. The maidens of Koofiord and of Aloen will look at you more than the pious Heinrick Sture, though he should shake the rafters with his eloquence. I think I am right. Is it not so, Ilda?"

Miss Ilda, in her high, black woollen dress, feather jacket, and fur cap, which rested coquettishly upon the side of her head, turned to the young nobleman, and nodded to him, with a smile. "I think so, father," she replied; "and Herr Marstrand will, no doubt, not take it amiss, if the young girls should forget the parson to look at him."

Helgestad laughed outright, in which Marstrand also joined; but Ilda's words carried with them a reproof, which he evidently felt, mildly as it was expressed. He helped the severe maiden into the eight-oared boat in waiting, which lay at the foot of the landing, and answered somewhat bluntly her inquiries as to whether he sat comfortably, and if his feet were well wrapped up in the fur.

The morning was dark and damp; the north-west wind drove into the fiord from the sea, bringing with it an icy-cold mist, and huge cakes of ice, rushing against each other, broke to pieces. Helgestad stood at the helm, and eight men plied the oars. A number of common people, with their wives, cowered upon the low seats; but before the rudder-head, where there was the most space, cushions and coverings, for Miss Ilda and the Danish Herr, had been placed.

After the stout boat, for a long time, had rowed against the wind, and availed herself of the shelter of every projecting rock, Helgestad conducted her in the midst of the high waves of the fiords. The morning twilight, in the meantime, disappeared; red clouds rose out of the mist, and, at length, this itself lifted up from the inlet, and a far-penetrating blaze of sun-light broke over the swelling water. This victory of day over night infused cheerfulness among all the passengers, and brought out the surrounding scenery with brilliant effect. The shores were distinctly visible, and the cottages, from which the smoke rose, circling in the air, as well as the church of Lyngen, upon its high rock. The people chatted together, laughed and looked delightedly into the devious windings of the side-channels of the fiords, out of which other boats, large and small, were seen rowing towards the same point as themselves. They were all filled with people. The bright red kerchiefs of the women fluttered gaily in the morning breeze; young fellows sprang upon the seats, and waved their hats and caps. Greetings were exchanged, sallies of wit and raillery were shouted to and fro, and bets were made as to which boat would first arrive at the landing-place.

After two hours' hard rowing, the boat was close on to the church at Lyngen, and Helgestad had just time enough to name the chief families assembled there. The whole aristocracy of traders and proprietors of Gaard, who dwelt in this bundle of sounds and fiords, of which the great Lyngenfiord, as it were, formed the knot, had already arrived, and were standing with their sons and daughters before the church in the sunshine.

It seemed as if the welcomes, inquiries, and shaking of hands would never cease; yet Marstrand was, as he could not fail to be, soon the subject of universal attention. Some had already seen him at Lofodden, and had spread the news into the remotest corner of this wild mountainous coast, that Helgestad would bring with him a stranger, who intended to establish himself in the country. Scrutinizing looks examined him from the crown of his head to the soles of his feet. Aversion and mistrust were expressed on many a face; but the greater part seemed to regard the stranger with a partial eye. Several of the young men took especial pleasure in running jokes on the Dane, and even his boots and coat underwent a sharp criticism; but Niels Helgestad presented him to the richest and most distinguished people with such flattering remarks, that the jokers deemed it prudent to withdraw in silence. "Nuh!" said the proprietor of Orenaes, so loud that every one could hear him, "Herr Marstrand, although a man of rank, has evinced a readiness and good-will in learning his future business such as I have rarely met with."

Such a testimony was sufficient to determine the public judgment in favor of Marstrand. The best people shook him by the hand, invited him to visit them, and inquired as to his views. The young girls found him a desirable person, and became absorbed in the observation of his dress and figure; and the mothers speculated, as all mothers are wont to do, whether they should live in Lapland or Denmark. Secret conjectures were made as to the intentions of Helgestad respecting the Dane and his land-patent. Among the women and maidens there was much question as to the views of Miss Ilda; and whether this proud heiress, for whom no one seemed to be good enough except the nephew of the Voigt of Tromsöe, would give her much-coveted hand to the young nobleman. A full hour elapsed before the parson made his appearance; and during this interval, many worldly affairs were transacted in the porch, and even on the seats of the little weather-beaten, wooden church. Sales and purchases of fish, cattle, oil, and provisions were concluded; bargains of the most various kinds were laughed over, disputed, and drunk; and, in short, it was a gathering of the people for many miles, who availed themselves of this occasion to supply both their spiritual and temporal wants.

Finally, came the pastor of Lyngen; a large, broad-shouldered man, in a leathern coat, lined with green frieze, and a wolf-skin thrown over it. After he had exchanged a dozen hand-shakings, and had complimented ladies and gentlemen, he put on the cope, and ascended the pulpit to deliver an interminably tiresome discourse. He had selected his theme from the fishing of the believer, who, trusting in the word of the Lord, had cast his net, and applied it to the prolific catch of that year, under thanks to a gracious God for the many large and fat fish which, by his command, swam in the Westfiord, there to fall into the hands of so many valiant Norwegian men.

Tired and bored by this monotonous discourse, Marstrand turned his attention from the preacher to the congregation, which he found much more interesting. He could not, in general, gainsay the opinion that a long residence in the inhospitable North, amid ice and bog, and tempests on sea and land, had impaired the beauty and strength of the Norman race. The weather-beaten, leathern-hued complexions, of most of the assembly testified to a continual contest with nature, against which no tender organization could maintain itself, and before

8

which the hardiest and strongest often sank to the ground. Here no one lived for pleasure, and no one could exist but for the fish in the sea. The fishy odor which filled every cottage reeked also through this church; and even the preacher himself, whose red face glowed with the fire of toddy, and whose eyes shone with enthusiasm, as he spoke of the fat fish, seemed to be a genuine worshipper of the great Fetisch, from whom came all the blessings of the land, and to whom all adoration was offered.

Several sprightly young men, with keen, strongly-marked features, distinguished themselves as advantageously among this mass of fish calculators and oil speculators as some young girls who, in their feather jackets and gold pins, were evidently conscious of their charms. Behind them, against the walls of the church, sat the fishermen, with their wives, as motionless as statues, and gazing with a fixed stare from beneath their long, falling hair, straight ahead. Gigantic Quanes, from the islands and the new settlements — ugly, stump-nosed fellows, with small, sparkling eyes — hovered in the corners, together with their wives, in red gowns and flaunting kerchiefs, and hideous, monkey-visaged children, by their sides.

Among all the women, however, in the church, who were modishly equipped in bonnet, cap, and ribbons, bought for them by their fathers and husbands in Bergen, but few could compare with Miss Ilda.

In her black, woollen dress, with her rich hair bound round with a velvet ribbon and fastened by a silver arrow, she was, as she sat by the side of Marstrand, in his opinion, the prettiest maiden in the assemblage. Here, for the first time, where many of her sex were gathered together, he recognised and confessed her superiority; and whether it proceeded from the fact that his eye was, for the first time, opened, never before did her commanding figure, her broad, arched brow, regularly formed face and large mild eyes, appear to him so commendable. He lost the standard of beauty which he formerly held, and received in its stead another in the region in which he was now living.

"Among the blind, the one-eyed is king;" said he, jokingly, to himself. "I shall, however, never be able to persuade myself that Miss Ilda, as she sits there, tall and grand, strong-limbed and motionless of eye, is such a charming being as to set blood and nerves in motion." His thoughts flew from Ilda's cold, severe countenance, to the nimble-footed Gula, revealing, with her pleasant smile, her white teeth, and nodding to him across the grass-plot before the door of the house at Orenaes. Yes, if she had something of the nature of that child, he thought to himself; if the pillar of salt could only move and breathe, life would awaken life.

Meanwhile, the preacher held valiantly on; and at length, as Marstrand congratulated himself he was nearly at an end, the discourse took a sudden turn upon his own personal concerns, and the holy man, in the most strenuous manner, reminded his audience of their obligations and duty to him after so rich a fishery.

"This is the day of offerings!" he shouted, as he thumped the pulpit, "and I advise you also not to be so miserly and niggardly as many among you, for a long time, have been. I will not mention names: you will understand me sufficiently, and will see to it, that I may be able to drink to your prosperity. Think of it, dear friends and neighbors; consider of the great care and trouble I undergo for your sakes, and that I am a Norman of good blood and family, and not a Lapp, who can live on fish-heads and frozen cheese. Search your pockets and bring out what you have designed for me; and if it be too little, add to it, and make it better than the last time, when it was a shame for Lyngenfiord Parish to see with what a light purse I went home. And now, receive the blessing; and I hope you will act properly towards your friend Heinrick Sture."

Marstrand could with difficulty suppress a laugh; and he was surprised to hear an approving grunt from the congregation, and to see that no one took offence at the admonition of the worthy pastor. The money-bag was handed around, and the large thalers rattled together. Every one watched the fingers of his neighbor, and graduated his gift to the like measure. Marstrand observed that quite a rivalry in generosity had sprung up, and he gave full vent to his merriment as he saw Ilda also take out her purse and drop a liberal contribution in the bag, and perceived the grateful nod with which it was hailed by the pastor.

"You have also suffered yourself to be moved by the appeal of the godly Heinrick;" said he, jestingly, as they both left the church.

"Do you think I did wrong?" she asked, with that reproving smile which she had so often manifested to him. "Confess that you are a very frivolous man."

"Frivolous? Wherefore?"

"Did you hear the sermon? Were you not rather peering over all the seats and corners of the church, instead of collecting your thoughts, and meditating on the necessity of God's aid? You break your jests on Heinrick Sture, and you have shown no respect to our opinion. You must know, that it is the custom and law in Norway, three times a-year, to give to the pastor, and that the greater part of his income is derived from this source. You have many trifling and giddy Danish notions yet to lay aside, my dear Herr."

Marstrand endeavored to excuse himself, and Ilda listened good-naturedly, and seemed to be reconciled by his apologies. Some time elapsed before the return voyage was thought of After the Norwegian custom, there stood near the church a number of small cottages, built of heavy planks, and which were designed to afford shelter on bad days, and also a night's rest, on the arising of a sudden snow-storm, or hurricane. The present day, however, was so mild and sunny, that all the families sat together upon the enclosure in front of the church, where the grass sprouted out of the clean earth, and where, with joke and laughter, the breakfast, which all had taken care to bring with them, was eaten with hearty appetite. The young people talked of the fine weather, when visits could be easily made, when the spring festival would be celebrated, and when they could dance, with sun-light, to midnight. The old folks gathered together, and made conjectures upon the issue of the voyage to Bergen, in that year, until finally the last glass was drank; and the boats, with the church-going voyagers, scattered in all directions.

The wind filled the huge sail of the cutter, which Helgestad expanded to its utmost compass, and she shot down the fiord merrily, tossing off the white foam from her bows.

"It was a fine sermon, and a glorious day," said Helgestad, as they got full headway. "Heinrick Sture will rejoice at it. He carries home pockets full of silver, which has not happened to him for a long time. Nuh! lucky for him that the hearts of his hearers were free from apprehensions of storms and snow-blasts; for, in such a state of mind, people give more, as he might discover, were it to-morrow."

He looked up to the sky, which was covered by light strips of cloud, and made a shrewd sign, as if to indicate that he was wiser than many of his neighbors, of whom he now related all kinds of anecdotes, until the boat reached the ware-house of Orenaes. Marstrand helped Ilda up the slippery stone-steps, and both looked around in vain for Gula.

"She has a visitor," said the steward.

"Who?" asked Ilda.

"There he sits at the door," he replied. "You will, no doubt, recognise him, Miss Ilda."

"Afraja!" exclaimed Helgestad. "What is the old rascal after? I could smell him, if I did not see him."

"It is curious, so early in the season," said Ilda. "What can it mean?"

"I do not know," said Helgestad, frowning, and quickening his pace; "but may I be hanged, if the old vermin brings anything good."

As they drew near to the house, Marstrand observed, with much interest, the man whose name he had so often heard. Bent double, and his head bowed deep, the old shepherd sat on a bench by the door. A brown robe of coarse woollen stuff covered his apparently decrepid body, over which he wore an open fur cloak of reindeer-skin, and his cap, of like material, he had taken off and laid upon his knee. His two meagre, sinewy hands clasped a long stick, the sharp iron point of which glistened on the ground. At his feet lay two yellow, shaggy-haired dogs, whose watchful eyes were fastened now upon their motionless master, and then upon the approaching strangers, whom they received with a low growl.

When Helgestad stood close by him, the old Lapp lifted up his head, and an humble friendliness beamed in his weather-beaten face, which was covered with wrinkles and furrowed lines. Half-grown grey hair overspread his low forehead, his nose was of a Mongolian flatness, his teeth unusually long, sharp, and white, like those of a wolf. From beneath the grey mass of hair, which the wind blew about his face, his small eyes flashed like the sun setting in a blood-red glow, but there was something uncommonly artful and lurking in their expression.

The old man rose from his seat, and made a profound bow to the trader. "May peace ever accompany you," said he, in the corrupt Danish of the coast language; "and your days be as joyous as the snow-flakes."

"I accept it," answered Helgestad; "every Christian man needs your greeting, and you have indeed brought it from afar. Your girdle is shrunken from the dampness, and your kommagers have been hardly used." He pointed to the half-boots of reindeer-skin, which Afraja, after the custom of the Finns, had tightly laced around his thin legs. "I have not seen you since the autumn," he continued; "I supposed you to be far in the Jauern."

"You are right, father," returned the Lapp, with an assenting nod "My cattle have pastured in the Tana, and beyond to the great sea."

"And what, by St. Olaf's beard! has driven you through the winter's snow to Lyngenfiord?" exclaimed the astonished merchant. "You must have had a fearful journey. Where are your sleighs and your Pulks?"

Afraja looked up to the mountains, and with a certain pride and dignity, stroked back the thick hair from his face, and replied; "You know that I own many cattle. My nephew, Mortuno, rests with a herd at the spring of Setzjok, which you call Old River. I came to him, to look after my property, and to fix his summer pasturage. From thence, it was not very far to you, father; yet how could you wonder that I have come here, when the bear and the wolf go out in quest of their young? My child lives in your house. I am old and infirm, and my heart yearns after her."

"Your heart?" said Helgestad, laughing. "Have you also a heart, old knave?"

"My heart," replied Afraja, with a stern look, "longs after my child, who is my greatest treasure."

"Nuh!" said the trader, "look after your treasure, then; no harm has happened to her. Stay until to-morrow, if you choose."

Afraja shook his head. "My time is short," said he. Before it is night, I must be far away. Gula shall go with me—I ask her back from you, Herr."

Helgestad regarded the Finn with a fixed and astonished look, for he had formed his resolution. "I see now what you have come for," he angrily answered; "and I anticipated nothing good from your visit. But it cannot be; you have a bad memory, Afraja. You gave me the maiden for a pound of tobacco and three pints of brandy."

"You are a Christian," said the old man, after a moment's pause, supporting himself on his staff. "God sees and hears all things. He knows that I did not sell my child; I let you have her, because you desired it. My *gamme* is desolate," he continued, beseechingly, "my eye is growing dark. I ask you, father Niels, what would you do, if your child were taken away from you?"

"I have no time to listen to your nonsense," exclaimed Helgestad, drawing his fur cap over his brows. "I have taken the maiden from misery, I have made a Christian of her; and I could never answer for it to God and man, if I should again let her return to the wilderness, to live among reindeer, dogs, and a cruel heathen people. It is a fact, I will not tolerate it, on any account. If I fill your Lappish pockets with tobacco, and your brandy-flask to the brim, that will be sufficient, I should think, to pacify you. Is it not so?"

Afraja lifted up his eyes with an angry scorn, and said, with a forced composure; "You know, Niels Helgestad, that I can buy what I need. I have left Gula with you so long as it pleased me, and I now reclaim her. You are reputed to be an honest man. You will not take that which is mine."

"Take what I offer you," responded the trader, "and do not be a fool. Where is the Lapp who would not sell wife and children into service, on the coast, for tobacco and brandy? Gula remains here. That is my last word. You must now depart, or I will force you."

"Have you a right to drive me from your door?"

"Complain to the voigt in Tromsöe," cried Helgestad, contemptuously. "Begone, or I will show you the way."

He went into the house, and left Afraja standing, who, gazing on the ground, did not seem to hear the mediating words of Ilda. "You know," said she, "that I love your child as my sister. What will you do with her on the wild mountains? She would fall sick and die — her life can no longer flourish there. Could you transplant the birch upon the Tjellen of the Kilpis? See, there is Gula. Let her remain with me, where she is contented and happy."

Gula, who, at this moment, was approaching, threw herself

into the arms of her intercessor. Afraja raised his eyes and extended his hands towards her.

"What do you say, maiden?" said he, slowly. "Will you not arise from the hearth of the stranger, and follow your father? Will you not be with him, when he is sick, and calls upon your name?"

With violent emotion Gula pressed her head on Ilda's bosom, and clasped her hands convulsively together, as if she feared to be separated from her by force.

"You see, old man," said Marstrand, moved to pity by this sad scene, "that your daughter prefers to dwell here."

A glance, full of hate and grief, was the response. "Jubinal sits upon his throne of clouds," said Afrajà, in a deliberate and expressive manner, whilst he lifted his eyes to heaven; "he sees and punishes the unjust."

Without a word of parting salutation, he turned away and ascended the rocks, which formed a crescent around the inlet and Helgestad's house, and, in a few minutes, with his following dogs, was lost to view.

"Is he gone?" said Helgestad, putting his head out of the window. "Come in, Herr Marstrand; the dinner awaits you, and must not grow cold on account of a Lapp and his curses."

Grace was said, and whilst the trader praised the culinary skill, docility, and intelligence of Gula, a considerable time elapsed, during which he was almost the only speaker. At length, Marstrand expressed his surprise that the old man had come alone, and without arms.

"Nuh!" said Helgestad, "his snow-staff is a weapon with which he can well defend himself when necessary. You may be sure, however, that he has concealed above there, in some hollow, his guns, sleds, his draught animals, and perhaps a half-dozen or so of scoundrels like himself."

"If the Lapps are such bold, good shots," continued the young Herr, "must not the inhabitants of a solitary Gaard have reason to fear their vengeance?"

"Who?" cried Helgestad, laughing. "We, here, in our houses? Nuh! the miserable people do not know it, but I tell you a Lapp is the more cowardly and cautious, as he is wicked and spiteful. In his mountains he is a master, and he who goes up to him must take heed. Many a one has never been heard of more there. Here below, however, is our kingdom; and we are as secure within it, as a king in his palace."

After the lord of Orenaes had stuffed himself with meat and fish, and drank as much old port as he could well carry, he sought his bed to obtain a blessed sleep. Marstrand remained sitting with the maidens in the room, who conversed together for some time in an under-tone, to which he paid no attention, his regards being directed on the red sun-light which overspread the brows of the high cliffs on the fiord, and gave promise of fine weather. When Gula had gone out, Ilda interrupted his meditations.

"I thought," said she, "that my friend had promised you, if the day were favorable, to accompany you in a walk. If you are willing, go now, Gula awaits you; it would not be right to leave her alone."

"Will you not go with us?"

"No," was her answer. "I have all kinds of things to attend to. Gula will conduct you to a spot which she has called my garden. It is beautiful there; and another time I will accompany you thither. You have no time to lose to-day, if you will return home for evening worship."

Gula stood upon the high rock on the edge of the fiord, and waved her white apron as he came out of the house. "How friendly and confiding," said he, musing to himself, "is this poor maiden in comparison with the monosyllabic Miss Ilda! With every succeeding hour I feel that I must leave Orenaes, and the sooner the better; but whither can I go without the assistance of these people, who are my only friends, and who yet inspire me with distrust?"

"Follow after me!" shouted Gula from the rock to him

below, as he climed upwards. "The way is steep and tiresome, but you will be compensated." When Marstrand arrived at the top, she was already a good piece ahead.

The rocky shore of the fiord rose precipitously to a considerable height, along which ran a rough, narrow path, until it sank, upon the other side, into a ravine, through which a brook rushed along into the sea. The melting snow had already swollen it to some height. It leaped in foam over cliffs and crags, and formed two splendid waterfalls, whose roar and spray filled the air.

"It is an Omnisjok, as we call it," said Gula, who stood by the most beautiful fall, rejoicing at the astonishment of Marstrand. "Do you see the dazzling snowy mountain-peak above there? That is the summit of the Kilpis, whence it descends. You will have a better view by following me; but take care, Herr; for in your country you have never seen such ways."

She bounded nimbly onward, and, despite all his efforts, Marstrand was not able to keep pace with her. It was a fatiguing climb, which Gula did not seem to feel, while the Dane, at last, for want of breath, came to a stand. She came back and gave him her hand. "There," said she, "on the black rocks, are steps leading upwards. Björnarne arranged them. Lean on me, and in a few minutes we shall be on the top."

And so it happened. Over blocks of stone, which formed a natural staircase, Gula led her friend to a small mountain shelf; where, as they passed through a cleft of the rock, a magnificent view suddenly presented itself to the eye. A thousand feet perpendicularly below them lay the fiord, and far beyond, the church of Lyngen. The eye wandered over a curious maze of dark, naked, and snow-glistening rocks, and smooth expanse of water, to the remotest sounds and outermost islands. At their feet they perceived Gaard von Orenaes, its warehouses and clay cottages, with Helgestad's great yachts, all dwindled into Liliputian dwarfishness. Over their heads, on the opposite side, a lofty wall of rock towered upward, whose overhanging crags threatened to fall at any moment.

"They will not fall," said Gula, laughing, as she observed Marstrand's mistrustful glances. "They have hung there since the world was created, and form deep caverns, in which we often find shelter against the wild weather. But look out there, Herr," she continued, pointing to the left; "you can overlook the peninsula which separates the Lyngenfiord from the Ulvsfiord. See how clear its rocks loom up; and there, where the high, sharp peaks rise, comes the Balself, out of deep valleys, full of fine tall trees, bringing pure sparkling water down from the glorious Tanajaure."

"You speak enthusiastically, dear Gula," said Marstrand, with a pleasant smile.

"I speak of the land of my fathers," she replied. "Sit down upon this bench, which Björnarne has made, and upon yonder side you will recognise the mountains of Tromsöe; and, when the atmosphere is clear, Hvaloen and the great, eternal ocean. Is it not beautiful, Herr? But glorious above all is the Ulvsfiord, and the Balsfiord next to it. I will tell you why it is so green there when all the land around yet lies buried under ice and snow."

Marstrand sat down and gave his attention. The sun stood over the high peak in the west, and its sinking rays fell on these two solitary beings. "Tell me, dear maiden, why this fiord is so blessed," said Marstrand, taking her hand, "and what good deity gave it its green garment?"

"You have, no doubt, heard much evil of my people," began Gula, after a brief silence. "It is a poor, forsaken, and ignorant race; but it was once great and powerful, and possessed all the land far to the southward, which was then much more beautiful than at present. Flowers bloomed high on the mountains, great trees filled the valleys, and many people dwelt everywhere along the sea-side. From time to time, according to the legend, Jubinal descended from his throne on the clouds, and wandered through the land to see for himself if his children were happy. He came once to Ulvsfiord, and found an old man, with his daughter, to whom all the land there belonged. Like me, she bore the name of Gula, and wonderfully beautiful was she. The shores of the bay were covered with grass and flowers, wild flowers sported in its waters, the whole valley was a garden with bubbling fountains, and in the midst of it stood the cottage of our grandfather, Afraja, more elegant and striking than has since been seen."

"The Lord of Ulvsfiord was then of your family?" asked Marstrand.

"Yes, Herr," she replied ingenuously, "Jubinal, the God to whom heaven and earth belonged, lived for a long time with him, and at length entirely forgot his heaven. Then he married Gula; but no one knew that he was a god. Through his power, he awakened love in the heart of the maiden; to the rich father he exhibited silver, and great herds, which came down from Kilpis under cover of a thick fog. You must not smile;" she exclaimed, while she herself laughed. "When I was a child, I have often heard this story told, and firmly believed in it. Yes; my father and all around him believe in it yet; although my father is wiser than many who ridicule him."

"But you do not believe it yet?" inquired Marstrand.

"Am I not a Christian, Herr?" she roguishly responded, lifting up her black eyes. "What would Ilda say if I were to believe on Jubinal, Ayka, or Pekel?"

"Yet listen further," she continued. "After some years had peacefully passed away, and Gula carried a son in her arms, the hour of suffering, of which she had not dreamed, arrived. Pekel, the base god, who hates mankind and entices them to sin, and eternally contrives how he may destroy the world, had sworn the ruin of my people and country. He hated Jubinal yet more because he loved the mortal maiden, Gula. He had formed an alliance with the giants, the children of night, who dwelt in the depths of the sea, which Jubinal heard of too late to change.

"The giants kindled a fire in their caverns, which bursted and melted the mountains to their summits by its consuming heat Pekel, the malignant deity, changed himself into the storm wind, which drove hither the sea before him; so that Norway is broken and torn as you now see it. It would all have been swallowed up had not Jubinal protected it to the utmost of his power. When he saw the water and flames coming, his figure towered up to the clouds. Afraja and Gula prostrated themselves trembling before him, but he snatched them up like feathers of the eider duck, and placed them, with their herds and servants, upon the summit of the Kilpis. 'I am Jubinal,' said he; 'fear not, for I will save you. Remain upon these holy mountains until I have conquered the evil spirit.' With the thunder in his right hand, he drove the giants back to their caves; and with his left, he repelled the sea. Thunder and smoke covered up the land of my fathers for nine long weeks; and as the sun shone out again, and the peak of the Kilpis rose above the smoke, Afraja and Gula beheld the frightful desolation. The whole land was rent in pieces; all fruitful earth had disappeared; black, naked rocks, everywhere emerged to view; and since that time, darkness and cold have reigned here. Storm and fog obtained the ascendency, and ice and snow lay heaped up on the mountains. Jubinal appeared not again to the outcasts; his voice alone spoke to them from the clouds. 'Go down,' he said, 'to your land on the Balsfiord and Ulvsfiord. You will find it green and lovely, and it shall be yours for ever. Dwell there. I will bless you; and, as long as you possess the land, Afraja's people shall not be lost.' So has it happened. The evil Pekel sent a people from the south, who slaughtered and drove away the Finns, so that they were obliged to flee to the icy mountains with their beasts. Poor and despised, there remained to them nothing but the freedom of their mountains, where they are masters to this day. The land, however, at Balsfiord, is to this day Afraja's pasture-ground. The herds descend thither every year from the Balself, and lay there, under the shade of the birch-tree, by the silvery fountain, till the autumn."

"Does Jubinal's blessing rest with your race, dear Gula?" said Marstrand; "and are you yourself a grand-daughter of the fickle God?'

"We are all God's children," she replied, laughingly. "Even Helgestad and Ilda say so."

"It is curious enough," said Marstrand," in a reflective tone, "that the cunning men from the south have not appropriated to themselves the pastures and springs of Balsfiord."

"Jubinal has blinded their eyes;" responded Gula. "There are but few fish there; either because the water is too sweet or too warm, or because the giants yet work at their fires in the depths. A long time ago, the father of the Voigt of Tromsöe built a house there; and when it was scarcely finished, in the night, the earth began to shake, all the beams fell, and the cruel voigt was killed."

"An earthquake," said Marstrand. "And has the Balsfiord been abandoned since that period?'

"It is Afraja's land. All know it; all fear him as a great sorcerer. Ask the Voigt in Tromsöe, and he will swear to this day that his father was circumvented by the necromancy of my grandfather. Inquire of the fishermen and the pastors, and they will relate to you the terrible history."

"But I have heard that, even among his own people, Afraja is reputed to hold intercourse with spirits and devils. Have you seen anything of the kind?"

Gula clapped her hands, and joyously shook her head. Before she could answer, a low, sharp sound was heard, which flew over their heads like the cry of a ptarmigan.

The maiden jumped up from her seat, and timidly looked around on all sides.

"Are you frightened at a Ripe?" said Marstrand, jocularly. "Behold, there is a great mass of them on the rocks."

"Let us go," she replied. "The ptarmigan screams when the night comes on; the way is slippery, and Ilda will grow anxious about you." She hastily bounded down the steps The birds fluttered above their heads, and flew screaming away over the fiord; the sun was quickly concealed behind a wall of dark clouds, which the gusty wind scattered over the face of the heavens. An uncertain glimmer shot over the peaks of the lofty Tjellan, as both reached the hamlet, from whose cottages the lights were already shining.

CHAPTER V

Miss Ilda sat reading aloud from an open Bible on the table before her. A dozen men and women from the hamlet were seated against the side-wall, devoutly listening to the explanations and comments of the pious maiden. Nothing could be more gratifying to them than, in their Sunday apparel, to hear their young mistress read to them in her soft, melodious voice, from the holy volume. Even Helgestad, reclining at ease in the huge arm-chair by the stove, and whiffing his pipe, found it pleasant to suffer her clear, full tones, to ring in his ears while he indulged in all kinds of calculations. As the belated pair entered, the trader nodded to them with a gratified look, and, with his pipe, pointed out a leather chair to his guest. Miss Ilda, however, did not permit herself to be disturbed. She did not look up; but quietly read on, in the wisdom of the prophet, Jesus Sirach, who has left so many beautiful lessons of wisdom and morality. When this was terminated, a chapter from the Epistle of the Apostle Paul to the Romans followed.

Heated and tired as he was, Marstrand listened without much interest. He would gladly have been spared this edifying exposition; but, by degrees, his levity yielded; for what he heard did not fail to make an impression on the susceptible heart of the young man. The harmonious tones, and the warning counsels of the prophet, conjoined to arrest his attention. The little congregation and the fair priestess formed a charmingly poetic picture. Without, the storm howled wilder and wilder, and shook the rafters with such violence as to sometimes interrupt the sound of Ilda's voice. The northern lights gleamed through the dark sky, and their phosphoric illumination trembled upon the countenances of the audience until a cluster of glowing clouds gathered around the snowy peaks to the south of the fiord, and lighted up the foaming waves with its wondrous fire.

Unmoved by all, Ilda read the exhortations of St. Paul to brotherly love and truth, and Marstrand listened with increasing interest. "Rejoice with them that do rejoice," read the maiden; "and weep with them that do weep; rejoice in hope, be patient in tribulation, receive the poor, succor the distressed. Bless them which persecute you; bless, and curse not. He that exhorteth, let him wait on the exhorter; he that giveth, let him do it with simplicity; he that ruleth, with diligence, he that sheweth mercy with cheerfulness. Abhor that which is evil; cleave to that which is good. Be kindly affectioned one to another with brotherly love; in honor preferring one another; not slothful in business; fervent in spirit, serving the Lord."

Here Ilda shut up the book, and the Sunday evening exercises closed. Marstrand remained sitting in deep meditation, whilst the people withdrew, having first been admonished by Helgestad to make fast their cottages, and to look after the fire and lights, as a wild night was coming on. Marstrand repeated to himself Ilda's last words, and his blood beat quicker in his veins. It appeared to him, as if she had especially raised her voice, and directed her regards to him. He felt that the admonitions suited him.

"I gladly hear the contents of the black book there," said Helgestad, while the table was being prepared, and the family were alone; "it is curious that men should have thought of uch things a thousand years ago — but Ilda can expound it etter than any parson in Finnmark."

All nodded assent, and the old man struck the table, as he set aside his empty glass, and continued, with a crafty smile; "He was a clever man, St. Paul; and one can, at this day, learn of him. He was a man to my liking, Herr Marstrand. Brief, concise, clear-headed, he knew what he was about; he saw everything with his eyes open, and when he speaks of love, belief, faith, and such-like matters, there follows always a proper admonition, as, for example—'Be industrious, and keep your mind and hands in motion.' 'Take heed that you do no harm, serve the time.' Had he lived in Finnmark, the holy apostle," he exclaimed, "it would not have been the unclean spot that it is — it would be profitable to many, if they would daily read him, to preserve themselves from evil."

"It would be well if people lived after Paul's precepts; and particularly where he exhorts all to live in brotherly love with one another," said the young man.

"I deny it," said Helgestad. "The apostle was too experienced and practical a man to have advised such things. He meant nothing more thereby than, perhaps; 'It would be good if it were so; the earth would indeed be a paradise, if all God's creatures lived with another in love and truth; but as it is little else than hypocrisy and deceit, the saying means only — Every one must take as good care of himself in this world as he can, until God takes us all into his keeping.' This the apostle Paul perfectly knew—for it was then as now, and will so remain from time to eternity. The whole may be summed up as follows — Keep your eyes and ears wide open, hold fast to what you have, and take care to increase your possessions. This is the only sound morality of life, Herr Marstrand, and no one can complain if he loses what was his."

Marstrand, at first, smiled at this spiritual and temporal philosophy; for it appeared to him to be founded on truly knavish principles. Helgestad, in the fundamental principles of Christianity, found only a confirmation of his sharp-dealing shrewdness, and the necessity of keeping eyes and ears open, and, instead of being the dupe, to become the deceiver.

"It is true," said he, "that St. Paul exhorts us to be wise and circumspect, and to adapt ourselves to men and circumstances, but he urges us also to strive after truth and justice, in order that God's voice, the voice of virtue and of conscience, may be strong in us, and preserve us from the sin of injustice."

"Nuh!" bantered Helgestad, "you have, as I observe, many of the humors of the great lords, who set honor and conscience above everything else, at the same time that they pile up burdens and taxes upon the peasants, wring from them their last penny, and hunt after titles and offices with large emoluments and no labor. I have seen and heard of many of these men of honor and conscience, who wear gold lace, and drain the purses of their fellow-men, that they may live in palaces, and revel in luxury."

"Indeed, Herr Helgestad," replied Marstrand, smiling, while he regarded his coarse dress, "I am not moved by these reproaches. As for me, I have only the humor of an honorable man, who would not overreach and defraud any one, to increase his own fortune. I have the same opinion of you, notwithstanding all your lessons of craftiness. You have acted towards me agreeably to the injunction of the apostle, with brotherly love: in my desolation you extended me a helping hand. Should I not, therefore, rejoice in full confidence at the same, and, as St. Paul says, love without dissimulation."

Helgestad blew the smoke of his pipe in thick clouds around his head, and raised his glass. "I thank you for your good opinion," he replied; "and I drink to your good fortune. You speak like a warm-hearted man, and you are young enough to give expression to your sensations. I adhere, however, to the belief that I am right. Every one is a being with one head and two legs, who feels and works for himself, and forms a world of his own. A prudent man will keep his wits about him, lest he may be overreached by better calculators. Life is game, Herr Marstrand, which we all seek to win. I wish you luck for the capital prize — but it is your affair to seek it. I have already, at the Lofodden, advised you to be wide awake, lest you lose the stake. Nuh!" he continued, as his guest did not answer, "enough has been said on this subject. Don't you think so, Ilda?"

"Yes, father," answered the maiden. "You have not concealed your thoughts, and you have spoken justly."

She arose, and bade the maids to close the window-shutters, and secure all the doors, for a snow and rain-storm, of the most violent kind, had now begun. Helgestad sent persons to his ware-houses, and he himself looked after the fastening of his yachts, by heavy iron chains.

"It is a dreadful night," he said, with an anxious expression, as he returned, dripping wet. "It blows from the south-west as if it would precipitate the old Tjellen of Lyngen into the sea: we shall have snow five feet deep to-morrow. Put out all the lights, and draw your heads under the coverlet, that you may not hear the infernal din. I suppose Björnarne is in Tromsöe with the yacht, or is lying securely at anchor in some inlet. He is a reliable young fellow—I have no anxiety about him, and I will enjoy a sound sleep."

Marstrand, on the contrary, for a long time, lay awake on the bed, in his clothes. The tempest howled without, with such fury, that it seemed as if cannon were discharged; and under its thunder, the house shook and tottered, as if about to fall. The small windows rattled as if they would fly into pieces, when the snow-gusts beat against them; the rafters groaned and creaked; and now and then, a pale light shone through the deep darkness, which mysteriously shot in rapid flashes from the zenith of the sky. At last the tumult overcame his thoughtfulness, and he fell into a sound sleep, from which, several hours afterwards, he awoke, stiff and benumbed with cold. He immediately jumped up, endeavored to throw off his clothes, to seek warmth and a new sleep under the down; at this moment, he thought he heard a dumb cry, which drove away all sense of fatigue. He stood listening for a moment. The storm yet raged, but the driving snow had ceased. The mass of clouds was not so thick, and a star twinkled among them. The cry was repeated, and two heavy blows seemed to fall; a murmur, as of human voices, arose directly under his feet.

With a few rapid strides, the young man bounded to the door, whose wooden bolt, however, resisted all his efforts; and whilst he was rattling at it, with all his force, he heard again a half-stifled wailing penetrating through the floor.

Bold men, in danger, resolve quickly. Marstrand sprang from the door, which he could not open, to the window, and tore it open. Deep snow covered the ground with its white veil; the storm beat in his face, and although he could hear nothing, he recognised a pair of figures, moving close by the house. Without a moment's reflection, he forced his body through the narrow window-frame, and slid down below. He fell down flat, and jumped up in pain, as he observed two men, upon whose heads he had nearly plunged, take to flight. The one disappeared in the darkness, and the other ran into the house, the door of which stood wide open. "Who are you?" shouted Marstrand, running after him; but instead of the one whom he laid hold of by his shepherd's cloak, he was suddenly seized by four men, who sprang at him out of the dark vestibule. He received such a powerful blow of the fist, that he tumbled back from the threshold: the guttural tones, and the forms of his opponents, left him no doubt that the antagonists with whom he had to deal were Finns.

For some minutes, Marstrand was in considerable danger. The assailants availed themselves of their vantage-ground, and struck him with their long sticks. But they were weak and cowardly enemies, for they had scarcely made a dozen steps, and the powerful Dane had hardly snatched a weapon from the hands of one, and given him a couple of blows, amid continual cries of help, when they all ran off, and left the first of their companions in Marstrand's hands.

After a brief struggle, he threw his prisoner down in the snow, and dragged him back into the house, in no little anxiety as to the fate of its tenants. His calls were lost in the uproar of the tempest. The man at his feet gave no answer to his threats. The house was as still and dark as if it contained no living being.

"Have you murdered them, you villain?" exclaimed the victor, with increasing fury. "Speak, or I will strangle you! What has become of them?"

"Be merciful, be merciful, Herr!" exclaimed a breathless voice behind; and two trembling arms clasped his arm, two cold hands endeavored to open his hands.

"Gula!" cried Marstrand; and whilst he unloosened the bound man, he continued; "It is your father!"

"Spare his grey hairs," she sobbed; "let him not fall into the hands of his enemies. No one has been harmed. He came to carry me off by force — I shrieked — they threw a fur-cloak over my head, and dragged me out. I will remain; Afraja, my father hears it. Let him go, Herr. He will not return. By the holy name of Jubinal!" she continued, "he will not. I swear it to you. Swear, Afraja, swear, and flee away."

Afraja had raised himself up, and, like a black shadow, he stood still and dumb before Marstrand; suddenly he sprang aside, and the night quickly concealed him.

"He is gone!" exclaimed Gula. "I thank you, Herr God's richest thanks! They stole in, opened the chambers, and surprised us."

"And where is Ilda? What did Helgestad do?" asked Marstrand.

The maiden answered not, but hurried into the house. He slowly followed her, and now, for the first time, he felt a strong pain in his feet. As he entered the sitting-room, Gula snatched a light which was burning on the table, and ran with it into Helgestad's bed-room. There lay the trader upon his bed, bound up like a bale, with hard leathern thongs of reindeer-skin, double and triple lashed together. His night-cap was drawn over his head down to his chin; the jaw-bones were pressed together with tightly-knotted bands, which put the whole man in such a condition, that he could not move a limb, and with difficulty could breathe enough air to escape suffocation. Gula tore off the cap, and, in conjunction with Marstrand, loosened his bands. Helgestad's dark red, swollen face, by degrees, resumed its natural color. He sat up, exhausted, on the bed, drew a deep breath, and gave no answer—until, suddenly springing up with a curse, he seized the light, and hobbled to his great bureau and chest; when he discovered that all was safe, he fell back into his arm-chair, somewhat tranquillised.

"It is a wonderful event," said he, after some moments' reflection. "I would never have believed it possible. But where is Ilda? where are the maid-servants?"

"They are asleep," said Gula, humbly. "I listened at their doors, and unstrapped the bolts. No one has harmed them."

"I believe it," responded the trader. "They sleep at the other end of the house, and the weather roared so that I could not hear the tread of the old scoundrel, until I was bound hand and foot, felt their villanous fingers at my throat, and observed, on the spot, with whom I had to deal. It was a master-stroke of the old devil," he continued, with a certain satisfaction; "he has more wit under his skull than many a Norman. He shall pay for it," he murmured, looking at the blood-red marks on his hands; "he shall learn what it is to lash up Niels Helgestad, like an old sail. I would never have believed it,

Herr Marstrand, that a Lapp would have dared to do this; no, not even if St. Olaf had said it."

He appeared, for a long time, not to be able to recover from this astonishment; he gazed fixedly before him, and shook his head. When he had learned all that Gula and Marstrand had to relate, he expressed his thanks.

"I say it every day," as he spoke to his guest, "you have a heart and head in the right place; you made a spring at the proper time. Otherwise, Gula would now be driven away in the little sled, through storm and snow, to the caverns of the Kilpis, and I had lain here bound until morning, and been a laughing-stock through all Finnmark. It is a curious adventure, Herr Marstrand. No one must know of it. I shall have some blue stripes from it, but nothing else."

With this assurance he consoled himself, and was not disposed to consume the remainder of the night in useless vexation about what was now beyond remedy. "Take the light," said he, "and if you will not join in a sleeping-cup, close all the doors, and seek your bed. To-morrow we can consider of the matter, and of what we ought to do. I hope you will sleep sound and safe."

Marstrand, however, slept not. When the morning came, he lay in fever. His feet were sprained and swollen, and pained severely. Helgestad came to inquire after his condition.

"Every one in Finnmark must be his own doctor; we have no learned physicians, Herr. We cure ourselves, and are successful in our remedies. Salt, vinegar, and clay will heal your feet — hensey-tea and lemon-juice will remove your fever — and in three days you will be in better condition than if the King's physician himself had you in hand."

It happened as Helgestad had said. The feet of the patient were enveloped, and bound up, and steeped in the bitter tea. Gula brought him cooling drink, and remained his untiring nurse. Helgestad came also from time to time, put on a new bandage, and assured him that no one had taken notice of the events of the night. A snow-staff and a Lapland knife were all that the rascals had left behind them, and not a nail of his property was missing.

"Nuh!" said he, "you must keep the affair secret, Herr Marstrand. It would be displeasing to me to have it known that Lappish fingers had touched my face and body. Ilda already laughs at me — and what would others do?"

Marstrand promised secrecy; but during these days, while the snow and storm still raged without, he would have found his uncertain condition very difficult to bear, had not Gula been his friend and attendant. She passed the greater part of her time with him, amused and cheered him, read to him from books which belonged to Ilda, and when the fever, on the second day, broke, she sang him songs, and played on the guitar, which she handled with great skill. She was eager for knowledge, and sensible; her questions upon a thousand things of which she had heard, were inexhaustible. For hours could Marstrand listen to her prattle, for it amused him. Whenever Gula came, she regularly brought greetings and instructions from Ilda, but she herself never appeared in the sick-chamber; for it was not proper for her, Gula said, as he made some remark on the subject.

"Ilda knows what is becoming," replied Marstrand, with a smile; "yet you know it also, little Gula. You come to your sick friend, and lay your cool hand upon his feverish brow. I thank you, dear little maiden. In the hour of need, we will always stand by each other. Is it not so?"

He reached her his hand. A gleam of joy broke from Gula's dark eyes, as she took it. "I will, oh, I will!" she merrily exclaimed; "but God preserve you from all trouble!"

A joyous shout arose on the fiord, and interrupted their conversation. Gula ran to the window, looked out, and exclaimed, as she returned; "They are coming, the yachts are coming from Lofodden. They are all coming—Björnarne, the fishermen, all!" She rushed to the door, but she suddenly

10

came to a stop, and with a look which seemed to ask pardon, she sat down, and seized her spindle.

"You must welcome your friend Björnarne," said Marstrand. "Take him also my greeting; you must not fail to do it."

After much persuasion, he induced her to leave; when she had gone, he tried, for the first time, his strength, and found that he could again walk. He sat himself at the window, to observe the landing. Two yachts were coming up the fiord under full sail. Boats, filled with people, went to meet them. Handkerchiefs, hats, and flags, were waved; the whole population of Orenaes ran down to the landing, giving vent to their joy with shouts and leaps. At last, the foremost yacht came to anchor, and Marstrand saw Björnarne jump on shore, and his father shake him by the hand, Ilda fall upon his neck, and Gula raise her arms in the air, and then turn around with her.

At the same time, he perceived that two other men were received by Helgestad; and he recognised in them, immediately, the nephew of the voigt of Tromsöe, the secretary Paul Petersen, and that iron-limbed Nordlander, Olaf Veigand, who had treated him so unceremoniously at the ball in Ostvaagoen.

The secretary conversed with Ilda in a confidential, and, as it seemed, jocund manner. All were pleased at his jokes. Speaking aloud, and laughing, they drew near to the house; when Marstrand withdrew from the window, as he observed that he was the subject of the conversation.

"What luck he has had, to fall sick," he heard the secretary remark. "I envy him the care you bestowed upon him."

"You would have done better to have turned to Gula," answered the maiden; "she had him most in charge."

"A worthy nurse—the little yellow princess!" exclaimed Paul, laughing; "and what dignified society for a chamberlain of his Majesty!"

The others approached, and Marstrand heard no more. Full of anger against the insolent secretary, he sat up in his bed.

Soon, however, footsteps were heard on the stairs, and, in the next moment, Björnarne sprang gaily in, followed by Paul and Olaf.

"God bless you, John Marstrand," said Björnarne, in his hearty manner. "Nothing is more painful to me than to find you sick. I hope, however, there is no danger."

"None whatever," replied the invalid. "Nothing but a false leap, Björnarne; to-morrow I shall be up again."

"Did I not," followed Paul Petersen, while he offered him his hand, "warn you to beware of false steps and leaps in this rugged country? I hope, Herr Marstrand, that the renewal of our acquaintance will afford me occasion to give you other useful counsels."

The three young men now seated themselves by Marstrand's bed, and amused him for some time with an account of the incidents of their voyage, which, however, were not very striking. They had come with Björnarne, to pass some time in Gaard von Orenaes; and both had their peculiar views in this resolution. Olaf Veigand was a considerable landed proprietor of Bodoen, and belonged to one of the principal families. The secretary of Tromsöe had arranged it with his uncle to remain as long at Helgestad's house as he would be tolerated.

"It would be better, on the contrary, Herr Marstrand, to say I will go out as soon as I can; but I think we will pass many pleasant weeks together, before you will look after your new kingdom."

"It must take place as soon as the snow melts," answered the young nobleman.

"It can scarcely be before the end of May," said Paul; "but have you yet selected your domain?"

"Not yet," was the curt response.

"Wherever it may be, it will be a warm little spot, and cost all kinds of strife," said Paul, laughing; "for there is not a meadow, where a spring runs, to which the Lapps do not lay claim, as their original property, with a great clamor about usurpation and injustice. Meanwhile," continued he, "we have here, in the house, the daughter of the mighty lord Afraja, through whose favor much can be gained."

"You are a fool, Paul Petersen," said Olaf, who, until now, had remained silent.

"My dear fellow," rejoined Paul, "I do not know where folly begins, or wisdom ends! If I desired, without trouble, to get the best piece of land, and to become rich quickly, I would make Afraja my father-in-law."

A general laugh followed this sally.

"I am in earnest," exclaimed the secretary. "The old sorcerer has, at least, six thousand reindeer; and, in addition, he has treasures, in secret chests, greater than the king of Norway, himself, possesses. All that his ancestors gathered, he has concealed by means of his sorcery; and, if the people are to be credited, he knows the rich silver mine which lies high up in the wilderness, and of which the old sagas make mention. At times, he disappears for weeks. The Lapps believe that he then works with his spirits in subterranean mines, and no one dares to follow him. Two or three times have curious people, who attempted to watch him, never returned."

"Idle lies and tales," said Björnarne.

"As far as I am concerned," answered Paul, "believe what you please; but no one can deny that Princess Gula is such a match as many a Baron might aspire to."

"Shame, shame upon you, Paul!" said Olaf. "Who would marry a Lapland maiden?"

"Not I, worthy Olaf, nor any of us," said the secretary; "but the enlightened people of the great world would trouble themselves but little whether the old Afraja wore *komagers* on his legs, and waded through the swamps with his beasts, if he would only furnish them with gold and silver enough to ride with the little stump-nosed Gula in carriages, to get up feasts, and to live in palaces. Ask Herr Marstrand there, if counts and barons would not gladly take Gula, if she came to Copenhagen with a yacht full of sacks of gold."

"It happens, indeed, sometimes, that men of rank marry rich citizens' daughters for the sake of money," said Marstrand; "but such actions are not spoken of with approbation."

"It is so, then," said Paul Petersen, gratified in the highest degree, while he maliciously regarded Marstrand. "There, you have heard what mighty lords, chamberlains and gentlemen of the bed-chamber can descend to. What difference is there between cultivation and rudeness, between fine manners and stupid commonalty? Here Gula, with all her riches and pretty face, could scarcely find the meanest fisherman to marry her; and yet, in Copenhagen, the noblest men would throw themselves at her feet, preferring her to a rich trader's or brewer's daughter — for Gula is of the highest nobility, which goes back to the time of Odin, and yet further, to Jubinal, and Ayka, the goddess of love. A maiden with such a genealogy, originating with the gods, could obtain a prince. Kings would declare her to be of equal birth; for, in Europe, it was never the fashion to deduce one's descent from divinity. The proudest, even, would be satisfied with a tiller of the soil, or a hunter who had sat in the ark with Noah. Is it not so, Björnarne?" he exclaimed, as he clapped his friend on the shoulder.

"What's the matter?" said the latter, startled.

"Now, by all the codfish in the Westfiord!" said the secretary, laughing, "he has not heard a word. Where were you, then, with your five senses, my young fellow? Were they dancing at the wedding of the Princess Gula with the Danish Baron?"

A deep blush suffused Björnarne's face. He stood up, and hastily and sharply said, "Hold your evil tongue in check, Paul. I will not suffer you to ridicule me or anybody else. Keep peace in my father's house."

The secretary smiled, and said, "Foolish Björnarne, why do you grow angry with me? I have only spoken a kind word for the despised. But you do not take a jest — so let us talk of other matters."

He then adroitly turned the conversation upon the resident families whom he knew, and intended to visit, and spoke of their landed properties, and their peculiarities, and united, with an exact knowledge of the subject, such good-humor and wit, that harmony was soon again restored. Only after an hour, when it grew dark, and the hospitable table of the lord of Orenaes awaited them, did the three young men leave the bed-side of the invalid, with a hope of a glad meeting on the morrow.

Marstrand succeeded in making his appearance in the family circle on the following day. He descended the stairs as well as he could, and was heartily welcomed in the *stuga*. The host sat at table, at breakfast, with his guests, and all were in the most perfect good-humor; and Helgestad gave Marstrand a place alongside of him. Miss Ilda spoke to him some kind words; and a venerable old man, who, in his black suit, occupied the seat of honor next to the stove, was yet warmer in his greetings.

"Nuh!" said Helgestad, "you have not, surely, Herr Marstrand, forgotten the pastor Klaus Hornemann. He has come from Tromsöe, to remain with us until he can go up to his foster-children, who longingly await him, like young birch scions."

"You must know, Herr Marstrand," said the preacher, smiling, "that for twenty years I have travelled over Finnmark, in summer; and have now received authority from the government, to complete, with some other helps, the conversion of the unfortunate, neglected people who inhabit this inhospitable mountain land."

"And are all the Finns not yet converted," inquired Marstrand.

"Nominally they are," replied the parson. "They are prohibited the worship of their old gods, and the most of them probably obey the mandate; but who is to look after them? Who nourishes their Christianity? Where is the love which supports and sustains them in their new faith? In Kautokaino and Karasjok, churches have indeed been built, and pastors appointed; which are frequented by the Laplanders during their gathering there in the winter months. Of what benefit is this, however? The preacher understands his hearers as little as they do him. His teachings must be translated as well as they can, and that with great toil. How can preachers convey instruction in a foreign tongue? How can the seed of salvation be made to flourish in such a manner?"

"Nuh!" grumbled Helgestad, "no Christian can be expected to learn Finnish. They should accustom themselves to the pure Norwegian."

With a kind smile, the pastor rejoined; "You see, no one will condescend to extend a helping hand to these outcasts; and yet they would receive all that could be offered to them."

"What can be done to effectually aid them?" asked Marstrand.

"But little at present, I admit," answered Hornemann; "but yet something. The government has directed me to report if it is advisable to build some new churches in the interior of the country; I shall advise to the contrary. The Lapps wander up and down with the herds, and even in winter they change their camping-grounds; and only in the very worst weather do they halt for some months, where they can best shelter their animals. Consequently, churches are of no use; they would remain deserted for nine or ten months in the year; and what sad influences solitude and seclusion produce upon the pastors sent thither, we have, alas! the most melancholy examples. Three in Kautokaino lost their speech and reason."

"The whole rabble are not worth the loss of one honest man," said Olaf.

"I shall advise the government, instead of building churches, to send thither pious servants of the Lord, who, as travellers and pilgrims, shall proclaim His holy word. Such men, filled with faith, and the inspiration of their sacred calling, would stand up against all trials and difficulties, and could accomplish much. They could wander from family to family, and travel with them from camp to camp, succoring the distressed, and protecting the weak, until the seed was sown from which fruit-bearing plants would spring up."

Paul Petersen, who, until now, had been silent, with the exception of an occasional jesting laugh, said to the pastor; "You are a worthy and pious man — but do you really believe anything good can ever be made of these reindeer herdsmen and hunters of the mountains? Every family there lives and dwells by itself — to-day here, to-morrow there. With their tents, they follow the reindeer; no effort is made by them after a fixed abode, more civilized customs, and orderly life. In their estimation, nothing is superior to their freedom, as they call it, and only those who cannot help themselves come down to the coasts, and become fishermen, at colonial settlements granted to them by the government. There they establish themselves; but they envy, even to the bitterest hate, their brethren of the wilderness; and whenever it is possible, they return to their mountain deserts. Reindeers and Lapps, like the ancient centaurs, have grown together; man and beast are united in one being, which inseparably lives and dies. It would be better, and nothing can prevent it, if they should all perish. In the last century, they numbered over one hundred thousand souls, and now they are reduced to nearly one half of that number; in the next century, they will not amount to twenty-five thousand people, and will finally disappear altogether."

"And who, Herr Petersen, is responsible for this decline of a race of people?" asked the pastor, in a kindly tone.

"Oh! I know," said the secretary, "you hold it to be our fault. We have taken away their pasture-grounds, introduced among them brandy and infectious maladies, impoverished and maltreated them—but all this is a mere dream. Instead of the perishing red-skins, the Normans and Quanes have increased, and with every year their emigration hither increases; they bring with them industrious habits, and make money. Tromsöe will soon become a fine town, and, in a hundred years, houses and churches will be erected on all the fiords and sounds. Let this shepherd race, which cannot be civilized, continue to melt away; such must be God's will, otherwise it would not happen. You must recognise it as a law of heaven; for it is repeated everywhere, and in all time. Civilization prevails, and makes itself room wherever it goes; inferior existences perish, because they deserve no better fate, and their organization is no longer suitable to their preservation."

"And thus," answered the missionary, "all the cruelty which has been perpetrated in the world could be justified. Thus the Spaniards ravage America, and with such a pretext of right are men carried into slavery, and treated like beasts of burden."

"The Lapps were never treated in such a manner," interrupted the secretary.

"No," said the pastor; "it could not be done with them, as in many of the civilized countries of Europe, with the great mass of the people; they are neither serfs nor vassals—for they, luckily, possess neither huts nor fruitful land. To them belongs only the boundless waste, whither no land-voigt and no tax-gatherer can follow them. They are left to their misery, and despised with a contempt worse than the deadliest hate; and yet they are a docile, intelligent, and reflecting people, endowed with many mental gifts, and various capabilites. There are among them men who, under other circumstances, would be renowned for their wisdom and capability."

"You mean Afraja, Herr Hornemann," exclaimed Petersen, smiling; "and I confess that the old fellow is more shrewd and subtle than all the rest, although none are wanting in malice and cunning when a Norman is to be cheated; you should however, say but little in praise of these wild heathen, as it is well known that but few believe in the word of God, and that only by threats of severe punishment are they prevented from offering further sacrifices to Jubinal, and their other cruel divinities."

The preacher, with a painful smile, bowed his grey head, and said to the secretary; "If we were all better Christians, Afraja might, at last, become one."

Petersen's face glowed with scorn. "That reminds me," said he, "of a story which I heard some time ago. Afraja was once converted. A pious man, (I forget his name), took the greatest trouble to soften his stony heart. He expatiated to him an entire day upon the teachings of Christianity, and related the wonders of the Lord, to astonish and edify him. But Afraja remained as incredulous as ever. He at length laughed outright, and said; 'Do you think, parson, that I consider such silly tales as true? They are written in your books, I know; but who has ever seen such things? What the old sagas report to the living is, for the most part, of not as much value as a reindeer-shoe; if your God is, indeed, as mighty as you pretend, and if you are his instrument, show me what you both ought to be able to do — change this stone into bread.' Thereupon he kicked at a great stone, and grinned like an ape — for he observed the embarrassment of the holy man, who had got into a tight place. There was, however, no hesitation. The parson threw himself upon his face, over the stone, which he covered with his long robe. He prayed for some time with holy zeal, and with the courage of a true believer, and at last jumped up, exclaiming; 'In the name of God, stone, I command you to become bread!' And behold! the old sorcerer was dumb from fear and astonishment; for the stone was gone, and a large loaf of bread lay in its place. 'Are you now convinced, obdurate skeptic? Do you not perceive what a Christian can effect?' Instead of answering, Afraja bent down, and took and broke the bread; which truly was, not only bread, but contained within it a baked fish, as is customary with the coast people, when they go on a long journey. 'Verily, priest,' said the heathen, 'your divinity is very gracious; for he gives more than is asked of him. Take what he has bestowed upon you, and depart! Your way is long, and you might suffer from hunger; but, before you go, see what my gods can perform.' At these words, he took up another stone, and as he thrust it with one hand into his coat, with the other he drew out a huge reindeer cheese. 'My stone has become cheese,' said he, 'as much as your stone, bread. Take it, and thank Jubinal. It will, no doubt, taste well, as it is of the best quality."

A shout of laughter rewarded the secretary, who regarded the pastor with a self-complacent look. Klaus Hornemann, however, lost none of his forbearance; he gently shook his head, and, with an expressive sadness, remarked; "An answer to your tale cannot be expected of me, Herr Petersen; but if a Christian and a judge, such as you are, can so frivolously make a jest of the High and Holy One, what may not the heathen Finns do, who are so despicable in your eyes?"

"Worthy man," replied the secretary, "your black coat gives you the privilege to be uncivil, I do not accept your rebuke; for, in this case, I can justify my jesting, as you call it. It is hard to remain serious, when one reflects how the Lapps, for some time, have been fondled and cajoled. They are represented to the government as unhappy, persecuted creatures, possessed of the most extraordinary qualities. They must first become Christians, and then their talents will be cultivated, and, in a short time, from this chosen people, not only merchants and landholders, but also judges, and voigts, and schoolmasters will issue, who will drive the Norman stock out of the land. What do you say to this? Is it not so?"

"Were there some truth in your remarks," replied Hornemann, smiling, "my heart would be refreshed at it."

"And is it not true," said Petersen, maliciously, "that you have sent frightful reports to the Governor of Trondheim, and to Copenhagen, of the misery and cruelty we inflict upon this wonderful people? Have they not especially spoken of the Voigt of Tromsöe and his nephew, the sworn secretary, as two of the bitterest enemies and persecutors of your unfortunate foster-children?"

"My office," replied the old man, with dignity, "obliges me to assist in exposing evil wherever I find it; to accuse is not my affair — I am neither a judge nor an avenger." His coolness, and the reproving earnestness of his defence, made an impression even upon Petersen. The tall, commanding figure of the pastor, his long gray hair floating in white locks over his shoulders, his friendly-beaming eyes, and his fine, proud countenance, altogether combined to form a most venerable and reverential presence.

Unable to make any reply, Paul arose and diverted the conversation to other matters. Immediately afterwards, he went out with Helgestad, who had two law questions to submit to him; Björnarne looked after the unlading of the yachts; his friend, Olaf, offered to keep company with Ilda; and Marstrand remained sitting alone with the pastor, who spoke to him instructively of many things, listened to his relations, commended his resolution, and gave him much useful advice thereon.

The presence of the missionary in the house of the trader already formed a peculiar division between the two different parties of the society who here dwelt together. Helgestad and the secretary evidently bore but little good-will toward the old pastor; who, modest and forbearing as he was, knew how to command respect and assert his opinions. Ilda, on the contrary, associated herself as heartily with her old teacher as her earnest character admitted; and Gula joined with her in the manifestation of a tender veneration and care for Klaus Hornemann. The venerable pastor, with his love of man and his mildness, and his faith in God, was, indeed, a heart-winning and consoling spectacle for Marstrand. How far was he elevated in his contemplations above Helgestad and all those avaricious, money-making proprietors of fishing-places and fiords; and what a sublime contrast his self-denying life presented to the excesses of these men, who, for the most part, found a compensation for their toil only in drunkenness and gluttony! The Lord of Orenaes would have more pointedly shown his dissatisfaction at a longer stay of the old fool, as he called him, if a great number of people had not clung to him with a sort of idolatry, and the government had not sustained him so effectually. In whatever cottage or stately residence the pastor entered, it would have been considered a gross shame and affront not to give him, gladly, the best place by the stove. That he ascended to the children of the despised race in the mountains, sought them out in the remotest recesses of the waste, to bring them love, consolation, and help, was a fact which greatly increased the sanctity of his name. No one ever smiled or spoke jestingly of him, without an apologetical remark that Klaus Hornemann's good heart led him too far, so that he made no distinction between man and man. But Klaus Hornemann was for the fishermen on the coasts, as well as for the colonists, and for all who had fallen into misfortune, a true friend and helper. He settled disputes, raised up the fallen, influenced the creditor to lenity, concluded contracts, assisted the poor, gave willingly of what he possessed, and improved the relations of the different classes of the population to such a degree, that no one in the land enjoyed so much consideration as this old man, whose only property was his pilgrim's staff and his travelling-pouch. He indeed possessed a tolerable parish on the extremity of Nordland and Finnmark, but he employed the greater part of the year in his wanderings; as the government, which then maintained no bishop at Tromsöe, had appointed him, both as their agent and general Vicar of Finnmark, to hold visitations, prepare reports, and make propositions. His official position was of importance enough to restrain the insolence of the voigts, sorenskriver, land-judges and under-voigts, and to induce them to seek his friendship; and the more so, as it was known that

Hornemann was befriended by the governor in Trondheim, the old General Munte, who ruled over more than an hundred miles of coast, and stood in high esteem in Copenhagen.

The old man was thus no inconsiderable person in *ultima thule.* He was, however, as well a subject of the most devoted affection and veneration as of secret aversion; which, of late, with many officials and rich traders, had visibly increased, since it was known that Hornemann's reports had spoken in a very decided and censorious tone concerning the state of things. The secretary had clearly enough expressed this aversion, and his own feelings were not withheld.

On the next day, as the weather was milder, the pastor visited the different settlements on both shores of the Lyngenfiord, and several times Marstrand accompanied him on these excursions; but they at last extended to a remote distance, and were necessarily undertaken in a boat. The young settler was glad in this manner to escape the society of the secretary, who annoyed him with his sympathy, and whose increasing power in Gaard von Orenaes was unpleasant to him. A reason for wandering with Hornemann was not difficult to find, as some families, who possessed trading-posts on the farthest fiord upon the island of Aloen, and even at Maursund and Kargoe, had often invited him to visit them. The old Helgestad had no objections to make; Björnarne, who stood between both parties, thought it very proper to seek to become acquainted with the people and the country; his sister, as usual, had no comments to make; and the only sorrowful eyes that followed him were those of Gula.

"Will you not return again?" she asked, as he took leave of her.

"Certainly;" said he; "my whole absence will, at most, last only two weeks; for it is near May, and it is growing green in the valleys."

"It will be lonesome here when you go away," she sorrowfully answered.

"Lonesome, dear Gula!" he exclaimed, smiling. "It will be more cheerful, I should think. Björnarne has almost finished his labors; Paul Petersen has overlooked all the account-books, and arranged with the debtors; the good-hearted, merry Olaf, will fish, hunt, and take you a walking, and the neighbors have promised visits. The Voigt of Kaaffiord will come with his daughters: you will dance and sing; and the evenings are now long; the beautiful clear nights, which you so much desired, already glimmer through the windows."

"What is that to me?" she replied, with her peculiar impulsiveness. "The good old man, who loves me, goes away, and takes you with him. It will be lonesome for me. I shall no more hear your voice; he will no more instruct me of evenings; I will sit in my corner and weep when the secretary makes jests on me."

"He will not ridicule you;" said Marstrand, encouragingly. "Björnarne, your friend, and Ilda are with you."

"Björnarne," she stammered, "is good, but——" she shook her head and looked on the ground; "we will all be melancholy, and Ilda too, for she loves you."

Her black eyes were upturned inquisitively to his; he smiled, and gently replied, "Ilda loves others better than me, and my return will afford her no greater joy than if I were to remain. You will, however, think of me, dear Gula, and receive me as a friend."

"I will always think of you!" she gaily exclaimed; "and will not be sad, because I know that you will return. Wherever you may be, you will see the lofty peaks of the Kilpis; and whenever you look upon them, will you not remember Gula?"

He promised it, and she was satisfied. Hornemann came in, spoke long and friendly with her, and benignantly laid his hand upon her head. "This child, Herr Marstrand," he said, "is a consolation for me, and reminds me that I have not lived in vain, and that it is not an idle lie, when, to the honor of God I offer her as a testimony that he has not rejected or forgotten any of his creatures. This maiden has proceeded from the Great Sculptor's hand adorned with beauty and understanding. And why could not many or all be like her if equal love and care were bestowed upon them? Therefore I tarry in this house, where I see before me the result of my labors — the intelligent Ilda, whose conduct is that of a true Christian, and the gifted child Gula, who, endowed with a wonderful quickness of apprehension, learns to understand what to others is difficult or impossible. But, alas! the pupils would be yet better if there were better teachers."

The following morning, the boat proceeded up the fiord to the next trading establishment; where they were gladly received, and entertained with Norwegian hospitality. Besides commercial spirit and the love of gain, Marstrand found everywhere, also, the virtues of the Norman people — simple, quiet habits, an industrious life, a hospitable hearth, and an open hand for the stranger and the oppressed. When Hornemann wandered through the cottages, giving counsel, hearing complaints, and affording aid, Marstrand, who remained behind, was frequently questioned touching his relations with Helgestad. "He is a man," was the concluding remark of these conversations, "who knows how to carry a thing through. He will advise you of what is proper; for if there be one in the land who can overcome difficulties, it is Niels Helgestad." On such occasions, Marstrand also heard speculations upon the pecuniary resources of his patron expressed, many of which seemed extravagant. At that time, the business with Bergen was almost entirely conducted by barter, and the merchants in Bergen acted almost in the same manner with the fish and oil purveyors of Finnmark as the latter with their dependants. They did not give specie for their products, but merchandize of all kinds. Every fish-trader and proprietor of a trading-post had his account and credit with one of the great houses in Bergen; who, firmly adhering together, rendered it impossible for the fish purveyors to liberate themselves from their absolute rule. The prices were fixed in common; no one of the rich *Signors* upon the German bridge gave one farthing more than another; and if any one showed a refractory spirit he was put under the ban. No merchant would take his goods until, rendered wise by losses, he suppliantly promised obedience and amendment. Helgestad had found means to release himself from this tyranny of the merchant lords of Bergen. He had formed connections with the merchants in Flensburg, whom he invited to export brandy, grain and flour, and all kinds of merchandise, into Finnmark. The traffic with the enterprising port of Schleswig rose to a flourishing and profitable condition. Helgestad became their agent, and loaded the vessels of Flensburg with his salt and cod-fish, which now traded directly with Spain, and Italy, and the Mediterranean. Ships of these countries were, by this means, first attracted to the fishing-grounds of Lofodden, and the Bergen merchants grew alarmed lest the greatest part of their important commerce should be taken away from them.

Had the Norwegian traders all possessed the enterprising spirit and perseverance of Helgestad, the merchants in Bergen would have been reduced to a sad condition; but most of them were too indolent, and too much addicted to custom and a love of ease, to unite in such vigorous measures. They could, at least, have compelled the Bergen despots to pay them in specie, and to abandon the right of forcing upon them merchandise of their own selection—a state of things such as prevails at present, and to which Helgestad, by dint of resolution, had already arrived. To pacify him, it was agreed that he might buy and sell with any one; and he selected a person through whom he could most cheaply purchase his goods; and every year he returned to Lyngenfiord with large quantities of specie in hand, by which he was enabled to make highly profitable purchases; he thus became so rich that he did not know the extent of his wealth, according to common repute, and had more money than he knew what to do with. He had lent out a great deal of capital—great and small people were in his hands—and he possessed land and trading-posts down to the Quanarnerfiord and the islands. Upon the rocky island Loppen, which was then famous for its countless swarms of birds, which produced the best feathers for exportation, he had put up an establishment, and had monopolised almost all that business. In summer, his sloops caught rayfish and seal on the remotest cliffs of Hvaloen; and he had once sent his son Björnarne as far as Spitzbergen, in quest of walruses. All this, and much more, mingled with admiration and fear of old Helgestad, who was considered to be the richest and boldest speculator in the country, Marstrand learned touching his friend. He saw, also, that Björnarne was esteemed as a jovial, good-natured person, entirely subservient to his father's will, and industrious in his habits. His sister, however, held a much more uncertain position in public opinion. She was much commended, as a young lady who, although a child at her mother's death, had presided over her father's house with skill and energy. She was also far better educated than any other of the maidens of the country. She could write, and keep accounts better than Helgestad and his son, both together; she read both Danish and Swedish, played and sang on the guitar, and was mild and kind to the poor, and such as suffered from her father's severity; but amid all this praise of her virtues, Marstrand clearly saw that there was much prejudice and censorious feeling against her.

As he once made a remark on this latter point, the pastor smilingly said; "You must not be surprised at such judgments upon a maiden like Ilda. Here, as everywhere else, people judge by themselves; and what they do not understand, they condemn. Helgestad is a man of great wordly prudence, which he has often demonstrated, and which his friends, as well as his enemies, fear. Björnarne is true and loyal, open-hearted and cordial, as his father is subtle and calculating; and as to Ilda, with her strength of mind and character, and goodness of heart, she is so much superior to most of them, that she excites their jealousy and animosity"

"You extol both the heart and intellect of this cold maiden," answered Marstrand; "but how is it possible that Ilda" — and here he hesitated a little — "how is it possible that she can find pleasure in the society of the secretary of Tromsöe."

"Is she pleased with him?" asked Hornemann.

"She accepts his low homage," said Marstrand. "He is constantly at her side; she has a ready ear for his jests, and a complying eye for his wishes. Do you not think that a dispassionate person, like myself, can see when a man is favored?"

"Are you then dispassionate, dear friend?" said the preacher, with a penetrating glance of his large eyes.

Marstrand could not suppress a certain embarrassment. "I believe so," he replied; "yet is it not true, that Ilda will become this man's wife?"

"You do not use the right word. Say, rather, whose wife will she be?"

The Danish baron good-humoredly replied; "That he did not think a maiden of such strength of mind, and such influence over her father, could be forced into a marriage not agreeable to her."

"You are in error," was Hornemann's answer. "Helgestad, for some years, has been agreed with the Voigt of Tromsöe on this matter, who rendered him a very important service. By means of Paulsen, Helgestad obtained the concession of the Loppen island, and its profitable feather product; while, at the same time, a costly law-suit was thus settled. The voigt is, moreover, a too important person not to give him reason to hope for other favors from him; and as to his nephew, who will be his successor, he is the only man who can take position with Helgestad; and, indeed, in many points, he excels him."

"I believe you are right," muttered Marstrand.

"When two such men meet together, they must quarrel, unless they prefer to conduct their affairs in common," continued the missionary. "Both know their own interests, and both, perhaps, conceal their real sentiments; but Helgestad could never deny his daughter to the secretary, if he should ask for her hand. Ilda cannot, also, refuse—because the union would be honorable; no maiden in Finnmark would do otherwise. Children in this country, Herr Marstrand, are accustomed, moreover, to yield implicitly to the will of their parents. It would excite an universal horror, if any one should oppose the parental wishes in such a matter, on the ground of dislike to the suitor. We never hear of such cases here. I myself would lose all my consideration, if I should protect or defend such a child. If you consider these things, you will judge Ilda differently. I do not know if she is satisfied with her lot; but I am certain that she has enough good sense to do what, after mature consideration, appears to be right. She will seek to win the affections of the man who is destined for her; and she will believe that his faults may be ameliorated by her love, and she will make every effort to secure the happiness of her future life. This," said he, "is my opinion of Ilda's conduct, and it has my entire concurrence."

After two weeks had been passed in these excursions among the fiords, the pastor came to the resolution to extend his journey farther than he had at first proposed. The weather had become so uncommonly mild and warm, that he could, with but little trouble, extend his visits into the swarm of fiords and sounds, which here seemed to converge, like rays of light. Marstrand was not disposed to follow him; for, however pleasing was the society of the old pastor, the monotony of this long excursion was tedious. Both of them ascended together the precipitous rocks which enclose the narrow Maursound, and after some hours they reached the summit of a mountain chain, which runs between the two great fiords. The misty sides of the Kilpis loomed up in the distance, and, for the first time, Marstrand remembered his promise to Gula.

Hornemann pointed to both sides of the fjeld below. "There," said he, "you see the watery mirror of the Lyngenfiord; here the way descends to the Quananger, to which I must direct my steps in the performance of my duty. Active as you are, before the night sets in you will be in Gaard von Aloen, and to-morrow you can be sitting by Helgestad's fireside. I think," he continued, smiling, "you feel a longing to be there. Am I not right?"

"I will not deny it," said Marstrand; "but where is my home? What will become of me? I am full of anxiety and mistrust as to the issue of my undertaking."

"All issues are in the hand of God — all peace is his work. I will see you again when I return, a month hence. What I can do, by counsel and deed, will never be wanting to you; and as to advice, receive this one in parting. Learn as much as you can in Orenaes; accept Helgestad's aid; but never forget that you have to deal with a calculating trader. The more independent you are the better; and the more you show him, to use his own favorite saying, that you understand the thing, the more inclined he will be to treat you fairly. With joy, Herr Marstrand, I see you in this country, which, alas! is sadly deficient in magnanimous and enlightened men. Hearts appear also to grow benumbed under the ice; but, no, no!" he exclaimed, lifting up his eyes, "it will grow better — we are advancing, not retroceding. The manners ameliorate, men become more just, and the Lord sent you hither, I am sure, to effect many good and great things."

"What can I do," said Marstrand, "forlorn and poor as I am?"

"A man, such as you, can accomplish much," replied the pastor, as, with beaming eyes, he looked upon the face of Marstrand. "You are young, intelligent, high-minded; and this will procure you respect. Your name, your descent, your fortune, will help thereto. Look around over this wide expanse of islands, mountains, coasts, and yonder angry sea. I am not the tempter," he resumed, with a smile, "who carries you to a high rock, and says, 'Cleave to me, and all this shall be yours.' I have no lands nor power to give away, but I appeal to you, young man, who have come to this wild, solitary land, where there is so much unrighteousness and misery — I appeal to you, as a just and true man, to receive the forsaken, to suffer no wrong which you can prevent, and, as far as in your power may lie, to promote the progress of all that is good. I desire no answer. Of what avail is yea or nay, where the power and the deed are wanting. Strive after truth, my noble young friend, and God will be with you in all your ways."

At these words he pressed Marstrand's hand again, and proceeding to the edge of the swampy fjeld, descended from rock to rock, until he finally disappeared.

CHAPTER VI.

Marstrand reached Orenaes only on the third day, where he was cordially welcomed as a long-missed guest. Helgestad came down to the water's edge, and received him with the strongest marks of affection.

"Nuh!" said he, after the first greetings, "I have been at work for you in the meanwhile. I have engaged carpenters and laborers from Tromsöe and the fiord, to aid us in erecting your house. Dry beams and planks are bought for the construction of the interior; and a dozen men are engaged, in the meantime, to fell trees, that the building may commence with the summer."

Marstrand quietly listened to all he had to say, and at last laughingly demanded where, in truth, his house was to be built.

"At the Balsfiord," replied Helgestad; "on the beautiful Balsfiord, which joins with the Ulvsfiord; there, by right of your royal patent, you will take possession. If the weather holds good, we will go thither as soon as you are rested. You shall see the little place, and I know it will please you. Nuh! say nothing more!" He turned and pointed to his largest and newest yacht, which lay by the warehouse, apparently deeply laden. "Look; there," he proceeded, "is the fair Ilda, with whom you are already acquainted; this time, however, she has no salt under her ribs; but barrel on barrel of clear liver oil. He related how many more casks he had made this year than the preceding one, and how he hoped to be the first arrival and to get a good price. The yacht, in a week, at furthest, was to go to Bergen, and on the way to touch at Lofodden, to look after the fish-scaffolds, and to set to rights whatever might be in disorder. At last he closed with an invitation to his *protegée* to accompany him on this voyage, and to inspect in person his own fish, and to learn the important trade at Bergen. "You will thus have gone through your year's apprenticeship," he said, as they went towards the house, "and you can further take care of yourself as you deem best."

"Is the house empty?" asked the Dane, as he saw no one at the door or windows.

Helgestad smiled. "You have, it seems, no ear now for the most important affairs; you would hear of lighter matters, and you shall have them. They are all there above, at Ilda's seat. I calculate you have a good eye and fine ear. I will not conceal from you that Olaf and Paul have their views."

"I think so," replied Marstrand, jocularly.

"They are both excellent fellows, and it is difficult to say which is the best;" continued Helgestad, thoughtfully. "Olaf has a rich property at Badoen; Paul Petersen, with God's permission, will soon be Voigt, and the Voigt in Tromsöe can become Amtmann, if Finnmark has its own separate administration. Paul is the finer, more learned man, has much understanding and sound sense, and there is no superior to him in the land. Olaf has a better leg and arm than head, can do the work of three persons, and is upright and true. I am perplexed, Herr Marstrand," he hummed, with a shake of the head, "and have thought about it for many an hour. It is like a thread in a cable, to which no end can be found."

"But the end must, however, be found;" replied Marstrand.

"Because Ilda needs only one man," said Helgestad, laughing. "That, I calculate, is a just conclusion; but I should like to have your advice in the matter, Herr Marstrand."

The young man was surprised at this information and request. It seemed to him as if he were especially honored. As Helgestad never did anything without an object in view, he suspected that his purpose was to ascertain if he himself would not like to be a third suitor.

After a moment's reflection, it seemed to him the best policy to coincide with Helgestad's mode of thinking. "If I were to advise in such a case," he said, "I would permit two such worthy suitors to press their claims until one of them retires before the evident success of his rival and leaves him a clear field. Both are useful, and may be made use of in various ways. Wherefore should you, then, offend such valuable friends, and convert one of them into an enemy? A prudent man will not be in a hurry where he has nothing to lose by waiting. By the time you return from the Bergen voyage, Miss Ilda will be able to determine who deserves her preference."

"Nuh!" said Helgestad, regarding Marstrand, while he spoke, with increasing satisfaction, "you judge with the wisdom of Solomon. Sit down here, Herr; mix a glass of welcome and drink to good luck! The best treasure for a man on earth is a good wife, who understands housekeeping, and can bring a suitable dowry with her."

He next asked all sorts of questions touching the families whom Marstrand had visited, commended the comfortable ease of some, and the good breeding of others. "And is there no maiden among them that pleased you?" he inquired, with a smile.

"My situation is so peculiar," said Marstrand, after a pause, "that I shall not think of taking a wife until I can do it with propriety. I have observed the distrust with which I am regarded. The principal families will not compromit themselves with me until they see how I succeed. I will at present remain single, and will show what I am capable of, and the time will come when I can ask the hand of some maiden without fear of refusal from the father. Years may elapse; but I am young, and have courage. I can do what others have done. I will faithfully follow your advice, Herr Helgestad, and merit your aid as well as I can."

"I calculate," said Helgestad, with an approbatory nod, "that you are right. For the present, establish yourself at Balsfiord in your new house; there will be no lack of visitors there; make a couple of good hits, and you can get whoever you choose."

"The main point," said Marstrand, "is, that I shall have need of your assistance; for without it I cannot begin."

"Nuh!" exclaimed Helgestad; "no one ever heard it said that I deserted any one to whom I had once given my hand and word. You shall want nothing at Balsfiord. But here comes Ilda," said he, rising, "with the others, who will all be glad to see you again."

This was the case; and the evening passed off as agreeably as it was possible in Gaard von Orenaes. Marstrand related his adventures, the secretary cracked his jokes, and Ilda appeared to have grown much more cheerful and talkative with the return of the guest. He sought in vain, however, to get near to his friend Gula. She kept at a distance, and coyly turned her eyes away from him. He could with great difficulty exchange only a few words with her, and during the whole evening she was constantly engaged, or seated close by the side of her protectress.

On the following day, the industry of the house resumed its accustomed activity. Marstrand helped Björnarne and Olaf in the warehouses, and in the lading of the yacht.

Paul Petersen was engaged with Helgestad; and Marstrand observed that the influence of the secretary had increased considerably during his absence. He decided all kinds of matters; and Helgestad yielded to his opinion much more readily than was to be expected of him.

The little journey to the Balsfiord was now to be accomplished; for the weather was good, and he was anxious to fix himself in his new settlement and commence his efforts for future success. As he was to set out on the morrow, many preparations of various kinds were to be made. From Lyngenfiord, a high and difficult fjeld was to be crossed, which forms the dividing line with the Ulvsfiord. Two horses were to be laden with stores, and provisions were to be carried for several days' use. Marstrand helped Ilda to pack up all sorts of wares and things, which were also to be taken along for the woodcutters.

For a long time both Marstrand and his assistant preserved silence; for there was something between them which closed their lips. When he looked upon Ilda, he thought of the secretary, and what Hornemann had said to him. He was oppressed with a deep dejection of spirits, he knew not why, and he could not speak. Ilda also said only what was necessary to facilitate their mutual labor.

"Who is there above?" he asked, looking up to the window on which the evening glow of the sun was shining, and perceiving two figures on the rock by the fiord.

"It is Gula and my brother;" answered Ilda.

"Is Gula sick?" he continued.

Ilda responded in the negative, and both were again silent until the basket was filled, and then she took up the inquiry again. "Gula is not sick," she began, "but I can imagine what induces you to think she is so. She formerly treated you with much confidence, but now you find her conduct changed. She avoids you, and that appears strange."

"It is so," replied Marstrand, "but what has induced her so to act?"

"My advice and her own good judgment," was the answer. "You must know," she said, as she resumed her work, "that her passion for you has brought her into ridicule. In the simplicity of her heart, and in your kindness towards a poor, forsaken being, you did not think how falsely men would judge of the relations between you. When you left us, deep sadness settled upon her countenance. She who formerly laughed so heartily and ran about so light of foot, wept at every word and jest. After some days, I spoke with her; and, as I think, I did right. I showed her that her conduct was foolish; and I think, in so doing, I rendered you, also, a service. I have thus explained to you why she avoids you. Do you not admit the propriety of my course?"

"I must confess you have acted wisely;" said Marstrand, with emotion.

"Reflect upon it," said Ilda, with the same tranquillity, "and you will find that if you are Gula's friend you must be severe towards her."

"How hard it is!" he said, after some minute's silence, with a sigh, and in a barely audible whisper; "the only being who has gratefully and trustingly approached me in this land, I must keep at a distance."

She turned her eyes upon him without uttering a word, but it was an eloquent and reproving glance. "To-morrow," she resumed, "you will go to Balsfiord; and when you return the yacht will be ready for sailing. You will need six weeks for the Bergen voyage, when your house will be completed, and you will leave us for a long time. I hope while you are far away that Klaus Hornemann will visit us in Orenaes. Gula is his pet, and he will take good care of her."

With these words she left him. After some time, Marstrand went forward, and leaning on the railing of the pilework of the ware-house, contemplated the dark water and the yacht, as it rose and fell upon the heaving sea. He was alone; the workmen had ceased their labors, and he was left to the undisturbed enjoyment of his thoughts. The communication of Ilda was a frank confession that the poor child of the wilderness had bestowed her affections upon him. Therefore, was her face so pale — therefore, her eyes so unsteady and sunken. For this reason she avoided him, and averted her glance, and, at Ilda's command, had scarcely entered the room the whole day. He angrily reflected upon the fact, that Ilda must have acted to her with great rigor, to have enforced her to such conduct. His blood fired at the cold-hearted wisdom of this female judge, who, in this uncalled-for manner, meddled in his affairs; and he felt a proud compassion for the poor girl who, under her domineering constraint, had been alienated from him; and yet a thought came over him, that Ilda might be right. If Gula loved him, what should he do? How could he repel her from him, or how cherish a passion which carried evil with it? Curious speculations agitated him. He thought of what Paul had related of the old Afraja and his treasures, but he jestingly laughed over it, and shuddered, as he suddenly heard, not far off, the voice of Helgestad, in conversation with the secretary. Marstrand stood under them, on the lower story; it was deep dusk, and he moved not, while they talked of the business of the day, the voyage, and the work which was to be done in Helgestad's absence.

"Where is, then, our Dane?" asked Paul. "Is he sitting at Ilda's side, and learning how to lay the packing-paper smoothly?"

Helgestad laughed. "You are blind with jealousy, Paul—I thought you would become good friends, but I see it is not so."

"No?" said the secretary, jovially — "and why not? He pleased me from the outset; but when I first saw him, a voice whispered in my ear — 'Beware, he will give you trouble.'"

"You are a fool, Paul," replied Helgestad, who appeared to

be amused at his minion's anxiety. "John Marstrand is a man who pleases all the maidens—attractive, as he is, in figure, and with a smooth face, unharmed by the rude blasts of the Nordland winters. You need have no fear of him. I have felt him by the teeth, and all is right."

"I wish," replied the secretary, "you had not acted for his sake alone at Tromsöe. Had you not have persuaded my uncle to register the royal letter, we could sing another song with him now. Take care, Helgestad, that the bird does not break through the net, when you would draw it. He is a stubborn fellow, who knows how to make his way, and help himself, more easily than you imagine."

"Nuh!" responded Helgestad, "I do not exactly understand what you are aiming at, Paul. I give the Dane my hand, place him where he ought to be, and ask nothing of him but what is right."

The secretary smiled; and, clapping Helgestad on the shoulder, he exclaimed, in his arrogant manner; "I will make one remark, which I beg you to remember. No one should attempt to be too cunning; for it will happen to him as to king Olaf Trygeueson, the bow broke in his hand, and the arrow fell in the water. Conduct him to-morrow to Balsfiord, let him put up his house, take possession of the tract of wood there, and we will quickly deliver him a title."

They both left the building, and Marstrand heard no more. As he went back he found the honest Olaf at the door of the house, busy with his gun and hunting-bag, and Petersen driving his jokes with him, as he cleaned a gun, to which he ascribed some rare qualities, and which, externally, was a noble weapon. It had been bought, according to the secretary, of a celebrated German manufacturer, and had been tried in many a chase, where it had performed wonders. Marstrand now, for the first time, learned that both the young men had resolved to accompany him to Balsfiord; and he secretly smiled at the shrewdness of Helgestad, who would not leave both or either of them at home with Ilda.

Early in the morning they set out on their journey, with the good wishes of those who remained behind. For a long time Björnarne's powerful voice echoed after them, and Ilda's white handkerchief was seen fluttering in the air, until the boat turned the promontory, and directed its course to the church of Lyngen. There, they found the two horses which Helgestad had sent over the previous evening, and the little caravan prepared for its march across the elevated fjeld. The horses were packed, and led by two guides; Helgestad, in his leather jacket, and a long, sharp-pointed staff, took the lead, and the young men, with guns and hunting-sacks, brought up the rear. The morning was fresh, and the sky blue and clear. The summits of the Kilpis gleamed in the early sun-light, and from its sides numerous brooks burst out, and fell down the precipices in dusty foam, shaking the air with the thunder of their reverberation. The ascent of the fjeld was, by degrees, overcome. The peninsula which separates the two fiords is not high enough to retain the snow to the latest moment. Most of it was melted, forming in the middle a spacious lake, from which the brooks filled their channels; and on the edges, moss and grass had already shot up, forming a soft green carpet. Beyond this, the travellers labored up and down through an alternating succession of swamp, water, hollows, and precipitous ravines, until they reached the high border of the Ulvsfiord, which expanded, far below them, into a beautiful mirror of water.

It was a long and difficult way, yet it was prosecuted with a cheerful disposition. Paul Petersen kept up a continual good-humor, relating anecdotes, and trying his wit on Olaf, or making music with his flute, to stimulate the flagging limbs. The smaller the fiord, the wilder were its shores, which rose up in steep and jagged cliffs, intermingled with huge masses of rock, confusedly piled together. Here and there a little friendly spot opened between this chaos of rock, covered with tall trees and birch-bush. At one of the larger of these beautiful ravines or dells, the travellers made a short rest, and then resumed their journey; for Helgestad was anxious to reach Balsfiord before night-fall. Before them lay a steep mountain comb, which must be crossed, and whose heights were covered with deep snow-fields.

"Be of good courage, Herr Marstrand," said Paul, smiling; "for on the other side of those white walls lies the paradise. When we are on the summit, you will feel like the children of Israel, when they descried the promised land."

"I hope," replied the Dane, "that your paradise is, at least, more fit for habitation than this dark and gloomy fiord."

"Bah!" responded the secretary, "that depends upon the feeling with which you regard it. If you ask the Lapps, they will tell you that there is nothing more beautiful than this little spot. There runs a story — perhaps the little witch Gula has already related it to you — according to which, this land was once a blooming garden, in which Jubinal, like Jupiter in Arcadia, passed his shepherd life. The evil spirits, children of night, and other rabble, acted like the giants of the Grecian fable. They sought to destroy Jubinal's kingdom, who indeed defeated them, but he could not prevent the desolation of his garden. Fire broke out of the earth, and the giants pitched up these rocks, under which the beauty of the spot lies buried. The god promised, however, to his favorites, the Lapps, that this fiord and the waste peninsula should be of service to them; and a god, also, must keep his word. The Lapps, in the summer season, come down hither from their wild mountains; and the reindeer never fail to find abundance of excellent pasture. At the same time, the water of the fiord is so wonderfully tempered, that the horned milk cows prefer it for drinking: in short, it is a holy spot, which is held in high regard by the superstitious thieves."

"Are they never disturbed in their possession?" asked Marstrand.

"They know that no honest man can live there," replied Paul, laughing; "and the fiord is, moreover, either too cold or too warm, or it smells too strongly of Jubinal's descendants; whatever may be the reason, the fish are wise enough not to venture there, and this is sufficient reason to keep off the fishermen; for the Norman follows the fish, as the Lapp the reindeer. My grandfather is the only one who attempted to build a house at Balsfiord, and he paid for his presumption with his life."

"Was he killed?" inquired Marstrand.

"Slain by the cruel Jubinal and his spirits, or by unknown villains. Masses of rock rolled down upon his house, and buried it up. Since that time the fiord, for most people, has become an object of terror, and none have ventured to establish trading-posts there. I hope you have no fear, Herr Marstrand."

"At least not from Jubinal and spirits," replied the Dane.

"Right," said Paul; "we must know how to deal with such creatures. Afraja and his worthy companions will give you trouble enough."

Thus conversing, they ascended the precipitous and snow-covered mountain, with painful effort; but, upon scaling the summit, a milder air was wafted in their faces from the Balsfiord, whose clear expanse of water was visible between green shores, and the small, dark valley in which the shattered dwelling of the voigt had once stood. Monstrous rocks lay strewn around; and a place, which was marked with ruins and rubbish, was pointed out as that where Petersen's grandfather had met such an unlucky end. Melancholy looking fir-trees overhung it with deep shade; tall bushes sprang luxuriantly out of the clefts; deserted, wild, and voiceless, lay the forsaken spot, enclosed by splintered walls of rock on one side, and by the crooked arm of the sea, and dark, naked mountains, on the other. A shudder came over Marstrand, as well as his companions; for they all kept silence as they went along, as if they feared to disturb the dead, or to awaken evil spirits.

"Afraja is universally believed to be the author of all this desolation. His magic it was that hurled down the rocks in that night of terrors, and, although he was then a very young man, he was abhorred and feared as a sorcerer."

"Do you believe in witchcraft?" asked Marstrand.

"Foolery!" answered Paul. "If the old wretch could play the magician, we would all be lying there with my grandfather, who was silly enough to build beneath loose masses of rock, which, in a stormy night, or in an earthquake, rolled down upon his head. But what is that? Is it not a man, who is sitting there under the firs on the highest stone? Marius on the ruins of Carthage, or Afraja upon the triumphal monument of his vengeance! My grandfather had him whipped and driven away, whenever he showed himself, and now he laughs at him, and takes his ease."

All looked, and they seemed to see a human figure on the ruins, in the obscurity of the old trees. Olaf's sharp eyes recognised the cap and hair, but Helgestad prevented a nearer examination. He hurried on to reach, before night, the cottage which stood far on the end of the fiord, and reminded them of the difficulties they would be involved in, if overtaken by darkness."

"It is, besides, an idle conjecture," said he. "How should a man come there, and, least of all, a Lapp, whose people are now on the high Yauren with their herds? Clear as may be your vision, you can see nothing but moss, stones, and dark fir branches. We have scarcely an hour left of day, and we must make good use of it in order to ascend the *Strommenbucht*, and see the Balself and its shore rise before us." So it happened; and the last red sunbeam fell upon the lofty mountain-brow, as they perceived the foaming stream; and at their feet a panorama expanded which was romantic enough in its contrasts to fascinate even these rough men. Deep down lay the Balsfiord, with its broad, open flood, and soft shores, which, beautifully covered with grass, stretched into meadows and slopes. Dazzling and foaming brooks plunged, in milk-white streams, from the clefts, and over projecting rocks, down upon the green sward; tall trees skirted the southern edge of the inlet, at the end of which the Balself noisily poured out of its valley; here, the eye roamed over many little dells and hollows; there, over an extensive wood, through which were occasionally to be seen the stream and its falls, and, far in the east and north, the boundless ranges of the Lapland Alps, with their beds of snow, stretched out and seemed to mingle in the distance with the clouds.

"Nuh!" said Helgestad, when the first excitement was over, "here shall you dwell, Herr Marstrand; and I think it is a happy little spot for one who can appreciate it. Many a one has built here and there, but without discretion. They overlooked the best places, and had, also, no right of property, and several little spots lie untouched to this day, and no one has opened his eyes and taken the purse."

"As to trading-posts," said Olaf, "there is much better business to be done at several other places. You have there in the neighborhood the great Melangerfiord, where far superior situations may be found."

Helgestad answered with a contemptuous grunt; and while the company approached the cottage, which was roughly constructed of broken stones and logs, for the wood-cutters, Olaf made the additional objection that the shore of the Balsfiord was the original pasture-ground of the Lapps, who would complain loudly against its being taken possession of.

"As to that," replied the secretary, "there need be no apprehension. Herr Marstrand's royal patent is unlimited. He can select land and establish trading-posts wherever he chooses —to be sure, without invading others' rights. Nothing is taken from the Lapps, for they find everywhere subsistence for their herds. Wood and fertile land is as useless to roving tribes as fishing and brooding-places. If Herr Marstrand, to-morrow, says "Here will I build my house; the valley of Balself shall be mine, with the surrounding territory, as far as the water of the Elf runs," no one can say aught against it. In two weeks he will have the deed of possession from the Voigt of Tromsöe."

"But Klaus Hornemann and the Governor of Trondheim?" responded the stubborn Olaf; "what will they say?"

"It is a long way to Trondheim," replied Paul. "For only five months in a year, at most, could orders reach us, and only once a year from Copenhagen. In this case, however, neither the governor nor the querulous parson do anything; for a royal patent, once recorded, can never be touched.'

The cottage was built on the deep cove of the fiord, and near at hand lay a number of huge trunks, which, in part, were divested of their limbs, or hewn on the sides, and lay where they had been felled. A dozen or more of stalwart men came in, one after another, and welcomed the unexpected visitors with great joy. A boat, which lay alongside of the shore, was immediately fitted out with nets and angling-rods to catch fish; and while preparations were being made for the lodging of the guests and horses, and the baskets were unpacked to provide a supper, Marstrand listened to the accounts of the workmen who, for several weeks, had been busy here.

All were satisfied with the result. The fiord had abundantly supplied them with fish, no one had molested them, and they had seen neither Lapp nor Norman. Once only a bear had made his way, during the night, to the hut, but he fled back again to the forests of the Balself upon the first alarm. Of the mighty trees and overgrown thickets of these woods, many curious accounts were given, which pleased Helgestad much.

"Nuh!" said he, "to-morrow you will see what God has here created, and I think you will be satisfied. Serve up now what you have; let us eat and take some rest, for a tired body has no room for an active mind."

After a long and refreshing repast and many a hearty drink,

a sleep followed which was in conformity with the fatigues of the day. Marstrand was the only one of all who was in a wakeful mood, when a loud snorting of the horses, which were stabled in another division of the building, entirely awakened him. The moon had risen in the sky, and its blue light shone through the door and the openings in the roof, and illuminated the plank partition, behind which were the beasts. Whether it was deception or reality, the listener thought he recognised a face which, motionless and staringly, observed the sleepers through the chinks of the wall. Long hair overflowed the brow, and furrows and wrinkles gave this vision of the night a Medusa-like aspect. For some minutes it fixedly directed its gaze upon Marstrand, who, as if under a spell, felt incapable of moving. It seemed to him as if two eyes, glowing like those of a bird of prey, were fastened upon him. Before he could shake off his fears, the continued panic of the horses had awakened two other persons, who immediately sprang up, under the conviction that a wolf or bear must be in the vicinity. Several seized their weapons and examined the premises, and others pacified the horses. After some time, as nothing could be discovered, quiet was restored, and Marstrand fell asleep; taking care not to reveal what he had seen, as he would have found but little credence in such a narration.

In the morning, the disturbance of the night formed the chief topic of the conversation at the breakfast-table. It was admitted, that in the woods on the Balself, many stout robbers had their hiding-places; and although bears did not run about as plenty as hares, and many a one could live and die in a land where they were not rare without ever seeing one, yet the Dane heard frightful tales of the chase, and adventures which had had a calamitous issue. The grey-brown bear of the high north is one of the most formidable kind. Paul Petersen related how such a monster swims with ease over all the inlets and gulfs, and sometimes unexpectedly makes his appearance on the remotest islands, killing the cows and horses, and exhibiting the most incredible strength and courage. The fishermen and settlers, colonists and Quanes, have but few firearms in their houses. Entirely dissimilar from the chase-loving peasants of the south of Norway, who make their own guns, as their ancestors forged their own swords, they know only the art of casting the net. The proprietors, only, keep arms; and among them are tc be found young men, like Björnarne and Olaf, who know how to use them well, particularly in the chase of the wild reindeer or birds of prey. In general, however, the proprietors remain with their account-books, in the shops, and with their yachts and business, and use their weapons only to shoot a gull or a snipe, or to frighten a bear from the neighborhood of the house.

Marstrand perceived the great difference between these proud traders, with their dependants, and the despised Lapps, every one of whom possessed a firearm, and of whose sharp shooting he had so often heard such boasts. Wherein, therefore, lay the superiority of these fish-traders over that degraded shepherd race, which intrepidly contended with the most savage beasts and of the wildest nature? Among the twenty men of pure blood here gathered together, he could find but few who were raised above the lower degrees of education and refinement.

What were these wood-cutters, fishermen, and laborers, but needy wretches, who dragged out a painful life in the service of those who maintained and oppressed them? and what were these rude aristocrats in comparison with the merchants of the capital and great cities? What was their pomp and arrogance in contrast with the splendid nobility and court of the king? All was servitude; yet one haughtily harassed the other, placed his foot on his neck, and was, in turn, tormented and despised. A feeling of disgust came over Marstrand. He looked up to the blue, icy wastes of the mountains, and he felt as if there was to be found the only untrammelled freedom on earth. While the early dewy morning broke, and the sun enveloped the high snow-fields with its rosy light, and chased away from wood and valley the thick fog, the whole company of travellers proceeded to the shore of the fiord. The air was sharp and invigorating, the scenery rich in grandeur and beauty, and the waterfalls tumbled with the sound of thunder from the rocky ledges. From a deep, blue lake, the Balself plunged into the fiord, where huge fishes leapt into the air. Youth, and a love of freedom, inspired Marstrand's soul. He felt vigorous in body and light of heart. His gun in hand, before him the forest, no lord over him, and independent of time and dependant on no man's will, he was immersed in a happy state of mind, which he, for the first time, experienced. Was, then, the life of those free shepherds so miserable? Did it deserve the contempt of the people who sat in their damp, dreary houses, and tormented themselves to catch fish? A Lapp, wandering with his herd from mountain to mountain, encamping by the springs, where his beasts reposed, which he guarded, gun in hand, when the stars were in the heavens, watching the midnight sun and the ptarmigan, and restlessly roving over the boundless waste—was he not a much more poetical sight than Helgestad, as he stood calculating before his oil-press, or sitting in his leather chair with a toddy-glass at his lips. The young man felt something of the longing of these free-born men, who, at no price, would descend to their oppressors and revilers; and as they reached the sunny mountain wood, with its mossy carpet and its voiceless solitude, he was almost resolved to dwell there, and was enthusiastic at the thought that all this was to belong to him.

The forest which covered the valley of the Balself was a primitive Norwegian wood, which had rarely been trodden by the foot of man, and had never been touched by the axe. There were here no gigantic magnolia or mahogany-trees, as in the forests of the tropics; no clinging plants of wonderful strength and beauty; no flowers with monstrous cups; and no fresh, variegated foliage. Mountain-firs, only, covered the sides of the valley, and the wide hollow between them, through which, in a deeply-furrowed channel, the wild mountain-stream madly plunged. Now it appeared to the eye as a cascade falling over tremendous precipices, now, veiled in foam, it was forced into an abyss, from which a cloud of mist rose in eddying whirl; soon again it flashed with the beautiful blue of its glacier-water half pacified, in a broad bed, and then disappeared under the rocks to spring forth again, in a milk-white sheet of foam, from black, mysterious caverns. Marstrand had never seen a Norwegian mountain-stream in such glory as here; and his senses were so thoroughly fascinated by the magic beauty of the spectacle that he could hardly tear himself away to follow his companions, whose thoughts were engaged on widely different matters.

The forest skirted the stream for miles, and wound its dark girdle around its swift-flowing waters. Thousands of years must have elapsed since trees grew here, from whose mould a soil was by degrees produced, which, washed by the rains and melted snows, could never form a deposit deep enough to cover the rocky ground on all sides. In some places, in the hollows and ravines, this, however, had perfectly taken place; and here enormous firs uplifted their dark tops to the clouds and storms. Weaker companions leaned for support against these mightier ones. Thick rows of magnificent trunks formed lines and walls of the most desirable wood that could be found anywhere. In other spots, the need of growth and nourishment was greater. A net-work of roots clambered over mossy stones and blocks, from which slender trees, with difficulty, were produced; in all the clefts and crevices they thrust their tenacious fingers, ran up the splintered sides of the rocks, and had even taken firm hold of the sharp cliffs in the middle of the boiling stream. The whole horror, and the innermost nature of this creation, its continually renewing power, and destruction, exhibited themselves under every form. Prostrated over one another, broken, split up, and weather worn, lay numberless trunks, as they had perished. Many had long resisted decay, and others had fallen in the spring of their existence. Here they lay close together, and there was prostrated a giant, dismembered by a fall from the heights above. They covered with their royal bodies the rocks upon which their crowns had been shivered; tottering and sighing in the wind, stood others with torn and separated roots, awaiting the shock which should put an end to their existence. Of many, which were once mighty and powerful trees, nothing now remained but a confused and corrupt mass; stretched out over them lay their children and grand-children, upon which the worm of destruction had more recently gnawed. Here were wanting branches, there the bark, there the sap was yet fresh; here the entire hull had fallen off, whilst alongside of them, covering their misery, were green, juicy companions, which but yesterday sent out fresh branches, upon which a wandering bird had sought rest and peace, but, shrieking, flew off, as the spirits of the night, howling through the ravine, prostrated in death these life-loving brethren of the wilderness.

It was no easy task for the travellers to continually clamber over these heaps of slippery trunks of trees, and the loose rocks and stones; but Helgestad was difficult to tire, immersed, as he was, in speculations upon the advantages which could be derived from this wood. While Petersen and Marstrand plunged into the depths of the valley, and followed the Balself, he and Olaf went up to the high ground to obtain a freer point of view, whence the whole territory might be overlooked. The Nordland proprietor was no speculator, and cherished no favorable idea of a speculation in this woody tract. He considered the difficulties, as well as the considerable expense of felling trees here, and bringing them to the fiord, and came to the conclusion that it would be much cheaper to transport wood from the south, where there was a superabundance. Helgestad listened quietly, striking, from time to time, with his great stick, on the largest trees.

"You cannot understand it," he said, at length. "You

belong to those who must see, before they will believe. You may rest assured, Olaf, that it would be the easiest thing in the world, to cut up the whole wood into planks and building materials, and load the yachts with the same at Balsfiord, and send it to Holland."

Olaf looked at the speaker with surprise, and replied, with a shake of the head; "It is possible that it may be done, but it requires a great deal of money and trouble. If the land belonged to you, I would believe in it; for you could venture upon it, for better or worse; this Danish lord, however, will not think so lightly of such difficult speculations, and he will hardly find any one fool enough to lend him large sums for this purpose."

"No other fool than I," replied Helgestad, with a cunning nod.

"How!" exclaimed the Nordlander, "you would indeed do it? It may appear enticing, but I warn you. You have made more than enough money, and you are at that time of life now, when you should repose."

"Nuh!" replied Helgestad, "I thought, indeed, that you would have grasped at it with both hands, if you had been offered a share in the business. It will cost money, as you say, but the profit will be great. Look here, there are twenty suitable places for saw-mills; and the sawed wood may be floated over all the falls of the Balself to the fiord, where it can be fished up. All building timber must now be brought from Trondheim, and even from Bergen. You would, in future, like it better, and, at least, cheaper. I hope you understand it now. Is it not so?"

But it was not so. Olaf declared, with much firmness, that he would have nothing to do with this speculation. Helgestad now enlarged upon the fact, that no such trees were any more to be found in Finnmark, that the best ships could be built out of them; and besides, that the little valleys, on the sides of the fiord, lay so sheltered, and were so full of fertile ground, that colonists would everywhere establish themselves. Olaf stubbornly shook his head, and underrated the whole enterprise.

Their conversation was suddenly interrupted by a wild cry from the ravine. In the next moment a shot followed, the report of which awoke all the echoes — then a howl of terror, and immediately afterwards another discharge. Smoke rose up between the trees, a man, in the greatest haste, flew over the rocks, shouting for help as he ran. All this happened almost simultaneously; yet Olaf, as well as Helgestad, both understood its meaning.

The Nordlander, with gun in hand, ran towards the fugitive, who was no other than the secretary, and when he reached him, he held him fast; for Paul Petersen appeared to have lost his senses from fright. His face was panic-struck, his hat had fallen off in the flight, his hair flew dishevelled from his head, and his eyes glared wildly around.

"Stand still!" cried Olaf. "What was it? Where is Marstrand?"

"The bear!" screamed the secretary; "it has torn him to pieces!"

"And you, cowardly man," replied Olaf, "you ran away. Shame upon you!"

With these words he sprang up the edge of the valley, to help or avenge his friend. Several times he shouted Marstrand's name with all his might, and at last, to his great joy, he heard the responding voice of his friend. Where the stream made a deep bend, lay an almost entirely level ground, which was enclosed, as with walls, upon three sides, by broken, overhanging rocks. Thick birch-brush, wild vines, and young firs overran the clefts, and the open space was covered with young, sprouting grass, in the midst of which Olaf found Marstrand leaning upon his gun. With a glance he saw what had occurred. At Marstrand's feet lay a powerful bear, in his last agony. Blood flowed over his tongue, and gushed out from the mortal wound. The gallant Olaf rejoiced aloud, and shook Marstrand's shoulder with reckless violence.

"My true one! The cowardly secretary might well run off, you had no need of him; you have indeed found the right spot to plant a bear-shot. But, heavens! it is one of the largest and stoutest beasts I have ever seen."

He measured the length of the body of the animal with renewed astonishment, amid encomiums on Marstrand, and shouts to Helgestad. The latter, at length, came up with Paul Petersen, who, with much composure, gave an apologetical description of the event. He had arrived, with Marstrand, at this plain, and was approaching, without any foreboding, the rock, as he suddenly heard a deep growl behind him. On looking around, he perceived the huge head of the bear protruding from the bush, and immediately afterwards he saw him stand up on his hind legs, as is the custom of that animal, when on the point of making an attack.

"I cried aloud," said Paul, "seized my gun, and fired. That my aim did not fail, the wound on the head and neck is a proof. But he was not killed. He uttered a fearful howl, while I left to seek help, and leaving it to Marstrand to complete his death."

"That he, indeed, did do," replied Olaf, jestingly; "although you are a hero without an equal."

Helgestad prevented dispute and reproaches, and, while he assented to the statement of the secretary, he gave all praise to Marstrand. "Body and life to stake upon a worthless creature," said he, "which, in this season of the year, does not afford a good roast; for it is lean and tough — no man can call reasonable. Nuh! the Lord has turned all to good; for it was designed that some one should slay the monster — John Marstrand was, no doubt, the man whose cow will, for this, be able hereafter the more securely to pasture."

With this application, the affair was disposed of; and it remained only to return to the cottage on the fiord, and have the conquered foe dragged thither. The wood-cutters had no sooner heard the news, than they zealously set to work to secure the valuable spoil from the wolves and foxes. The bears'-meat was boiled for some hours in a great kettle, and Marstrand was obliged to recount, a dozen times over, the story, and as often to celebrate his victory with an interchange of hand-shakings, and salutatory bumpers. The cheerful repast lasted the whole evening; and it proved a real advantage to Marstrand, in rendering Paul Petersen more modest and subdued. Partly on account of his prolonged anxiety, and partly for fear of Olaf's raillery, he found it most advisable to be as silent as possible, and not to mingle in the conversation; Helgestad, in the mean-while, walked up and down before the cottage with Marstrand, pointing out to him the advantages of the settlement.

"You know," said he, after the young settler had agreed with most of his assertions, "that we can put the whole thing in order, through Paul Petersen, before any one can hear of it. The fools no longer believe that the Balsfiord does not produce fish, because Jubinal gave it to his people. See the green streaks there in the water—there are herring; swarms of young seyfish are playing on the rocks, and salmon are leaping on all sides. The level island Strommen, on the sea close by Tromsöe, also belongs to the fiord, and it is too important to be omitted from your deed."

"Is the naked island, then, so important?" asked Marstrand.

"Nuh!" exclaimed the old man, "it is the best piece of all. As you are a man who sees clearly, you must observe that all ships going to Tromsöe pass close by it. It is the best place for a ware-house. You have with it, also, the fishery in the Stromung, and the whole sound. It is a spot where the stones can be turned into silver by him who understands it: you could, from thence, carry on an immense trade in wood, on all sides, to Nordland and farther."

"In earnest, however, Herr Helgestad, I have some serious scruples on this subject, which Olaf has confirmed."

"Because his thick head cannot think," said the trader. "You mean the money — make yourself easy on that subject. I have a good quantity of *species* waiting for you; and, if it is not sufficient, I will increase it. Begin when you choose; you may have ten thousand as soon as we return from Bergen."

"On what security?" asked Marstrand.

"Your bond alone—nothing more," replied Helgestad. "I trust in your brains. You shall have credit, at eight per cent., year out and in, until the stream flows back into your pocket."

"Enticing as it may be," replied Marstrand, hesitating, "it is, however, not the money which troubles me. Has not the government promised to preserve to the Lapps their pastures, and do they not claim these fiords and peninsulas as their ancient property? The Governor-General, Munte, has solemnly given his word that no more wrongs shall be perpetrated upon this persecuted people; the Voigt of Tromsöe has already, on one occasion, been held to account with considerable severity, and Klaus Hornemann——"

Helgestad would not allow him to proceed farther. "I have a word to speak with you," he said, lifting up his hard face, while he stood still between the rocks; "do not be in a hurry to answer; you can wait until to-morrow; but you must then decide. Should you know of a better place to build at than the Balsfiord, follow your own wishes. Take the workmen with you, and let what has happened remain as it is, and say no more about it. Would you be a man, who understands what is to be done, take firm hold of that which you would have. Tenderly to think, and weakly to resolve, you cannot. What do you care for the worthless rabble on the mountains, who perpetually wander to and fro, and to whom no spot on earth can belong? Why trouble yourself about the old general who sits in Trondheim and writes letters which are nothing more than pieces of paper? What, also, have you to do with the parson; who may bring women, not men, to tears, do what he may?—Look there! Herr Marstrand, you can have it all; and no one can take it from you. If necessary, you can write to Copenhagen, or go thither, with gold, with which you can adjust everything. You may laugh in defiance at the outcry which may be raised over power and injustice. With your royal letter of possession in hand, let them raise their arms and voices; and were they angels' voices, they could not avail them. Reflect upon this, and then say to me yea or nay; more is unnecessary."

Marstrand remained behind, among the rocks, which, with their mossy and bramble-covered surfaces, in chaotic wildness, covered the shore of the fiord. The evening came on with heavy clouds, which, in dense masses, rolled over the bay, extinguished the last ray of daylight, and soared up to the cliffs. The water beat, with a heavy sound, against the steep rocks, and the young Dane stood musingly gazing upon its dark and agitated billows. With one hand, Helgestad offered him the means of winning riches; and with the other, he thrust him from the door if he refused his money. The advantages which he had presented to him were real. He perfectly understood what this property was worth; and yet a voice within admonished him that all right-thinking men would condemn him. Another voice chased away his distrust, and impelled him, at last, to exclaim, half aloud, "He deceives me! It cannot be otherwise. That is his purpose."

He suddenly heard a response to his remark: "Rest assured, young man, that you speak the truth;" said some one, firmly and clearly, behind him; and a few steps farther, he perceived a human figure, sitting on a stone, dimly obscured by the mist and darkness.

For some minutes, both regarded each other in silence. Marstrand had no doubts as to who the venerable individual might be, who, fixedly leaning on a staff, appeared like a statue. The night-wind agitated his long hair, and he slowly repeated, with emphatic solemnity, these words. "Rest assured that you speak the truth; for no one can boast of not having been deceived by Niels Helgestad."

"Afraja," replied Marstrand, "I thank you for my life to-day. You it was who killed the bear. Your ball penetrated him, when I had only wounded the beast. I came here for the purpose of appropriating this land to myself; but I will not do it. I will not invade your rights, but I will protect you to the utmost of my ability."

The old man made a gentle inclination, and waved his hand, as if to prevent the expression of thanks. "As far as you may be able," he said; "but you have no power. Your heart is tender, as I have already experienced. You despise not the children of Jubinal. I knew that Helgestad would bring you to Balsfiord, and I determined to await you here. I was near you and defended your life when assailed by the bear, and I will be with you, and protect you against your enemies. Live here in peace, because it is a pleasant spot. If you did not take it, a worse person would; for the thirst of gain is aroused among these hard-hearted men. The Voigt of Tromsöe, his wicked nephew, and Niels Helgestad, have already devised another plan, if you would seek to escape from them."

Afraja spoke composedly; and, to the surprise of Marstrand, expressed himself perfectly well in the Danish-Norwegian tongue.

"What plan have they devised for me?" he asked.

"Your royal patent," replied the old man, "is too precious a property not to excite the avarice of Helgestad and his companions. For many years he has known that the Balsfiord abounds in wood, fish, and fruitful valleys. He has taken you into his house, treated you well, and will help you farther, until the time has arrived to chase you naked away, and to take from you all that you call your own."

"You hate him!" cried Marstrand.

"I hate him," answered the Lapp, "yet I see through his eyes into his wicked heart. He will give you his money, with which you will fell the wood; yet you are inexperienced, will lose it, and fall into want. This is the time for which he is waiting. Then you will find his hand firmly closed up. He will show you your indebtedness, and will expel you, with the help of the voigt, with whom he will divide the booty."

"Is it indeed so?" cried the young man, in agitation; "is this his way, to cunningly proffer his aid for my ruin? It is possible, Afraja; indeed, I have already had suspicions of it; but Helgestad is esteemed as the first in the land."

"Do you think," asked the Lapp, "he will be less esteemed after rendering you a beggar? His fame will increase; he will be more highly regarded; his consideration will increase with his wealth; and no one will pity you. They will laugh at you; for, according to their view of right, you will have been justly treated."

"Ha!" murmured Marstrand, as he clinched his fist and vehemently raised his arm, "they shall not laugh!"

He thought of Ilda, and it seemed as if the old sorcerer read his thoughts. "Do not dream that Helgestad's children could protect you. They would say to you, you had eyes and ears; you heard many a word, and saw many a sign; wherefore were you not, then, a firm-footed man? Björnarne is a simpleton, and blindly obedient to his father. The maiden is of a better sort, but proud of disposition; and will, agreeably to the intention of her father, become the wife of the secretary, who at last will pocket what Helgestad has taken from you."

"He shall take nothing from me; by heavens, he shall not!" said Marstrand. "I will have none of his help."

"Accept it;" whispered the Lapp.

"And his money?" said Marstrand. "It cannot be."

"Let him, young man, give as much as he will."

"How can you give me such advice," asked Marstrand, indignantly, "when you yourself show me to what he seeks to bring me?"

Afraja was silent for a moment. His form was barely visible among the dark rocks, and his hoarse laugh penetrated the Dane like that of a spectre, when, on wildly looking around him, he heard Helgestad's voice calling upon him from the distance.

"Take the money of the avaricious man," whispered the Lapp, "and make use of it without apprehension. What can he give which Afraja cannot surpass tenfold? Go to him, and say, 'I will dwell here, and will do as you recommend.' I see your angry countenance through the darkness. You must not be angry, young man. Afraja is your friend. Should you need silver thalers, you shall have them. The hour will come when I will conduct you — your eyes shall see what has never been seen by a man of your race. Deceive the deceiver, and be bold. My gods, which are more powerful than your unrighteous God, will help you."

"Blaspheme not, old man; blaspheme not!" cried Marstrand. "Where are you? Answer me."

He groped around, but the Lapp had disappeared. "When shall I see you again?" he exclaimed, in a louder tone. He received no answer. A gust of wind plunged down from the high fjellan, shook the bushes, and resounded over the waters of the fiord. At the same moment, Helgestad's iron-shod shoes clattered upon the stones.

"Holla!" he shouted; "where are you, Herr? You are standing there, between cloud and darkness, and invoking the Nornes and Trolls to tell what is good. Is it not so?"

"It is indeed so," he answered, assentingly, to Helgestad's jest. "I have spoken with the spirits of the night, and heard their counsel."

"Nuh!" said the trader; "and what have they advised you?"

"That I should live at Balsfiord, and that they will help me to fill my house to overflowing with silver."

"Encouraging counsel!" exclaimed Helgestad; "and I hope they may make it true. Until, however, the good fairies load you with gold, take it from me; and now shake hands. It is a settled affair. John Marstrand, of Balselfgaard, will soon be a man who will make a noise in the land."

The next day, the way to Lyngenfiord was travelled over without difficulty; and late in the evening the company arrived at Orenaes, where they were cordially received by Ilda and Björnarne. The relation of the various adventures whiled away the evening hours. Marstrand was commended again for his gallant onslaught on the bear, and Olaf did not fail to utter many a jest upon the flight of the secretary; which, however, no longer moved him. "I think, my good Olaf," said he, "that the killing of a bear is no very remarkable feat of courage, if one has a good gun in hand, and the animal is only ten paces distant from you. It would, on the contrary, be an unpardonable folly, to suffer yourself to be torn in pieces if you had missed your shot and had not another weapon. Laugh at my cost this time, as much as you please; another time, we will balance the account; but nothing will induce me to believe that I did not take the wisest course."

"And no one will doubt," said Marstrand, "that our friend Paul always acts wisely."

"I am satisfied with my conduct," said the secretary, as he fastened his grey eyes upon the speaker. "He who knows how to act wisely always, will escape not only bears and wolves, but also the fangs of men, who, sometimes, are much worse."

Helgestad joined in the conversation, and diverted it to Marstrand's affair. He made known his resolution of settling at Balsfiord, of occupying the little valleys with colonists and serving-people, and of taking possession of the extensive territory, by virtue of the royal patent. The secretary was also solicited to have all the necessary formalities executed with all possible dispatch, agreeably to his promise.

Paul Petersen gave the utmost assurances. "I take all upon my shoulders," said he, shaking Marstrand by the hand, "and I hope soon to show you how precious your interests are in my eyes. You can travel without any concern; and when you return from Bergen, the title will be made out so that none can question it. I will go, myself, to Tromsöe, as soon as Miss Ilda gives me permission. My uncle will be as ready to serve you as I am."

CHAPTER VII.

THE yacht was ready for a voyage to Bergen, all the stores were shipped, and the cargo well packed and stowed away. Helgestad had long conversations with his son, to whom he communicated directions for the management of matters during his absence, and, at last, in Marstrand's presence, the family affairs were discussed between father and son.

Helgestad spoke of Ilda's impending marriage as a fixed fact. He jested about both the suitors, and advised Björnarne not to meddle in the question, but to leave Ilda to her own free choice; but it was evident enough, from his manner, that Olaf had but little chance.

"I think I can pretty surely divine how it will terminate," he said, with a cunning grin. "Paul Petersen is not a man to run away from Olaf, as from the bear. I calculate, Herr Marstrand, that children are curious creatures. When one has carefully raised and educated them, some one comes along, and carries them off, and him they follow over land and sea. I should prefer to have Ilda near me in Tromsöe, rather than far away in Nordland, where she will always be longing for the black rocks of Lyngenfiord."

He turned to Björnarne, chucked him under the chin, and looked pleasingly at the stout youngster. "Nuh!" he continued, "you are to remain with me at home; but there is no order where men alone live; so you must look to it, to make up the loss."

"What do you mean, father?" answered the son, while his face was suffused with a blush.

Helgestad laughed. "You know better than I, and I imagine you will be glad to imitate your sister. Speak frankly, Björnarne; have you never seen a maiden in Orenaes Gaard whom you might have, with her marriage chest?"

"Not one," replied Björnarne.

"You dunce!" cried the old man, pinching his ear; "there is one whom I will select as my daughter-in-law. You will be pleased, Björnarne. I know a maiden, fresh, young, and fine, sleek as a deer, and well made in all respects. I think you know whom I mean. Is it not so? I will sing you another song on this subject when I return from Bergen."

Björnarne turned quickly away, as if he would hear no more. Helgestad smiled, and said, "He has too little of what others have in too great abundance. Many a young fellow who, without sense or reflection, springs upon the neck of a girl, should rather jump into the water, to cool his hot blood. Björnarne is of those who could live with Eve in Paradise, without ever longing for the apple. I have never, Herr Marstrand, heard of his loving any one more than his sister, and have never observed that his eyes spoke more to one than to another. He is, in truth, what a son ought to be. He could have all of them; I calculate there is no door in the land at which he might not knock. He is too discreet, the young fellow; he is Niels Helgestad's son, and he knows it. Let the maidens sigh, and set their caps, until he brings home the right one, and all their faces shall turn as blue, from envy, as lobsters."

Marstrand was glad that Helgestad was called away; for his arrogant tone and manner offended him. "He will select a daughter-in-law as he has a son-in-law," he said, as he strolled along the fiord. "They will bring the greatest marriage-chests into the house, and their brothers and cousins will be solid people, who stand firm on their legs."

He laughed contemptuously to himself, and continued his way: now thinking on Ilda, who was accompanied the whole day by the secretary, having scarcely a word to say to himself—and now of Afraja, whose enigmatic words had made such a lasting impression upon him. When he recalled what he had heard, from so many persons, of the wicked and perfidious character of the Lapps, he feared to trust the old sorcerer; when he remembered how prompt was the aid of Afraja when in peril, his belief in the good-will of the old shepherd increased —when he compared him with Helgestad, he felt his distrust against the latter excited to such a degree, that all appeared possible which Afraja had declared of him.

So much was certain, that he could not have had any selfish views. A feeling of gratitude to Marstrand, for his treatment of him when he fell into his hands, had probably influenced his conduct, as well as vindictive hatred against Helgestad, the secretary, and the voigt. He, therefore, was confirmed in the conviction that Afraja would surely help him, in case of an attempt on the part of Helgestad to ruin him; if he did not, also, believe in the treasures of which the old Lapp had boasted, he, nevertheless, did not doubt, that in the boundless wastes enough silver might lie concealed to frustrate Helgestad's base views. A man who possessed such great herds, and spent so little money, must yearly lay up large sums; if it was true, that he discovered what his ancestors had so long in secret digged for, he must indeed have the command of vast riches. He found that the counsel of Afraja, to deceive the deceiver, to make use of him until he was unmasked, and to accept his help and his money, until he had no more need of either, perfectly just, wise, and adapted to the circumstances. And then, where was the proof that the cunning trader did not mean him well? Upon what good ground should he refuse such magnanimous sympathy and aid, which no other man could afford him? and how could he venture, through mistrust, to offend a man who had, thus far, only done him good?

He found himself in the happy position of being able to quietly await the course of events; and his active spirit impelled him to utilize the proffered help with the utmost energy. Helgestad was not wrong in recognising in this young man more aptitude for a clear-seeing trader, than for a gentleman of the bedchamber; as he mounted the steep rocks which lie at the end of the Lyngenfiord, he felt a longing after the fresh, green, and glorious woods of the Balself; and dreamed himself deep in all the glories which should arise there, through his own industry, his creative talent, and Helgestad's specie thalers. He saw the saw-mills already in motion, he heard the wood-cutters at work, he looked down into the little valleys, where dwelt his numerous colonists and liege people; and he pictured to his fancy his ware-houses, his yachts and boats sailing up and down the fiord, and his own stately *gaard*, under overhanging birch-trees, with a garden full of mignonettes, pinks, gilliflowers, and ripening corn-fields in the shelter of the blessed bay. His heart beat lively at the thought, that he would triumph over the cunning and power of his enemies.

"Am I not lucky?" he exclaimed; "gods and men are with me! Helgestad throws his bags of silver in my lap, and Afraja promises me the support of Jubinal, in whose paradise I shall dwell. If the one abandon me, the other will bring me his manna and Gula."

He stood still, and looking up to the cliff, where Ilda's seat was placed, he thought he perceived a figure seated upon the stone bench, behind the drooping branches of the dark fir-trees. Since the day that Gula had conducted him to that spot, his walks had never been extended so far. Then the ravine was filled with ice, and the summits and sides of the mountain were thickly veiled in their winter dress; but now only the high Tjellen, from whose midst emerged the jagged chain of the

Kilpis, wore their long, dazzling trains. The sun shone warm and friendly on the deep bays and promontories; young grass and slender shoots sprouted in the bottoms and clefts of the rock; and as Marstrand strode over the steps, and reached the little *plateau*, he found it covered with a soft, velvet-like turf. His next glance fell upon the seat. He had not deceived himself; Gula sat there, and, for some time, he hesitated whether he should speak to her, or retire. She did not appear to have seen him as he climbed up the rock, or even to observe him now. With her head bowed down, she held her hands folded on her bosom. Her beautiful, dark tresses were lighted up by a chance sun-beam which stole through the thick branches of the firs. In the midst of the bright green of the little spot, in this profound solitude, upon the platform of rock which hung high above the smooth fiord, in which the blue of the sky and the fleecy clouds of spring were mirrored back, her presence produced a melancholy impression upon the Danish nobleman. All the compassion and sympathy which he had ever felt for the deserted maiden, revived in his heart. He drew a step nearer, and, stretching out his hand, he softly called her name; at this sound, as if struck by an electric shock, she sprang up and looked wildly around her, made a movement as if she wished to flee, and then, as if exhausted and incapable of executing her purpose, her arms dropped by her side. In the next moment, however, the anxious expression of her countenance changed into joy. A happy smile played upon her lips, and she gazed upon her friend with a bright, sunny glance, which warmed the heart of Marstrand with the tenderest emotions, as he spoke.

"At last, dear Gula," he said, "I find you; and at last I see you as friendly before me as ever."

At this salutation she cast down her eyes, and a blush of confusion covered her face. "Is it you, Herr—is it you?" she lisped.

"And who should it be then, Gula?" he asked. "Did you expect another?"

She gave no response. Marstrand sat down alongside of her, while he took her hand, and continued to speak. "Unexpectedly I meet you; but I accept the happy accident, as a propitious sign for my long voyage. I have seen your father, Gula."

She nodded, as if she knew it.

"And I have spoken with him," he resumed. "He has promised to be my friend."

"And he will be so," she said, looking up with greater confidence.

"I believe it," he responded. "Afraja has already proven it. He is satisfied with my intention to build my house at Balsfiord."

"All that Afraja calls his own will he cheerfully share with you," was her answer. "Do not think ill of him; he knows how good you are."

"And whence does he know of my great goodness?" smilingly asked the young settler. "Have you confided it to him? Was he here? Have you told him that we made a bond of friendship, which you did not keep?"

Her eyes resumed their clear glow. Half-timidly, half-sadly and joyfully, she shook her head, and laughingly whispered; "They say I must not."

"Oh, poor little Gula!" exclaimed Marstrand, in his former confidential manner, "they have taken away your ingenuousness, and cast a stone between us, which we must roll away, because it oppresses and annoys us. Seat yourself close to me, here; do not draw back — lay your hand, as heretofore, in my hand, prattle and ask, and I will tell you how often I thought of you, when I looked upon the Kilpis in the morning light and the evening shade. Are we not both companions in sorrow, dear maiden? How often have I said this to you! Both among a strange people, who will force upon us their ideas of propriety, and of right and wrong. What care I for what they say? I love you, little Gula, in spite of all."

"You love me!" she said, fixing her dark eyes upon him.

"And you me, also," he continued. "Do we not understand each other enough to say this, and have we not promised mutual fidelity for all time to come?"

He continued so to speak, and to descant upon the future, when he should be established in his new house, where he alone would be master. He described how Gula would come to visit him, and how she would help him: her eyes, in happy oblivion, wandered over his face, and she snatched the words from his lips, and converted them into pictures and dreams, which she pursued with delight. Marstrand had folded his arms around her waist, but his thoughts flew far away.

"So, I think, dear Gula," he at last exclaimed, "we will sweeten labor. In my house, time shall pass cheerfully; I will not be as these traders. Your father shall be welcome with me whenever he comes; he is a man whose understanding I respect, and if you then"— At this moment something suggested itself of which he had not yet thought, and he left the sentence unfinished, looked below to the Gaard, and continued; "When Ilda leaves her father's house, will you accompany her to Tromsöe?"

"Never!" she promptly answered.

"Paul Petersen is not your friend," resumed Marstrand, smiling, "and he is as little my friend. Will you remain with Helgestad, to manage his house?"

"I will not remain," she replied.

"Would you return to the tent of your father?"

"No, no!" she vehemently cried. "Rather far away, where no one knows me."

"But where?" said Marstrand, meditating. "Yet give yourself no anxiety; the time has not yet arrived, and when it does, your friend will be active in your behalf. Klaus Hornemann will return, and I will speak with him."

"Speak not with him," she interrupted, "I know what he will advise. 'At my father's hearth is my place,' he said to me. He found it unreasonable that Helgestad should detain me, when my father reclaimed me; and only a few days since, he wrote me a long letter, in which he insists that it is my duty to obey the will of my father. I believe that Afraja prevailed upon him to do it."

"Who brought the letter?"

She hesitated a moment before answering. "A man of my race, my cousin Mortuno."

"Did Ilda know of it?"

"None knew or shall know it."

"And you, Gula — what is your resolution?"

She ceased speaking, and dropped her head.

"When I observed you," he continued, while he drew his arm closer around her, "it seemed to me as if it should not happen. You appeared to resemble one of those beautiful moss-flowers, which can never flourish again above there, when they have once been transplanted to, and cultivated in, the valley; it appeared to me that Afraja had no more right to reclaim you, let the pious Klaus say what he may to the contrary."

"He says," she replied, without lifting up her eyes, "that I am a torn-off branch, which cannot here find earth to take root. When Ilda, who has protected and educated me, goes away, I have no one left who loves me. Even the maid-servants and serving-people in Helgestad's house would rise up against the Lapland straggler. As Paul Petersen ridicules, and Olaf despises me, so would they all do. There, above, however, on the mountains, where my father dwells and is honored, shall I, also, be esteemed; there, with the outcast children of my people, can I do much good. I can teach them what I have learned; can bring their hearts to the fear and love of God; I can console and cheer them in their mortal darkness, and spread happiness and salvation around me."

"So said the pastor; that is his talk;" replied Marstrand. "He will make use of you for his plans as an instructress to your people; and he seeks to persuade you that all who live here participate in these prejudices against the Lapps. But does not he himself love you, as well as Björnarne, and many others?"

"You," she sadly replied, "are just and good, and do not know the hatred and malice which cowers in their souls. Oh! you know not how, in secret, I have wept during long nights, since Ilda bade me to avoid you. Tell me if it is true that an abyss lies between us, deeper and broader than this fathomless fiord? Tell me if it is true that your foot will drive me from you? Tell me if I must fly before your voice as it calls me, because that voice once penetrated my heart like a poisoned arrow?"

She tremblingly clung to him with both hands, and anxiously scrutinized his features.

"Who, dear Gula, told you this?" asked Marstrand, excited and disquieted. "Never shall an abyss divide us; never will I do you harm."

"I know it, I know it;" she whispered, in deep meditation, to herself. "I have thought over Ilda's words; I have learned to be humble. Yes, she is right! I belong to those who must never forget that they are rejected outcasts; but, Herr, when your maid sits upon your threshold, will you chase her away from you?"

He laid his hand on her brow, and said, in a mild and reproachful tone, "Have you such thoughts of me? Rest assured, poor child, no one shall injure you; and if all forsake you, I will remain your friend and protector."

He held her in his arms, and looked in her smiling, reanimated face. Her heart beat under his hands; his fingers gently smoothed her rich, silk-like tresses, and his lips bent down to her lips.

She suddenly started up with a scream, and stood upon her feet. Marstrand followed her eyes: above, on the peak of the the rock, he observed Björnarne; who, unmoved, looked down upon them, and then disappeared.

"He is descending the steps," said Gula, hastily. "Farewell, Herr; wherever you may go, God be with you!" Before he could prevent it, she ran to the farthest and steepest edge of the rock, clambered and leaped from stone to stone, and thus gained a shelf of the cliff, from which a precipitous path led down to the shore of the fiord.

Marstrand looked anxiously after her, and was still standing here, as he heard Björnarne's footsteps, who, a moment after, came up to him.

"Where is she?" he asked, looking around with a sinister aspect.

"There;" replied Marstrand, as he pointed to the flying form.

"And you," resumed Björnarne, with a menacing look, "what were you doing with her?"

"You ask in such a tone, that I must decline to answer;" haughtily responded the Dane.

"Answer!" cried Björnarne, doubling up his fists, while his eyes glowed with passion. "I saw her in your arms. What did you say to her? What lies did you tell her? Shame upon you for what you have done!"

"You are out of your senses," answered Marstrand. "What entitles you to impeach my honor?"

"Is it compatible with your honor," asked Björnarne, "to ensnare a maiden who is under my father's protection — under my protection, John Marstrand? Were you a king's son, you should not lay your finger upon her; or do you suppose, because her father is a Lapp, that you may attempt it? Know that I will not rest until I have avenged myself on him who may have injured Gula."

"I would enter into a compact with you for such a purpose;" said Marstrand, as tranquilly as he could.

Björnarne surveyed him with a scrutinizing gaze. "What will you, then?" he exclaimed, after a pause. "Will you persuade me that you could so far forget yourself as to take Gula for your wife? You could not; for, in this strange land, you must have a wife who can promote your happiness; and you are too sensible not to know, that in the event of such a marriage, no one in all Finnmark would offer you his hand."

"I know it as well as you;" said Marstrand.

Björnarne was silent. His eyes sank slowly to the ground, and he said, in a subdued tone, "Do you, John Marstrand, love Gula with all the might of a human soul?"

"I love her as a friend—as a sister;" replied the Dane. "Believe me, Björnarne, that my affection for this poor maiden springs from the purest and best motive."

Björnarne shook his head. "Then you do not understand what I mean. If you do not love her with a passion which renders you indifferent to the opinion of people, be it what it may, why did you draw her to your breast? why did you put your arm around her waist? why did you kiss her lips? and why did she drink in your looks? that was not right! And why—John, tell me that—why did she tolerate it all from you? and I—— dare not touch her!"

Marstrand was now certain of what he had formerly only imagined He seized the hand of his friend, and, with much feeling, said, "You love her, Björnarne! Tear out this love by the roots!"

"Bid me to uplift the Kilpis on my shoulders and plunge it into the sea! bid me to tear up these firs by the roots, which have intertwined themselves with the rocks!" answered Björnarne, violently. "Speak not; I know all that you would say. My father would rather see me devoured by a shark, than allow me to marry Gula; my nearest relatives would spit upon me; my best friends spurn me, as one contaminated by the plague; and the poorest wretch in the land would drive me from his door. You see, I know all; and yet——" he laid his hand on his brow, and murmured something indistinctly to himself.

They both remained silent, until Marstrand said, "Is Gula aware of your affection for her?"

"Ask her; maidens know much," he replied; "yet no; she may not know it. For years I have lived with her in the same house, and I have seen her grow up; no one was nearer to her than I. I went and came without care; but now, I am entirely changed. She was a merry and trusting child; now, she trembles at my voice—not at your voice; not at your arms; not at Ilda; — but at me, who would follow her even into the wilderness."

"Heaven preserve you from such thoughts!" exclaimed Marstrand, in alarm. "I see it clearly: Gula perceives the state of your mind, and seeks to save you."

He drew Björnarne down upon the seat, and, for a long time, endeavored to persuade him, at every cost, to shake off this foolish passion. By degrees, his reasons appeared to work conviction; Björnarne listened patiently; but, at length, he raised his head, and replied, with renewed earnestness.

"All that you say is true," said he; "but is she not good and beautiful? and has she done anything but good to those who despise her? She belongs to a bad race; but my father, hard as he is, loves her. And do you not think, John, that there are some means by which he may be conciliated?"

"I see, only, the necessity," replied Marstrand, "of restoring Gula to her father, who has the best right to her."

"Restore her to him!" cried Björnarne, with excitement "Shall she perish in misery? She trembles at the idea of the *gamme* of her father, the miserable old sorcerer."

"How," said Marstrand, "can you hold Afraja in such aversion, and yet think of a love-match with his daughter?"

"What has his daughter to do with him?" answered Björnarne, roughly. "She is a being of another kind than these filthy, disgusting animals. But Afraja is vain. He is old and rich; he can dig silver out of his caverns, as much as twelve reindeer could hardly carry. Must I stay here at Lyngenfiord? Is there no other place in the land? Can I not go away to the south—to Denmark or Sweden? cross over to Iceland, or to the

Shetland Islands, if necessary?" He looked keenly upon Marstrand, as if to penetrate his thoughts.

"I fear, dear Björnarne, that your plan would fail, for want of the consent of Gula."

"No!" he cried, in a distrustful and violent tone; "how do you know that? She will, and shall. I will compel her to it."

"Compel her, Björnarne? use force with a woman!" said Marstrand. "You ought to be ashamed of such ideas. Could I credit all that you say, I would not hesitate to appeal to your father. But this is not your plan; it cannot be." He looked at him with a penetrating gaze, and, in a low tone, said, "Does Paul know the state of your love?"

"Paul knows nothing of it," he replied; "he only said to me that you secretly sought Gula for the sake of her father's silver."

"And he has thus set your blood in motion, and dropped poison in your ear," was Marstrand's answer. "Be yourself again, Björnarne. Undeceive yourself; and, above all things, do not trust him who, in this evil affair, will serve you with ill-designing aid."

"Will you not serve me?" asked Björnarne, looking at him.

"No;" replied Marstrand. "If I were to pursue what I deem best for you, I would reveal all to your father."

"Betray me!" exclaimed Björnarne, with a dark frown. "Then would I this day abandon my father's house, and for ever!"

"You are ashamed of yourself," replied Marstrand; "you fear a discovery. I implore you, Björnarne, recover from your madness, or it will ruin you."

He spoke further of his father's grief and anger, which would know no limits; and this time, Björnarne heard him without interruption. He gradually appeared to admit that his friend was right.

"I see," said he, more tranquilly, "that you have taken my confession in too great earnest; and I shrink back myself from the consequences of it, which you have so forcibly depicted. Gula's conduct annoys and distresses me; and, at times like these, I find it difficult to endure it. Why should I not say that I love her; and that, for her sake, I could dare the worst? In the mean time, I have not done it, and I now see the folly of it."

"I am glad to hear you speak thus," said Marstrand, half-credulously. "If Gula is no more near you, and if your father keeps his word, of selecting for you a fair and proper maiden, all will result for the best."

"Bah!" said Björnarne, with a sinister laugh, as he removed the hair from his brow, and, in a frank and good-natured tone, replied, "I know at what my father is aiming, and I will wait. Only one request I have to make of you, John. What you have seen and heard is the result only of a violent passion, which had seized upon me, I know not how. It is now past, and will not return again. Gula is right in fleeing from me, and I commend her for it. I shall have time to reflect upon it; but promise me, however, not to communicate it to anybody." Marstrand promised it, and Björnarne arose. "You are going, to-morrow, to Bergen; and in six weeks, at farthest, you will be able to return. When you come back, you will find great changes; and if you are then still of the opinion that Gula must leave us, I will myself induce my father to give his consent. Now let us return, and separate in reconciliation."

Marstrand deemed it best to agree to this proposition, and the two young men descended the rocks. Björnarne spoke of the yacht, of the voyage, of friends in Bergen, and that the wind, in that season, generally blew from the south-east, rendering the passage always short and agreeable, until at last he came to a halt, and looked down upon the *Gaard*, in the vicinity of which they now were. Marstrand saw the cause. Upon the little area in front of the house, stood three strong-built, stag-like animals, with large forked antlers, which he immediately recognised as reindeer, although he had never seen any before

They were browsing on the short grass, and upon their broad backs lay pack-saddles; the bells upon their slender necks tinkled merrily. Upon the bench by the door sat Paul Petersen, and before him stood a man in a brown over-coat, with a broad belt around his body, and a high, pointed cap on his head, from which a number of long white and black feathers dangled in the wind. He was a Lapp, that was certain; and upon Marstrand's inquiry, Björnarne said; "I know him—he is called Mortuno, and he is the nephew and favorite of Afraja. What is the fellow doing here, with his beasts? He is a disagreeable, puffed-up creature, who takes upon himself great airs. Come quickly; we must see what is going on. He has not surely come here for nothing; the old man has sent him to look after Gula."

He hurried forward, and, as Marstrand reached the place, the secretary hailed him with a loud laugh. "Here is something novel for you," Petersen cried to him; "here you have a new demonstration of the distinguished qualities of our dear brethren, who occupy themselves with the care of the reindeer. I present to you the young Herr Mortuno, nephew of the wise chief of a kingdom whose limits no one has yet traced. He unites the artist, poet, singer, and guitar-player in his own worthy person, is a hunter like Nimrod, a lovely Adonis, who charms all hearts; a young nobleman from the mountains, who conquers all his rivals by his grace and beauty."

The Lapp turned round to Marstrand, with a smile at the encomiums bestowed upon him. His face was purely national; Mongolian-like, broad, and flat, with high cheek-bones, a low forehead, and small, turned-up nose; but his eyes glowed with a fiery and searching expression. His whole figure indicated health, strength, and agility; and the evident care bestowed upon his toilet justified the ironical wit of the secretary. A girdle of green leather, ornamented with silver bells and various colored embroidery, braced up his stout frame. From it was suspended a pocket, composed of the feathers of many rare birds, artistically twisted around in radiating lines, with intermingled colors; his shoes, or komager, were of the finest kind, interwoven with green and red threads in elegant arabesque, which was repeated also upon his cap. Shining, black, and luxuriantly rich hair fell down both sides of his head in curly locks. His cap sat jauntily upon his head, and the nodding plume of eagle and cormorant feathers gave him quite a romantic aspect.

The comparison which Marstrand involuntarily made of this stately young fellow with the figures of the bystanders, did not result to the disadvantage of Mortuno. The gigantic Olaf, in his buttoned jacket and huge boots, as little as Björnarne, or Paul Petersen, in his frieze-lined coat, could stand a comparison with him; and it was evident, also, that this scorned son of the wilderness had as little to fear from the mental qualities of his assailant. He answered, without embarrassment, in the Norwegian tongue, and repaid jest with jest, in a manner to elicit Marstrand's applause.

"Mean what you may with your praise," he said to Petersen, "I will accept it as it is expressed. You call me a poet and singer, and you speak truly. Visit me in my *gamme*, and I will receive you with a song which will please you."

"I invite you, worthy *skalde*, to Tromsöe, where you may one day gratify me with your poetical effusions, much better in a firm-set house, than in your airy tent."

"You have unlearned to be *skalde*," answered Mortuno, "in your houses and towns. In your fish-taking and liver-pressing, you have lost the science of song. Did you live, like us, on the mountains—did you chase the yellow wolf—did you follow your herds through the birch-woods, and lie down with them by the cool springs, you would, perhaps, have less money, but more joyous faces and glad songs."

"If you have so much enjoyment in your swamps," interrupted Björnarne, "why have you descended to us here?"

"Because I had a longing for you," said the young Lapp,

smiling; "and because I knew that old father Helgestad is glad to see me when I come," he continued, as he observed the countenance of Björnarne darken into a frown at the laughter of the others.

It was not certain that the saucy and half-savage fellow undertook to ridicule the proud Norman; but Olaf laid his sinewy hand upon Mortuno's shoulder, shook him once or twice, and whirled him round like a top, to the great amusement of the spectators.

"Let me see how you look," he exclaimed. "You are a jester, as I perceive. We had a Lapp in Bodoen, who was a watchman, and would fall into the drollest rage, when he was obliged to work. Now he is dead; I could put you in his place, and procure you a becoming coat, and a cap of otter-skin."

With this, he crushed the pointed, feathered cap so recklessly together, that it sank down over his eyes and nose, and could with difficulty be raised up again by the victim of the joke. This rough usage excited Marstrand; but before he could give expression to his displeasure, the Lapp joined in the laugh which had been raised at his expense, and said, with some comical bows; "I thank you, Herr — I thank you for your kindness. I will watch for you late and early; and my eyes shall not grow weary in affording you all the service which the dwarf Bugo rendered to the giant Yulpus."

"What kind of a story is that?" asked Olaf.

"A long and merry story, which I will tell you another time. Look, there come my friends with little casks of brandy and vinegar, and other good things."

Two Lapps, at this moment, brought out of the shop of the trader all kinds of stores, in casks and baskets, which, under Mortuno's inspection and assistance, were fastened upon the pack-saddles of his reindeer. At the same time, Helgestad came out of the house, with Ilda and Afraja's daughter.

The trader spoke, in a friendly manner, to his acquaintance

from the mountains, permitted him to shake his hand, made a couple of remarks on Mortuno's gay costume, and allowed him to relate his news. The young Lapp informed him, that, with his herds, and more than a thousand reindeer, he had approached the coast from the interior of the country, because his beasts were troubled by the unusual heat of the season. Marstrand now learned that the reindeer exercised a tyrannical influence over his master; for, as soon as spring commences, the roving animal longs for the cool sea-coast, where it may escape the oppressive heat, and the swarms of stinging flies; and if its wishes are not followed, it runs thither itself. On the approach of winter, a longing for its icy mountains returns, and it will flee thither, should its master stay away too long. Mortuno reported that the snow was almost entirely melted, that the winter had been mild, that the birch-trees were putting forth young shoots, and that his herds gambolled, fat and merrily, upon the fresh grass.

"And because your reindeer happily put on their new skin," said Helgestad, "have you yourself donned your new *komagers* and your holiday girdle."

"Right, my good old father!" exclaimed Mortuno, in a jovial tone. "Why should not a man be glad, and adorn himself, when Nature puts on her best attire, and his beasts announce that a good year is in prospect for him."

"You are a fellow with more brains in your flat skull than many that I know of. I have always said so," replied Helgestad. "You must know, Herr Marstrand, that Mortuno comes down from the mountains every year with his herds, and gives us a call now and then. He is a dashing fellow, who possesses his good qualities, and he flutters many a heart in the mountain tents when he goes out a visiting, and sets his cap on his right ear."

The Lapp appeared to be much flattered by this praise. His eyes expressed the liveliest pleasure — he laughed aloud, and gave repeated cause for further jests upon his vanity.

"What the deuce!" said Helgestad, "will you do with that pretty feather-pocket? I will buy it of you, Mortuno. It is a rare piece of work that, and can be sold at the Lyngenfiord fair for four *species*."

"I will not sell it," said the young Lapp, as he detached the gaudy pocket from his belt.

"You will not, dunce?" said the trader, in reply. "I will give you five, six hard, smooth thalers. It is such a thing as the Lapps alone can work. You will not? Have you a sweetheart around whose brown neck you would hang it? Or, perhaps, you have brought it for Gula, out of old love and affection?"

Mortuno responded negatively to all these inquiries with the childish and wild laughter which makes the Lapps so contemptible in the eyes of the grave Normans. "When I want a maiden," he vauntingly exclaimed, "I need no feather-pocket. Five, ten, twenty come at the sound of my voice. But Gula has no right to it. She may hang a fishing-net on her apron when she wants a pocket."

"You will have nothing more to do with her, because she will hear no more of you," cried Helgestad. "You are right, my dear fellow; seek some one who rewards you better. You are a sensible man. Look here, six new *species*."

The desire for the acquisition of the pouch was excited in Helgestad; and Marstrand afterwards learned, that this elegant feather-work, which was often carried to Trondheim, and even to London and Paris, was considered very valuable. In Nordland and Finnmark, feather-pouches and collars were the highest ornament of the richest and most distinguished ladies; the old avaricious speculator was, therefore, most agreeably surprised, as Mortuno, with more gallantry than was to be expected of him, presented the precious trifle to Ilda.

"Are you pleased with it, Miss?" he asked, as she turned it round and round, to let the light pass through it.

"It is very pretty," said Ilda.

"It is a bridal-pouch, such as no one could so easily procure. Take it and wear it, Miss, is the request of the poor Mortuno."

Ilda would, perhaps, have refused it; but Helgestad put an end to all scruple. He took possession of the gift, and expressed his thanks by a hearty shake of the hand of the Lapp, and a promise to fill his flask, which, however, the latter disdainfully refused.

"Very well," smiled the trader, "we will make it up another time between us. Where is the old scoundrel, Afraja? Is he with your herd, or is he spying around here?"

"I know nothing of him," was Mortuno's answer. "When I saw him last I was deep in the Yauren, in the Tana, where he was sitting in his tent with the good father Hornemann."

"He found him out!" cried Helgestad. "Nuh! the parson will send a pretty report to Copenhagen this time. You will also be paraded in it, Herr Marstrand; but I suppose you can bear it."

When Mortuno was ready with his reindeer, he gave him a parting volley of jests, which the Lapp took as good-naturedly as Olaf's rudeness.

The others pressed around the poor fellow, for all were eager to give vent to some cherished witticism. One surpassed the other in ill-natured jokes; and even to the fishermen, women, and children of the place, was the tormented Mortuno a subject of heartless raillery. Imperturbable as was his good-humor, Ilda at last begged her father to put an end to the malicious sport.

"Let him go!" cried Helgestad. "Mortuno, you are a jewel; you laugh at a joke. Come again, and bring with you another feather-pouch; for which you shall have the same payment."

"I thank you, father; I hope to give you much joy—but my cap is torn."

"Let your lovely bride stitch it up with Lappish thread—reindeer-sinews;" cried Petersen.

"And my feathers are ruined."

"There flies an eagle; get yourself some new ones;" said Olaf.

Mortuno seized his gun and looked above him. He took aim, and, in a moment, an eagle fell headforemost at his feet. It was a large fishing-eagle; and the ball had passed through his body. A feeling of surprise at such wonderful skill and sureness of aim produced a universal silence."

"Had I not seen it, I would not have believed it," said Olaf; "although I knew that the rascals could shoot."

"You shall not be a watchman; but I will make you my huntsman!" exclaimed Petersen.

Mortuno tore out some of the largest feathers of the eagle, and attached them to his cap. "Good Sorenskriver, I will be your huntsman, and will go to the chase with you. Until I can give you something better, take this." Throwing the bird at the feet of the secretary, he bounded after his companions with a triumphant yell.

Several of the people of the place ran after him; and even if they had not been called back by Helgestad, they could not have reached him; for he leaped over the rocks like a chamois, and in a few minutes he had crossed the ravine and ascended the opposite heights, where he stood, waving his cap in the air with a shout of derision.

"Let the monkey run," said Helgestad. "It is, jesting aside, a sad thing to see one of God's creatures, endowed with a human form, so far beneath us as to excite only ridicule and contempt."

"He is, nevertheless, a fellow whose nails must be cut in time. The malicious dog will certainly soon fall into my hands, when I will make him wash my bloody stockings."

The bleeding eagle had daubed the stockings of Petersen, at which there was no little wit perpetrated, until Helgestad called the whole company into the house to the parting meal; for, with the earliest dawn, the ebb-tide would flow in, and with it the yacht was to sail.

After a plentiful repast, and frequent toasts to a happy journey and good business, song and dance were introduced. Old and young were on their legs; and Ilda, amid universal applause, danced a Halling-dance with Paul Petersen, to the accompaniment of a pair of yelling fifes. Marstrand was the only one who did not fully participate in the general joy. The day, in many respects, had been an eventful one for him. He made several fruitless efforts to speak yet once more to Gula; but Björnarne's eyes were constantly fixed upon him, Petersen stuck close to him, or Ilda intercepted him. It seemed as if they all conspired to frustrate his purpose; and at last Helgestad got hold of him, and edified him for the rest of the evening with his plans and speculations, good advice and cunning suggestions.

CHAPTER VIII.

At sunrise, the fair Ilda spread her huge sail to a favorable breeze, under which she soon made her way out to sea.

We pass over the leave-taking, which was accompanied with many hand-pressings and good wishes. Helgestad himself stood at the helm; six active seamen executed his commands; and Marstrand, who, unoccupied, from the middle of the deck could exchange adieus with those left behind, remained there until the yacht made a turn, and Orenaes, with all its cherished objects, disappeared behind the rocks.

He now had time enough to meditate upon the past events and the future. Helgestad reigned supreme the whole day over the great, heavily-laden ship, which, tossing off the foam from her bows, gaily dashed along before a stiff south-easter. The numberless passes of rock and broad water-basins which lay in their course required great skill on the part of the helmsman; and Helgestad was unwilling to confide the safety of his precious ship and cargo to any other hand.

Such rapid progress was made, that by evening Tromsöe lay before them. The trader avoided touching there, however. With wind and tide he swept through the sound; and by the expiring twilight he pointed out the island Strommen, a part of his proposed possessions, to his passenger. On the second day, the yacht lay under the red cliffs of the Ostvaagoen, close on to the fishing-grounds, which Marstrand, three months before, had seen in the full uproar of an abundant fishing. Now all was deserted and empty of men; but the rocks resounded with the cries of the sea-geese and auks, of the great gulls and countless divers, which, in immense swarms, covered the cliffs and waves. The boats were launched, and the fishing-scaffolds examined. With the satisfaction of a prophet who sees his predictions happily fulfilled, Helgestad pointed to the numerous perches; many of which were undisturbed, while others were empty, or exhibited only some few remains of the rows of fish with which they were once covered.

"I told you truly," he triumphantly exclaimed, "that fishermen are a reckless and negligent race. The more blessings the Lord casts into their laps, the less they know how to profit by them. Look there, what snow-blasts, storms, and worms have done! More than half of the fishing is lost. The price will, consequently, be doubled in Bergen. And now look there," he continued, as the boat steered to the point where his own rich booty and Marstrand's purchased stock were preserved; "not a tail is missing, and every head is on its proper shoulders. All is dry and sound. Luck is with you, Herr! I should not be surprised," and here Helgestad's mouth was distorted into an exulting smile, "if you have complete success."

It is not our purpose to accompany the yacht in her voyage

through the rocky labyrinths of these mountain coasts. We satisfy ourselves with stating, that after twelve days, the fair Ilda had traversed more than two hundred miles; and that the good fortune of this quick voyage remained so true, that she sailed up the Bergenfiord in the finest weather; and, notwithstanding the almost continuous rain of that place, the city of Bergen appeared before them in a glorious blaze of sunlight.

Helgestad's yacht was, however, by no means, the first Nordlander which had arrived that year. Close on to the German bridge a number were anchored; but she was the first craft from Finnmark; and, as she reached the harbor, shout upon shout welcomed her arrival.

Bergen was then, as now, the most frequented and the richest trading-town of Norway. It extends, in a crescent-shape, between seven high mountain-peaks, around the spacious basin with which the fiord here terminates. In the middle ages, and during the Hanseatic league, it was the seat of a very extensive commerce. The German traders, who founded Bergen, had made it almost entirely a German town. Great German fleets often anchored here to sustain the power of their countrymen. The commerce with Hamburg and Lubeck drew thousands of traders thither every year to exchange merchandise and wares for fish and wood. Although Germany yet chiefly supplies Norway with foreign importations, at that period, the trade, to a much greater extent, lay in German hands. Although Bergen could no longer be called a conquest, and no German man-of-war visited its harbor, and the power of the proud Hansa was broken, and the Norwegians themselves had subdued the haughty German trading-lords into peaceful fellow-citizens, yet the larger part of the merchants were Germans, who owned the great warehouses, and monopolised the principal part of the business of the place.

The long row of houses on the west side of the harbor, before which lay the places for discharging cargoes, was called the German Bridge. Here anchored the Nordland fleet several times during the year, with codfish and salted fish, liver-oil, furs and feathers; here the numerous herring-boats unloaded in the midst of winter, when the rich fishery of Skudenaes was in activity; here, in small, dark, arched counting-houses, had a profitable and extensive business been carried on with the adjacent and remoter countries of Europe. The whole sea-side of the harbor was surrounded by monstrous ware-houses, which were so built as to overhang the water, and enable the anchored vessels to take in their cargoes from the numerous stories. When the yachts had landed their contents, they came to anchor under the magazines; where they took in the various assortment of articles which made up a cargo for Finnmark and Nordland. In the midst of the broad basin lay ships of all nations — Italians, French, Spaniards and Portuguese, together with many German craft, all of which were awaiting the arrival of the Nordland fleet, whose crew they hailed with far-echoing shouts.

Marstrand, from the deck, surveyed with glad sensations, the valley, the city, the forest of masts, and the crowds of people. May had now introduced the spring in full maturity. There before him lay flowery gardens, and green meadows, and villas, under shady trees; beautiful plantings and fertile trees stretched from one mountain-shelf to another, up to the naked summits, from which the Bergenhaus and Friedrichsborg forts loomed up, with their dazzling white walls. Two cannon were fired from the harbor-battery; flags of all colors waved from the trading-houses, and from the schooners, brigs, galeots, barks, and ships; to whose compact line the yacht steered to take her place by the bridge. Everywhere was activity; the song of sailors at the windlasses and cranes, shouting and greeting from the boats, welcomes from old acquaintances, inquiries and questions, laughter and wishings of good-luck. Marstrand found himself suddenly transferred from rocks and waves to the civilized world; and he stretched out his hands as towards an old friend upon whom he had unexpectedly fallen in the wilderness.

Before, however, the Fair Ilda had fastened her cable to one of the great harbor-posts, her deck was thronged by a number of old and young men, who had rowed to her, or had got on board by jumping from yacht to yacht. They were brokers and traders in search of news; they stormed Helgestad with questions touching the result of the fishery at the Lofodden; and his answers, dubious as those of the Delphic oracle, were received with laughter and gravity, jests and imprecations.

The Dane had looked on the tumult from a distance, until his attention was directed to a person who came on board only when the others had mostly withdrawn. He hastily stepped over the scattered ropes until he approached Helgestad, to whom he advanced with outstretched arms, and spoke in a tone of the fondest intimacy.

He was a small, stout-bodied man, with a red face, heavy hanging cheeks, puffy lips, and round eyes. A brown frock coat, cut short, after the fashion of the time, black velvet breeches, reaching to the knee, an immense waistcoat, covering his round belly, and a white cravat, supporting his fat double-chin, gave evidence of a rich and notable person. A wig, with a richly-bound cue, powder upon his side-curls and his coat-collar, a little three-cornered hat, with a band of gold lace, and polished boots, in which his bandy legs were stuck, completed the picture of a well-to-do and reputable merchant of the last century.

"Oho, Niels Helgestad! oho, my man! how bravely you came in!" he cried out to the trader. "Thunder and lightning! you look as young and sleek as ever. A good cargo, Niels. I looked at the side of the yacht — she is ten inches over the white line in the water, and that makes a clear hundred and fifty centner more than last year; I am in a terrible perspiration," he continued, puffing and blowing. "I was sitting with the captains, Normans, and brokers, as I saw your sail. I am sorry that I have come so late."

"The last shall be first, and the first last," replied Helgestad, with a laugh, and a hearty shake of the hand. "Peace to your house, Uve Fandrem! I bring a rich cargo; and what is to come after this will not be worse."

A long conversation ensued between these business friends, which revolved over family affairs, and all kinds of news touching trade and traffic. The liver-oil cargo came at a better season to be appreciated, than would have been the case a little later. The Bergen merchants desired to send the article immediately to Hamburg, before the prices should fall. Dried codfish and salted fish were certain of an extraordinary profit; for the news of the loss and ruin of the greater part of the catch had already got wind.

"Bring what you have as soon as possible into market, friend Niels," said Herr Fandrem. "For four successive years fish have been cheap, which has, of course, increased the consumption. Already many vessels have arrived from the Mediterranean, and yet more are expected. There will be a competition for the fish, such as has not been seen for a long time; I hope we will get the prices up beyond all expectation. Heh! you have no objections to that, Niels?"

The merchant had probably received a wink from Helgestad, for he suddenly came to a pause, and looked over his shoulder at Marstrand, who was standing near them, with no very friendly regard.

"What kind of a jackanapes have you brought into the country, Niels?" he asked, between his teeth.

"He is a friend, Uve Fandrem," answered Niels, aloud. "Look here, Herr Marstrand, there is a man who will help you."

He related, in his own brief and concise manner, Marstrand's condition and intentions, spoke of the trading-post at Balsfiord, praised the young settler, and a dozen times calculated that

John Marstrand would soon become a man before whom a hundred doors would fly open in Bergen, when he visited it.

After this account, which Fandrem listened to with frequent nods of approbation, all the while regarding more the face of Helgestad than the Dane, he stretched out his hand, and touched the corner of his three-cornered hat. "Before other hands are proffered to you, I offer mine. I have never had anything to do with young beginners in business; but when Niels Helgestad speaks a recommendatory word, I say Amen! and I shall be pleased to serve you to the utmost of my ability."

Marstrand felt that there was some security in this assurance, upon which he might rely, and Helgestad confirmed it with the remark, that Fandrem's hand-pledge was worth more than the sworn friendship of kings and princes.

There was no hotel at that time in Bergen, and it is doubtful if there be one now, although the town numbered already thirty thousand inhabitants. Every stranger who came there was obliged to depend upon the hospitality of some family: strangers, indeed, unconnected with business, did not visit Bergen in particular; for pleasure travellers were then unknown in Norway. The Nordland traders lodged with the brokers and merchants with whom they had intercourse in business, and the sea-captains remained on board their vessels. It happened, as a matter of course, that Uve Fandrem conducted them, as his guests, to his house on the German Bridge, where he gave them the guest-room, in the upper story. The dwelling of the merchant was one of those old houses which are yet occasionally to be met with there. The upper stories rested on huge beams, upon the massive substructure. Balconies and bow-windows increased its elegance, and produced quite an imposing effect. Deep and wide passages penetrated the under space on both sides of the compting-room, which occupied the middle. In the first story resided the family of the merchant — in the second was the guest-chamber, all simply furnished, but with a fine prospect of the harbor, the ships, the movement, and the great ware-houses on the other side of the basin. This building, so limited in lodging-room, was only during the winter the residence of its proprietor; at the beginning of mild weather, every one who possibly could, withdrew to his country-house; Bergen was surrounded by summer villas of every variety, overlooking the fiord, the city, and built on the woody mountains, or in the lovely velvet green valleys.

When Fandrem retired, and his guests were established in their new quarters, Helgestad communicated to his companion what he deemed it advisable for him to know. "I have not yet," said he, "spoken to you of Uve, as I preferred to do it at the proper time and place. He is one of the first here in Bergen—is President of the Guilds, councillor, and, withal, a man who owes everything to himself—quick of eye, prompt in action, prudent and firm in all that he undertakes. Thirty years ago he had nothing. He began a small trade, at which he had no luck, until I made his acquaintance. We joined hands; at that time, no Nordlander could escape the fangs of the blood-suckers. It was an infernal spectacle; they wanted to hang me up alive, but it was of no avail. I gave them so much trouble that they, at last, left me alone; and since that time we have firmly held together, and have prospered."

"Are you also a partner in Fandrem's business?" inquired Marstrand.

"I have been," replied Helgestad, with a knowing wink; "I calculate all partnerships are foolish; never right in all points, and particularly when one lives at Lyngenfiord, and the other at Floyfjeld. I cannot read through those thick account-books, and study the long reckonings; it is not exactly to my liking to let another make the payments, and to take and give what he chooses."

Marstrand smiled. He thought that Herr Uve Fandrem understood accounts much better than Helgestad, with his

He promised to prepare a list, and Fandrem gave his word to select the best, and to sell them at the lowest price. The whole affair was arranged with a shaking of hands; and scarcely more time was necessary to purchase the cargo of the Fair Ilda of Fandrem. The Guild President sent for a broker, for, through the medium of such persons was all business in Bergen transacted. The broker paid for a half-dozen purchases, which were effected that day, and this affair was also settled with another hand-shaking.

"And now, gentlemen," said the merchant, as they arose, "yet another glass, to our lasting friendship. I hope to see you twice a-year in Bergen, Herr Marstrand; and, as is the custom, the next time with a young wife. Ha!" he exclaimed, in a jovial tone, "how do you stand in this respect? There are in Nordland and Finnmark many pretty maidens; I can sing a song on that head myself. But the handsomest maiden, far and wide, at Lyngenfiord, is my niece Ilda. Am I right, Herr Marstrand? Let us drink to your prosperity."

Helgestad deemed it advisable to interrupt the conversation at this delicate point, by declaring that Ilda would shortly marry the nephew of his old friend Paulsen, in Tromsöe; but that Marstrand could make the best match in the land, so soon as he was established at Balsfiord. There followed a long talk between the relatives, with abundant wishes of good luck, and questions and answers, which was at last terminated by Herr Fandrem's drawing out his thick gold watch, and holding it under the nose of Helgestad, with the remark, that there was no time to lose, to save his cabbage-soup and loin of veal from growing cold or burning up, in his garden, on the signal basin.

"Forward, gentlemen!" he exclaimed; "my Hannah will show you a pair of pretty eyes. I have told her I should bring some guests with me, cousin Niels. I think you will hardly recognise her. A fine child, Herr Marstrand, well brought up; she is perfect in her education. I had her a year in Hamburg, and before that in Copenhagen."

"You had better have left the tree where it grew up," hummed Helgestad, with a squint at the speaker.

Fandrem was silent for a moment, as if he were not averse to recognise the truth, for he said, with a smile, "It may be, that maidens are best kept by the side of father and mother — you will see, however, Niels. She has become a proud girl, fine and sensible, and of strict propriety of deportment. She has also learned many things abroad which are rarely to be found here. She works, with gold thread and colored silk, with enamel and spangles, the most curious things, of which you can see many specimens in my house, such as birds and flowers, upon cushions and hangings, full of beauty and elegance."

In the meanwhile, they had arrived at the harbor, when an officer met them, who saluted the worthy merchant, and then remained standing; Marstrand looked at him with profound astonishment, and called him by his name.

"Heinrick Dahlen!" cried Marstrand.

"Is it possible that you are in Bergen," said Dahlen, "and what a costume! The proudest cavalier of the court," he continued, "in Nordland frieze jacket, and in company with the most avaricious and narrow-hearted old usurer of the German Bridge!"

Herr Fandrem had, in the meantime, walked on with Helgestad; but the sight of the Danish officer had evidently disturbed his good-humor. He gave him a sullen look, and his brow darkened with a deep frown, as he observed the satisfaction that this unlooked-for meeting gave to Marstrand. Both young men followed, arm-in-arm, and mutually relating their respective adventures. Heinrick Dahlen commanded a company of Danish infantry, which lay in garrison in Bergen. He had served with Marstrand in the Guards at Copenhagen; but was suddenly transferred to Norway, whither all were sent whom it was sought to get rid of. The young officer had complained of the ill-treatment of a superior in rank, whose influence had brought about his removal to Norway. He was sent deep into the interior of the country; but General Munte soon called him to Trondheim, took him as his adjutant, and employed him on military duty. In a short time, he gained the good-will of that severely just man, who, finally, to rectify evil with good, gave him, last Autumn, the company in Bergen, with a promise to recall him to his own neighborhood as soon as it could be done.

"And the sooner the better," said the captain, as he finished his story; "I am hoping for it every day. It is insupportable, this headquarters of herring and codfish, where no one has any sympathy for anything else than the round, salted merchandise; I should have died from weariness and desperation, if not——"

"If the sweet voice of an angel had not kept you alive," interrupted Marstrand, smiling.

"You were born for a privy-counsellor; but tell me how you have fallen into this wilderness."

Marstrand related his story, to which Dahlen listened with an incredulous and bantering air.

"You, settled among Laplanders, reindeer, beauties of the polar circle, and ignoble fish-traders!" he exclaimed, with a roar of laughter. "You, a so-called trader at Balsfiord, come to Bergen to stock his shop! Are you mad, Marstrand; or will you become so? Many a one has, indeed, procured one of these royal patents who knew how to make money, and has thereby bettered his finances."

Marstrand at first blushed at the laughter of the captain, but he soon resumed his tranquillity. "I thank you for all your propositions, but I cannot avail myself of any of them. Jest as much as you please, and I will remain the trader of Balsfiord. My destiny is irrevocably fixed. I have chosen it, and will submit to it. I wear this blue coat with a lighter heart than I once did the embroidered uniform. I will be a free man; will lead a hard, laborious life; but I will also have my pleasures and my ease. You know not what a fascination clings to those naked wastes; I feel it in my veins. Upon my word, Dahlen,

I would just as little think of living here in Bergen as of returning to the glittering halls of Christiansburg."

The captain looked at him amazed. "I can imagine only one solution of this riddle," he said: "you are in love! An especially lovely sea-nymph has stretched out her hand to you and turned your brain."

"No one has proffered her hand to me, that I know of," replied Marstrand.

"Then Satan has done it!" cried Dahlen; "for only love or the delusions of the devil could induce a man of your name and standing to condemn himself to such wretchedness."

"My good friend," replied Marstrand, with a smile, "ask the men there what they call misery, and they will point to you and your profession. Your life, and your want of independence, appear to them intolerable. Misery is only that which we recognise as such. A man may be unhappy in the midst of wealth and surrounded by all the enjoyments which earth can afford. I am not miserable, for I have a future before me full of industry and schemes. I say to myself that I must suffer every kind of privation; but I can also work, gain a livelihood, and do good. My ambition, also, has a stimulus; for in that country I can be one of the first, which I could not be elsewhere. Smile not, Heinrick Dahlen. I will catch fish, and sail my yacht to Bergen; but I hope that my fellow-countrymen will receive me with respect, that all upright people will give me their hands, and that all doors will be open to me: this is all that I need, not to be miserable."

The captain, who for some moments mused in silence, at last said, "You are right; every one should know what his happiness and misery is, and go his way, and not deviate from it. But there stand your honorable friends and patrons, on the top of the Signalberg, impatiently beckoning to you. The deuce take the dried-herring souls, who think of nothing but their money-bags. Go on, Marstrand; I commend you for your wisdom; but stick to the good path; for old Fandrem has a snake in his paradise above there which may easily fascinate you."

"I fear no Eve," said Marstrand.

"No?" said the officer, laughing, "so much the better. To-morrow I will make you a visit; let not our old friendship be impaired."

When Marstrand reached the height, he found the Guild-master alone, Helgestad having gone on ahead. His apologies were received with a sullen shake of the head; and Fandrem said, mistrustfully, "I will give you a piece of good advice, Herr Marstrand. We have no respect in Bergen for soldiers, and such like useless people; but we hold in high esteem a man like you, who has thrown his braided coat in the corner and become an industrious citizen. The perfumed and bedizzened dandy no one likes to admit to his house; and I least of all. It is no good sign for a respectable man," said he, with a side-glance, "to be seen promenading arm-in-arm with such fellows. A merchant has his reputation to take care of, as well as a maiden. If you only exchange a friendly greeting with such a windy fellow, evil reflections are made upon it. Let a merchant show himself in such society, and his reputation—that is, his credit—is at once damaged. And now," said he, lifting up his stick, "may all the captains, by land and see, be hanged, who would prevent me from eating my soup warm! There is my house, Herr Marstrand; and Hannah, God bless her! has set out the table under the old walnut-tree, where we may enjoy our dinner in the shade."

CHAPTER IX.

From the Signalbecken, a projection of one of the seven piles of rock which surround Bergen, the road descended to a lovely valley, which formed the property of Fandrem. The pretty villa, with balconies and wooden pillars, stood on the side of the mountain, which rose behind it. A grass-plot, ornamented with beds of flowers and odoriferous plants, stretched out before it; venerable old trees expanded their thick foliage over it, and full in view lay the fiord, the harbor, and city — a charmingly beautiful panorama.

Helgestad was already seated at the table under the great walnut-tree, and Hannah stood before him. She went to meet her father, and began to scold him for his long delay.

She was, as it seemed to Marstrand, no great beauty; but she was slender, and possessed the delicate hue of skin and the regular features for which the women of Bergen have always been celebrated. It appeared as if she made a powerful effort to suppress the fire of her large brown eyes, and a rather scornful expression played around her mouth, which was not calculated to please an observer. The dress of this young maiden was very pleasing. She wore a white and blue star-spangled gown of Netherland muslin, closely attached to her bodice, over which was a spencer of the same material, with broad sleeves and trimming. Upon her lightly powdered and puffed hair sat a small lace cap, with a crown of silver stuff; and around her neck she wore a finely-worked collar, from beneath which a heavy gold chain fell down to her breast.

The Guild President regarded his gaily-dressed daughter with pride; and she was, undoubtedly, the first lady of fashion in

Bergen; he patiently tolerated her scolding, while he stroked her chin and pinched her neck.

"Softly, maiden; softly!" he said; "I am hungry and tired enough. If any one is to be punished, it must be John Marstrand, here; who kept me standing and roasting above, at the Signal, while he was gossiping with the captain of the loungers and do-nothings, whom we must support here in Bergen."

A cold, scrutinising glance of the young lady, was directed to the stranger, followed by a rather insolent laugh, which increased the unfavorable prepossessions of Marstrand.

"What do you think of it?" asked Fandrem, who desired an answer.

"I think, father," she replied, "that we could do better than to waste our time thus."

"You are right, my jewel! you are right," said the Guild-President, with a laugh. "There sits Helgestad, like a half-dead man. Bring in the soup, and wake him up with my welcome."

The soup was served up, and with it a smoking-hot piece of beef. Green peas, brought from Holland in boxes, a loin of veal, cooked in its own sauce, eels from Hamburg, and a stuffed turkey, which a French captain had brought the day before from Dieppe for Fandrem, constituted the chief dishes of the meal, the daintiness of which none esteemed less than Helgestad. He seemed to find a pleasure in playing the unsparing critic; and, while he greedily helped himself to all good things, he made light of Fandrem's sweet-toothed extravagance, and swore that a single dish of fresh seyfish or redfish, and a shoulder of reindeer, such as Ilda prepared, was worth more than all these foreign delicacies.

Ilda's approaching marriage with the secretary was the next intelligence that Fandrem communicated to his daughter; but Miss Hannah listened in silence to all that was related by him of these interesting family affairs. Two or three occasional words, a nod of the head, or a smile, was, for the most part, her only response. Only once she ventured upon a more extended remark, which was expressed in a disagreeably haughty and assuming tone; for the residue of the time she sat immovable, or played with her gold chain.

"Now, niece," at length said Helgestad, with his accustomed grimace, "you have become a fine lady among the Germans in Hamburg, you have acquired good manners, and know how great people conduct themselves."

"There is nothing like a proper education!" cried Fandrem to Marstrand, as he raised his glass.

"It is a stout saying," said Helgestad; "I calculate, however, that you have brought with you some things which do not suit our Norwegian land."

"What means cousin Niels?" she asked.

"I mean your painted skin," said the rough man, with a laugh, the French bodice, there, the shining cap, and the flour on your head."

Hannah looked proud and offended. "At Lyngenfiord, they do not know what the world appreciates,' she replied.

"It may be, maiden," was his answer, "that we are not as wrong in our judgment at Lyngenfiord as you suppose. I am thinking of your mother," he continued, as he saw the blush upon her face; "she was a genuine Nordland woman; had head and feet in the right place, and, to her blessed end, she wore her plaited apron, as in her young years." He stretched his coarse hand across the table to the angry maiden. "Bah!" he exclaimed, "you will permit a word from old Niels Helgestad. You know what your mother's wish and desire was, and I have already spoken of it to-day with your father. Give me your hand, Hannah; you shall make the voyage with us and see how the Gaard von Orenaes is managed. Ilda will be rejoiced to meet you; you will make us all glad; and Björnarne, on the second voyage, can bring you back: you can safely trust yourself to his care."

This request was so suddenly made, and was pressed with so

much earnestness, that Hannah dared not refuse. She accepted the invitation, laid her hand in that of Helgestad, and calmly said, "If my father approves of it, I will go with you."

"It is an old agreement, Hannah," said her father, embarrassed at the declaration; "you know it." She nodded. "For some years, indeed, nothing has been said on the subject; but to-day Niels has spoken his word," he continued.

"I hope it is a word which has pleased you?" spoke Helgestad.

"Old friendship and old truth," replied the Guildmeister; "I have long looked for this word."

They both raised their glasses. "Herr Marstrand," cried Helgestad, "you are a witness here, to speak for Björnarne. Look here, maiden," he continued, "and you shall hear a friend speak who knows the state of Björnarne's heart."

But Hannah ran into the house, amid a roar of laughter.

"You will not run away from us when we have you on board," said Helgestad; "and you will yield to everything when Björnarne puts the ring on your finger."

Marstrand had supposed that Helgestad was speculating for the daughter of his friend; but he was, nevertheless, surprised at such a sudden declaration and agreement. While he was speaking with Dahlen, Niels must have broached the subject, and have met with a ready answer. Now he learned that, according to the old custom, a family conversation on this subject had been held years before. At that time, Hannah was just born; but her mother, as a true Nordland woman, desired her child to live in the cherished home in the north which she had been obliged to give up. Fandrem, who owed Helgestad everything, willingly joined in a promise to this effect; when, also, changes had taken place, and the family connection with the rich cousin was not so desirable as formerly, yet was the marriage an advantageous one, and the compact itself too sacred to be broken.

After much had been said on the subject, the joviality was increased by the old Madeira, which the Guildmeister produced from his choice wines. A tobacco-box of China porcelain was set upon the table, and Hannah brought in long Holland pipes, bound round with silver threads. At her father's bidding, she was obliged to drain a glass to the prosperity of Björnarne, and to light the pipes with a wax candle; all of which was happily accomplished under Helgestad's encouraging sallies of wit.

"Such is the custom in Nordland and Finnmark, when a young woman wishes to do honor to her guests!" exclaimed Helgestad, as he embraced her. "You have three days left to show your pretty clothes, chains, and rings to the young gentlemen in Bergen; after which, Paul Petersen can admire them, who is a judge of such matters, and John Marstrand, also, who has seen the court ladies in Copenhagen."

"I need no one to admire my ornaments," she said, as she liberated herself from his grasp.

"You like it enough, but would rather be admired yourself. You are a cunning vixen, maiden, but Björnarne has eyes."

"If he has eyes," she responded, "let him open them."

"I calculate you will help him thereto," he cried after her.

"I will do what I can," she answered.

"Take care of yourself, Hannah," said Fandrem, delighted. "There is nothing better than a proper education, gentlemen; and whatever you may say, Niels, it is an advantage for her to have been in Hamburg, where she has learned so many things."

Helgestad bit his lips, but his cousin's equanimity was not disturbed. He had her embroidery brought from the house, related how fluently she spoke German, and that she could even play the spinnett.

Helgestad heard all quietly, and confirmed the long eulogium of her attainments with some guttural expressions and his most cunning grins.

"She is a fine maiden," he said, "and too good for Bergen; but a father cannot keep his daughter always by him, were she his greatest treasure. I have thought of this; and so shall I do with Ilda, and receive Hannah in exchange for her."

"You will not lose by it," said Fandrem.

"I hope to gain," said Helgestad; "and for that very reason, in order that no one may recede in the affair, I bind myself to pay you thirty thousand smooth specie thalers, in case Björnarne does not ask for your blessing; if you refuse him Hannah, or she him, then you must pay as much."

Marstrand was a witness of this curious bargain, which, begun in jest, had ended so earnestly. The Guildmeister smiled in the outset at the apprehensions of his relative that a father could not separate himself from his child; he shook hands and accepted the forfeit-money.

The evening had come on. The sun illuminated the mountain summits with a red glow of fire, and below them hung a bluish mist, which covered the city and harbor with a soft twilight veil. Confused cries arose from below, and died away on the clear, still air. A more beautiful picture could hardly be imagined than this animated valley, spanned by a cloudless and deep-blue sky. The crescent moon hung over the edge of the highest fjeld, and far in the distance flashed the sea, with moving ships and fluttering sails.

Marstrand ascended to the top of the garden, whence the rocks sunk in a perpendicular line, and here, also, he again found Fandrem's daughter. She leaned over the railing, and threw a stone below, after which she gazed; she rose up ill-humoredly as she heard Marstrand's steps so near at hand.

He spoke some words in praise of Bergen, which she heard with indifference, and then turned to the observation of her Nordland jacket and the gold chain about her neck. After answering his inquiries for some time with a yea or nay, she left him standing and again leaned over the breastwork, until she at last turned round, and, without any salutation whatever, went to the house.

"There is nothing better than a good education and a knowledge of the world!" exclaimed Marstrand, looking after her.

"Heaven protect poor Björnarne from this fine maiden — this disagreeable composition of chintz and gold."

With these words, he returned to the two old gentlemen; who, disputing and reckoning, yet sat at table; and the stars shone out in the sky before it pleased Fandrem to recommend his guest to sleep to begin the morrow with renewed strength.

"And where is Hannah?" asked Helgestad, who seemed to keep himself on his legs with difficulty.

"Where a discreet maiden should be at this hour. She is lying under the cover, and sighing over the godless father-in-law who cannot be satiated with the sweet poison."

"And dreaming of Lyngenfiord, and of the happy day when Björnarne shall press her to his heart!" cried Helgestad.

"Be silent, you old sinner, lest she awakes and hears what you say. She would never forgive you for thinking that any man could press her to his heart."

"And if all the others allow it, I calculate she will do the same;" replied Helgestad, with a grin.

"I calculate that your brain is too hot, Niels," replied Fandrem, joining in the laughter; "but it is now time to get to bed. Give him your arm, Herr Marstrand, and conduct him in. There is nothing better than a good education and temperance!"

Helgestad took up the candle, which was standing before him on the table, and held it before the red cheeks and blazing face of his relative. "You are a specimen of temperance," he said. "Hold fast to temperance, Herr Marstrand, or it will break to pieces."

Fandrem had taken the other light and illuminated the yellow, wrinkled features of the Nordlander. Thus they stood, facing each other, making faces and staring at one another, amid shouts of laughter and all kinds of provoking words, until Fandrem fell into the arms of his housekeeper, who put him to bed, and Helgestad, under Marstrand's aid, found his way to their sleeping-chamber.

To all appearance, Helgestad was in a sadly drunken condition, and his companion with difficulty helped him along. No sooner were they alone, than all signs of intoxication disappeared.

"I am as temperate as you, Herr Marstrand," he said, extricating himself from his helping hands, "but I preferred in this manner to get Fandrem to bed and preserve his reputation. It would be a great shame with him if his head went round and his guests did not do honor to the entertainment. I hate and despise drunkenness; but it is an heirloom of this people which centuries will not eradicate. Bergen is a temperate town, and Fandrem rarely drinks more than he can bear; when you go to Trondheim you will see what feats thirsty throats can perform."

What he said was, indeed, only too true; but it applied as well to Norway as to the other countries. In the best society of that period, drinking was the chief enjoyment, and intoxication in no wise a shame. The marriage-feasts and christenings in Norway too often terminated in scenes of blood and murder; and Helgestad related how, for such occasions, the women sewed the winding-sheet at the same time as the bridal-shirt for their young husbands; and no law had yet been sufficiently powerful to prevent these knife-fights, which had cost so many persons their lives.

"It is equally wicked and foolish for men to kill each other like brute beasts, and on the morrow to cry over their deeds like women."

"Always better," answered Marstrand, "than never to repent of evil actions."

"False, Herr," replied Helgestad. "What a man does, he should think of beforehand; but what he has done, should never give him pain. I have a head and hands which cannot act without the consent of my reason. He raised himself up on his elbows in bed, and, looking at Marstrand, said, "Before you go to your room, wait a moment. Tell me, how did Fandrem's daughter please you?"

"I have had no opportunity of forming an opinion."

"You are a Dane," spoke Helgestad; "that is, a man who knows how to bend and cringe when it is prudent. I read in your countenance your real opinion. She is a proud, lazy maiden; vain, and spoiled of disposition."

"Then, Herr Helgestad, I cannot understand why you wish to introduce this doll into your house, to which she is so little suited."

"Why is she not suited to it?"

"Ask yourself if such a woman is a fit wife for the simple, good-natured Björnarne. When you spoke of Lyngenfiord, she answered with a contemptuous sneer; and your accounts of the life in Orenaes Gaard were received with ridicule and laughter."

Helgestad nodded assentingly. "You have a good eye; it is exactly so. But Fandrem's daughter is a bird with golden feathers, and he were a fool who would let her escape out of his hands. Fandrem is a weak father, wise as he may be in his counting-room on the German Bridge when dealing with Nordlanders and Spaniards. An owl has rested upon his roof and warned him to be watchful. I have heard something of this alarm, Herr. Do not question me about it. I see, only, that I addressed him at the right time as we walked to the Signalbecken. He fears scandal to his name and reputation, and is heartily glad to send Hannah to Lyngenfiord. They will there accustom her to habits of industry and order; I have no apprehension but that she will be virtuous and obedient."

A grim smile distorted his mouth, and hate and scorn flashed from his eyes.

"And will solitude, grief, and home-sickness do more than her education?" said Marstrand, compassionately.

"Bah!" answered Helgestad, "let her grow pale and thin; there is Finnmark blood in her veins which will assert its rights. If it should not turn out so — if Fandrem is weak enough to indulge her vain, spoiled temper, so let it be; but he shall pay me for the voyage and my trouble. You heard that half her fortune, as forfeit-money, would go to Björnarne."

Marstrand now understood Helgestad's whole plan, the low shrewdness of which disgusted him.

"But if the needle turns," he exclaimed, "and pricks your own finger; if Björnarne will not have her, whom he neither loves nor esteems, what then, Herr Helgestad?"

The trader fell back on the pillow, drew the night-cap over his ears, and hummed, turning over on the other side. "All nonsense, Herr. Take the light and go to your chamber. Björnarne will not have the maiden that his father presents to him — Uve Fandrem's daughter, from Bergen? will not have her? The fish will sooner cease to swim in the Westfiord. Will not have her? A pretty story, indeed! I tell you Niels Helgestad wills it, and that is enough."

The merchant had slept away his intoxication by morning; he was gratified to hear Helgestad say that he had been in no better condition, that he had not passed such a night for years, and that he hoped not to see another such until Hannah and Björnarne's marriage-day.

The Guildmeister, to this remark, did not respond with the same cheerful countenance as the day before; and his eyes roved from the coffee-cup to the closed window of his daughter's room, above; but, after some reflection, he brought the affair again in order.

"Hannah shall go with you, hard as it is for me to part with her. It is good for her to go and see, for herself, where she is to live in future. May Björnarne win her heart, that she may joyfully say, 'Yes;' and both can come and receive my blessing. She will have her inheritance; and, on her wedding-day, I will pay such a dowry as becomes Uve Fandrem."

"You pay the thirty thousand, one way or the other," replied Helgestad, giving him his hand.

"Let it be so," said Fandrem. "It is, indeed, a large sum," he continued; "I will, however, satisfy you, and render Hannah happy. If an obstacle should arise from your side, you are bound to me in a like manner."

"You know Niels Helgestad," was the answer.

The treaty was further confirmed by the usual hand-shaking, and, during the breakfast, business alone was discussed. The yacht was that day to be entirely unladen, and she would, immediately afterwards, be ready to take in the new cargo. By the fourth day, Helgestad was to commence the voyage, and, until then, much was to be done. All Marstrand's necessary stores were to be selected and packed up; the experienced trader, on casting an eye over the list, discovered that it would amount to the sum of eight thousand thalers.

His fish on the scaffolds at Westfiord were allowed to Marstrand in the account, and it was stipulated that they should be delivered to Fandrem on the next voyage. The merchant offered to immediately close the transaction, and proposed a certain price for the vaage of forty-eight pounds, consenting even to add a quarter thaler also; flattering as was the offer, and many as were the arts employed to recommend it, and which Helgestad supported with his endorsement, Marstrand would not come to any determination on the subject.

"With you," said Fandrem to his cousin, "I could not make such a bargain, for evident reasons. Fish may be bought cheaper; for it is not as bad as reported. Your large stock would then bring me great loss; besides this, I must pay in cash; while, with this young man, who has won my good-will, I keep an account. He is also a beginner, to whom I cheerfully make concessions; you, on the contrary, have full chests, and will fill them to overflowing."

Helgestad put his finger on his nose, and calculated that wisdom flowed like honey from the lips of the honorable Fandrem. "It is possible," said he, "that fish may be yet higher; and it is also probable that they may be lower. A great quantity has been taken on the whole Nordland coast up to Trondheim, and salted fish are prepared in great numbers

Whoever can hold on may do so; but he who desires to be secure, must prefer the snipe in hand to the goose on the cliffs. It is a fine business for a beginning, Herr Marstrand, when one can, after a short time, button up his pocket with his money trebled. Establish yourself first at Balsfiord, and then you may in future venture upon what you will; now, the surest is the best for you."

"Accept my thanks," replied Marstrand, who was not uncertain as to what he should do. "I am young and inexperienced, and have great gratification in the counsel and good-will of such men as you."

"Shake hands upon it, then," exclaimed Fandrem.

"With all my thanks," replied Marstrand, modestly, "I do not wish to be the cause of loss to you; and would rather take less, than injure a man whom I esteem so highly. For this reason, I will wait until my fish are lying at the German Bridge, and will then take the price which is fixed, between Nordlanders and merchants, by the commission. Should there be a loss, it will be mine; should there be a profit, I will enjoy it."

Fandrem looked at Helgestad, who, with an expression of the greatest good-will, nodded to Marstrand, and said, "Every man must know what he is doing, and never lament the consequences. You know this is my motto, Herr Marstrand."

"Agreed," said the Guildmeister. "Every one after his own manner. It is no wonder that every man seeks his advantage where he can find it. I will pay you the price of the commission."

An hour after, they were on their way to the city. The clocks were striking seven, and the morning was charming. Birds sang in the trees, warm and sunny came on the day, but Hannah's shutters opened not; and the little stumpy merchant drew out his huge watch three times, held it to his ear, regarded windows and house, turned round, stood still, and, at last, followed the two others, who were already at the signal-tower awaiting him.

The labor of the harbor was in full activity. The Guild President gave the overseers, who awaited him before his house, their commands; and he then introduced Helgestad into his counting-room, where the business accounts lay ready, and where also Marstrand's contracts were signed, and the obligation entered into, to carry on trade and traffic exclusively with Uve Fandrem, in Bergen.

The counting-room of the rich merchant was small and dark. One old book-keeper alone sat at an equally old writing-desk; for, notwithstanding their large business, the merchants had not much writing to do. They had much more need of overseers in their magazines, than of assistants in the counting-house. In a corner stood two ponderous account-books, behind a lattice-work which had probably not been dusted for half a century; and the narrow windows let into the vault just so much light as to bring into relief two nail-fastened Russia leather-chairs, with high backs, and a clumsy old paying-table. The remaining space was taken up with chests and boxes, seal-skins, and well-stuffed feather-bales, and against the wall stood a tower-like pile of casks, which Marstrand, in his efforts to wind his way through this labyrinth, had nearly brought down upon his head.

Fandrem called out to him, in warning. "It is a fine house," said he, "with a thousand nooks and corners, which a wise man can make more use of than a larger space. Everything has its place; and there are nice dainties for good friends — anchovies of this year, syld of the right kind, honey from Herdermarken, and butter from Flensburg."

His laugh was explained by the information that these delicacies were destined for the crews of the Nordland vessels whose cargoes Herr Fandrem bought, and who, after the old custom, must be presented with something to eat. The best and freshest were, naturally, not selected for these spoiled stomachs, and thence came it that the odor of fat and meat formed a combination which was no attar of roses for the unconsecrated.

"All smells gold that brings money," said Fandrem; "and when jestingly it is said of Bergen, 'It is much better to smell than to see it,' we could only wish that this saying was never dishonored; for the farther they smell us, the more yachts lie in our harbor, and the higher will rise, at the German Bridge, the piles of dried cod-fish, herrings, and oil-casks, the odor of which is as grateful to us, as the smell of their burnt-offerings, rams, and bulls, to the ancient deities, and which were not, certainly, as odoriferous as amber and myrrh"

After this display of wit, Fandrem drew Marstrand to the writing-desk, where the contract was read through and signed. Thereupon Helgestad took the pen, and subscribed as security for the indebtedness of Marstrand for the articles received from Fandrem in the first year.

"How?" asked the young man, astonished; "am I to understand that another must go security for the credit which is offered me?"

"Such is the custom in Bergen; and I willingly do it. Without security, you could not easily find any one to supply your house with merchandise."

"I should think," replied Marstrand, "that my property, if not my word and honor, would be sufficient security."

"Nuh!" said Helgestad, unmoved, "you talk again like a Danish nobleman, not like a considerate man, who looks at things as they are. Who knows the value of your Gaard at Balsfiord, when we have built it up? Who knows if the Balself will furnish a log or a plank? Much means and skill are requisite for that purpose. Think of what Olaf said, that any one was a fool who would spend one shilling for such a property. I calculate that you have no friends in Bergen but me alone."

Marstrand was in a high degree displeased at the discovery,

that also through this affair his dependence upon Helgestad was increased. He had, on the contrary, proposed to himself to follow his own designs; he now saw, that only through Helgestad's security could the hard hand of the Bergen merchant be opened, and the various schemes founded upon his credit be accomplished. Helgestad's reply clearly demonstrated how completely his welfare lay in his hands; and he thought he discovered, in the avaricious eyes of the old man, an expression of contempt for his helpless condition. The wild Balsfiord was nothing without the money of Helgestad. He appeared to be a fly between the fingers of this cunning speculator, who would let him flutter until he should see fit to crush him. This distrust overmastered him to such a degree, that he forgot all foresight.

"I cannot, in this case, accept your security," he replied, in his irritation. "My obligations are, moreover, so great, that I will not increase them."

"And why not, John Marstrand?" asked Helgestad.

"Because I hold it to be my duty, now I stand upon my own feet."

"I think so," coolly responded the trader; "and it is wisely determined — but who will take my place? Who knows you here?"

This question embarrassed Marstrand. "I know no one here but Captain Dahlen; and he, as well as all other persons of quality of my acquaintance, would, if circumstances required it, pledge their word for me."

Fandrem, who had listened to the conversation, thus far, without interruption, bounded from his seat at the desk, and struck the huge account-book such a blow that the dust flew about on all sides. "Who will go your security?" he cried. "The young swaggerer of the Bergenhaus? Proudly enough the cockerel struts through the streets, gaping at the young girls, in his brushed-up feathers and lace. Do not jest, Herr Marstrand. I esteem you as a worthy young man; but I would not lend a farthing or a doit to your friend, the gallant captain."

"And why not, most excellent Herr Fandrem?" asked a clear voice from the back-ground, as the slender figure of Heinrick Dahlen was seen emerging from between the mountain of casks and chests.

For a moment, the merchant was visibly disturbed at the unwished-for presence of the officer; but he was not a man to lose his courage so easily. He placed himself behind his counting-table, whilst Dahlen victoriously pressed forwards, and reached the other side of this division line. "I know not, Herr, what can induce you to visit my house and counting-room; but as you have come, you can stay. I am always ready to repeat my words."

"I have sufficiently understood you, Herr Fandrem," replied the young man, with a contemptuous laugh; "and I can myself answer my question."

"I calculate," said Helgestad, stretching his iron face over the table, "we are engaged in a transaction in which we had better not be disturbed."

"Exactly so," answered Fandrem.

"I calculate," replied Dahlen, imitating the manner of the trader of Lyngenfiord, and putting his finger on his nose, "that I should vacate this pleasant abode?"

"Yes, Herr officer; yes, if you please," exclaimed Fandrem, peevishly. "I do not think your visit concerns me."

"No, Herr Fandrem," responded the captain, with a polite bow, "I desired only to hunt up this bewildered and forlorn man, who calls himself John Marstrand, and whose presence excites my especial sympathy."

"I think Herr Marstrand would rather not be disturbed in his business," said Helgestad.

"I imagine Herr Marstrand has no need of a spokesman, when he is on the spot himself," was the answer: with a haughty glance at the darkened countenance of the Nordlander,

Dahlen aid his hand upon the arm of his friend, and turning to him, continued; "If you are busy, hear a few words General Munte recalls me to Trondheim. To-morrow I must leave Bergen, and, as I could hardly expect to see you again to-day, I bid you farewell, unless you prefer to accompany me."

"You know that I neither can nor will do that," was the decisive reply.

"Then God be with you!" said the captain. "May he protect you from all hypocrites and sharpers; preserve you from loss and shame, and drive all the fish of the sea into your net. Herr Fandrem, I am ready to leave your house, never to re-enter it, without your wish."

"You can hardly expect me to make so presumptuous a wish," said Fandrem.

"Who knows?" cried the arrogant young officer. "I am, on the contrary, of the opinion that you will one day take me by this right hand, and ask me to increase the honor of your house."

He extended his right hand to the merchant, who angrily drew back, and, with a scornful inclination, replied, "It is a sad thing for Bergen to lose so valiant a soldier, who could, more easily even than Thor, have vanquished the giants and their king. But my house is more difficult to conquer than Yolena, and my feelings are of such a kind, that I would rather the seven Tjellen of Bergen should overwhelm me and mine, than I should live to see the day when you should be welcomed here by this, my right hand."

"Nevertheless, it will happen, Herr Fandrem; it must come to pass—but we will not dispute about this matter. I must be gone."

Fandrem wiped the perspiration from his brow; he trembled from anger, and his fists were clinched together, but he made no reply.

"Since when is it the custom in this country," asked Helgestad, "for a man to suffer himself to be insulted, in his own house, by one whom he will not tolerate?"

"Good friend," said the captain, who was on the point of going, "wait till you are asked, and do not meddle in my affairs."

"Nuh!" grumbled Helgestad, "go your ways, young gentleman; only do not come in my track."

"As I am no codfish, herring, nor haddock," exclaimed the young officer, "and also no unfortunate Lapp, and have not the means of making your nearer acquaintance by a royal patent, I hope always to be preserved from that honor! Peace in your house, Herr Fandrem — remember me kindly; and you, Marstrand, keep your eyes open until we meet again."

As he pressed his friend's hand, the latter felt a small note within it. Dahlen immediately beat a retreat, pitilessly kicked aside whatever stood in his way, and disappeared with a curse at the foul odor, and with a roar of laughter at the sight of the tumbling and rolling casks and barrels, precipitated from their artistically-constructed position against the wall.

"Look at him," said Helgestad, contemptuously; "these are the men who think themselves superior to us in name, position, and honor. Nuh! let him run. I wish never to face him again; it might have ended otherwise to-day. There lies the paper, Herr Marstrand, and here am I. Shall I go security, or do you intend to dispense with my aid in future?"

The tone was so decided, and so menacingly earnest, as to leave no doubt that Helgestad had taken his resolution. He knew well enough that his *protegé* was a considerate person, and could not do otherwise than abandon his opposition. After some discussion, it was settled that Niels should sign as security; Fandrem and he again both assured Marstrand that it was right and customary, but that it was in truth a mere form, as no one doubted the ability of Marstrand to discharge his debts within a year, and then he could obtain abundant credit, without security.

The whole day was passed in the great magazine of the Bergen merchant, in examining and selecting the goods with which the Fair Ilda was to be laden. Helgestad himself bought a quantity of lines and angling-rods, scrutinised and proved what was assigned to Marstrand, and gave him some useful instruction touching the character and qualities of goods. The weighing, packing, binding-up, and making entries, occupied several hours, and left the young settler no time to think over the late events. His friend's strange behaviour in Fandrem's house, and his bitter and scornful remarks had amused him some; but it seemed as if he had some secret aim. The billet which Dahlen thrust between his fingers, contained a couple of lines, which yet more aroused his curiosity. "I must see you again to-day," it ran, "to inform you of various matters which concern us both. When the two old fellows have completed your cargo, come into the garden, where you will find me."

In Fandrem's house, and by night, Dahlen thus sought an interview with him — what could he have to reveal to him? Marstrand turned the matter over in his mind, without being able to come to any conclusion. The noise of the workmen, the uproar in the harbor, the tumultuous activity of so many men, and the continual vicinity of Helgestad, combined to stimulate Marstrand to his new duties in the magazine. His assiduity, and skilful manner of working elicited much applause from Helgestad. Fandrem, at last, came to call off his guests, and take them with him. They took the same road to the pretty villa, found the table set, and Hannah waiting, attired in a yet finer dress, but as silent and motionless as the preceding day. Fandrem tried some kindly words, but these had as little effect as Helgestad's jokes. The maiden manifested not the slightest sympathy, and answered only what she was obliged to, but in such a repulsive and distant manner, that her father could hardly repress his anger.

Trade was the chief subject of conversation; the bottle went merrily around — Fandrem had recovered his good-humor, and said many flattering things to his young friend. "A man like you will soon rise. Labor sweetens life."

"I will do my best," answered John; "I will be industrious—and I believe I have some talent for business, and know how to help myself, where others, without experience, would fail."

"Good!" exclaimed the Guildmeister, "self-confidence is necessary to success in business."

"Every one must have self-confidence, if he would not be ruined, in difficult situations."

"But foresight must not be wanting," continued Fandrem. "The golden rule of every merchant is, not to undertake that for which he has not sufficient strength. Speculation is the soul of trade; but he who ventures risks, without means, is a giddy-brained fool. Slow and sure, that is the word."

"Speculate as carefully as you may, all will be in vain, if fortune abandons you; undertake the boldest risk, and it will succeed, if fortune favors you."

"Ha! and you are, I suppose, a favorite of the blind goddess," cried Fandrem, laughing.

"I have, at least, the courage to be," replied the young adventurer. "Formerly, I experienced the frowns of fortune; and why should I not now believe that she will be more propitious to me? I will not suffer any antagonist to surpass me. He who does not fear misfortune, has always the best chance of success."

"I wish you every good," cried the merchant, raising his glass, "and that your ship of fortune may never run on a rock."

In the coarse, red face, a rising sympathy was evident, which Marstrand increased, as he remarked, "Everywhere, where men struggle for an object, fortune is opposed to fortune. Every one has his part therein; the only question is, who shall have most? They who seem to be the proudest and most secure, who contrive their plans with the greatest secresy and skill, are often the most easily overcome by antagonists, of whom they scarcely took notice. One must do right, Herr Fandrem; the conscience must always be in order; and not only the head, but the heart also be kept at the right place; for thus can we cope with every enemy. It is written in the Bible, 'Be wise as serpents, but harmless as doves;' this is a just saying, which helps us in many extremities."

This last reply made a various impression upon his table companions. Fandrem hummed to himself, and drained his glass, and his daughter's countenance grew more animated than it had been. Helgestad, however, met the eyes of the speaker, and both sought to interpret their respective thoughts.

"Nuh!" exclaimed the Nordlander, in his short, sober man ner; "I calculate that every one will do what he can. He is right, who keeps his head above water, and executes what he begins. Every one must determine with himself what is conscience; one says this, another that: Herr Marstrand must prove his proud words in many kinds of storm and weather."

"Time will prove if I shall deserve your praise," said Marstrand.

"Or whether your luck holds out," said Niels, with a grin.

"I think, Herr Fandrem," replied Marstrand, "it will soon be evident that I have profited by Helgestad's instruction."

"I do not doubt it," cried the Guildmeister, holding out his glass. "Were the captain a man of your stamp, by heavens!" — he struck a heavy blow with the handle of his knife on the table — "he should sit at my table, and be welcome to my house."

"Heinrick Dahlen, as far as I know him, is an honorable and upright man," he said, on behalf of his friend.

"A Danish blusterer, a Jack in red hose — a misfortune is it for the country that it must support such idlers," cried Fandrem, with passion. "Would to heaven," he continued, with a sigh, "Norway was what it once were, a free and independent kingdom, and Bergen again a city, framing its own laws. Then it would be better than now, when Danish bloodsuckers of all kinds, tax-gatherers, judges, priests, and profligate soldiers, lord it over us."

"The beautiful maidens of Bergen will judge of this in a milder manner," cried Marstrand, with a laugh. "What says Miss Hannah thereto?"

"Bah!" cried the father, angrily, "behave properly, Herr, and do not ask a modest maiden questions about such matters. Bergen is, thanks to heaven, not such a Sodom as Trondheim, where the Danish officers go into the houses of the best families; and balls, with other sinful amusements, ruin the young people."

"Is there no dancing, then, in Bergen?" asked Marstrand.

"We live in an honest city," answered Hannah, "where such follies are unheard of. Here, happily, we hear only of codfish and herring; and instead of music, the roar of the winds among the warehouses, and the song of our dear friends, the Nordlanders, whose society gives us so much pleasure. Our innocent pleasures consist only in passing the summer here on the heights, and of sitting by the stove, in the winter, at the German Bridge. It rains, regularly, two hundred days in the year at Bergen, when it does not snow, by way of change: we recognise every ray of sun as God's especial gift."

Although the maiden spoke with apparent earnestness, Marstrand was yet convinced that she was only indulging in some quiet satire; her father, however, appeared to be much edified by the description. "You are right, maiden," he said, "still and God-fearing is our modest life, without theatres or disorder. The families never meet together," he continued, with evident satisfaction, "and it is a rarity for them to visit and eat a dish of fresh sey or syld."

"Genuine Bergen blood does not let the right hand know what the left hand does."

"Excellent! maiden, excellent!" continued Fandrem. "Such is our existence, our own society suffices for our happiness. There is nothing better than a good education, Herr," he ex claimed, with a look of parental affection at his daughter. "Fill your glass, and help yourself to the best rib. We drink with our guests, as long as they will; but we would rather invite Satan into our house, than a Danish red-coat."

"Nuh!" said Helgestad, "I see you have the same prejudice against the red-coats in Bergen, as we in the North against Finns and Lapps."

"It is worse, Niels; it is worse!" said Fandrem, as the wine mounted to his head. "A Lapp is a filthy creature; but he is, nevertheless, an useful being, that can work, and is also able to drive a trade and business, to gather money, to employ his time acceptably to God; one who costs nothing to his fellow-men, but rather affords them opportunity of gain and profit. Of what utility was ever a soldier to human society? They are the drones in the beehive, Niels, and must be treated like them. Women, indeed, are easily fascinated by tassels, epaulets and other such like foppery; but were I to choose my son-in-law between a Lapp and a red-coat, may I be cursed if I would not give the preference to the former!"

Laughter and a renewed dispute followed these passionate remarks, and, as on the previous evening, the glasses were filled and emptied until Fandrem was carried to bed, and Helgestad tottered to his room. The latter appeared, on this occasion, to have taken his full proportion without troubling himself about his companion, who, with considerable difficulty, helped him to bed; he sank in the down, and in the next moment was sound asleep.

Some time after, Marstrand extinguished the light, and opened the window. In the house all was quiet; under the trees it was dark; but the sky was full of stars, which cast a faint light. After a long observation, listening and looking around, Marstrand descended to the garden, and proceeded with cautious tread to the furthest path. A figure was leaning there, in the same spot where Hannah had cast the stone down the precipice, and it advanced towards him, as he emerged from the trees. At the first word, Marstrand was convinced that it was the captain. He was enveloped in his cloak, and held his drawn sword in his hand.

"How!" he exclaimed, "are you armed with a drawn sword?"

"A necessary precaution," answered Dahlen, thrusting his sword in the sheath. "I should be treated with little ceremony, if I were found here at night-time, alone and unarmed. A sudden push would send me over this parapet here; and when I should be found in the morning, a hundred feet below, they would lay me in my grave without much regret."

"And who do you think capable of such villany?"

"Candidly, the thick-pated, knavish scoundrel who brought you here, if he could gain anything by it."

"And what would it profit him, to send you out of the world?"

"I will tell you. He lets you live for the present, because it is to his interest; me, he would throw to the shades, because my pockets are empty — but his sack shall fill them."

"I do not understand you, Heinrick," said Marstrand.

"Wait a moment, and I will make it clear to you. I hold the grim old fellow for a gallows'-bird of the worst kind; for a scion of those children of night whose whole aim was the ruin of men. He dragged you hither, in the first place, to talk you out of your fish at the lowest price, in order to share the profit between them. You have frustrated both the honest men, but he has got you upon the credit-book of Fandrem, for which he has given his security, that is to say, for as much as Fandrem has lent him; and he can, any day, say to you, get out of your shop, for it belongs to me, and not to you."

"Nonsense," muttered Marstrand. "Could that, indeed, be his object?"

"Satan take the scoundrel," exclaimed Dahlen, in a louder tone; "but I would rather see him turn you out to-morrow, and thus put an end to your madness, than that you, a free man, should live among sharpers and polar bears."

"And who has advised you of all this?"

"I could answer, a Kobold, or the beautiful goddess Gnu, who rides on the sunbeams, and exposes all secrets, or that I had dreamed it, — but here begins my own story. What I know, John, I know from a being who takes a lively interest in you, and yesterday heard your magnanimous patron swear that he would soon be done with you, although no one could despise your talents. But a young nobleman from Copenhagen was one spy more in Finnmark; that you were, at bottom, an excellent person, but with all kinds of fancies in your head, touching honor, right and justice, and that you were already putting your nose in matters with which you had no business. Is there not a fellow of the name of Paulsen or Petersen?"

"There is one," answered Marstrand.

"He is his accomplice. Endeavor to escape him; do not suffer yourself to be treated by this rabble like a seal, whose skin is stripped off his living body. Apply to the Governor, and, if necessary, at Copenhagen; you can reach Trondheim soonest, where I will give you my assistance."

"And who is the being who takes this interest in my behalf?"

"That is a direct question," replied Dahlen; "yet I will give it a plain answer. Hannah is the name of your friend."

"Fandrem's daughter! I thought so."

"Thus, you know all. I have been acquainted with her for three months; and for the three weeks she has resided here above, I have every night visited this spot."

"And, to all appearance, not alone."

"I never loved solitude," said Dahlen, smiling; "and happily Fandrem follows the good Bergen custom of going to bed early, after a stout meal and a good sleeping-draught."

"He has no idea of your love passion?"

"He knows all; but he wishes to be ignorant. I have, in

vain, attempted to approach him. It is an unheard of thing for a soldier, a Dane, and a nobleman, who has nothing but his uniform and sword, to be received into the house of one of these kings of the German Bridge. In vain has Hannah dropped some favorable words in my behalf; it has had no other effect than to render him more eager to deprive her of every opportunity of seeing me."

"And now?"

"Now comes the Finnland porpoise, to drag Hannah into his hole, as a dainty morsel for a churl, who looks upon the fishing girls, in their bright frieze gowns and leather jackets, as the first beauties of the world."

"You are unjust," replied Marstrand; "Björnarne is a different person from what you suppose."

"How unjust? I only know that a jewel, like this, is not fit for the hand and log-hut of a half savage trader. He shall not have her, and upon that I stake body and soul."

They had, in the meanwhile, arrived at the wall, and had conducted their conversation in a suppressed tone. Only the concluding words did Dahlen pronounce aloud, and with some emphasis. Marstrand laid his hand on his arm, and gazed inquisitively into the bushes——"Hush," he whispered; "did you hear nothing?"

"Nothing," replied the other. "Make yourself easy; no one hears us, of whom we have to fear. Hannah must be mine at every cost."

"Do you know that, by the law of the land, he who carries off a young girl is punishable with death?"

"Only he is hanged who is caught," replied the captain. "I will not steal my treasure, but I will deliver her from her kidnapper. There would be a great outcry in Bergen, if the Guildmeister should, some morning, find his nest empty; and if I should be taken, their old statute-book of the time of Christian the Fourth would be opened, and heaven knows what one of its penalties would be applied to me, before I could obtain assistance. I will not afford these dirty fellows such a pleasure. I will act openly and above-board, and neither morals nor reputation shall be infringed upon by me. A government lugger carries me to Trondheim, and to-morrow morning, early, I go on board. Would it not be possible for my nimble little vessel, in the middle of the night, to draw up close alongside of the shapeless box, dubbed a yacht, and if a boat were quietly lying at its side, could not a prisoner be liberated, especially when there was a helping friend on board?"

"Is this your plan?"

"By heavens!" cried Dahlen, "I know no other, and it is not difficult to accomplish. If I once get Hannah on board, and carry her to Trondheim, I am safe. General Munte will protect us, and things done cannot be undone. Fandrem will see that the affair is beyond remedy; and Helgestad will believe his victim has jumped overboard to escape from his murderous hands. I rely upon you, Marstrand; you can aid me to success."

"You are mistaken; I can do nothing."

"How?" asked the captain; "have I deceived myself?"

"Ask yourself, if I can help you in such a transaction."

"Could you refuse me your coöperation to free a lady, who prefers death to a miserable, hopeless life,—to render your friend happy,—to deceive a heartless sharper, who wants Hannah's money for his heir, and who looks upon her in the same light as a cargo of codfish?"

"Is, then, this vain, giddy maiden, a person to render you happy?" answered Marstrand. "Is she not a mere doll, with whom you would regret to have shared your destiny, be it what it may?"

"Hold," cried Heinrick; "now you speak unjustly!" He immediately turned to the dark bushes, and continued, laughing, "Come forth, sweet Hannah, and show him that he abuses you, without knowing you——There she is; she has heard all, but she forgives, in advance, your sins."

The Dane was astounded to see how near the maiden was, when he expressed his opinion of her; but his surprise increased, as she jested upon it in the most good-natured manner. "I have nothing to forgive," she said, "for how could Herr Marstrand have formed any other judgment than that which I richly deserved by my conduct. It seemed to me the only means of preserving myself from Lyngenfiord, by showing my detestable father-in-law that I was not suited to it. I was, when quite young, deprived of my mother, sent to an educational establishment at Copenhagen, afterwards lived in Hamburg; and now, in pursuance of a family compact, which I abhor, the rest of my life must be passed in a desert. I will not," she cried, leaning on her lover, "permit myself to be sold. Since my childhood I have thought with horror of this Helgestad, who has often threatened me with the honor which he now proposes. My father is good-hearted, and loves me; but nothing in the world could induce him to make a Danish officer his son-in-law, so long as he could prevent it. All my entreaties have been in vain. The reports in Bergen concerning Heinrick and me have aroused his pride, and I have been subjected to cruel scenes. Now, he has gladly accepted the proposition of Helgestad, to carry me to the end of the world; he would rather that I should perish, than not thus save himself from what he calls shame and disgrace." She paused a moment, and then resumed in a milder tone; "Since this, I have lost my cheerfulness of disposition, but I have not given up all hope. Isolated as I am, I have patiently fulfilled my duty; but a cheerful face I could no longer show to my father, who unfeelingly thrust me from him, and whose anger broke forth, whenever he heard Heinrick's name. We have, nevertheless, often in secret seen each other. God forgive me the sin, if it be one; but has heaven bestowed such power on parents? Are children so entirely their creatures, as to be disposed of, body and soul, like slaves? The laws say so — the holy commandments threaten disobedience with eternal perdition, and custom requires submission and despises the transgressor. I do not, I cannot, believe that my love is a crime. How could it be? Where is the stain that it has inflicted? Where is the shame in his intimacy? Who knows anything evil of him? This is our story, Herr Marstrand, and it is a sad one, full of sorrow and unhappiness. What did you say to-day at my father's table? You said, 'One must trust in the great goddess Fortune to defend him against falsehood and cunning.' I have lost my heart, but my head is filled with the thought of being where my heart is, and of never leaving him who has taken it."

"Now, friend, can you hesitate to assist us?"

"No," replied Marstrand, "I will help you as far as I can; but is there no other way than the dangerous and uncertain one you propose?"

"There is no less dangerous one. My plans are well laid. I am protected against the punishment of their accursed laws. Pursuit is not possible; and I shall spoil the old scoundrel Helgestad's sport, where he least expected it."

They walked up and down in anxious conversation as to what should be done. In three days the yacht could put to sea, and the lugger would await her at the mouth of the fiord. Signs were agreed upon for mutual understanding; and Marstrand undertook to favor the escape, on the condition, however, that Hannah should previously employ every effort to change her father's mind."

"It will be in vain," she replied; "but I will try it, that I may convince myself there is no other choice left."

A yellow light hung over the summits of the highest mountains, as Marstrand turned to leave the lovers. "Take her with you," said Dahlen, "otherwise the sun will find us here, and betray to all Bergen what has passed. Be her protector, Marstrand, and in return, I will be your true friend in all events." He laid both hands on Hannah's head and endeavored to scan her features, and then drew her to his breast. "My heart will beat for you to its last throb," he said; "do you firmly believe it?"

"Forever, my Heinrick," she whispered.

"Then farewell and be ready. Trust my luck and your fortune."

He rapidly hurried to the wall and down the steep path which conducted below, and soon disappeared.

"Farewell!" cried Hannah, after him, and she listened until she heard him clap his hands from beneath. "He is gone; he is quick and prudent, and I fear not. Yesterday, he lay there under the bushes waiting for the stone to which I had tied my note. Thereupon you came up to me, and I did not know how to endure the unacceptable society except by silence."

"Will I in future be more welcome?"

"My friend's friend is my friend also," she responded; "though, for the present, she remains the same vain doll as formerly. We are acting certain parts, Herr Marstrand, and we must not be indifferent actors, if the conclusion is to gratify the spectators. To-morrow evening, when we meet again, we can resume our natural characters."

They separated, and some moments after he climbed into the window, from which he had descended to the garden, and cautiously glided to his chamber.

CHAPTER X.

On the next day, the fair Ilda had shipped her cargo, the goods were stowed in the hold, and a quantity of iron bars piled up against the mast. The Guildmeister was in an especial good humor. He privately informed Helgestad that the Danish swaggerer had left the city, and with a hearty curse he wished him a good voyage. In the evening, the merchants gave the captains a feast in the old tower hall, where, formerly, Christian the Second, that cruel enemy, and subsequent victim of the nobility, had first seen and danced with the beautiful Dyveke. On this occasion there was no dancing. The ladies of Bergen withheld their presence from the banquet; but there was great eating, and drinking deep into the night. Fandrem plied his glass with such zeal, that Marstrand was obliged to see him home, before midnight, amid the jests and laughter of the company at his early discomfiture.

Helgestad returned only with the dawn; but he possessed such an inexhaustible fund of strength, that an hour after he was again at work, and did not desist until the yacht had drawn out into the middle of the harbor, and everything was in readiness for sailing, as soon as the ebb tide should begin to run.

During the whole day, many people had been at work on board; boats had carried provisions and stores, and at last the old speculator showed Marstrand the cabin and its arrangements. He had put up a curious little chamber, furnished with all kinds of comforts. A bed with curtains was secured against the side; a mirror and a table, a carpet and a pretty bureau, with several soft, easy chairs, presented an unaccustomed elegance in the fair Ilda. The rough woodwork was everywhere covered with yellow cotton stuff, and flowers and ornaments of various kinds had not been forgotten.

"Nuh!" said he with his finger upon his nose, "no one shall say that a Nordlander is deficient in taste. I will show the proud maiden that we are people with whom she can live; and, if it pleases her, Björnarne, on his marriage-day, shall put on bright green breeches, and a red coat, with lace, like a nobleman at court."

He laughed aloud; but as he saw that his companion did not sympathize with him, he begged Marstrand, for that day, to assume a cheerful countenance, and dismiss all thought of himself — "I well know," he said, "that Fandrem's daughter does not please you, and I also have but little inclination towards her; I have, however, considered the question on all sides, and I am certain that what I am doing is right."

"I hope so," replied Marstrand, "but"——

"Lay all buts aside," cried Helgestad, "I know the women better. If you, a fine gentleman, with white hands, in so short a time have acquired a love for the life of the fiords and rocks, what can she not do, who is attached to them by blood? You have nothing to do the whole voyage but to pass time agreeably, as young people ought to do. I should be sorry for people to say that I had compelled her to enter my house. Now, let us go to Fandrem's, to eat his bread and drink his wine for the last time."

All preparations had been made for this purpose; for, when they reached the villa, the table was already set out, and the Guildmeister was seated before it; by no means, however, as a joyous host with a smiling face; he appeared rather to be absorbed in deep thought, and shrank back as he heard Helgestad's voice. His daughter sat opposite to him, and between them both lay a letter, which Hannah took up, and went into the house.

"Nuh," said Helgestad, as he stood before his relative, "all's ready for sailing, and with the earliest dawn, I shall raise anchor. Why has Hannah left us?"

"She will return," said Fandrem. "We have received letters from my son, who will return, at the latest, in three months."

"Will you, in future, keep him here?"

"I think I am old enough to require help," murmured the merchant. "He has a longing to see his sister, writes to her as tenderly as a lover, and urges me to take good care of her, and to wait for his return."

Marstrand had retired to a distance, and the two old men were left alone. Helgestad took off his tarpaulin, wiped the perspiration from his wrinkled brow, and crossing his legs, scrutinized Fandrem with a penetrating look.

"Nuh!" said he, "I think I comprehend all, and can speak frankly with you. Do you believe, Uve, that I do not know what the people in Bergen whisper in the ear? I have heard of it, and know more of it, but it is not my business to trouble myself about matters of which the least said the better."

"What do the people in Bergen say? What do they know?" shouted the excited man.

"I may not repeat it," replied Helgestad quietly, "I do not like to put my hands in pitch, when I can avoid it, Uve. Hannah must be gone, if you would silence this talk and ridicule."

The little thick merchant gave vent to a long-drawn sigh, without replying.

"I observe from your words," said Helgestad, "that Hannah has turned to her brother, and I should infer from your countenance, that the young Herr had persuaded you to his wishes. It is an evil thing with children, Uve, who, among foreign people, learn to forget what is proper. Another race is growing up in the world, different from that of our young days. The egg will be wiser than the hen; but the question is, if it is not the duty of a father to keep his house in order, and to teach his children obedience."

"You are right, you are right," exclaimed Fandrem.

"You should know," continued Helgestad, as he bent down to him, "that Ilda would prefer another man to the one I have destined for her."

Fandrem turned inquiringly to Marstrand, who was walking with Hannah in the garden, and then looked at his cousin, who responded with a nod, and a twitch of his grey eyes.

"I have thought of this," continued Helgestad, "but not a word ever escaped her lips on the subject. There is a happy intelligence in the girl, which informs her of my wishes. She is ready for what is determined upon; I have already the bridal ring in my pocket—and in a few days after my return to Lyngenfiord, Ilda will place it on Paul Petersen's finger."

"It must be so, to obtain a father's blessing," said the Guildmeister, in an unctuous tone.

"You have all in your own hands, and can do as you please. Old friendship and ties of blood, old promises, with new pledge of hands, stand on the right hand, and on the left the wishes of your children; you must choose between them."

"I hope you know me," replied Fandrem; "I have never broken my word."

"Then act like a man. Listen no more to sobs and sighs, as a woman. Call her here — I will tell her what is to be done."

Fandrem clapped his hands, and Hannah left her companion, who slowly followed, at a distance.

"Come here, maiden," began Niels, extending to her his huge hand, "there is something serious between us." In a dry and positive manner he said that, at ten o'clock, he was going on board, and that she must accompany him. All is ready for your reception, and before the day breaks the yacht will have left the signal tower behind her.

For a moment Hannah's face assumed a paler hue. She looked at her father, who nodded to her, with a kindly smile. "It is necessary and indispensable, Hannah," he said. "You must go to meet your bridegroom, and you will return, blooming as a rose. Ha! ha! blooming as a rose, Niels. You must give her back to me fresh as a rose. Heaven protect you! Hannah, heaven protect you! It is irrevocably settled."

"Is there no retreating, father?" she asked.

"None, Hannah, all is for your happiness, child; all for your true happiness."

"And my brother's request, my prayers, father?" she resumed, clasping her hands.

"There is no help, Hannah!" cried Fandrem, grasping his wig. "I hope you will respect your father's wishes, and will act as becomes you."

"Yes, father," she calmly replied, "I know that all supplications are useless, and I am ready."

"It is the result of good education," said Helgestad, with a grimace. "You have received a good understanding from heaven; pack up your treasures, Hannah, and fear not. I will protect you, maiden, as my own life; I will bring her back, Uve, fresh and red as a rose. You will make a journey, Hannah, which you will remember all your life. Fine weather, a good vessel, and a nice little cabin; also a fine gentleman, who has sworn to serve you like a courtier does a noble dame. So shake hands, Hannah, and let us cheerfully pass the last day."

"Let us be merry and happy," cried Fandrem, "merry and happy forever!"

"That I hope, father; yes, I hope so, cousin Helgestad," replied Hannah. "I hope our return will be more joyous than our departure."

Fandrem was glad to see that his daughter made less opposition than he had expected. He drew her to his arms, kissed her, and whispered in her ear all kinds of promises and consolation. "It is hard enough," he said aloud, "to let you go, but it must be so; sit down now, Hannah, by my side, and all shall be forgotten and forgiven. You will return with Björnarne, to be married here. May I be denied eternal happiness, if it will not be such a marriage ceremony as Bergen never yet has seen! Children, and children's children, shall relate how Fandrem's daughter walked under a canopy, how magnificently she entertained her guests, and what gifts she bestowed upon the poor, the hospital, and the church."

Amid such remarks the repast went on, the wine was not spared, and with jest and laugh it closed. Helgestad observed, with especial satisfaction, that Hannah had packed her trunks in advance, and had bespoke a costly wedding-dress of rare elegance. Two Nordlanders next came from the yacht, and carried the travelling chests on board. When it was dark, Helgestad put on his hat, and tapped Hannah on the shoulder.

"Nuh!" said he, "everything in this world, as is best, has an end. Come then, maiden, take your cloak, and give the old man your hand. Say no more, but give him a kiss and a good-night, as you are wont to do. In a few moons you will be here again; act, then, as if you were going on a pleasure trip."

"It is a pleasure voyage, a bridal trip, and may it be a glad one," cried Fandrem. "Every year I must have you. You will come with the first voyage, and remain with your old father until Björnarne, in high summer, takes you away again. This is all written in the marriage agreement, Hannah; and now go, my child; I must console myself the best I can. When I see you again, your lover will be with you, and I will take you both in my arms, and hold you as fast as I can."

"Your blessing for me and him," lisped the daughter, laying her head on his bosom.

"Take it, child; take it upon all your ways," replied Fandrem, laying his hand upon her breast.

Helgestad interrupted this leave-taking, whilst he drew Hannah back, and grasped Fandrem's fingers between his own.

"Good-night, Uve," he said. "Enough for to-day; to-morrow you must drink your wine alone."

"Remember me to all at Lyngenfiord," cried the merchant, falling back in his chair, "and hurry with the fish, Niels. The quicker they are here the better—first price, the best price. A pleasant voyage, Herr Marstrand! May the Balsfiord do you honor, and bring you no harm. Light them, Lars, as far as the tower. Are they already ascended there? — so much the better." He stretched himself out in the chair, covered his round belly with his hands, and laughed quietly to himself; then he filled a large glass several times, and drained it drop by drop, holding it before the light to admire the ruby wine with his leering eyes, which every moment swam more and more in giddy gaze. "It must be so," he murmured to himself; "the maiden must go—I could no longer bear the disagreeable face. All must be settled, as it ought to be, before Christmas. Helgestad is the man to arrange everything. He is the richest man in Finnmark, and will become richer. Marstrand, the Danish fool, it's a pity for him—ha, ha! Would I had the royal patent; but it has fallen into the right hands, and Hannah will have her share in it. All is good, all as heaven wishes it!——"

Hereupon the worthy Fandrem leaned his head against the cushioned arm-chair, and fell into such a sound sleep, that his housekeeper and his old servant Lars could with difficulty arouse him, and conduct him to bed.

The morning had hardly yet dawned upon the peaks of the Floyfjeld, as the Fair Ilda lifted her anchor, and sailed beneath the signal-tower. All was still in the harbor; the city yet slumbered, a light mist rose from the fiord, and the smoke hovered over the huts of the fishermen, and the lovely little valleys were buried in the darkness. As the heavy vessel, with many windings, made her way, now through narrow water-passes, and then across the great basins, she awoke the sleeping water, whose swelling waves, as they plashed against the yacht and the rocks, seemed to say—Whither are you going, and why do you disturb our tranquillity? Helgestad, in his great oiled cap, and thick sailor jacket, stood at the helm, and guided the vessel through this labyrinth. Now and then he cast a glance over the low rocks, where the church of Hammer already showed its spire, and the Sound of Alvesund opened to view. A light breeze drove the vessel forward at a tolerably rapid rate. Behind, the sun shone over the icy summits around the Hardangerfiord, and shot its beams over woods and bold masses of rock, which bathed their feet in the sea, and lifted their cloud-covered heads to the heavens. The day advanced, and Helgestad was glad to perceive that there was no stir yet in the cabin below. "Nuh!" he muttered, "it is a good sign of a healthy sleep. I wish they would both sleep until the old church of Lyngen wakens them with its bell."

It was now become broad day, and nothing more was to be seen of Bergenfiord, when Marstrand showed himself, and Hannah soon after followed him.

"You are welcome, maiden," cried Helgestad, offering her his hand; "you can stand the sea, as I observe. And you have done well to put that on," as he remarked her dark woollen dress, and hat of oiled silk.

"I hope you will be satisfied with me, cousin Niels," she replied.

"And do you not look back, Hannah? Do you not ask where Bergen stands?"

"I look forward," she replied, as she boldly raised her eyes. "What lies behind us must be forgotten."

"It is a fact," he cried; "you have calculated aright. As soon as you are out in the open air, and on the broad sea, your Nordland blood, maiden, will awaken, which longs after freedom."

"After freedom, cousin Niels—that is the right word. I almost feel it already in my veins, and it makes me feel better and lighter of spirit and body."

"Are you glad to be here, Hannah?"

"Glad indeed, and I hope to be yet more so. It is beautiful here. What a curious nature—what innumerable rocks! And how huge those mountains! how green those ravines and valleys!"

"You will see much more beautiful, maiden," he said, with a pleased nod. "The farther to the north, the grander is creation. It will imperceptibly fascinate you, so that you cannot leave it again: as the invisible chain of Osla, which winds around every one who touches it, without observing it, and draws him into her grotto. You shall see the deep caverns at Lyngenfiord, where the witch once dwelt, and yet dwells," he continued, with a smile. "Björnarne shall take you to the rapid whirlpool, where the waters are sucked into the abyss, no one knows where, and from which no boat has ever returned, that has once been drawn in."

Hannah's lips trembled so that she was obliged to turn round, concealing her emotion under inquiries touching the churches, towns, and high mountains, which seemed to form a gigantic wall around the ship.

Helgestad placed a man at the helm, caused a table, chairs, and breakfast to be brought on deck, and satisfied at ease all her questions. For half a century he had voyaged over this sea, and it was all familiar to him. He could name the family that inhabited every house he pointed out. All these numerous fiords, sounds, and devious tracts of sea were old friends to him; and there was no mountain peak the name of which was unknown to him.

He laughed aloud as Hannah expressed her fears that the yacht might lose herself in this labyrinth, or stick fast, so as not to be able to move farther.

"It seems likely, but rarely happens. Often, cliffs and dark walls lie around us, at sight of which the anxious heart exclaims there is no escape. He, however, who stands firm, and moves his hands and keeps his eyes and ears open, always again finds a road which leads to open water. Is it not so?"

"It is so," said Hannah; "no one should despair."

"Nuh!" spoke Helgestad, "we are here before Indre Sulen, wild rocks without number, and there is the way into the great Sognefiord. Many kings have dwelt there, and Norway's history there begun. King Nor founded his kingdom there after the great battle with the Aasen; there King Harald Harfager conquered the bloody Wickinger, and the great Jarl of Mar, and many good folk yet dwell around that blessed water. Without, it is full of rocks and narrow; within, however, it is magnificent and rich in fertility. No one should fear a rough beginning, Hannah; for what lies behind often appears the more pleasing for the contrast."

Helgestad spoke with more knowledge than he was credited with of the history of his native country; and related to his auditors many tales of the olden time, when the interior of this great fiord, with the islands, was inhabited by that savage and warlike race who, living on piracy, spread the terror of the Norman name throughout Europe.

Several hours were thus passed, during which the yacht glided through the insular chain of Indre Sulen. To the astonishment and horror of the maiden, the vessel sometimes ran towards piles of rock, which it almost grazed with the bowsprit, before a sudden turn of the rudder directed it into an unobserved, narrow pass, through which, by the force of the current and the sail, it was driven into another maze of the scattered rocks.

At last the smooth water expanded to a breadth of several miles. The high coasts receded, woody mountains formed deep bays, and to the westward lay a chain of islands, between which the waves of the Atlantic rolled in all their might. It was here that another vessel, with two slender masts, steering nearer to the coast, came into sight behind some flat, naked rocks; but it soon after disappeared from view under the high shores.

Hannah's eyes discovered it first. "There is a yacht," she said, pointing with her finger.

Helgestad cast a glance at the object, and smiled. "Nuh!" he cried; "you seem to me like a Nordlander in Copenhagen, who, upon seeing some goldfish in the king's pond, said to his companion, 'Peter, look at the herrings; they are the same as with us, only smaller; but, by St. Olaf's beard! they have painted them yellow.' As the honest fellow held every fish with which he was not acquainted to be a herring, so you think every sea-going craft is a yacht. You will soon learn the difference with your good eyes, maiden."

"And how do you call the vessel?" asked Hannah.

Helgestad looked again, and then morosely drew his cap over his brow. "It is one of those," said he, "which, like sharks, prowl up and down; and wherever they are seen, honest people thank God if no harm is done by them."

"How! is it a pirate?"

"Nuh!" exclaimed the trader; "one might think that the

fellow had plunder in view. Look at him, how he shoots out of the gulf. He is long, sharp, and slender, and flutters a signal at his mast-head to caution people to beware of him."

"It is a coast-guard on a cruise," said Marstrand, as he recognised the government flag.

"One of the many bloodhounds that are now sent out to embitter poor peoples' lives."

The government at that period maintained a high tariff on imports, and exercised unusual vigilance to prevent smuggling from England and Germany, especially of brandy. The presence of numerous revenue-cutters was of course ineffectual to completely accomplish such an aim on this island-lined and broken coast. These cutters had the right to detain all vessels at pleasure, to overhaul their cargoes, and to compare them with the bill of lading. The Danish luggers and sloops, for this reason, were deeply hated; and a round of curses accompanied the fleet sailer as she ran up, on the main-yard of her mainmast, the Danish flag, and, hauling sharp on the wind, steered to the yacht.

As a bird of prey, circling round and watching its victim, she ran, in wide sweeps, around the heavy craft. Two officers stood upon the deck of the lugger, who, with their glasses, examined the yacht for some time; and it seemed as if they would content themselves with this inspection. All at once, the lugger turned round; and, to Helgestad's great displeasure, he was in a few moments at his stern and hailed him.

"I could tell you where I wish you were," said Helgestad; but his rage increased, as a boat was let down from the stern of the lugger, and a half dozen sailors and two men, in the uniform of custom-house officers, sprang into it and rowed to the yacht, the sail of which was lowered. The coast-guard, in the meanwhile, lay at cable's length from the Nordlander; her deck was well-manned, and the long guns on her bow admonished obedience to her commands.

A minute afterwards, half of the sailors, with their leaders, had climbed up the rope-ladder of the yacht, which rose up from the water like a giant alongside of the little lugger. As a bound giant, Helgestad also obeyed the request of the officer for his papers. With a sullen look he descended into the cabin, followed by the officer, who narrowly scrutinised every nook and corner.

His companion remained on deck, and while the crew were engaged in conversation with the stranger sailors, it pleased him to approach Marstrand and the maiden. A fall or a wound must have injured his sight, for he wore a black plaster over his eye, and a red, bushy beard covered his chin.

"We know," he said in a rough tone, that this ship is full of contraband. You will do well to conceal nothing."

"Does the Herr take me for something of the kind?" asked the young lady.

"Oh, Hannah," he replied in a whispering tone, "how gladly would I press this contraband to my heart, and carry it off with me. My mask, indeed, must have been successful, to have deceived the penetrating glance of love."

"Heinrick," she replied, trembling with joy and fear, "what a surprise! I did not expect you here to-day, at least in the person of a revenue officer."

"All that can help, must be made use of," said the Captain. I wished to see you, and to say that I am ready, and near you. The coast-guard cruises at the mouth of the Sognefiord, and Lieutenant Hansen, my friend, whom it pleases to aid me, had the old dress of a revenue officer on board; and as we discerned your floating prison, a visit was determined on. It has succeeded, dear Hannah; he will detain the old scoundrel below, with the papers, as long as it may be necessary. Be prepared, my life! Sleep sweetly and soundly to-night, but to-morrow watch and hope.

"Marstrand, my friend, stand by her," he continued, turning to him. "The wind is good, and will grow stronger. The yacht will, to-morrow, be at the entrance of the Eidfiord, where I will await you. During the night you will anchor, for this heavy-laden box cannot sail through the confused maze of rocks of Staatenland in the darkness. Be ready then, my Hannah, for my coming. All is arranged for a rapid flight to Christiansund."

"You will find me," she said, grasping his hand, but which, without answering, he released, as he saw Helgestead's head emerging from the cabin.

"I hope, Herr Helgestad," said the officer, "you hold the service in too much respect to be offended. I will look no farther. Up sail, 'bout, ready! Happy voyage, Herr!"

The two officers immediately jumped into the yawl, and with a dozen pulls of the oars they were again on board of the lugger, which instantly shot ahead of the yacht. The polite officers saluted from their deck; Hannah modestly responded, and Helgestad, who raised his cap, muttered loud enough, that they might be hanged with all the prying, good-for-nothing spies, who, out of mere pastime and insolence, waylaid honest people.

The little adventure had passed off so quickly and pleasantly, that it was soon forgotten; and the lugger, laying close to the wind, in half an hour had entirely disappeared. The yacht continued her voyage the whole day through; and Helgestad mixed his grog, and was in the best of humor at the favorable wind and weather. Occasionally, the fair Ilda traversed open ranges of the sea, where she was tossed about by the great waves; but she soon again lost herself among the endless small sounds, until darkness came on, and Helgestad deemed it best to cast anchor in a little quiet bay.

Hannah could not complain of a want of friendly attention. Helgestad was as constantly engaged with her as possible, and Marstrand was always ready for conversation and amusement. What was the subject of the former is easy to conceive. Whenever she could, the maiden spoke of her plan of deceiving Helgestad, and how she might best manage, at night, to go on deck. The room in which Hannah slept formed the innermost part of the cabin, and she must go through the latter to reach the door of the staircase. A lamp burned there, and Helgestad and Marstrand slept on either side. She had the most hope of overcoming the danger, by loitering upon deck until Helgestad, overcome by fatigue, should seek his couch, and leave her there also.

In order to accomplish this, Hannah already set to work. After supper, when the old skipper had taken his sleeping draught, and was nodding in his chair, she put on her bonnet again, and requested Marstrand to accompany her in a promenade on deck.

"You are very foolish, maiden," said Helgestad, opening his eyes. "We are lying here between steep cliffs, and the fog falls as heavily as lead upon the breast."

"I love the night," she replied. "It is consoling, in the middle of the sea, to be watched by the light of a single star, and to confide in it, when the evil spirits descend in the fogs—when sparkling light flashes from the clouds, and the hollow tones of the wind sound like the voices of spirits from the clefts and caverns of the rocks.

"Nuh!" cried Helgestad, angrily, "I have heard enough of such nonsense. It is called poetry, and it is made by people who have time to imagine things, not as they are, but as they might be. You will soon be cured of all this; you will feel the rough reality, and will be glad to seek your bed and house, when the stars without appear like twinkling sparks in the clammy fog. Go with her, Marstrand, and show that you, also, have some of the fantastic stuff in you, of which Paul Peterson possessed such an abundant stock; but look to it, that you bring her back when her dress is dampened by the fog."

With these remarks he dismissed them, and was already in a sound sleep as Hannah, some hours after, glided by to bed, and Marstrand softly whispered good-night.

The next day passed as the first. The weather remained fine, but the wind, from time to time, blew up masses of cloud, and swelled the sail with its violence. The sea basins, this day, appeared full of life. Seals and dolphins swarmed around the vessel; over the brooding-places of the sea-birds fluttered flocks of ravens and auks; and a fin-fish spouted its jet of water high into the air, and announced the herring swarms, in the catch of which numerous fishing-boats were busily engaged. Helgestad bought lobsters and red-eyed Ure from one of these boats, for the dinner; and, by dint of jest and persuasion, induced Hannah herself to take charge of the cooking of the meal, a thing which she had always left to the housekeeper, at home.

"You will learn, child," he said, "therefore is man sent into the world; and they are right who say that necessity is the best teacher. You will see how Ilda conducts the house; and there is something in your face which assures me you can do much, if you choose. There is a proud expression in your eyes, of a disposition to shrink from nothing, and to yield to nothing."

The jesting of the old trader was so far effective, that Hannah, to escape further importunity, set to work and proved herself sufficiently expert for a beginner. In part it arose from her desire to gain Helgestad's good-will, from its enabling her to conceal her mental agitation which prompted her to continually scan every inlet and opening of the islands, and with Helgestad's glass at her eye, to sweep the horizon in quest of the peaked sail of the lugger.

The nearer approached the evening, the more intense was her anxiety. Where was the rescuing boat, and what would become of her, if it did not appear? Marstrand pacified her as much as he could. — "I do not doubt that the lugger passed us in the night, and is lying concealed under some promontory for our coming."

"And if it should not appear? If I should hope in vain? If some harm has happened to him?" she anxiously murmured.

"He will come to-morrow, or send us a message."

"He must come, or I shall despair," was her answer. "I could not conceal my feelings a day longer, with this anxiety of heart,"

"Helgestad was wrong, then, in attributing to you such strength of mind?"

She paused, and then more placidly said, "He does not know me, but he is right in expecting something from me. I have need of all my firmness to withstand his cold icy looks."

The darkness was coming on, and red evening clouds lay scattered over the sky. The yacht flew faster before the wind, and before her opened a broad arm of the sea, dotted with island groups and isolated rocks, behind which the coast stretched out in dim lines in the distance. To the left rolled the boundless sea in wide swells, upon whose billowy crests the evening light trembled in a soft dazzle.

Helgestad stood at the helm, scanning wind and waves. "Nuh!" said he, smiling at Hannah, who had placed herself near him, "you will soon see a merry dance. Look there at the long dark ledge, upon which the surf is breaking, that is Staatenland. Thence we steer out into the open sea, where the south-west wind will give the fair Ilda a jolly shaking."

The navigation along the coast of Norway, almost always, lies among the innumerable islands and rocky groups, which have survived the revolutions of nature, and form most curious passages and sounds; sometimes they suddenly cease, and the waves of the Atlantic and the Polar sea then dash in unbroken fury against the mountains of the continent, and a vessel must often lay by for several days in some sheltered nook, until the sea is calmed.

Helgestad also would not undertake to double Staatenland by night, although the wind had considerably abated. "You shall sleep quietly, child," said he. "To-morrow morning, you had better remain in bed, if the spray breaks over the bow. Do you see the sharp rocks before us? That is the island Silden.

No one can securely dwell there, but it is a gift of God; for, in its bay, twenty yachts could lay at once."

Half an hour after, the fair Ilda ran under the high wall of Silden; all motion ceased, and gently impelled by a light puff of wind to the sure harbor, the vessel was made fast to one of the great iron rings, inserted in the rock. The crew were yet occupied in securing the yacht, when, almost imperceptibly, a boat glided before the bay in the darkness, with its sail furled, and two men at the oars. A third stood in the bow and hailed the yacht; "God's peace be with you. Where do you come from?"

Helgestad looked over the taffrail keenly at the boat, and replied, "From Bergen. You are late on the water."

"We are accustomed to it," returned the man. "We are fishermen from Selloen."

"If you have any fish, bring them here," said the Nordlander.

"We must first make our haul. Our nets are ready, and at eleven o'clock comes the flood tide."

"*Helm* and *stern*," said Helgestad, laughing. "You must have good eyes. I advise you to go home, it will be a wild night."

"Night or not, we will find in darkness what we seek," was the reply.

A laugh accompanied these words, while the boat disappeared in the canal, which, running out of the bay, opened into the sea, between a tortuous line of rocks.

"Gallant fellows!" exclaimed Helgestad. "It is a hard life, before which many a stout heart would shrink with fear; they will have luck to boast of, when the morning breaks upon them fresh and jovial."

Hannah trembled slightly against Marstrand, and when Helgestad had withdrawn, she excitedly whispered, "It was he, it was his voice! Now, Herr Marstrand, we must summon up our courage. What time is it?"

"It is ten o'clock," he replied.

"At eleven, Heinrick will be here. Yet a long, anxious hour! My heart may break, but it will obey; hear me. When we are sitting at table, drink with him, amuse him with stories, speak of your plans, and keep him seated, while I go out. Employ all your ingenuity to prevent him seeing or hearing anything but you."

"You must do what I ask of you," she continued as Marstrand objected. "You remain in his power, and cannot take any part in my flight."

"I would not deny my participation, if he should seek to know it," said John.

"No suspicion will be raised, if you are not near me," she answered. "Engross his attention; that is all I ask of you. And now, worthy sir, let us descend. Think the best of me. And if I ever meet you again, suffer me to be your grateful friend."

The table was standing in the cabin, covered with meats; and upon the stove, the tea-kettle was boiling. Helgestad was more tender and attentive than ever to Hannah. He laid his hand on her brow, and felt her hands. "Nuh!" he exclaimed, "your head burns like fire, maiden, and your fingers are icy cold. You must keep yourself from harm, in order to arrive at Lyngenfiord with a blooming face; but I have a remedy here against frost and fever."

He pointed to the bowl, in which he was preparing some punch, the Norwegian nectar, whilst Hannah laid the plates, cut the meat, brought the bread from the side closet, and exhibited so much activity that the old trader could not refrain from a hum of satisfaction.

"You will surpass them all," he said. "It is the effect of blood. Pure Norwegian blood is better than all your education."

"I hope to fully satisfy you to-day, cousin Niels," she responded with a smile.

"You have a good heart. I will pledge myself for you as a good daughter. Take your glass and pour out; you shall always be as happy as to-day. May all our wishes be fulfilled!"

"To-morrow as to-day, and forever," she replied, heartily emptying her glass.

"Amen!" said Helgestad. "I look upon your eyes with joy, Hannah, they shine like stars in heaven. Does the wish come from the bottom of your heart? I think so. Is it not so?"

"Yes, cousin, from my soul, I wish that my happiness may also be yours."

"I calculate it must be so," he said, laying his finger upon his nose, with a cunning grin. "You look like your mother, Hannah, spruce and trim, and truthful. Nothing is wanting but the green Nordland dress, and the plaited apron."

"I will wear them both, as soon as I am in Norway," she replied.

"I will hold you to your word, maiden. You will be an ornament of Tromsöe and the fairs."

The conversation went on in this gay tone, while Helgestad poured out the smoking punch and jested at Marstrand's serious face, which, to his idea, resembled an icefield on the Kilpis.

"Nuh!" said he, "I know not what troubles you that is so hard to bear. Return to Balsfiord like a man who has his pockets full. You have wisely held on to your fish; you carry home a yacht full of goods; your house stands ready and you have only to enter and sit down. But I observe," he continued, "that he is dissatisfied with his loneliness, which is, indeed, acceptable to neither God nor man. We must take care of him, Hannah, and endeavor to find for him some one who will smooth the wrinkles from his brow, and if nothing else succeeds, we must invoke the interposition of Afraja with his incantations."

These remarks of Helgestad aroused Marstrand from his

silence. For two days he had been divided with himself. Lively an interest as he took in his friend's happiness, and heartily as he wished him success, he, nevertheless, felt some compunction at the thought of being associated with him in his daring scheme. He despised the motives of Helgestad in thus procuring a daughter-in-law, and he felt the greatest pity for both Björnarne and Hannah; but his sense of justice protested against opposing the man to whom he owed so much. With all his distrust of Helgestad, it seemed to him an act of the grossest ingratitude, even to thwart evil with evil. He would, according to his character, have afforded Hannah every assistance, if she had openly resisted Helgestad, as he would have supported the son against the father, if Björnarne had solicited him; but it appeared to him to be reducing himself to his level, to deceive the old speculator by a deceitful trick.

"And yet," said he, to himself, "this is the only means of defeating Helgestad's intentions and of uniting the two lovers." Whatever might be the consequences, certain it was that he would have acted in the same manner, were he situated as Heinrick; and it was equally certain that there was no more hope of escape for Hannah after Helgestad had got her to Lyngenfiord. He saw the misery which awaited her, and he felt himself bound by his promises; yet he was heartily rejoiced that Hannah had declined his active assistance, although she had assigned him a no less influential part.

He thus reconciled himself to assist Hannah; and he was thinking how he could entertain Helgestad during the critical moment now at hand, when the latter indicated the way, by resuming his jesting humor.

"Afraja," said he, looking up, "is indeed a man whose assistance is desirable. And as we are speaking of him, answer me, Herr, a question. What do you think of doing with Gula, when your house is empty?"

"Nuh!" answered Helgestad, eyeing him with a cunning

look, "I think she will stay where she is, unless she prefers to emigrate to Balsfiord."

Marstrand smiled. "I have lately had a dream," said he, "which, if Afraja is indeed a sorcerer, was probably sent to me by him."

"I would not swear to the contrary," replied the old man. "Dreams are curious things; they often come into men's minds as secret signs, and are sent by a power which nobody knows. Let us have the dream, Herr Marstrand."

"I dreamed," said he, "that I was living at Balsfiord, well established, had much work, but was sitting down under a load of care. It had been discovered that all the little valleys around were fruitful. Many colonists could settle there. Yet despite of all my efforts I could not succeed in rendering the wood on the Balself available. It happened that the trees could not be carried away from the wilderness. They could not be floated over the deep falls of the stream, no saw-mill be put up, and, after a series of fruitless efforts, I saw all my labor and money spent in vain."

"I can imagine it," cried Helgestad, with a satirical laugh, while he drained his glass.

"I found myself in a sad condition," resumed Marstrand; "and it appeared to me, in a most wonderful manner, as if I saw hands stretched towards me, and heard voices sharply calling me a fool. The darkness, which was so intense that no light could be discerned, suddenly became bright as day, and I recognised Afraja standing by my bed, with his little red eyes glowing like fire."

"I know them," said the trader, "I know the thievish eyes of the grey lynx."

"He grinned at me, and danced around with wonderful bounds. 'You are a wise man, from the great white people who think themselves wiser than we,' he cried, in his vehement voice; 'but I will show you what you must do to convey away the trees, and to build a saw-mill.' He led me to a spot where he waved a long staff, and instantly a mill, with double wheels, arose above the water. Then he pointed to the steep precipice below, and I saw a curious fabric of beams, standing upon props, which was kept slippery by a spring of water, and down this channel the trees were slidden and gathered up, without much difficulty, for sawing."

Helgestad listened with breathless interest to the narration. "It is a remarkably curious dream," he muttered; "but I cannot precisely understand the sorcerer's plan."

"I will explain it to you," said Marstrand; "for all the particulars are so clear to my mind's eye, that I can sketch them for you."

"I am anxious," said Helgestad, opening the drawer of the table, and taking out some writing materials, "to see this contrivance of the magician."

At the same moment Hannah arose. Marstrand gently nodded, and as Helgestad raised his head from the search in the drawer, she had slipped out.

"Sketch it here," said the trader; and Marstrand took the pen and drew the rocky valley, the Balself, and the stream in the ravine, then the steep precipice, and the ingenious construction, which was, indeed, nothing else than a wood-slide, such as is everywhere employed in mountainous countries, to send down trees from great heights. "Look here," he said, in explanation, "here the trees are felled, stripped of their limbs, and then placed upon this smooth inclined plane, which is kept wet with water, that the wood may not be heated. In cold weather it freezes, and upon the ice the trees descend with greater velocity to the point where the saw-mills must be built. It is evidently the best position; for it lies before the falls of the Elf; and from here to the fiord the stream presents but few obstacles."

Helgestad had leaned over the table, and was regarding the drawing with a greedy interest. "It is right," he said; "I calculate it must succeed. It was a wise dream, Herr Mar strand, come whence it might." He raised himself up, and looked at his companion. "You are a wise man, and I must praise you; you are a true friend, who conceals nothing from me. I think so. Is it not so?"

"Certainly, certainly," replied Marstrand, a little confused.

"What fell on the deck?" exclaimed the old trader, starting up.

"I heard nothing," said Marstrand.

Helgestad was at the door. "Remain!" he exclaimed; and his eyes assumed a fierce expression. "You are heated, and you might take cold."

"Let me speak, Herr Helgestad, hear me," shouted John, grasping at his arm; but before he could reach him, Niels had shut the door to, and turned the key in the lock.

He quickly sprang up the steps. The sky was covered with heavy clouds, the wind moaned through the rigging of the yacht, and without, the breakers dashed in fury against the cliffs of Silden. Helgestad glided along in the darkness to the mast in the middle of the ship, where he stopped; for, at an arm's-length before him, he discerned a form, to which another was closely clinging.

"Let us hurry, Hannah," said a manly voice. "The boat lies alongside, and the ladder is down; all is ready."

"I also am ready, my Heinrick," she replied. "Oh, eternal thanks to heaven, that I have you at last!"

"Here," whispered Dahlen; "give me your hand. Has Marstrand fast hold on him? May he keep him securely. Forbear!" he suddenly cried out, clinching her firmly; for, in the same moment, he felt himself suddenly grasped by some one from behind, and raised in the air. Hannah was torn from his side, powerful arms held him, in spite of his utmost resistance. His fingers let go their hold on the bulwarks of the yacht, and with a shriek, which was quickly stifled, he sank into the dark billowy grave, which closed over him.

With a jump, Helgestad was at the iron bars around the mast He seized a heavy piece with both hands, and threw it with all his might upon the boat beneath. A cracking and breaking followed, a cry for help arose from below, and a red fire flashed over the sky, illuminating for a moment the black water.

Pieces of the boat floated around, and a pair of oars drifted upon the agitated sea. A furious gust of wind followed, and an arm, raised above the deep, convulsively clutched at the air, and sank again. Helgestad looked at the spectacle with a face full of hate, and beaming with satiated vengeance and triumph. "You have met your fate, you fool!" he said, with a savage roar of laughter. He then turned around. Hannah lay, without a sign of life, in the arms of a sailor.

"Oho!" muttered the trader, "you hold her so fast, that you have squeezed the life out of her."

"I believe so, Herr," answered the long-haired man. "She does not move a limb."

Helgestad took the sleeping body, like a child, in his arms. "Call the men," said he, "slacken the cable, double-reef the sail; I will return in a moment."

He carried Hannah down stairs, pushed the door open, and entered. Marstrand sat at the table, with his head buried in his hands. When he saw Helgestad, and the pale face of the maiden, he sprang up and remained standing, without uttering a word. Anxiety and horror closed his mouth.

Niels laid his burden upon the bench, against the ship's side. "Take water, rub her hands, Herr, help her, and lay her on her bed."

"What has happened, what have they done?" asked John, hurriedly.

"I will tell you, in reward for your trouble," answered the rough man, stroking back his hair, wet with dripping perspiration. "Thank God for his gracious aid, Herr. The yacht is under sail; I must be at my post. An inch too much to the right or left, and we will have a wet bed below there."

He dashed his cap on his head, and, as he went out, closed

the door with lock and bolt. Marstrand leaned over the powerless maiden, in embarrassment as to what he should do. There was a heavy trampling to and fro on deck; lanterns moved about, and loud voices rose above the noise of the wind and waves.

Suddenly, Hannah opened her eyes, and stared her friend in the face.

"Speak, maiden, tell me; was Heinrick with you, and where is he?" asked the Dane, with a palpitating heart.

She gazed upon him with a wandering look; and, as she heard the name of her lover, her body shook with a convulsive shudder. A scream rang from the inmost depths of her breast; her hands clasped together, as if in prayer; and she endeavored to spring up, but fell back again.

A whistling and shouting mingled with this scream. The yacht plunged, as from a mountain, into the abyss; her beams trembled, the timbers creaked and groaned, heavy blows thundered against her sides, and the water trickled down through the deck.

The vessel had passed out of the sheltering channel into the open sea.

LIFE AND LOVE

IN

NORWAY.

SECOND PART.

CHAPTER XI.

HELGESTAD'S yacht ran along the coast of Trondheim, for the next two weeks, close by the mountain of the seven sisters, which keeps watch at the entrance of Nordland, and the other wild and curiously-formed cliffs and insular groups, to which the imagination of the Norwegian poets has given name and shape.

It seemed as if the old trader had purchased a good wind, and the finest weather, of some sorcerer; for, from the stormy night in which the fair Ilda had sailed around Staatenland, the sky had remained blue, and a fresh, favorable breeze from the south had urged the ship nearer home.

June was come, and the further the yacht ran to the northward, the longer were the days. In the vicinity of the Lofodden, the sun scarcely sunk, any more, below the horizon. It described a circle in the heavens, and its beams, on all sides, illuminated the high glaciers of the Grimfiord, and the Tinden peaks of Salten; at last, Tromsöe lay before the travellers, and the church clock was heard in the distance, striking the midnight hour.

Yet another day and night were passed, before the fair Ilda steered into the Lyngenfiord. The lofty mountains rose up in a long and shining row, and out of their depths the Kilpis lifted up its colossal peak, and alone exhibited a glittering bed of ice and snow, which gleamed like a collar of diamonds around its black neck. The sun, for the first time, lay upon the waves to the west. It sank not below, but stood up like a fire-darting ball; and sent out, from this point, its red, glaring light, as if it were tired, and would rest, but could not, like a man who would gladly close his eyes and sleep, but is prevented by an internal fever.

The midnight sun lighted up the Lyngenfiord, upon which it would now shine, without setting, for four entire weeks. If, however, the light was not extinguished, there was yet something in nature that indicated the missing night. A mysterious silence rested upon the wide waters. The wind died away; the swarms of birds sat still upon the cliffs and the rocks in the sea, with their heads under their wings. No cry was heard in the air that indicated life; none of the great robbers of the deep raised their finny backs from the dreamy, motionless sea. The yacht, with her loose sails, which now and then flapped with a breath of wind, seemed to be moved by spirit hands to the Aloen island. The little church of Lyngen next came into view, upon the great rock which overhung the fiord. From the stone tower a large flag fluttered in the air; and below, in the bay, many boats were discernible with colored streamers or green branches at their mast-heads. The church upon the hill shone bright in the sun-light; and, from the deck of the yacht, the crew looked joyfully upon the scene. The men had thrown off their jackets, for it was as warm as the bay of Naples. They shook hands, and exchanged wishes of good luck; for rarely had a Bergen voyage been accomplished in such a short time; and God had so ordained it that they should return home on the very day when the feast of Spring is celebrated in the high north; on the day when the sun, for the first time, does not set; when all nature rejoices, when all labor rests, and when singing, dancing, and banqueting last as long as human legs and strength can hold out.

But no feast without the Lord, no rejoicing without the Christian consecration, no gathering in these wide deserts without the church and its plot of ground. Therefore lay here the many streamer, leaf, and flower-decked boats, which had brought the proprietors, with their families and people, from all the nooks and corners of great fiord; therefore waved the flag from the spire of the first house of God which had been erected more than five hundred years ago in this wilderness, by great king Olaf, of holy memory; therefore, the little church houses of the various families stood wide open, and gaily adorned for their guests.

The whole population of the fiord and the islands sat in the church, to sing and pray in the holy night, and to praise God, and to invoke a good and fruitful year; and then, amid games and amusements, to pass the glad hours, to settle disputes, to strengthen old friendships, and to form new ones over full plates and glasses, until all were satiated with pleasure.

As the yacht, borne along by the flood tide, reached the church, no person was to be seen; yet the crew, without awaiting orders from Helgestad, unlashed the great anchor, and stood ready to let go the cable. The old trader stood at the helm, and appeared to have surrendered himself to thought. He looked earnestly towards the church, among the flags, in quest of a boat from Orenaes; and when he descried one, a glad smile lit up his hard weather-beaten features.

"We have come at the very nick of time to join in the Spring festival," said he. "Let go the anchor. We bring joy to joy."

The anchor fell, and in the next minute the yacht lay behind the boats. With the same celerity the yawl was lowered, the best ladder hung out, and the men hurried aft to put on their holiday attire.

While they were dressing themselves, Helgestad went down to the cabin. He stood a moment at the door, listened, and then entered with a friendlv countenance. Hannah Fandrem had just placed the coffee-pot on the table, and Marstrand was arranging the cups and saucers. Both were ready dressed, which seemed to gratify him.

"Nuh!" said he, "you have everything in order, and you are sprucely and gaily attired, maiden. We are laying close under the church of Lyngen in the clear sunshine; but no one is to be seen there. I calculate they are all in the church, listening to Heinrick Sture's thanksgiving sermon, which, although it closes the eyes and ears, opens the hearts."

He sat down, took a cup, and poured it full, while he spoke on—"The celebration of the July festival is an old custom of the heathen times. It would have cost much time and blood to procure its abandonment; and the Christian priests could never get it transferred to Christmas. More than one king was compelled by the peasants to visit the July festival; and Haken the good was obliged to eat there mare's meat, in honor of Odin and Thor, much as it disgusted him. Christians and heathen, for many generations, dressed up this meat, and offered it in sacrifice on the summer solstice."

"Was the July festival in the olden time the Spring feast?"

"It was the greatest festival, when men prayed the holy Father to be merciful to his children," said Niels, "and we have here preserved it unchanged, except in a Christian sense. But let us sit no longer. We must to land and surprise them in their prayers. You will see them, Hannah; no one is wanting, I think. My great boat is lying at the rocks, and carries the gay flag, which Gula embroidered last year."

He threw off his jacket and put on his blue-lined coat; and when Hannah went into the adjoining room, he spoke with Marstrand. "Nuh!" said he; "all kinds of distrust have entered your head; you have become moody and melancholy. There should be no misunderstanding between us. I offer you my hand, Herr; let all between us be as it was. I esteem you as a man who knows how to explain his purposes; but you, also, must esteem what I calculate aright; put reckoning against reckoning, and take word and hand upon it, that Niels Helgestad will remain, as he has promised you, your friend and helper."

Marstrand accepted the proffered hand. "I thank you, Herr," he replied; "I have no disposition to break the peace between us."

"I think you must be glad to be here to-day. You will find all the maidens gathered together at the church. You have only to cast your net to catch the best among them."

Marstrand smiled, while he shook his head; but Helgestad continued, in a confidential tone. "Look around you, and fasten a ribbon on the wings of her who pleases you most. It is a primitive custom to form acquaintances at the July festival, to be succeeded by marriage. I hope your house at Balsfiord is ready by this time. In a few days, I will carry your goods there and see what further is to be done. Now, forward! Here comes Hannah, modest and pretty, in her lawn dress and plaited apron; and they are calling to us from the yawl; they can wait no longer."

He put on his cocked-hat, tied a silk neckerchief around his throat, and led Hannah and Marstrand to the boat in waiting. With a few pulls, she flew to the stone landing at the foot of the shore steps, and returned to the ship to bring on shore the whole crew.

Hannah hastily mounted to the platform above, followed by Marstrand; but Helgestad was at some distance behind when they had both overcome the ascent.

"Nuh!" he muttered, looking up and observing her, "she is indeed no dove, that will take food from everybody's hand. She looks at me like a stone statue, or as one of those Nornes of whom the old Sagas speak, which sing to men their destiny. No finger of hers, I imagine, will do me harm. I have her now where I have long desired, and she shall no more escape."

He nodded to her, and thought that her large and imposing figure would please Björnarne. In her gay, festive attire, Helgestad was in doubt which was the fairer—his own Ilda, or his destined daughter-in-law.

As the sun rose upon the horizon, Hannah folded her hands and gazed over the fiord and the distant sea.

"How sweet and peaceful is this tranquillity! it almost subdues my benumbed soul to tears."

"Marstrand added, in a soft voice, "Wherever man may wander, and with whatever sorrows God visits him, he sends, also, the atoning angel with the command, 'Place your vengeance in my hands and obey my commandments.'"

"Certainly, I will obey;" she said, in a firm tone. "There comes the most horrible of men, the sight of whom I could not endure, if the voice of which you speak did not order me to follow him. I will follow him, and wait upon his nod as patiently as a maidservant. He will and shall have me."

"That cannot be, Hannah," exclaimed her companion. "You must return to your father. Helgestad himself could not resist the energetic remonstrances I would make in your behalf."

"Neither a father nor a home await me," was her answer. "Where could I live? Where is my future? my hopes? He whom I must now trust took from me all that I held dear. The black worm which he has planted in my heart winds around to my very feet. I have formed a compact with him which no one shall ever dissolve. I have sworn it with a thousand oaths, that as long as I live I will live for his sake. I will never separate from him, and will bring as much happiness and joy to his house as I can, under the assistance of heaven."

Her eyes glowed with an expression of the deadliest hatred,

while her lips smiled and her countenance beamed with a sunny glance.

At this moment, a soft hymn sounded from the interior of the little church:

"Oh! Lord, take from us all sin, and, after thy image, enable us to bear all things with patience."

The holy stillness of nature appeared to be filled with the inspiration of heaven. There it expanded in all its boundless grandeur. The gigantic mass of mountains, enveloped in a roseate glow, with their peaks stretching into the invisible depths of the blue heaven above, looked like a guardian barrier around this consecrated ground; while the fresh green of the earth, the bursted foliage of the trees, the broad-expanding fiord, with its tranquil waters, the islands sleeping in the warm sun, and the pacified surface of the dimly-visible sea, spoke of the return of summer with its pleasures, and of the beneficence of God.

Helgestad lingered yet awhile, bared his head, and folded his hands in prayer. The yellow-greyish hair fell over his shoulders, and the spirit of devotion seemed to soften his hard features. The strong man, with all his cunning and audacity, bowed his soul before an invisible power, and in a subdued tone, said, "I thank thee, gracious God, that thou hast preserved me from all danger, and restored me to this spot. I thank thee with all my heart, and will faithfully strive, as a man and a Christian, to walk in thy ways, that I may present myself before thee, just judge, without fear."

He looked askance at Hannah, who was motionlessly regarding him, and said aloud to Marstrand, "In my whole lifetime I have seen nothing more beautiful thau this blessed morning. It is a holy feast, when we should put off the old Adam and open our hearts to goodness. Let us enter the porch and praise God. It is a long hymn they are singing, but we can, in the meanwhile, look within, without entering. I expect my good friend, Heinrick Sture, has no breath left, and will suffer from hoarseness the next week, unless the rich offering works wonders upon him."

From this unholy jesting, it was evident that the evil spirit had returned to Helgestad. He opened the low door and entered the dark space behind the screen. From here, he could see the congregation and the parson; he rapidly scanned the thickly-crowded mass, fixed his eyes upon his own seat, and frowned as he observed the silver-haired Klaus Hornemann officiating in the pulpit, instead of the stout red-faced pastor of Lyngenfiord. Then he looked around the assembly, which was composed of many well-known faces, in some of which a visible impatience was depicted, to see the ceremony at an end, and to escape into the open air; while others appeared deeply engrossed in, and moved by the service. Helgestad, for some time, looked quietly upon his children, who sat together, before he pointed them out. By Ilda's side was the red head of the secretary; behind them the tall form of Olaf loomed up; and next to Björnarne, a man was seated, the sight of whom drew from Helgestad a loud grunt. It was no other than the Voigt of Tromsöe, in person. The heavy face, with the small, forbidding eyes, the fiery nose, and double chin, belonged to him alone. Helgestad appeared undecided whether to be pleased or vexed at the presence of this worthy chief magistrate of Finnmark. He had intentionally passed by Tromsöe, upon his return, without touching there, for the purpose of avoiding the voigt; now he sat here before him, and had unquestionably not been drawn thither for slight reasons.

From Helgestad's countenance it was clear that he was debating his course of conduct; but at last, his inspection terminated with a satisfied "Nuh!" Hannah had been regarding the brother and sister, and she fixed her attention on Björnarne, who seemed to disappoint her expectations. When she had known him in times past, he was a frolicksome young man, with a fresh color, and clear, merry, glancing eyes; now he seemed to be a grave, reflecting man. He sat with his head bowed down, his eyes upon the ground, and his lips compressed, as if he were absorbed in some serious meditation. Ilda sang from the same book with her betrothed; but Paul Petersen's crafty eyes were incessantly in motion, and the first sight of him produced an unfavorable impression on Fandrem's daughter. Ilda's clear, arched brow, her tranquil countenance, and its soft smile, and her religious fervor, excited Hannah's keenest sympathy. As she looked around the meeting, she could discover no one that could be compared with Ilda. Marstrand had occasionally spoken of her. He had not described her as beautiful, but had praised her understanding, her mild disposition, and the goodness of her heart. Hannah now admitted that Helgestad had truly spoken of her as the flower of the fiord. And should this flower be wasted upon the ugly secretary with the mean face? A presentiment assured her that Ilda must be near to her—that her fate must be like her own; that it was impossible she could love him who was forced upon her; and she felt a longing for a confidential friend, who, full of her own misery, could sympathise with her's, and console and advise with her.

In the meanwhile, the hymn was ended, and Klaus Hornemann pronounced the blessing: as soon as the audience rose, and descried old Helgestad, they called out to him with terms of hearty welcome.

"Nuh!" exclaimed the trader, "here I am, friends and neighbors! I have offered my thanks to God, from the outside here, and I bring you good news from Bergen. Fish is greatly risen in price, and is going up, from week to week. It will reach four spezies and more; but now let me see my children, for I have been long separated from them."

With Ilda hanging on his arm, and holding his son by the hand, he went out in the clear sunshine. All wished to shake hands, and speak with him. Those who knew Marstrand, pressed upon him with inquiries and good wishes. Shouts and hurrahs hailed the crew of the yacht, as they clambered up the rocks; and it was some time before Helgestad could free his church cottage from the curious crowd, and form within it a circle of his friends and children, to whom he presented Hannah, with appropriate remarks.

He did not, indeed, say what his particular intention was—but every one could imagine it. "Hannah," said he, "wished to see the country of her mother, and it had required great pains to induce Fandrem to part with her for a couple of months; and Björnarne was to take her back." From this, every one inferred what seemed best. The rich merchant in Bergen was well known, as well as the relation in which Helgestad stood to him. No one also doubted that the crafty old Niels had brought his daughter-in-law with him, that she might become acquainted with his wealth, and her destined spouse. It could not fail, but that envy and suspicion should arise from all these speculations; but where did not the like always occur, under similar circumstances! Hannah was friendly received, and Ilda went arm in arm with her among her female friends, to withdraw from the men, among whom Helgestad's observations had excited no little jest and laughter. Marstrand, during these proceedings, had been taken in charge by Olaf, who had much to tell him of his new settlement; and with all the honest heartiness of his character, he gave vent to his joy at seeing him again at Lyngenfiord. How widely this differed from his reception by Ilda and Björnarne. The maiden had given him her hand, and bade him welcome in a few cold words; but Björnarne had hardly done as much, for he averted his eyes from him, and grumbled out something which sounded like a greeting. The chilliness of this reçeption offended the young man. Around was universal joy and gladness; groups of young people lay reclining upon the green grass; provisions of all kinds were brought out of the cottages; busy maidens and women hurried about with cups and cans, and fire flashed up between stones, where it had been kindled for cooking. Games and dances were arranged, fresh twigs waved from the hats and caps, songs were sung, and many families, whom Marstrand scarcely knew, saluted him with kind looks and words, and invited him to celebrate the happy day with them.

All his self-possession was necessary to conceal his feelings, and properly to respond to their cheerful acts of kindness. Olaf withdrew him from the crowd, and clapping him on the shoulder, while he looked in his face, said, "The journey has not been of particular benefit to you, friend John; you are, indeed, grown browner and stouter, but you have wrinkles on your brow, and you look as if a heavy weight of care lay upon your heart."

"Should I not have care, Olaf, seeing what lies before me?"

"You have a hard work to accomplish, but you are a ready man. Your house is prepared, and Helgestad can land your goods from his yacht, at the very threshold. It is true, I would not like to be in your place; and I have always thought you might do better elsewhere, than in attempting to make money out of the wood, in Balself ravine."

Marstrand paused at this honest confession, until he pressed the hand of Olaf in a sympathising tone; and continued, "So you have given up your hopes, my friend?"

"I must be gone," said Olaf. "You would not have met me here again, had I not promised Helgestad to assist Björnarne; and if I had not promised you, to take care of your interests, and—if I were not a fool," he exclaimed in a stronger tone, while he struck himself on the head, with a smile at his burst of temper.

"Were all folly like yours, good Olaf, nobody would complain of it."

"And if all blessed me, what good would it do me, if one was wanting. There has been much change since you were here, friend John. Look at Miss Ilda; you will not observe what my eye sees, and you will not know what her voice says to me, and how well she knows how to conceal her wishes."

"What does she say to you?" said Marstrand, walking on with him.

"That it is dark in her — here," muttered the Nordlander, laying his hand on his breast.

"She was always taciturn," he continued, as his companion made no reply; "but as a star does not speak, but shines — so formerly spoke her face, so beamed her eyes. Now the lustre has faded from her eyes; I hear her voice, and it grieves me; I look at her, and sadness rests upon her brow like a winter cloud on the mountains."

"Probably she is sick," added Marstrand.

"You understand it not, because you do not feel it," replied Olaf, impatiently. "No one, but I, seems to observe it. She is the same as ever — all her conduct is as sensible and good; she speaks as formerly, but yet I know that she is not what she once was."

"And what do you think of it?"

"See, there sits the Voigt of Tromsöe; he lays his hand on Helgestad's shoulder, and whispers in his ear. Look at the birch grove, and observe the secretary how he walks with Ilda; how he presses her hand in his, and endeavors to please the maiden who came with you from Bergen. There is no woman whom he cannot please — no man whom he would not deceive. The ugly, avaricious scoundrel has a thousand vices: he has neither honesty, nor truth; and yet he will place the ring on Ilda's finger, and before the winter comes she will follow him to Tromsöe. Look how the old fellows shake hands; they have agreed upon the contract."

"Do you think that this is the cause of Ilda's sorrow?" said Marstrand.

"What else could it be? Do you suppose that Ilda does not know the hypocritical secretary? Does she not know that he is made up of cheats and lies? Never would a finger of hers touch him, if it could be avoided. So says her eye, when she looks on me; thus speaks her voice, when she pronounces my name; this I read in every action."

Marstrand gazed in silence upon his friend, who continued; "You now comprehend why I do not go away; although she herself yesterday said I must depart from here, for my property at Bodoen, where my old mother pines for me."

"And Björnarne?" asked Marstrand, with hesitation; "have you not spoken with him of Ilda?"

"No," replied Olaf. "Björnarne cannot help matters; he is, as Ilda, a submissive child; and he himself is tormented by certain caprices of his own."

"We bring a wife for him, for whom he will abandon them all," interrupted Marstrand.

"I know not," replied Olaf; "it may be good for him, and restore his spirits. He returned a week since from an expedition which he made with me, and several others, through the Yauren as far as the Kilpis."

To the inquiring stare of his companion, Olaf indifferently replied; "That is also a novelty which you should be informed of. The Lapland maiden, little Gula, has run off, or fallen in a ravine, or in some other manner been lost."

"Gula!" said Marstrand. "Did you not find her?"

"Not a trace of her. Björnarne believed she had been stolen, Paul Petersen said she was in love, and Ilda wept like a child. Thereupon I resolved to go in search of the Lapland maiden, and ran over the swamps until we found her father, in the Kilpis-jauren, with his herds."

"Was she not with him?"

"If the old rascal does not dissemble, like a Christian, he knew nothing of her. He swore a thousand oaths, by Jubinal and Pekel, that his eye had not seen her, accompanied with some terrible curses for our particular benefit."

"Poor maiden! Poor Gula!" said the Dane, in a subdued

tone. "If I had been here, your fate would not have been so sad!"

Olaf shook his head. "You could not have done more, or be sadder, than Björnarne. The maiden was for a long time very melancholy, and it actually seemed as if what Paul Petersen said was true, that the little witch had gone mad with love."

Their conversation was interrupted by Helgestad, who called to Marstrand, and, as he approached, said to him, "I see you have already heard the news. Nuh! may she run and milk reindeer, or brew devil's drinks with the old villain, and, as far as I am concerned, lie in the swamps till the last day. I will not trouble myself about it on this festive morning. Sit down with us, Herr Marstrand, and give the voigt your hand. I calculate you must thank him, and receive Paul Petersen with a friendly countenance, for they have both united to serve you."

The voigt had, in the meantime, arisen, and advanced a few steps towards Marstrand. His blue coat, with standing collar and embroidery, announced the dignitary; the little three-cornered hat sat majestically upon his fiery brow, and buckled breeches of black velvet, and long, shining boots, together with a Spanish gold-headed cane, completed his imposing costume. In his younger days, the voigt had been an officer in the army, and yet wore a cross and ribbon in his button-hole; his carriage was erect, like that of a soldier, and his grey eyes were expressive of energy and firmness of character.

"You are welcome, Herr Baron; I have long looked forward to this agreeable meeting," he said, lifting his hat. "I have waited for you in vain in Tromsöe, and have at last resolved to come in person, and offer you my respects."

Marstrand excused himself, and expressed his thanks. The voigt held his hand firmly, and obliged him to sit alongside of him, reaching him a full glass, and drinking to his prosperity. He next took from his pocket-book a paper, regularly drawn up, with seal and signature, by virtue of which the valley of Balsfiordeif, the adjoining valleys on both sides, together with a considerable extent of shore, was granted to him forever, including the island of Strommen, near the coast of Tromsöe. This he handed to Marstrand, who could not refrain from expressing his warmest thanks for the complete and exact manner in which the document was drawn up.

"Is all arranged to your satisfaction?" asked the voigt.

"This act contains more than I had any reason to expect. The property is greater than I wished," said Marstrand.

"It is not too large, if well managed," answered the magistrate. "The king has here yet much more to give away, which, in good hands, would redound to the benefit of the country. For this purpose am I here, to seek out the worthy, and to take care that it is not wasted among beggars and vagabonds. I have not inquired, Herr Baron, if the allotment were too large, but I have given what was advisable."

"You have bountifully fulfilled my wishes; and now oblige me further, by calling me simply by my name. I left the Baron in Copenhagen, when I put off my laced coat; here, in my new country, I am John Marstrand, the trader of Balselfgaard, and will so remain; and, by the blessing of God, I hope to be of service to my fellow-countrymen."

"Nuh!" cried Helgestad, "bravely spoken, and may you prosper, Herr Marstrand."

The voigt gave an assenting nod, and glass after glass followed, accompanied with good admonitions, hints, and sayings. They sat in the shade of the gently waving birch trees. The sun rose higher in the firmament, and before them was spread an animated scene, on the green-sward before the church. The young men and maidens gathered together on a smooth, level piece of ground to dance; in other places, groups were engaged in throwing heavy stones at a mark; and further on, there was firing with guns at the painted head of a bear as a target, for a prize. There were trials of strength, running and leaping matches, accompanied with plauditory clapping of the hands for the victors, and mocking roars of laughter for the vanquished. While the multitude were thus variously engaged, single couples were occasionally seen stealing off to retired nooks; for, as Helgestad had said, at this feast many tender declarations were made and future resolutions of matrimony formed.

The voigt, after a pause, raised his stick and pointed to the side of the church, where he saw his nephew with Ilda; Hannah and Björnarne standing in the midst of the circle which surrounded the old parson.

"You must know, Herr Marstrand," said he, "that it is a fine old custom to call out the bridal pair on this holiday to be blessed by the minister. I have just been talking with Helgestad of this. My nephew Paul, and Miss Ilda, could thus calm the agitation of their hearts. A more handsome and stately pair I have never seen than they are. Do you not say so yourself?"

"I wish them all possible happiness," responded Marstrand.

"Paul is your friend," continued the voigt; "a truer one you could not have, Herr. I must inform you that I was prevailed upon by his praise of you and his arguments, to grant the deed of possession without any further delay. He himself drew up the writing, studying it point by point, and arranged it in such exact terms that it can never be questioned."

Marstrand returned his thanks; the voigt gave a cunning wink to Helgestad, and clapped the Dane upon the shoulder. "I thank you, heartily," he said. "A word is a cheap thing, but I know how you could render a valuable service to Helgestad's house."

"What do you mean?" asked Marstrand.

"What do I mean?" said the voigt. "I mean that it would be a fine thing if we could have Björnarne, also, blessed to-day. All are here on the spot, bridegroom, bride, and parson; a few minutes might accomplish what may otherwise be spun out for months."

Marstrand shrank back. And what can I do in such an affair?" he asked.

"Speak a proper word with Fandrem's daughter. You can set her right; show her the way to make her father, Helgestad, Björnarne, and all of us, happy. You alone can do this, Herr. I have heard of the confidence which she so justly entertains towards you; so go to Hannah as she stands alone there now, and persuade her to do her duty."

The young man observed Helgestad, with a dark, inquiring, and almost threatening look, as he sat listening with apparent indifference, his legs crossed, and with a Holland pipe in his mouth.

"I calculate," said he, as the voigt ceased speaking, "it is good advice, and you will cheerfully acknowledge it as such, Herr Marstrand. Speak with Hannah; if there is any one who understands her, it is you. I observed that she took Björnarne by the hand, as Ilda presented him to her, and there was something in her eyes and bearing expressive rather of satisfaction than aversion."

"Ha! ha!" exclaimed the voigt, laughing; "no maiden could look on such a spruce fellow like Björnarne but with pleasure."

"Could you expect a promise of marriage from her on this day, when they have scarcely seen each other?"

"Nuh!" said Helgestad, sullenly; "you know, as well as I, that it must take place sooner or later. Long reflection is of no service to such a maiden. Everything to-day wears a cheerful aspect. A half dozen of young couples will celebrate it with pledges of love. To her all is new, and she rejoices in the land and the people, in the sunshine. I see that her heart is glad, for this is the native country of her mother, where she often danced and sported.—I calculate, therefore, she will not say 'no,' if you address her properly. It is a speculation, Herr Marstrand, which, like all others, has its peculiar hour, of which advantage must be taken. You must bring us back her consent, Herr Marstrand."

It seemed to Marstrand that he could not refuse. He arose, and declared that he would do all in his power to bring about a successful result.

When he had left, the red face of the voigt contracted into a frown of deep scorn. "It seems to me that the fellow takes no pleasure in serving you. Get rid of him as soon as you can."

Helgestad made no other movement than to pour out a new glass. "I am nevertheless of the opinion," said he, "that he will do his best. He is cool and clear-headed, and knows that I can crush him with my finger. She cannot go back to old Fandrem; her heart, as she called her lover, lies in the depths of the sea of Staatenland; and now this or that one, Björnarne or Olaf, are all alike the same to her."

"A woman without a heart is a curious thing," said the voigt, laughing; "for they have generally too much of it. You cured her for ever, Niels, in the night at Silden. Are you certain, however, that the Danish robber and his associates did not escape?"

"I am sure of it," muttered Helgestad. "The cliffs there are a hundred feet high, which no human foot can climb. I hear yet the crash, as the boat broke in pieces, and the cry of the drowning men, which, curious as it may appear, Paulsen, frequently resounds in my ears."

"Does it frighten you?" asked the voigt, jeeringly.

Helgestad looked at him moodily.

"No law can ever lay a finger upon you," resumed Paulsen. "You found robbers upon your deck in the foggy night, and you threw them overboard. The less said upon the subject, however, the better."

"No one knows of it but you and Helge, my helmsman, and he will not speak of it."

"I hope it may turn out so. The morning after this event,

when you again stood before the maiden, must have been a glad one!"

"I did not see her for the three following days. She lay in her chamber, as if dead, and no one came near her but Marstrand."

"And then?" asked Paulsen.

"And then she made her appearance, and I gave her my hand. There was no allusion made to that night, and nothing shall ever be said of it between us."

"Has she not attempted it?"

"She has not," responded Helgestad. "I saw that her heart was consuming with grief; I did all that I could to show her that I would make it up to her."

The voigt replied in a bantering tone, "You are an excellent father, Niels. You have a mild, conciliatory disposition. But I understand it all, cunning old fellow; there is less question of the feelings and wishes of the girl than of the connection of Fandrem and the rich inheritance. I would never, however, forgive the Dane for his interposition in the affair."

"His hour will come," muttered Helgestad.

"I believe it; and it will be a good hour. You have him already in your hands, and must not let him run too long. Paul thinks the sooner the threads are torn the better, lest he may have time to fasten them together again."

Helgestad made no reply, for at this moment he saw Marstrand advancing, and leading Hannah Fandrem by the hand.

"I will bring my answer in person," said Hannah, as she stood before him. "Herr Marstrand has made known to me your wishes, cousin, and it needed no long persuasion. If it will give you pleasure to have me declare myself to-day your son's bride, I am ready to gratify you. If Björnarne will ask me, as it is seeming, I will yield to his prayers."

"Will you, girl of my heart, do so? Will you enter Orenaes Gaard as my daughter?—Call Björnarne here; he shall fall upon his knees and kiss your hands. Call him hither, and old

Klaus also. Bring Ilda and Paul, and all of them There shall be such a wedding at Lyngenfiord, that it shall be talked of, for fifty years to come, in every cottage in Finnmark."

Helgestad was in such an extraordinary state of excitement, that the voigt looked at him with surprise, and in doubt as to whether it were true or false. Several, who were in the vicinity, drew near; and there was no little agitation when they learned the cause of their neighbor's clamorous rejoicing. Good wishes were offered on all sides; and next, two young men appeared, leading Björnarne by the arm, who, while shooting at a mark, and with his gun yet in hand, was suddenly dragged off by his merry friends, without any explanation of their object.

"Come here, Björnarne," his father shouted to him, "and throw aside the gun; for another kind of game is awaiting you. You shall shoot directly to the heart, without powder or lead. I calculate you understand the art. See, here is Hannah, who has no objections to go with you to Klaus Hornemann. Nuh! you fool; are you changed to stone for joy? Take hold of her; she is of flesh and blood; fall down; she will raise you up."

Helgestad was not wrong in comparing his son to a stone; for Björnarne seemed to be paralyzed with astonishment. For some minutes he was of a deadly paleness; then his whole face glowed with a dark red; his gun fell from his hand, and his eyes wandered despairingly around. The paternal authority obtained a quick victory over his rebellious feelings; for, at the last words of Helgestad, he made a movement as if he wished to bend his knee.

"Dear Björnarne," said Hannah, taking him by the hand, "it is our parents' desire that we should belong to each other, and this is not the beginning of our acquaintance. Years ago, in our childhood, we saw each other, and, as I think, you loved me."

"It is a fact," interrupted Helgestad; "is it not so, Björnarne? For years you have desired to see Hannah in Gaard von Orenaes. Your wishes are now fulfilled. Look in her eyes, and fall upon her neck. Lay aside this bashfulness, and tell Klaus Hornemann yourself there, what you want of him."

Marstrand was not a witness of the last part of this scene, around which a large circle of spectators had gathered, who raised a loud shout as Björnarne, in obedience to the injunction, kissed Hannah, and stammered out some words. While Ilda and her near relatives were mingling in the expression of good wishes and in the embracings, Marstrand withdrew to meet the parson.

"I am glad to see you back again, dear friend," said the latter. "A hearty welcome, after your journey, of which you will have, no doubt, much to relate to us. And what is going on there? Has John Marstrand brought a pretty young lady with him from Bergen?"

"Not for myself, worthy Herr," interrupted Marstrand. "She is Fandrem's daughter, and is destined for Björnarne. Prevent the betrothal, I beg you, from taking place here to-day."

"And wherefore?" inquired the pastor. Is the maiden constrained to this match?"

"Not that," answered Marstrand; "she is ready for it, but Björnarne"—— he speechlessly gazed before him.

Hornemann shook his head. "The pastor of Lyngenfiord, Heinrick Sture, is sick, and I am administering his office; and that commands me to bless the couple who present themselves to me. Björnarne does right in giving his hand to this virtuous maiden, and in complying with his father's will. The friends of this young man should not oppose what tends to his happiness."

"Can he be happy," replied Marstrand, impressively, "who, pallid and confused, says yes? They know not what I know; they are ignorant of what has happened, and in what manner this happy pair have come together, and what Helgestad has done to bring about their meeting."

"I do not believe that this is the worst act of his life," said

Hornemann. "Her heart may suffer from it; but remember my young friend, what I once said to you of the customs of this country. Children here follow the commands of theii parents; this is a stringent and inviolable law. Have you not thought of this while you were in the travelling intimacy of this bride of another?"

"Rest assured," said Marstrand, blushing, "that I have entertained no forbidden desires for Hannah, and that I am not interested in any degree in her marriage."

"And if this be so," replied the pastor, "what induces you to raise objections?"

"My sympathy for both, and my fear of evil."

"Curious," said Hornemann; "could you not inform me upon what this fear is based?"

"No, not now, nor here," said Marstrand; "I have promised Hannah to be silent. But do you prevent this precipitate betrothment."

"Hither with the pastor, hither!" was heard Helgestad's voice exclaiming. "I think no one has a greater longing after him than we." Leading Hannah by one hand, and Ilda by the other, and followed by Paul Petersen and Björnarne, he strode out of the circle, with the voigt at the head, amid the applauding shouts of the bystanders.

"I can neither change nor prevent anything, Herr Marstrand; but I can wish that God may give you as much joy and resignation as I perceive in the faces of this young couple."

"Amen!" murmured Marstrand to himself, as he turned away.

"Forward, music! and let us have the best piece you can play," cried Helgestad. "Then three times round the church in procession, according to the old custom. And now, Klaus Hornemann, take them and conclude the compact, that it may never be broken."

"Is it so, my dear children?" said the old man. "Will you

in joy and sorrow, cleave to each other, and truly adhere to what your hearts in this hour promise?"

He looked at Hannah, who stood smiling by the side of Björnarne. "Yes," she said, with an amiable inclination of the head; and Ilda also pronounced her "yes," but without changing a feature of her face.

"Come, then," said Hornemann; and the bridal pairs arranged themselves, with their relatives and friends surrounding them; the music sounded, and wreaths of fresh spring flowers were placed upon the hair of the young maidens. In the first hour of the morning, with the clear beaming sun over head, Klaus Hornemann pronounced the blessing of heaven upon the betrothed.

CHAPTER XII.

THE next day, the Gaard von Orenaes was full of guests and activity. The voigt was there, and wished to remain a few days, in order to return to Tromsöe with Helgestad; for the old trader had resolved to proceed immediately to Lofodden, and to carry the fish himself to Bergen. All had gone off so quickly and so well, that he must communicate the result in person to Fandrem, and at the same time secure the dowry; and upon his return, the marriage would take place. He had now pushed the affair so far, that Hannah could not again leave Lyngenfiord but with Björnarne, and as his wife.

The maiden conducted herself to his satisfaction. She had scarcely got warm in her new nest, when she acted as a bird long accustomed to it. She assisted Ilda in all her domestic labors, was to be found in the kitchen and store-room, stood in the shop, weighed and measured, and scanned the account-books, as if she had managed them for years. Her fine clothes ornaments and rings were laid aside, and she was kindly and active; not like Gula, who jumped about, singing and laughing; but all her actions were regulated by good sense and discretion, and every one in the house spoke well of her. Paul Petersen only appeared not to be particularly pleased with his sister-in-law, for he found her a very different person from what he had anticipated. He had taken her for an indolent, supercilious maiden, who would not suit her new position, or for a young girl with a heart full of grief and eyes swimming with tears, or a conceited and arrogant person, likely to call forth Helgestad's anger and severity; to his astonishment, he beheld the rough man full of tenderness and affection to his daughter-in-law, who sought to win his approbation by all the efforts in her power. Paul Petersen's brain was sadly disturbed. When he was gone, and lived with Ilda in Tromsöe, and Hannah managed Helgestad and everything to her own liking, what might not happen? His eager eyes already saw how nimbly she plied her fingers, and how her kindly looks and smiles were observed and appreciated by her father-in-law, as if he himself would marry the sly and pernicious witch; as for Björnarne, he wandered about like a dreamer, and spoke to her only when encouraged by others. For these reasons, Paul felt a strong prejudice against Hannah, which was evidently reciprocated on her part.

Paul Petersen at first employed humility and hypocrisy; but he soon saw, from Hannah's looks, how little he recommended himself by these arts; he next tried raillery, but Fandrem's daughter had so much wit and malice, that he always suffered in the encounter. He was jeered, reproved, and laughed at; and when he showed a desire to make peace, Hannah would not consent, but she prosecuted the war with the more earnestness, to the great delight of Helgestad and Olaf, who were both glad to see the secretary paid off in his own coin.

In the meanwhile, the yacht had discharged the articles that belonged to Orenaes, but a great number of other materials and goods were put on board, which Marstrand bought of Helgestad, in order to provide himself fully for the exigencies of his new settlement. His house stood ready for him at Balsfiord, and all had been done for him that was possible; but he must now go to work with his own hands. Helgestad reckoned with him for two days; everything was delivered to him, the lists examined, and his whole indebtedness amounted to ten thousand specie dollars, inclusive of the money borrowed of Fandrem.

Helgestad was to sell the fish at Lofodden, and to deduct the product from the account, but it was plain that this would not cover half the debt.

"Nuh," said Helgestad, "it is always a gallant beginning, which does not fall to the lot of every one; your main reliance is the wood on the Balself; and from that, with your good head, you ought to realise your most sanguine wishes."

He opened a huge chest of iron, and pointed to six great leather bags. "Here," continued he, "are six thousand spezies, which are now at your service. They are all correctly counted, for which I will be responsible. With these, you will owe me sixteen thousand; but, I say again, let it be fifty or sixty thousand: whenever you need money, come to me, and I will supply your wants."

As Marstrand expressed his thanks, the old man laid his finger upon his arm, and, with a sly wink, said, "Look to it, Herr, that you follow the words of St. Paul, 'Keep your eyes open, and take care that no one be wiser than yourself;' sit down now, and sign the bond. Debtor to Niels Helgestad of Orenaes in Lyngenfiord, for sixteen thousand spezies, at eight per cent. lawful interest."

Marstrand subscribed his name, without uttering a word, and Helgestad, after reading it, silently thrust the paper in an old brown leather pocket-book among other money documents. Then they both went to the packing and ware-houses, where the lading of the yacht was completed; thus passed the last day of the stay of the possessor of Balsfiord, at Orenaes.

Upon returning to the house, he met Ilda by the way. "I have awaited you," she said, "to speak with you again, and to wish you well."

They passed over the green-sward in front of the house, whose borders had been planted with birch bushes, over which the evening sun shed a soft purple light. Two maidens had been hired by Ilda for the new Gaard to manage the house, and to take charge of some cows and other animals; there were, likewise, several young men among the families at Lyngenfiord, who were willing to become Marstrand's vassals, if he would provide them with board and lodging. Ilda gave him some good advice for the first arrangement; and at last the conversation came to a pause, and both stood among the fresh, odorous bushes, silently regarding the sleeping waters of the fiord.

"To-morrow," said Ilda, smiling, "you will see this sun shine at Balsfiord. May it never set for you, John Marstrand; and when, next year, the fine season returns, and the god of day does not withdraw his light from us, may many, if not all, of your hopes be gratified."

"And what shall I wish you, Miss Ilda?" answered Marstrand.

His eyes met hers; he seized her hand, and fastened his gaze impressively upon her face; but he dared not accompany his thoughts with words.

"Wish that it may go well with me in Tromsöe; and when you visit it, do not forget us."

"How could I forget you? May Tromsöe never hold a happier house than yours!"

They were again silent, until, after a while, Ilda turned and looked upon the distant Kilpis, whose gigantic head heaved up in the crimson blaze of the declining sun.

"Yonder wild mountain-range reminds me that I must speak

to you of Gula. Do you know that she suddenly left us, and that Björnarne and our friends have sought after her in vain?" Marstrand nodded a silent response; and Ilda continued, in a sharper tone, "She left us because her heart's peace was overpowered by the evil which is implanted in our nature. God so willed it, and he is almighty."

"I have not," said he, with emotion, "disturbed the peace of Gula."

"No," was her quiet answer; "I know it was not you. Heaven's mercy upon the poor child! When you are established at Balsfiord, you will have occasion to see many Lapps. Afraja's herds pasture on the peninsula, and he possesses others which roam as far as the White Sea. Inquire after Gula, and you may probably hear of her."

"Do you know, then, if she lives?" he asked; "her relatives deny having seen her."

"She is alive," she said, drawing a folded note from her pocket. "This paper I found yesterday in the bean-arbor, when I went, as usual, to my little garden."

She handed it to Marstrand.

"Do not trouble yourself about me," were its contents; "I must be gone. No one compels me, but I must away! How beautiful it is here! All the red and blue flowers are blooming, and all beings love me. The young animals come and lick my hands, birch branches bow down to me. I tremble no more, my sister; I am glad. God is good, and his power is great; his golden sun shines on me as I sit by the falling stream and think upon you."

"She raves!" said Marstrand, as his arms fell by his side.

"Her soul is with us," replied Ilda. "Solitary she sits in the boundless waste, where no one understands her. Her bosom is decked with flowers and birch branches; do you know what that signifies? She is to choose a husband."

"Mortuno!"

"I have spoken with the pastor; do you, also, talk with him.

Klaus Hornemann, in a few days, goes over to the Alten river. He will seek after Afraja. Give him some intelligence of her; help him as much as you can; for I fear our worthy friend will seek for her in vain. Afraja will conceal his daughter from him. He will dissemble and lie, so as not to deliver her up."

"Is this the object of the *Pfarrer's* journey?" asked Marstrand.

"We have considered of it," said she. "You know, in Trondenaes there is a school; thither Hornemann wishes to carry her. Do you not see that the paper is stained with tears? and cannot you perceive that Afraja stood by and dictated to her the words as she wrote?'

Marstrand was moved by these conjectures, yet he rejoiced that Gula was with her father.

"If Afraja will positively keep his daughter, and if she fled to him, what expectation can I have of discovering her retreat, or of interfering with her destiny?"

"When you are living at Balsfiord," replied Ilda, "the crafty old man will visit you. You have acquired his fullest confidence."

John blushed. What knowledge had Ilda of his various meetings with Afraja?

"A wise man can draw profit as well from the blade of grass as from the great tree; I do not blame you if you do this. You know what you may do, and you will not go farther than your conscience and judgment authorize."

In these words there was a mixture of admonition and accusation which increased his embarrassment. He could not speak with Ilda of his distrust of her father, of his expectations from Afraja's friendship; and as little could he endure an unjust suspicion. With a certain pride of manner, he said, "I thank you for your good opinion. I will do nothing against my conscience, and I heartily wish I may never have need of Afraja's services. As to Björnarne——"

She interrupted him, and pointed to the house. "There he

stands, with his beloved. Before three months are past, he will be lord of Orenaes, and will give you all the aid you can expect of him."

Marstrand looked there with a gloomy expression. "Your father," he murmured, half aloud, "is a hard man; and he is hardest towards his own children."

"It does not belong to you to censure him," she answered; "and, least of all, in my presence."

"You always know what is proper," he cried, with bitterness. "You are an exemplary daughter, and will take along with you the blessing which builds up houses. Let us leave here. I thank you, Miss Ilda, I thank you. You have no sorrow, no wounded heart. Whatever may happen is God's will, and what your father may do against you, against me, Björnarne, or any one else, is well done."

"You shall not go, John Marstrand," she cried after him, "without knowing that I pardon you, and that I think better of you than these angry words merit."

The tone of her voice was so soft and plaintive, that Marstrand turned to her, quickly reconciled: but he sought in vain for a reflection of her words in her eyes. She coldly and tranquilly looked upon him, and then composedly said, "Let us part good friends, with the assurance that we are doing right, to the best of our knowledge."

In the evening, according to the usual division of time, although the sun shone warm and bright in the windows, there was merry-making in the Gaard. Helgestad had invited several neighbors to celebrate the departure of his guest, and Klaus Hornemann also, although uninvited, came over from his brother Heinrick Sture's, who was recovering from his indisposition. The people of the Gaard also gathered on the *Vorplatze*, where they were entertained. In the *stuga*, there was dancing, and in the garden, by the side of the house, the tired dancers rested themselves under the shade of the thick bean-arbor, from the scorching rays of the midnight sun.

Marstrand had danced, played, and drunk, and was overflowing with excitement and good-humor. He had never been seen in such a state. His eyes were flashing with pleasure and enjoyment; his hand was ever willing to accept another glass, or to whirl a maiden in the giddy maze, and he was prompt at repartee and jest.

He sat with the men in the circle, and discussed the arrangements which he had devised for Balsfiord; at which many gravely shook their heads, in anticipation of a sad end to such inconsiderate plans of living. To the young people he promised invitations to feasts, dances, and hunting-matches; and to the maidens he had a polite word for all, leaving each under the impression that she had won his preference.

His gaiety became contagious. Paul Petersen strove to maintain his reputation of being the merriest boon companion; many young men heated their brains with strong drinks, emulating each other in extravagant laughter, songs, and mummery of all kinds; even the serious Olaf lost his gravity, and the old Gaard of Orenaes shook again with the wild uproar.

After a while, Marstrand encountered Hannah in the arbor, to which she had fled from the tumult. "I would have never believed, Herr Marstrand," she said, as he stood before her, "that you could have so gaily and lightly taken leave of us."

"Why should I not be gay," he replied, "when I leave you all so happy behind me?"

"And what is concealed beneath this happy exterior?" she said, with a piercing look. "Grief which, in its desperation, makes a jest of its misery."

"The deception will not, at least, continue much longer; for, in an hour more, the morning wind will carry me and my vessel to sea."

"To the wilderness of Balsfiord, where there will be no leisure for laughing and jesting."

"So much the better, Hannah: when tired with labor, I

I can sleep and wake, free from every thought incompatible with my life of a settler."

"I hope," she replied, "that however you may forget the rest of the world, you will remember us, and a few others: although the way over the wild fjeld is difficult, yet I trust we shall shortly see you here again."

Marstrand replied with a dissenting sign. "I shall not return here for a long time. I have fifty workmen to look after; and Olaf has refused me his aid. He will have nothing to do with what he considers a waste of money and time. But I will not be here to see how happiness and contentment will flourish in Gaard von Orenaes. I will not see how Helgestad calculates, how the vulgar face of the voigt, in which all vices are depicted, daily grows redder from his deep potations; and I will not also see his vile nephew making himself secure of his prey; and, last of all, I will not see how Miss Hannah associates with him, and casts away all hopes of earthly happiness, notwithstanding my efforts to prevent the sacrifice."

"And Ilda?" she whispered in his ear.

Marstrand drew back, and his face reddened with displeasure. "At this last moment, hear me, Hannah Fandrem; although you have avoided me for several days. What horrible object is it which induces you to give your hand to Björnarne, and to consent to Helgestad's plans, and so indefatigably to strive after his approbation? After having inflicted upon you the deepest injury, he seeks your forgiveness; and you take his bloody hand, and aspire to the honor of becoming his beloved daughter! You pretend affection for him, and love for Björnarne; but deadly hatred and vengeance are burning in your soul, and you are willing, for their satisfaction, to involve yourself and an innocent person in the same sacrifice. What prevents me from going before Helgestad, and telling him what I know?"

"Nothing but the consciousness that no one would believe

you," responded Hannah, smiling. "You saw how the vener able pastor answered you, and what improper suspicion you brought upon yourself."

"True," said he; "but have you no compassion on Björnarne? Do you not see with what repulsiveness he receives your manifestations of love?"

"Am I then so repulsive?" she replied, with a loud laugh. "What a picture you draw of me, Herr Marstrand, and how politely you speak! If it were true, I would be sorry for it; but I would only redouble my caresses, to cure him of his aversion."

"Unhappy maiden! tempt not God. Björnarne must obey his father, whatever his own feelings may be. You will live by his side at Lyngenfiord, and in this house, until you die. He will reconcile himself to his lot, Hannah, but you will not. Your vengeance, with all its torments, will recoil upon you."

Her face turned pale, and her hands convulsively clasped together, but it was only for a moment. She immediately resumed her equanimity. "I have chosen my lot," said she. "Heaven help me, I could not do otherwise. Consider, my friend, what was left to me. For me, there was no retreating, and I could only look forward. I suffered my betrothment to take place because I could not prevent it. Am I guilty, if Helgestad's son does not love me? What opposition could I, a weak, forlorn woman, on this savage coast, without friends, make to Helgestad's powerful will? I can do nothing else, but endeavor to ameliorate my destiny by gaining his love and favor. This is my honest purpose, and why should I be blamed for it? I seek to gratify those with whom I am to live, and manifest a friendly and pleased inclination for my betrothed. I wish to convince him that I will be a true companion, and that I honor and esteem him. These are my purposes, and I swear to you by all that is holy, I will always faithfully fulfil my duty."

Marstrand made no answer, and for a while stood in silent

contemplation. He could not gainsay what Hannah had said, but yet he knew it to be false. A pause ensued; the flowers in the garden awoke from their sleep, and a breath of air rustled the leaves above them, reminding him that the morning had come.

"Björnarne's heart is heavy with sorrow, and his eyes are red with secret weeping. It is ridiculous, and at the same time shameful, to speak of it. He cannot forget the fugitive Lapland maiden. Gula is always in his mind."

"Do you know that?" exclaimed John. "Who told you so?"

"Softly," she interrupted, with a smile. "A friend, an upright friend, who wishes me well, and who trusts me, like you; in a word, my dear brother-in-law, Paul Petersen."

"The miserable hypocrite," muttered Marstrand.

"The good Paul," continued Hannah, without noticing his remark, "who gives himself the greatest trouble to chase away Björnarne's sadness. Around the whole fiord, and wherever his influence extends, he urges the most experienced men to hunt out the place of concealment of the maiden. He will finally succeed in discovering her retreat, and I almost believe he knows it already."

"There is mischief in whatever this man meddles with. Beware of him. Why does he seek Gula? What will he do when he has found her?"

"What care I?" was her reply. "If he brings her here, I will receive her; or do you think I ought to be jealous of her? I believe the rascally secretary has himself rather lovingly looked upon her black eyes; at least he speaks of her with wonderful enthusiasm. Ilda must take care that he does not carry her to his house in Tromsöe."

"Gula," replied the Dane, "does not deserve such jests."

"And what does Ilda deserve?" she asked.

"Your esteem, Hannah Fandrem."

"More than that, I admire her. She is as cool, resolute,

and intelligent, as the best fish-trader in Nordland; as submissive to God's will as a missionary; as humble as a Lapp: this pious, discreet maiden, has also a warm, tender heart, and is prouder than many a privy-councillor's daughter."

Marstrand's face was in a flame, he turned around and arose. Hannah took his hand—"There comes the wind, rippling the smooth surface of the fiord," she said. "So will the morning come over us, and chase away the heavy air. They are seeking us. Farewell, dear friend, every one plays his part as well as he can; may the deceivers be deceived."

Klaus Hornemann stretched his head around the corner of the house; he held Björnarne by the hand. "There she sits, the fair bride, in vain awaiting the sad bridegroom. The last dance is now to come off."

"Not the last, dear Björnarne," said Hannah, as she hurried up to her betrothed, who gazed at her with an irresolute and distrustful air; "we will have many dances before the last comes; but you will always find me ready to do my best."

She drew him away, and Marstrand took the arm of the old, laughing parson. "Do you yet doubt," said the latter, "that this will be a happy pair. Such an active, bustling wife Björnarne ought to have. She will bring a blessing on his house, and lead Helgestad to good works and repentance."

Marstrand had no reply to make, for at this moment the whole body of his young friends took possession of him, and brought him back in triumph to the *Stuga;* here he made his farewell speech, and received his full share of toasts to good luck, hand shakings, and parting hints of good advice.

An hour later he was standing on the quarter-deck of the yacht, which, with her bellied sail, was gliding rapidly over the fiord. Reiterated huzzas followed the vessel, as she bore out to sea under a fresh wind.

A curious sensation came over him, as he sat alone in the cabin of the vessel which carried him to his uncertain destiny. A little while before, he was surrounded by people who all entertained more or less sympathy for him; now he was altogether isolated, and thrown entirely upon himself, without the assistance of any one related to him by blood, or near to him in affection.

He cast a glance at the heap of chests and stores that filled up the cabin, and laid his heated head in his hands; he courageously lifted up his eyes again, and repeated his vow of indefatigable industry, and his resolution to overcome all difficulties. Fortune had favored him, and he had found friends and support; his royal patent had obtained him a vast tract of land; the whole vessel was his, with all its contents; and stout men stood ready to serve him. It would be easy to procure others, for by him in the corner were the iron chests full of specie thalers; and what could not be had for money? He impatiently watched, the whole day long, the run of the yacht, as she sailed along the coast; the next morning she cast anchor before Tromsöe. The voigt had named to him some laborers, carpenters and wood-cutters, who, for good wages, might be induced to accompany him; he was more successful with them than he had expected. The report of the new settlement at Balsfiord, and of the Danish lord who was to build mills there, and to saw up the Balself wood into logs and planks, had already arrived at Tromsöe; although most made light of it, yet they were not unwilling to join in the expedition, and obtain their share of the wasted money. The Balsfiord was a desert place, but little known, of no repute as a fishing ground, and visited only by reindeer and Lapps. But there was, also, in these poor idle men, enervated by want and the climate, something yet left of the bold, adventurous spirit of their Norman ancestors; and when the yacht got under way again, the number of laborers shipped was nearly doubled.

On the third day the vessel ran into the winding and constantly narrowing bay, but the view was more pleasing. Lovely meadows stretched out on all sides before the eye. The naked, black rocks receded, and gave room for little valleys, into which numberless cascades might be seen tumbling from the heights above. The platforms of the mountains were covered with thick green grass and groves of birch trees; and at last the new-built *Gaard* loomed up before the ship in stately dignity from its elevated site.

The sight of the house was hailed with a triple hurrah; and from the various huts men and women came out to meet the new comers. A pile work had already been commenced between the rocks on shore, where the packing-house was to be built, and it had advanced so far, that the yacht could make fast to it. Marstrand was the first to touch the shore, with a desperate leap; he stood there, as Helgestad would say, upon his own feet, his hat on his head, the picture of a man who knew how to take care of himself.

The unloading of the cargo went under his immediate inspection; and the first day was for Marstrand one of incessant confusion and toil. The rooms of the house were filled with chests, and boxes, and bales. It required no little judgment and attention to see that everything was put in its right place; but with the assistance of some expert men, whom he had selected for the purpose, Marstrand was enabled properly to arrange the various articles.

After a week, the household establishment was put in order, boats prepared for the fishery, places sought for the building of huts for the different families, and every where the laborers were hard at work, and joy and hope beamed in all faces. The yacht had brought a considerable quantity of flour and provisions of all kinds, and Marstrand distributed them bounteously, without thinking of repayment. For this first time he made no charges against his people. The fishermen were to take care of themselves, the wood-cutters must first prepare dwellings, the Gaard and its shop be completely established, and the whole curious machinery of this new life be first set in motion, before trade could be commenced.

With the combination of all his forces, Marstrand began the

building of his store-house; where wood was not at hand, it was felled in the forest; but he soon saw the difficulties with which he had to contend to gain a practicable access to the rocky valley of the Balself. It was necessary to build bridges over deep ravines; a road was to be laid out and graded, and it often required considerable ingenuity to overcome obstacles which only succeeded after repeated failures.

This road to the mountain forest was the chief effort of the enterprising proprietor, who procured additional laborers from Malangerfiord, and especially carpenters who understood the mode of constructing saw-mills. With great difficulty two Nordlanders were obtained from Lenvig, who boasted of having built mills in Trondheim and other parts of the north. When they saw the valley of the Balself, however, the deep, furious stream, the precipices, and the rugged ground, they declared it impossible to find a place where a mill could be erected. Marstrand's cash could alone induce them to set to work, and at last make the attempt.

The more the difficulties increased, the greater was the energy of the young settler. From morning to night he was constantly busy. Now, he was with the workmen, who were finishing the warehouse; now with the mill-architects, or with the road-makers and the wood-cutters in the side valleys on the fiord. New requisitions upon his time and strength were made upon his return to the house, where he found many in quest of provisions, money, and instructions. He had strifes to settle, discontents to appease, and, at the same time, he was obliged to take care of his domestic concerns, and keep his accounts as a trader.

The mountains of the peninsula around the Ulvsfiord were peopled with wandering families of Laplanders; the tinkle of the reindeer's bell sounded from the mountains; the report of the gun echoed over the bay; and, in the evening, men in brown shirts, peaked leather caps on the head, and kommagers on the legs, came down to the valley, and curiously looked at the new works. They brought with them birds, reindeer horns, and skins, which they exchanged for powder, lead, and knives, twine and needles.

Thus stood matters, when one day, to Marstrand's greatest joy, Olaf Veigand entered his house. He received the honest, single-minded Olaf, as a being of a superior order, who as cordially responded to his hearty greeting.

The news which he brought with him was of no particular interest. Helgestad had not yet returned, and the secretary exercised unlimited sway, which had given rise to all kinds of scenes. Ilda could only influence her lover by her submissive gentleness; but Björnarne was entirely independent of him, and by devilish arts, as Olaf said, had been so entirely changed, that no one knew him any more. He troubled himself about nothing, and passed most of his time in coursing over the high fjeldes like a wild animal, from which he came back famished with hunger, and with his clothes in tatters. A poisoned drink must have been given him, or a witches' spell have been pronounced over him, for his eyes glared like a madman's, and his limbs shook like one in a fever, when he was questioned upon his conduct. "The only one who makes head against the secretary, is Hannah," said Olaf farther, "and it is amusing to see how she gives him his dues. She shows much love to Björnarne, whom she caresses and flatters; but he deserves it not, for the fonder she is, the more rude and uncivil he becomes. In my vexation, and because I could no longer support these proceedings, I ran off, deep into the Jauren, where I nearly lost my life."

He took off his hat, and showed Marstrand a bullet-hole in the crown. "See how close the lead passed to my skin. May the hand be withered that made that shot! But may I be hanged if I do not know the rascal who fired it."

"Who could attempt your life?"

"Were you ever up there," asked Olaf, "where the great cone rises, which they call the Kilpis?"

Marstrand replied in the negative.

"That is a curious place," continued Olaf. "A woody, broken fjeld leads up to it. Now you meet deep ravines, covered with trees, with thundering water-falls and streams; then naked clefts, black, thunder-riven, and scorched; then again, level plains full of monstrous stones and blocks, sometimes curiously arranged in a circle, as if disposed so by the hand of man.—A herd of wild reindeer sprang over these rocks, with half a dozen wolves at their heels, I behind them all, seeking to get to windward of the animals, who always run against the wind. It was all in vain. The whole pack plunged down into a ravine, and far in the distance I heard the rustling of their antlers and the howl of their pursuers. As I clambered up the other side of the gorge, the Kilpis stood before me, a jagged mass of rock, full a mile long, and more than a thousand feet high. It rose up in the midst of a sea of ruins; at its feet, the water was gathered into a black lake or swamp, covered with innumerable quantities of malf berries and yellow gentian flowers. No living being was to be seen, and no sound agitated the air, except when, occasionally, a stone breaking loose from the summit rolled down into the water with a heavy splash.

"As I was observing the curious mountain, I remembered that the Laplanders revered it as the holy seat of their god Jubinal. I looked around to see if I could discover any of the dirty, lurking scoundrels; for my sack was empty, and my tongue cleaved to the roof of my mouth. It was all in vain, however. I climbed up to a projecting ledge, and surveyed the whole country. Nothing was to be seen but deep gorges, overgrown birch-thickets, and the bare, desolate fjeldes of the mountains. I tore off a gentian-stalk and put it in my mouth, as the Laplanders do to relieve thirst, when, to my great joy, I observed, over an opposite ridge of the mountain, a thin smoke rising in the air. It was a severe undertaking to reach it through swamp, wood, and water. More than once I lost the direction, as the way lay through a perfect labyrinth of rocks, rubbish, and wild bushes; but I at last overcame the ascent, and looked down into a green valley beneath, which appeared as if slit with a knife in the body of the Kilpis. I saw no human beings, but it was too beautiful not to be inhabited. A clear brook flowed between overgrown banks; tall trees grew on the edge of the mountain-sides; and the faintly-sounding tinkle of reindeer-bells was distinctly audible.

"I had often heard that such lovely little spots existed in the midst of these savage wastes, like the oases spoken of by the books in the deserts of the hot countries. As I was looking about for a place to descend, I heard a report, from above or below, I was not certain which; but my hat fell from my head and my hair stood on end. With a bound, I jumped behind a rock. I pointed my gun in all directions, but nothing moved. I saw no smoke. Probably the scoundrel had shot up from the ravine without my observing it. It was no shame if I set out at full run. Behind me there echoed an infernal laughter, as if it were Jubinal himself, shouting down from the top of the Kilpis. I waded in the swamp knee-deep through the jungle, and was heartily rejoiced when I again reached the black lake and had found the right direction. In the evening, I was at the sources of the Balself, which gush out from the Tanjaure; and who should I meet there? No other than Mortuno, the cross-eyed rascal; his plumed hat on his left ear, and grinning as maliciously as a blue fox when he has scrambled upon the fish-scaffolds. His herds lay around the springs; four tents were pitched within an enclosure; and a whole band of men and women hovered over the fire in the stones, each uglier than the other."

"And was there no trace of Gula there?" asked Marstrand.

"Not that I could learn. The foolish fellow obliged me to enter his *gamme* and rest; but if he had not been so polite, and if this whole tribe of thieves had risen against me, I could not have left the spot, because I was completely exhausted, and hungry enough to have eaten a reindeer cheese."

"Did you not make any inquiries after Gula, dear Olaf?"

"Certainly I did; for Ilda is always making a bustle about her; and Björnarne, also, cannot forget the yellow, black-eyed witch. I asked after her; but Mortuno grinned, like a monkey, from ear to ear, spoke and screamed in his miserable tongue, which nobody understands, bent himself double, shrugged his shoulders, and shook his head in denial."

"He lied," said Marstrand; "Gula lives."

"He certainly lied; for immediately afterwards, he laughed; looking, for all the world, like a skarfe on the rocks dressing its feathers, and said that as soon as Gula was found, he intended to buy her of Afraja."

"Buy her! Is he mad?"

"Ha, ha!" roared Olaf; "you do not understand it. To buy, in good Lappish, means to marry. The maiden's father receives a number of reindeer, or some other kind of present, for which he leads his daughter into a holy circle of stones—a Saita, as they call it—where he delivers her to her husband, who conducts her into his *gamme*. This is all the marriage ceremony among this wretched rabble. In spite of the efforts of the government and the pious Klaus, there are rarely any among them who will act, in these matters, after a Christian fashion."

"Afraja will never give his daughter to this Mortuno," said the Dane, with much warmth. "Gula will not permit herself to be sold to this filthy villain."

"Bah!" replied Olaf; "what else can she do? Mortuno is a fine gentleman among his equals; but I believe him capable of the worst things. May I be hanged if it was not he who sent a bullet through my hat.

"I could read the exultation in his rascally face," continued Olaf. "You remember how we broke our jests upon Mortuno, when he was in Orenaes Gaard. He took all in good part, and laughed at our tricks; for these scoundrels are very humble when they are among us. As I now sat in his *gamme*, he reminded me of how I proposed to make him a watchman in Bodoen, and how Paul Petersen would have him for his body guard. 'Now look,' said he, amid all kinds of grimaces, I have not forgotten it, good father, 'Mortuno forgets nothing; when you come to the country of the children of Jubinal, he will be as vigilant as the dwarf Bugo over the giant Yulpus.'

"The look with which the villain surveyed me was of such a character, that I involuntarily laid my hand on my knife; but he clapped his hands like a madman, leaned back, and muttered something through his throat, that set all the rest in the same ecstasy. They looked at me with their round, red, wicked eyes, as so many devils incarnate. A shudder ran over me, and I was obliged to summon up all my energies, to prevent my fear from being seen. Mortuno next laid his hand upon my arm, and disgustingly fondled me about the head and neck, as I would do to a dog, all of which I bore in patience, without uttering a word. Snatching the hat from my head, and observing the holes in it, he exclaimed: 'Ha! ha! my dear father, this is a pair of ugly holes. Take care the next time. I will relate to you how Bugo, the dwarf, did with his lord, the giant.'

"He took the pipe out of my pocket, the tobacco out of my bag, and coolly set to smoking. 'Bugo,' said he, after a while, 'was a Finn, a wise and discreet man, who lived here. Yulpus, surnamed the giant, dwelt by the sea, and was such a monster, that he could cross the Lyngenfiord with a single stride. Bugo had been instructed in the use of the bow by the god Ayka, in which he was so expert that no wolf, bird, or even fish in the water, could escape him. 'You must watch over my house, and keep it in order,' said Yulpus to him, and Bugo assented. He watched and hunted for him; and when Yulpus slept, he stood near him and shot the flies from his face with his arrows, without moving a hair. This he did for a year, and then asked for his compensation; but Yulpus laughed at him. 'You simpleton,' he cried, with the point of his finger throwing him upon his knees, 'speak another word, and I will crush you to powder.' Bugo supplicated for mercy; but when Yulpus went to sleep, he took his bow and shot a mighty arrow through his head and hair, which was several feet thick. The arrow sank deep in the side of the rock, and nailed the giant fast, who awoke in great terror, and imploringly begged Bugo to set him at liberty. 'Will you leave the land, and never again return?' asked the dwarf. Yulpus promised all, and Bugo then drew out the arrow; but this had hardly been done, before the giant sprang on his feet, and squeezed the dwarf so hard between his fingers, that the blood ran out of his mouth and ears. 'You fool,' said the giant, 'if you jest again with me, I will hurl you seven miles over the mountains and islands into the sea.'

"'Will you not keep the oath you have sworn?' asked Bugo.

"'I will not observe it,' cried Yulpus; 'but I will break your neck if you do not become my servant.'

"Bugo then took his bow and arrows, and ran to the Kilpis; and when he saw the giant coming to take him captive, he said, smiling: 'I warned you, little father, to keep away from my country. I shot within a hair of your head; now I will take a lower aim,' and as he spoke his arrow flew through the head of Yulpus. He plunged into the black lake, and never appeared again. There lies he yet; and at times roars so by night, that all flee away who hear him.'

"So," said Olaf farther "spoke this long-haired scoundrel, and he looked at me and my hat with such a horrible grin, that I understood well enough what he meant. The whole evening he jeered me; and how it happened that I awoke the next morning with a whole throat I cannot yet comprehend. I slept soundly enough among dogs and men in the *gamme;* and, as I was aroused by a shake of the shoulder,

I sprang up, and beheld the grinning creature standing before me with a bowl of warm reindeer's milk and bread, both of which tasted wonderfully good. He then showed me the nearest way through bush and rocks, and how I must follow the course of the stream, all of which he did with as much dignity as a monkey in red breeches.

"'Farewell, Olaf Veigand,' he exclaimed, in separating, 'and do not forget the giant Yulpus and the dwarf Bugo.'

"I would have liked to have given him a remembrancer," said Olaf, closing his story; "but for the apprehension that some one of the roving thieves might be concealed behind the rocks. If, however, the black brute ever falls into my hands, I will pay him up for his jokes."

Marstrand could not refrain from smiling at the rude manner in which Mortuno had exercised the right of retaliation, and how deeply he had humiliated the Nordlander. He endeavored to pacify him, and led him into the gaard and around among the various laborers, and deep into the woods among the wood-cutters and mill-constructors. The more Olaf saw and heard, the less satisfied he seemed to be; and, at last, he could not withhold the expression of his anxiety.

"It is, indeed," said he, "the custom in Nordland for no one to undervalue another's works; but, as your friend, John Marstrand, I cannot be silent and see you going to ruin. Your settlement is large, and by all appearance, you would soon make your fortune, if you would act as other men. You have fish in the fiord, and the sea belongs to you as far out as the Strom menbucht: but you have no fishermen. Where are your fish-scaffolds, which should already be full? Where are your warehouses and your presses? What are your household arrangements? All is neglected, imperfect, and no provision made for the winter. Nowhere do I see any signs of cultivation; you squander your stores, and support a great number of indolent people, who do as little as possible. The beautiful little valleys where industrious colonists could dwell, lie as wild as ever;

miserable huts have been erected, instead of solid log-houses for your working-people. You are throwing away your strength, your money, and your provisions, to make a road to the woods, whose trees will strike you dead. You are building your happiness on vain calculations that can never be realised."

Marstrand unsuccessfully attempted to defend himself, and Olaf continued; "I cannot praise the man," said he, "who walks in the light of the sun, and yet stumbles and falls over every stone. Let us examine your stores, and make an estimate of the quantity you have used, and of what you stand in need of for future exigencies."

The examination took place, and it was found that the young settler had consumed six times as much as was necessary, according to Olaf's calculations, and if he continued so to manage, the stock would be exhausted before the autumn. His ready money had also greatly diminished, and his account-book showed that he reckoned badly, and it was evident that his good-nature had been taken advantage of.

"In fine," said Olaf, "you have begun badly, and you will soon be a ruined man, if you do not immediately correct your faults. Drive away a fourth of these idlers, let the trees lie where they are, and throw your mills and saws into the fiord. You must go over to Lyngenfiord and ask aid and stores of all kinds, and then be wiser. I will take your place here, will put things in order, and finish the building of your storehouse; dismiss, however, the useless people who are consuming your means, and laughing at the stupidity of the Danish fool."

Although Marstrand felt the truth of these reproaches, he could not resolve to admit their justice. His pride prevented him from confessing, before all the world, that he had, indeed, acted like a fool. All around the country, as far even as Finnmark, the new undertaking was talked of. From Tromsöe, from the Malanger islands, and also from Nordland, came people, who looked at his operations with astonishment. Many had their own peculiar notions on the subject; but they were all convinced that these woods could, if converted into logs and planks, become extraordinarily profitable. Marstrand had no doubt on the subject. He was satisfied with what he had done, and he knew that he could overcome all difficulties. He could not consent to abandon his plans, to cease operations, and expose himself to ridicule and contempt.

He slowly wandered along in solitary meditation, until he arrived at the meadow where the bear had been formerly killed, and as he looked up, he perceived Afraja sitting on a rock.

The old man wore his summer dress, a short blouse of brown cotton stuff. A reindeer of extraordinary size, with monstrous antlers, stood alongside of him, upon the back of which, a kind of saddle, with high cushions, was strapped. The two yellow dogs of the sorcerer, as before, lay at his feet, and he, himself, was nearly bent double, with his chin resting upon his staff.

As the dogs started up with a growl, Afraja raised his head, and, without any appearance of surprise, awaited the stranger, whose countenance suddenly lit up with joy as he beheld the man who could help him if he chose.

"I am glad thus unexpectedly to meet you," he exclaimed, as he approached.

"Sit down by me," answered the Lapp; "I have been waiting for you."

"How did you know that I would come?" asked Marstrand, with an incredulous smile.

"I knew it," said Afraja, impressively; "I know much."

"Tell me first," continued the young man, "how is Gula?"

"She is well," was the answer.

"Where do you keep her? Is she in the neighborhood?"

The old chief suffered some minutes to elapse before he made an answer. Leaning with his hands clasped upon his staff, he appeared to be in deep meditation. "My child," said he, "is sitting in her gamme upon the border of the stream, where the good Gods suffer flowers to bloom. She is glad, and rejoices that she can run around under the young birches, light-footed as the reindeer, and that she no longer dwells in the confined house of the avaricious trader."

"Helgestad has been a benefactor to her," said John. "I do not believe you, Afraja; you are a hard father; you have carried her off by stealth to some part of the wilderness, where you compel her to remain."

"Did she not," answered the old man, "of her own accord leave the house at Lyngenfiord, to dwell again with me?"

"But she longs to return thither."

"Believe me," said the Lapp, "her eyes are bright, and her lips laugh."

"What will you do with her? What will be her lot?" said the young man, with agitation. "Shall she, year by year, rove about with you, even to the polar sea? Such a life will kill her, and you are old, Afraja. What will become of her when you are taken from her?"

"She will take the husband that is destined for her."

"Whom? Mortuno, perhaps?"

Afraja bent down, and answered not.

"Is such a man fit for one of the education and training of your child?" continued Marstrand. "You will see the flower which God gave you wither and die before the winter comes, and you will then repent in vain of your folly."

"Have you reflected upon what you say? Gula is a daughter of an outcast people; where shall she dwell to be happy? With you, perhaps? Shall she be despised and scorned as a maid-servant? Shall she inhabit the house of a filthy Quane? Who has driven us into this wilderness? Who robbed us of the land of our fathers? Who compels us to wander with the reindeer?"

Marstrand could not contradict the old man. "Your complaint is just, but all do not deserve your reproach."

"You," answered the Lapp, "are milder than these hard-hearted, avaricious men. You are a sensible, friendly-disposed young man; but would you introduce Gula into your house?

Would you place her at your hearth, and eat out of the same dish with her?"

He laughed aloud, and crouched upon his staff, as he observed the effect of his inquiry. "You see it," he exclaimed. "Are you more just or better? But you could not be, for they would treat you as they do us. They would thrust you out like a dog; they would bring shame and disgrace upon you, and chase you away like the grey wolf, so that nothing would be left to you but to flee into the desert where the outcasts dwell."

Afraja spoke with a clearer, fuller voice, and without the usual ambiguity and signs of the Lapp. In an intelligible manner, and with the dignity that Marstrand had often observed in him, he described the misery of his race; he remarked the deep impression which his descriptions made upon his sympathetic hearer.

"Therefore," said Afraja, "you cannot wonder that my child does not go down to you again. Leave her, I pray you, with those who love and honor her as Afraja's daughter, and tell the fools who blindly seek her, that they had better remain quietly at home than to pursue her among our deserts."

"You astonish me," said Marstrand. "Were all of your race as intelligent as you, the opinion of their persecutors would be changed."

"I would not change it, young man," replied Afraja. "Whom do they hate most? Me, because they call me wise. If all my people were like me, their hate would consume every one of us."

"They hate you," said Marstrand, "because they fear you; your people, however, despise and laugh at them. It would be better if they did not do the latter. Hate may be reconciled or destroyed by hate; he who laughs and despises is not an enemy to excite apprehension."

Afraja listened in silence. He sat in deep meditation upon the stone, rolling his little red eyes wildly about, and lowering upon his counsellor. "Let us talk of your affairs," he said, in reply, as Marstrand ceased speaking; "for that purpose have I come hither. Often, in the sleepless hours of the night, your lips whispered my name. You called me."

"You know more than I myself," said Marstrand.

"You called, because you had need of me," continued the old man. "You expend much money, and maintain a great many people. Your bags and chests are empty, and your silver thalers flow into other men's pockets."

"You are right," answered the young proprietor. "I have myself feared that I should be obliged to desist, and leave my work in an unfinished state."

Afraja laughed aloud. "Do not so," said he, "your work is good. Helgestad will commend it when he visits you"

"Will he supply me farther with money and goods, despite your warnings."

"Your saw-mills and your industry will please him."

"But if Helgestad withdraws his aid, can I rely upon you, Afraja?"

The sorcerer replied with a nod. "Let us see first what he has to say. Go then, if you desire, to the fiord below, until you come to the spot where Jubinal once outstretched his hand, and crushed the voigt in his house. Go thither in the starlight, and call upon me. Wherever I may be, I will hear your voice. Speak my name softly, as when Syda, the wind-god, dances over the surface of the young grass, and Afraja will be with you."

It seemed to the Dane as if he were forming a compact with the Evil One; and yet the old, mysterious man, of whom he asked assistance, and who, with all kinds of jugglery, maintained his reputation as a sorcerer, was rather encouraging than intimidating.

"May I trust in you, Afraja?" he inquired, as earnestly as he could.

"You must do it, young man — you will do it," he replied.

"And what do you ask of me, in return for your service?"

"Nothing, nothing!" said the Lapp, as hypocritically as the arch-fiend himself. "I have as much money for you as you may want. Yet, let me go. My way is far. My land is endless. No one knows it—they call it a wilderness. Come and see for yourself, if it does not produce better fruits than grow at Lyngenfiord. I will show you what no one has seen: farewell, and remember what I have told you. I am sitting on a grave-stone, my eyes are open. I know and can do much."

With these words, which he spake in a half-singing tone, he mounted his beast, and seized the halter which dangled from its neck. With a gentle jerk, he set it in motion, and followed by the two yellow dogs, the reindeer quickly clambered up the steep rocks from which the Balself precipitated itself.

Marstrand looked after him until he was lost to view. He then turned away in deep thought, but evidently composed in mind. Afraja had money for him, in case Helgestad should entertain evil intentions against him; but why should he leave him helpless, after he had done all in his power to assist him?

When he reached the Gaard, he resolved to go over to Lyngenfiord, as Olaf was certain that Helgestad must have returned. He had to fulfil his promise to Olaf, to give him, for a time, the supervision of affairs—to finish the ware-house, and to prosecute the work in the woods, until he himself should return from Orenaes.

Olaf was ready for all this. "I will," said he, "put up a fine ware-house for you; but you will have no stores. Do as you please, however; I will not oppose you. Every one must know what is best for himself."

The careful Gaardherr allotted the work to the carpenters, and, on the following morning, selecting the best among the eight horses, which he had purchased for his establishment, he set out upon his journey. The young, strong animal soon carried him over the mountain ridge which separates the Balsfiord from the Ulvfiord, and by noon he had reached the fjeld which leads to Lyngenfiord.

The scene was much different from what it was when, in wading through snow and swamp, he had first learned the difficulties of this pathless waste. Wild grass, moss, and green spots now abounded; birch-bushes and briery thickets grew in sheltered localities, and everywhere the prolific mountain bramble cast a scarlet hue over the broad, high plain, upon which the swamp was, for the most part, dried up.

From the higher elevations, he looked down upon both fiords, with their coves and bays, into which the Omnisjok and other mountain waters plunged with a sullen roar. Through many ravines, and over many steep slopes, and boundless mossy swards and stoneless wastes, his sturdy horse bore him safely along. From time to time he saw rising smoke in the distance, and the wind bore along the faint sound of tinkling bells. In several of the deep, bush-covered ravines, which ran down to the sea-shore, he thought he saw herds of horned animals. He was sure that the Lapps wandered there with their cattle, and were passing their summer pastoral life in his neighborhood without his being able to see a single gamme.

And was it, then, a misfortune to live in this illimitable freedom, and to be a son of the boundless waste? The air was fresh and pure, the sun sparkling and warm; springs gushed out of the rocks, which were thickly covered with blue and red mountain-flowers and fragrant shrubs. The cares of men who called themselves refined and civilized, did not reach there, where nothing more was necessary for the support of life than reindeer's meat and milk, a gun for the chase, a net for fishing, six props and a piece of coarse cotton cloth for a tent. The musing traveller left his horse to take his own course, while his thoughts reverted to Gula, who lived in some of these deep-sunken valleys, where anemones bloomed, and a foaming brook rushed through the gentian-bushes, and where she, probably, was sitting by a waterfall, thinking of him.

Thus meditating, he looked anxiously around; for he seemed to hear his name called. It was only imagination, however A snow-hen, colored brown by the summer, flew, with a shrieking cry, through the birch-bushes. Far in the distance, upon a rocky peak, which rose up like an isolated column, a motionless figure was seen, leaning upon a staff.

He could not discover whether it was a human being or a rock. It was, probably, Afraja himself; but the traveller had no desire for a nearer examination. When, in his romantic dreams, he praised this pastoral life, the reality advised him that it must, however, have many disagreeable features which a cultivated man could with difficulty support. Swarms and clouds of scarcely visible gnats, together with stinging flies of every kind, and the great reindeer-fly, which inflicts the most acute pain, gathered around his horse. He could now appreciate the truth of what he had often heard of these torments. Men and animals, in the summer season, suffer almost insupportable pain from the myriads of winged insects with poisonous stings that infest these high plains. For this reason, the Lapp fills his gamme with a dense smoke, to drive off these tormentors; for this reason, the reindeer compels his master to follow him down to the sea-coast; where, on the cool fiords, the breeze blows away his winged plagues.

The traveller was glad enough when he reached the yellow edge of the fjeld, and the Lyngenfiord lay beneath his eye. There, deep down before him, expanded the blue sea-basin; and in the rocky cove he discerned Helgestad's red house, peering out of the green grove of birches. A home-sick feeling rose in the breast of the young man. The Balsfiord, with its lovely little valleys, woods, and the rushing stream, was, no doubt, a more romantic, and, at the same time, a more fruitful scene; yet all there below appeared to him much more beautiful and friendly. He guided his horse down into the steep-sinking ravine; and in half an hour he had descended, and could wave his hat, with a loud hurrah, to his female friends, when his horse climbed up the rocky ridge. Ilda and Hannah, who were sitting at table in the middle of the grass-plot before the mansion, had no sooner perceived him than they rose to welcome him, each after her own manner.

Hannah ran towards him with loud expressions of gratification; Ilda laid aside the work she was sewing, but advanced not a step; yet, when the long-desired guest stood before her and extended his hand, her eyes and face warmed up with such a genuine glow of welcome, that he gazed upon her with unwonted delight.

How much was there to talk about! He could not have hit it better. Paul Petersen and Björnarne had, a week before, gone a bird-hunting to the Loppen Island. The two young maidens were alone at home. Hannah brought Helgestad's arm-chair, with the Holland tobacco and stately pipe. Ilda prepared the coffee in her careful manner, and now, sitting between his two protectresses, he was obliged to describe his mode of life and adventures at Balsfiord. In return, amid jest and laughter, he received a full account of all that had occurred at Orenaes in his absence. It was not, in truth, much; but yet it gave him pleasure to hear it. Ilda had made an attempt to plant potatoes in her little garden, which had waxed into strong weeds; behind the windows were a couple of pots with green herbs, and Hannah believed that Olaf had not in vain sowed oats, which had shot up in thin stalks. Otherwise, nothing had changed. A new maid-servant had been hired, an old man had died, and pastor Heinrick Sture had again preached on the last Sunday.

"And where is my old friend Klaus?" asked Marstrand.

"Quite near at hand," said Hannah. "We have news that he was at Tromsöe some days since. Now he is travelling around among the islands, and will soon be here — soon be here," she repeated, with a glance at Ilda.

Marstrand made some inquiries after Helgestad, and learned that the day before a neighbor who had returned from Bergen had met him there, in good health and spirits. The fish-trade was extraordinarily good; and the oldest people scarcely ever remembered such prices; Niels could be expected back every hour; for both his yachts were laden when the neighbor left the harbor.

All seemed good and favorable for the young settler. He sat smiling and calculating in Helgestad's chair, as if his spirit had taken possession of him. He reckoned over his profits, and quietly strengthened his hopes of success. As he surveyed the naked, poor, rocky soil, from which with difficulty a few oat-stalks could be gathered, he recognised, for the first time, the superiority of the land at Balsfiord. The sea was there more prolific in fish than any one had dreamed. Olaf himself was astonished at it; and then the woods, with their great trees, extended for miles; while only here and there a scanty growth of birch was to be seen in the hollows and on the slopes. The more he thought of it, and the more comparisons he instituted, the more assured was he that he owned a choice spot; and when Helgestad should bring back the fish-earnings, money would abound.

He had thus far only carelessly inquired after Björnarne and Petersen, and their journey, satisfied with the good-luck of finding the secretary absent: he now learned more of this subject. The rocky island of Loppen belonged to Helgestad; it was the brooding place of innumerable swarms of birds. At this season, when there was so little to do at home, Björnarne had fitted out a sloop to carry off the stock of feathers, which, in the latter part of autumn, were to be sent for sale to Bergen. Petersen had accompanied him, to assist in the gathering of the rich product; or, as Marstrand secretly thought, to examine it more closely, in order to estimate its worth.

The absence of the repulsive bridegroom was so pleasing, that he could not suppress his feelings. "So, I have come in good season," he exclaimed, "as I find the house occupied by forlorn women, whom I can protect, if necessary."

"It is to be hoped that our tranquillity will not be disturbed," answered Hannah; "but we are gratified that our solitude is animated by the presence and sympathy of so chivalrous a gentleman."

"Willingly do I enter upon my former duty," continued Marstrand, smiling; "and will remain until Herr Helgestad anchors at the packing-house. I will help where I can, and will forget that I am banished from Orenaes, and think the time has come back again when my kind protectress Ilda took me under her teaching, and gave me her favor."

"Has she then withdrawn it?" mischievously inquired Hannah. "Herr Marstrand has left such a good character behind him, that everybody speaks of him with love and gratification. The old fishermen have almost as much to tell of him as the young ladies."

"And what says Miss Ilda?" resumed Marstrand.

"She says," she replied, "that Hannah is a mischievous prattler; yet she is right in saying that no day passes by without talk of you. We have all missed you, dear John; and now that you have returned, we hope to hold you as long as we possibly can."

"At best, we will bind him in fetters, so that he cannot go," exclaimed Hannah, while she took Ilda's thread, and tied him fast, placing the ends in her friend's hands.

"Presumptuous maiden!" said Ilda; "we must devise another means to keep this young lord in good-humor. Sing him a song of home, while I put the house to rights."

CHAPTER XIII.

What delightful days Marstrand passed in the quiet mansion, alone with his female friends! When he awoke the next morning, the sun was shining in his chamber—the same which he had formerly occupied. How clean, bright, and friendly was all — how noiseless was the house — how beautifully green lay the green grass-plot before him, with its fringe of birch-bushes. There was no sound of Helgestad's rough voice, no hammering in the warehouse, no cries on the fiord; but everywhere the reddish sun-light and blue sky, so pure and mild, as if this cold land of the north, by some magic, had been transported to the south. He remained standing for a long while at the little window; and never did this retired settlement appear to him so fair. He suddenly saw Ilda leave the house, and, at the same moment, the golden day-star rose over the rugged rocks on the Kaafiord, and threw its rays upon the little garden, its flowers, and the young maiden, who, with folded hands, gazed around upon the beauteous picture. A light glimmer played round her long brown tresses; the slender form, in dark attire, stood reverentially still, until her serious countenance broke into a smile, as she plucked some flowers, and arranged them into a bouquet. After a few minutes, she disappeared again in the house, and then Marstrand heard her light tread on the steps, and in the next chamber; when he opened the door, he found a glass upon the table, from which the various-colored flowers welcomed him with their sweet perfume.

He regarded them with deep emotion. They were pinks and mignonettes, dark red gilliflowers, and, in the middle, a bunch of bright forget-me-nots. He bent down to them, pressed them to his lips, and then looked around to see if no one was observing him. A strong excitement agitated his heart; he was, several times, on the point of fastening one of the flowers in his coat, but he replaced it; as he descended the stairs, he was met by Ilda, who chided him for his long sleep. "I was standing by your wards, and what they said to me was so grateful, that I forgot everything else."

"You should not forget; but let us be happy. The days come and go, and if they have joy for us, we will draw from them consolation against the sorrow that may follow them."

Five times the sun rose and sank in short night, which had now again drawn on, for August had arrived; the weather was that of the fair summer, and when the darkness, with soft shadows, overspread the fiord, and the highest mountain summits alone wore their roseate crowns, the moon rose over the dark horn of the Kilpis, and, wonderfully clear and gleaming, scattered its mysterious beams over the dark waters of the fiord and the bays and inlets.

No one, during this period, visited the settlement. The men had all gone with Helgestad to Bergen, or with Björnarne to Loppen. Such of the old fishermen as remained in the vicinity, were catching sey fish in the gulf of Aloen. There were only two maid-servants in the house; and, as on the estates of this remote north, there is as little to do with cattle as agriculture, Helgestad's three cows and two horses pastured in the mountain gorges under the charge of a boy, who drove them out and in. The warehouses were all closed, and the shop did no business. The shepherds on the mountains had bought what they required; it was only in the autumn that the people provided themselves with provisions for the winter: in this season of rest, there was nothing for industrious women and girls to do but to put the linen, beds and furniture in order, to clean the houses, or to travel with their husbands and brothers, and to take as much recreation as they could.

During the forenoon, John assisted his friends at one thing or another, who banteringly solicited his aid in small services; or he sat in the great-leaved bean arbor reading from one of the books which Klaus Hornemann had lately sent from Tromsöe. Holberg and Tullin were then the favorite authors of the Danes. Holberg, a Norwegian, from his birth in Bergen, was highly esteemed; the worthy parson, for the first time, sent to Lyngenfiord a number of volumes of plays, poems, and the satirical romance of Nicholas Klimm's subterranean journey, which Holberg had written in Latin, but of which a translation was immediately made.

Marstrand enthusiastically fell upon these treasures, for he had long been deprived of the pleasure of reading books, and of perusing the semi-weekly little half-sheet gazette of Copenhagen, some copies of which Hornemann had also added. He was personally acquainted with the intellectual professor Holberg, and he entertained his attentive listeners with some interesting sketches of the life of his original and witty friend. When the domestic labors were over, he read one of the droll, keen, characteristic plays, which from beginning to end was accompanied with peals of laughter. When the evening came on, he walked with both the maidens over the rocks to the fiord, or he took the oar and rowed the little boat over the mirror-like gulf, to a picturesque waterfall, or to a promontory, upon which stood a solitary tree, and from whence the view extended to the distant islands and to the snowy mountains of Senjenoen. In one of these excursions, darkness came on before they started homeward; when the moon arose, the sea, gently agitated by the evening breeze, broke in silvery cascades against the rocks; the little boat drove before the breeze, and Marstrand, laying aside the oars, spoke and jested in respectful confidence with Ilda and Hannah. The guitar sounded soft and sweet over the gently-heaving water, accompanied with songs which awoke the poor fishermen and their wives from their sleep; it seemed as if the mermaids and trolls had ascended from their crystal palaces and grottoes, and sat singing upon the waves.

During these charming days, Marstrand was frequently alone for hours at a time, with Ilda or Hannah, but he had as little chance to speak of his own affairs as of those of others. At last, however, on one occasion, when he was sitting with Hannah in the arbor, he asked in a subdued tone, if the hearts of the two betrothed had grown nearer to each other.

"Do you ask after my heart?" replied Hannah, after threading her needle. "What I possess of it lies in the sea, whence it can never be fished up."

"Have you heard nothing since from the south?" asked Marstrand, agitating another subject.

"But little," she replied. "Two weeks ago, a sloop arrived at Tromsöe, with letters for me from my father and brother, who are now again in Bergen. My father sent me his blessing, and my brother wrote me that he regretted he was not on the spot, when, as he supposes, I was forcibly carried off. If any force should be used to make me marry Björnarne, nothing could prevent him from rescuing me. The good Christi has always loved me tenderly, but he does not know all the facts."

"And what answer did you make him?"

"What should I answer him? I sent a note to Tromsöe for the sloop on her return voyage. In it I wrote, 'Dismiss all care, dear Christi, I am Björnarne's betrothed of my own good will, and long for the day when Helgestad's son shall be my husband. Then we will come to you at Bergen, where you yourself can see how it is with me.'"

"Oh, Hannah!" murmured Marstrand.

"What is this warning word, my friend John?" she answered. "My life is bound to that of Björnarne; and what is written must be fulfilled. The Lord has given, and the Lord has taken. He took from me, and he gave to me. And what say the holy books: 'Honor the will of your father, that it may go well with you, and your days may be long on earth.' What say the laws and customs of men? They require submission, and know nothing of the feelings of the heart. Helgestad"—— she drew a long and deep breath; "I saw him when in that fearful night I lay on the deck, and a cry broke upon my ear, which I yet hear waking in broad day. His face was over me, his eyes full of fire; his breath hot as hell upon my cold forehead. I awoke, and heard him laugh, and exultingly exclaim: 'Now you are mine, and neither God nor Satan could have you, were they to seek you. You leave not Orenaes Gaard but as Björnarne's bride!'

"Observe, John Marstrand!" she said, with reanimated countenance, "these words strengthened me wonderfully, and yet support me. Helgestad's greedy eyes, his cruel laugh, and the iron, God-defying will of this powerful man, made a strong impression upon me. If God can bear it, you also must bear it, said a voice within me. Raise yourself up and obey him. That have I done to this hour."

"And Björnarne?"

A triumphant smile played around her mouth. "I believe all my friendship has availed but little with him. The closer I endeavor to approach him, the more he draws back. Now he is entirely dependent upon his friend, Paul Petersen, who persuaded him to the journey to Loppen, and is his secret adviser in all things."

"Be then on your guard, Hannah, for you may be sure mischief is brewing."

"What could happen to me?" she replied; "I am an humble, submissive maiden, and await God's will. Let him come who has been selected as the master of my destiny. I am no victim, John Marstrand. I'm as tranquil as a priestess. Victims suffer from fear and pain; I suffer not, but am, as you see me, cheerful and of good heart. I praise God's wisdom and mercy; look around me, and recognise the way of the Lord. There are victims in this solitary house, and I see them suffer;

but I am not one of them. Ilda"—— she looked at him with a penetrating stare; "she has the noblest, truest heart."

"A strong heart, which is never too warm, and will bear whatever God may inflict upon her," murmured Marstrand.

"The strongest heart may also break," said Hannah; "Ilda is unhappy."

"Unhappy!"

"Do you not see it? Is not the secret, despite all her efforts to conceal it, revealed upon her face?"

"What secret?" he asked, astounded.

"That she loves where she ought to love, and that she hates where she should hate."

Hannah left Marstrand completely confounded.

Late in the evening he went with Ilda alone in the little boat across the fiord, to visit a curious chasm, where the water formed a whirlpool, which lost itself in the deep recesses of the rock. The moon illuminated the tranquil sea, and its fine clear light glimmered in the dark cleft, where the waves dashed themselves into feathery surf. A heavy sound burst from the cavern, now swelling into thunder, and then subsiding into a soft, plaintive moan. Without, all was silent; only the blue, mysterious light of the night hovered over the eternal, gigantic mountains, guardians of this wild coast.

The boat had for some time floated around the chasm, upon the surface of the gently heaving sea. Marstrand had laid the oar aside, and sat by Ilda. Both listened to the wonderous sounds which issued from the dark ocean caves.

"I remember," at length said John, "that a saga relates a curious history of this cavern. Is it not an unhappy sea nymph which weeps and sighs there beneath the water?"

"A poor, beautiful fairy, whom a giant holds in chains that cannot be broken," replied Ilda.

"Now I know it. The giant had carried off the fairy, and compelled her to become his wife. He was a wild, malicious fellow; but he was great and powerful, and a king in the watery dominions there beneath. Sometimes he permitted her to leave the cavern, which formed the entrance to his crystal and golden palace, and then she sat in the moonlight, upon the peak of the rock, twining wreaths of grass and flowers, and singing songs, and enjoying herself in the earthly air, until her gloomy husband sounded his horn to recall her to her sea home. It happened that a young fisherman met her; and every night when the sweet queen ascended the rock, he sat by her side. Then he gazed in her soft, clear eyes, smoothed her golden hair, smiled, and fondled with her little white hands. He said not a word of that of which his heart was full; but she was conscious of it all; and when the sullen horn sounded, and she sadly rose to depart, he knew that she also loved him."

While Marstrand thus spoke, he had taken Ilda's hand, which he held fast in his own, and leaned towards her.

"It happened that once she did not hear the horn as they sat together," said Ilda, softly.

"Because," continued Marstrand, "the fair water-witch had lain her head on the bosom of the young man, who embraced her with both arms."

"After the horn had sounded a third time, so that the mountains shook to their foundations, an arm was extended from the cavern, followed by a monstrous head. The giant raised himself up, reached round over all the rocks, and with a finger he crushed the poor fisherman, and with a grasp drew the unfaithful one into the dark abyss."

"It happened so," said Marstrand, "because the fairy could not resolve to be free and happy. I love you, had the youth whispered to her; come, accompany me. Do you see the grey streak in the East? It will soon be red there, and the sun will come; the children of night have then no more power over you. Trust me; my arm is strong, and I will bear you away; let us live to be happy. She thought of the oath she had taken; she removed the dark hand that clasped her waist; and now lies she there in white glowing chains, weeping and moaning, and the fiendish giant laughs at her misery."

With a gentle exertion Ilda loosened John's hand from her waist, for he held her in his arms.—"She did right," said she, "and her punishment was not undeserved. Ply your oar, or we shall be drawn into the abyss and be swallowed up."

"In death with you, Ilda!" he hastily exclaimed.

"Shall that be your end, John?" she replied. "Have you nothing more to hope and desire; and do you not believe God has yet much to require of you?"

"You will live!" he bitterly exclaimed aloud.

"Yes," she responded; "I will live, because it is my duty; because I have received life to do good, and cannot commit sin."

He gazed in her eyes, upon which the moonlight was shining. She tenderly responded to his glance. Suddenly a loud laugh was heard above their heads, and a voice began to speak, which penetrated to Marstrand's core. — "By heavens and the holy Olaf!" shouted a man from the summit of the rock," it is Ilda, hovering around the witch's cave. Here, Björnarne, come up hither; it is your sister, who is praying to the Nornes for us. And who is that? Herr Marstrand, as sure as I live! Good luck to your house, Herr; or rather to your hand! Bring your little boat out from among the eddies and rocks, and keep my dear treasure until I can kiss her fresh lips."

"Is it you, Paul?" exclaimed Ilda to him. "Where do you come from? Where is the sloop?"

"If she is not here yet, she will come. We landed in Maursound, because a vessel without wind is like a wife without a heart, cold and monotonous. I beg you, Herr, come-to there in the cleft, and take me on board. Björnarne has run on, but I am tired with this break-neck tramp over the rocks."

With an inward regret Marstrand directed the skiff to the designated spot, to which only a sure-footed and light-limbed man like Paul could descend, and jump into the boat.

Paul threw his gun and leather pouch aside, and took the seat alongside of Ilda, which Marstrand had left to ply the oar. He unceremoniously clasped his arms around his betrothed, and kissed her, amid all kinds of jests and tender oaths, and shook Marstrand by the hand, all the while inquiring after the cause of this unlooked-for visit.

"Five days already here!" he exclaimed. "Had I dreamed of it, I would not have given myself so much anxiety and trouble. I was always harassed by the thought of Lyngenfiord and Orenaes Gaard, where my beloved Ilda sat grieving in loneliness. How oft have I stood upon the high cliffs of Lappen, and gazed into the distance! It seemed to me as if I could see you with eyes full of devotion, and your heart longing after your true Paul; but instead, it appears your guest has rendered the time short enough."

"We have passed many pleasant hours," said Ilda.

"That I believe," said Paul, smiling. "I know that Marstrand understands the art of amusing the ladies, and that none can resist his fascinations. Even the little Gula fell into danger, and was turned to a pillar of salt. Have you heard nothing of her, worthy friend? Has she not suddenly appeared at Balsfiord?"

"I know nothing of her," said Marstrand, with as much composure as possible, to conceal his anger. — He had thus far not said a word of Gula, and Ilda had not asked after her, for good reasons.

He now joined in the conversation and inquired after the events of the journey and the residence at Loppen, while he applied himself to the oars.

"Were you ever there?" asked Paul.

"Never."

"By heavens, a blessed little spot! High precipices surround it, against which the raging sea beats in heavy surges. There is only one practicable landing, and in the interior, the rocks are torn and split asunder, as if riven by a thousand thunderbolts. A man might lie concealed in its fastnesses and caverns for years, without being discovered. Sweet Ilda! how glad I am again to be at your feet, to press you to my beating heart, and to sail with you over this smooth, moonlit fiord! Herr Marstrand, you seem to me like Saturn, carrying Cupid and Venus through the sea of life; I pray you only to be slower, that we may prolong the enjoyment of the pleasure."

Paul laughed. "What say you to that, my Venus?" he exclaimed.

"I say," replied Ilda, "that the boat will upset, unless you keep quiet."

"That would be romantic, poetic, dramatic!" said he. "What think you of such a ducking, Herr Marstrand?"

"Are there any bears in Loppen?" asked the latter.

"The devil take all bears!"

"There are none there; otherwise the valiant Paul had remained at home," exclaimed Hannah, who was standing on the shore steps at the warehouse awaiting the boat, which was now close to the landing.

"Received as always," said the secretary with a laugh; "by my magnanimous friend with a somewhat stale wit."

"Which, however, is always good enough," she replied, as she turned round and with a loud shout of "Björnarne!" hurried towards him as he entered the courtyard of the mansion.

They were soon sitting in the stuga, where Petersen entertained them with a description of the journey, and the bird-hunting at Loppen. The expected sloop was laden with bags of feathers, for an unusual number of birds had been taken in that year. The great three-toed gulls, the Auks, the many species of ducks, the northern pelicans, together with innumerable divers, sea-pigeons, rotten and lummen made up the rich booty. Paul described, in animated style, the dangerous taking of the birds; upon the highest and steepest cliffs, where the young were stolen from the nests, the nests themselves divested of their soft feathers, and the old ones were beaten to death by thousands in the air, with poles. For these simple birds are stupid enough," said Paul, "to fly screaming in thick swarms around their nests, instead of putting their heads in security."

"It is cowardly, inglorious murder," exclaimed Hannah; "I do not see how men can find associates in it. Hunt the wolf, snare the fox, overtake the swift reindeer, and measure yourself with the bears—but the bear, Paul Petersen, the bear is a terrible creature, which should only be approached by one who has swift legs."

Paul joined in the laugh against himself; but in his false eyes, anger flashed at the jest. "In future," said he, "we will send you to Loppen, where you can harangue the assembled birds, and persuade them to pluck and roast themselves."

"Let every one apply himself to what suits him. It is not proper for a woman to do what may put anxious mothers in fear."

"Oh! tender-hearted daughter of the herring-king of the German bridge," exclaimed Paul, laughing; "how much I admire your noble heart! For the benefit of your nerves, you should make a voyage to Loppen, and take instructions from Anga, the wife of the honest Egede Wingeborg, who excels all others in whipping off heads, and skinning birds."

"Who is Anga, and who is Wingeborg?" asked Hannah.

"Wingeborg will have the honor to present himself to you to-morrow, if the sloop arrives. He is sole lord of Loppen, placed there as viceroy by Helgestad, a man to whom I unquestionably owe my life, and without whose aid I would have been dashed to pieces on the rocks."

"Then blessed be Wingeborg!" said Hannah, "for we would have died from grief."

Paul made a scornful bow.

"Were you in danger?" inquired Ilda.

"A little," he replied; "but God was merciful to me, and Egede near at hand. You know," said he, "that the lummen build their nests in the holes of the rocks, on the face of precipices, often a thousand feet below the summit of the cliffs, and as many above the surface of the sea. There they nestle by dozens, and crowd upon each other, so that when you have one by the neck, you have all. One seizes the other by the tail, and in this manner the whole chain is drawn up. Such sport is highly exciting. A rope, about twelve hundred feet long, is let down over a kind of wooden roller, the bird-catcher sits upon a cross-stick at its end, and beneath him swings a basket to receive the birds; six or eight men lower him down, until he is suspended before one of the brooding holes. If he cannot reach the birds with his hand, he sends a small dog which he carries in the basket, into the cleft, to seize the first bird and draw it out until he can reach it. He then pulls in the dog, who, holding on to the neck of the prize with his teeth, drags the rest along also.

"The occupation is not, indeed, free from danger. The men above will not very easily let go their hold, although it has happened; the bird-catcher will hold fast to his cross-stick, although many a one has lost his balance and broke his neck; the worst is, when the rope begins to turn round, and the bird-catcher is whirled about, like a top, until senseless from giddiness, he falls into the abyss beneath, or dashes out his brains against a projecting crag. And that would have been my fate but for Egede. I was hanging to a cliff by a seven-hundred feet rope; I was seven masts high above the sea, when a gust of wind set me whirling. At first I laughed; then I swore, and at last I raised a death-shriek; for it was dark around me. Suddenly a man slid down the rope and stood with his legs right and left on the cross-stick, snatched the grappling-stick out of my hand, stuck the point in a crevice of the rock, and, with a spring, leaped upon a ledge no broader than a hand. In the next moment, he drew near the rope, held it fast, then cautiously settled it by swaying it to and fro, and burst out into a rough laugh. In a minute more, I unconsciously stood alongside of him. We advanced along the ledge to where it widened. There were holes and clefts, and auks and lummen, in swarms. It was a wonderful haul. Above us, was the splintered precipice; beneath, the sparkling sea; shrieking swarms of birds flew around our heads, beating us with their beaks and wings, until we were bespattered with blood. We took and killed great numbers until all was quiet. Egede then bound me fast, gave the sign, and I was drawn up without difficulty. We hauled him up afterwards, and he brought with him a basketful of game; so much, indeed, that Anga did not know how she could preserve and salt it all."

"Anga is, I perceive, the housewife of your worthy friend Wingeborg," said Hannah.

"She is the most charming and most thick-headed beauty, of genuine Finnish stock, that ever wandered about in Finnmark without shirt or stockings, in a blouse of sheep-skin;" said Paul, laughing. "You must know, Herr Marstrand, that the Ausen islands are a kind of paradise for innocence and tranquillity, and that no one visits them who would take umbrage at such a costume. My friend Wingeborg, his Anga and children, all alike rough and shaggy, live there in undisturbed freedom. Anga herself does not need the sheep-skin; for she might cover herself with her own hair, as the fair Countess Genovesa once did. Wingeborg has no cause for jealousy. He is a magnificent fellow. If we were Greeks, we would chisel him in marble. Tender hearts must beware of him when he comes to-morrow."

Björnarne took but little part in this conversation, and all that he said appeared to be the result of a reluctant effort. Marstrand manifested the most profound indifference, as well to Hannah's efforts to divert him, as to Paul Petersen's talk; and he leaned back in the arm-chair with half-closed eyes. Instead of an improvement, which Marstrand supposed had taken place, matters had actually grown worse. He gazed upon his once gay and reckless young friend, Björnarne, with secret sadness. His features had now grown sharper; his eyes were sunken, and their expression was restless and unsteady and apparently incapable of fixing their attention upon anything.

These observations, which Marstrand made in the evening, he continued in the morning. No sympathetic inquiry crossed his lips. He avoided the lord of Balsfiord, and buried himself in the warehouse; leaving Paul Petersen to seek an explanation of this unwelcome visit to Lyngenfiord.

Marstrand was reserved, but the secretary was too sagacious not to conceive the state of things from the answers which he elicited. He knew more than Marstrand himself; and, with secret satisfaction, observed how much Helgestad's plans had been advanced—much further, indeed, than he had hoped.

There was no order in the new settlement; the provisions were wasted, the money squandered, and Marstrand had come over in quest of aid; the simpleton, Olaf, had sent him away, while he exerted himself to reduce the confusion to some system. Paul listened to all with great interest, gave good counsel, and, because he justly concluded that Marstrand would believe exactly the contrary of what he recommended, he eagerly sustained the opinions which Olaf had expressed.

"I can readily conceive," said he, "that the honest fellow is amazed at your proceedings, and there are but few, of a truth, Herr Marstrand, in the land who do not regard your undertaking as a very rash one."

"You seem to share in their opinion," said Marstrand, contemptuously.

"They are right," replied Paul. "I formerly thought differently, but I now look at the matter with a closer and more practical eye."

"I thank you for your advice."

"I give it to you with pleasure," continued the secretary jestingly; "and am of the opinion that we all may be benefited by counsel, even if we are endowed with an extraordinary share of wisdom."

The indignation of the young settler would have elicited

from him a more violent response, had not the expected sloop suddenly appeared upon the fiord. The mansion and surrounding huts were instantly in commotion; women and children shouted to the new comers — for the six men who formed the crew, were on the deck, and as soon as the anchor was cast, the usual boisterous scene of welcome greeting took place. Every one had brought something for his family, a plume of feathers, bird-skins, or whole casks of salted bird's meat, which was neither agreeable to the smell or taste. Marstrand also walked down to the landing. His female friends were accompanied by Paul and Björnarne; with no little mortification he observed the change which had all at once come over his prospects, and he would gladly have returned to Balsfiord. He looked on the animated scene before him with profound indifference, and it was only after a while that he observed a curious short-legged creature with small shoulders, very long arms, and a thin body, whom Paul was presenting to Ilda. The fellow wore a black tarpaulin hat, from under which his dirty yellow hair fell in wild disorder; his head, which was disproportionably large for his body, increased the grotesqueness of his appearance. From his red and pock-marked face a small, stunted nose projected, and his mouth was adorned by puffy lips, and two rows of long white teeth, which he showed like a grinning ape. His ugliness was increased by his eyes, which appeared to have been completely inverted, and which rolled about so incessantly that it was almost impossible to divine upon what they were fastened.

"Here, Ilda, is Wingeborg: my friend Egede, dearest Hannah," exclaimed Paul, smiling. "A distinguished man, on account of his various qualities of body and soul! Look at his legs, meagre, agile, and indefatigable as those of a mountain goat; and these arms, long enough to reach to the bottom of a well, and attractive enough to draw a chain of auks from their hiding-places; and that incomparable head, which ought to be placed on the shoulders of a diplomate to render him inscrutably profound. His swan-like neck is in keeping with the rest of his body; and as to his heart, we know enough of it, from the fact that he holds the unworthy race of Lapps in abomination, with whom he refuses all companionship, neither permitting them to visit the Loppen with their herds, nor to settle there as colonists. All this demonstrates a keen and refined sensibility."

During this raillery of the secretary, Wingeborg kept rolling his eyes about in all directions, and exhibiting his teeth. Now and then, he thrust his spider-like fingers in his blue neckerchief, twisted his tarpaulin several times around his head, and burst out into a self-satisfied laugh.

"I hear, Sorenskriver Petersen," said he, "all that you say; and although I understand but little of it, I am much obliged to you for it."

"Dispense with ceremony, friend Wingeborg, as it comes from the heart."

"Good! do as you please," said the Quane; "but I hope the maidens will believe what you say of me and the Lapps. I have had much to do in my life-time with the thieves, and I can smell them for miles."

"And if you do not smell them, dear lord of the winged creation, your faithful leopards will. Where are they?"

"Here," said Wingeborg, pointing to the sack at his feet, which he shook until two little yellow and dark-spotted dogs made their appearance. They had sharp, weasel-like heads, long and slender bodies, stumped ears, very long tails, and were extremely nimble in all their movements.

"Are they not," said Paul, "charming creatures? They belong to the precious race of bird-catchers, which God in his goodness has especially created to ferret out the brooding holes, and to whom he has given a keener scent than any customs-inspector can boast of. They can track a Lapp by his foot-print, or the odor of his garment."

Both the little dogs occasioned many inquiries and caresses, to which they responded with lively demonstrations of gratitude in yelling and leaping upon their fondling friends. This scene was suddenly interrupted by the appearance of a stranger upon the summit of the fjeld, waving his hat and shouting to the spectators below. From his long white hair, black pilgrim coat, broad-brimmed hat, and his staff, he was easily recognised as Klaus Hornemann. Ilda went to meet him, but the sorenskriver laughed aloud, and leaned on Björnarne's shoulder.

"Truly!" he exclaimed, "we are a favored people. We are scarcely at home, when the pious bore, of whom we have already seen too much, makes his re-appearance. I assure you, Björnarne, it is time to discover some means of getting rid of such people."

"We shall probably," said Björnarne, thoughtfully, "get some information from the pastor."

"Do you believe he will tell the truth? Guard yourself against him, and treat him coolly, or he will inflict upon you all kinds of moral lectures. I tell you the old fellow with his unctuous wisdom knows how to manage us. If you listen to him but for a moment, you are lost; be prudent, Björnarne, or you will soon fall into his clutches."

They advanced to meet the pious man, who was coming toward the house, accompanied by Marstrand and the young girls.

"Here I am again, my dear friends," exclaimed the old man, "and God has granted me a great favor in finding you all together again, in good health."

"We have had a pleasant time in Orenaes," said Hannah, "and, above all, the rare favor of the presence of the witty Paul; but you, worthy man, you have not spared your gray hairs in wandering over the wilderness in this sweltering summer heat."

"No, indeed," responded Klaus, with an affectionate smile; "I cannot think of myself. I have come by a circuitous route from Tromsöe. I was at Balsfiord, Herr Marstrand, and met there the honest Olaf, the faithful guardian of your property; thence I passed over the peninsula and the fjeld to the Kilpis-jaure, and have now come to pass a few days on the borders of the cool fiord, with the permission of my dear little daughter, Ilda."

"You are heartily welcome, dear pastor," replied Ilda. "It will give us all pleasure to have you among us, as long as you see fit to remain here."

The old pastor, unstrapping his knapsack from his shoulders, proceeded to the house where Egede Wingeborg was sitting on a bench by the door. Upon his approach, the dogs of the bird-catcher jumped up with a loud yell, and sprang towards him with open mouth, and would have bitten him, but for the inter position of their master.

"An inhospitable reception, Wingeborg," said the old man, smiling.

"It may be," replied the thick-headed Quane; "but a beast's nature springs also from God. The reception was not on your account, but on that of the society you have kept. Have you not, lately, been with the Lapps?"

"Yes," replied Hornemann; "Mortuno accompanied me, and carried my knapsack to yonder point above there, where he left me."

"Am I not right?" exultingly exclaimed Wingeborg. "My dogs knew that a Lapp had been with you. It is the voice of God, that speaks from the animals."

"My good friend," said Hornemann, "let the voice of God be heard by you, which says: 'Love all men, for they are created in the image of God.' But what are you doing here at Lyngenfiord?"

Wingeborg replied that he was waiting Helgestad's arrival, to deliver him his annual stock of feathers, to settle his accounts and to make some purchases. The pastor, leaving Wingeborg outside, entered the house, where the whole settlement gathered around him, to greet him with respectful salutations.

Hornemann's presence was a source of much gratification for Marstrand. His good star had unexpectedly brought him to the man of whose counsel and assistance he had much need, and whose presence held Paul Petersen in proper check. He was sure that the secretary had more dread of the old pastor, than of anybody else. He dared not interrupt the edifying discourse of the pastor in the evenings, or jest upon his zeal for the conversion of the heathen. Paul Petersen regarded him as a fool and miserable fanatic, who was honored only by foolish people; but this reverential respect towards the pastor was so deep and universal, that Paul did not dare to oppose it openly.

He sat in moody silence in the corner, revolving over his plans. He withdrew, as soon as he could, followed by Björnarne, leaving Marstrand alone with the pastor. The young Dane poured out his heart to his friend, and conversed with him far into the night, touching his affairs.

"Friend John," said the pastor at length, "I have no practical experience in such matters, and my advice must be one of questionable propriety. Had you spoken to me earlier on this subject, I would have advised you against engaging in so costly and extensive an undertaking, on account of your youth and inexperience. As Helgestad has encouraged you to it, it is his duty to assist and sustain you, and I believe he will do it, as he must be convinced that your labors were necessary to the success of your schemes."

"I am satisfied that I have accomplished more than Helgestad could have expected, and that by the next summer such progress will have been made as to render success certain."

"Then, be of good cheer, and work on steadily, without giving heed to envious and censorious remarks. I must always compare you with myself," he continued, with a smile. "You are, indeed, in all the bloom of youthful strength, and in your whole character there is an energy that warms my old heart. But we are, nevertheless, alike. Ignorant and malicious men misrepresent and reproach us both. Narrow-minded people always despise and blame what they cannot understand. Do not be disquieted, my young friend. Even if a part of the reproaches cast upon you for indiscretion and rashness were true, you are yet a man, like all others, liable to err. Can there be light without shadow? Superior minds err most and need examination, for they do more in one day than others in a lifetime. Go on your way: it is a good one, I am sure."

"Olaf has shown you my faults," replied Marstrand. "I have had too little care, heretofore, for my property; my expenditure has been profuse, and there is a great deal of disorder for want of proper attention. But I will, henceforward, be more prudent."

"It is too much for you," said the old parson, laying his hand upon his shoulder. "To set your house in order, there is but one sure means — to obtain a true-hearted, devoted wife, who will bring with her peace and joy."

Marstrand made an admonitory sign, while he cautiously looked around the quiet room, lest some one should be listening.

"I could give you some information," continued Klaus, "did I not think I should displease you in reviving disagreeable recollections."

"Disagreeable recollections," said Marstrand, with a sigh; "I have many such."

"It relates to a poor, deceived maiden," said the pastor, after an expressive silence; "not intentionally deceived by you; no, I do not mean so; but by her own heart. It is a sad story of grief and misery, for which there is no relief. Children bear the sins of their parents; a curse descends from generation to generation, and the hated and despised must unjustly suffer, innocent as they may be in soul."

"Of whom are you speaking," asked Marstrand, whose face crimsoned with apprehension.

"Of one," replied the old man, in a soft voice, "whose heart is filled with your image.

"I speak of Gula," he continued, as Marstrand kept silent; "I have seen her."

"Seen her! and is she unhappy?"

"Do you think that Gula can be happy?"

"Your voice sounds reproachfully," said Marstrand, "and I deserve it; but God knows my fault is not so great. Compassion for her fate, gratitude for her sympathy, a humane sensibility for the abandoned creature, and a solicitude for her welfare, led me to excite feelings, the existence of which I perceived when too late."

"I know all," replied the pastor, "and I do not blame you; but Gula lives and hopes."

"How can she hope?" murmured John to himself.

"Because she loves," said Klaus. "Love is a plant which never dies, even though it be deprived of light and air. Its head droops, and its leaves wither; but an immortal, celestial seed exists within it. She fondly dreams of past happiness, and with inflexible confidence trusts in the future. If you could see the poor child in her solitary sorrow, sustained by but one thought, and her eyes beaming with joy when she speaks of you, you would be deeply moved at her condition."

"Where is she? where does Afraja conceal her?" asked Marstrand.

"What avails it for me to name the place?"

"Is she in the valley that Olaf discovered?"

"Let me pass this over in silence," replied the pastor; "I must not give occasion for new hopes. Afraja desires his daughter to marry Mortuno, and I am satisfied he acts wisely. Gula will give up her opposition when she is convinced there is no hope of the realisation of her foolish preference for you. You, yourself, need a bosom companion for your own happiness. Poor young friend! I know what hopes your heart once cherished; but can you not find a substitute among the maidens whom you know? Choose one, and I will support you. All that I can do for you by word and deed is at your service. A true wife will adorn and regulate your house, and Gula will, at the same time, be saved. She will no longer consume away her existence in fruitless sorrow and longing."

"She will die," said Marstrand, burying his face in his hands.

"No! no!" replied the pastor; "she will live, if the only man of a strange people who has ever pressed her to his bosom, and called her his own, for ever separates from her."

"And shall I thus purchase a joyless and frightful existence? If you could, father, only see into my soul!"

The pastor bowed his white head, and folded his arms. "God has willed that his children should suffer from pain and affliction. Praised be the Lord!"

"Not God," said Marstrand, in anger, "who is love. No, it is these miserable, avaricious men, with their hatreds, who are responsible."

"And where are the pure and just?" asked the pastor, with uplifted hands.

"I feel it! I feel it," said the young man, with downcast eyes; "but what prevents me from becoming just?"

Klaus Hornemann ceased speaking, but his eye beaming with kindness, fell upon his friend. After a long pause he said: "Tempt not God a second time! He who would defy the prejudices of his age, must be panoplied in seven-fold brass! Where is the armor that would not melt before this fire of raillery, hate, contempt and shame?"

"I love only one," responded Marstrand, earnestly; "and my heart has no room for another. That one is lost to me!"

The pastor looked upon him with compassion, and kindly said, "I hope you will overcome this passion with manly resolution, and the more so, as the maiden seeks to please her betrothed; and we all hope that Björnarne's heart may be turned to her."

"Björnarne?' replied Marstrand, standing up. "You were formerly in error, as now. I have never thought of Hannah Fandrem but as a friend. There is another, father, one who loves me — yes, who warmly loves me in secret, and whom I would rather possess than the daughter of a king. But it is impossible. Between us is her father and a miserable, common man, a scoundrel of whom I expect the worst. To him has she been sworn, and to him must she belong."

"Is it so! my dear young friend? I have thought as much, but have not believed it. Ilda——"

"Hush," said Marstrand; "let us not speak of that subject. I cannot hear the name without deep pain. Happy days have we passed, days of forgetfulness and hope, until we were suddenly awakened from our dreams."

"Be vigilant and prepared when the tempter approaches," said Klaus, pressing his hands.

"Awake and prepared! Yes," answered the Dane. "You know the strong sense of duty that governs the incomparable maiden; but believe me, she despises the wretch who is forced upon her more than I do. Björnarne is in his hands. Do you know what has broken down the spirits of this once happy young man?"

Klaus Hornemann nodded assentingly. "I know all," he said. "Gula took to flight to escape his passion."

"And this passion is yet nourished and stimulated by Petersen," continued Marstrand. "I do not know his plans, but they must be directed to Björnarne's ruin. You would do him a favor to undeceive him."

"I am come on purpose to speak with him," said the pastor.

"Then, delay not," replied Marstrand, as he extended him his hand. "I will think upon what you have communicated to me."

CHAPTER XIV.

On the next morning, Paul was sitting alone in the counting-room of his father-in-law at the writing-desk, carefully examining the figures and items.

"None but those acquainted with the subject can form an idea of the productive value of the naked craggy rocks of Loppen; but here it stands written. Feathers of Loppen produced at market, in the first year, 2340 specie thalers; and in the following year, 3785 specie thalers; and in the third year, 4512 specie thalers; and so forth, and so on," said he; "for in this year the trade is yet better. Loppen must be mine! Especially—but"——his eye fell upon the spacious warehouse, and then upon the packing-houses and the vessels—"I do not see why all that the old fool has amassed in his lifetime should not be mine."—At this moment he observed Marstrand accompanying Ilda and Hannah to the garden, where he sat down and read to them.

Paul Petersen's countenance assumed a bitter expression. He smiled, while he menacingly shook his fist. "Wait, my noble youth!" he exclaimed, in a suppressed tone; "you will awake from dreams of love." For a long time he stood behind the window, observing how the maidens in the garden gazed upon him as he read; how they inclined the ear to him; how their faces glowed with pleasure; and how joyously they laughed. "Between the brown stately Dane and the wizen-faced secretary of Tromsöe, there is indeed a great difference. But you shall learn to know this difference, severe maiden, pattern of women, soft and patient as you may be I will see you at my feet begging for mercy. I will reward your Christian, pious disposition, and your contempt; for he is right, the Danish rascal;

you despise me! yes, more than he does, and yet I have a body and soul."

While he was thus speaking, Björnarne entered. Paul turned and nodded to him.—"Open your eyes and do not look so gloomy, my young fellow," he said; "I have many things to speak to you of. Were I like you, had I a beautiful maiden sitting there, who was up to the eyes in love with me, I would be happy beyond measure."

Björnarne frowned, looked through the windows, and said, "Would that I may never see that face again!"

"Patience, my son; patience!" said Paul. "We shall get rid of these faces if you are prudent, and follow my advice. Collect all your senses and listen to what I say. As for that high-nosed, stiff-legged youngster, I think it is the last time he will show his face in Orenaes. As soon as your father returns I will speak a word with him, and I am convinced he will acknowledge that I am a sensible fellow. As to the worthy maiden of Bergen, you can easily shake her off."

"May I be hung if I ever speak a friendly word with her!"

"Whenever you see her, you look as if you had swallowed a dose of rhubarb. Do not suffer yourself to be read through by every shallow-pated fellow; be as cunning as the craftiest, and act like a man who knows how to execute his own plans."

"What shall I do, then?" asked Björnarne.

"You should do as the fox," said Paul Petersen, smiling, "when he heard mass with the hens. He read with them out of the same book, and put on such a devout air, that they admitted him in full confidence to their nests, and asked him to dine with them; which he did so effectually that nothing was left of them but their feathers. Believe me, my dear fellow, he will be deceived; that is a law of heaven. One betrays the other; and he who is not betrayed belongs to the betrayers. Be keen and bold in all you undertake, and cunning and sly, and set your sails to every breeze. Unless you can act so, submit to fate and your father's will. Be a good son; let Hannah Fandrem kiss you, and draw the night-cap over your ears."

"I do not understand your meaning," said Björnarne. "I cannot lie and deceive."

"That is easily said," responded Paul. "Do you know why old Klaus has come, and what he wishes? He comes directly from Gula, and has his leather pouch full of sighs and greetings; but none for you."

Björnarne's face was flushed with a deep red, and his inflamed eyes glared on the secretary.

"Not one tender sigh for you!" repeated Paul, bursting into a laugh; "but ten thousand for the faithless Dane there."

Björnarne convulsively clinched his fist. "How do you know that?" he asked.

"I heard some of their conversation yesterday, when they supposed they were alone. The little black-eyed witch told the pastor that she had run off on account of your passion. Now she is sitting there, where Afraja has confined her, weaving wreaths and weeping for the dear John who is to free her from the filthy Mortuno."

"Where is she? Where does he keep her confined?" exclaimed Björnarne, in a violent pitch of excitement.

"I do not know; but you may rely upon it I will learn;" replied Paul.

"The pastor will reveal it to me," interrupted Björnarne.

"You are a fool," said Paul. "Utter not a word on the subject, but seem as if all had passed away. You must control your countenance; you must be able to laugh when he speaks of her, and must say to him it was a momentary act of forgetfulness, and that the simple Lapland girl must not imagine that you have any further thought of her."

"Oh, that cannot be!" exclaimed Björnarne, clasping his hands to his forehead.

"No?" said Paul. "I am sorry for it; for I will tell you what the result would be: Klaus would deem it a duty to communicate all that he knew to your father; and you can readily divine the consequence. Your father will treat you as a demented person. He would strangle you before he would pardon you. Ask yourself if you can resist his powerful hand."

Björnarne furiously gnashed his teeth; but the wicked secretary was perfectly right in his calculation that the name alone of the father would exercise a wonderful influence upon the son.

"Will you now listen to my counsel?" said Paul, after observing him for a moment with unsuppressed scorn.

"Speak on," said Björnarne.

"And will you also follow it? for only on this condition can you hope for success."

"I will do as much as I can."

"A man can accomplish all that he wishes," exclaimed the secretary; "and believe me, when you have made a beginning it is easy to continue. What signifies lying, dissembling, and deceiving, of which foolish people profess such horror? It is nothing else than to be circumspect and cautious, and to take advantage of circumstances. And do you suppose the virtuous do not act on these principles? The old gray-headed pastor knows where Gula is concealed as well as our man of honor and conscience, the Dane. Ask them where the maiden is hid, and they will assure you, with the most honest faces in the world, that they know nothing of her. The Danish vagabond has undoubtedly spoken with the devil's son, Afraja, more than once, and he told me to the face he had not seen him. Let a man do what he may, he must not suffer himself to be surprised. Undertake whatever you please, but do not perform it so as to provoke ridicule. Pursue your aim, whatever it may be; employ every means; lie, blame, deceive, whenever necessary; but do not be a man of whom it can be said, 'he has been caught at his tricks like a school-boy.'"

Björnarne had listened with great attention. He felt ashamed at the satirical admonitions of the secretary. "Do not believe, however," said he, "that I will suffer myself to be so easily taken."

"Act so then," answered Paul. "An ignorant man shows himself as he is; an educated man uses his understanding. You must desist from your present behavior to Hannah, but you must be polite and agreeable, as her beauty merits. Deceive them all, or give them up. Say yea to all, laugh and excuse yourself, be of good cheer, and think you are lying in Gula's arms, when you kiss Hannah. The pastor has undertaken to convert you into an amiable bridegroom, and to reconcile you with your friend John; do not resist his efforts."

"I hate him the most," angrily murmured Björnarne.

"Do you think that I love him?" said Paul, smiling; "but what signifies hate, without the hope of revenge? The day will come when we shall be able to revenge ourselves; when he shall be driven off like a dog, and shall be pursued with universal infamy and shame."

"And at last, Paul Petersen?"

"Have no fear. Play your part well, and I will help you. In a few days, I will know where Gula is concealed. We will free her from the villain Mortuno, and you shall have your little treasure again. See!" he exclaimed, looking up to the window, "there glides the worthy Klaus about among the warehouses. He is seeking you, Björnarne. Would I were in your place! I have a great desire to play the old fellow a trick. Go, my dear fellow, and if you are indeed the son of your father, and if there be a spark of his spirit in your brain, you will pass a precious hour."

He accompanied his pupil to the door, and joyously rubbed his hands together, when he saw him soon after, hatchet and saw in hand, proceeding to the warehouse.

"He is not so dumb as usual," whispered Paul, looking after him. "I would wager that he will move the godly Klaus to tears."

Björnarne, meanwhile, cast his tools down among the casks and barrels, opened the water door of the great warehouse, and gazed over the fiord. It was a bright, clear morning, the pure and fresh air rendering the most distant objects visible; the whole scene was soft and tranquil. The lofty mountains, piled up on one another, were enveloped in a warm veil of mist. The nearer mountains smoked from the summer heat, and a gentle plash of waves was heard beating beneath, on the pile-work. With melancholy earnestness, the unhappy youth gazed into the deep water, and sadly whispered to himself: "Would that I lay there buried in the sea-weed, that I might neither hear nor see more. God knows how it has happened, but I have neither rest of body or mind, and I shall never see her again. I cannot bear to think of it."

He suddenly turned round, raised his axe, and began to whistle an air, for Klaus Hornemann was standing without and looking in. After a while, as Björnarne hammered and knocked, he drew near and said to him; "You are at work early, dear Björnarne, and, as it appears, with a right good will."

"Why should I not be happy," exclaimed the young man. "I am young, strong, and healthy."

The missionary took his hand, led him out to the porch, and sat down with him on a bench. "How pleasant it is," said he, "to sit on an old familiar seat and to think of past days and pleasures! Upon this same bench I have sat with your mother, and chatted away many an hour in friendly conversation. You hardly knew your mother, and you were too young to understand and appreciate her character. She was a most kind-hearted and sincere woman, with warm sympathy for the poor; very intelligent, and strongly attached to her children. I distinctly remember the time when she sat here with you, then an infant, in her arms. Your father was far away upon the sea, and heavy, dark clouds hung upon the Kilpisjaure. It was a profoundly calm day; we spoke of the uncertainty of human happiness, and of God's inscrutable providence to man. All at once, your mother seized my hand, and looking full upon me with her large piercing eyes, she pointed her finger to you. 'When I am no more,' she said, 'look after the boy. Do not suffer him to wander into evil ways, but speak to him, for his disposition is good and he will understand you. Promise me, as a true servant of God, and as my friend, to watch over and guard the child as much as you can.' I said in reply; 'You may rely upon my efforts to fulfil your injunctions, as long as I live.'"

Björnarne listened uneasily: the allusion to his mother moved his feelings; but he thought of Paul's advice, and when Klaus ceased speaking, he smilingly replied, "My mother, I hope, will never hear any evil of me."

The pastor fixed his eyes so intently upon him, that he could not endure his gaze. "What have you, then, to do with me?" he contemptuously asked, to conceal his confusion.

"I find you paler, and much changed, since I was last here; and because I know the source of your trouble, and on account of my promise to your mother, I have sought to speak with you."

"Fear—no, fear not for me," exclaimed Björnarne. "The summer heat is injurious to me; I had a fever in Loppen, drank bad water, and over-exerted myself. All this has enfeebled me."

"That is not all," rejoined the old man, in a gentle tone; "you do not tell the whole truth. I know more than you suppose, Björnarne; for Gula, less than three days since, informed me of the reasons for which she had fled from your society."

"What did the foolish creature say?" asked Björnarne "That I reproached her for being found in the arms of John Marstrand; and that I also once loved her? I was foolish, and did wrong; but I am young, and have warm blood. What does she want now? She ran away from this house, and she has nothing more to do with us. I am here; I have a bride, and will soon have a wife. Does the girl imagine that I yet think of her? What is a Lapland maiden to me, and what could I wish of such a creature?"

The good pastor listened with astonishment to these short

and bitterly-spoken remarks. He had expected something different, and had resolved to employ all his powers of persuasion to bring his young friend to his senses; and now he found that he exempted himself from all suspicion.

"All that you say is true, dear Björnarne," said he, rejoiced; "and all is right, if you have seen the evil of your ways."

"All is over," said Björnarne.

"She willingly forgives you," replied Klaus; "and it was quite natural that your heart should turn to the good, friendly creature. You both grew up together; you saw her bud and bloom under your own eyes; and were Gula the daughter of a rich nobleman, he might be proud of her. She is light and graceful in shape, and her eyes are as pure and bright as her heart." The old pastor smiled as he said this. "As I love her, how could I condemn your love? Mortuno himself is become a poet, and at evening sings to her his own compositions, with no little effect."

Björnarne had silently listened to the pastor; but a deep passion was expressed in his features, and the dark, fiery glances, which Klaus either did not understand, nor observe: when Mortuno's name was mentioned, the blood mounted to his face, and he furiously clinched his fists.

"Love her as a brother," continued the old man, taking Björnarne by the hand; "she deserves to be your sister. Protect her in the hour of misfortune, and listen to her prayers. 'I beg, my dear friend,' she said to me, 'not to be angry with the poor Gula. I pray to God that he may be happy; and when he possesses a true and loving wife, he will extend me his hand, when I knock at his door, and will receive me, when I am persecuted.'"

"That will I!" exclaimed Björnarne, with flashing eyes. "Yes, as sure as I am a man, I will! But is she happy, my father? Does she yet love the Dane?"

"Marstrand," said the pastor, evasively, "is as little capable as yourself, of responding to her love."

"He folded her in his arms, with declarations of love, kissed her lips, and now he betrays her. I——" he menacingly shook his head.

"You, my son," interrupted the missionary, "would not act differently from this generous-minded and intelligent man, whose friendship you should prize much higher than that of many others."

"He loves her not, and yet she clings to him; for this reason he desires her to marry the rascal Mortuno," said Björnarne, whisperingly, to himself. "He abandons her, but I will not. Where," asked he, aloud, "does Afraja keep the poor creature concealed? I can conceive that she suffers much."

"She is sad at heart, but she suffers no evil; and the valley in which she lives is the most beautiful of all those above there."

"There, above!" exclaimed Björnarne, with a rapid glance at the lofty mountains. "Does she wish that I should not know it?"

"What could it avail?" replied the pastor; "you must both fulfil the destiny which God has ordained for you. You, dear Björnarne, will live in happiness and peace here; she will lead a wandering life with Mortuno and his herds, but will also be happy, because the eternal being bestows upon all his creatures, after their manner, the means of felicity. You know that the Lappish people are never so contented as in their own mountain home, and that Gula herself has not lost her preference for the freedom of the wilderness. She will accustom herself to it again, without destroying the nobler seeds in her heart, and will endeavor to implant them in the hearts of others. Let her overcome her sorrow; but do you, my young friend, bestow all your affection upon the excellent maiden who loves you, and show her that you merit her tenderness and confidence."

Björnarne sat musing. His blood boiled in all his veins, and he was on the point of laughing at the pastor in derision, and of rejecting the hand of the mediator; but Paul was right.

In good as well as evil, the first step is the most difficult. When the first lie and deception is accomplished, the others follow like the rings of a chain; he must either deceive the pastor, whom he had already half-beguiled, or he must make him an accuser and judge, without hope of pardon.

Klaus Hornemann spoke earnestly again concerning Hannah's excellent qualities, and upon his rude and unbecoming behavior to her. During this discourse, Björnarne had time to smooth his frowning brow, and to consider of his answer.

"It is true," he said, looking up, "I have not been as friendly as I ought to have been; but do not think I have been insensible to Hannah Fandrem's excellencies. I am also accustomed to follow the will of my father; but it disgusted me to be sold without my own consent. I was obliged to betroth myself to Hannah at Lyngen church, where I met her for the first time for many years. My friends laughed at me for being treated as a child. My father called me to seek Hannah's favor on bended knee; and she, who should have hesitated, and, according to custom, have demanded time for reflection, smilingly said yea, but with such a scornful and malicious expression, that I shall never forget it."

"And this is the cause of your coldness and foolish conduct," exclaimed Klaus, rejoiced. "But, my son, if your father, after his manner, acted too rashly, how could you be angry with Hannah, who followed you with a good heart? Would it have been better for you if she had contemptuously frustrated the wishes of your father, and have left you kneeling? What ridicule and jesting, to your discredit, it would have given rise to! No, you foolish youth, Hannah did the best she could; and instead of going off in a pet, you should have loved her twice as much as she deserved."

"I almost believe that you are right," said Björnarne, smiling.

"Come, Björnarne, be kind towards her, and she will forgive you. I will not say a word; you yourself must atone for the wrongs done. As to John Marstrand, he has begged me to express to you his regret that your friendship for him has changed into aversion. You avoid him, and reject his proffered hand."

"Because I believe," said the young man, "that he advised my father to his precipitate measures with Hannah."

"No, no," said the pastor, "therein you are wrong. I can, in all confidence, assure you that Marstrand would not hear of this marriage, and that he most urgently implored me to prevent it if I could."

"He did so?" said Björnarne, amazed; "and on what grounds?"

"Because he had formed all kinds of fearful apprehensions on the subject of your unhappiness and Hannah's misery. Let us go, my son, and wear a cheerful countenance to all."

The effect of this conversation was precisely what Paul Petersen could have desired, for another spirit appeared to have passsed over the mind of Helgestad's son. He accompanied the pastor, sat down by Hannah's side, and listened to Marstrand, as he read the works of Ludwig Halberg. He was thinking of other matters, however, for his thoughts roved beyond the summits of the bold cliffs which encompassed the Lyngenfiord. Far over the mossy surface of the measureless fjeld he sought the secluded valley where Gula was concealed, where the softly waving birches overhung the brook, where she, with that gentle voice which he so well knew, sang songs of truth and love, and where she ran to him with outstretched arms, as he suddenly appeared before her to free her from Mortuno. A glad smile overspread his face as he looked up and met the gaze of Hannah. A cold shudder passed through his frame; but Klaus, looking over Hannah's shoulder, nodded encouragingly to him. The whole truth and deceit shot through his brain like cold steel; with almost superhuman force of will he took the hand which Hannah offered him, pressed it softly, and looked upon her with a kindly eye.

This was an unexpected surprise. A sudden blush gathered on Hannah's face, she opened wide her eyes, as if doubtful of the truth, and an involuntary tremor shook her hand; Björnarne held it fast, and laid his arm upon her shoulder. It gave him a secret pleasure to see the anxiety of Hannah.

In a moment, nevertheless, Hannah's alarm had passed away. She cast a long, searching, and inquisitive glance upon him, and then turned round to the good Klaus, who, with a face beaming with delight, was regarding the young couple with the tenderness of a father.

The whole day was cheerfully passed away; and even Paul Petersen deemed it proper to appear amiable, and to contribute to the general amusement. After he had busied himself for some time with Helgestad's books, and had made extracts, he joined the little circle, and at a glance he discerned the successful conduct of Björnarne. He assumed a serious and modest aspect, sat down by Ilda, and spoke with Marstrand touching the new and unexpected revival of Norwegian literature with so much knowledge and good sense as to excite the admiration of all the company.

"We have had too long a repose in the dominion of poetry," said he, "and we consequently so much the better feel the storm which Halberg and his friends have raised. No people has such abundant resources for a genuine popular poetry. Innumerable are our treasures in old Sagas and songs, which will be collected as the progressive development of the language, and a more refined cultivation, shall generate a taste for them. Mere natural poets no longer exist; original genius must be combined, now, with taste and artistic rules. I blame Halberg for the roughness and bluntness of his satires; his works form a treasure which may probably survive a century. He has given the impulse to a new literature. He will be succeeded by others, who, although they will not, probably, equal the master in spirit, may yet surpass him in form and skill of composition; beautifying and improving our tongue to such a degree that no one will thereafter write in Latin who desires to be read. Books will then be more generally diffused, and the people will read and profit by them."

"I see the time coming," said Hannah, smiling, "when there will be a printing establishment in Tromsöe, and the Gazette of that world-renowned town shall be read in all the fiords."

"And why should not that take place?" asked Klaus. "Paul is right. With the increase of cultivation, schools will be established for popular instruction; when every one can read, the newspapers and books will find many readers. Then will men grow more enlightened, and prejudices will be dissipated."

"And they will be troubled by new prejudices, plagues, and imperfections," interrupted the secretary.

"Certainly, humanity has a long way to travel," said the pastor, in a kindly tone; "but increasing culture will render prejudices less cruel and bloody."

"Every age," said Marstrand, "will have its own devices. Men will torment men, selfishness and avarice will sacrifice their victims, and the just and good will continually sigh for the Redeemer promised to the sufferers and oppressed."

Petersen looked at him with a scornful expression; but the old pastor gently replied, "He will at last come, bearing palms of peace. Is it not a fact that we are continually progressing in knowledge? But a few days since, I read that in Prussia, in Germany, a young prince has ascended the throne who has proclaimed liberty of conscience and the abolition of torture of criminals."

"I have also heard of this young visionary," said the secretary. "He will introduce a beautiful confusion into his country."

"How?" said the pastor. "Do you not desire to see this noble example imitated throughout the world, where men and Christians are to be found?"

"No," replied Paul; "my conscience as a judge revolts against it. We have no other means of bringing obstinate villains to confession."

"Confessions extorted by pain convert justice into a cruel mockery and wrong;" interposed Marstrand. "How many innocent persons have suffered death as witches and sorcerers!"

"Is the torture yet in use with us?" asked Ilda. "I never heard of it."

"It exists," said Paul, "but it has not been applied for a long period. Happily, great crimes are rare in the country; so that we have no need of thumb-screws and racks to bring the truth to light."

"And they were never necessary!" exclaimed the good Klaus. "I have heard that efforts have been made in Copenhagen entirely to abolish the question and prosecutions for witchcraft. Our humane sovereign will not hear of these cruelties; and but for the opposition of his ministry, they would have already been put an end to. My humble voice shall be exerted to increase the horror which every feeling man entertains against the old, cruel forms of justice."

"If you succeed, I shall rejoice for the victory of humanity; but as a judge, I should like to know what is to be done in desperate cases?"

"It is better that ten guilty should escape," replied Klaus, "than that one innocent man should suffer."

Paul laughed. "Zeal must not be pushed too far," said he, "and too much must not be expected from the revival of letters. To get rid of the question, you will introduce other forms of torture. Heavy chains, severe and solitary confinement, starvation and the lash, all kinds of moral mortifications, which, in their degree, are tortures of no light kind. You will not only not be able to abolish them, but they will extend and become universal, until, at length, the rage for reform will be pushed so far, that the half of the costs will be put into the hands of the criminal, with the order to kill himself when he chooses."

With this jest the secretary withdrew, and at the same moment an event occurred which diverted the attention of all to another subject. Above in the mountains, a shot was heard in the distance, which resounded from rock to rock; and while all eyes were turned upward, a man appeared upon the summit of the crags, in full run; in wild flight, he sprang from rock to rock, until in breathless haste he reached the edge of the ground upon which the Gaard was built.

He was recognised before he reached the company, as Wingeford the Quane, with one of his little dogs under his left arm, and his glazed hat in his right hand. His long hair flew about his heated and perspiration-covered face; and, as he approached, his wrath and fear broke out into disjointed expressions, oaths, and a kind of brutish howl.

He threw his hat and the dog on the ground, upraised his long arms, shook his fists in the air, stamped with his short legs, and rolled his eyes about in such a frightful manner, that Hannah concealed herself from fear behind Ilda. He foamed at the mouth, and his long white teeth lay like wolfish fangs behind his retreating lips. Marstrand was alarmed into the belief that he had been seized by a sudden frenzy.

"What has happened to you?" exclaimed Paul and Björnarne together.

"There! There!" he cried, pointing up to the fjeld. "Oh, Herr, he lies there dead!" — He uttered a fearful curse, beat his forehead like a madman, and tore his hair by the roots.

"Who is dead? Who lies dead?" — As he had left the house with a young man, Björnarne thought of him. "Has something happened to Feddersen?" he asked.

"May he rot under the stones!" cried the bird-catcher. "No, no! cursed be his mother! no snake was ever so false. He is a crawling worm, Herr; I will tear his throat with my nails."— He continued to pour out a volley of unintelligible exclamations, until Paul grasped him by the arm, and held him fast.— "Speak, now," said he, in a severe tone, "like a man of sense;

I can guess what has happened. There is one of your dogs, but you departed with both—one of them is dead."

Wingeborg nodded to him.

"And the shot which we heard was aimed at your dog?"

"Close by me; not twenty steps off. Oh, Herr, never was such another dog born!"

"Who shot him?" asked Björnarne.

"A thief, a robber, a red-haired scoundrel, who lives on reindeer blood!" shouted the Quane, in a new fit of fury.

"I thought he was a Lapp," said the secretary. "Did you see him?"

"Not a shadow of him! I was clambering along among the rocks, through which, in various directions, there ran channels with flowing water. My dogs were ahead, but they scented nothing. They can smell a Lapp at a hundred paces; and it must have been the devil himself! Suddenly, I saw the dog running at full speed, and howling, and at the same moment a flash and shot from behind a rock, about eighty steps off. I am a man who understands the Lappish tricks, and I now knew with whom I had to deal. One concealed himself in the gulley before me, another behind a great rock, and God knows how many more there were. Gilf lay dead; he moved not a limb. I raised a cry; ha! ha! a cry, which they knew, snatched up Yern, and ran as hard as I could. Behind me I heard a laugh—they laughed, the yellow wolves, the hogs; but they shall howl like women, and I will stamp them under foot."

"The boldness of these wretches becomes every day more reckless," said Paul. "They have shot Wingeborg's dog from mere malice. Who can it be? Mortuno accompanied Herr Hornemann hither yesterday; the scoundrel wanders in security above there, and is base enough to perform such a trick."

"And dexterous enough," said Hannah; "for, as I hear, he has shot an eagle on the wing."

At this reminiscence, the secretary avoided her vindictive glance.—"If we could take the rascal, he should be tied up to the post in Tromsöe, and be thrashed until the flesh was scored from his bones."

"On account of a miserable dog?" interrupted Hannah.

"Who knows if it was Mortuno?" said Marstrand, "and whether the story we have just heard, is to be relied on?"

"And whether the dog Gilf is actually dead," said Ilda.

"Whatever may happen," angrily replied Paul, "the rabble will not want advocates here. Let us go up there, Björnarne; we may probably succeed in taking the fellow, or discover some sign by which we can bring him to account."

Accompanied by the three fishermen and the Quane, they set out on their expedition. The maidens went into the house, followed by Klaus Hornemann, after an interval of some minutes.

"I think this excursion will all be in vain," said the latter; "if indeed Mortuno has shot the dog, he will not wait long. Do you believe that he fired the shot?"

"I believe so," replied Klaus.

"But wherefore this insolence, and pleasure in doing ill?" inquired the young man. "Have not these persecuted people already provoked enough hatred and enmity, and why should they give new cause for vengeance?"

"Rather wonder at the mild disposition of these rude shepherds," replied the old man.

"Do you call them mild?"

"Yes, mild," continued Hornemann. "No one has so much tormented and persecuted the Lapps, even to the imbruing his hands in their blood, as this Wingeborg. More than twenty years ago, this man came and settled here on the Lyngenfiord. Then the Lapps pastured their herds everywhere, only the Gaard proprietors drove them from their neighborhood, shot their cattle, unmercifully beat women and men, and stole their children to make them servants. They put a bottle of brandy in the hands of the old men, made them beastly drunk, swore then that they had bought the vermin to rear then as Christians, and the cruel voigt of Tromsöe caused every Lapp to be whipped, who ventured to complain. Wingeborg drove away the unhappy people from Lyngenfiord at that time, without any justification whatever. He was Helgestad's serving-man and steward. Even then, a bird-hunter of rare skill, he kept dogs, which scented not only the breeding holes of the auks and lummen, but also Lapps, against whom they manitested a peculiar aversion."

"If these dogs were as large and strong as blood-hounds, Wingeborg and Helgestad, and alas many others with them, would have employed them for the pursuit of the savages, as the Spaniards, but they rendered a similar service. They found out the gamme of a Lapp in the most secluded gorge; they scented the slightest track of a Lapp, and behind them was Wingeborg with his companions, who beat down whatever they found. More than one poor creature has thus perished; it was only when the report of these cruelties had reached Copenhagen, and provoked an order not to harm the Lapps in future, that an end was put to these tyrannical acts. There was of course no investigation. Helgestad sent the Quane to Loppen, where he has lived for ten years, to the great profit of his master. But the Lapps have no more pasturage grounds at Lyngenfiord; they only come to the great autumn market, which is held around the old church of Lyngen, and buy of Helgestad, because he is the most extensive and cheapest trader. They have not forgotten these barbarities, and to this day, if a Lapp meets Wingeborg, he takes to his heels as quick as he can."

"Think," continued the pastor, "that this man suddenly comes here with his two dogs, which the Lapps almost believe have been given to their cruel enemy by the devil himself. Remember that with his infernal comrades, he scours the fjeld exactly as formerly, when he maimed or killed outright every Lapp whom he could reach, and then ask yourself if it is not evidence of a very mild and forbearing disposition, that

Mortuno's ball only struck down the dog and not the godless master. Short as the time is that he has been here, I am yet convinced that it is known far into the land by the Lapps; for it is very remarkable how quickly they learn all news that concerns them."

"How is that possible?" said Marstrand, astonished.

"It is only to be explained by the fact that Afraja has reduced them to a sort of society, and has obtained a kind of despotic influence over them."

"Has he acquired their love and affection?"

"No," said the pastor, "but he is respected and feared. If many superstitious Normans regard the sly, rich shepherd as a sorcerer, there is no one of his people who does not believe him possessed of supernatural knowledge, and in communication with spirits. I perceived upon my last journey, that Afraja understands the art of increasing this delusion and consideration. He makes visits to all the families, and he is by far the richest; this increases the universal esteem."

"And even these children of the rocky waste hold the possessor of wealth in awe!" exclaimed Marstrand, smiling.

"All is united together — property, money, and wisdom," responded Klaus. "Afraja has a number of young men with his herds, who might be called his guards and courtiers. As his eight or ten thousand animals are scattered over the remotest pasture grounds, he frequently sends out messengers, who bring and carry news. His sister's children and cousins are his dependants; he has bound to himself many other heads of families by various benefactions, and there are but few indeed of these roving people who are not in some degree under his influence."

Marstrand listened attentively to what the pastor had to say of these matters, with which he was perfectly familiar. He thought of how he also should be subjected to Afraja, if he accepted his proffered aid; and he thought of the words of the cunning Lapp, that he should hear, in time, of his conditions.

"This seems like a regular scheme to raise himself to the supremacy," said he, giving vent to the reflections by which he was occupied.

"So I think," replied Klaus. "There can be no question of a civil authority; but a moral supremacy Afraja has, indeed, already obtained; and this I am glad of, because his intentions are good and just."

"Has he also communicated his plans to you?"

"We have often spoken of them. He endeavors to prevent the realization of Paul Petersen's predicted extirpation of his people. He seeks to discover some means of uniting the separate tribes and families; and of providing them with one common language, instead of the dozen and more different and mutually incomprehensible dialects now spoken. He encourages the young people to learn the Danish, and all useful knowledge; but, at the same time, he restrains them from evil habits and vices, and particularly from the use of brandy, that curse of his people — that terrible poison with which the European discoverers and conquerors have debased and destroyed so many people."

"But he has not yet made much progress, notwithstanding all his efforts!" said Marstrand, reflecting upon the miserable condition of the Lapps.

"My son," replied the pastor, "if it is difficult to redeem one depraved man, it is yet more so to elevate and improve a debased people. Afraja has, already, converted many a one; he possesses a remarkable moral power, which commands respect. He cannot work miracles, but he has done wonders. His successors can perfect what he has not been able to carry through. Gula is gentle and intelligent; and Mortuno — do not smile so contemptuously — Mortuno has something of the spirit of his uncle, and is, withal, a young, courageous man."

In the meanwhile, they had reached the Gaard, where the two maidens were expecting them: in an hour after, the men also returned, without having found anything, not even the dead body of the dog, or any sign of his tragical end, but a blood-stained stone.

"We will, in the course of time, erect a monument to his memory, which the scoundrels shall long remember," said Paul. "I give you my word, Wingeborg, that you shall have satisfaction. If such rascality is tolerated at our very doors, the villains will grow bolder. My uncle and I will make a rigid investigation; and the Lapps are too loquacious to conceal the affair. Now let us be gone, and be merry. Do not fair eyes and full glasses invite us? What could we do better, than to revel in love and wine, and compassionate those who are deprived of them?"

Paul, accordingly, endeavored to fulfil what he had commended; but he was too temperate to perform great things with the glass. He devoted himself the more to his betrothed, whom he took the greatest pleasure in entertaining with tender conversation, and solitary walks. What he had heard only confirmed that which he already knew. "She hates me, she holds me in contempt," he murmured to himself; "and so much the better, as I shall not, hereafter, impose any force upon myself. But I must recompense her for it; I must show her that I am a passionate lover; and I must keep this Danish fop away from her!"

"To-morrow, dear Ilda," he said, "your father will be here. The fishermen have seen a large yacht off Reenoen; and how shall I rejoice, again to press that hand which is to unite our own."

"Blessed be the day of my father's return," responded Ilda.

"The only thing that troubles me," resumed Paul, "is, that we shall then lose our friend from Balsfiord, who appears to be particularly full of anxiety and secret care; for which, in truth, he has good reason."

Ilda's eyes flashed: "Why should he have care?" she asked.

"Oh," said the secretary, smiling, "there are many reasons Firstly, he has entered upon a bold undertaking; secondly, he has managed his affairs in a careless and indiscreet manner; and, thirdly, he is in love. What say you to that?"

A light blush overspread Ilda's face; but she proudly raised her head, and looking at the malicious man with a severe and reproving expression, she replied, "I have nothing to say to it, Paul Petersen, and as little to hear of it."

"Nothing?" he scornfully exclaimed; "but the worthy Dane is your friend; and we sympathize in a friend's joys and sorrows. You could, at least, inquire who is the loved one of this fine gentleman."

"I will not ask, because he himself has not spoken to me of it."

"Has he not," said the secretary, "spoken of his love? He keeps it a profound secret; but have you not observed it, or are you not curious to know it? Shall I whisper in your ear the name of her upon whom this gallant gentleman has bestowed his heart?"

He smiled maliciously, as she turned away to hide her face. "Hear then," he cried, "you will dispute it, and yet you know the sweet little treasure as well as you know yourself, who, behind the back of her father and her betrothed, has listened to the love-vows of the seducing Dane."

Ilda stood still, and with proud contempt looked at Paul. "Speak on," she said, "I will answer you."

"Zounds!" exclaimed Paul, "how you stare? You have probably heard that the princess Gula is the favored object."

Ilda breathed freer, but she changed not a feature. "That is a lie of your own manufacture," she replied.

"Lie!" he exclaimed. "And if it were a lie, why should it disturb you so? Of whom were you thinking, when I spoke of a maiden who could so far degrade herself as to cling to this impudent beggar?"

"Not disturbed, but offended in the name of the injured; I felt the calumny as if it had touched myself."

"You!" he exclaimed. "Who would dare even to think of it? Be quiet, sweet Ilda, I know you. You love me, and I worship you. You know who you are, and who I am. You are Helgestad's daughter, the first maiden in the land, and I am a man, who, will soon, Ilda, soon—be Amtmann in Finnmark. You are too proud, intelligent, and discreet, to think of this vagabond, who will have soon reached his end."

"You speak with such bitter hate of a man whom I esteem, that I will hear no more."

"Why so sensitive? There is more truth in my words than you suppose; but as to my lie, you can readily test it. I accidentally heard a secret conversation which this estimable John had with his father confessor, the worthy Hornemann. Gula sits in a mountain cave, weeping her eyes out. Afraja has selected Mortuno for his son-in-law. Marstrand confessed that he loved Gula with all his heart, that she had lain in his arms when she was here, and had gone half-crazy with passion from his kisses. On his account she ran off, yet he swore not to desist until he could lead her into his own house before all the world, as his wife. Shame, infamy, and ridicule, are all alike indifferent to him. For a Lapland maiden, to whom no fisherman would give his hand, the foolish lover is willing to risk universal contempt."

"You have become quite pale," he continued, as he jeeringly looked at Ilda. "If you yet doubt, ask the pastor, who will tell you the whole truth."

Paul was satisfied that Ilda would make no inquiries. She could not conceal her agitation; a deep, secret pain filled her soul. She dared not speak further, or offer any objections, as Paul continued to break his sarcasms on the Danish lover; it was only to the jest upon the beggar, to whom nothing would be left, but to frequent the palace of his noble father-in-law, and to lead a pastoral life with Gula, that she replied with a reproving earnestness :

"You might deceive yourself," she said, "for this man whom you call dreamer and fool, and whom you so bitterly scorn, may yet be able to laugh at his enemies."

"Out of mere friendship, you ascribe him too much sagacity."

"Less sagacity, than truth, fearlessness, and a considerate understanding."

"These are certainly fine qualities, and I wish him all possible success. I question his understanding however, beloved Ilda, or he would have acted differently."

"What should he do?"

"He is entirely in the hands of your father. If he had not given him money to begin the wondrous establishment at Balself, he could have done nothing. If he refuses to lend him any more money, the undertaking must fail."

'I dare not ask you what advice you give my father."

"Certainly, you may ask," said Paul, smiling, as he put his arm around her and kissed her; "for there can be no secrets between us; your father, however, will know what to do without my counsel. Helgestad began the chase when the Dane first appeared at Lofodden with his royal letter. He took his money, and gave him fish in exchange. The speculation was as likely to fail as to succeed. Then he introduced him into this house, that he might know him better, for he had gone so far as to prevail upon my uncle, against his custom, to grant him the registration of the royal patent without delay. I, my dear Ilda, could have rendered the matter more difficult. But Helgestad whispered in my ear: 'I think you know me, learn what I wish. Paul will not take it amiss to find the patent in his own pocket, when he takes Ilda home. I know a great piece of good land, which will well please you.'"

"I hope my dowry will be clear of it," responded Ilda.

"My pocket is large enough to hold all that may fall into it," exclaimed Paul in an exulting tone. "When your father returns, he will decide whether he will throw him another sack, or whether he will refuse to assist him farther. What can the poor devil do, in the latter case? His money is gone, the goods and provisions which he bought on credit are likewise wasted and lost. There is no order nor care in his house. Olaf will do his best to set things to rights, but the Dane will undo all the good he may accomplish, and your sharp-sighted father will hesitate to throw away any more money upon what already belongs to him."

"Do you expect to have the Gaard so quickly?"

"Bah!" exclaimed the secretary; "in two weeks I will look to it. Your profoundly wise friend did not secure his money for a certain period. If Helgestad reclaims it to-day, and he cannot procure it, the property will be sold, and to whom but Helgestad? Now, my little heart, how does that please you?"

"It pleases me so little, that I pray to God only to show me some way by which I may prevent it."

"Ah!" said Paul, laughing, as he looked to the house where Marstrand sat by the door with the pastor, "you can admonish him, in your virtuous indignation, of the prospect before him. Your father, however, would thank you but little for it, and I indeed do not know what course he may take. The noble youth will not believe it, and if he would, he cannot change matters. He cannot find the sums which he should pay. Where is the man who will lend him anything? The report of his folly is universally diffused throughout the country, and there is a general conviction that he will meet with a bad end."

"They end badly who do evil," she responded. "Shame upon your conduct and counsel against an innocent person, who needed your assistance."

"Which he rejected," said Paul, "and reviled me for it. May he enjoy his wisdom! I do not hate him, I laugh at him."

"You hate him, because you envy him."

"I envy him? You reverse the matter. He envies me."

"You envy him, because you feel that a better man stands before you than yourself."

"How jocular you are!" he whispered with a tender smile. "Will my charming Ilda find a better person than I am?"

"Many, indeed," she replied. "God knows it."

"Then I must change myself," he said with a smile. "When you are my wife, dear girl, you will understand me. I will endeavor to clear your little brain of caprices, and I will show what it means to belong to me. We shall be so happy, that you will worship me in the very depths of your heart, yet more than that virtuous gentleman there upon the bench, who turns towards us his melancholy face." His eyes were fixed upon Ilda with a malicious expression, and every word that he spoke was full of bitterness.

"Paul Petersen," said Ilda, "I bow to the will of my father, and I promised at the church of Lyngen, before all our friends and the people, to follow you. So shall it be done, and I will faithfully cleave to you, as it is meet and proper. Cease with your jesting, and let us sign a truce. I know you, and what I have to expect; but you will not intimidate me. I will perform my duty in all things, and I will unflinchingly pursue the path of duty, and He will sustain me, who holds the just and unjust in His hands. Smile not, and study not how you may vex me and others. I can see deep into your heart, and must warn you, for what you build up will fall to pieces. Take care that you are not killed by the rock, as your grandfather was."

Bold as the secretary was, he dared not push his jesting further, for Ilda's keen, clear glance seemed to penetrate to his very core. She stood before him as cold and white as a statue of ice. He assumed a sad and troubled countenance, and with an anxious air, said; "I did not believe that you held me in such low estimation; but I hope you will recognise the great injustice you have done me. You excited me by contradiction, and your defence of a man whose conduct and follies provoke me. I said nothing of him but what was true. Wait awhile, and you will confess that I have not misrepresented him. Givo me your hand and let us be reconciled. I ask your pardon for whatever fault I may have committed. Let us chat together as cordially and merrily as Hannah and Björnarne there. I am heartily glad that I have persuaded your brother to change his behavior to his betrothed."

Loud laughter echoed from the other side of the ground, where Björnarne, sitting by Hannah, held the wool which she wound around a large ball.

"Hercules at the distaff!" said Hannah, laughing. "Will you be as good a husband as the penitent bridegroom you have suddenly become?"

"I hope you will never have reason to complain of me," replied Björnarne.

"But I will be a spoiled wife, and will give you difficulty to manage me. No, fear not," she continued, as he gave a forced smile, "we shall lead a different life from those below there. Ilda is of a serious disposition; I am more cheerful, and it shall be my task to make you happy. You have to-day, for the first time, shown me your heart, and confessed that you have done me wrong. Fine days are in store for us."

"Fine days!" mechanically repeated Björnarne.

"When your father comes, he will see how you are changed. I doubt not that he brings with him my father's permission for the celebration of the marriage here. Helgestad will urge him to it. But a few weeks will elapse before we are man and wife."

"Only a few weeks! — Few weeks!" exclaimed Björnarne.

"And until then, we shall have much to do. From morning to night, we shall consider of our arrangements. We will dream of the future — of love and happiness; and we will sit upon Ilda's seat, above there — your former favorite haunt, when you were accompanied by Ilda and Gula."

A cold and unnatural smile played around the lips of the

young man; and his eyes, which were directed upon Hannah's face, appeared to gaze into the farthest distance.

"And when our eyes sweep over the wide sea, over Senjenaen's peaks, beyond Tinden," she said, raising her hand, "then will peace come over us; and with peace, ardent feeling and warm love. Have you already loved?"

"I love now!" he replied; and in his eyes there glowed such a consuming fire, that Hannah suddenly turned deadly pale.

"You love," she resumed; "but will your love never grow cold?"

"No," he said. "If all these rocks were piled upon my heart, they could not crush my love. If I lay in the depths of the sea, with the ice-cold Trolls, I would melt their diamond chains and rise again."

"What lies beneath the waters never returns again. No love softens death; no will can bring back the heart which we have lost."

"We will never find again," continued Björnarne, "what we have lost. If love is truly love, it must be able to wake the dead. What say you, maiden? Can you doubt, when you love? When I observe how beautiful you are," he continued, as his eyes roved wildly over her features, "ought I not to venture all to possess you? What could be too difficult? What obstacles could the devil place in my way, that I could not surmount! I love you, I love you! And if voices in heaven and earth should exclaim you are lost for ever, I would laugh in your arms!"

Hannah Fandrem regarded the excited man with a mixture of fear and pity. He seemed, from his wild and haggard eye and features, to have been suddenly struck with madness. His countenance was of a dark-red; and she had never before remarked the fluency of speech with which he was all at once endowed. As long as she had known Björnarne, he was a merry, careless fellow, of but little sensibility of feeling or depth of thought. Then, again, she had seen him moody in temper and monosyllabic in his answers; looking darkly upon her, and rejecting her offers of friendship. Now, he seemed to be filled with a burning passion, as if he had drunk a witch's love-potion. She had heard much of such charms, without believing in them. Björnarne spoke, as it were, in a strange tongue, and with images and thoughts in striking contrast with his previous simplicity of conversation. She listened with astonishment to his comparisons, and his oaths of love; and at length, with a certain degree of force, she released herself from his embrace, as he pressed her to himself and kissed her.

"I think you are sick," she said, as she drew back.

"He stroked the hair from his forehead, and looked at her as if awakening from a dream.

"Sick?" he asked, in deep meditation. "Why do you call me sick? Do you not love me?"

"Do you doubt it?" she said.

Björnarne shook his head. "It is all right!" he exclaimed. "You see how it is with me; and there comes my father, in good season to participate with us in our happiness.—Hallo! I see the flag of the fair Ilda fluttering in the distance! She brings us a matrimonial bond which will firmly unite us together for ever."

CHAPTER XV.

HELGESTAD'S return from Bergen set all the Gaard in movement. Great was the joy as the old speculator sprang on shore, and was received by children and friends. He had never appeared more active or stronger. His countenance was beaming with contentment, for he had safely brought home his richly-laden yacht; he had left behind him a happily-concluded and profitable business, and the future promised all that he could desire.

He embraced one after the other, not even excepting Hornemann. "It is God's suggestion that you are here, Klaus," he joyfully exclaimed; "and you must not leave the house until your work is completed with those who have more need of a parson than their daily bread. All is arranged, Hannah. I bring with me your certificate of baptism, maiden, and an attested authority from Uve Fandrem for the performance of the marriage ceremony at Lyngenfiord. I would have brought him along, but your brother Christi is travelling around the country, to make large purchases of wood. He is expected from day to day, and old Uve could not consequently stir from his closet on the German bridge. You shall make a trip to Bergen with Björnarne, when all is over here, and shall have a marriage banquet, as Uve has sworn, which will long be remembered in Bergen."

He clapped his son on the shoulder, and with a cunning laugh, said, "Does the thing please you, Björnarne? Ha! Fant, you have become pale and thin; you have rings about your eyes, passion-signs, you good-for-nothing fellow. The time seems long to you. Ha! ha! I guess so! Is it not so?"

Björnarne smiled, and took Hannah's hand. "It goes well with us," he said, "and the longest time will have an end."

"Nuh!" said Helgestad, "time comes and goes. Look at your sister, she is a pattern for all. Never too little or too much; neither pale to-day, nor red to-morrow; neither sad nor exuberantly gay, but always careful and discreet. While we are chatting and standing idle, her eyes and hands are everywhere. Let Paul Petersen take care of himself, and do you bring us all something to eat and drink."

He stretched himself at ease in the great arm-chair, mixed his glass, listened to all, and had a good word for every one; with Marstrand, however, he had no intimate conversation. He contented himself with general inquiries, and with a nod of the head, replied to the remark that Olaf was at Balsfiord, kindly accepting the assurance of the Dane that he was laboring with all his power and industry for the success of his work.

The family remained in glad converse together late into the night. On the following morning, Marstrand deemed it proper to seize the first opportunity to make Helgestad acquainted with his wants. The trader had arisen very early, and had resumed his accustomed activity. He had been engaged since the break of day, in his little counting-room at the shop, scrutinizing all the books, to satisfy himself of the state of his affairs. He entered into a long conversation with his steward from Loppen, touching the product of the island; and when Marstrand awoke, he saw him engaged at the yacht with twenty and more people, adjusting the tackle to hoist the cargo from the hold.

With the coming of Helgestad, the quiet Gaard had put on another face. There was no more sitting at ease in the garden to talk and while away the time. All were occupied in something or other; Helgestad could not bear to see any one idle, and his presence seemed of itself to incite every one to activity. A glance of his long, sharp eyes, or a grin of his leather-like face, was sufficient to stimulate the most flagging.

Noon had passed, and night was coming on before Marstrand had an opportunity of introducing his own concerns to his attention. Helgestad was also not in so jovial a mood as upon his arrival, and it sometimes seemed to his guest as if his eye rested upon him with a profoundly penetrating expression. An anxious feeling agitated the young man, which he in vain endeavored to allay, for his conscience whispered to him all kinds of reproaches, that he could not entirely remove. He remembered that he was entirely in the hands of Helgestad; when, towards evening, still hesitating, but impelled by necessity, he determined to visit the trader in his counting-room, he was yet more confused upon finding Paul Petersen with him. He opened the latched door a little, and remained standing in a state of irresolution as to what he should do. Helgestad was leaning upon the old writing-desk, among a mass of papers, and before him stood Paul, shaking with laughter.

"You will not believe it, but it is so. I tell you, this fool must be chased away. Do as I tell you, and in a short time all will go on smoothly and regularly."

"Nuh!" muttered Helgestad, "we will think of it." As he turned his head aside, he discovered the Dane in the half-opened door. "Come in, Herr, come in! You do not disturb us; I am ready to spin a thread with you. Close the books, Paul, and seek your little treasure. Ilda has already waited a long time for you. It is a peculiar fact that people in love, Herr Marstrand, see everything double. It is a very curious world, that of the loving; and it sometimes confounds the cunning of the sharpest wits, and puts the wisest in fear of their own shadow."

"Even people not in love," replied John, smiling, "miss their reckoning."

Helgestad beat a cloud of dust out of the ledger with his fist. "What you say, is not true," he exclaimed. "He who reckons rightly, cannot make a mistake. He who does not, has no right to call himself wise. With love, however, it is another affair. It disturbs the strongest brain, and pours liquid fire into it, which burns out its contents."

Paul, in the meanwhile, had gone out, and Helgestad looked after him with a roguish twinkle of the eye, as he placed his finger on the side of his nose. "Do you know what is called jealousy, Herr Marstrand?"

"No," said the young man, "I have no knowledge of that passion, which, in my judgment, is nothing else than selfish envy."

"Nuh!" exclaimed Helgestad, "another true saying of yours. A jealous fellow is always full of envy, and speaks ill of his rival. When will you return to Balsfiord?"

"I hope to-morrow, if I can."

Helgestad interrupted him. "You are a witness of what is

meant by good calculation," he continued. "Look there at Björnarne and Fandrem, how happy they are together; how he runs after her, and how he carries the spindle for her. Confess, Herr Marstrand, that you never believed in this, and that you shook your head in doubt."

"I might yet do it," he muttered.

"Nuh!" said Helgestad, "I know the women better than you. There was, in Bergen, a young gentleman—I know nothing of him, and wish to know nothing of him; it would have been a misfortune, if Fandrem had not consigned the maiden to me. Shame comes upon a house, as a cloud at mid-day; but it may be averted by timely precaution. All grief and sadness is passed; Hannah is happy and contented at Lyngenfiord, and no one knows what has become of the stripling." He smiled, while he fiercely regarded Marstrand, as if seeking to penetrate the inmost recesses of his soul.

"Herr Helgestad," said the young man, gloomily, while he fixed his eyes upon the false face; "call not the vengeance of the dead from their graves, to awaken the conscience of the living."

"Is your conscience moved?" asked the trader, "or what do you mean? I am responsible for my actions. You look at me as keen as a knife, but I am not flesh which you can cut. I am prepared, Herr Marstrand, to hear from you unpleasant remarks, although I think you ought to be satisfied with me."

It appeared to Marstrand as if his patron sought to commence a quarrel, into which, for many reasons, he was unwilling to engage. He mastered his anger, and said, "I have no wish to dispute with you. You have rendered me so many favors, that I will never repay them with evil, even if I had it in my power. If Hannah Fandrem contentedly looks forward to her marriage-day, that is her own affair."

"Yes," murmured Helgestad, "you have nothing to do with it."

"No," proudly rejoined the Dane; "and I shall never have

anything to do with it; for a good work is not accomplished with a bloody hand"

Helgestad extended his hard, yellow hand, without uttering a word.

Marstrand continued, in a suppressed tone, "Do you believe such a maiden could be so frivolous? You vaunt of your happiness; it may, one day, crumble to pieces. You boast of your judgment and skill in speculation; it may fail, when you least think of it. I see a shadow near you, a black shadow — and is not your heart cold from the hand which lies upon it; can you always sleep soundly, when the night is dark, and the wind howls?"

Helgestad's countenance, for a moment, was pallid with fear; but he arose from his seat, and nodding with his customary crafty assurance, said, "Let every one trouble himself about his own concerns. I have lived a long life, Herr Marstrand, and expect to live many years yet. No one can say that Niels Helgestad ever did anything which he repented of. You came into my house as a blind man; may your eyes find the right road. Care not for me, but for yourself. It is not my business to admonish, and to waste my words in the air; every one must look to it, that his roof is tight. Think as you please — my foot shall not budge, my hat shall not fall from my head; but do you beware of evil report. Ilda," he resumed, with a sharp glance, "is a maiden who is differently formed by God, and educated to other notions of propriety than a half-heathenish girl. In a few days she will repair to her husband's house, in Tromsöe; and Hannah will dwell here, in Orenaes Gaard, with Björnarne. There will be a couple of happy marriages, and I hope you will dance at them, Herr Marstrand; sit down now, and let me know what you want, and how I can help you."

Marstrand accepted the invitation. He had perfectly understood Helgestad's hints; he could imagine what Paul had related of him, and he could not conceal the truth. He described at large the actual state of things at Balsfiord, boasted of his industry and success, but could not deny that his money was wasting away, and that he had need of a farther supply of provisions.

Helgestad listened without expressing any reproof or objection. He seemed to be glad to learn that the saw-mill was in construction, the difficult road almost completed, and that every thing was prepared for the wood-slide, by means of which the largest trunks could be conducted from the summit of the rocky precipices to the stream.

"Nuh!" said he, "I have heard much of your doings; but I will come to Balsfiord and see for myself in a few days, when I have finished my labors here. I calculate it is no easy matter; I have always, however, regarded you as a person able to carry through a difficult undertaking." With a pleasing smile he gave him his hand, and then musingly said: "We will consider of all these matters when we are at Balsfiord. Come, now, let us pass a merry evening, that you may be able to start out on your journey to-morrow with renewed strength, over the high fjeld, where the Lapps are already killing their fat beasts, gathering skins and horns, and making kommagers and covers, to be able to come down to the market at Lyngen church with full sacks. Will you visit the market?" he asked.

"I think not," said Marstrand.

"You think not!" exclaimed Helgestad. "The autumn market at Lyngen is the greatest of all. It brings in money, and we receive in barter many hides, feathers, and horns, together with reindeer meat for the winter, bear hams, and other dainties. There is no trader far and wide but may be found at it."

"But you know my affairs," replied the young proprietor, embarrassed; "and, besides, as I am entirely alone, my goods are not yet in order."

"Nuh!" said Helgestad, shaking his head; "it must be a strange sight; order is more precious than bread. You must not neglect the market; many things may happen in four weeks. Ask the pastor, and he will tell you that the thick-headed Quane there, would on no condition return to Loppen before he had spent his last penny at Lyngen market. Men and women resort to it from the Aussen islands, and expend there the earnings of a whole year."

He continued to chat on in this strain with Marstrand; and when the latter sought to turn the conversation on his views touching his settlement, he was always met by the curt reply that he would come and see, and assist in person. The best information that the young settler had received, was an accurate account of the condition of the fish trade in Bergen, and the certainty that he had acted wisely in not making an immediate sale. The price had gone up over four species, and Fandrem had credited in his books a handsome sum to Marstrand's account.

"It is a lucky year!" exclaimed Helgestad; "and I would lay a handful of silver thalers upon it that it ends happily. Uve Fandrem opened wide his round eyes as I forced him to give you the highest price. I will not boast, in this particular, of my friendship, Herr Marstrand," he continued, as he observed the sceptical expression on the face of his guest. "I say it openly that it is my advantage that your accounts, for which I am security, should be as favorable as possible. You understand trade and traffic well enough to know that friendship is of no significance in it, and that every one will take whatever he can, even from his brother or father." He chuckled with evident satisfaction at the soundness of his views on this subject, which he followed up with some humorous remarks upon his relative in Bergen.

"Nuh! the Guildemeister has a sharp eye for many things. He has a high opinion of you; he thinks you are a man who will prosper in Finnmark; in trade he is as hard and firm as a shark's tooth. As a father, however, Uve is as tender and yielding as the reeds in a breeze of wind. His son fell in love in Hamburg, and has brought home a daughter-in-law without a dowry-chest, or a bag-full of mortgages and papers. She has nothing but her heart full of love and goodness, as Christi writes in a letter which I read. She is small and lean, like a lamb in spring. She is a poor orphan girl, who lived in the house of a merchant, who has children enough, and is not even one of the first of his class. What do you suppose Uve said to this story?"

"I suppose," answered Marstrand, "he approves of the love of his only son."

With a face like a cat that has tasted vinegar, Helgestad exclaimed, "He is too clear-headed not to act judiciously. He has lost about thirty pounds in a few weeks, but he has not the courage to say 'no,' because he is afraid, the old fool."

"He will recognise his son, and provide against misfortune."

"Nuh!" said Helgestad, "Christi is indeed a different man from his father. He has the Nordland blood of his mother, is proud of temper, and, in addition, addicted to all kinds of frivolity. He esteems not old customs and laws. He holds he has a right to think for himself, and select his own wife. He bluntly writes that he does not wish to return to his father's house, and renounces all, if Fandrem will not countenance his folly."

"And you made no opposition?"

"No," said the trader. "Let him have the puppet; my door shall not open to her. Were he my son, he might run to the end of the world, but not to my arms. You know my principles, Herr; I thank God for my children! Ilda is the apple of my eye; but I would rather see her steeped in misery, before she should suffer a man to enter her chamber who was not agreeable to me. Nuh! Were I to say to Ilda, the squint-eyed Quane there shall carry you away to Loppen as his wife, she would bow assent, and would say, 'Thank you, father.' And if I were to send Björnarne to Afraja's gamme to fetch Gula away from there as his wife, he would answer, 'Your will shall be done, father.'"

He regarded Marstrand, who smilingly replied, "I do not doubt, Herr Helgestad, that Björnarne would comply with your request; but it may be questioned if Afraja and Gula would give their assent."

"We will not dispute about trifles," exclaimed Helgestad; "let every one hold on to what he has. I would not indeed marry Ilda to the changeling there from Loppen, although the ugly creature, who is as true and faithful as a dog, would be more acceptable to me as a son-in-law, than a man who flies over the earth like a snow-flake, until it is trodden down in some corner. — That fellow," said he, in an exulting tone, "is far and near the best bird-catcher, and is a treasure for any one who knows how to profit by him. He brings me in a handsome quantity of species, much more than the island formerly produced, when its value was not appreciated. It was a wild rock in the midst of the stormy ocean; Afraja and his knavish companions frequented it every year, and claimed it as their property from the time of Jubinal.—Ha! ha! Wingeborg got the better of them; he threw them out of their nests, and plucked them as bare of their feathers as young auks. This is the thing, Herr Marstrand. Many a one has a good nest, but does not know it is lined with down, until some one comes who understands how to use it. So was it with the miserable people to whom all the land once belonged. Had they been more active and intelligent, it would have remained their property for all time to come."

He accompanied these remarks with so many confidential nods and winks, and with such a mixture of frankness, rough truth, and knavish cunning, that Marstrand was at a loss as to what he should believe. At last he threw his books aside, and invited his guest to join him in a fresh glass.

On the following day, the young proprietor set out, with a heavy heart, on his return to Balsfiord. Ilda had not afforded him a single moment of confidential leave-taking; and if she had, what wish or request had he to leave behind him? — It was a dark gloomy morning as his horse toiled up to the high fjeld. All the rugged isolated cones which rise out of the mass of splintered rocks that strew these elevated plains, were enveloped in heavy clouds of fog. The dense masses revolved around the mountain ridges, and all the pagan gods and witches appeared to revel in them; and fog, cloud, rain, and sunshine, to be struggling for mastery. — The signs foreboded a change of weather. The sun's rays could not penetrate through the misty vapor, which fell cold and damp upon the traveller.

An experienced person would not have regarded all these signs without apprehension, and he would have quickened his speed to the utmost. Marstrand, however, troubling himself but little about the weather, only occasionally turned his eyes upon the clouds. The icy shower fell soothingly upon his flushed face, tranquillising his troubled heart.—"Never," said he to himself, "will I touch what is forbidden to me; never more will I disturb the peace of this maiden, who rejects me because the voice of duty is stronger with her than the voice of her heart.—And do I know, then, that she loves me? Has she ever said so? Has she not repulsed me; and to-day, yes, this very day, as I took leave of her, was not her face as insensible as this flinty rock? — And yet," he exclaimed, in such a loud tone, that the horse started with fright, "yet she loves me! I know it; and a glance on her deep eyes, and these flowers, tell me so."

He took out the nosegay which Ilda had presented to him, and looked upon it; but he hurriedly replaced it as he heard a cry in the distance behind him. As he halted his horse, he thought he perceived a figure on the rocky ridge, beckoning to him; to his surprise, he saw the venerable pastor hastily advancing towards him.

Klaus Hornemann, in his black over-coat, broad-brimmed hat, latchet shoes, and his long pilgrim's staff, was the very image of a preacher in the wilderness. He carried a leather knapsack upon his shoulders; the brave old man laughed good-naturedly as Marstrand blamed him for leaving Orenaes Gaard in such threatening weather.

"My dear friend," said he, "we must all be gone, when the Lord calls us, and have you not yourself set out to fulfil your duty? Your presence induced me to tarry there below, where I do not willingly abide; but I think now of passing some days with those by whom I am always kindly received." Marstrand alighted and offered the old pastor his horse, but Hornemann declined it.

"Keep your seat," he said, "we shall not travel far together. I must soon turn to the right, to reach the four families who pasture their cattle at Ulvsfiord; you must, on the contrary, turn to the left, to ascend the high saddle of the fiord, in order to reach your house in good season." He squeezed the water out of his long white hair and continued in his mild manner. "For forty years, I have wandered around here, and my strength has not yet failed. The Lord has protected me in many storms. With this staff in hand, I have travelled farther than a horse could carry me; delay not now, for we must both hurry on."

Thus speaking, he went ahead and showed Marstrand that he had lost none of his activity; for he often travelled faster than his mounted companion, moderating his pace, when the sagacious horse carefully picked his way over the stones. As he walked along, he had much to tell of his foster children, the Lapps, which excited the sympathy of Marstrand. The venerable man vividly portrayed a picture of shepherd life in this wilderness. "But you will see all with your own eyes," he said; "when old Klaus can do nothing more for the protection of the forsaken, you will take his place, and one will at least bless you for it, and in spirit be with you."

"This one," replied Marstrand, excited by the remembrance, "has more need of protection against her destroyers, than all others."

"No," said the old man, "the Lord is with her, her soul is pure and her enemies can do nothing. I saw her to-day before

I left. Her whole mind and character were as transparent before me as a clear brook. Ilda will never be unhappy, for her heart is strong, and her courage unyielding; it grieves her that a man who is dear to her, could not be so firm as she herself."

"She spoke and thought of me?" asked Marstrand.

"Do you think she could do otherwise?" answered the old man. "You will live in Ilda's thoughts as long as she breathes on this earth."

"Did she say that? Did her lips confess it?"

Klaus Hornemann nodded affirmatively with a melancholy smile. "Why should I conceal from you the noble, loveful sympathy which Ilda takes in your welfare? It is proper that you should know that you possess a female friend who will cling to you with the purest and holiest sympathies of her heart. You know Helgestad, and you have yourself heard him say that he would rather tread his children under his feet than permit them to oppose his will. He fears Paul Petersen much more than he loves him; but he is in his power, and cannot liberate himself from him; he has promised her to the secretary before all the people, and it would be dishonorable to be false to his pledges. My dear son, I say and repeat to you all this, to inspire you with Ilda's strength to overcome strength. She saw your grief, but she dared not trust herself with a smile or friendly look. She will never change her feelings towards you, and you must act as a just man, as you are."

"Accept my thanks for all your consolatory information and admonitions," replied Marstrand. "Say to her that I accede to her request. Who knows how long I may yet remain in her neighborhood? But wherever I may be, and if I again see her, no look of mine shall ever cause her sadness, and no word shall ever betray to her my feelings."

The mild and venerable countenance of the pastor shone with kindly sympathy. "God's will must be fulfilled," said he; "his strong hand heals the wounds which it inflicts. My dear friend, all will again become clear, if we remain strong in faith and restrain the violence of our passions. Even this waste, over which the wind drives the cold fog, is it not a picture of our hopes? Yesterday, it gloried in sunshine, variegated flowers, and mosses; to-day, they are level with the ground, and will soon disappear under ice and darkness. But where the roots are good, they cannot be injured; and when sunlight and fair weather return, the strong young shoots put forth again."

"Amen, father; amen!" exclaimed Marstrand; "every human being has his sorrow; I will bear mine."

"Listen to an admonition which comes from good authority — not from Ilda," he continued, smiling, "for she is too obedient a child to warn against her own father. Paul Petersen is your enemy, and exerts all his influence to persuade Helgestad to ruin you. His efforts are opposed, but you must take care not to anger Helgestad yet more. In this world, the good, according to the apostle, must be as wise as serpents to defeat the cunning malice of the wicked."

"I am prepared for all," said John; "Helgestad shall find me all right. If he thinks to throw a noose over my head, he will be disappointed."

"Let us separate," replied Klaus. "I find the combatant awake and ready, and my soul rejoices in this young, undismayed strength. With God's help, forward, then, Herr Marstrand! Would that he had ordained that I should place this hand in that of Ilda at his altar, on St. Michael's day, instead of wedding her to a false and faithless man! Now, as we separate, take this as a last remembrancer."

With these words, he drew out of his great-coat a piece of paper, folded as a letter, placed it in Marstrand's hand, and proceeded on his way with the bounding steps of a young man. For some moments, Marstrand stared at the paper, which was without superscription; as he opened it, he recognised the handwriting of Ilda. He lifted up his eyes and looked after the pastor, who was already concealed in the dark mass of fog

Alone in this dreary waste, he began to read the writing, while he held his cloak over it to shelter it from the driving rain and the wind, which threatened to tear it out of his hands.

"John Marstrand," he read, "suffer me to say a few words to you, which you may keep, if you choose; for they are farewell words, although I hope soon and often to see you again. You are a strange man, with strange customs; but you understand me, nevertheless; for God has created a keen and lively sympathy between us, as universal as human nature itself, and unaffected by distance of separation or the lapse of time. We have both felt it. You have wished to give it speech; but I prevented it, because I dared not listen to it. I have perceived your bitter pain, the reproachful expression of your eyes, and your anger. Had I turned my ear to you, or proffered my hand, a voice of cursing and infamy would have pursued you and me. Therefore I freed myself from you. Know that I have eradicated from my heart all that should not be there, and it would be a criminal act of folly if you do not the same. I earnestly implore you to it, as I wish you happiness and peace. Do not suppose that I could think you would ever forget me, or that I shall ever cease to be your friend. My marriage will be celebrated on St. Michael's day. Come and be the most welcome guest at it. I shall see you on my wedding-day, and do you be kind towards my husband, to whom I belong, and whom I wish to honor. Be cautious and prudent in your transactions with my father; for you have, indeed, need of it. Rest assured, from me, that I gladly look forward to my future destiny in Paul Petersen's house. And now, may God's blessing always rest upon you!"

Marstrand held the letter a long while in his hand, as his horse moved along, contemplating its firm-set characters. No tremor of the hand had betrayed her feelings; no word was badly written, and no sentence was out of order. The whole of this letter of adieu was as composed and cool as if it were an affair of perfect indifference. "There is no warm pulsation of the heart in it," he said, as he folded it up; and, moved by a sudden impulse, he tore it to pieces, and scattered the fragments to the wind.

"No! I have done right," he exclaimed, drowning the voice of self-reproof; "let the wind carry away these pieces, and the rain destroy them; so will I rid myself of this folly. She has driven me from her heart, as if I never had a place there! She joyfully looks forward to her future! She dissembles; she will soothe my wounded feelings, while she deceives me." He laughed aloud, and wrapped his cloak more closely around him. The fog gathered so dense and heavy about him, that he could not distinguish twenty steps ahead. "Yes," he exclaimed, in the wild roar of the elements, "I will dance at your wedding; Paul Petersen shall have joy in me."

It seemed as if his laugh was answered by another, or was it an echo? Marstrand paid no attention to it, but rode on, leaving his horse to seek the way, which he could no longer find; he grew alarmed, however, as the snow began to fall in heavy flakes, and his snorting horse suddenly came to a halt on the brink of a declivity. It was evident that he could not descend it; but whither should he turn? He deemed himself to be on the right course; but his most searching glances could discover nothing. The mist seemed to grow thinner, but it yet closely enveloped him; clouds and whirlwinds of fine snow drove around him, benumbing him to the bones. He had heard of the Fana-rauk — the snow-storm which destroys all living things — and a dismal feeling came over him. In the few minutes that he stood on the brink of the descent, he was covered with snow, which clung to his damp clothes, and froze them stiff; his horse had become perfectly white, and as far as he could see, the atmosphere was filled with the soft, white snow, which was whirled about in eddies by the violence of the wind. There was no standing still, or hesitating; but it was necessary to seek out some place of shelter, and to persevere in the pursuit of it with unflinching courage. There was no help to be looked for in that desolate waste, and no use in outcry, or attempting to turn back. Marstrand knew that he had nothing to hope from others, and that human energy and patience alone could contend with the terrors of the elements: upon a sudden impulse, he sprang from his horse, seized the bridle, and was endeavoring to discover some place where he could lead the animal down into the steep, when, in the midst of the snow-gust, a figure rose up, which, at first, struck him with terror, but afterwards inspired him with hope.

At first, it appeared to be a frozen human form, on a rising rock in the snow. A peaked cap was drawn over the head, a brown fur jacket enveloped the body, on his arm lay a shepherd's staff, and a musket projected over his shoulders. It was a Lapp, who did not stir until Marstrand reached him, and recognized him as Mortuno.

"Hallo, friend!" he shouted to him, "do you desire to become a snow statue! Assist me in my need; and if you know any means of finding a place of shelter in the storm, speak, and let me hear of it."

"Would you go below there?" asked Mortuno, as he pointed with his staff to the ravine.

"It seems to me there is nothing else to be done, unless you know of something better."

"If you succeed in it, very well! You are young, and have much success," exclaimed the Lapp, with a laugh.

"An hour or two since, Mortuno, Klaus Hornemann, the pastor, left me, who assured me you were a sensible, well-disposed man. I bless the chance by which I find you; but it would certainly be unjust for you to refuse me your services, which I will reward to the best of my ability."

The Lapp, at first, did not seem disposed to give up his propensity for joking, and he grinned and made faces; but he soon assumed a more serious mood, and at last he jumped from the rock, and took the bridle of the horse.

"What would you do down there, Herr?" he inquired

"You could hardly have got to the bottom in safety; and if you had, it would not have availed you anything; for it is a steep and narrow declivity, which ends in cliffs and clefts, through which a wild elf plunges down to the Ulvsfiord. No one can get out of it, and even I would not attempt it," he said, with a proud air; "when the snow-storm ceases, the hollow may be half filled up. Follow me, and I will hunt you another place, which will suit us better."

He surprised his companion with his intelligible and quite tolerable Norwegian; he drew the exhausted horse along over the rocks for a quarter of an hour, until they reached a high rock, bent like a horn, with a narrow chasm opening into a cavity in its interior.

This was, doubtless, one of the spots where the Lapps were accustomed to seek rest or shelter with their herds. Great stones lay in a semi-circle around, and the ashes and soot indicated that many a fire had been lighted there. Mortuno threw off his coat of reindeer skin, turned over a stone which covered an excavation, and drew out some dry moss, birch twigs, leaves, and grass. In the next moment he kindled a light from his tinder-box; a comfortable sensation came over Marstrand, as he sat by the fire and felt its vivifying warmth on his body. Upon the saddle of his horse, who appeared to be better pleased here than without, hung a bundle, which was filled in Orenaes with bread and meat, and a flask of good Holland gin; what better could the traveller do than to spread out his treasures and divide them with Mortuno, who did not wait to be pressed, but valiantly helped himself. John next took out his travelling cup, made in Bergen of the hard knot of the Norwegian birch; but, to his astonishment, Mortuno could with difficulty be persuaded to taste a drop of a liquor which his brethren coveted with such insatiable avidity.

"You can do it," said he, as Marstrand took a deep drink; "but I dare not. My people have not the cool head and the sluggish blood which yours possess; at least, I believe, that all depends on this. For how otherwise could a Norman drink a quart measure full before his entrails burn. His head may shake to and fro, and his legs totter, and yet he knows what he is about. With the Samoyedes," he continued, "the blood flows fast, and the head is hot. When they drink, they fall down and wallow about like swine. A Norman needs the fire-water to warm him when he is cold; a Samoyede needs only his reindeer and his cover. Although the breath freezes on his mouth, he does not feel the cold; and when he has lost his way in a Fana-rauk, he does not crawl into a ravine where he must perish."

He burst into a laugh at his own wit, and Marstrand joined with him. "You are entirely right, friend Mortuno," he replied; "but tell me, now, what we shall do if the weather continues as it is."

The Lapp shrugged his shoulders, and looked cunningly at him with his little round eyes. "I do not know, my good Herr," he considerately replied; "snow-storms often last a week; and if the white sand is deep enough, we dig a hole and sleep until it ceases."

"What!" asked Marstrand, terror-struck, "can that happen?"

"It has often occurred," replied Mortuno. "I have myself lain nine days in a snow-hole, and have eaten up half my fur in hunger. Whither will you go?" he continued, as Marstrand arose and went to his horse.

"If such be the case, we had better get out."

"Not I," laughed the Lapp. "I am no fool, and will keep my neck and legs sound. Look out; you cannot see a dozen steps ahead. You cannot long hold out, and so you will lie down, tumble into a ditch or chasm, and your benumbed horse will be unable to go on. If he were a reindeer, he could easily make his way. If you were a Samoyede, you would carry your head in the air, and you could see. Ha! ha! you are a proud Herr, a Norman, and you would be a Samoyede! Is it not so? Speak, Herr, tell me, would you not like to be a Samoyede?"

He stretched himself out upon the warm stones, and laughed to his utmost, while Marstrand anxiously looked at the weather, which appeared to be wilder than ever.

"Why did you come up to us here?" continued Mortuno "What do you want in our land, where you are as children who do not know what to do? Sit down here by me, Herr, and be patient. You can do nothing."

"If I were Olaf or Helgestad," said Marstrand, "I would compel you to guide me on the way."

"If you were Helgestad," responded the Lapp, with a reckless levity, "I had left you drown in the elf; and if you were Olaf, who has already two holes in his hat, I would have sent a third shot into your heart."

"Beware, Mortuno; you have a sad account to settle. If Olaf meets you, it would be better for you to be lying in the elf; if the Sorenskriver lays hands upon you, he will scourge you at the whipping-post till the blood flows; and if Helgestad catches you, you will not come off much better. You killed Wingeborg's dog, and he has sworn to be the death of you."

"Has he, the poisonous wolf, has he Mortuno already by the ear?" exclaimed the Lapp, clapping his hands. "Let him come here, let them all come, we have nooses enough to take them by the horns."

At the very moment he said this, a dog barked directly on the outside of the rock, and the curious, tall, and slender form of Egede Wingeborg, the Quane, appeared at the entrance. His slender body was enveloped in a leather coat; and from beneath his glazed hat, covered with snow, peeped out his red, broad face and distorted eyes. He rushed by Marstrand like a shadow, and with a grip of his long arm he seized Mortuno by the throat before the latter could get on his legs.

The whole proceeding was so sudden, so surprising, and so noiseless, that Marstrand only came to his senses as Wingeborg drew a long knife out of his girdle, which, in a moment more, he would probably have plunged in the throat of the Lapp, who was so tightly grasped that he could not utter a word. Marstrand seized Egede's arm in time, and with all his strength tore him away from his victim. Mortuno quickly profited by this timely aid. He rolled off the stones, sprang up, and, with his short gun in hand, he uttered a cry of fury and vengeance.

The two enemies stood facing each other, and Marstrand between them; the little dog lay howling before his master. "Why do you hinder me?" cried Egede. "Why did you lay hold of me and kick my dog away? Fine thanks to a man who offered to seek you in the storm, when the maidens in Orenaes were anxious for your safety."

"You shall not commit a murder, as long as I can prevent it," replied Marstrand. "If you have a complaint against the Lapp, present it. He is a man like you, and the laws are made for all."

"A man!" exclaimed the Quane. "He is a Lapp, a beast, not a man. Out of your corner, you thief! I will slice you like a fish, and salt you like a herring."

Mortuno naturally declined to comply with this kind request. He crept down yet closer behind the rock, and laid his finger upon the trigger of his gun, without uttering a word in reply.

"He would be a fool to obey you," said Marstrand, laughing.

"Good, so he will go with me, we will all go," said Wingeborg. "I will present him to the Sorenskriver, as you recommend. Take the gun away from the cowardly dog, and we will bind his hands."

"I fear, my friend Wingeborg," answered John, "he will not be satisfied with this arrangement; as to me, I have no desire to return to Lyngenfiord."

"Ha!" cried Egede fiercely, "will you not help me to take a scoundrel whom my masters are seeking, and who has treated us all so scurvily?"

"He has done me good," replied Marstrand. "Without him, I would yet be wandering about in the storm, and might have perished. I have broken bread with him, and have shared my drink with him, so be satisfied, Egede Wingeborg. We are sitting together here in a free haven; do as you please with the fellow when you find him again; to-day, however, let there be peace. Come, Egede," he continued, "sit down alongside of the guest-fire. You, Mortuno, lay aside your weapon, and take your place on the other side. Between you be the fire, and here stands the bottle. Drink a full glass, lord of Loppen, and drown your trouble in the consolatory draught."

He handed the Quane his glass; but he drew back with disgust. "Cursed be my hand, if I touch it!" he exclaimed. "Has not a Lapp drunk out of it? Are you not ashamed to offer it to me?"

"Have I not, myself, drunk from it, you fool?"

"Have you?" rejoined Egede, contemptuously. "The Devil! I would not tell anybody. Are you a Norman, a man of good blood, and will you drink with a filthy lubber, a reindeer driver, more stupid and malicious than a hog? Ho, ho!" he cried, swinging his hat in triumph, "God be thanked! You are a Dane! I will tell them in the Gaard, where I met you. I would rather be ten feet deep beneath the snow, than pass an hour in such society. You thief! You murderer! Beware of Egede! He will find you again, and so true as I have tapped more than one Lapp, will I mark you, that all may avoid you."

With this fearful threat, he turned his back and left his companions, without being recalled by any one. Marstrand was vexed at the idea of what this miserable churl might report of him. Mortuno stood for some time more with his cocked gun, as if he feared that Egede would return; but he, at last, laid it aside and approached Marstrand, who sat on the rock, gazing in the distance.

The Lapp knelt down, and suddenly taking the hand of his protector, raised it to his lips.

"What does that mean?" roughly exclaimed the Dane.

"Permit me, Herr, permit me!" said Mortuno, whose dark eyes beamed with a gratitude which mellowed his features into a soft and friendly expression. "You are good and true, and much better than I. Mortuno will always serve you to the utmost of his ability."

"If you could only, my poor Mortuno, procure us good weather, and stop the snow!"

"Have no fear," replied Mortuno, springing up, "it will not snow long; and if you choose, we will immediately set out, and I will guide you. Snow-clouds cluster over the fjeld, but they do not descend to the valleys. In a few days all will be water, and it often melts in a few hours. You will see that no one at the green Balsfiord has heard of this."

"So you brought me here without any particular necessity?"

Mortuno was embarrassed. "I brought you here," said he, humbly, "because I cannot bear the men of the fiords. They ridicule and despise us; what shall we do? We jest with them when we can. Punish me, if you choose."

"You would also drive your joke with me," answered Marstrand, "although I treat you so much more mildly than Olaf. Beware, Mortuno, you have seen what you have to expect."

The Lapp cunningly rolled about his little eyes. "Let them come up to me, I shall not go down to seek them. The Quane is a wicked churl, and his dog a devil; but I sent one to his father in hot hell, and if he again goes a-hunting——"

He struck the barrel of his gun, and, with a loud laugh, leaped in the air. He ran up to the horse, fastened the saddle on, again packed the provisions, slung his gun over his shoulders, and all was made ready for the journey. As he took off his ugly cap, and bound together his shining black hair, his young face appeared quite handsome. It glowed with a happy expression, and he seemed to rejoice at what he had done, and to think of his powerful enemies with an undismayed spirit.

"Curious!" said Marstrand, in a half audible tone, as he regarded the merry, active being before him. "Many a one has good understanding and talents, but they are, nevertheless, too bad for such a monster as the Quane."

Mortuno heard the remark. "That," said he, while he was tying a long leather loop on the bridle, "comes from our bearing all that these proud men inflict upon us. There is no wrong too great not to find patient necks. How could they respect us, when they see that we are miserable women? Do we respect the dog which we kick with our feet, and who, in return, crawls upon his belly and licks our hands?" He threw his hat in the air, and his eyes flashed again. "Men esteem men!" he exclaimed, "and they are just towards each other, when they know that wrong is retaliated."

"If such be your principle of action," said Marstrand in a musing mood, "travelling over the fjeld will soon become insecure."

"You may travel as much as you choose," replied the Lapp, "you will be welcome everywhere. Afraja protects you."

"And it was this high protection, my dear Mortuno, that prevented you from sending me into the fearful abyss, and induced you only to play off a little less perilous joke upon me."

Mortuno burst into a laugh. "Had the secretary or Helgestad stood there, I would have pushed them in. I hate them all, for they deserve it."

He drew the horse by the halter out of the place of refuge, and although it yet stormed and snowed with violence, he resumed the journey in a somewhat different direction from that which Marstrand had taken. Mortuno declared that it would soon cease snowing, a prediction which was realised. Half an hour later, the sky was clear, and the wind blew mild from the south; the Lapp conducted the traveller with great prudence and care, sounded with his long stick, where it seemed insecure, and was indefatigable in assisting the horse, all the time running about hither and thither, laughing, jesting, and relating anecdotes of one kind or another.

His companion amused himself with his remarks, which were sometimes very droll and sharp-witted; and when he described

Helgestad and the traders, he was sure to hit the nail on the head. He was, on the contrary, profoundly silent touching his own life and the affairs of his people, and he said not a word of Gula. As Marstrand at last inquired after her, he professed to know nothing of her, and ran ahead to escape further questions. When he came back, he had considered upon an answer.

"The birch droops its head," he said; "it is no time to think of a maiden. When the leaves become green again, Ayra the goddess of love stretches out her red hands! Then will my gamme look beautiful — young grass and flowers are strewed about, and Gula will sit at the hearth-stone, and offer me the bowl of rich milk. The clouds lift up from the mountains, and the sun shines brightly. So beams the face of Gula on my coming."

He began to whistle and sing a tune, looking all the while with a curious smile at Marstrand, and exclaiming that it was his marriage-song, which he had composed himself. He suddenly came to a pause, and pointed through a rift in the fog. "Behold the Balsfiord!" he shouted. "There it lies; that is your land, Herr, there can you dwell and take fish. Leave us to pasture our cattle, here above, in peace."

Marstrand looked down into the depth below, which opened before him, and descried the green fiord. Not far off he recognized his own house, which, at that moment, was illuminated by a ray of sunlight that broke through the cloud.

"I thank you, good Mortuno," he said; "and you are right in all. We must remain there with our claims and vexations; to you belongs the mountain kingdom, with all its contents. Accompany me, and rest with me."

The Lapp shook his head. "Thanks, Herr," he exclaimed. 'you have spoken it; we remain in our land."

"Have no fear of Olaf," resumed Marstrand. "I will reconcile him with you."

"You cannot persuade him to give me his hand, as you do,"

said Mortuno; "and I would not take it. If you alight, and give your horse the bridle, you can pick your way down, and he will follow you. Farewell; Mortuno will not forget you." With this remark, he sprang back into the darkness of the mist, unheeding the call of Marstrand to return.

CHAPTER XVI.

Marstrand had, on the next day, abundance to do, again to accustom himself to his solitary, yet active life. He found that Olaf had gone to work with practical earnestness. The warehouse was finished, the dwelling was put in order and completed within, and furnished with all kinds of domestic articles; and the wares and stores were properly arranged. Marstrand proceeded to examine his works, the success of which had, indeed, not been promoted by his absence. The saw-mill was not yet ready, and his directions had not been properly carried out. His plans of improvement had been frustrated by the opposition of the mechanics, who would not deviate from their ancient habits, and these were inapplicable to the present case. The young proprietor endeavored, by greater exertions, and more persevering patience, to accomplish his plans; and it was only when he himself set to work, and was actively engaged from morning till night, that he succeeded in giving the right direction to his plans. He had found the means, by his knowledge of mechanics, to erect his mills in a better manner than was the custom; and in the ship-yards and wood-yards of his native country he had also obtained an acquaintance with timber, and the mode of handling it, that was of material assistance to him now. The Norwegian workmen had derided the Dane, who seemed to think he had all the wisdom in his own pocket; but they now saw, with half-credulous astonishment, that a well-arranged pulley could raise more than twelve men, that every thing could be better secured by pegs and screws, and that much manual labor might be obviated by the ingenious appliances of art.

Marstrand now looked upon his labors with the most confident hope. All his experiments succeeded; he had his head full of plans, and he wished that Helgestad were on the spot to witness the progress he had made. But little more was necessary to crown his labors with triumph, and to put to the blush his enemies and revilers. As he contemplated his works, he could imagine how much better they would appear in another year; and, as he walked through the little valleys which belonged to him, he proudly thought of what they might be made to produce, when occupied by industrious colonists. At that time, also, many Finlanders emigrated from the east into the unsettled country, where they gave full scope to their indomitable activity, and love of agriculture. An attempt was made to introduce colonies into the waste places of Norway; and Olaf desired to obtain such colonists, who, in his opinion, would here find the best situation in all Finnmark.

With such hopes, the young settler, after a week's absence, returned from his excursion; his heart beat stronger as, in the distance, before his door, he discerned a little caravan, which had just arrived. He perceived Helgestad, Paul Petersen, who was shaking Olaf by the hand, and the uncouth Egede, standing by the horses, and waving his hat, with a loud hurrah, as a sign of greeting. Marstrand hurried on to his guests, to all of whom he gave a hearty welcome, not even excepting the secretary himself.

"I thank you heartily, Herr Helgestad, for having so promptly performed your promise to visit me at Balsfiord. Seat yourselves, while I see what I have in the house. It is some time past noon; but whatever I have, shall be set before you."

"Nuh!" exclaimed Helgestad, after him; "it will be little enough. Olaf has grown lean. I think so; is it not so?"

With this witticism he clapped the Nordlander on the shoulder, who, indeed, was much leaner than formerly, when at Lyngenfiord, and appeared to relish but little the laugh at his expense.

"Heaven defend us!" said the trader; "you look as sour as an unripe cucumber in Ilda's pot. I bring you greetings from her, and from all. Ilda has a deep longing after her Ole; she will not rest with fresh syld and sweet groat-soup, until he again stands full and stout in his coat."

"Let her make the experiment on Paul," said Olaf, "if that can be done."

Helgestad put his finger on the side of his nose, with a cunning look at the secretary, who was, truly, thin enough.—"Nuh!" he exclaimed, "if he were cooked in all the fat which comes from the Lofodden, none would nevertheless adhere to his ribs. It is another thing with you, Ole. You are made of stouter stuff; you have young, firm flesh, like a stag; and you always had a pleasing face, which wrung sighs from the maidens."

Helgestad knew that he vexed them both, and he was secretly as much amused with Paul's feigned good-humor as with Olaf's sullen grumble. Turning to the Nordlander, he said, "Have you heard that on St. Michael's day there is to be a marriage in Orenaes Gaard?"

"I have heard of it," was the answer.

"Ilda can scarcely bide the time," said Helgestad.

"I do not believe it," said Olaf, as he turned round to go away.

Helgestad held him fast, without moving from his seat.—"Nuh!" he said, "I would have been satisfied if Ilda had said, 'I will have this one and no other, father.' But she has said nothing of the kind. I hope you know now what she sends you, Ole."

"I know the message that is sent," replied Olaf; "it is to go home, and before St. Michael's day I shall be shooting snipe in Bodoen."

"Good!" continued the trader; "the snipe there are the best in the world, and as large and fat as ducks. I have eat many a one with your father, Ole, who was my friend as long as he lived; and your mother cooked them famously."

"Come when you will," said the young man, "my door will be open to you."

"Orenaes Gaard will ever have a willing welcome for my friends," replied Helgestad. "I hope you will not forsake Björnarne, the companion of your boyish days."

"I will never," answered the Nordlander; "but with him there" — pointing to the secretary with his extended finger — "with that false man I will have nothing to do."

Paul, who had quietly listened, shrugged his shoulders with a smile. "You are an old Berserker," said he, "who neither sees nor hears anything, suffers himself to be used by everybody, and, like a true slave, runs into the fire for his master, without thinking that it will burn."

"Hush!" exclaimed Olaf, with a dark frown. "You lie."

"You will come to your senses sooner than you think," continued Paul.

"Will you not go with us?" asked the trader.

"No!"

"Nuh! remain then. You have no great estate in Bodoen that calls you thither. I will place you in the new Gaard; you shall take care of it, and administer it; and I assure you, you will be satisfied with me."

Olaf looked at him with astonishment. "What do you mean?" he roughly inquired.

"You shall hear," responded Helgestad.

"Let me speak a word with him previously," said Paul. "I will open his eyes, that he may learn to see."

Marstrand reëntered the Stuga, followed by a maid-servant, bringing what she had been able to find. The fragments of a leg of mutton were set upon the table, with a loaf of black bread. With the addition of coffee the entertainment was completed; for the poverty of which Marstrand apologised.

"It is curious!" said Helgestad, laughing; "you have game enough here, birds of all kinds, a sea full of fish that swim up to your very threshold. You are a careless fellow, as I see; but I hope you have bestowed more attention on other matters."

"Truly!" answered John, "I have not had time to look after my table, and Olaf has forgotten it. We have both worked from morning till night, without thinking of fishing or hunting; but we will take care to provide better to-morrow."

"I hope so!" said Helgestad, drawing the dish towards him, which he obliged Paul Petersen to divide with him. The meat disappeared in a few minutes, and both then attacked the bread.

"Have you no butter in the house—no?" asked the trader.

Marstrand was obliged to confess he had not.

"And not a slice of cheese?" asked Paul.

There was none.

"Why," said the secretary, laughing, "why did you not beg your good friend Mortuno for a Lapland cheese, or plunder his hunting-bag, as you sat with him under the rock? Did Herr Marstrand bring you nothing, Olaf?"

"What should he bring with him?"

"A new hat, at least, in place of the one torn by the bullet. Mortuno is a polite man."

"I will teach him!" said Olaf, menacingly. "It is a pity that he met such a magnanimous friend. Wingeborg cannot forget it yet."

"Nuh!" said Helgestad, interrupting, "I must say, Herr

Marstrand, your conduct has not been acceptable to any of us. For Olaf's sake, you should not have protected the scoundrel. You ought to have taken and bound the fellow, that he might receive his reward."

"Do you know nothing of it?" asked Paul of the Nordlander.

The latter shook his head in denial.

"You must admit that it is high time to make an example; for the rabble every day grow bolder and more lawless. Complaints are also made of the Lapps from other places. They cruelly beat a man at Maursund who was hated by them; they fired the house of a fisherman at Quanearnerfiord; and robberies have been committed such as were never before known. The villains laugh at us below; when they are among their mountains, they rattle their guns about our ears and howl jesting songs after us. It is all a soup brewed by the infernal churl, Afraja. The old scamp spurs them on, and Mortuno is his best helper. They might set Orenaes Gaard on fire by night, and might no longer content themselves with sending their bullets through hats merely. They are wicked, heathen people, without any tender feelings; they hate all Christians, and those most, who do them good. An example must be made of some of them, to humble the rest. Mortuno shot Wingeborg's dog, he put Olaf's life in danger with his accursed hand, and for this he should be taken and delivered up, instead of being protected."

"Did you help him?" asked Olaf, angrily.

"I did;" replied Marstrand. "Shake not your arm against me; hear me; for you would have done the same."

He related what had happened; and in conclusion, he exclaimed, as he observed that his remarks produced but little impression on his hearers, "Should I have suffered a man to be murdered before my eyes? Ought I to have taken, and helped to bind and deliver to his enemies, a man who received me when I had lost my way and was in danger? Never will I raise my hand for such a purpose! You complain that the Lapps are hostile to you: treat them with humanity, and they will be conciliated. The Voigt of Tromsöe will make an example; but it will only be a new inhumanity. I cannot change this cruel system of treatment — alas! I cannot; but I will not aid in its maintenance."

"But you will rave against your own friends," said the secretary.

"Revile as much as you please, Herr Petersen," rejoined Marstrand, with increasing warmth; "I can bear it. I have become acquainted, among these persecuted and despised Lapps, with better men than——"

"Than we are!" interrupted Paul, striking his breast.

Marstrand made a repelling, contemptuous gesture.

"Cursed be he who can be the friend of a Lapp!" exclaimed Olaf, with a tremendous blow of his fist on the table.

Helgestad rose and requested peace. "Young blood always runs too fast, and never knows discretion. Let Herr Marstrand do what he deems best. The people in the south think differently from us in the north. We will go, Herr Marstrand, and look at your operations. As you have taken but little care of your house and table, your external industry must probably be so much the greater."

Marstrand followed him, and he summoned up all his self-possession to overcome his anxiety of mind and his angry feelings.

"I must be cautious," he whispered to himself, "and remember that this man has my fate in his hands. I will not forget the admonitions that I have received. He can hardly be well disposed, or he would not have brought the secretary with him. Yet, I hope to reconcile him. He must, when he sees it, commend what I have accomplished at Balself, and what I shall offer him will gratify his thirst for gain."

He smiled as Helgestad looked into the great shop, which seemed tolerably bare, and grumblingly shook his head at the confused mass of goods.

"You have forgotten my instructions, Herr," he said, as they walked on. "A trading-post is the true foundation of every establishment in Finnmark. If this is not conducted with order and attention, there can be no prosperity. You have done nothing which shows you to be a practical man. You have no account-book, no fishing-grounds, no drying-stands; you have instituted no system of barter, and made no provision of cattle; nor have you procured any colonists."

"Only be patient, and all will come, Herr Helgestad," answered the gaard-proprietor. "What you have mentioned shall be my next care. Already I have made preparations thereto, I pledge my word! In another year more, you will be satisfied with it. Think only that I am alone, and that I have not a thousand hands. I have attacked the greatest difficulties first, and I have succeeded. See what I have accomplished. Observe the troublesome road hewn out of the rock; look at those bridges, the dam which I have built, the sawing-machines, and what exertions I have made to render the wood-slide serviceable for the next spring."

He conducted Helgestad further on, and with eloquent words explained to him his difficult labors, and the advantages he expected to derive from them.

The countenance of the crafty old speculator gradually brightened up, and his increasing satisfaction was manifested by a prolonged "Nuh!" from the depths of his throat. The new structures for the saw-mills received his especial approbation. He suffered Marstrand to explain his improvements and inventions, and with much satisfaction, witnessed the easy process of cutting the blocks, exclaiming it was the best he had ever seen.

"So I trust," said Marstrand, "that your confidence in me will not be shaken, and that your own hopes will be realized."

"God grant it! I think so," answered Helgestad. "I have always said you have a head which can effect something."

"And I will," rejoined Marstrand. "I am inexperienced

in shopkeeping, and in many other matters which appertain to a trading-post, but I will learn, and shall be as grateful to you for your good advice and just censure, as for your assistance. This help I cannot dispense with. I ask for additional aid. Will you listen to what I offer you in compensation."

"Nuh!" answered Helgestad. "I have two ears; go on."

They had arrived at the brink of the wooded chasm, where the Balself, with a bold leap from the rocky basin, in which it has gathered its foaming waters, plunges into the fiord. Here, Helgestad halted, and surveyed the bright, sunny shore of the gulf, which, covered with trees, and green strips of meadow, stretched to the red porphyry rocks, which formed a precipitous wall behind Marstrand's peaceful Gaard. The little valleys, opening on all sides, revealed their glittering brooks and waterfalls; the mill-wheels, lashed by the stream, scattered drops of spray and mist about; the woods rang with the cries of the workmen and wood-cutters, and the echoing blows of the axe. Everywhere were activity and industry, and the whole evening picture looked so beautiful, that Helgestad himself regarded it with pleasure. His imagination, which was not remarkably sensible to the charms of nature, was incited by this prospect to another course of reflection. He calculated, and his eyes, as Marstrand spoke to him, assumed a penetrating expression. He nodded and grinned as if he was wondrously pleased, turning his attention every now and then, below, where Paul Petersen, with Olaf on his arm, ascended the rocky hill, between the trees, and approached them, while engaged in animated conversation.

"What I offer you, Herr Helgestad," said Marstrand, "is, in return for your generous aid, to divide with you the profit which may flow from this undertaking. You have hitherto advised me; you have perceived the treasure which is here, and through your influence it has fallen into my hands. Without your powerful support, it would not have been possible for me to gain it, and as I have further need of your assistance, it is but proper that I should offer you the half of the profit."

"The half!" exclaimed Helgestad, leaning on his stick; "I have no wish for the half. I am also not magnanimous. I set but little value upon a thing which seems as full of holes as a barrel."

"Give it whatever name you please," continued John, with a smile. "Say that you laid your plan to obtain a real profit, and that you knew that I would succeed as I have."

"You have guessed it to a hair," replied Helgestad.

"You also knew that I would gratefully divide the profits with you."

"May be," answered Helgestad, "but it is an old saying; he who takes a pleasure in dividing, will also to deceive. I will therefore neither share, nor be deceived, Herr Marstrand; I will have what is mine, and in a word, I tell you I am come here to look after my rights."

"What do you mean, Herr Helgestad?" asked Marstrand, astounded. "What do you call your rights?"

The trader grinned at him, took off his hat, and smoothed back his tangled, pale-yellowish hair. "Nuh!" said he, "we must look things in the face. I have become acquainted with your housekeeping, Herr Marstrand, and I calculate matters cannot go on much longer in this way. Experience is another thing than the will and love of labor. You have wasted your provisions, squandered your money, and neglected my counsel. There are eight thousand *species* to pay in Bergen, eight thousand in Orenaes, and you will borrow more; but it will go the same way. As I look at the Gaard there, I expect that it will have to be sold at Tromsöe, with all its dependencies, woods, mills and the costly dam upon which you have lavished my money; I should like to see the man who will lay the twelve thousand *species* on the table. I calculate also, it need not be sold unless you insist upon it."

"I — Herr Helgestad — I," exclaimed Marstrand, in amazement, casting a rapid glance on the secretary and Olaf, who had come up at that moment, and then staring at the old speculator as if he did not understand him.

"You," resumed Herr Helgestad with a nod; "for if you do not accept my proposition, it must be sold to the highest bidder. It will then be seen what is left, and it depends upon me to decide what proceedings shall be resorted to, if the proceeds do not cover your debt. I can imprison you, compel you to labor, and hold on to what you have; but I hope we shall settle matters amicably. I am not a man of cruel and despotic temper, and will let you off as easily as I can."

"If I understand you rightly," said Marstrand, who had become deadly pale, "you will refuse me any further assistance?"

"Nuh!" replied the old man with a grinning laugh, "my skull must be as flat as the head of a Lapp, if I give you a penny."

"Then I must see where I can find another man who has more confidence in me."

"Do so," said Helgestad, "but procure my money—I must have it back."

"You shall have it," responded Marstrand. "Give me a respite, and I will endeavor to obtain it."

"A respite! There is no agreement for such in the bond, Herr. It is settled by our law, however, that when it is not otherwise provided, every debt must be covered and repaid between one day and the next."

"How!" violently ejaculated Marstrand; "can this be your intention? It seems to me that you have sought, with studied cunning, to accomplish my ruin."

"Consider your words, Herr Marstrand," said Petersen, joining in the conversation. "You make grave charges against Niels, who, if he seeks to punish you, can bring you to a bitter repentance."

"Nuh!" said Helgestad, "I desire nothing but my money, and to this I certainly have a right. Here stands the country judge; ask him, if you do not believe me. I notify you to-day, in presence of both these witnesses, that you owe me the sum of sixteen thousand silver species; and, according to the custom and law, if it be not paid by to-morrow, I intend to confiscate your property and take it out of your possession."

"By the law, this request must be complied with without delay," said Paul Petersen. "By virtue of my office as a sworn secretary, I can step in, and oblige a sale within a week, if security is not offered, or the debtor is proven to be destitute of means, of which in this case there can be no doubt."

Marstrand heard all in silence. His face, at length, glowed like a flame, and his heart swelled with indignation. He endeavored to repress his feelings, and to preserve his self-possession. "It is difficult for me, gentlemen," said he, "to believe that what I hear is true; for it seems to me as if I have, from the beginning, fallen into a net which was contrived for me, to which every one of you has lent a hand I would have relied on your friendship, Olaf, to the end of time, but you look upon me as if you rejoiced in my distress."

"If you are in distress," replied the Nordlander, "you have deserved it."

"How have I deserved it?"

"You are a Dane, and are false! Go where you came from, you fool, or seek your darling in the gamme of the Lapps."

"Are you so heartless as to insult me?" said the forsaken man. "Oh! you have quickly verified my saying, that there are better men among the persecuted and outcast, than you are. What more do you require of me?" continued he warmly, as he turned to Helgestad. "You want my property—you will reduce me to beggary! The thought has often enough flashed upon me, but I have dismissed it, as too base and unworthy to be cherished for a moment. You devised your plan when you first saw my royal patent, and you obtained a suitable coadjutor. Take then the booty if you can; injustice and infamy can never bring a blessing."

"Nuh!" said Helgestad, entirely insensible to these reproaches, "you are as choleric as ever. I have advised you, as a son; I have not concealed from you how a prudent man should act. You have not heeded my warnings, and you have no right to reproach me for your negligence and indiscretion. So it seems to me. I have nothing to fear from a judge, or from the opinion of all good people. Go, and carry your case before them. They will laugh at you, and drive you from their doors; I advise you beforehand. They will only be vexed that Niels Helgestad struck the blow, and not themselves. I show you things as they are, and I yet offer you a hand for your benefit," he continued, as he observed Marstrand standing speechless before him, with downcast countenance. "I will buy the Gaard from you with all its appurtenances. I will pay you twenty thousand species cash, deducting the sixteen thousand, and taking in compensation the property as it stands, and discharging all the debts with which it is charged. You can have the four thousand at any moment, to employ as you see fit. You may again resume your merry life in Copenhagen; the experience you have here gained will seem like a dream, and will furnish an interesting topic for narration over the glass, with your bedizzened companions. You can make fun of the old sharper of Lyngenfiord, or profit by what you have here learned."

"I will never return to Copenhagen!" said Marstrand.

"Nuh!" said Helgestad, "you are a considerate man. Here is Paul Petersen, who will put our compact in legal form, before an hour has passed; and it will depend upon you, whether we shall, henceforward, live together in peace and friendship. You have begun the work in the Balself woods, and you may continue it; for which you are admirably capacitated by your ingenuity and intelligence. It will yet cost many a thousand species; but I have a chest, which cannot soon be exhausted.

You can do as you please. You must see that your means were inadequate for such a work."

"I see, too late," replied Marstrand, "how you have led me on, step by step, to this point."

Helgestad smiled. "It is a lesson which will serve you for your whole life. Years hence you will thank me for it; but you may remain here, and supervise the property; I will not haggle about profit and compensation."

The shamelessness with which Helgestad spoke of his own base purposes, and his proposition to allow him to remain as supervisor, drove Marstrand's blood to his brain. But, at the moment he was about to give vent to his indignation, he reflected how fruitless it would be. The old speculator stood before him, with outstretched hand, but with a face of iron, in which nothing could change a feature.

"I cannot give you an answer on the spot," said Marstrand, with an effort. "Taken by surprise, as I have been, I require time for deliberation."

"Nuh!" responded Helgestad, "you have a right to it, and sufficient time until morning. We must not hurry, in good things. We will both consider of the matter. I will not be bound by my proposition."

"If I were in your place," said the secretary to Marstrand, "I would gladly embrace it."

"If you were in my place, Herr Petersen," answered the young man proudly, "you would not submit to injustice. I will, however, remain master in my property, at least until to-morrow; and until then I beg of you to be my guests, and accept of what I have to offer you. Between to-day and to-morrow lies a night, and there is many a slip from the cup to the lip."

He heeded not the laugh of the secretary, and Helgestad's grumble.

"Nuh!" exclaimed the old trader, "we must be patient; do as you think fit, Herr. Much has been accomplished in a single night; but do not suppose that Niels Helgestad will change by morning. To-morrow, as to-day, I will sit at your table."

"I certainly hope so," said Marstrand. "The Balselfgaard is a more secure place than a vessel, from which one, by night, may fall overboard into the sea."

A look, full of hate and unutterable menace, was Helgestad's answer. With his companions, he followed the Gaard proprietor, and occasionally Paul Petersen's croaking voice and loud laughter might be heard behind them. On reaching the house, he ordered a servant to man a boat, and catch some fish; and he held a consultation with the maids in the kitchen, as to the contents of his larder. It was evident there was but little left, and the lateness of the hour rendered it impossible to procure a satisfactory repast for his guests.

Nothing was left to Marstrand, but to make the best apology he could under the circumstances, which was received with jesting and laughter. A few fish were at length obtained; but they were small, and of the commonest kind, and only added to the disappointment of his friends. By way of consolation, Helgestad, after consuming his share of the meat, and lighting his pipe, gave a sketch of the improvements which he intended to introduce at the Gaard. First of all, one of his yachts was to be despatched to the Balsfiord, with a full cargo of provisions and stores: Wingeborg, the Quane, was to be left behind, to provide brooding-places for the birds; and people were to be brought from Orenaes, to build huts for themselves, and to establish a fishery, for which he had already selected locations: Olaf was called upon to give his opinion, and invited to hunt in the Balself valley: an estimate was made of expenses; and the property was spoken of by Helgestad, as if it were in his undisputed possession.

Marstrand listened in gloomy silence. He made no reply to the sneering observations of the secretary; for his thoughts were engrossed with an eager desire to extricate himself from the hands of his betrayer. In the dim obscurity of the room, his eyes burned with an unwonted intensity of expression, and lowered fiercely, from time to time, upon Helgestad's countenance. The hypocritical old sinner appeared to him to be one of the meanest and worst of men. In the pursuit of money, he trampled on honor and conscience; and spared no means, however base, to attain his ends. His long, bony fingers, which were drawn together on the table, like the claws of a wild-cat, would have strangled his son and daughter, had they opposed his will; and his remorseless face would not have changed a single feature, if, from desperation and shame, Marstrand had seized his gun, and blown his brains out on the spot.

The deceived young man was well convinced of all this, and that he had no chance of changing the mind of his oppressor. Helgestad was right in declaring that all the speculating fish-traders would laugh at and jeer him if he should make public his complaints. He knew no one of whom he could expect anything better; and in his more sober moments he reflected that Helgestad only followed the universal custom of the country, that he acted upon principles which he had often proclaimed aloud, and that the greatest fault was committed by himself in not giving heed to the various hints and admonitions which he had so frequently received.

His anxiety, however, grew more intense to frustrate the designs of Helgestad; and he felt as if he could even sell himself to the arch-fiend to be delivered from his difficulties. All his thoughts were now directed to one point, the finding of the only man who could assist him — Afraja!

The mysterious figure of the old sorcerer hovered before his eyes. When he looked at Helgestad he saw the head of the Lapp suspended over the table; at Paul Petersen's laugh the misshapen greybeard, crouching in the corner, totteringly raised himself up, and over Olaf's broad shoulders he extended his little withered arm. Marstrand could scarcely wait until his guests were ready to retire to the humble chamber prepared for them.

"Nuh," said Helgestad, "it is an old saying, 'as one is

bedded, so he sleeps.' You have given us hard beds, Herr, but our sleep, for that reason, shall be more sound and healthful. I wish you such a night as the holy Olaf had. He went to sleep surrounded with enemies; but when he awoke, they were all subdued."

"I believe," responded Marstrand, "that such predictions are verified when it is God's will."

"Nuh!" said the old man, "you are of a pious disposition, and you have a friend in Klaus, to whom many wonders have come to pass. I would advise you, however, not to dream, but to hold fast to Niels Helgestad's hand."

"Ask to-morrow what I will do," replied the vexed young man, as he withdrew; "to-night I will be master in my house."

A shout of laughter rang after him. "Let him for one night more dream of the money-bags which the Balsfiord was to yield," said Paul Petersen; "to-morrow we will eject him, and then he may look out for a house wherever he chooses."

Marstrand threw himself in the chair where Helgestad had sat, and waited an hour without moving; but this hour seemed an eternity. He constantly muttered to himself the words which Afraja had spoken to him: "Go to the hillock under which the wicked voigt lies whom Jubinal crushed; ascend the stone, and softly pronounce my name, as when Syda, the wind God, dances over the surface of the young grass. Wherever Afraja may be, he will hear you!" He had, originally, secretly made light of this solemn injunction of the sorcerer; but now, with all his heart, he wished Afraja might listen to his summons, and lead him to some divinity who protected the oppressed in their darkest hour of need. His faith was weak and distracted by a thousand doubts, notwithstanding his proudly-spoken words to Helgestad. How could Afraja know that Helgestad was at Balsfiord? And if he should appear, how could this old man immediately procure such a quantity of money? Probably he possessed it, and possibly it was his wish, out of hatred to Helgestad, and good-will to the man who had rendered him a service, to give it to him. Afraja's silver must certainly be buried in the far wilderness; and before it could be dug out of the rock and swamp, all would be over. And what danger was connected with Afraja's money gift? No one durst know that a free man — a Christian — a person of pure blood, had borrowed of a Lapp. Marstrand himself, pressing as was his need, felt that now in particular, when the animosity against the Lapps was greater than ever, it would be impossible openly to acknowledge the aid of the sorcerer without being regarded as a plague-contaminated person.

Engrossed in these reflections, he quietly slipped out of the house, and descended to the fiord to seek his last helper. It was deep night; heavy leaden clouds hung over the *Wasser-spalt*, which lay dark and motionless in its rocky bed. No fish leaped, not a star was to be seen, no sound to be heard; and it required no little caution to be able to walk without a light on the pathless edge of the fiord, among the rocks and broken stones. Marstrand's eyes were, however, excellent, and as much accustomed to darkness as his flexible body to great exertions. After an hour, he stood on the *bucht*, into which the rock-strewn bottom opened, in which Paul Petersen's grandfather had met his fate; after climbing over the wall of rock which closed up the the entrance of the valley, he found himself at the hillock of huge stones, composing the grave of the cruel voigt. The tall firs which had grown upon it hung down with their dark branches to the earth, and with the bushes and briars canopied over this chamber of the dead. Their gnarled labyrinth made an impenetrable darkness; and as Marstrand, with beating heart, entered this mysterious enclosure, he heard the hollow sigh and moaning of the wind through the top of the trees.

With firm steps, he wound his way through these obstacles,

gliding over the smooth moss, and climbing from stone to stone, until he at last attained the summit of this mass of rubbish, capped by a huge rock. Here, he breathed alone in the midst of the wildest solitude, separated from all living things; under him were the shattered remains of the dead, which would repose there to the last day, while his wandering spirit affrighted the fishermen of the fiord.

A deep depression of spirits came over the young adventurer. "It is not the dead that I fear," said he, to himself, "it is the living who drive me to madness. Who would wait for me here, in such a night? But even a wise man, hanging over an abyss, grasps after his amulet, and pronounces a witch-spell. What avails the wisdom of the wise, when it cannot procure help? Either God's angel, or the devil's comrade, will appear to me. Let us see, old sorcerer, what you can do."

"Afraja! I call you!" he said, in a slightly contemptuous tone, twice repeating the name.

"Here am I!" responded a voice from the other side of the valley, followed by a rush of stones from the mountain side. It seemed as if a figure arose from the earth, through a fissure in the granite rock.

Courageous as Marstrand was, he could not resist the impression of this overpowering, mysterious vision. A shudder came over him, his hair stood on end, his tongue cleaved to the roof of his mouth, and his eyes glared wildly. He thought of the ghost of the voigt. It seemed to him that lightning flashed through the trees, that the earth shook under him, and that a strange breathing issued from its depths.

"You called me," resumed the voice. "Are you afraid?"

"No," answered Marstrand; "are you Afraja?"

"I am," said the Lapp. "Sit down by me, give me your hand."

Cold, slender fingers grasped Marstrand's right hand. He heard the hoarse laugh, which he knew, close by his ear; he thought he perceived the bright little eyes of the sorcerer, glittering through the deep darkness.

"Tell me, what drives you to me?" spoke Afraja; "I was far off when you called. I came, because Jubinal willed it."

"If you have such power, you will also know why I am here."

"You say it," was Afraja's answer after a long pause. "In this darkness I see into your heart, I know your thoughts, nothing is concealed from me. A wolf sleeps in your gamme, who digs his teeth in your flesh, and has driven you out in the night. When the day dawns to-morrow, he will tear you to pieces."

"I am come, that he may not succeed," replied Marstrand. "I seek your help, Afraja. If it be true that you are willing to protect me, prove it now. Procure me money, that I may satisfy Helgestad. Upon my honor! by all that is holy, I will give it back to you."

Afraja suffered some time to elapse, before he inquiringly answered—"How much do you want?"

"A large sum!" exclaimed the younker; "but I know that you can give it, if you choose. Helgestad requires sixteen thousand species of me; but I have a credit in my favor, for the fish which he sold on my account in Bergen."

"Sixteen thousand!" muttered the old man. "It is a great deal of money. Sixteen thousand! If I give it to you, what will you promise?"

"You require a high interest, I believe. Eight per cent. is the customary rate; yet ask what you please. As true as God helps me, I will pay it!"

"I want no interest!" exclaimed Afraja, in a hoarse laugh. "I am not a Lyngenfiord trader, an usurer, or a voigt."

"If you will take no interest," asked Marstrand, "what will you have then? mortgage-bond on the Gaard?"

"Your bond is of no use to me, and I do not want your Gaard. No one must know of my silver, and your word; but you must pledge it to me. Will you?'

"What security is my word?"

"But little, young man, but little! Promise me that you will come, when I call you."

"Whither?" asked Marstrand.

"You will learn."

"And then—what more do you ask?"

"Nothing farther," said Afraja, as he appeared to meditate for a minute. "Give me your hand. Swear to me that you will come, when I send for you."

"I swear it."

"In Jubinal's name!" murmured the Lapp. "Call upon him."

The Christian young man hesitated to call on the pagan divinity; but he overcame his reluctance. "Good," said he, "if you believe that you are thereby better secured—in Jubinal's name, then!"

"He will help you, young man. He is mighty, as you will learn."

"But say now," said Marstrand, in an urgent tone, "how shall I obtain the money? You know that I must pay it at break of day. Have you it here?"

"No," was the answer.

"No? Where then? Speak, Afraja; where is it?"

The Lapp stirred not. The stars which broke through the clouds revealed the outlines of his bent form. Marstrand extended his hand to him, and, in an anxious tone, said, "You cannot deceive me; so come then, and show me the place where I shall find you."

"Listen to me, young man," muttered the sorcerer; "listen and trust. Return to your house; look neither to the right nor left; sleep quietly till morning; Jubinal will stand by you. When Helgestad requests his money, go with him to your writing-desk; yet do not open this before — mark it well — before the insatiable man stands by you. Then say to him, 'You shall have what you desire;' grasp within, in Jubinal's name, and you will find what you want. Now go, and think on your promise."

"How?" exclaimed Marstrand, in angry surprise; "must I believe this? Is this your help? — Do not trifle with me, old man; no juggling tricks. Where is the money? You have buried it in this mound; but, wherever it may be, you shall not go until you confess the truth!"

He grasped anew at the place where Afraja was sitting, but he seized only the hard stone.—"Where are you?" he shouted in desperation. "Answer, deceiver, liar! You mock me!—Oh, fool that I was, to believe you!"

"Trust!" whispered a hollow voice, which appeared to issue from the tomb behind him. A gust of wind swept through the darkness of the firs; a light glimmer, as a flash of lightning, broke over the solitary hillock; and above, upon the peak of the rocks, Marstrand thought he discerned a tall and powerful figure, enveloped in a great-coat, with a Danish hat on the head.

An insupportable terror seized him. The night, the solitude, hell with its kobolds and demons, set his hair on end, and bewildered his brain. He jumped down over the rocks and ruins, pursued by a loud shout of echoing laughter.

CHAPTER XVII.

It was an anxious, sad night for the abandoned man. When the morning dawned, he was sitting sleepless and motionless in a chair by the table, staring at the writing-desk in the corner He had returned without being observed; but ten times at least in every hour had he jumped up, seized the key, and laid his hand on the writing-desk; and yet he had not opened it. He did not believe in Afraja's witchcraft, yet he dared not despise it. The superstitious credulity by which even fearless men and heroes in danger were attacked, excited his imagination.

His ruin or salvation depended upon the question whether the writing-desk contained the money or not; and around this point revolved all his speculations and doubts. Now it seemed to him a perfect folly to entertain any hope whatever; and then again he deemed it improbable that Afraja would so shamefully deceive him.

"What hinders me from opening the desk, and ascertaining if I am deceived? Why should I wait for the sneering laugh of the miserable secretary? If the heavy, hard silver is indeed there, it will not disappear; if it is as empty as I think it is, nothing will certainly enter it before morning."

The more his judgment attempted to assert its rights, the stronger were his secret fears and hopes. The old man, with great knowledge of human nature, had fixed his conditions and injunctions; and at last the morning came without any attempt on the part of Marstrand to violate them.

Exhausted by so much care and anxiety, he had fallen asleep, when Helgestad opened the door of the chamber and entered. The reflection of the red morning light shone upon the countenance of the young man, with a peaceful and happy effect. His long light brown hair flowed over the shoulders of the arm-chair, as he reclined at full length; he breathed quietly, and a smile of contentment overspread his features.

"He is dreaming," said Niels, "and I would not awake him. He looks different from when I first saw him. He was then full-bodied, rotund and soft-featured. In a short time he has grown lean, and his face has sharpened, and all for nothing!"

He leaned over him, and drew back as the brow of the sleeper contracted, and his countenance assumed a sombre expression. — "He observes that I am standing by him, "he whispered, with his hard smile; "it will soon be worse with him, but I cannot yield. It is a long-prepared and studied work. It is not my business to catch a fish and then throw it into the sea."—He turned to the door, at which Paul made his appearance, and pointed with his finger to Marstrand.

"Wake him up!" said the secretary; "it is time."

"He has certainly had a hard night," whispered Helgestad.

"And a harder day consequently awaits us," exclaimed Paul Petersen aloud. "There comes the boat with the officers; I see *Lovman* Gulick at the helm. We have no time to lose, if we will finish by noon."

"I will yet once more try kindness," said Helgestad, shaking Marstrand by the arm.

The latter opened his eyes, and stared wildly around.

"You come from another world, Herr," said Niels; "but you are yet here in Balselfgaard. Look around; it is nothing else. There is the morning for which the living must provide, until they die.

"You have had time enough for reflection," he continued, as he received no answer; "many think they have time enough, but time comes and goes, even though we do nothing. You are a man, Herr Marstrand, that thinks understandingly of matters. You see clearly what must happen. Women cry and wring their hands; but men weep not, and avoid useless words. I repeat my proposition of yesterday. You may remain, if you choose, and help me; you will not repent of it. If you decline it, go; but you must not go with empty hands. There is the boat with the voigt's officers, in which you can proceed to Tromsöe; I will myself provide you with an opportunity of reaching Trondheim or Bergen. You have made a good business, you have acquired some experience, and I hope we separate as friends. Is it not so?"

He extended his hand, which, however, Marstrand did not take. He looked frowningly before him, and his lips were firmly set together with a contemptuous expression.

"Will you, or will you not?" asked Helgestad.

"The younker desires it not!" said Petersen. "There is

Lovman Gulick, with the two officers. The time for negotiating is past, Niels; let the law take its course."

The *Gerichtsvoigt* came forward; a little, broad-shouldered man, in a long official coat, a laced hat, and with the coat of arms on his breast. Behind him were his two companions.

"Look there, Herr Marstrand," said Niels. "Those are the officers of justice, who have come to perform their duty. They may attach all your property, and can even put you in arrest, if it does not cover your debt. I again offer you, for the last time, my proposition of compromise. Accept it, for you have no other means of escape."

"Do you think so?" replied Marstrand, rising up. "I will not dispute with you, Herr Helgestad, nor utter reproaches or complaints; for I know I might as well attempt to move the woods of Balself. You say I have no alternative but that which you propose. We shall see. Have you my bond and the security-bond of Bergen at hand? Let me see them."

Helgestad looked at him as upon a man who had suddenly lost his reason.

"Nuh!" said he, "you want to see my evidence. Come here, *Lovman* Gulick. Here is the bond for six thousand species, received in cash; and here is the other, of over two thousand, for wares and stores. The name is subscribed. I trust you will not deny it?"

"Certainly not," responded the younker. "I acknowledge the debt, as well as the security granted me in Bergen; but, as I have a credit with Fandrem, the half, at least, will be liquidated by the proceeds of my sale of fish; and I cannot possibly, therefore, pay Niels Helgestad the whole sum."

"A security must be covered when it is required," added Paul Petersen.

"By no means, Herr," said the *Lovman;* "the security must only be covered when the bail sees no means of indemnifying himself. If Herr Marstrand cannot pay, and his *hof* is seized, the security falls into the general debt; if he remain in possession, it must first be shown if he cannot satisfy the claims against him."

"Nuh!" said Helgestad; "it is a dispute about the king's beard (about trifles). We will not insist upon the reimbursement of the security-bond of Balself. I am well-disposed to you, and you shall not say that I am a hard man. I offer you, here, before the *Gerichtsvoigt*, once again, twenty thousand species. I will pay your debt in Bergen, and satisfy myself with the product of your fish-sale. That will make, in all, twelve thousand species, and I will pay you eight thousand in cash."

"Accept it," said Gulick, who spoke as a friend; "it is the best. A word is a word."

"A word is a word! You have heard it," exclaimed Helgestad. "Take your pen, Paul Petersen, and write it down."

"Wait a moment!" interrupted Marstrand. "And, if I pay you the sum which I owe you, what further have you to ask?"

"Nuh!" said Helgestad; "I prefer my money as I have given it. I have nothing to say to the contrary, if you can pay it."

"You shall have, then, what you desire!" said Marstrand; and, with the key in his hand, he went up to the desk. His heart beat violently, and his limbs trembled. "Help me, mighty Jubinal!" he ejaculated to himself, and his trouble instantly changed to joy.

As a dreamer who suddenly finds a great treasure, he beheld, in the deep chest, a row of tolerably large bags, standing close together. They were made of reindeer-leather, appeared to be quite new, and were bound round with thongs. On every bag the number one thousand was distinctly written.

He hardly knew, at first, whether it was truth and reality, or a trick and a delusion. He was agitated by contending emotions of doubt and hope, joy and fear. He clutched the first bag with his hand, as if he feared he might lose it; he then took it out and threw it on the table, so that the silver rang again. When he heard this sound, his nerves shook; and when he looked on Helgestad and the secretary, his heart swelled with unwonted delight; for both these persons, struck with surprise, gazed at the treasure in speechless amazement.

"Take your money, Herr Helgestad," said Marstrand, with as much composure as he could muster; "here it is. Eight bags, each containing a thousand species, all counted. *Lovman* Gulick, I call you to witness that I have satisfied the bond, and am discharged from every obligation."

"A knife here!" cried Helgestad, tearing the cord.

Marstrand cut through the knot, the bag opened, and the silver thalers lay there, as smooth and bright, as if they had just issued from the mint.

Helgestad seized some of them, and let them fall. "It is all right," said he; "it is silver, beyond a doubt."

"They are made of reindeer skin," added Petersen, as he examined the bags. "This is the best specimen of Lappish workmanship that I have ever seen. Princess Gula cannot sew more elegantly."

"It is not my business to ask from whence you obtained it," said the trader. "Count them, and take the bond."

This operation was soon performed, and all was found to be correct. Helgestad touched thousand after thousand, and no one said a word more. Every one seemed to be occupied with his reflections, and these all concurred in the certainty of the fact which Petersen had maliciously suggested.

The cold, morose countenances of the bystanders, from time to time, turned with redoubled mistrust to the young Gaard proprietor; when he had finished the count, he tore the bond to pieces; and approaching the kind-hearted *Gerichtsvoigt*, took him by the hand.

"I wish to express to you my thanks for your assistance," said Marstrand; "and for all time to come I call you to witness that I have extinguished the debt."

"It is my duty, Herr Marstrand," answered the official, "to look after the right. The affair is concluded; Niels Helgestad has declared he has no further demand against you; and I can, consequently, return to Tromsöe."

"But not before you have sat at my table," rejoined Marstrand. "My housekeeping has not been very liberally conducted; but I will take better care of it in future."

The men were hungry and tired, and the invitation to breakfast was not, therefore, to be despised. The *Lovman* said nothing; and Marstrand went out to see what he could hunt up. There was almost nothing in the house on the preceding day, so he had but little expectation of anything eatable; but it would have been a shame not to have invited them to remain. He now had much money in his chest. He had paid sixteen bags; but he would joyfully have given one of them for a full larder. He anxiously unbolted the door of his provision-room, to observe its empty shelves; but if he was ever grateful to Afraja, he had increased reason to be so now. There lay a great leg of reindeer meat, carefully cooked, and packed up in fresh leaves; also several of the little, savory cheeses, a bundle of moorhens, and three huge loaves of bread.

The sorcerer had carried his beneficent foresight, in this instance, to a great extent; Marstrand eagerly ran to call the maids, delivered to them the mutton and cheese, to be warmed in the oven, ordered coffee to be prepared, milk to be procured, and the table to be set.

While he was occupied in these active preparations, his guests, whose society he had not courted, were engaged in endeavoring to discover some explanation of the strange solution of his difficulties.

The two companions of the *Lovman* were enjoying themselves in the sunshine, before the house; the other three, however, remained sitting at the table in the stuga, discussing the subject in all its aspects.

The costs of the judicial expedition from Tromsöe were not inconsiderable; Helgestad had them to pay.

"It may be," he said; "I do not know; but I would never have believed it."

"You have been too quick," answered Gulick, with a slight smile.

The trader gave him a sudden side-look. "Rashness has never been a fault of mine," he murmured. "I have always had my rights in view; but as I saw no safety in this enterprise, I wished to get back mine own."

"You have got it," said Gulick.

"But from what source has the blessing been derived?" asked Paul Petersen.

"There was not certainly, yesterday, a hundred dollars in the whole house; and now there is a pretty number of full bags in the chest. Where did he get them from? Who is the fool that lent them to him? Who meddles in Niels Helgestad's affairs? It was not a Norman, or a neighbor. A man of practical sense would not place so much money in the hands of a Danish adventurer, to be wasted upon his senseless projects. There is no one in the vicinity who would lend it to him. I know of only one who can, and who may have done it out of malice and hatred; one who contrives evil, but who, indeed, does not give without expecting some good service in return."

Gulick nodded assent, but he inquired who was meant.

"Oh!" said the secretary, "you know as well as I. Who else can it be but Afraja? This Danish younker and the pastor Hornemann have for some time been in secret alliance with the old sorcerer, who must be burned as a terrifying example. There is treason in it, I am certain. The pastor, for years back, has made reports to the government in favor of the Lapps. He raises a great clamor about every little event; letters of complaint and menace against the voigts and sorenskrivers come from Copenhagen and Trondheim; and only a few days since, a letter has been received from General Munte, filled with complaints of cruelty and injustice, with the assurance that the old blade will come in person, or send a commissioner to restore order."

Gulick seemed indifferent. "The Herr may say what he will," said he, "but the pastor is an agitator; and if it were true that the Dane had contracted a secret alliance with the Lapps to harass us, he should be expelled from the country."

"Nuh!" said Helgestad; "signs enough have been given us. A Dane is never a Norman; he is as fanciful on the subject of rights and laws as the pastor himself."

"I cannot, however, yet bring myself to believe it," said Gulick. "A Lapp would suffer his hand to be cut off before he would draw a species from his pocket; and a man of good blood would never debase himself by accepting it from him, even in his worst extremity."

"Money is money," replied the trader; "silver does not smell of the source from which it springs. But Paul Petersen is right; there must be treason brewing when the old scoundrel opens his money-pots. It is the duty of all of us to protect ourselves against ruin."

The maids now entered with coffee, dishes, and the table-cover, and immediately afterwards followed bread and meat, and finally Marstrand himself, with some glasses and bottles.

"Take heart, gentlemen," he said; "it is not much that I have to offer you, and I know you are accustomed to better fare. Accept it, however, as a proof of my good will."

Helgestad was too good a judge of the juicy meat not to enjoy it. He took his knife and cut off two large slices, saying: "Such tender and lovely meat is a rarity, Herr Marstrand. You have found means over-night to stock your chests and larder most abundantly."

"For such guests," said the *Gaardherr*, "one must do the best he can."

"I hope," said Helgestad, with a laugh, "it will not turn out as with the honey-combs mentioned in revelation. They tasted deliciously, but they were followed by the stomach-ache."

"I hope not, and here is a bottle of old Port, which is a sovereign antidote against all such complaints."

"Meat and drink," said Helgestad, "are the gifts of God. I take my glass, Herr Marstrand, and drink to your success in all good things."

The conversation now took a general turn, and the rich fare seemed to have produced a favorable influence upon the guests. Helgestad said that it would give him pleasure if the enterprising settler should succeed in completing his work; although he himself had lost all pleasure in it, yet he did not wish it said that he did not believe in its success. He sought to excuse himself for his proceedings with the declaration "that every one should look after, and endeavor to save his property when he considered it in danger. But you know that from the first day when you entered this country I proffered you my assistance, and I hope to live to see you do me justice."

There was no use in a fruitless dispute, and Marstrand, therefore, replied in a conciliatory manner; and as one word suggested another, a kind of treaty of peace was at last concluded, the articles of which were arranged to suit each person's notions.

"I hope, Herr Helgestad," said Marstrand, "that I shall never forget my just indebtedness to you. You have had some cause to be dissatisfied with me, for the Gaard has been neglected. I have failed to accomplish all for want of strength and hands. But I hope soon, with God's help, to set my wood business in order, and then the mansion and dependencies will be put in good condition. My property is large, and has many sources of wealth, and my means are sufficient to develop them."

"You have found a rich partner," rejoined Helgestad. "Is it not so?"

'You may be right," smiled Marstrand.

"Nuh!" exclaimed the trader, turning to the secretary;

"there is probably some business for you to arrange by a written contract."

"It cannot be concealed with whom you, Herr Marstrand, have entered into partnership," said Paul; "and great surprise will be excited throughout the country when these facts shall be divulged. It would, indeed, be to your benefit if you would give some information on the subject; or is it a secret, Herr Marstrand, that must not be revealed?"

"I do not see the necessity of my being as communicative as you desire," said Marstrand. "The man who received me in my great need, and saved me from the shame of being cast out of my house, wishes, for the present at least, to remain unknown."

"Is he, however, a good Christian?" said the secretary, jestingly.

"Better than many who bear the name, and whose conduct belies their professions," said Marstrand, rising up, for he felt the blood mounting to his head, and as at that moment also, a noise was heard from without, which attracted his attention.

He was followed by all, for it was the voice of Egede, the Quane, that was heard. The uncouth fellow with his short-legged dogs, which had been searching around about the house, was relating something to the justice, officers, and workmen, amid a volley of curses and threats.

The first word that Marstrand heard was Mortuno's name.

"Look here," said Egede; "he stood here. See how my dog tracked him step by step. Mortuno was here, so sure as I am the son of my father! Here is the entire print of his kommager in the soft earth. This is a Lappish foot, and I know the rascal by his large heel."

"Seek him! Take him!" cried a couple of laughing voices.

"If I had him, the murderer!" replied Egede, doubling up his fists, "he should never prowl around another house. But there he is above there, where my dog stands and barks; the devil himself will not take him now."

"Nuh!" said Helgestad, "what's the uproar? Have Lapps been here?"

"Yes, Herr," said the Quane. "Three reindeer stood in the bushes, eating leaves, and round here the grass is trodden down."

"How long can it have been?" asked Paul.

"Not eight hours," replied Egede, "for the grass has not sprung up again, and the tracks are fresh."

"Were the animals loaded?" continued the secretary.

"Heavily laden," cried Egede, "otherwise their feet could not have made such a deep impression; but, Herr, he who led them to and fro between this place and the house six times, was no other than the accursed scoundrel, Mortuno."

"Pshaw! Egede," laughed Paul, "you will not insinuate that Herr Marstrand receives nightly visits from the Lapps. They could bring him anything they pleased—fat reindeer hams, or bags full of silver."

Marstrand cast an angry look at the secretary. "I despise your jest," he said, "but put a guard on your tongue in my house."

"Why deny your friends and helpers?" exclaimed Paul. "That is not becoming in an honorable gentleman. What is there to conceal? Mortuno made you a visit, and three reindeer brought the silver treasure; Niels Helgestad is paid; what you have promised in return, is your affair. Good morning, *Lovman* Gulick—happy voyage! Greet my uncle; I will myself come to Tromsöe. Bring the horses, and let us depart. Where Lapps make secret alliances, I will no more set foot—where a cut-throat like this Mortuno finds protection and friendship, no Norman can any more sit down to table. There comes Olaf!" he exclaimed, as he saw the Nordlander approaching from the shore of the fiord. "Ho! Olaf! what a pity you were not here! Mortuno was; probably he wanted to see your new hat; you have missed much, my dear fellow. I will tell you, on the way, a merry story of how debts are paid by professing Christian men."

"It is difficult to believe," said Helgestad; "and it grieves me to go away with an evil opinion of you. Mortuno has fallen under the ban of the law; he made a murderous attack on Olaf, and is a wicked wight, whom every good man should arrest, wherever he can find him. But it really seems as if you had held intercourse with him and Afraja, whom everybody curses."

"I have no answer to make to such accusations," said the young man.

"It is an affair from which you must exculpate yourself, and it is more serious than you suppose," replied Niels. "The Lapps are brooding mischief in their mountains; and a court-day will soon be holden, to gather evidence. No Norman, humble as he may be, will trust a man who holds intercourse with his worst enemies; no one will believe him, nor even eat his bread. It may be, also, Herr Marstrand, that you may have to deal with judges and the law; give your word, therefore, that you have seen as little of the heathen sorcerer, as of the scoundrel Mortuno."

"I will speak before the judge and law, if necessary; but I will not tolerate constraint. Many things in this world, Herr Helgestad, are regarded as right and honorable, which are knavish and dishonest; I shudder when I observe the judges who are appointed to administer justice, in good and evil report, in this country."

"Go then with those of whom you hope better things," said Helgestad; without speaking another word, he caused the horses to be brought, packed up his money and effects, and departed from the Gaard with Paul and his serving-men.

The *Lovman* had also gone off in his boat, and Olaf was the last, who went out of the house, after he had gathered together his hunting-tackle and gun.

"And will you also, Olaf, leave me, as a stranger," asked Marstrand, as the former, in a sullen and proud manner, strode by him.

Olaf halted, and set down his gun. "Know," said he, "that to-day, when all were asleep, I went out to hold counsel with myself. I would not be a witness of the manner in which you were treated. Were you an innocent sufferer, I would have taken a stand for you, and would not have tolerated it; I even would have thrown money away for you, as little as I sympathise with your follies. You are inexperienced, however, and your credulity has been abused. But you are false, and have betrayed me."

"How did I do it?" exclaimed Marstrand. "I let Mortuno run; and I said nothing of him to you, because I did not wish to vex you."

"I speak not of the scoundrel," said Olaf. "Can you look me in the eyes, without shame?"

"There is nothing to prevent me."

"You are a Dane, and you know how to dissemble," answered Olaf. "No one on earth knew how I felt but you, to whom I told it. I complained to you of my trouble about Ilda; and you—you, yourself, went to Lyngenfiord to play a dishonorable game. You employed all kinds of artifices, you bemoaned about your love until she repelled you from her, as she ought to have done; and I—I was working and providing for you, while you were protesting your vows of love. Do you deny it? do you yet dare to say no?"

"I do not deny it," said Marstrand, "for I loved her, and love her yet, Olaf, although I have ceased to hope. But I have not betrayed you. I know not how to conciliate you; yet can you be angry that I love a woman, whom you love, and who has listened to neither of us? Can you hate me that I found words, when my heart spoke, and when looks told me I was understood?"

"You lie!" cried Olaf in a passion; "Ilda never lifted up her eyes on you. Vain as you are, you dreamed from mere fancy, and you betrayed me." He lifted up his arm with a wild, murderous look. "Do not come in my way, or you may rue it, and never speak of me, as of a friend—my hand shall be against you, wherever I meet you!"

With these words, he proceeded to meet Helgestad, who awaited him on the heights of the ridge that encompassed the fiord. The latter then mounted his gray horse, and looked down upon the valley beneath. His countenance was full of hate, and as he surveyed the woods and the elf, he broke out into a fierce laugh; "My efforts ought not to have been in vain," he muttered, "I must yet have the Balsfiord. What will the fool do with it? I will sing another song with him, and it will be one which will suit him better."

CHAPTER XVIII.

THE caravan reached the Lyngenfiord by evening. Helgestad had had an understanding with his stepson and Olaf, to pass over in silence these events, as not suitable for female ears. It was also suggested that the Danish younker was much too sweet a little heart not to have left behind him a sympathising remembrance.

"You know well, how maidens are," said he, "they love a smooth face and a lisping speech; he who can the most politely address them, is the surest to win. You must admit that the Dane understands such like things better than I or you, Olaf, as well as Paul himself, refined and well-bred as he may be."

The secretary merely smiled, and said; "The end praises

the master; practical success, the man. I shall trouble myself but little about the sighing and lisping of the Danish younker. In a few weeks my marriage takes place, and my house in Tromsöe is in order; but he shall be driven from the land, and if he falls into my hands, as I hope he will, he will have no reason to complain of a want of politeness on my part."

"Have you prepared a plan?" asked Niels, as they rode together, Olaf being some distance ahead.

"More than one," answered Paul, "and"—he continued with an expressive look—"it is precisely the same as your own."

"So," said Helgestad, with a grumble, "do you also know my thoughts?"

"Exactly," said his companion. "Hold on to the security. It will be useful to us. I think it will not be long before we have brought the younker, whom we both love so tenderly, to a place where no sorcerer can help him."

"Will you do him bodily injury?"

"By no means," said the secretary, laughing; "I will defend his body and immortal soul from all harm. He shall, moreover, remain near his friends, from whom I do not wish to separate him."

"Nuh!" murmured Helgestad, "look well to it; you are upon a road the end of which is not very clear to me."

"The end must be as we fashion it," said Paul. "I have already made an agreement with my uncle in advance. We must take the birds as they are fledged. Let the Lapps carry out their intentions; disturb them not; do not threaten them more, but be as friendly as you can. In three weeks, the great market begins; when they descend from their rocks and deserts to buy winter provisions. On that occasion, we can seek out the rams which we desire to get possession of."

"You will not take Afraja so easily," responded Niels.

"No," said the secretary, "we must fetch the cunning old rascal. We have no soldiers, but we do not want in strong arms and legs. I have already quietly spoken with a number of resolute men, who are ready to assist us, and we can reckon on several more."

Helgestad, with an approving smile, replied, "Look well to what you do."

"Certainly," said Paul; "I have my own spies among the Lapps. I know a fellow who will give me accurate information of the hiding-place of the wolf; and I hope soon to make him a proper visit. A hunting-party!" he exclaimed, laughing, "with Björnarne and Olaf, upon the Kilpis. There he lies concealed. We will track him to his gamme, and I hope to manage it so that he will not escape."

Niels nodded approvingly. "And then the younker," he said; "you will have them both at one haul."

"The fire which burns the sorcerer, will at least," said Paul, "singe his skin and hair."

Helgestad grew serious at these words. "Do not drive matters too far. A Lapp is a creature which may be whipped to death, or be thrown into the fiord with a stone around his neck, without creating much sympathy for his fate. The younker, however, has a voice which reaches far over the water. He may be driven out of the land by the jeers of his equals; but friends will arise to shield him from harm."

"Have no fears," said the secretary; "where are they who could help him? Who assisted the fool who boarded your ship around the rocks of Silden?—and yet he was a younker."

"Hush!" said Helgestad, morosely. "I preserved my life and property from a robber."

"It is a question if that will be believed if an accuser proceeds against you. I would not like to be in your position if they bring you before the criminal court at Copenhagen. You are, however, four hundred miles distant; and no accusation could be made here, but by this Marstrand or Hannah. You have the maiden safe enough; and we must, on that account, deprive him of the power of working mischief."

"What will you do with him?" asked Helgestad.

"With him? What is done with a traitor?"

"Nuh!" exclaimed the trader, in astonishment.

"This is the way," softly continued the secretary, "to securely place the Balsfiord in your hands, and to free us from all apprehension. The impudent younker must be condemned as an arch traitor, and then we will send him to Trondheim in chains, with all the proceedings pertaining to the case, or not, as we please. You must come forward with your security-claim. No one will come to dispute the property and rights of Paul Petersen's father-in-law. Say nothing of it. The matter is well considered, and I will bet my neck that you have calculated in a like manner."

"You have an eye," replied Helgestad, amid the laughter of his companion, "which penetrates the inmost secrets of the heart. I have thought of it, and must say that we are of the same way of thinking. Seize the accursed sorcerer, and force a confession from him which we can make use of."

"I verily believe," said Paul, "my uncle has already, for this purpose, set up the old thumb-screw again, and has had it repainted and repaired."

"He does well," continued Niels; "and Afraja will open his mouth and become communicative touching his silver treasure in the wilderness. You have to-day seen a specimen of the riches of the old villain."

Paul Petersen's eyes sparkled with mirth as he said, "It is curious how closely we agree in our views and thoughts."

Helgestad offered his hand, which the secretary grasped in return. They said nothing more, but regarded each other with a friendly expression, and yet there was no love or truth between them in the depths of their hearts.

They were joyfully received at the Gaard, and Hannah brought a letter, which had just arrived from Tromsöe. It was from her father; after repeated coquettish denials, she permitted it to be read. The Guildmeister had heard, with genuine pleasure, that not only the air of Lyngenfiord was beneficial to her, but that she had also become deeply attached to her beloved Björnarne. "I always expected this," the letter ran; "and I now learn from your confession, as well as from Helgestad and other sources, that your affection for the rare treasure is extraordinarily great. I may come to the wedding, Hannah, if my legs are better; but I can scarcely, any more, get up and down the Signal-becken; and I shall be obliged to procure a carryall, which brings all kinds of expenses. But I should be as glad as a king to see you here, and if it gets too late in the autumn for you to return, to keep you and my handsome son-in-law at home with me here the winter through. Embrace him for me: your brother Christi can, probably, go to the wedding; but, at all events, he will come to the celebration of it in Bergen; and Helgestad also must spare no pains to be present at the festivity. You have money enough, Hannah; you are Uve Fandrem's daughter; and there is so much lying in my chests for you, that Björnarne will be envied by everybody. I will load his yacht full with the best that I have — chests, and boxes, and costly furniture; you, yourself, however, are the choicest of all my possessions; and I know that Björnarne loves you as the most precious blessing on earth."

At these fatherly remarks, Helgestad raised his eyes, and beheld his son entering the room, who had also heard the reading of the concluding words. Hannah went up to him, and drew him nearer.

"I can confirm what my father writes," said she. "Björnarne loves me as much as I do him."

"Right! maiden!" exclaimed Helgestad; "it is a woman's duty to shield man, and hold him to her heart. It is scarcely three weeks yet to the great market; and in one week after that, your marriage will take place. Then, in God's name, you may go down to Bergen, and pass the winter, if you choose, in the house on the German bridge. It will do the fellow good to live among the fine people, and he can deck himself out like a swallow on its flight to the south; before the summer comes when he hears, at night, the cry of the sailors from the Lofodden, he will long to return to his Norwegian home."

The time whiled away in such conversation. Björnarne was as quiet as ever, and soon sought to escape the approaches of his bride: he went out with Paul to show him the various preparations made for the Lappish market. Helgestad spoke of Marstrand in general terms, and that he had found him well; and he appealed to Olaf as a witness of his wonderful activity, which promised to be so productive.

The Nordlander could not deny this; but he had not much skill in the art of dissembling. His answers were short and blunt, and his whole demeanor evidenced that there was something wrong with him.

An understanding between Paul and Björnarne ensued, as soon as they found themselves alone in the warehouse. Björnarne passionately seized his friend's arm, and with a bitter, desperate expression of countenance, said, "I cannot bear it any longer; happen what may, I cannot endure it. Help me, Paul, for you are the only one to whom I can appeal for aid. Two days had not elapsed, after your departure, before I discovered how miserable I was. She was by my side from morning till night; and as she recognised the anxious state of my mind, she never ceased to speak, as if in mockery, of our future life."

"You should have rewarded her tenderness," replied the secretary. "Why did you not follow my advice?"

"Because it was impossible for me!" exclaimed Björnarne. "There is something about her, I know not what, that impels me to shrink back with aversion, when she lays her hand upon me."

"And yet it is a fine, delicate hand, you fool," said Paul, laughing. "Far and near, you could not find a lovelier one."

"Believe me," said Björnarne, "she knows my thoughts; for she is too sagacious, not to see the state of things. But the gloomier my face is, the more friendly she grows, the softer is her voice, and her mouth overflows with jests and smiles."

"She will oblige you to be as happy as herself."

"No," muttered Björnarne, "she hates me; but she lies. She cannot love me. How can a woman love, when she knows that she is despised? And she was dragged into it; my father and her's compelled her to it. She cannot escape, and she has resigned herself to her fate, like a wolf, with a halter about his neck. Her eyes, as they gazed upon me, were like those of a witch, who would suck out my blood. Yesterday she held me firmly by the hand, as I could no longer bear to be near her. 'You are impatient,' said she, 'and so am I. Be contented, my dear friend; for what can we dò, if it does not suit the wills of others? Children must be obedient; and it is also written, that they must bear their parents' sins. We must endure it: you are Helgestad's son, and I am Fandrem's daughter. As angry as you may be, you must take me upon your shoulders; it may be that you have more courage than I have given you credit for.'"

"That was spoken plainly enough," said Paul, laughing. "That means, begone, and say openly, I will not have you."

Björnarne remained silent, and his head dropped on his shoulders. "I cannot," he muttered, "oppose my father."

"You are too good a son," answered Paul, "to do behind his back what would offend his eyes. I will help you as well as I can to restore the fresh color to your grief-sunken face; as a beginning, know that I have made every arrangement to deliver the princess Gula to your arms."

The eyes of the young Helgestad flashed with delight at this announcement; but his confidant, laying his hand on his shoulder, said, in an admonitory tone, "Not a word, nor a syllable of this, or all will fail. Leave all to my care; I will take all upon myself. Olaf and I now know where the maiden is hidden, and Egede shall help us to seek her. I have spoken with your father of a hunting party to the Kilpis to seek Afraja. The wild reindeer are fat now, and the bears also; Afraja is yet fatter, that is, in treasure; for of flesh, he has not half an ounce. Wait two weeks more, when we break up. Upon the way I will tell you all. Speak with no one, but hold yourself in readiness. Agree with what your father may say, and trust your faithful Paul."

When he was alone, Paul said, "It must so be done. Unless I help the clown, nothing will be accomplished. In the bitterness of his disgust, he dares not yet oppose the will of Helgestad. He will not jump into the fiord, nor run away; and, to crown his troubles, he will take the insolent maiden; but that must not be. He shall have the miserable vermin, until at last" — here, in a subdued tone, he whispered to him self—"until all falls into my hands."

The Gaard was now full of bustle on account of the approaching market. The stock of goods was examined, and various expeditions made into the neighborhood, to consult with other traders on the prices, to barter, and probably to secure certain advantages in advance. Helgestad had bought a great quantity of flour and provisions in Bergen, which he now, in part, bartered at considerable profit for hemp and iron-wares, which he could use; he returned well satisfied from the smaller trading-posts, which were tributary to him, because he supported them for the market, and fixed the per centage of profit. The goods were gradually selected, which were to be shipped to Lyngen; the boats were laden, and the church-house of the trader filled with the articles which required the greatest care in handling, and to be protected against dampness. Another yacht was dispatched with the more common articles. The weeks thus passed in constant labor.

Meanwhile, the secretary had gone to, and returned from Tromsöe. Olaf had accompanied him; and as Helgestad and all the occupants of the Gaard believed, not to return again. Olaf had become perfectly pliant in his hands. His jealousy was the chief cause of the urgent request he made to the Nordlander to travel with him. In Tromsöe, however, with much apparent heartiness he represented to him how sorry Ilda would be, if he should now leave Lyngenfiord; and that it was not courteous in him to go home before the wedding.

"I know, good Olaf," said he, "what wishes you have cherished, and by God's throne! if I were not myself too deeply interested, it would give me pleasure to favor you; but I cannot change matters now. You are aware that Helgestad knows what has occurred. It is possible that Ilda would choose differently; I cannot deny it; circumstances have so determined it; and we ought not to be any the less friends on this account."

Olaf gladly returned, for he had no longing for any other place in the world. Upon the journey, Paul employed all his powers of flattery to dissipate mistrust from his mind.

They were fully agreed in one point, hatred of Marstrand; and upon this he built his hopes of enlisting Olaf in his new undertaking. After diligently preparing him for its reception, he communicated to him his plans. — "I will tell you how I will take the arrogant youngster in his own noose, and punish him. You know how the Lapps act now, and that no man can leave his house in security; you, yourself, have become acquainted with their audaciousness."

"The dog, Mortuno, shall not do it a second time!" exclaimed Olaf, excited by the recollection of his adventure.

"I think you will get hold of him," continued Paul, "but you shall, moreover, take vengeance on his helpmate, Marstrand; but for whom the miserable scoundrel would never again have offended you. Marstrand holds secret conference with Afraja under a roof, and all the atrocities which the old villain contrives, he is abetted in by the Dane. I have heard him say that he would not be surprised to see the Lapps driven by desperation to vindicate their rights. This condition of things must have an end, he says, and protection be given to the oppressed."

"Will he probably put himself at their head?" asked Olaf.

"Bah!" answered the secretary; "he is not so foolish as that. But remember what I said to you, when I first saw him. He will take princess Gula; go with her to Copenhagen — set heaven and earth in motion; and I know what can be done there with money. Let Afraja load his yacht with silver, and you will see how the birds of prey will be procured to fall upon us."

Olaf looked at him with an incredulous countenance. Paul, however, in an earnest tone, said, "Afraja possesses immense treasures; of this there can be no doubt. Part of his riches are in coined money, gathered by himself and his ancestors; but the greater part consists in the silver-mines which lie in the desert, and of the situation of which he alone knows. What I tell you, I have from persons of unquestionable authority; Afraja's own people also relate most wonderful tales upon this subject."

Olaf was Norman enough quickly to feel a rapacious desire for the silver, and his face glowed with an avaricious expression.

"You see, my dear fellow," said Paul, clapping him on the shoulder, "that we must have the old fellow, if we wish to get possession of his secrets. The best mode to effect this, is to capture Gula, and then he will come and deliver himself to the knife. At the same time, we will destroy all the plans of the noble younker, and will finish with him. Therefore sits she above there in the Kilpisjaure. You must be our guide, and show us the valley, where Mortuno found you, and you will play off a capital joke."

The two young men soon agreed upon a plan, to which Olaf promised his assistance. Bold and eager of adventure, he was ready to hunt the old sorcerer, or to carry off Gula, and deliver her into the power of Helgestad. Paul gave him, in return, to understand that Afraja's treasures would be fairly divided, and he imposed the strictest secrecy, warning him to beware of treachery.

They returned to Lyngenfiord in the midst of all the bustle of the Gaard, to the great satisfaction of Helgestad; for Olaf's strong arm was of material assistance, and Paul's skill in accounts was highly serviceable in the counting-room.

"Now," said he, when he was alone with Niels, and had made him a report upon his journey, "you see all is right in Tromsöe. My uncle has given me up half his house, and it will not be long before he will surrender me the whole of it."

"Do you also think of becoming his successor?"

The secretary laughed. "He frequently feels himself that he is growing old. When I reside with him, with my young wife, I can again take all the business upon my own shoulders, as I have already done. It is known in Trondheim and in Copenhagen that I conduct the duties of the office; and if I am rightly informed, the new organization to which, at the request of government, I have forwarded a plan, will not overlook me."

"Nuh!" said Helgestad, "I am gratified to know that you will be Amtmann. The hand of the laborer cannot be blamed for seeking its just compensation. You will take care of your uncle."

"As well as I can," replied Paul. "You know that my uncle has enough to satisfy his love for toddy, punch, and gin."

Helgestad nodded, and as they both laughed, their cunning eyes met each other.

"And now," continued Petersen, "we can begin to-morrow or the following day, our hunting-party to the Kilpis. I have already prepared everything; Afraja is cared for, and will fall into the snare — for what object do not trouble yourself now."

"I shall be satisfied, if you take him; and will be silent and wait."

The secretary passed his hand over his brow, and continued, with a smile, "There is yet another business to be settled between us. According to custom, when a man marries, he must ask after the dowry. That Niels Helgestad has made provision for it, I do not doubt; but nothing is yet fixed."

"It is right," answered Helgestad; "I should have done it; but look here." He opened a chest, and showed him its silver contents. "There are ten thousand specie thalers in it, which you will take home with you to Tromsöe; and as long as I live, two thousand shall annually be given to you for household expenses; and when it is God's will to call me away, Ilda will have a rich portion of my inheritance."

"I hope so," said Paul. "Have you made all your arrangements to that effect?—for the end of man is uncertain."

"I have," replied Helgestad, opening another compartment and taking out a writing. Paul looked at it. His father-in law pointed to many passages, and said: "I hope you are satisfied."

"I am satisfied, and only in one point I would make an objection. You have bequeathed various properties to Ilda, but not Loppen. Let the island pass to us."

Helgestad peevishly shook his head. "It is a hard-acquired property," said he, "and it must remain with the inheritor of my name."

"But if I request it of you, father-in-law," said Paul, smiling. "It is a rude rock; the birds are diminishing in number, and it is worth almost nothing. Take something else back, and give me the rock; remember you would never have obtained it but through my instrumentality."

Helgestad was out of humor. "You seem to me," said he, "like a Wal lying before a herring swarm. The more they run into his open jaws the wider he stretches them, and appears never to have enough. It is especially for your services in obtaining Loppen that I have given you Ilda"

"And you mean by that, that I have been sufficiently compensated," exclaimed Paul, in a jocular manner. "I think it is as great an honor for you to have me your son-in-law. Let us, however, be frank, and speak calmly. You are unhappy with your children, Niels, for you married her, indeed, agreeably to your own prudent calculations, but against the promptings of her heart. Bah!" he continued, as he saw Helgestad's darkening face, "I do not blame you; you calculated as a man of experience; but what I have said is, nevertheless, true. I know that, in many respects, I am not fitted to win the affections of Ilda. That is a fate which falls to the lot of many a husband. I must bear it; and I foresee my marriage state will not be particularly happy."

"Do you mean that Ilda is forced upon you?" asked the excited father-in-law. "You can give up the marriage; there is yet time."

"You are in error, Helgestad," replied Paul, smiling; "the time is past; neither you nor I can recede. You have need of me, and I of you; Ilda and this marriage are the bond of our union. I don't care a button if this Danish younker has found a lodgment in Ilda's heart; I know she will, as my wife, fulfil her duties; but do not imagine that you make her happy," he continued with a sneer, "my dear papa."

Helgestad made no answer; he bowed before the superiority of the secretary.

"I do not think, however," he smilingly resumed, "that you are spinning a better thread with Björnarne; it may, on the contrary, strangle him. Björnarne bears the strongest antipathy against the bride whom you have forced upon him, and he is not prudent enough to call his judgment alone in counsel. I foresee, father Niels, that your son is of different stuff from you or me. He has little brain, but much blood; do not delude yourself, by way of consolation, with the idea that Hannah Fandrem could be thankful to you. She hates and despises Björnarne, as well as he does her; but she is more cunning than all of you; she knows how to dissemble, and she takes pleasure in it."

"You are a devil!" muttered Helgestad; "can you prove what you say?"

"Prove? Reflect; the thing proves itself." He tapped Hel gestad on the breast, and jestingly said: "You are so wise, you calculate to the bottom; but there is always something within there which deceives you. I will tell you how that happens. With your bloody hand you have torn all love from the maiden's heart; you have taken from her the solace of her life, and you would now too eagerly give her another, who is of your taste, that you might, as far as possible, appease your conscience, and acquire true love where you have sowed hate. Ask yourself frankly if that be possible. She hates and abominates you, for it cannot be otherwise. I warn you again, not to deceive yourself." He paused a moment, and then, in a low voice, said; "If you will give me Loppen, I will do what I can to assist you to ward off every source of unhappiness."

"I will give nothing!" cried Helgestad, withdrawing his hand; "keep your wisdom for others. I think they know us both, but would——" he raised up his arm as if to pronounce an oath, and his eye glared wildly on the secretary.

"Hold!" said the latter, "commit no folly; we have not separated from each other. Consider, and let us stand peacefully together, we may fear each other; or, if you choose, hate. Prudent people know how to be friends, and to preserve themselves such. Keep Loppen: I say nothing more. To-morrow, we will begin our hunting-party; we will see what we can take. And now smooth your brow, and let me know how I can perhaps yet help and advise you in your account-books."

While this scene was enacting, on one side of the house, Ilda had a solitary conversation with Olaf, on the other. The maiden was sitting and sewing the marriage linen, as her suitor entered, and offering her his hand, sat down by her.

"Are you surprised," said he, after the usual preliminaries of a conversation, "that I returned with Paul Petersen?"

"I am not surprised at it," she replied; "but I am glad, for I could not believe you would leave us without taking adieu."

Olaf, for some time, spoke not; at length, he said, "If I

could have left you, I would have done it long ago. Have you heard of the story which took place in the olden time, when Haken Jurl was ruler in Trondheim? He had a mistress of the name of Thora, whom he set aside for the sake of another woman. But Thora would not leave him. She sat dejectedly on his threshold, from which the cruel Jurl drove her away, but she always returned. 'I only desire to see your face,' said she; 'God's blessing upon you, if you grant me this favor.' When all forsook the fearful man, Thora concealed him; when a hundred swords threatened her with death, if she did not reveal his hiding-place, and Olaf Trygeueson promised her as much gold as she could carry, she remained firm and chose death."

"My dear, true friend, Olaf," said Ilda, pressing his hand; "Oh! do not cease to be my friend."

"In every extremity," he replied. "I am a man, and I know what I ought to do. I envy not Paul Petersen his happiness; I hope he will show himself worthy of it. But whenever trouble threatens you, come from whence it may, let me stand by you, and lay your sorrow on me."

Ilda promised it to him, and then turned the conversation upon Marstrand. "I am grieved to learn," said she, "that you separated from him in anger. What has he done, that caused you to leave his house in such a passion?"

The Nordlander, at first, could find no suitable answer. He fixed his eyes upon the floor, but lifting them up again, he said, with violent emotion. "The false Dane has betrayed me! He has not only betrayed and mocked me, but he has done yet more to you. Let him beware of his tongue, for my knife might cut it out."

"And what terrible thing has his tongue said of me?"

"He has calumniated you," he replied; "he has spoken of you with a vain and proud foolishness."

"Did he?" said she, letting her work fall in her lap, and folding her hands. "What did he say of me?"

"That you loved him — him, no other, him alone!" said Olaf, in great anger, "and that he will never cease to love you, never!" He paused and looked upon her.

A strange smile animated her features. Her face was pale, but she looked like one in ecstasy, and big round tears burst from her large eyes.

Olaf, for a moment, was struck with this curious change. Something then arose in his mind, which set his blood in disorder, and his heart in commotion. He jumped to his feet, and his lips trembled. He wished to ask a question, but he had not the power. He suddenly pushed the chair away from him and upset it, and then quickly rushed out of the door.

The hunting party left the Gaard on the ensuing morning. Paul Petersen, Olaf, and Björnarne, all well armed, Egede, the Quane, with his dogs, and two pack horses, with provisions for several days, composed the expedition.

CHAPTER XIX.

MARSTRAND had, in the meanwhile, to contend with many heavy difficulties, in his secluded settlement. He had money enough, but he wanted provisions, and these were not easily to be procured even with silver. He could not leave the Gaard himself, without exposing it to great disorder. He made every effort to supply his deficiencies from Tromsöe and other points, but he was daily more and more convinced that distrust and suspicion were spreading among his workmen and the people of his household. Hitherto, he had enjoyed a certain influence as the friend and confidant of the great trader of Lyngenfiord, the first in the country; but he had openly separated from him in anger and hatred; all kinds of rumors began to circulate, that the old sorcerer Afraja had lent him money for building, in return for which Marstrand had renounced Christianity, and had forsworn all honor and truth. The consequence was, that the greater part, who already liked not the Danish lord, denounced and ridiculed him as the purchased dependant of Afraja. All respect was lost. When Marstrand complained, he received impudent answers; when he wished to urge, he met with opposition and rudeness; and after two weeks, things had arrived at such a pitch that most of them demanded their money, and left under bitter threats, saying they would not have anything further to do with a man who associated with Lapps. There remained scarcely any in whom the young proprietor could confide, and none but the refuse of the laborers, who could not get employment elsewhere. To add to his embarrassment, the settlers and traders on the neighboring fiords, likewise, turned their backs on him. At every attempt he met with opposition, instead of assistance. Those who were once friendly to him, now closed their doors against him, and no one bought of him or would sell to him. No laborer, notwithstanding the assurance of high wages, would enter his service; everywhere he was subjected to humiliating treatment, and those to whom he had rendered the most favors, seemed to take an especial pleasure in insulting and vexing him.

It was evident that he could not continue his labors, and what would become of him, and how could he support his seclusion, privations, and discomforts? No friend would knock at his doors; no human being would show him any sympathy, and his desolate house would be his only place of refuge. It was doubtful if, indeed, he could retain any of his workmen; and in such a case, how should he be able to provide himself with food.

When he looked forward to February, when half of Finnmark repaired to the fishery, what comfort could he derive from the prospect? It seemed impossible for him to take any part in it; for what did he possess of the necessary equipments, not to speak of provisions for the crews, for such an expedition? Had he settled colonists in the valleys and along the sea-shore, and suffered the woods to remain standing until he could have engaged in speculation without risk, it would have gone differently with him. Helgestad would not have dared to lay hands on such a secure property; and had he done it, help could easily have been obtained. More than one of the rich traders would then have lent him money; but now, he was laughed at as a Danish fool for his reckless and senseless management. He saw it all, but it was too late.

It required the most unyielding courage and energy not to give up to despair in such circumstances. The only friend from whom Marstrand could expect any genuine sympathy and assistance, was Klaus Hornemann. But where was the old pastor? Probably in the depths of the wilderness, at the northernmost cape, or on the Tana. And when, indeed, he should come to Helgestad's house, to witness the performance of the double marriage, could he deny that he had taken money from Afraja? and could the pastor allay the universal animosity against him, and enable him to reëstablish himself in public esteem and overcome his powerful enemies? It was Marstrand's firm resolution not to yield, or to suffer himself to be plundered and driven out of the country. He was sustained by the consciousness that his honor was unblemished, and that no taint rested upon his character. In all his speculations on the means of procuring assistance, he could discover none that promised success. Afraja's money could not help him, and yet this old man was always the concluding point of his reflections; all his minute inquiries reverted to him; and when he lay awake, and the wind rattled the window-frames, he would joyfully spring up in hopes of seeing the sorcerer.

One day, however, as he was walking up the valley of the Balself, and had gone beyond the waterfall, he suddenly heard a voice calling him from behind; and through the dense woods he beheld Mortuno, bounding towards him with the agility of a deer, his gay cap with eagle plumes jauntily set upon his head. Mortuno was buoyant with delight as he approached him. "Joy be with you, Herr!" said he.

"I have not seen you for a long while, Mortuno," said Marstrand.

"You see me now," said the Lapp, "because one sends me who wills it so."

"Afraja!"

"You say it," continued Mortuno. "He has an important communication to make to you. For this reason, he prays you to come and listen to him. Will you follow me?"

Marstrand immediately promised it.

Mortuno sat down upon a stone, and said, "I will wait for you here. Tell your house-people that you will be gone for two or three days. You will find two men at your door, who will buy vinegar and powder. Give them what you have; they are Afraja's serving-men. In the panniers of their animals, they bring you meat, as a present; your proud Gaard-people will not refuse a dish of reindeer's-meat."

Marstrand left him laughing in his merriest mood; and upon his return, he found, indeed, two Lapps before his door, who desired powder, of which they bought a small cask of twenty-five pounds, as well as scissors, vinegar, linen, and hatchets. They gave cheese and meat in part exchange for these articles, and then departed.

Two hours after, when the sun began to sink, Marstrand was ready for his journey. He recommended the management of his house to the maid-servant in whom he most confided, and gave orders to send to the Melangerfiord in quest of flour. He found the expectant Mortuno at the Elf, who immediately rose as he saw him coming, and, waiting for him to come up, began to climb the precipitous rocks.

He did not halt until he reached the point where the fjeld began; and then he conducted the Danish lord, for several hours, eastwardly, through the still desert. It was curious to behold how the red sunlight, and blue, gold-tinted clouds, lay around the gigantic summit of the Kilpis, and set off its weather beaten ravine and slopes. The wind blew sharp over the wide, unbroken expanse. In some places, the earth was richly carpeted with moss; in others, it was strewn with flowers and thickets; and occasionally an immense swamp appeared, in which Marstrand carefully sprang from one tuft of grass to another to keep his feet dry. Mortuno displayed much more agility; never stumbling, and, while his companion soon heated himself and grew weary in the mud and stones, he ran with monkey-like ease down the steep banks of the brooks, which had here formed deep and narrow valleys, with equal light-footedness clambering up the opposite sides.

The Kilpis gradually grew nearer; but it was yet distant as the night came on. The illimitable ranges of the Lappish mountains were seen rising one above another, to the farthest extremity of the horizon, veiled in cloud and shadow. Here and there rose a colossal mass of rock, not a peak, but, as is the nature of this country, a mighty mountain-block, huge and dark, with smooth walls, its summit terminating in a wide, extended fjeld, or a monstrous cone. Upon the other side, however, lay the red, dazzling surface of the sea, a glowing mass of fire, in which the sun's disk sank; and a wondrous array of islands, glittering strips of water, glaciers and remote ice-fields, involved together in labyrinthine confusion.

After contemplating the magnificent spectacle for some minutes, Marstrand questioned his guide as to the terminating point of their journey. He was right in doing so; for if these wastes could not, indeed, be traversed by daylight but with great caution, the difficulties of travel were much increased by the darkness. Towards the Kilpis lay a frightful swamp, and stony wilderness, intersected by deep sunken ravines, and broken by lakes of water, such as are frequently found at the foot of mountain masses, serving as the feeders for the brooks and streams, and as reservoirs of the melting snows. To wander here by night, where a false step might be fatal to life, was fearful enough for a novice; but Mortuno had good consolation at hand.

"This is, truly, not a land for your feet and eyes," said he, laughing; "but be patient for a while, and we cannot fail to obtain help."

Thereupon, followed by Marstrand, he strode forwards as well as he could in the deepening darkness, which soon enveloped all objects, remote and near. After about an hour, they descended into a deep ravine. Here grew birch thickets and gnarled brushes, through which it was almost impossible to penetrate; Marstrand soon after heard the barking of dogs, and a peculiar grunting, which indicated the vicinity of a herd of reindeer. There must be, he said to himself, an encampment here, and herds at pasture, with men and tents; but he could not recognise anything. When they stood by the water, which flowed in the ravine, Mortuno directed his companion to wait; but only a few minutes elapsed, when he returned, leading a horned animal by the halter.

"I bring you here," he said, "a riding animal, the best and strongest that is to be had, far and near. Mount him, and he will carry you safely."

Our adventurer promptly complied with the request of the guide. A soft cushion lay upon the back of the animal, and a little bell hung from his neck, whose soft tinkle was heard in the stillness of the night; Mortuno gave him a gentle blow, calling to him with some guttural sounds. The animal bent his way through the bushes to the heights above; the young Finn sprang forward; and Marstrand thought that this was the same great reindeer upon which he had once seen Afraja in the Balself woods.

Every preparation seemed to have been made for his reception; and it secretly gratified him, that the old sorcerer had sent his own riding animal to meet him. Mortuno was very reserved upon the subject. Marstrand could extract but little information from him; and he would scarcely admit that Afraja's herds were at pasture in the ravine, with an encampment of his people.

"You will see where you are, when it is day. Afraja will then be with you, and will show you many reindeer."

"Are you carrying me, also, to his gamme?" asked Marstrand.

"Afraja lives everywhere," answered Mortuno. "Wherever he goes, he finds what he wants."

"Serving-people, tents, and riding-animals," said his companion, smiling. "But your reindeer are so strong, that I am surprised you do not hunt them all upon the fjeld."

"You are in error," said the Lapp. "An animal is seldom found, which does not, in a short time, roll with his rider on the ground. This one is a rarity. He comes from the White Sea, where there is an island of the name of Kala, where the largest and stoutest are found. You must not believe," he continued, "that the reindeer, gentle and patient as he appears, will submit to all the injustice which may be perpetrated upon him. They will carry burdens, draw sleds, and bear tent-posts and household utensils upon their backs with the utmost good-will; but if they are overloaded, they fall into a passion, attack their master with the horns and feet, pursue him, and throw him down." He burst into a loud laugh, and exclaimed, in a merry tone, "The reindeer is wiser than we are, and he enforces his rights; God knows where we have had our eyes, that we have learned so little from him."

Marstrand made no comment on this remark; but asked Mortuno, "Is it far from here to the place where your uncle expects us?"

"You are nearer to him than to the Balsfiord."

"And Gula is with him?"

Mortuno was silent. After awhile, he began to sing a song, which did not sound bad. It appeared to have been originally composed in his mother-tongue; but he translated it, as he sang, into Norwegian, in order that Marstrand might understand it.

"Oh, sun," it began, "when you shine in the heavens with your golden light, would that I could see the Urevand, the blue, wave-beating lake; but I see the stars which beam in its clear water, and I know of one who looks down into it, and seeks to know where I am.

"If I could look down from the high top of the fir-tree, I would ascend it to see under what flowers my loved one is sleeping. I would tear up all the brambles, and all the branches; the green branches would I cut away that opposed me.

"I want wings, I want feet; wings of the swift bird, feet of the slender reindeer, to bring me to you; and alas! does she not see me? does she not hear me? I know not. But my eye sees her, however dark the night may be, and my ear hears her breathing.

"I have waited for you so many, many days, so many good days; I have waited to see your most beautiful eyes, and your lovely, soft smile; but alas! how pale is your face, how feeble your foot, which was once so light and delicate, as the foot of the young lynx.

"Oh! tell me, sweet one, what ails you? Fly not from me, for whither you fly, I would hurry to overtake you. What can bind stronger than a rope of twisted sinews; what holds firmer than a chain of iron? Stronger, stronger, maiden, love binds my head and limbs, prevents me from thinking, makes me weak.

"The will of the wind, the will of the child, the thoughts of youth, are all idle thoughts. Were I to reason with them, they would lead me astray. But you alone shall decide. Do what you will; close your eyes; listen not to me! However my heart may tremble, it will obey.

"Peace shall you have, love; peace and consolation! Your cheeks shall again be red; your foot, joyous and light, shall run over the nodding flowers; and your heart shall beat as in happy days."

Mortuno here became silent, after his voice had sunk into a soft whisper.

"Did you compose the song?" asked Marstrand.

"Yes, Herr."

"It has not been long since you made it."

"It was yesterday."

The night waned away. The overhanging heaven was bespangled with countless stars. The reindeer plashed through the water, which seemed to cover a large basin, and in which the glimmer of the stars was reflected back.

"And is this the Urevand?" asked Marstrand.

"So it is called by your people," replied Mortuno; "it is Jubinal's holy lake." — Suddenly a red light was seen in the distance, and the beast mounted with his rider out of the water on to the firm ground, which constantly rose higher and steeper. Dogs barked loudly, but Marstrand asked no more questions; for he knew that he was in Afraja's neighborhood. Some time afterwards, several men came to meet them with burning torches of wood, and exchanged a few words with Mortuno; who, taking the halter of the reindeer, led it between huge masses of rock to a peaked tent.

Marstrand was assisted to alight, and was politely conducted to the brown gamme. The floor was thickly strewn with birch-leaves; and in the middle was a fire-place, over which a double iron lamp, attached to a chain, was swinging in the air. On one side was a seat of birch-wood; on the other, a soft bed of moss with linen sheets; and near by it lay a number of warm counterpanes and furs.

"Tarry here," said Mortuno; "Afraja invites you to repose."

"And where is he?" asked the Dane.

"Who knows? When the time comes, he will be with you You are tired; sleep in tranquillity; if you are hungry or thirsty, you will here find what we can give you." He pointed to the hearth-stone, where there was bread and meat, with bottles and pitchers, and then left the tent, while he repeated his request to Marstrand patiently to wait for his uncle, and to accept his hospitality.

It was deep in the night, and the long wearisome journey had not a little fatigued the traveller. He sat down upon the great stone, and tasted of the rich, fresh milk and meat, and then surrendered himself to his reflections, listening from time to time when he heard steps or a noise on the outside. But it was nothing but the hollow moan of the wind; and as he opened the door and stepped out, he found nothing but darkness and deep silence. No object was visible, and he knew not also where he was. No gaard was to be seen, and no noise betrayed the vicinity of the living. Marstrand said laughingly to himself, that he was better secured here than a man who, in the civilized world, is shut up behind bolts and bars. The prisoner who there succeeded in breaking his chains, knew where to flee to; but here, nothing apparently prevented an escape, and yet not a step could be made without danger. Afraja had cunningly arranged to have his guest brought to him by night, and where was he now? where was Gula? Why did he leave him alone, and what did he want of him? A long series of questions connected themselves with these first ones; but at length, when his patience was perceptibly exhausted, he threw himself upon his bed of moss, covered his head in the soft skin, and fell asleep. Sometimes he awoke again, looked timidly around, sought his old protector, and listened and fell back again into a profound sleep; from which, when he awoke, the lamp had gone out, and the day was dimly dawning.

His curiosity was great, when he opened the tent door, to observe the unknown world; and yet he was surprised again to find himself alone. Nowhere was there a reindeer, or a gamme; nothing but the broken, frightfully desolate wilderness. He turned round, and raised up his head to the mountains. Behind him lay the jagged, monstrous rocks of the Kilpis, his gigantic, black brow illuminated by the early beams of the morning. As he scrutinizingly looked around, he observed that the place where he was, was a mountain platform, at the foot of the mighty mass, from which it was separated by a deep ravine. Upon three sides, the little fjeld fell with almost perpendicular sides into a tolerably large lake, which expanded itself between scattered blocks, and tongues of rock; upon the fourth side, it was connected with another mountain platform, to which the reindeer must have climbed in the night, after having waded through part of the lake. But where was it now? where was Mortuno? where was the brown herd? And where, above all, was Afraja and his child?

Marstrand sprang upon a high block, and he observed, with astonishment, that the circle in which the tent stood, was quite regular in appearance. All these pieces of rock appeared to have been hewn square, and they were marked with curious lines and furrows, which could not be the result of accident. He had often before heard of the magic and sacrificial circles of the Lapps in the mountains, and he doubted not that this was a Saita, which was dedicated to some one of the many deities. At the same time he was surprised that Afraja had erected a tent, and lodged himself in such a place. The great, smooth stone upon which he had taken his repast, was certainly not a hearthstone, but a stone of sacrifice; and there where he slept, and where he stood, cruel worship had probably but a short time before, been performed in honor of the pagan gods.

All these conjectures led to nothing. The day had grown brighter, the distant bank of cloud had divided itself, and Marstrand looked over a wide tract of land, without being able to make any new discovery. As, however, he went to the ravine, which lay between the projection and the high wall of the Kilpis, it seemed to him as if the stones were there arranged like steps, one above another, so that it would be possible to descend below. He hesitated not to make an attempt, which succeeded beyond expectation; upon arriving at the bottom he saw that this continued to a gap, which, as a deep, cavern-like gate, broke through the Kilpis and the adjoining mountain-mass. It was impossible to perceive anything of it from above; but the ravine here arched over into a passage, and its depths were filled with a wonderful splendor, which Marstrand was soon conscious was nothing else than the bright sunshine, that glimmered against him. He was convinced that a natural connecting road lead through the great mountain saddle, which rose up precipitously to the Kilpis, and it seemed to him that this must be the wall before which Olaf came to a stand on his exploring journey, as he just looked down into a great valley. He eagerly pushed on. A presentiment assured him that there Gula must dwell; there he would find Afraja; and yet he stood surprised and hesitating, for the scene before him, surpassed all expectation.

He saw a valley lying before him, greener and lovelier than any which he had ever seen in that country. A milder, happier nature seemed to reign within it, and a warmer sun to pour upon it its light. Nowhere was any rocky surface, but the earth was universally fertile; great trees sprang up in all directions, which, although the birch and northern fir, yet they were not so dark and gloomy as those upon the fiords; but they had the strong, green, and bushy appearance of those of the more southern latitudes. Through the middle of the valley, streamed a brook, whose banks were covered with overhanging bushes. Dense grass grew in abundance; moss flowers of various colors shot up from between, and wherever Marstrand gazed, he seemed to look upon a garden cultivated by a diligent and careful hand. He suddenly heard, as Olaf had also, the distant tinkling of bells; but how his heart beat when he saw a maiden emerge from out of the thick foliage, behind which he drew back, and approach the brook; it was no other than Gula herself.

Marstrand's inmost sympathies were aroused, and his heart

trembled with joy. The delicate little figure was dressed in a light brown gown; her face was perceptibly consumed and sickly — her long black hair fell over her shoulders, and alongside of her walked a white tame reindeer, whose red collar grazed her hand. She looked down before her, and went towards the sun, which was just sending its first beams over the rocks; the beast suddenly stood still before the thicket of bushes, and as she slowly lifted up her head, she saw the stranger standing before her.

"Gula!" exclaimed Marstrand, outstretching his arms, and her eyes lighted up, and her alarm changed into sudden delight; her lips opened speechlessly. Tremblingly she ran towards him, and clung to him tightly, as if she did not believe that it was actually he. Her large eyes looked at him with an inexpressible tenderness, and tears rolled down her cheeks. She spoke not — a painful tremor passed over her face and through her whole body — then the sweet certainty returned. The moment, with all its holiness, engrossed the poor child, and while Marstrand spoke to her, her head hung down upon her neck; her eyes were fastened upon his mouth, as if she would never take them from him.

"My dear Gula," said Marstrand, excited by this reception, "how long have I desired to see you! Tell me how you are, and if you are sick? But no — you smile, your eye is bright, and you live in peace!"

"Peace with you and me!" she replied. "I see you, and I feel not. But what is that?" she continued as she regarded him. "You have become pale, and your face denotes trouble. Oh! my father told me they persecute you, because you are better than they. They have betrayed you; Helgestad has deceived you — all, all are against you."

"Do you know what has happened to me?" he asked; "how your father has assisted me?"

"Did he!" she joyfully exclaimed. "God bless him for it! No, Herr, I know nothing of it; it was only yesterday that he spoke of you. Oh! now I perceive why he did it. He wished to prepare me for your coming — he related anecdotes of you, and he praised you; and here you are now, before I thought of it."

"By his will," replied John, musing and smiling.

"By his will! Say, rather, by your will," she said, interrupting him. "Did you not say that you had a longing to be here? Did you not ask how I, many days, prayed — how I, every day, looked up to the Kilpis, when the fiery vapor hung around him—and how consoling it was to me, when I thought, Now, indeed, he looks up here, and remembers his poor little Gula. Name me so again—call me, that I may hear it. Oh! oh! you do not know what good your voice does me! You do not know how much I have suffered in solitude," she whispered, tremblingly.

She hung on his arm — her smile, her look, was love — new hope, and that divine credulity which rejects all doubt. He kissed her lips—he pronounced her name, and called her his dear little Gula. What could he have said to her? Who would have had the courage to repel such unreserved love?

"You should not grieve," said he. "Have we not made an agreement to remain true to each other?"

She nodded to him, with glistening eyes. "I am true to you," she exclaimed. "Tell me what I shall do—shall I live or die? But forsake me not — reject me not!" She placed her hand upon her brow as if she called something to her recollection, and continued, "My father is well disposed towards you; he is mightily rich—richer than Helgestad. Ask of him what you will, and he will secure it to you."

'Where is your father?"

"Here!" answered a voice from the hollow of the rock, and there stood Afraja, leaning upon his tall staff, his sharp-pointed cap upon his large, ugly head, looking sharply at him with his cunning eyes.

"You are welcome to my land," said he; "and I thank you

for coming." He extended his right hand to his guest, laughing after his manner. "You discovered the way, which is difficult to find; but I was certain it would not long remain concealed from you Now you are here in Jubinal's paradise; I hope it may please you."

"Did Jubinal once dwell here?" asked Marstrand.

"He dwells here yet," replied Afraja, earnestly. "He suffers the flowers to bloom, and stretches his protecting hand over all that lives in this valley. When the Kilpis lies buried in ice and snow, and all the springs are frozen, the brook flows on, as it does now, and my herds find as much food as they need."

Marstrand could have made many objections; for he knew of a certainty that this secluded valley must, as well as all the other valleys, be covered with snow; but it was surely a lovely, sheltered spot, and he heartily expressed his surprise, which the old chief seemed gratified to hear.

"You speak truly," said he; "but there is many another that would please you better." His eyes lighted upon Gula; and, while he smoothed her hair with his hand, he whispered some words to her, and then continued, aloud, "We will go; I will show you my animals, while the maiden will take care to prepare for your proper reception."

Gula ran away, at a sign from her father, with a warm glance at her friend. The tame white reindeer bounded after her, and Afraja conducted his guest through the windings of the valley, climbing with him up a high wall of stones and broken rocks, by the side of which the rushing water forced its way in a deep, overgrown gorge. Marstrand now found himself upon the high, mossy plain, opposite to the Saita-stone, where he had passed the night. The tent had disappeared, having only been put up for him; but at his feet, upon the edge of the woody ravine, five other tents were erected, and before them extended an enclosure of birch-branches and hurdle-work, within which was a crowd of antlered milk-cows.

For the first time, he was in the midst of the domestic moun tain life of a Lappish encampment. The great herd within the enclosure was more than a thousand head strong; and on that day the autumn mustering was held. More than a dozen men and women appeared to be engaged in milking, while many others were driving the refractory animals to the milking-ground. Only a part of them voluntarily came forward to have their swollen udders emptied, most of them seeking to run off; but no South American Indian could more surely throw his lasso than these shepherds their forty to fifty-feet long nooses, which never failed to fall upon the horns of the animals at which they were aimed. They were then led, without any further resistance, into the enclosure, where they were milked and set at liberty; or Mortuno, accompanied by two experienced aids, went around, and, selecting out the fattest and largest for sale at the next market, designated them by a mark on the skin. The young animals stood in a close heap; the calves gambolled around their mothers, chasing each other, and bleating for joy, until recalled by the old ones, who impatiently waited until the herd was set at liberty. The bells of the guiding-beasts sounded melodiously, and the men and women sang at their labor. Laughter and rejoicing prevailed everywhere. The shepherds ran, with great vessels of milk, to the storehouse-gamme, and then again to a double-built tent, which seemed to be the family or dwelling-house, and from which, as the covering was thrown back, the bright glow of the fire was seen, beneath a column of smoke. All these tents or gammes were built simply; for they consisted of nothing but eight or nine tolerably high posts, uniting in a point, and forming a circle beneath. A roof of coarse brown canvas overhung the whole structure, which was further secured by some strips of twisted leather and wooden pins, to render them better able to resist stormy gusts of wind. In some gammes, the tent-covers were oiled; all were in good condition, and near the largest were suspended articles of furniture, wooden bowls, and pieces of clothing. Marstrand looked upon this spectacle of the shepherd and domestic life of the dwellers of the desert with a curious pleasure.

The day was clear, the sky beautifully blue, and the sun warming and golden in its light, in spite of the earliness of the morning and the movement of the wind. Afraja left him to his own reflections; for he was soon called back, by Mortuno and the other men, to decide upon the choice of animals.

"Thus passes human existence," said Marstrand, after he had sat some time on the stone and looked around; "there in palaces, here in huts; with one on silk cushions, with another on the rude rock and snow; and what seems, to the spoiled child of luxury, frightful misery, is happiness and enjoyment to the son of nature. But I can now comprehend," he continued, as Afraja returned, "why the poor Bö and fish Lapps on the coast envy you so much. There is a great superiority in such a free shepherd life over the dreary life in a clay hut."

"Those below there," replied Afraja, proudly, "are beggars, who support themselves by alms. I have selected a hundred beasts from this herd, which I will sell on the market-day, together with feathers, hides and horns. My other herds will not bring me in less; my pockets will be full of smooth thalers; and with that we can procure good food, of all kinds, every year. We wander up and down in our broad land, live where it seems good to us, suffer no want, and know no privation. How multifarious are the vexations of the men who think themselves wiser and better! How great are their wants! And the further you look, the more will you find that I speak the truth. Men were happy as long as their wants were but few; the farther they advanced in cunning arts, the more avaricious and unscrupulous they became. We live, at the present day, as our ancestors long years ago. We seek not to divest others of their property; but your people has oppressed us, and taken from us our own, and they give us no peace."

"If what you say were true," answered Marstrand, "there would be none but shepherds and hunters on the earth. We would be as the animals of the wilderness. But man has received from God a disposition to strive after improvement—to learn, and to create, and to employ his understanding."

"Must he use it to do injustice?" asked Afraja.

"No," replied the Dane. "Enlightenment will render us better, and make us more humane and just."

"Look what those have become, who think their God is the God of truth," said the old man. "But come, my herd is going to their morning pasture. You are thirsty; break bread with us, and thank the universal Father, to whom every creature belongs."

While he was speaking, the thick throng of animals had begun to move. A dozen of the small, shaggy dogs, which had previously vigilantly surrounded the whole troop, and had driven back every reindeer fugitive, set up a loud yelping. The leading animals placed themselves at the head of their numerous families, and they all proceeded, first, to the lake below, to drink; and then to the woody ravine, where there was rich pasturage. It was a gladsome march into free life. The reindeer ran and leaped, in frolicsome delight; the dogs barked merrily; and the shepherds, with their long staffs, shouted on all sides. Those who remained behind, assembled in the great tent, where a kettle was suspended by a chain over the fire on the hearth-stone; and an old woman, ugly as a witch, sat boiling the rich, fresh reindeer milk for breakfast.

Women, children and men crouching in a circle, received their share, eat the flour cakes, as they came hot from the hearth, and looked with sly, peering glances upon the stranger, who wondered at their great appetite.

Afraja took one of the wooden bowls, which the old woman filled with the drink, and handed it to his guest: "You must accept what we have to offer; no one, here, receives any better or worse."

The bowl did not look very inviting, but the sweet milk had an excellent taste. An animating warmth came over him, and he felt himself refreshed, which Afraja observed, with great gratification.

"I hope," said he, "you will be yet better satisfied with our fare; for even men like Helgestad do not disdain it."

This name reminded Marstrand of the peculiar motive of his visit. "You sent for me," said he; "and I fulfilled my promise the more willingly, because I have need of your advice. You certainly know how it is with me — that my house is forsaken, my works are arrested, and that I really know of no means to extricate myself from the position in which I have been placed by the treachery of Helgestad."

"I know," replied Afraja, looking in the distance, as if he was considering of his next word, until he pointed to an object which was visible in the chain of rocky hills that stretched out on the other side of the lake. Willow-bushes grew there; and whether it was a delusion, or the truth, Marstrand thought he recognised Olaf, and with him Paul Petersen and Björnarne.

"Helgestad's son!" he exclaimed, in surprise.

The Lapp nodded, and seemed to be in no wise concerned at the sight. His eyes were sharp; and as he bent forward, it seemed as if he held his ear towards them, and that he could overhear their conversation. In a few minutes, the strangers descended the hill, and rapidly approached the tent.

"They must not find me," said Marstrand. "What do they want?"

Afraja lifted up with his staff the thick cloth partition of the other compartment of the tent, and said, "Conceal yourself there, and you will hear the reason of their coming."

At his shrill whistle, Mortuno, with some men, came out of the provision-gamme; and he had scarcely beheld the three Normans, when his eyes flashed, and his face assumed a wild and vindictive expression. Marstrand could not understand the subject of the conversation between the uncle and nephew, but he perceived, from gestures and signs, that Afraja commanded caution and peace; and he finally seemed to speak in a most imperative tone, as Mortuno seized his gun, which hung upon the post by the entrance.

He obediently laid down the weapon again, and silently listened, with the other men, to the commands of the chief. They all then immediately withdrew, and Afraja sat down by the hearth upon the birch seat, until the barking of dogs, and rough laughing voices, close at hand, announced the arrival of his guests.

"Call away your beasts!" cried the secretary, as he observed Afraja; "do not let them attack your best friends and patrons. There sits the wise high-priest on the bundle of straw," he continued, in a jocular tone, "and hardly takes notice of our insignificant presence."

Afraja made another whistle, and immediately called off his dogs.

"Now, verily," said Paul, as he pressed forward to the tent, "we have him, and our ardent desire is gratified. Peace be with you! all glorious Afraja; heaven protect your dear head! You look upon us with stoical indifference, and yet you are curious to know to what you are indebted for the honor of our visit to this blessed gamme. I will advise you of that in a few words. Yesterday morning early we left Lyngenfiord, to make an autumn hunt, as the grouse, and snipes, and other game are now in the best order. We have had abundant success, and a heavy-laden horse has been dispatched to the Omnisjok with the prey; we, however, pushed on through the Pitsasjauren, where we slept, and from thence came on to the Kilpis. When we saw your tents, wise patriarch, we deemed it indispensable to make you a visit, and recommend ourselves to your friendship."

"You are welcome," said Afraja; "I am glad to see the sunshine in my gamme. Sit down by me; all that I have is yours."

"You have heard it!" exclaimed Paul, laughing; "all that he has belongs to us. We take you at your word, and here are the witnesses. Will you acknowledge then, old miser, where you conceal your treasures?"

"Seek them," replied the Lapp, joining in the merriment, "and take what you find."

"You also give your permission to that; who knows, now, what may happen?" He raised up the curtain of the tent, and looked into the next division; but as he perceived nothing within it but covers and household effects, he asked; "Where are your people? are your gammes depopulated? Where is the amiable Mortuno, who was formerly so quick of hand when he saw a Norman hat?"

"My beasts are at pasture in the valley," replied Afraja, "and my young people are with them. Let me see what I can set before my guests."

He went out before the door of the tent, and clapped his hands as a summons to some women and children.

"If the old rascal were indeed alone, we might speak an earnest word with him."

"Do not make a bad joke, my dear fellow," answered Paul, whose eyes restlessly roved around; "I thought you knew well enough what a Lappish ball signified. No, peace and friendship with the old sorcerer, who must not, on any account, distrust us. Let us drink his milk, and do not thwart my plans. Be of good heart, Björnarne, think of your sweet love, Hannah, who anxiously expects you to-morrow; and you, Olaf, do not begin any dispute, for I see, just as I thought, Mortuno's yellow face peering out of the storehouse gamme. Afraja will certainly be polite enough not to bring him into your neighborhood, to disturb your good-humor and cool blood."

The three young men seated themselves at the hearth-stone, with their guns and hunting-pouches alongside of them; and Paul drew out a well-filled bottle, which he held up before the returning Afraja. "Take this drink of the Gods," he exclaimed, "which Jubinal would not disdain. You are a connoisseur, I consecrate it to you. Excellent raki from the fire-land of the south. Do not refuse it, worthy chief; your slaves, there, are bringing milk, reindeer meat, and flour cakes; at present we have nothing else to offer in return; but our indebtedness shall be discharged when we meet again. Are you coming to Lyngenfiord in person?"

"I am coming," replied the Lapp, with a smile of satisfaction. "I shall carry thither more than an hundred reindeer." He enumerated his other articles of sale; and a conversation arose touching the markets, while three Lappish women and children brought in some food, which they placed before the guests.

Marstrand lay concealed under the cover, and could hear every sound; but no allusion was made to what he was most anxious about. Not a word was said of him, and no inquiry or remark of any kind was made touching the sudden moneyed aid he had received. The hunters were hungry and thirsty; they relished much the juicy meat, and laughed at Paul Petersen's wit, who extolled in high terms the delicate fingers which had prepared and brought it.

"You must come to the Lyngen market," said the secretary with a full mouth, "and you will thus obtain the thanks of the voigt of Tromsöe. All kinds of disputes, petty thefts, brawls, assaults, and other improprieties, have occurred. To speak the truth, it is on this account that I have come to you. You have influence with your countrymen. Keep them in order, that they may not commit any excesses. You are a reflecting, intelligent man, and you can foresee the consequences."

"Am I to blame?" asked Afraja.

"None censures you," continued Paul; "but your own nephew plays sad tricks. Where is he? Is he here?"

"Not here," said the old man, with a Lappish laugh. "Do not mind him; he is young, and will grow better."

"Has he a wife?" said Paul. "Has he not led Miss Gula home to his gamme?"

Afraja shook with laughter, and took a hearty draught from the rum-bottle.—"It is a long way to the Enare," he exclaimed; "Mortuno has time to whip the top, when the winter snow has fallen."

"That means, in the language of civilized men, that you have hidden Gula at the Enare lake, and her marriage will take place as soon as you have fixed your winter encampment."

"You are a wise man; a wise man!" said the Lapp, smiling.

"Why did you steal Gula away from my father's house?" asked Björnarne, impatiently.

"The deuce!" interrupted the secretary; "therein he is right; every father must look after his child. What could she do in Orenaes Gaard? Ilda cannot take her with her, and I would not like to have her in Tromsöe; and your young wife has as little need of her. She could be useful to none but Olaf, who might take her as housekeeper with him to Bodoen. Will you give her to him, Afraja?"

"Let him seek her gamme at Enare."

"Rather wolves and bears, than such a brood!" replied Olaf.

"Do not take it ill, Afraja," said Paul; "it is with this unfeeling man as with a nut; his shell is hard, but his kernel is sweet. He loves you more than you think, and would carry you on his back to Lyngenfiord, if you would allow it. He has, however, previously to make a request of you. In a few days he will set out on a distant voyage, for which he has need of good wind and weather. You are a sorcerer; all the world says so. In the old books it is written of the saidmen or sorcerers whom king Olaf caused to be burned, that they made a profession of dispensing, at will, storm and sunshine, and good and bad weather. Tell us, then, wise Afraja, if you really have this power. Out with the truth, and do not sit there in such a brown study. Will you give my good friend Olaf here his wind, and thus procure him a quick voyage?"

Afraja shook his head, with a cunning laugh.

"Why will you not do it, old sharper?" asked Olaf, pushing

up the butt-end of his musket. "Write your hocus-pocus, and I will give you a dollar for it."

"You call it so," replied the Lapp; "but what will you do with it?"

"Don't trouble yourself about that," interrupted Paul; "he believes not in your wondrous art, and I beg you to convert him. Fishermen have told me that you have sold them good fortune, and that you have rendered their fishing abundantly successful. Tell me if it is not true."

Afraja laughed to himself, and then, without further reply, he took out of the pocket, suspended from his belt, a small angular-shaped piece of brass, which bore a resemblance to a rudely-formed human head. He held it by one end, and Olaf by the other; and, whilst he muttered something to himself, he wound it round with a thin sinew, which he likewise drew from his pocket. When this was done, he tied three knots in it, each accompanied by a certain saying, and handed it to the Nordlander, who all the while exhibited a most incredulous face.

"What shall I do with the trumpery?" inquired Olaf.

"Carry it with you," said Afraja; "wind and waves will be at your service."

"Nonsense!" exclaimed Olaf. "Do you suppose that I believe in your tricks? Enough of the joke; let us go."

He was about to throw the amulet in the smoking ashes on the hearth, as the secretary held him by the arm, emphatically saying, "You should not so reward Afraja's willingness to serve us with his sorcery. You should thankfully accept it, and you can try its utility."

He thrust it in Olaf's coat, and put on his hat. "Give Afraja your thaler," he continued; "let us be gone, if we would reach Lyngenfiord by night. We shall meet you again at the market, Afraja. You will be satisfied."

They left the gamme after the restoration of harmony and good feeling by the secretary, and a general shaking of hands

Afraja accompanied them. When Marstrand issued from his hiding-place, he saw them all standing on the edge of the woody ravine, where the reindeer were at pasture. They looked down into its depths, and Petersen's eyes followed the course of the water and the high wall of rock which rose up against the Kilpis, Afraja appeared to be advising them as to their route, and they then crossed the fjeld, and disappeared between the masses of rock on the other side of the water.

Marstrand was disquieted at this strange encounter. Was it indeed mere accident which had brought his former friends there? or what secret motive had inspired them?

"They are gone!" he exclaimed to Afraja, "but are you certain that they did not suppose me here? and have you no apprehensions concerning them?"

"They know nothing of you," responded the old man; and, with a significant smile, he added, "they wish to have me at their market; and Afraja will go—he will go and settle his account with the wise voigt."

"Beware!" said Marstrand, who felt a presentiment as he looked upon Afraja's mysterious countenance. Scorn and anger were expressed in its deep folds and wrinkles, and his reddish eyes looked towards the point where the Normans had disappeared.

"Let me know," said he, "what is your will. I am indebted to you, and will maintain my word; but I will not remain in doubt any longer touching what you desire of me."

Afraja stood up. "You are impatient," said he; "let us go to Gula; she is expecting you."

"Only tell me when to go."

"Not now," answered Afraja. "Come and follow me." He went forward; and close on the steep precipice which the lake bathed, he conducted him to the platform of rock upon which lay the circle of huge blocks of rock in which Marstrand had passed the night. When he reached the first, he bowed himself humbly, and folding his arms on his breast, muttered some thing to himself which was, undoubtedly, a prayer or an invocation. He then kneeled on the smooth, table-like stone of sacrifice, in the middle, and speaking aloud, raised his head up to the black summit of the Kilpis, which, in the sunlight, now looked almost like a colossal head, with long hair and a wide-extended mouth, from which the red sunbeams streamed forth.

"Sit down here, by me, young man," said Afraja. "You are at a place which neither permits falsehood nor deceit. This is the holy Saita of Jubinal; where the father of all things for many years has been worshipped. Jubinal's hands placed the stones here as they are; his eye sees into the hearts of those who come and call upon him; his ear knows what they think; nothing is concealed from him."

The old man seemed, as he spoke, to grow stronger; and his voice sounded earnest and solemn, and what he said was simple and penetrating; very different from the usual manner of speaking of the Lapps.

"I speak, in the first place, of you," he resumed, "in order to show you that I am sincere. You come here to a land of strife and poverty, to associate with those who are entirely absorbed with their greedy thirst for money. They oppress all who have any relations with them, and much more, us who, before they came, possessed this land. You are acquainted with books and writings; so you must have heard that this extensive land was once the property of our fathers. Their bones are yet found in rock graves in the far south, on the shores of the Baltic; but we rove over these treeless fjelds, and even these deserts are envied to us by these cruel men.

"Do not think," he continued, after a melancholy silence, "that the reindeer formed our only care and sustenance. Many sagas have related that we once lived in light, beautiful valleys, where fruit-trees and grain grew. We were driven away from them by force; we were hunted and persecuted, until nothing was left to us but the naked waste, and the creatures which can alone live there. Your books relate, that your wise men went to the Finns, to learn what they knew; they will also inform you how queen Gunnhild acquired her knowledge of sorcery from two Finn brothers, and how she betrayed these, her tutors, to become king Erick's wife. The Finns were not then despised; their boundaries extended beyond Nordland to Helgeland.

"This was all so," he said, raising his head; "but what avail complaints? Every generation has seen worse times; and if it continues so, there must soon be an end of us. Our best pastures are lost; there is neither right nor conscience in our persecutors; our presence only provokes ridicule, and our name contempt. How is justice to be expected from those who hold us in less consideration than the meanest animals, and who would slay us wherever they could lay their hands on us, if they had not a double advantage over us in the markets, in buying and selling.

"You, young man," he said, with a grateful look, "have been born with a mild heart. Your soul was fashioned by Jubinal's hand, and baptized in the fire of justice. You interested yourself for the outcast, and what has happened to you, in consequence? He who assisted you to your property, did it to ruin you. The men who govern the country united with him to chase you away; and when I lent you my helping hand, they detested you as one whose neighborhood was worse than death itself."

"What you say is all true," interrupted Marstrand; "but how can it be helped? Let me know what I can do to put an end to these outrages."

Afraja remained silent for some time, and then replied, "Whatever you may do, you cannot escape their vengeance. You will find none to offer you a hand; every door will be closed against you, and none will trade with you, or eat your bread. You will find only miserable people to serve you, who will deceive you; you cannot take fish; and where you show yourself, you will be insulted; and whatever you undertake, will be injured and destroyed."

"You are right," answered Marstrand, keenly excited; "I have received too many proofs of the ill-will and malice enter tained against me; many also act with great secresy and deliberation, the better to conceal their evil intentions."

"Do what you will," said the old man, "they will be quicker than you. The voigt and sorenskriver are the most powerful men in Finnmark; they are your enemies, and will give you no rest. They will contrive plans to ruin you, and will reduce you to poverty. You know," said he, "of what worth judges and laws are with this people. Him whom they would ruin they deliver to justice; when they seek to divest a man of his property, they send the sorenskriver to his house. You may be sure that Paul Petersen has already devised a mode to accomplish his base purposes against you."

"And is there no means of escaping from this brotherhood?"

"There is but one means," answered Lapp, looking fixedly at him, "but one means; there is no other, and it will help us both. Listen! How many traders live in the sounds and fiords? Not five hundred. Who loves them? None! Are they stout, valiant men who can chase the wolf and the bear? They are lazy, drink, count money, reckon, and sit at home by their firesides.—What are we, on the contrary?—a people of more than ten thousand men, all of whom are armed, indefatigable, and untiring alike in the chase and in the storm."

"How?" exclaimed Marstrand, astounded and alarmed, "will you excite an insurrection against the king and his government?"

"Not against the king and his government," said Afraja; "but against our enemies, who abuse all authority in the name of the king."

"He knows nothing of it. Did he know it, or was the governor in Trondheim informed of it, much would not happen, that is complained of. I hope that Klaus Hornemann's efforts will soon bring efficient help."

"He knows it not," said Afraja, "the worse for him. How can he wish to be king, so many hundred miles from here? No, Herr, I hope for nothing. Nothing from your king—nothing from his servants, and nothing from the old pastor, who thinks we must become Christians; and thus the heaven will be open for us, in which our tormentors wish to enter. I do not desire to be where they are; and if your God were mighty, how could he permit his children to act in such a manner?"

Marstrand had found time for reflection. "I admit what, in your bitterness of feeling, you have said, but you must prudently consider what the consequences would be. The traders and settlers, the Quanes and fishermen, would not suffer themselves to be overpowered so easily. Your people are scattered over the whole north, as far as the Frozen Ocean. You have no power over them. Even the two hundred families on this fiord are each for themselves; often in hostility, and never capable of being united. Should you succeed in burning the houses in some places, or, what is altogether improbable, in destroying all the settlements, there would soon come ships full of soldiers who would take fearful vengeance."

Afraja laughed to himself—"Let them come," he answered; "it is far to the Enare Traesk, and to the Bumanafiord. A Lappish ball can be fired from every rock, and your soldiers are not men, who would wade for many days through swamps, and climb through the Jauren, without being well supplied with good meat and drink."

The Dane was obliged to admit all this; but the more he saw that Afraja spoke in earnest, the more his feelings were excited against his views.

"If I knew," he said at length, "that you could resort to such bloody and ruinous measures, I would do all in my power to frustrate your plans."

Afraja answered with a look full of meaning, and which Marstrand thoroughly understood. "You would never," said he, in a deliberate tone, "see the Lyngenfiord again, if you should seek to betray him who has done you so much good. But you could not do it, if you would."

"Will you force me? Will you hold me prisoner?"

"You have laid your head in Jubinal's holy Saita, you have taken your bread from his altar. I have not asked in vain the universal father, if you should be his instrument: all the signs have answered that he has taken you into his alliance."

"What have I to do with your horrible pagan sorcery!" replied the young man, with a secret shudder; "I am as little disposed to serve your God as I am to participate in your insane schemes."

"You are destined to it, and will fulfil the command," replied Afraja, unmoved. "Do not suppose that I inconsiderately expose myself to danger. Mortuno is a fearless man; the young men of all the gamme are ready to follow him. We have powder and arms, and everything necessary."

"And at the first shot they will run off," exclaimed Marstrand.

"You will be with them," said Afraja, "and your presence will give them courage."

"Who? I?" exclaimed Marstrand; "may my hand rather be palsied! But cease with your jesting," he continued, as he seated himself again on the block of stone. "You wish to tempt me, but you must see that I can never assist you in such designs, although I am ready to help you in all proper undertakings."

"You are skilled in the art of war, and many fear you," said Afraja. "When my brethren see you at their head, they will be firm; but you are also mighty in your own land, and can make your voice be heard there. It is said that he who has money can do anything in Copenhagen. Jubinal will give you these arms, young man. You shall satisfy their avarice with as much money as they desire. Let them fix the price for which they will sell us our land."

"If you possess so much money," said the Dane, astonished, "much may be effected through negotiations. At all events, a better and more just government may be obtained, together with larger privileges and a strict supervision of the traders and voigts."

Afraja shook his head in derision. "They must all leave; we will not tolerate them any more. Were you to give them our silver in bags, they would come to-morrow to seek for more. Have you not yourself advised that we must inspire them with fear, if we desire them to respect us? They shall learn to fear, for you have spoken truly, young man. Jubinal's children shall go down to them, and Jubinal shall have his victim!"

The fierce looks which he cast upon the stone, the witness of many a bloody sacrifice, startled the Dane. A frightful thought passed through his brain, that perhaps he himself might be sacrificed to the dark god, if he refused to fulfil the will of Afraja; but his pride and honor struggled against a hypocritical submission. He, therefore, began with much composure again to dissuade Afraja from any lawless act, and to show him in a dispassionate manner that there was no possibility of the success of an appeal to insurrection. He demonstrated to him, on the contrary, with impressive truth, the consequences that would ensue. All the odious complaints and accusations against his unhappy race would, for the first time, meet with general belief. None would thereafter raise their voices to defend it; all the horrors of fanatical persecution would now break out, to end, amid the greatest cruelties, in its annihilation.

"You will offer silver to purchase the freedom of your country, but, as you admit, you will thus only add new stimulus to their greedy rapacity. If it were true, as Paul Petersen asserts, that rich silver-mines lie concealed in the bowels of these mountains, with which you alone are acquainted, take care not to give increased credence to the tale. To possess themselves of the silver of Peru, the Spaniards destroyed whole nations of people, and the voigt of Tromsöe would readily find companions to join him in your spoliation. Great bands would come in search of these treasures, and of what advantage would it be to drive off the fish-traders, and give place to worse successors?

Afraja listened attentively; and he, several times, seemed to recognise the truth of his guest's remarks, "Be patient," resumed the latter, "as I am. My condition is, indeed, unhappy enough, and you have not been able to give me any comfort; but you have, on the contrary, shown that I am a lost man. I do not, nevertheless, despair. I will seek to hold out, and God, who is the help of the weak, will indicate to me the way that I must go. I will find help — will go in person to Trondheim and Copenhagen; and you may rest assured, Afraja, that I will raise my voice to the utmost of its power in your behalf."

The old chieftain, after a silence of some minutes, resumed, as if he had heard nothing of Marstrand's assurances, from the point at which he had ceased.

"When we have driven them away, we must then look to it, that no others come. Your words are in my memory, and you are right in saying that we can only possess this land when we ourselves engage in trade, and live in fixed dwellings. But why should we not be able to do it? We can handle the net, as well as the noose of the shepherd and the gun of the hunter. We received our understanding from the great Father, and we know how to use it. Our hands are apt for many things. Who sews such fine shoes — who makes such beautiful girdles, pockets, and collars? Why should we not build vessels and houses? Why should we not be able to go to the fishery at Lofodden, and even to Bergen? Why should we not prosper, and be respected?"

Marstrand regarded him with astonishment. What Afraja said sounded well; but it was, nevertheless, a dream — a tale impossible to realize. How could these half-savage reindeer shepherds, these hunters of the mountain, this deeply-despised, and from time immemorial, oppressed and degraded race of men, be civilized, as would be necessary, in order to become a trading, tilling, and fishing people?"

A feeling of the warmest sympathy seized the young man; for Afraja's questions were deeply affecting. His countenance took another expression; and the thoughts, which agitated his mind, beamed from his eyes.

"Oh! Afraja!" he exclaimed, "would to God that I could believe that all could really happen, and that your people could be raised from their degradation! Were all like you and Mortuno! but alas! reflect what the most of them are. Desist, old man: it is too late!"

"Too late!" muttered Afraja, as he dropped his head; he then looked up to the crags of the Kilpis, and its sun-illumined peak, and in a resolute tone said: "Jubinal helps you and me, you must not despair. You have won the heart of Gula; her lips have grown pale, and her eyes are dark with tears. You have found the way to her affections, because God willed it so. Take her as your wife, with all that I have, and give me your hand as a pledge of fidelity." He extended his hand, but Marstrand did not move.

"Listen to me, and do not be angry! Gula is dear to me; I could venture much for her, but she can never be my wife—never!"

Afraja stared wildly at him, and said, "What did you do to her?"

"Nothing! I honor her, I esteem her as a sister, and now ask no more; another woman has my love, and will retain it as long as I live."

"Do you repel her from you who has kissed your mouth?" ejaculated the old man, clasping his hands.

"You do not understand me," answered Marstrand. "I will speak with her in person; she will justify me."

"Hold!" exclaimed Afraja, seizing him by the arm. "Are you a wolf, to strike your teeth in her flesh, without regard to her grief? She will die if you speak to her."

He sat down again upon the stone, and fell into a deep meditation; but his eyes roved restlessly around, and his lips softly muttered words. Marstrand did not interrupt him; he wished himself far away from this mysterious spot. How could he take Gula from this father, who offered her as a reward for a treason which would dishonor him forever, and must drive him into the wilderness with the Lapps and reindeer? Were he possessed by an all-forgetting love, it would have delivered him into Afraja's hands. Björnarne was right; only the most ardent passion would bring a Norman into the gamme of a Lapp. Marstrand had nothing but good-will, pity, and what is called friendship.

Sad and disconsolate, he buried his face in his hands. Afraja commenced to speak to him in a mild and gentle manner. "You know," said he, "that I have only this child, and I am old. How long will it be before Jubinal sends his messenger? At the desire of the pastor, and because I believed it would be well for her to learn some things, I gave her in charge of Helgestad. It was not wisely done; you know, Herr, what happened. Gula fled, but her heart was with you; and I saw her grow pale, saw Hangir, the dark messenger of death, scatter the white flower over her head and lips. I prostrated myself, then, before the great father, and struck my head upon his holy stone. He spoke to me; the smoke of my sacrifice rose high, and steadily, and his commands filled my brain.

"I had destined Mortuno to be my heir; I knew that he kissed the dew from the grass which Gula's feet trod. I told him Jubinal's command, showed him the way he should go, and he went it without complaining. I sent him to you, to bring the man for whom Gula's eyes longed.

"Do not interrupt me," he continued; "hear me. Jubinal lies not; his will is mightier than the will of men. I could say much to seduce you, or to move you, and could show you that I have power; but peace and love shall always be with you. Speak kindly with Gula; to-morrow I will again question you.

Jubinal is omnipotent; he will turn your heart. Be silent, young man, and let us go; Gula is anxiously awaiting you."

This was an escape, a respite until morning, which was eagerly embraced by Marstrand. What change could be made, he did not know; but he required time for reflection and preparation.

"I will think of it," he said, "will examine myself; but if the power of your God does not prevail over me, then let your promise be true, Afraja; let love and peace exist between us."

The Lapp nodded his assent with a cunning smile. "Ayka, the goddess of love, will fix herself on your head; and when you awake, she will hover over you." Thus speaking, he preceded Marstrand down the steps of rock.

CHAPTER XX.

How lovely was now the secluded valley, fragrant with the perfume of flowers, and illuminated by the warm noonday sun! Gula flew with a cry of joy to meet her friend, as he came forward under the mountain arch. All his gloom and anxiety disappeared at the sight of her happy, animated face.

Gula had dressed herself out as she had not done for a long time. She had left her Norwegian fur jacket, the plaited gown, and the white apron in Helgestad's house; for Afraja would not have permitted her to wear it. She now appeared in the romantic costume which the young maidens of the mountains sometimes yet wear, when they belong to the more fashionable classes, and are rich, taxable heiresses.

She had interwoven her rich, dark hair, with red ribbons, which was fastened by a golden hoop, that encircled her brows.

Her short-gown, of blue, light woollen stuff, was elegantly embroidered with red threads, and secured around the waist by a long, falling sash. White trowsers descended to the half-boots of fine, soft reindeer leather; and these were ornamented with various-colored stripes. A feather pocket, of the finest kind, hung from her girdle; and around her neck she wore a collar of gold pearls, which glittered in the sun-light.

But nothing could be more radiant and ravishing than Gula's countenance, full of love and tenderness. Her eyes beamed forth her heart's happiness; they flashed with delight when she saw with what increasing pleasure Marstrand gazed upon her. She wished to please her lover; she sought his approving smile, his admiration, and his praise; she tremblingly clasped his hands, and hung on his lips with the fervent faith of a saint, who awaits the command of his God.

"Where were you?" she exclaimed. "How long I have expected you, adorned myself, and asked myself if I am as I was when I first saw you. Oh! then I was more pleasing to look upon. Is it not so? Tell me, if you did not like me more then?"

"No, Gula," replied Marstrand; "never have I seen you with greater pleasure, or found you more beautiful."

"Oh, how kind you are!" she exclaimed, with an inimitable expression of the love which engrossed her heart; "what consolation and strength you bring to my anxious bosom! Come now, and I will show you my dwelling, and the waterfall, where you will gladly sit. When Klaus Hornemann was with us, he used to gaze upon it for a long time, declaring it the most beautiful that the human eye could see. But are you fatigued? Your eye is dark, and you smile not. Have I done you harm? or does something give you pain? Has my father vexed you?"

"No one has vexed me, and you, least of all," he answered.

She was satisfied, and led him on. Afraja held back, following leisurely behind.

The valley turned in the form of a crescent to the mountain declivity of the Kilpis, gradually rising to a greater height. Everywhere it preserved a garden-like appearance. Luxuriant, thick grass covered the ground; and where it opened towards the south, it was full of sunlight, which diffused an agreeable warmth. Strong mountain firs mingled with the birch trees; and behind a beautiful grass plot, under protecting rocks, was a small, firm-set house, like the log-houses of the Norman traders, but incomparably more elegant. Its exterior was covered with birch bark, lapping over in separate pieces, like shells. Over the door Marstrand perceived a row of huge reindeer horns, and his astonishment was yet more increased by the sight of a couple of windows. Gula said, laughing, "All this is the patient work of Mortuno. He bought the windows at a dear price, and arranged the house as you see it. But look here, at what is more beautiful," she continued. "Sit down upon this bank by me, as formerly in Ilda's garden; no one is here to disturb us."

She had conducted him past the house, through the birch-wood, where the foaming brook forced its way; and already, before he perceived the wonder which he was to see, he heard the sullen thunder of a great waterfall, which now burst upon him in all its glory. Some hundred feet higher than the valley, the stream fell down from a cliff of the Kilpis, like a mass of molten silver, and plunged into a black cauldron of rock, from which the water-dust (wasserstaub) rose in eddying whirls. Millions of dazzling sparks, scattered in the sunlight, formed rainbows of the richest hues. It was fascinating to perceive how the sparkling clouds flew against the wall of rock, and sank down; how the thunder continually roared through the air; and how new, changing, and variegated pictures formed and dissolved over the valley. The damp mist had called into existence a most luxuriant vegetation. Mountain flowers grew there, such as Marstrand had never seen there before. He looked upon a garden full of blue and bright red beds, and his eyes were charmed at the beauty and grandeur of the spectacle.

Upon the bank, opposite the dark grotto in which the column of water-dust fell, thence to make its last spring like a cascade, he sat and listened to the prattle of Gula. Here had the gods of her fathers dwelt; here had Jubinal's mighty hand rescued his beloved when the giants and the wicked Pekel began their combat; and there, above, in secret, deep-hidden gardens, yet lived the universal Father, with his blessed spirits, who nightly descended in the soft moonlight and wandered through the valley.

He dreamingly listened, and looked up to the stone shapes to which Gula gave form and meaning, and then upon her animated countenance, radiant with joy and happiness. It seemed to him as if he could sit and gaze there for ever; as if he could renounce all which lay outside this little world, and that Jubinal's arm would close up the valley by insurmountable rocks, and for ever prevent his exit from it. He breathed deeply, and looked around; as it were, in apprehension that this event had already taken place, and then laid his arm around the yielding maiden, who bent towards his embrace. A gentle moan of the wind swept over their heads. The trees bent lightly, and voices whispered from them, and a cloud of sparkling mist rose up from the waterfall and surged towards them.

Gula pointed to the rainbow which stood over them. "God speaks to us," said she; "that is his sign."

"And what does he say to you?"

"That I shall never leave you."

"Shall I dwell with you?" he continued, laughing, "sit under the birches, hold your hands, and conceal you from all the world, and adorn you with flowers?"

"The flowers fade," answered Gula, "the brook freezes, the valley is filled with snow, and Afraja wanders away to the lakes of the Tana. I will go wherever you wish."

"Oh, poor little Gula!" he exclaimed, "I do not yet know

where I shall find a resting-place. You have heard what is my present condition."

She bowed to him, laid both her hands upon his breast, and confidently looked upon him with her lustrous eyes.

"Must you, then, dwell at the Balsfiord?" she inquired. "Must you live in this rough land among such rude men?"

The suggestion came upon him unexpectedly. "Whither shall I go?" said he, surprised.

"To your native country," she replied. "Is it true what I once heard Paul Petersen say, that none will hold me in contempt there if I bring riches with me?"

"Money!" exclaimed Marstrand: "it secures respect and consideration everywhere."

"All, then, is right," she confidently said. "Afraja will give you as much as you wish. We will take passage in a vessel for the south. You have told me so much of Copenhagen, and now I will see it." She clapped her little hands, and her eyes grew bright at the idea with which her head was filled. "I will learn everything, and you will see that I can accomplish anything I choose. Tell me what I am to do. God bless you! God bless you, dear, good John!"

How could he pour a black drop in this stream of hoping love? The happiness which he could awake reflected its glimmer upon him; and, as he observed her with a long, tender look, he said, half to himself, "Trust in me. I will do all that a man can do to requite your true friendship."

"You will never forsake me, nor cast me off!" she exclaimed, in a tone of unshaken confidence. "When I saw you again, to-day, the thought seized upon me as a wild beast, and a terrible anxiety commingled with my joy. Now I know, for certain, that it was childish and foolish. I could not bear it," she said, with a gentle smile.

"But what will your father say if you desire to forsake him? Will he consent to it?"

"He will, he must!" she answered, joyously springing up

"There he stands, expecting us. Speak with him on the spot; he will gladly listen to you."

Marstrand soon saw that she knew nothing of her father's plan, but he easily pacified her with the assurance, that on the next day he would speak with him.

"He will be glad to see you," said Gula, "and I can think of but you alone. What you do is good, and that is all that I know."

Hand in hand, in happy conversation, he led her to the hut, before which the old man sat in the sunshine, seeming to hold conversation with the two dogs, which stood regarding him with uplifted ears.

"They are wise beasts, Herr Marstrand," said he, "they are just asking me why no fire is to be seen on the hearthstone, as the sun has already cast long shadows there; and I answered them that it is not good to be there, where there are men who are satisfied with mere words." Laughing after his manner, he stroked the soft hair of his daughter, and in his angular face there shone something which appeared like a tender, parental satisfaction. "Flowers live on dew," he continued, "fishes on water, and maidens on love; but food also is indispensable to the existence of every human being."

Gula ran into the house, and Marstrand sat down by Afraja, who related to him much of his wanderings, which had extended for more than a hundred miles to the north, and far into the land. He described the family arrangements, the domestic life, and the labors of the Lapps, and said with a certain pride, that in this land without law, officers, and bailiffs, there was hardly ever a crime committed.

"They abuse us as thieves and hypocrites," said he, "and yet I never knew a theft or robbery committed but by the coast people. They are bondsmen—a poor, wretched, and oppressed people, who miserably eke out their life. Here, you find only free men, who have no lord over them but the Almighty, and none under them, for all are equal. We live in a gamme, eat out of a kettle, and clothe ourselves in the same dress; we are brothers who share all, and will never surrender their freedom."

He could speak so. Even Helgestad himself had recognised this indomitable love of freedom, and that no Lapp would exchange his mountains, his gamme and herds, for all the luxury and wealth of a king. And this old man wished to cease from all this, and to drive away the enemies of his people, in order to establish them in their trading posts. It was incredible of belief. Afraja himself, who had long lived a shepherd's life, could not possibly transform himself into a fish-merchant and navigator, and how could it be otherwise? How many centuries were required to change such a people from hunters and shepherds to cultivators, and how could this degraded race find a place among the family of nations? He looked with esteem upon the old man who, in his desperation, could imagine and begin such an undertaking. There sat he, before him, in his brown, coarse robe, and reindeer shoes, more wretched and naked than the meanest beggar at the palace-door of Christiansburg; and yet he was a king, and if fate had placed him on a powerful throne, he would, as Klaus Hornemann asserted, have been a great and wise prince. What a difference between this grey old chieftain in reindeer skins, and the velvet-apparelled, embroidered and ribboned monarch in Copenhagen! Where were here the guards, the halberdiers, the luxurious palaces and gardens, the ladies in trailing brocades, the pages and soldiers in scarlet and gold! Nothing but men in wooden shoes, and women shaggy and wild as the yellow dogs; nothing but rocks and wastes, the forest of horned cattle, and princess Gula in her blue, fluttering gown, flying through the valley, the white reindeer her only companion.

But what would King Christian give, if he could only transfer one of these waterfalls, and a majestic mountain like the Kilpis, to his park? That was not in the power of man to accomplish, but Gula could be transplanted. Gula could weave her rich hair in curls, envelope her elegant figure in purple and satin, and cover her little feet in shoes with red heels. Was then indeed the difference between a wild and tame king, between a princess behind mirrored walls, and this one behind the hearthstone, so immeasurably great? Put jewels upon her, bind her shining black hair with white pearl strings, and let us see who would play her part best. Dress this old man in ermine, place a crown on his broad brow, and how would the younkers and all the people stare at him! And he has money, much money, despite his rags; and what cannot be done with money? Who yet asks after me? Where is the hand that seeks me? What restrains me yet? Ha, Ilda!

While Marstrand muttered all this to himself, and with open eyes dreamed wonderful things of palaces, feasts, and vain splendor and glory, Afraja continued to describe the past condition of his country, without receiving much attention from his only listener.

The Danish government had given itself hardly any trouble about Finnmark down to the end of the sixteenth century. It was only when the fisheries developed their importance, when the codfish trade had increased, and the settlers had considerably augmented in number, that a regular government was introduced, with voigts, writers, officers of all kinds, pastors, and rising taxes. But all efforts to reduce the independent Lapps to subjection had been made in vain, and equally fruitless were the attempts to convert them by persecution to Christianity.

Already the chivalrous king, Christian the Fourth, who made a romantic voyage to the North Cape in 1599, had issued a severe edict that all the Lapps should renounce their gods, and become Christians; sorcerers, however, were to be taken and burned alive.*

"And was that done?" asked Marstrand.

"To be sure," replied Afraja; "many were burned for a century and more, and many priests came and poured water on the heads of the heathen. But the water dried up, and the priests died. Down to this hour, the teachers of your God have been able to effect but little with us; for what can the priests do, who do not understand our language; and of what use are books which we cannot read? The holy Saitas yet exist everywhere in the mountains; and no Lapp, were he even a baptised Christian, would pass by Jubinal's altar without laying his forehead upon it."

"Will you not become a Christian?"

The old man crouched upon his staff. "Are they who call themselves Christians," said he, "so good and just as to induce me to the adoption of their faith?"

"My God is strong and just; he mercifully protects those who believe in him, and helps them in the hour of need. People are no longer burned for sorcery, and we no longer believe in such folly. Milder manners bring more humane laws, and noble-hearted, pious pastors, such as Klaus Hornemann, will no longer preach in vain to your people."

Afraja remained silent for some time, and then mildly replied, "Let us not dispute. Hold fast to your belief, and hinder no one in the enjoyment of his own. You see that Gula is a Christian; Mortuno prays with the old Klaus when he comes to us, and I have never opposed it. But know, young man, that your Christians are not better than the children of Jubinal, but are, on the contrary, more cruel and unjust. They murder and burn when they can, yet, and practise as much outrage and barbarity as the mild customs, as you call them, permit. You see by their treatment to yourself, what they call law and right; beware of them, for you may have much sad experience to undergo."

At this moment, Gula bounded out of the door, joyously exclaiming that her table was ready; and Mortuno, who was coming along the brook, approached his uncle, with whom he exchanged some words. The poor fellow looked much more serious and reflecting than formerly. Of his merry jesting manner as little remained as of the idle foppery to which he was so much addicted, With a downcast air, he silently gazed upon the happy Gula, who was conducting Marstrand, without seeming to observe him.

The apartment in which the guest entered served the double purpose of kitchen and sitting-room. A bright fire burned upon the hearth, and a savory odor arose from the kettle. The floor was strewn with fresh leaves, a low table stood in the middle, upon which lay wooden spoons and plates, and on both sides were seats of moss. Although nothing more was to be seen in the modest room than a couple of shelves with the customary household articles, and some chests in the corner, it nevertheless presented a friendly appearance; for it was clean and neatly dressed up, Gula having arranged fir branches in the windows, to which were suspended festoons of cowslips and bell-flowers.

This was her palace, her only possession. Of what use was money to these people, who buried it in the earth, to whom this hut appeared an uncomfortable luxury, and whose choicest delicacy was the dark-greyish food which Gula poured from the kettle upon the plates, and which was so eagerly looked for by her relatives? The white reindeer and the shaggy dogs lay around the fascinating Hebe, who selected the best for her friend. It seemed to him, as he sat in this patriarchal circle, as if he were in the ark of Noah, in the midst of the flood; but no dove entered with an olive-branch, and he saw no land where he could save himself. He shuddered with disgust at the first sight of this delectable meal; but, after a spoonful, the shepherd's fare did not appear to him to be so bad. It consisted of the blood of the animal, which had been killed in his honor, of the heart, liver, and choicest pieces of meat, which were cooked with rich milk, flour, and fragrant herbs.

Gula was indefatigable in her assiduous care for her dear guest, and delighted at the satisfaction it gave him. He was further informed by Afraja that the Wald-Lapps lived upon nothing else than meat and milk, blood and the entrails of their beasts; and when he compared this fare with that of the poor fishermen of the coast, the children of the wilderness appeared to revel in Lucullian luxury. He also thought of the peasants and poor people in Denmark and other countries, who had received from civilization little else than the privilege of being oppressed by princes and official personages to such a degree that the most miserable existence could hardly be maintained. The peasantry, at that period, were everywhere in a state of bondage, and the prejudices of caste divided, with their iron barriers, every condition of society.

Were not these free shepherds, in many respects, to be envied, with their illimitable hunting and pasture-grounds, and exemption from the plagues of civilised people? Marstrand expressed this aloud in an emphatic manner; and the descriptions which he gave of the peasants, and the poor people of the towns, of the prerogatives of the nobility, and the great power of the princes, appeared to gratify Afraja much.

He listened for some time, and then said, with a peculiar glance of his lowering eyes, "So falls the rat upon the mouse, the marten upon the rat, the wolf upon the marten, and the bear upon all. In the water, the air, and everywhere, it is the same; but it is a consolation to see that one robber is torn to pieces by another, until, at last, Jubinal sends his black messenger, before whom the boldest tremble. Bring us a drink, maiden. Let us drink, that the unjust may mutually devour each other, until not one of them shall remain."

Gula brought wooden goblets, and, to Marstrand's surprise, a bottle of good old Madeira, which Afraja had bought, with some others, at the last market.

The sun, in the meanwhile, declined, and the valley was covered with shadow. They sat together, and the hours passed away, and the stars rose in the heavens. The waterfall thundered, and flashed like a white light through the night. Marstrand walked through the driving spray of the fall, which cooled his heated face. His eyes sought those of Gula, which were glowingly fastened upon him, when he spoke of his father's old palace at Seeland, and of the days which should come there; of the hunts in the beech-woods; of the lovely hill-slopes reflected back in the blue Oeresund; of horses with yellow manes, rode by fair ladies; of gorgeous halls, with crystal lights, and pealing music executed by Moors, with silver armlets, and pearls in the ears.

Gula saw it all. She saw the towers and the bridges, the brilliant cavaliers, and the fair damsels, with long trains. She saw the glass palaces, and heard drums and trumpets calling to festivity; then she saw herself on the arm of a beloved husband; and as she lifted up her brow, and the night-wind cast withered leaves upon it, she thought she felt the weight of heavy gold chains and diadems.

All her thoughts were engrossed in these speculations. Inexpressibly happy, she sat by the side of her lover, and observed not the poor Mortuno, who, from a corner, mutely watched every smile and movement. At length she brought her guitar, at the request of Marstrand; and sang so sweetly, and with such expressive grace, that, although he could not understand the language, he perfectly comprehended the meaning.

"They are songs of love," said he.

"They are the laments and prayers of a maiden expecting her lover," she replied.

Marstrand looked at Mortuno. He had bent forward, as if he heard something which greatly pleased him. His arms were crossed, his face was illuminated by the hearth-fire, and a smile, such as Marstrand had never before observed in him, played around his lips. Afraja, on the contrary, after his custom, crouched down, and stared in the flames, which gave a sharp and red appearance to his fierce, angular features.

After some moments, Marstrand said, "Now, Mortuno, how is it with you? Will you not sing again the song which I heard yesterday, or have you composed another?"

With the same gentle, smiling face, Mortuno nodded to him; then he stood up, took the three-stringed guitar from Gula's hands and commenced a song, of which Marstrand long afterwards remembered one strophe.

"Take the flower of the Kilpis," he sang; "ah! I see well that it blooms for you. When the young birches are again green, my hand will not pluck it; when the lambs cry and spring around their mothers, I shall no more hear them. Take the flower of the Kilpis, and press her to your heart. To no one would I give her but to you. What is man's will is the will of God! His voice speaks to me. Fly, white dove, fly over sea and clouds — my eyes will accompany you; my heart will be with you."

At his last words, Afraja's hoarse laugh was heard, as he rose up. He thrust his pipe in his belt, filled his goblet again, and offered another to his guest.

"Enough for to-day," said he; "I offer you the sleeping draught. To-morrow, let us see if the white dove sits on your shoulder."

But it must indeed have been a strong drink which Marstrand had taken, for he felt his head become as heavy as lead, and he was hardly conscious that Gula yet held him by the arm; her tender adieu for the night sounded to him as if from a great distance. He laughed as he stumbled, and Mortuno supported him; then he went with the two men, and they led him, as he thought, through the ravine, and up the steps to the tent, which was again erected on the Saita. He thought he saw the lamp burning, or was it a flaming torch which glimmered before his eyes. Then it seemed to him as if he was mounted on the monstrous reindeer upon which Jubinal nightly rides around the earth. Suddenly he fell into a fathomless abyss, and was conscious of nothing more.

CHAPTER XXI.

In the middle of the night, several men stood around the stone of the Saita, talking together in a low tone.

"We will, without doubt, break our necks," said one of them, who was Paul Petersen. "I wish Egede may break his first, and we may thus, probably, get off with the fracture of an arm or a leg."

"Where is he?" asked Olaf.

"He is climbing the rock down below there," replied Paul, "because his dog or the devil incites him to it, and shows him the way. There he comes. Is it you, Egede?"

"Yes, Herr," whispered the Quane. "An important discovery. Steps lead down below there; underneath is a wide hollow, through which the wind whistles. The dog drew me by the line; I followed him, and at length heard the noise of running water and rustling trees. Then he stood still and growled; I turned round."

"It must be the valley that you have seen, Olaf," said the secretary. "It must lie behind the steep rocks. You said it is precisely there where Afraja has established himself with all his rabble. I will bet my head that princess Gula lies concealed below there."

Björnarne, who was sitting on the stone altar, stood up and said, "Go on, for we are losing time."

"My young friend," said Paul, with a laugh, as he took hold of him, "you will either yourself dash your brains out, or get it done by others. Stop a moment, and let us consider. It is possible that this is a secret entrance to the woody ravine, where we think that the old rascal keeps his stolen daughter; and it is also possible that we may find her; but it does not appear credible to me that she is sleeping there without being surrounded by dragons and witches, and other frightful creatures; were only the amiable Mortuno, with some other gallant gentlemen, lying at her threshold, we could certainly count upon seeing our hats or coats ruined by a couple of unbecoming bullet-holes."

"Why have we come here, if we fear?" answered Björnarne. "I will attempt it at every hazard."

After a brief consultation, it was resolved to make a closer examination, and when they had succeeded in reaching the ravine, they discovered that a passage led through the rocks. They soon distinguished what their guide had heard; they stood at the mouth of the gorge, and below them the moaning of the wind through the trees, and the roar of the cascade and the brook, were distinctly audible.

After another consultation, Olaf remained standing in a deep corner of the cavity, with his hand on his gun, and eyes and ears open on all sides. The others clambered yet further down, until they arrived at the bottom of the valley, and the brawling brook, where Egede's tracking dog did not seem to know where to begin properly; for he scented some hidden object both on the right and the left.

The heavens were covered with whitish stripes of cloud, through which, in several places, the stars were to be seen; and through the midst of this soft veil of the firmament, lights of dazzling brilliancy flashed out, shone for a moment, and then disappeared. These eccentric flashes sometimes revealed the wooded declivities of the valley, together with the wall of rock, which appeared to close it up. Paul Petersen laughingly whispered, "The devil's fire is at least good enough to show us where we are. It must be a lovely little spot, and there must be their gammes."

They glided cautiously to the left along the brook; and, as a brighter light gleamed over the valley, Paul exclaimed, "What is that? It seems to me that I saw a hut, a house with windows. By heavens! there it is again."—The red glimmer fell upon the birch-covered walls, clearly exposing them to view, and then ceased. It seemed as if a demoniac power wished to show the way to evil.

The three men carefully followed the windings of the water. Egede held his dog fast, which uttered a light growl, then glided over the grass-plot, and stood still before the hut, in which not a sound was to be heard.

"Who can it be?" muttered Paul. "No one!"

"Feel here, how high his hair rises," said the Quane, laying his hand upon the neck and back of the dog. "Lapps are sleeping in it.—Afraja! Mortuno! I will awaken them."

He slowly drew a knife out of the leather sheath hanging at his left side, and listened.

"Fool!" said the secretary, "Afraja sleeps in no wooden house; if any one is here, it is Gula. They have built the palace for this tender beauty."

At the same time, he held Björnane fast, who had raised his hand to the door. "Stop! if you do not wish to lose all," he continued, in a whisper.—"Here is the little lantern and the tinder-box; strike a light, Egede; you understand it best."

The Quane executed the order with great dexterity. In a moment, a light was struck, which was so well covered up, that only a few rays fell upon the door, which had neither bolt nor lock. It was noiselessly turned upon its hinges of birch, and Paul entered with the uplifted light in hand, closely followed by his companions. He opened the lantern sufficiently wide to light up the apartment. There was the hearth-stone, and there stood a table with all its furniture; he suddenly pointed in silence to a corner, where a bed of cushions and skins had been arranged, upon which a human being was soundly sleeping. The gleam of light fell upon dark, long, dishevelled hair; the head rested upon one arm, so that the face could not be seen; and the other arm lay extended upon the lynx-skin, and appeared to be of fine skin and well-formed. He could not recognise the person, but all doubt was soon removed; for Gula, probably disquieted by the light, or from some presentiment, turned in her bed and resumed her sleep.

Upon her moving, Paul had entirely closed the lantern. After some minutes, he opened it again, and held it so that the light did not fall on Gula. He stood still when he saw Björnarne approach the bed, kneel down, support himself upon his hands, and regard the sleeper.

Björnarne was pale and care-worn; but, at this moment, his face was glowing red with excitement, and his eyes beamed with joy and hope. There she lay, gently breathing, before him; and, as his breath discomposed her, her lips smiled, and the black arched eyebrows lifted up, as if she perceived something which excited her surprise.

A tremor shot through the heart of Björnarne. How beautiful she was! Her little white teeth shone in all their brilliancy—her brow was petulantly knit, and she appeared as in the fairest days of her life, when upon his return home she would spring from the corner to meet and surprise him. Agitated by these reminiscences, and distracted by his feelings, he seized the hand, which lay before him; at the same time, Paul exclaimed in a suppressed but sufficiently loud voice, in which his smothered laugh was distinctly audible, "Kiss her awake, you loving fool, for we have no time to lose!"

He accompanied these words with a rapid turn of the lantern, throwing its full light upon the helpless sleeper.

The effect immediately followed. As if struck by an electric shock, Gula suddenly started up. Her hair flew back—her eye glanced upon Björnarne, and the hut echoed with her affrighted and piercing cry.

"Stop her mouth!" exclaimed Petersen; and Egede threw one of the coverlets over her head, held her down, and with his murderous hand, grasped at her throat. Before, however, Björnarne could hold him back, he received from the other side such a powerful blow, that he fell headforemost to the earth, and a white kobold rose over him, who, with curious grunting, knocked his head about. It was Gula's reindeer, which had sprung from its corner to assist its unfortunate mistress; and, after the custom of these animals, butted against him and kicked him.

Egede was terrified to such a degree, that he could not move a limb; as soon, however, as he recognised his opponent, he plunged his knife into the ribs of the faithful creature, which immediately turned round, tottered, and fell down at the head of Gula's bed.

"Hear me, Gula!" said Björnarne. "I beg you to hear me. Do not fear, it is I, Björnarne, your friend. No one will harm you."

"Blood! Blood!" cried the poor maiden, looking upon the Quane and the dying animal.

"Be still!" fiercely muttered Egede, "or I will cut your throat."

"Oh! have pity!" exclaimed Gula upon her knees, uttering a piercing shriek, and calling "John! John!" as she endeavored to liberate herself from Björnarne.

"Put an end to it," said Petersen, coming forward, "or there will be an end with us. The ear of a Lapp can hear this cry for miles. Will you keep still, darling, or shall Egede lay his fingers upon your throat? Draw the jacket on, quick! The cloth about her mouth — her hands behind her back. Forward! And if you make a noise—— Egede! seize her by the arm, and hold your knife ready."

But Gula seemed to have lost her voice and all power of resistance. As soon as she observed the presence of the secretary, her blood ran cold. She trembled in every limb, and a cold perspiration covered her face. She cast an imploring look upon Björnarne, but her cry for help to "John! John!" had filled him with such hate and fury, that he motionlessly looked on while Paul and Egede carried out their plan. In a moment, the maiden was bound in the clothes, and her mouth sealed up

Nothing moved without. Petersen listened on the outside;

and turned once more around the hut with the light. The dying reindeer made a last effort to raise himself up to follow his mistress; but it was in vain. The rays of the lantern fell upon its soft, still eyes; Paul jestingly whispered, "Let every one take an example from this intelligent creature, how to die with grace." While he was thus speaking, he examined some chests, the contents of which excited his surprise. In one of them were more than two dozen short guns, all new and in good condition. In the other, he found two small kegs of powder, and a number of bars of lead. The kegs bore the name of Marstrand; after examining them for a moment, he called Egede to take them and throw them in the stream. He then went ahead, the Quane carrying the prisoner, and Björnarne following after. Olaf stood under the dark arch, and was advised of the successful issue of the expedition. He himself had neither heard nor seen anything; he observed the pale and terrified face of Gula with comparative indifference, as the secretary cast a light upon it.

"What shall we do with her?" he asked.

"You will soon hear, my dear fellow," replied Paul. "At present, the chief thing is to get to our horses as soon as possible. Did you conceal them securely, Egede, and can you find them again?"

"Certainly, Herr," said the Quane. "Their feet are chained, and neither bear nor wolf will seek them."

"Then let us be gone! We have full two hours to travel. The girl must be in the saddle by daybreak, for she has tender feet. Carry her up the steps."

Egede had no taste for this service. "She can walk," said he, rudely.

Björnarne handed him his gun, lifted the maiden on his own shoulders, and carried her up the steps to the Saita of Jubinal.

Hence, the way led down the steep declivity to the lake at the bottom, which was to be waded; the wild, high plain stretched out, with swamps and thickets, intersected by innumerable springs, and streams, and jagged ridges of rock.

After a rest of a few minutes, Björnarne again took the burden on his shoulders. Her gentle struggle was soon overcome. It seemed as if Gula endeavored to tear the ligament which bound her arms; and as she was laid down on the stone of sacrifice, she was heard to exclaim, from beneath the thick cloth, "Jubinal! great Father, help! help me!"

"Ha! ha!" laughed Paul, "as John cannot help, and Herr Jesus shows no disposition to aid, you now call upon Herr Jubinal. Shame upon you, you little heathen! Do not try to hold fast to the stone of sacrifice. Tear her away, Björnarne. Whatever harm you may invoke upon us, Björnarne wishes you nothing but love and kindness, and we laugh at your avenging Jubinal."

At this moment a crash was heard on the summit of the Kilpis, followed by a sullen roar; then came a gust of wind, howling through the crags and clefts of the mountain, and the lake beneath heaved with its agitated waters.

"Do not call the devil and the spirits to awake," said Olaf.

"What a fool you are!" said Paul. "It was nothing but a stone plunging down from above into the water; or do you think Jubinal may have been awakened by this weeping girl, have raised himself on his pillow, and drawn his night-cap off? Alas for the pious Klaus! What will he say, when he hears that his convert, in whose fidelity he so firmly believed, has, in her extremity, worshipped the golden calf!"

The steep declivity was descended without any accident, and then the march proceeded through lake and swamp, and the rugged country, as quietly as possible. Björnarne did not let go of his beloved; he carried her for hours, with the indomitable strength of a man accustomed to great exertion. At length a grey coloring spread over the sky, before which the darkness of the night gradually vanished. Single peaks and ridges rose out of the inhospitable waste, in turning around one of which Paul Petersen descried the glowing red brow of the Kilpis, rising up through a mass of clouds.

"There lies the Pitsasjaure," he exclaimed; "and hereabout, in the bottom, our horses must be hidden. You can now set down your precious burden, and rest from your fatigue; Egede will procure you a four-legged carrier."

But Egede did not execute the order. He stood still, and listened; for his dog, which, up to this time, had followed in his steps, stretched his nose in the air, growled, and showed his teeth.

"What does that mean?" said Paul. "Is the devilish rabble on our track? Away with you, behind the rock! The horses, there, you ape. Look there, verily — no I do not deceive myself — Mortuno, as true as I live! Come on, my dear Mortuno. By heavens! He is alone; I see no other. He is running like a lynx. We must take him, alive, if possible. Should he be uncivil, think then, Olaf, on the hole in your cap."

Paul Petersen stood upon an open space, behind which great blocks of stone were strewn around. An arm of the Snibotjok, which descended from the Jaure, wound through this labyrinth, rushing and roaring along its deep bed. A human figure was visible on the edge of this stream of the wilderness, which immediately disappeared again: soon after, there appeared in sight, on the opposite height, another, which was no other than Afraja's nephew. He ran directly up to the secretary, who put himself in readiness to receive him; but the Lapp suddenly came to a halt before him, as he endeavored to recover his breath.

"How?" cried Paul, "is it you, my sweet friend, that seeks us at this early hour of the morning? Where have you left your cap, and how do your kommagers look?"

"Where are your brothers?" asked Mortuno.

"Come here, I will show them to you," said Paul. "Sit down by us; our fire will warm you."

"Where have you left Gula?" continued the Lapp, as he raised his gun.

"Has your darling run away from you, poor fellow?" replied the secretary. "I will help you to seek her."

"False man, you have stolen her!" cried the Lapp. "Give her up. Where is she?"

"Here, Mortuno, here. What a foolish fellow you are, and how fearfully you turn your eyes about! Gula, herself, invited us; she gave us information of her place of abode, for how else could we have found her out? Her inmost wish is to be again with us, and to live with her benefactor, Helgestad, and her friend, Björnarne. Why should you be so angry at it?"

"You lie!" exclaimed Mortuno. "A cry awoke me; I found Gula's faithful animal, which you killed. Wherever you tread is blood, and wherever your eye looks the grass and flowers wither."

"I have always said," said Paul, laughing, as he slowly raised his gun and cocked it, "that you are a poet; you have promised me a song. I will have it now, my dear fellow, or I will teach you to sing another tune. Do not stir, I beg you; for as sure as you raise your arm, you will repent it. Heda, Egede, Olaf! go to him, and give him your brotherly hands."

As he said this, Mortuno heard a piercing shriek. He stood facing the mouth of the gun of the cunning secretary, not doubting that the least movement would cause his death. At the cry, however, his eyes turned behind the stone. He did not see Gula, but it was her voice, and with the rapidity of the lightning he stooped down, made a spring towards the hiding-place, and wrested his weapon, in the same moment, from Paul, as the prisoner ran towards him from between the rocks. Paul discharged his gun, with a curse, at the Lapp, who would have escaped unharmed, had not a better-aimed shot been almost simultaneously fired. Mortuno fell down without an exclamation, and Gula threw herself upon him without attempting to fly, which would have been in vain, for Björnarne was behind her, and Olaf sprang forwards with his smoking gun. All stood still, and Paul himself, wicked and unfeeling as he was, uttered not an insolent word, when he saw the poor child kneel at the side of the unfortunate young man. She stroked back his hair, and discovered a couple of bloody streaks upon his forehead. As she looked into his fixed eyes, and laid her hand upon his head, she suddenly began to hope. The body made a struggle, and the feet quivered, as if he would stand up; it seemed as if she had recalled him to life and understanding.

"Oh! awake," she exclaimed to him; "do you hear me, Mortuno; do you hear me? Has my call, which once you could hear over lakes and mountains, no power on your ear?"

The dying man once again opened his eyes, and while they were intently fixed upon her, he fell back a corpse.

"Help him! help him!" cried Gula, weeping, as she pressed the head to her bosom, and sought to lift up the body.

"Why did you let her cry and run?" said Paul, in anger. "But for that, we would have taken him alive."

"She had entreated Björnarne, with tears in her eyes, to unloosen her arms," said Olaf; "and she raved like a madman when she heard the fellow's voice."

"She will never hear him more," muttered the secretary. "You have repaid his shot through your hat full an inch deeper, and that will suffice him for all time to come. But really," he continued, as he felt his side, "I think the rascal has not only ruined your hat, but my coat and shirt."

He now perceived that Mortuno, as he ran, had fired a ball, which had grazed his left side; for his fingers were bloody after feeling it.

Olaf examined it, and said, "The skin is torn off with a considerable piece of flesh."

"How can a man be so basely vindictive," said Paul, in jest, "to wish to lessen the rest of the little flesh I have? But we must now put an end to this scene. Here comes Egede with the horses; observe his exulting smile, when he sees his ancient enemy lying still before him."

"Here, our road divides," he continued. "I must go directly to Lyngenfiord, where the market is to be opened to-morrow, and you will draw off, with Egede and this weeping doll, to the left, to the high Jaure, which is already visible in the morning light. It is the Reisajaure: behind it lies the Quanerfiord. Egede is well known there, and has a kind of cousin or friend living at the Lachself, whose boat is at your disposition."

"And then?" asked Olaf.

"Then in God's name, down the fiord to Loppen, where we will conceal the precious treasure for the present."

"Will you not take her with you and give her to Helgestad?"

"No," said Paul, "I have determined differently, and for good reasons. The market must first be over. Were we to carry Gula there, it would give rise to great uproar; to-morrow morning every stone in Finnmark would speak of it. She must disappear until we have the old villain in our power; and the more secretly we act, the sooner will it be accomplished."

"And Björnarne?"

"I would most willingly take him with me," replied the secretary, "but he will not go. You must go along with her, Olaf, for Egede would strangle the poor thing before she saw the Quananger. Björnarne must, in his turn, guard you, lest the fiery eyes of the little witch may do you harm."

"Listen," replied Olaf, with a menacing look; "I am not a fit subject for your jests. I shot the fellow down because I could not help it, and because he deserved it; but I can neither make light of it, nor of the grief of the maiden. You are responsible for all the evil in this affair."

"If you cannot laugh, weep then, on my account; I will take all the consequences upon myself. Where is the holy image which the old scoundrel sold you?"

"In my pocket."

"Good! keep it securely, Jubinal will take excellent care of us. From the appearance of the sky, it will give us wind. You will return to Orenaes Gaard for my wedding. Ilda would otherwise miss the best dancer; and the gallant younker, moreover, will not be there."

The Nordlander felt the point of this sarcastic remark, but he made no reply; for at that moment, Egede burst into a diabolical laugh, and twisted his eyes about, so that nothing but the white could be seen.

He stood before the dead body, shaking his fist, leaping, and laughing like an insane person, and uttering volleys of reproachful expressions which Mortuno no longer heard. Gula heard them, however, as she was praying and weeping on her knees, and she sprang up and advanced before the corpse.

"Shameless man!" she said, "dare you look on him? As long as he lived, you feared him, and he despised and derided you. Go and leave this dead body, to which you must answer before the judgment-seat of God!"

The dignity and severity of her rebuke was so startling, that the Quane, although he shook his fist and gnashed his teeth, shrank back in terror; for the thought of the judgment had, at least, produced a momentary impression on him.

"Bravo, little moralist!" exclaimed Paul; "old Klaus could not have done better. Retire, Egede, you have received enough, and you, Björnarne, seat the princess on the best horse, and depart; or will you accompany me, and consign her to the care of Olaf?"

"I, myself, and none other, will take charge of her: tell my father what you choose," replied Björnarne.

Paul nodded to him, and said; "Forwards, then! Take her away, and be happy!"

"Whither?" asked Gula, drawing back; and as she received no answer, she continued; "Who gave you the right to drag me off by force? What have I done? Where is the law or authority? You surprised me, like robbers, in my sleep, and you have shed blood. Answer, you who are to be a judge. Shame upon you, and upon all of you, to bind and maltreat a helpless woman."

"Charming!" laughed the secretary, "old Klaus was right; she has something of her father's spirit. We will answer your inquiries on another occasion; be satisfied now, and go with Björnarne."

"If you persist in your violence," said Gula, "carry me to Helgestad and Ilda. I will go there, and nowhere else. If I committed a fault in abandoning his house, I will declare the cause which induced me to it. I was born free, and no one has any right over me. You are all subjects of the king, and the laws protect me also. Severe orders, Paul Petersen, against your arbitrary conduct, have lately arrived. Do not suppose that I will remain silent. I will find friends to assist me."

"The younker of Balsfiord!" cried Paul.

"Would that he were here!" answered the unhappy maiden, as she turned her burning eyes on all sides; "you would tremble at the sound of his footstep. But no," she continued, "no! You would, with your cruel helpers, lay him by the side of Mortuno there, and then laugh, as you do now. God in heaven preserve him! Preserve him!"

Gula acted as if she could call Marstrand to her aid from the air and mountains.

"Charm him hither, you wicked witch; we will receive him properly. But I smell no brimstone, and I see nothing."

"One Being, at least, sees and hears you," replied Gula; "and he will find you sooner than you think, wretched man!"

"Jubinal, or your fiery devil, Pekel, or you yourself, little snake."

"Almighty Father of all things!" said the maiden, as she fell upon her knees, and folding her hands, lifted her eyes to heaven, "do not permit him to scoff at your sacred name.

Protect me, help me, punish him! Show him that you cannot be mocked with impunity."

"The devil!" exclaimed Petersen; "why are you standing there, listening to the idle prattler! I give you permission to curse me as much as you please. Begin now, for it is daylight. Seize her, Egede, if Björnarne will not do it. To horse with her, and stop her mouth!"

Björnarne pushed aside the arm of the Quane, and took Gula's hand. He appeared downcast and melancholy, and his eyes were timid and unsettled in expression. "Come, dear Gula, come with me," he said, in a gentle tone. "I will not abandon you; you have nothing to fear."

"Oh! Björnarne!" she answered, "is it then possible that you are with these men? Have pity on my misery; carry me to my father; let me see my father. Dear Björnarne! dear, dear Björnarne!"

She looked beseechingly at him, but he stood speechless and pale. Paul answered in his place, and said, "Go with him; he carries you to Paradise, and will sit with you under the apple-tree."

"I cannot carry you to your father, Gula," said Björnarne. "I have sworn it."

"Sworn, Björnarne? Sworn to do evil?"

"I cannot do otherwise," he murmured. "You shall hear all; take consolation, and believe me."

"And if he may not console you, we will then send you the younker Marstrand," said Paul.

"If he knew it," she exclaimed, he would stand by me. How base and wicked you all are! John! John! Help!"

"You have lost your senses," cried Petersen. "Are you a man, Björnarne?"

Björnarne's face was now glowing with fury. He lifted up the light body as a feather, as if he would dash it to pieces against the jagged rock. But, in the next moment, he placed

Gula on the saddle, and, seizing the rein, he ran with the horse through the rock-strewn fjeld to the Reisajaure.

Egede sprang forward with his dog to seek the best road, followed by Olaf; and, when they were some distance in advance, Paul mounted the other animal, and patted its neck in his gratification. "We are at last rid of her, and now carry me to my mistress, old Nic, in time for a sweet welcome this evening." He cast a glance at the corpse, before which the horse startled. "You are a fool, Nic; a dead Lapp does not bite; he is worth just as much as a dead Norman. Love, and obtain what we desire, that is the aim of life. And now I have them, —Helgestad's money, Afraja, the miserable Dane, and all. I have them all in my fingers; and, by Jubinal and Pekel, no power shall open them!"

He listened, for it seemed to him that he heard a distant cry; then, he urged the beast on; and, as it was young and active, it rapidly made its way across the rocks and thickets of the fjeld, until the Snibotjok was reached, when his rider urged him into a full gallop.

CHAPTER XXII.

When Marstrand awoke from his unconsciousness and opened his eyes, he gradually became convinced that he was in a high and spacious chamber, the extent of which was lost in the distance. A singular jagged and dark vault hung over him, and a red light occasionally burst through the darkness; but nothing broke the voiceless silence.

After some reflection, Marstrand recollected what had happened to him; but this was not the tent at the Saita stone, nor Gula's hut, the valley nor the woods. He sat on the ground against the corner of a pillar of rock, a couple of fir branches were burning in a cleft, and before him crouched a figure, which he easily recognised as that of Afraja. The oppressive drowsiness left him, and the more he collected his thoughts, the more was he convinced that he was in a great cavern. At the same time, he remembered what he had frequently heard of such caves, and he gazed in astonishment on all sides. His unsatisfied looks at last rested on his silent companion, and he said:

"Is it you, Afraja?"

"Yes," was the reply.

"And what is this? Where are we? In a cave?"

"You say so," responded the old man.

"Why have I been brought hither?"

"Jubinal's messengers brought you, at his command. Arise, and follow me. Speak not, ask not, but behold—and hear."

He took the burning torch from the cleft, and went ahead. The softest whisper re-echoed with ten-fold force from the vault, and the torch lit up the clefts and passages, causing the adjacent sides to glow as if set with numberless stars and diamonds. Stalactites descended from the yellow roof, forming the most fantastic shapes; as Afraja, at a point where two natural passages divided, entered one leading outwardly, his companion could not suppress his astonishment.

It seemed to him as if he had been introduced into the most brilliant jeweller's shop in the world. His eyes were dazzled by the sparkling light, which was nothing else than genuine, solid metal—pure, crystalline silver! He had read in tales, of grottoes, where all was silver, where grew trees and flowers of silver, and where silver moss covered the earth; but he now saw the wonderful spectacle before him. Leaves and tendrils hung down from the roof, intermingled with flowers and branches.

Immense riches were to be gathered here without any trouble. This deformed old man possessed more than had ever been stowed away in the treasure-vaults of a king, and yet of what value was it to this houseless wanderer of the desert? Afraja lowered his torch and silently exposed to view a row of large pots and old chests, standing within a recess of the vault. They were filled with large pieces of money, green with dampness. This must be the treasure accumulated by his ancestors; from these old pots he must have procured the specie thalers for the Balsfiord, without any perceptible diminution. He looked at Marstrand without uttering a word, showing by his exulting laugh that he was satisfied with the impression produced.

"It is not a dream!" said Marstrand, striking his forehead; "I actually see it. These are my hands and this my head. Could you produce all this by magic? Is it imaginary or real?"

"Convince yourself," replied the old chief, as he kicked against one of the chests. "Take what you please and examine it in the sun-light." He tore off one of the twigs from the roof and laid it in Marstrand's hand. "What you see," he continued, "is not the best I know of. In Enare Traesk, there are larger caves than this, traversed in every part by veins of silver; and you shall have all, all shall be yours. You have seen what I have shown to no other man. I have brought you here, that you might be satisfied that I have the means to accomplish my undertaking. Help me; you are bold and I love you. I will be more grateful to you than your own offspring."

"What I see is wonderful!" exclaimed Marstrand. "I am astonished beyond comprehension; were, however, all the silver of the earth here collected together and offered to me, I would refuse it, rather than do what you wish me."

"Will you not?" asked the Lapp, as he fixed his lowering eyes upon him.

"I cannot commit a crime," replied Marstrand.

"No one will punish you," whispered Afraja.

"But my conscience! I am a man, a Christian! I have sworn to help you in all proper things. I will go to Trondheim, Copenhagen, and will prostrate myself at the feet of the king, and tell the story of your wrongs, and what the power of truth cannot effect, will be obtained by the influence of your silver. Desist, Afraja, or you will ruin yourself, and all who depend on you. You are wise, and you must act wisely."

The old man gazed upon him with a crafty and incredulous stare. He did not seem to comprehend how Marstrand could refuse him, after this unlimited proffer of treasure. He eyed him closely, and raised the torch on high, while he again whispered his tempting propositions.

"I will give you all. All that I possess and know shall be yours. How can you help yourself? You must be ruined. You will be mighty before them; you will take vengeance on your enemies; they hate and betray you, young man. Will you suffer yourself to be trodden under foot? Are you a man? You counsel me to wisdom — be wise yourself. Will you not? And Gula — do you think of Gula?"

"No! no!" exclaimed Marstrand, in a voice which was triplicated by the echo; "you shall not have me, even for Gula's sake!"

Afraja angrily shook his head. In the red glow of his torch, he looked like one of those wicked, necromantic dwarfs who once dwelt in similar caves and clefts in the north. Probably he was whispering to himself a magic spell, while he turned his flashing eyes upon the refractory Dane, who shuddered with secret terror.

"Let us see," said Marstrand; "I will do all that I can."

"Will you betray me?" cried Afraja.

"Never; I am not a traitor."

"Have I not done you good, and are you not a Norman?"

"I hope to prove to you, that I am grateful."

"You shall not go!" shouted the Lapp.

Marstrand stood still. The wild and threatening face of the chief inspired him with apprehensions of evil. "What will you do?" he asked, as he grasped him by the arm.

But Afraja sprang back, with youthful agility; and as he

waved the torch above his head, he gave vent to a diabolical laugh, rushed out of the passage into the middle of the cave, and all was suddenly involved in profound darkness and silence. After a few tottering steps forward, Marstrand gave up all attempt to follow. He groped along to the walls of the cavern, and laid his hand upon one of the projecting crystals. The thought suggested itself to him, that he might miserably perish here, in the midst of treasures; but he kept silent, and repressed his rising sense of despair; for it did not appear credible, that Afraja would use his power so cruelly. Nowhere was a ray of light visible, or a cleft in the rock, through which might be seen a star of hope, or any means of discovering the way out. He could form no idea of where he was, whether far from, or near to, the Kilpis; whether in the bowels of that sacred mountain, or in the depths of a fjeld. His reflections suggested no explanation, and not a whisper was to be heard. With increasing horror, he imagined that Afraja had withdrawn from the cave.

"I do not know if you hear me," he, at length, said, in as firm a tone as he could; "but I hope so, for the sake of your honor. I came here as your guest; and even those who hate and despise your race, praise your hospitality and honesty. What a shame it would be, if you had enticed me here to destroy me! You wish to intimidate me, but you will not succeed; I would a thousand times rather perish, than peril the salvation of my soul. I cannot, and dare not. Remember that this deed will follow you; and what will Gula say, when you stand before her? What will you answer, when she asks after me?"

He ceased, and some time elapsed without hearing a sound. The abandoned man dared not move from the place where he was standing. He did not know whether he might not, at the next step, plunge into an abyss; or in seeking an outlet, whether he might not lose himself in these subterranean halls, which appeared to be of immeasurable extent. The more he reflected, the less he could understand how he had got there; so much only was certain, that Afraja must have given him some deeply-intoxicating drink, and that he had profited by his unconsciousness to carry him to this secluded place. Probably he was close by the valley; probably in Gula's neighborhood; and she could not hear his call. Possessed by this idea, he suddenly shouted her name with all his might, and it was repeated by the echoes.

"Come to me, my Gula, come to me! Oh! do you not hear me? You are the only one who would not forsake or betray me!"

"Come!" said Afraja, as he shook him by the arm. He must have been standing close to him.

This single word poured another stream of life into Marstrand's veins. At this moment he felt all the horror of his forsaken condition, and he seized the faithless Lapp with a feverish grasp.

"You call upon Gula," said the old man. "I will bring you to her. May she soften your heart, stubborn man, which is harder than the iron mountain in Enare Tracsk."

It would have been superfluous to reply. Marstrand surrendered himself to the guidance of his leader, who strode rapidly forward through the darkness, without making any effort to procure a light. He doubtless had his reasons for this, and the distrustful prisoner divined them. Afraja wished to conceal from him all possible knowledge of the entrance to the cave. He followed patiently, and suppressed inquiries and reproaches; for what could these have availed him, when a stab would have sufficed to get rid of him forever.

The way was followed for a long time in silence by both, to judge from which the cavern must have had a great extent. Sometimes there appeared to be spacious halls; and then again narrow passages. The Dane several times struck his head against the low roof; and then again, he entered places where the arch of the rock was many feet higher. Sometimes he groped outwards; and then he descended — but finally he thought he perceived that the cunning Lapp often led him the same way, to bewilder him the more; and it was only when he deemed he had done enough for this purpose, that he conducted him through a narrow side opening, in which Marstrand suddenly felt a strong draught of air. Soon afterwards he saw a star above him. He breathed freely, for he was again in the open air. The darkness of the night was yet intense. On both sides rose up smooth precipices of rock, and the bottom of the ravine, which continually declined, formed the bed of a stream, the roar of which, although it was not visible, could be distinctly heard. They were at last obliged to descend into this channel, and wade through it, until Afraja turned into another cleft, and reached one of the mossy and swampy fjelds through high rocks, thickets, and deep little valleys. Here the grey of the morning was breaking through the darkness; but Marstrand endeavored in vain to guess where he was. The fjeld sank again into the steep bed of a mountain stream, and when another ascent was gained, the thick fog prevented anything from being seen. It was day, yet this veil of cloud shut out the light, as if Jubinal had sent it to blind their eyes. Marstrand did not know whence he had come, or whither he was going; and he had already opened his lips to ask a question, as one of these phenomena took place, which are frequently witnessed in the north. The fog lifted itself up and disappeared as quickly as the rising of a stage-curtain. The wind scattered it over the firmament, and the high summit of the mountains, with the crimsoned brow of the Kilpis, burst full into view.

Marstrand was now again entered upon the waste; but he could not discern in what direction lay the caves from which he had so lately issued. Afraja had led him through such a devious way, and the fog and darkness had been so intense, that all his speculations as to the situation of the silver-mines were completely baffled. The old chief conducted him in silence towards the Kilpis, which was yet several hours distant, when he suddenly came to a halt, and, leaning on his staff, listened, as if to sounds in the distance.

"Whither must I follow you?" asked Marstrand.

"To her who is expecting you. Did you hear nothing?"

"No," said Marstrand.

"It was a cry," muttered Afraja. "Yet again! Heard you nothing then?"

"It sounded like a shot; but the wind is against us. It may be a mistake."

One of the great brown-colored and white-breasted möven, which fly from the fiords to the sea, flew screaming against the wind, circled round their heads, and rose higher and higher in the air, until, with a wild and mournful cry, it went off in the same direction from which it had come. The Lapp looked after it for some time, and then said, "Who sends you? Are you a messenger of Ayra, the dreadful God, who holds the threads of life in his hand, or was it a soul bringing me a farewell greeting?"

Marstrand was not surprised at these questions. He had heard of the superstition of the Lapps, according to which, the soul of a lonely dying man enters into the body of an animal, to announce his death to his relatives, before Jubinal's heaven is opened to it; but he reluctantly followed Afraja, when, instead of proceeding towards the Kilpis, he pursued the flight of the bird; and without heeding his call, took his way through a steep, rising fjeld, full of broken masses of rock. The Lapps are all active and persevering pedestrians, and they easily climb the sharpest heights. Marstrand had frequently seen the superior power of endurance of these apparently weak men over the coast-people; and he now found that the old man was more active and agile than he himself. He felt exhausted from the adventures of the night, and the many hours of wandering, and he was both hungry and thirsty; while Afraja's strength, on the contrary, appeared to have redoubled.

A full hour had elapsed. Afraja had attained a high projecting platform, and disappeared on the heights of the fjeld, leaving his tired companion to pick his way as well as he could. When he finally stood above, nothing was to be seen. Huge fragments of rock, which, thousands of years before, had been scattered there by some natural cause, or by Pekel's giants, covered this lofty mountain-plain. Dark, weather-beaten masses rose up from the swamp, or lay piled upon each other in confused heaps, and were covered over with pale green grass, moss and gnarled roots.

When Marstrand had, for some time, in vain looked around, and called for his companion, he thought he perceived the impress of his footsteps in the soft ground. He followed these, until they brought him to a small open space, in the midst of which Afraja was seated, contemplating a human figure which lay stretched out before him. It was the spot where Mortuno had expired, a short time before; Marstrand stood upon the same point where Paul Petersen had been, less than an hour before.

When he looked upon the bloody face of the dead, he uttered a cry of horror. Who could have killed him? Who had done this deed? How came Mortuno there? His skull was shattered, his blood formed a pool, and the trodden earth around showed that the struggle and death must have taken place on that spot.

A presentiment suggested itself to him; but he dared not speak of it. Afraja's countenance was serious and dignified; his grief must be great, but yet he endured it. He seemed to be buried in thought, as he regarded the corpse, until, at length, after the custom of his people, he broke into a death-wail in praise of the departed.

"Here you lie," said he; "and but yesterday I saw you bounding as lightly and joyously over the fjeld, as a young stag at dawn. Who had feet and eyes like you, or a heart so full of courage and truth? Wherefore have you left us, Mortuno, and why did not Jubinal protect you? Woe to my old head! Woe to your wounds! Let him who has tears, weep over you; even your animals themselves will shed tears; only your murderers will rejoice. Fly, soul, fly to the arms of Jubinal; he will lead you to ever-blooming gardens, where his daughters will surround you; but care not — they who slew you will be slain; snakes shall consume their bodies, and their souls shall be frozen to ice."

"Of whom are you thinking? Who may it be?" asked Marstrand.

Afraja arose, and pointed to several foot-tracks. "Look," said he; "here were men who wore thick soles on their boots; and here are the hoof-prints of horses. There were two horses, and four men." He stooped down, and examined them attentively again, in silence, and then turned to the rock, and regarded the blood-stains upon it. "Mortuno shot," he said; "but his head was heavy." From the position of the corpse, it appeared to him to be certain that the fatal ball had come from another side.

He now ran to the rock, from behind which Olaf had fired, and picked up something that lay in the corner. It was a small, blue handkerchief, embroidered with red threads, the ownership of which he immediately recognised. The staff fell from his grasp, as he held it up before him, incredulous as to the reality of what his eyes looked upon.

Dogs barked upon the Elf, and men, in brown frocks, sprang out of the depths of the ravine through which it flowed. The dogs howled loudly, as they leaped towards the old chief, as if to announce something evil; and their masters looked wild and horror-struck.

"Good father!" cried the foremost, "what has happened? Your gamme is empty; robbers have carried off your daughter; and the white beast, which was the joy of Gula, has been killed with a knife! Oh! woe! woe! What shall we do?"

Afraja summoned up his spirits. In impotent fury, he shook

his clinched fists at the heavens. Fury and despair were depicted on his face; his eyes were distended, and red with rage; his lips trembled, and he could not speak. "Cursed be you all!" he, at last, shrieked. "Cursed in your heaven, and on your throne of clouds! If you betray your descendants, Jubinal, help me, then, you who live in the subterranean fires!" He uttered a wild cry, fell on his face, and convulsively grasped the stones and earth with his hands.

Marstrand lifted the old man up; but he appeared to be in an almost insensible condition, and he made no reply to the remarks addressed to him. His attendants carried him to the Kilpis; while Marstrand, and some of the Lapps, with their dogs, pursued the tracks of the robbers.

CHAPTER XXIII.

Two days later, the great autumn market, at that time the most considerable in the country, was holden at the church of Lyngen. Multitudes of the small cultivators, Quanes, agricultural Lapps, colonists, and fishermen came from all the sounds, and fiords, and islands, as far as Sorven, to make their winter purchases in part with the traders; but more with the fjeld Lapps, who descended from their mountains with great herds of fat reindeer, with furs, hides, otter-skin caps, kommagers, pockets, girdles, and strong leather cords. They carried on, also, an active barter; selling their articles for cash, or trafficking them for powder and lead, pieces of linen and woollen coverlets, needles, and thread, and twine, steel and iron wares of all kinds, but more particularly for flour and brandy, to supply their winter encampment. The autumn market was the chief epoch of the year, and the source of constant anxiety and hope. Every effort was made to hoard up and economise, in order to be able to buy and sell; the Lapps were the most important frequenters of these markets, and thence the designation of Lappish markets, which they bore; at that time, when this unfortunate people numbered eighty thousand heads, the commerce was yet greater than it is now, when they scarcely reach the sixth part of that number.

The Lapland herd proprietors came with their wives and families; and the markets were not devoted exclusively to trade, but they were also holidays, celebrated with feasting and dancing. They were also occasions for the administration of justice, and the collection of taxes, and the adjustment of old feuds. The Voigt of Tromsöe had erected his throne in the middle of the market, surrounded by his lensmen and bailiffs; the sworn secretary, his nephew, declared the law in the name of the king, with the great statute-book alongside of him, together with piles of acts, papers, and other legal instruments, which excited no little astonishment and awe. The Lapp market was no less advantageous for both these persons, than for the traders; for it gave rise to abundance of litigation, which was a favorite passion with the Lapps, colonists, and Quanes. The Lapps had always complaints to prefer of encroachments on pasture-grounds, and the people of the Gaard accusations of malicious mischief; but all brought money into the pockets of the judge, whose decisions were always suitably paid for.

On this occasion, the market presented a singular appearance. Enough Lapps had repaired to it, but there were comparatively few women and children; and they had brought a much less number of fat reindeer, and other things, with them than usual. With their long, iron-pointed staffs, and occasionally with short guns saucily thrown over the shoulders, they moved up and down, or gathered in squads, and anxiously peered around, as if they expected something strange. The northern traders had put up tents before their small church-houses, in which the whole wealth of their goods was temptingly displayed; but there was little business transacted. The principal traders were from Tromsöe and the fiords, among whom was Helgestad. The waters of the bay were covered with yachts and great boats. No one rightly knew what was the true cause of this bad market; but the dissatisfaction was universal.

Some attributed it to the weather; for a fearful storm, which had raged in the night, had thrown down Helgestad's tent, and torn it to pieces. Heavy clouds yet drove over the sky, and from time to time sent down showers of rain; and the wind howled around the tower and little square, obscuring the glory of the market. The wives and daughters of the traders, with the voigts, pastors and sorenskrivers, were accustomed to promenade about in their best attire; and it was, in truth, a rendezvous for the whole aristocracy of the north, when the ladies expected and received elegant gifts, the value of which was in proportion to the success of the market. But few had come, on this occasion, on account of the weather; and those who were on the ground, sat in their little houses, complaining of the cold and wind.

The wives and maidens of the Lapps could, indeed, better endure such weather; and some other reason must be assigned for their absence from a scene, where they were accustomed to invite their husbands and fathers to make liberal purchases for their sakes. Many were of the opinion, that it was feared in the gammes that the thefts, and other crimes, laid to the charge of the Lapps, would be severely punished at the market, and they had, therefore, remained at home. No one, however, knew what was true or false: on the other hand, there was a considerable number of young men, of good blood and family, at the market, who had not frequented it before; friends and acquaintances of the secretary, from Tromsöe, and of the family of Helgestad; they were seen but little in the market-shops, their time being devoted to the young ladies in their tents.

A numerous society had gathered in the little house of Helgestad, where, despite the discomforts of the weather, a general cheerfulness prevailed. The daughters of the neighbors and of the pastor, Heinrick Sture, had assembled around Ilda and Hannah; the pastor himself sat in a corner, with a full glass, awaiting patiently the hour when the tenth part of the market-tax, which he silently counted over, should be paid him. A half-dozen of the sons and cousins of the landed proprietors entertained the maidens, and from time to time others came in, laughing and jesting, and related incidents of the market, or complained of the impudence of the Lapps, who asked double for their animals over the preceding year, and stood before the shops of the traders, looking as if they would devour them, at the same time scarcely asking after the prices. Brandy was usually the most efficient means to inspire them with a desire for buying. Every transaction began with offering a full glass of it to the Lapp; if he did not find the price acceptable, a second glass was given him; and a third generally made him perfectly pliant. There were indeed some crafty fellows who would not get drunk until the trade was concluded and the species was placed in their belts. As theft was almost an entirely unknown vice among their race, they felt sure that nothing would be taken from them, even in the most senseless state of intoxication. This time, however, the full glass was everywhere refused, and the small colonists, who came forward with full bottles, were turned back and laughed at. All kinds of abuse were showered upon the Lappish rabble, for not drinking and suffering themselves to be swindled.

"It is a shame!" exclaimed one of the traders, who had just entered; "such a day has never before been seen here. It is a market in which no shout, no laugh, no merriment, and no drunkenness is to be heard or seen. Last year, they lay there at the church in whole rows. They sat in a circle, bellowed until they fell down and were carried out, and many a one of the poor islanders and colonists bought a fat beast for a species, a fur for the half, a cap for eight shillings, and a pair of excellent kommagers for a fresh dram. To-day, the rascals stand grinning at us, devour our wares with their eyes, as if they would run off with them, and will sell nothing but for cash, and at a high price. I cannot blame the men, who, in their fury, fell upon a couple of the scoffing scamps, and gave them a regular thrashing."

Helgestad entered at this moment, but the face of the great fierce man was more expressive of scorn than anger. "It is well calculated, but it will not help us. They are obdurate creatures, who cannot be rendered better by cudgelling. We must have patience with them; they will come to their senses before night. Go out now, maidens," he continued, as he turned to the society. "Help to enliven the market, and accompany Ilda, who expects Paul Petersen. He will buy her the most elegant marriage gift he can find, and you must assist her to look for the best feather cloaks. You may, perhaps, meet with the merry Mortuno, who always brings some good things."—He laid one of his huge hands on Hannah's shoulder, and smiled.—"You are anxious in mind," he said, "because your sweet-heart has not arrived. Comfort yourself, maiden, for he will not be long absent. It is yet right and proper that you should be compensated, and I beg of you to accept a present from me. Select whatever you desire, the most precious you can find, and the money shall be at your disposition. You are Niels Helgestad's daughter-in-law, and Ilda herself must yield to you."

Great was the astonishment, that the crafty trader, in spite of the bad market, should voluntarily incur such great expenditures. But he was indeed the richest in the country, and Fandrem's daughter brought full chests to his already wealthy house. The young maidens envied their friend the privilege of being able to select at will the choicest and dearest articles; and as the weather had become better, they accompanied her in the search.

Helgestad remained standing at the door, and from there

looked upon his store-tent, where his agents in vain called for purchasers. He paced to and fro, stamping violently; but he repressed his impatience until Paul Petersen entered with a happy smile and inquiries after Ilda.

"They have just gone out to seek you," said Helgestad. "Wait a moment, Paul. I have some apprehension as to the result; would that Björnarne were here, and that they only had the infernal scoundrel safely secured! I doubt if he will run into your net."

"Dismiss your doubts," replied the secretary. "Wherefore do the Lapps wait and put their heads together? They are expecting him, with the idea that they can commence the dance with his arrival. From what I have learned, it is evident that they have come from all sides, to lay their complaints before the voigt. Afraja and Mortuno, together with their assistants, have labored for weeks in the gammes to set the rabble in motion. You see what has been the effect. The women and old men have been left at home, and some two thousand lusty fellows are moving about here; many of them would wring our necks with pleasure, and plunder the market. The only reason why they do not buy, as true as I live, is because they believe, in some hours, to be able to break up the whole market. It would be no joke if Mortuno were to come with his band, and especially if there were only a couple of courageous, death-despising men among them."

"You cannot convince me that the Lapps would assail us in open market."

"But circumstances have changed," said Petersen. "Mortuno will neither shoot the voigt from his seat, nor Niels Helgestad from his bales of merchandise. No other dare attempt it."

"Have you brought the maiden to Maursund?"

"She has been secured."

"The nights were stormy," said Helgestad. "Did no mishap occur?"

"How could any happen? We have succeeded in our plans, and our measures are devised to obviate all fear. Leave all to me. As soon as we have the bird, it shall be put in a good cage. There lies the craft which will carry him to Tromsöe; with a sign from me, he will be placed on board. Go, father-in-law, and look after your business. When we get hold of the old rascal, we will extort silver from him, and I shall then have some other propositions to make to you."

"Nuh!" said Helgestad, "are you sincere?"

"As sincere as a Dane," replied Paul; "but there is Ilda. I will go to her; see how her eyes rove around, and who can she be seeking but me?"

Helgestad looked after him and muttered to himself, "I can imagine whom she is seeking; but she will never find him. The Danish lord, I believe, has run off; and, indeed, he had nothing else to do."

With this consolatory remark, he went back to the market, which had indeed increased in animation. The Lapps did not appear to know how to account for the absence of Mortuno and Afraja; and, as the greater part of them knew nothing more than that Afraja was coming to defend their rights before the voigt, they ceased to believe that it would take place.

They were well aware of the animosity entertained against Afraja, and if he had renounced his complaints, it was no doubt through fear of ill treatment. But few knew that it was proposed to call them out, to vindicate their wrongs by force of arms, and the rest had only formed vague conjectures of such a design. Mortuno had thrown out some intimations of the kind; but he had not communicated any plan to them, nor had a conspiracy been maturely devised. He had advised them to carry their arms with them, to fill their powder-horns, and line their belts with bullets; his words glowed with hatred against the oppressor, and he described in animated terms what would be the condition of the country, if the Normans were expelled, and the possessions of their ancestors should be restored to them. His remarks had aroused their cupidity, but there was no patriotism. Yet, had he shouldered his unerring gun, many would have followed him, who would not have trusted in any other leader.

If he should not make his appearance with his wise uncle, what would become of the market and the trade? Here were reindeer hams, skins, and hides in heaps; and there, stood the living beasts of slaughter in whole rows. Quantities of venison, and birds of various kinds, were bound to their backs by birch branches, and upon the ground lay gay colored garments, heaps of half-boots of reindeer skin, sewed together by sinews; bear and wolf furs, fox and otter-skins, antlers, and bags filled with feathers from the breast of the great, dazzling white moven; eider ducks, and other rich and warm-feathered birds. All these articles could not remain unsold, and why should they wait any longer? Many were seized with a secret fear, some longed after the brandy of the traders, others remembered that they had need of flour, cotton stuffs, iron-pots and hatchets, and it seemed to most of them, that these desirable articles, and the silver species of the Norwegians, were preferable to entering into a conflict with them, which would end in broken heads, punishments, whippings, and bloody wounds.

An active trade sprang up, by degrees, in many places, accompanied with shout and laughter, and flowing glasses; and only a small troop of young men stood apart, with guns on their shoulders, and knives in their belts.

When the maidens entered among the crowd, the market was already in full activity. Gigantic Quanes haggled, with savage curses with malicious grinning Lapps, who would not abate their prices. Their wives crouched together, smoked the pipes of the men, or mingled clamorously in the bidding. The reindeer were handled, their weight questioned and doubted, and the offer responded to with a scornful laugh, or the vender was brought to reasonable terms by the aid of a bottle of brandy.

In other places, the clamor turned upon fur coverlets, and kommagers, fox-caps and bear-skins. Fires were kindled, around which Finns and Bölaps, fishermen and colonists assembled, to eat, warm themselves, drink and frolic, while others gathered about roughly constructed tables to feast on mutton swimming in onion-broth. The Lapps cooked fish in their tinned vessels, which they devoured half-raw, or roasted flesh and birds.

It was a remarkable fact that while the Norman fishermen, as well as the Finns and other colonists, could not present a man or woman of prepossessing appearance among their rough and weather-beaten faces and forms, the despised Nomads, the Lapps, had sent to the market some quite elegant and pleasing young men and maidens.

These small-statured young girls were, indeed, regarded by the proud daughters of the traders, with contemptuous glances, and they were hardly looked upon by the men of better blood; but they were, nevertheless, much prettier, and more elegant of shape, than many who affected to hold them in contempt. In their blue jackets and full gowns, embroidered with red lace, and their white caps and plaited aprons, their neat feather pockets, and laced gaiter-boots, they tripped along, like fawns, through the crowd, presenting in their vivacious eyes and fresh color a striking contrast with the coarse figures of the Normans.

These graceful maidens, in their attractive national costume, were the heiresses of opulent families, or women in their early bloom. They were probably possessed of two or three thousand reindeer, and had a dozen of buried pots, filled with specie thalers, in expectancy. They were young aristocrats, who knew well their worth, and coldly turned their backs upon their poor, dirty countrymen, who sought to be intimate.

Among the young men who strutted about in their new, brown hunting-shirts, broad girdles with silver bells, and caps adorned with the feathers of the eagle and skarve, from beneath which their dark locks escaped in careless profusion, there were many stately and fine looking figures. They had all indeed something wild and striking in their appearance, and their small, flashing eyes roved timidly around, yet many a form was admirably shaped, and they were exempt from that tottering walk, so peculiar to the Lapps.

Many of these young men had brought various articles for sale, but they were only objects of art, consisting of Lappish pockets, precious baskets, collars, and overcoats, ornamented with the finest feathers of different birds, arranged with a taste and skill that would have done credit to the most ingenious artist.

With Ilda on his arm, and accompanied by her friends, Petersen had entered on the busy scene to make a selection from among this dazzling array of articles of taste. He urged his way through the dense throng of Lapps, who, as they yielded him a passage, scowled upon him with furtive glances; no hand, however, was raised against him, and no threat was uttered in his hearing; but the secretary looked upon them with a scornful expression, as if he knew their malicious thoughts and cowardice, while his keen penetrating glance struck every heart with terror.

On this day he wore his official costume—a blue coat, with gold embroidered collar, and laced hat. His powdered hair was bound with a ribbon, and by his side he wore the long sword of justice. This costume was a subject of fear and admiration to the Lapps, investing the secretary in their eyes with a mysterious power and authority.

The young maidens were bargaining for a beautiful feather mantle of a young Lapp, as Paul came up. The Lapp demanded a rather dear price, which had excited general surprise. Paul examined the cloak on all sides, and placed it on Ilda's shoulders, saying, "In your whole life, you fool, you have never beheld such a sight. The fairest maiden in Finnmark puts on your bad work, and for the first time gives it some value. Is there nothing better than this? Is there no richer and more elegant gift to be had in the market? The mantle does not please me. Is there no more skilful hand in your gammes, which can produce a better work than this?"

A throng had gathered around the group of purchasers, from the midst of which some one suddenly called out the name of "Mortuno!" in answer.

The exclamation was so instantaneous, and uttered in such a shrill piercing voice behind Petersen's back, that he was startled, and let the mantle fall from his hands; a moment after, his attention was called, by a loud cry, to the neighboring church, from which a curious procession of Lapps, bearing something on a bier, was issuing. The men at its head particularly excited his notice, and afforded him a malicious triumph; for one of them was Afraja, and the other Marstrand. Pushing aside the bystanders, he hurried to the official tent of the voigt, in the middle of the market-place, and there gathered also the friends and confidants of the sorenskriver. The arrival of the dangerous Lapp was announced from mouth to mouth. Petersen was prepared to receive him, as he had held a conference with his uncle as soon as he saw the funeral train. Universal silence prevailed, the traders and their assistants left their shops, and the Lapps stared with open mouths upon their prophet. All eyes were directed upon the old and decrepit man who was supported by the proprietor of Balsfiord. A Norman, one of the ruling caste, giving his hand to a Lapp, and walking by his side, was a spectacle which excited the frowns of some, and the joy and astonishment of others. Ten or twelve of the family and tribe of Afraja followed the old chief and Marstrand, four of whom supported the veiled poles of the bier, while the others walked with bowed heads, with a number of dogs with drooping tails, at their heels.

When Afraja reached the steps, he took off his cap, and clasped his bony hands. He made a low bow, and lifted up his head towards the seat of the voigt. His saddened eyes, red with weeping, immediately assumed an indignant glow, when he beheld the secretary. Extending his shrunken arm, he exclaimed, "Where is my child? Where have you concealed her? If she is here, let me see her. Have pity on me!"

"What does this mean?" said the voigt, with a fierce frown. "Have you a complaint to make? So have we."

"I complain," said the old man, in an humble but fearless manner, "that my child has been stolen from me; that robbers have entered my gamme, and carried off all that they could find; and not content with this, Mortuno——"

Paul Petersen sprang from his seat, and exclaimed with the full strength of his powerful voice, "Hold! a villain and traitor like you neither deserves to be heard nor believed. Before you make your complaint, learn what you are accused of. Travellers have been robbed and maltreated, dwellings fired, and cattle stolen and driven off. Besides all this, you have obstructed the pious efforts to spread the Christian faith. You constrain your people, by force and threats, to continue the worship of pagan gods; and you yourself are a heathen, whom no influences can convert to Christianity. You sacrifice to Jubinal, pray in the Saitas, curse and ridicule the Christian ministers, and have entered into partnership with the devil as a sorcerer. I accuse you of all these scandalous offences, and I will prove them against you. I, the judge of Tromsöe, arrest you in the name of the law. Seize him, and lead him away!"

This command was given to a crowd of officers of justice, and young men, who were placed on both sides of the Lapps, and had separated him from his companions; the last words were hardly pronounced, when Marstrand had thrown himself before the old chief, and his strong voice was heard replying to Petersen. "I protest against such arbitrary proceedings; if this man is not to be believed; I will be a witness for him."

"Spare your testimony for yourself," said the secretary. "You will soon have need enough of it.. Seize him, officers!"

"First look here!" replied Marstrand. "Here lies the victim, and there sits his murderer!" He advanced with a rapid stride to the bier, tore off the covering, and exposed to view the corpse of Mortuno, with the bloody wounds upon the forehead.

"Voigt of Tromsöe," said Marstrand, in the midst of the breathless silence; "in the name of the king, I demand justice of you. You are the highest magistrate in this country; and you must pursue every criminal, even though your own nephew should be among the number."

The voigt sat motionless upon his seat. His hands convulsively clinched together, and his face was inflamed with rage: he could have annihilated the accuser.

"It is," said Paul, "a false and abominable accusation. I am not obliged to answer it; but I will do it, that my friends and countrymen may not think ill of me. Bring the witnesses, John Marstrand, to sustain your charges, that they may be heard in the presence of all."

"Two days ago," began the accuser, "three men appeared, early in the morning, in the vicinity of the Kilpisjaure, hovering near the tent of Afraja, and who, finally, entered it. They were the sorenskriver, Paul Petersen, Olaf Veigand, of Bodoen, and Björnarne Helgestad. They pretended to be on a hunting excursion, were friendly received and entertained, and about an hour after again left the gamme. They returned, however, in the night, accompanied, without doubt, by a fourth, for the foot-prints of four persons have been discovered, and a broken knife, with the name of Egede inscribed upon the hilt.

"These four men, accompanied by a dog, forced their way into the secluded valley which lies at the foot of the Kilpis. The daughter of Afraja, called Gula, who is known to many, was sleeping there. They surprised the maiden, bound her hand and foot, as these torn bands prove, laid the hut waste, destroyed property, and carried off the captive. Some hours afterwards they were pursued and overtaken. Mortuno, the nephew of this old man, appears to have first discovered what had occurred. He endeavored to liberate the prisoner; but he was shot down, if not by Paul Petersen, at least by one of his companions. Here is a half-burnt paper, the wad of a gun, which is part of a letter written by Paul Petersen. It is his handwriting; let him deny it, if he can."

"I do not deny it," said Paul, contemptuously, as the fragment was handed to him; "but I do deny, upon my honor and conscience, and in the presence of Almighty God, that this Lapp fell by my hand. Before I defend myself, I have some inquiries to address to this accuser. You certainly can tell the whole story. Were you close at hand, or were you present, when the dead body was found?"

Marstrand was silent.

"It is not possible that Afraja sent to the Balsfiord to seek you. The time was too short for that; and it is also known that you left your residence several days previous, ostensibly on a journey to the Malangerfiord. But you were not there. You went, instead, to this Lapp, at the Kilpis, with whom, for some time, you have been in such intimate intercourse, as no Norman practises.

"I have no explanations to make to you, touching my conduct," said Marstrand, amid the disapprobatory murmur of the bystanders.

"For the moment, no—but, hereafter, certainly," exclaimed Paul; "it is sufficient now to know that you were concealed in the gamme of this old malefactor. I frankly confess that you spoke the truth, and that I was at the Kilpis with my friends Björnarne and Olaf; and I am willing to avow the motive which impelled me to this journey.

"This slain man was a villain of the worst kind, and I can hardly believe that his end excites any commiseration, but among his associates. He was the near relative of Afraja, his right-hand man in all his schemes, and his confidant in all his plans against the peace and security of the country. As the servant of the king and the law, I was obliged to think of some means of getting at this scoundrel. For this purpose, I associated myself with my friends, Björnarne and Olaf, and I appeal to the best man in Finnmark, Niels Helgestad, as a witness of the truth of what I say, as he was made acquainted with all my views, and allowed his son to accompany me.

"We arrived at the Kilpis and met Afraja there. In his gamme I convinced myself again of his vile life and actions. I tempted him by some flattering words, and he sold us a piece of money, an idolatrous picture, wh'ch he assured us would procure us a safe return, and a good wind on the sea."

Afraja, upon this remark, fixed his eyes on the secretary with a most scornful and vindictive expression.

"Can you deny it, old heathen and sorcerer?" exclaimed Petersen.

"Strike him down, the accursed villain!" shouted a crowd of half-drunken Quanes and colonists.

"We withdrew, and lay concealed in a ravine until evening," continued the secretary. "Duty and conscience urged me to employ every means to deprive this vermin of further power of doing mischief; for it was evident that Afraja would never come down from his wilderness, unless we could find some mode of enticing him here. I had learned that he kept his daughter concealed in a valley of the Kilpis, the same Gula whom Helgestad once bought of him, and educated to be a Christian, until he stole her away, and forced her again to the worship of idols."

"You lie," said the old man, "and you know it."

"We found the valley and the maiden, and we took her with us. No harm has been done her; our object was simply to bring this crafty malefactor down here, in order to get him in our possession, and punish him. We have succeeded in it. As to this dead man, I do not know how he came to his end. He has merited it a thousand times. He was a malicious enemy of every Christian and Norwegian man. Some weeks before, he shot Olaf Veigand through the hat, so that he made a narrow escape with his life. I would have punished him with the utmost rigor of the law, had he not been taken away by the will of God. If Olaf shot him, he doubtless did it in self-defence. I separated from my friends, who carried the maiden to Quanerfiord, in order to deliver her to Niels Helgestad, her rightful lord, when this Lapp, her father, should be in our power."

"She has no lord," said Afraja. "By the great God of the Christians, I swear that I never sold my child."

"Nuh!" answered Helgestad, as he came forward; "I am also here, and can say that you are a liar and a scoundrel. I bought your child for more brandy and tobacco than she is worth. You stole her away, as Paul Petersen has justly said. All here know me, and will credit my word."

"It is false!" said Afraja. "Gula never belonged to you. She left you, because your son persecuted her with his love. He tore her away from my gamme to dishonor her."

These words made a painful impression as well upon Helgestad, as upon the whole circle. It was the most dishonorable accusation that could be made against him. The rich, arrogant man, the first in the country, could he see himself and his son so publicly disgraced? Could a miserable Lapland maiden have been obliged to fly from the passion of Björnarne? Was it possible that he had pursued her, and carried her off, and was now lying concealed with her at Quanerfiord, while his betrothed, the daughter of Uve Fandrem, was in vain expecting him? Helgestad stood like a statue of stone. His hands were clinched together, his face was suffused with deep crimson, from mere shame, and he could, with difficulty, control himself. "Wretch!" he at length exclaimed, "I would tread you under my feet, if it were not a shame to touch one who belongs to the hangman."

"Away with the old villain!" said the voigt; "he shall atone for his many atrocities."

Afraja fled to the Dane, and clung to him. "Hear him!" he

exclaimed, "ask him, he knows all. Ask the pastor, Klaus Hornemann, he will tell the truth."

"I will hear him," said Helgestad. "Silence, you people, and let him speak! Speak, Herr Marstrand; you are a fine gentleman and a stickler upon the point of honor. Whatever has occurred between us, you have lived under my roof; name and character are now at stake. Chastise this rascal for his lies, and shame him before the people here, as you hope for mercy hereafter."

"If it is necessary," replied Marstrand, "that the whole truth be told, then, Herr Helgestad, I can do nothing else than confirm Afraja's words. It is, indeed, true, that Björnarne drove Gula from your house. He persecuted her with his love; they who wished to ruin him, cherished his passion, and I fear it was a well-considered plan to carry off the maiden, to separate the son from the father, and thus to make all alike miserable."

"You have conspired with him!" cried Helgestad. "You have taken the heathen devil's money!"

"Not I, you—you sought to deceive him!" said the Lapp. "I frustrated your schemes. The young man speaks the truth. Your son, your only son, lay at the feet of my daughter, was willing to fly to the gamme, whenever she pleased; but she repulsed him; she would not accept his proffered love!"

Helgestad tottered, and was obliged to lean upon a bystander for support, but the blow which he had received was not the hardest that was to fall upon him. In the same moment, a man broke through the crowd, before whom every one gave way. His long hair floated in disorder over his neck, he was almost breathless from exhaustion and anxiety, and his countenance struck all with terror and apprehension.

"Egede!" exclaimed the secretary. "He comes as another witness. Where is Björnarne? Where is the maiden!"

The Quane clasped his hands together, and stood perfectly motionless in the circle that surrounded him.

"Speak!" shouted Helgestad; "where is my son? You have come at a seasonable moment from Quananger. You shall now, friends and neighbors, hear the truth, which will dissipate all falsehood and deception. I suppose you have left them behind, and that Björnarne and Olaf have sent you ahead to announce their coming."

The wild creature grasped the hair of his head, and twisted it into knots. His eyes were distorted, and a guttural sound issued from the bottom of his throat, as if his tongue was incapable of action, or as if he dared not give utterance to the words which pressed to his lips.

The voigt sprang from his seat, and with a menacing wave of his extended arm, he exclaimed; "Have you lost your senses? You must speak. Holy God! what has happened? —Hold, Niels Helgestad! hold! Let him alone."

Helgestad had approached him, and struck him so violently on the shoulder, that Egede fell upon his knees. He glared upon him with a stare that seemed to penetrate to the inmost depths of his heart, and he appeared to gather something from this scrutinising look, which struck him with horror. The iron-hearted man trembled in every limb; his hard face was red with the blood that pressed to his brain, and his eyes protruded from his head with affright. Ilda stood alongside of him, pale, but self-possessed. She held her father's hand with a convulsive grasp; upon the other side, Hannah clung to his body, while her eyes fell, like lightning, upon the Quane and Helgestad, and in her countenance was depicted a strange mingling of passion, scorn, fear, pity, and anxious expectation.

Various as were the feelings of this miscellaneous throng, the deepest silence prevailed among them. In breathless anxiety, they fixed their eyes upon the individual who for so many years had been regarded as the first and happiest man in the whole country. No one had ever seen him in such a state• whatever he had commenced, he had always accomplished; whatever he wished to acquire, he had obtained. His sagacity was proverbial; whoever opposed him was defeated. And, now when he appeared to have arrived at the climax of human prosperity, and his son and daughter were about to contract marriages of a rare and enviable character, Afraja had hurled the first stone at his proud head, and here was a messenger who had something yet more fearful, to announce.

No one knew what it was and what it could be, that would cause such a being as Egede Wingeborg to tear his hair and beat his breast in such a fearful manner!

All these rough people were oppressed by the same emotions as those which agitated Helgestad. Paul Petersen alone felt an internal satisfaction; and while, with a saddened countenance, he endeavored to induce his father-in-law to retire, he saw that his projects were unexpectedly realized, and his most covetous expectations surpassed — and heaven itself seemed to have come to his assistance; for he was perfectly cognizant of the news which Egede had brought with him. The whole prey had now fallen into his hands, and the certainty of this was so gratifying, that he could easily feign a grief which he did not feel.

His eyes were moist, and his voice faltered, as he laid his hand on the shoulder of Helgestad. "I beseech you, dear father," he said in a lachrymose tone, "go with your daughters, and leave us alone. Lead your father away, Ilda. For heaven's sake! take him to your embrace, and console him with your tender sympathy."

But Helgestad lifted himself up like a lion, who, awaking from his sleep, beholds his lair surrounded by dogs and hunters. The bold pride of his youth returned—his head was erect, and his eyes roved sternly around. "I am able to suffer whatever must be submitted to. Go on, Egede, and let us know what it is; I can almost divine the truth — but uncertainty is worse than all. Where is my son?"

Egede's head sank down upon his breast, and as he clasped his hands before him, he exclaimed in a deep-toned voice, "Dead, Herr!"

Not a sound was heard. Helgestad clinched his fist — a fierce smile hovered around his lips, and his eyes opened wide, without a quiver. "He was a noble youth," he murmured to himself. "And where is Olaf?"

"All gone — all dead!" howled Egede, throwing up his hands. "Herr! Herr! all dead!"

The old man slowly raised his eyes to the stormy clouds overhead, and a prolonged heart-rending "Oh!" burst from his bosom. His looks wandered round upon the faces of the spectators, many of whom wept; and in a broken voice, he said, "He was a good child, my son Björnarne, and this is the only sorrow he ever occasioned me."

"You have yet a daughter and a son, Niels," said the voigt.

Helgestad laid his hand upon Ilda, who regarded him with a look of tender compassion, which moved his keenest sensibilities. Almost at the same time he observed Hannah, and he comprehended the defeat of all the hopes he had formed in relation to her marriage with Björnarne. She was free. He had no other son, who could bring the money of Fandrem to Lyngenfiord. All his projects were frustrated; his cunning was foiled, and her eyes seemed to glow with a demoniac expression; and he imagined he heard again the frightful laugh which she uttered, as her lover was plunged into the sea.

He drew a deep breath—the blood rushed from his heart to his brain, and he shook off Hannah's arm as if he had been touched by a snake. Turning to Egede, who had again risen to his feet, he said, in a commanding tone, "Relate the circumstances of the death of these brave men."

"You know," replied the Quane, upon whom all eyes were now riveted, "that we had gone to seek the daughter of the sorcerer of the Kilpis, to bring her to Loppen."

"I know it," said Helgestad. "Who set her free? Who killed Björnarne? They were Lapps. Thieves! Murderers! The old hell-hound sent them for that purpose."

He pointed to Afraja, and as Egede observed him with a face of exulting rage and vengeance, he exclaimed, "You have him! you have him! Send him where she lies, pale and cold, with the water-sprites and the trolls — down deep in the waters, where the sharks greedily await him. Oh! Herr! would that your son had not held on to my arm, and that he had not heeded her cry. I would have quieted her." He gnashed his long teeth, and stretched his arm towards Afraja. "All his charms and spells would never have found her again; they ought not to have set out for Loppen in the storm."

"It was the raging sea that did it," said Helgestad, "and not the hand of man."

"No human hand could save us," responded Egede. "We took a boat at Quananger. I saw the cloud caps around the Jakülnfjelle, and the long streaks of foam that broke upon the Arenöen islands; and I warned them, but, alas, in vain. The maiden fell on her knees, wept, cried and threatened; wished to go to you, Herr, and to Miss Ilda; she implored God and man, the witch! Olaf also spoke; but nothing availed—Björnarne was determined to go to Loppen. We went down the fiord. The evil one had entered into your son, Herr, and blinded his heart and eyes, so that he would neither see nor hear. The storm assailed us in the Kaagsund. A whirlwind seized our boat, whirled it about like a top, lifted it up above the waves, and plunged it beneath them again. Olaf struck against the cliff with his head, and never came up again. I clung to the shattered boat for my life; I saw your son as he rose above the billows, with the maiden in his arms; and I sought to save him, by grasping his long hair. 'Let her go,' I cried, 'let the witch go?' He would not separate from her. She clung around his neck; he pressed her to him, and endeavored to raise her on high. Thrice I called to him, and then came a furious wave. 'Throw the brat to the devil!' I cried. 'I will live and die with her!' he responded; and these were his last words."

Helgestad had listened, till now, with apparent equanimity; but his whole face gradually crimsoned, and he suddenly exclaimed, in a voice of thunder, to the Quane, "You lie, miserable wretch! Björnarne, my son! Cursed be your tongue! Gula! You lie, traitor, he never wished to live with her!"

He was overwhelmed with shame and confusion; for it was now evident to all that Björnarne had loved the Lapland maiden, and that Afraja had spoken the truth.

"You villain! you robber!" cried Egede, shaking his fist at the venerable old shepherd; "you sold a charm to Olaf, which was to bring fine weather; you conspired, however, with the spirits of darkness, to destroy him."

Helgestad looked at Afraja, who had also lost his child. A revengeful murmur ran through the mass of people around the Lapp; but he stood erect, fearless, and calm. A wild enthusiasm, and an expression of triumph glanced in his fiery, red eyes.

"Accursed sorcerer!" exclaimed Helgestad; "you betrayed him, and enticed him to the sea!" He raised his powerful arm; his brow frowned, like the head of Medusa; and he sprang at his enemy. But he tottered before he reached him, and fell into the arms of the bystanders, who hurried forward to catch him in their arms.

A wild cry, and a confused discord of jarring voices, now arose. Helgestad's huge form sank into an apparently lifeless state, and he was carried off, to procure help. A vindictive and clamorous band gathered around Afraja and his companions, muttering the most sanguinary threats, and they were only restrained from violence by the active interposition of the voigt, the secretary, and other persons of authority.

"And now," said Paul, when the first confusion was over; "now, Herr Marstrand, I turn to you. I arrest you as a confederate of this criminal."

"You arrest me?" replied Marstrand. "Upon what grounds?"

"As an arch-traitor," said the secretary. "Your trial will prove it. You have sold a considerable quantity of powder and lead to this Lapp; you have been made acquainted with his treasonable intentions, and you have made common cause with him."

"I hope," said Marstrand, as he quietly looked around, "that no one believes this nonsense."

But his eyes fell upon dark and frowning faces; threatening words reached his ear. "Right! sorenskriver Petersen!" cried many voices confusedly; "clear out the whole nest! He has had intercourse with the Lapps. Away with the vagabond! Away with the Dane! Down with the dog, the traitor!"

"Will you obey?" said Paul.

"I am a single, powerless man," said Marstrand. "Do as you please, but I will hold you responsible for your conduct."

The whole fraternity of young men, about forty or fifty in number, that surrounded the secretary, were armed with guns and knives. A part of them had thrown Afraja down, and bound him, and others had seized and led off the Dane; but the greater part threw themselves upon the throng of Lapps, and mastered those who were armed.

Afraja's immediate attendants were next beaten down. The tall, robust men met with but little opposition from the poor, weak people, who took to flight, in their fright falling over one another, while shots were fired at some, and blows showered upon others. The Quanes, Bölapps and fishermen fell upon the abandoned stores, carried them off, and divided them; and pursued the retreating fugitives to the summit of the fjeld, behind the church.

Paul Petersen protected the prisoners from injury, and had them all conducted to the vestibule of the church. From time to time others were brought in, who had been taken in the flight, most of whom had been severely beaten. The poor creatures lay trembling in the corners; and when the clamor from without grew more menacing against them, they crowded together like affrighted sheep.

The only Lapp left upon the place was the dead Mortuno, who slumbered upon his bier, undisturbed by the coarse jests of which he was the subject. Those who once feared him, now kicked him with their feet, and threatened his impotent form. What was to be done with him? No one sufficiently compassionated his mortal remains, to give them a decent burial; and it would be considered a sacrilege to give them sepulture in the graveyard of a Christian church. After some moments' deliberation, a couple of fierce-looking Quanes slung a rope about his legs and neck, fastened some heavy stones to his body, and when the sorenskriver, and the voigt, and others, were called off to a consultation, they pitched the body of the unfortunate Mortuno from a steep cliff into the sea.

"That was, indeed," said Paul, to himself, "the best thing that could have happened to him. The *Groundhais* will soon finish him below there, and we shall be rid of him forever."

He blamed, aloud, however, the precipitate proceeding, and forbade any one to touch the property of the fugitive Lapps — a command, however, which came too late; for whatever was to be found, had already met with new owners. The voigt then caused the doors of the house to be opened, and entered with his companions. There were some thirty prisoners, who threw themselves on their knees, and howled for mercy, when they perceived the dark and sinister faces of the visitors. Afraja sat against the wall. His feet were bound, and his hands were tied together on his back. The voigt looked at him, and shook his fist at him, in a threatening manner.

"You old rascal, you shall not escape from the hands of justice this time," he said. "For many years you have practised your jugglery and witchcraft; but we have you, at last. You will devise no more mischief, nor stimulate to more plots and insurrections. But," he continued, "I will yet spare you, if you will confess the truth. I will bring the truth out of your wicked head, you may rely upon that. Think upon this, until you arrive at Tromsöe. You must go thither, and testify. Forwards with you all! and woe to him who makes a noise, or attempts to escape. Take the old beast, and drag him away!"

There was no talk of escaping. Their hands had been bound; some of them were now loosened, to carry Afraja to the cutter of the voigt, which was ready to sail. The old chief spoke not a word, and no feature in his face betrayed fear or pain, although he was cruelly treated, and very tightly bound.

Voigt Paulsen now went into the church, where Marstrand was sitting on a chair. He had been separated from the Lapps, and an armed sentinel was stationed at the door, to prevent any conversation with Afraja. He had had time enough to think of his fate; yet he was much less concerned for himself, than for what had happened around him.

The sudden death of Björnarne, Olaf, and the poor Gula, had deeply grieved him. He thought of Hannah and Ilda, of Helgestad's sorrow and shame, and upon the unhappy old man who had fallen into the hands of his merciless enemies. What would become of him? For more than a hundred miles there was no power which could put a stop to their cruelty. His only friend, and the only protector of the unhappy Afraja, was Klaus Hornemann. Where was he now? Why was he not here? Who knew whether he was sick, or dead? That he would come, if he was alive, was certain; and this thought was the only ray of hope which sustained his drooping spirits.

When the voigt entered with his companions, he turned away in disgust from his red and vicious face.

"Stand up, Herr!" said Paulsen, with all his official pomp.

"By what right am I maltreated, and bound in this manner?" he replied.

"You will learn that in Tromsöe," said the voigt; "where you will be judicially tried."

"I demand to know my offence?"

"You have heard it. You are accused of high treason."

"If it is really so, and any one is foolish enough to bring such an accusation against me, no one here can be my judge. I am a nobleman of the kingdom, and must be judged by the supreme court. I am an officer; and as such, the right of judgment belongs to the governor of Norway."

"You are entirely mistaken," replied the voigt. "You live, and are settled in Finnmark, which has its own supreme court of life and death. No one is excepted from its authority, not even a nobleman. In important cases, the court in Tromsöe is assisted by six judges, selected from among the principal men in the country, and from whose decision there is no appeal."

The confusion of Marstrand's countenance called forth a smile of triumph from the voigt. "I have given orders to carry you to Tromsöe," he continued. "You were an officer, and a nobleman; and I also have worn the sword. I will treat you according to your former rank, if you will give me your word to submit with patience, and to make no attempt at escape."

"And if I do not?"

"Then I must take all proper measures to prevent your escape. All your confederates lie bound in the ship's hold."

"By heavens!" cried the Dane, while he clinched his fists; but he suddenly let his arm fall, and calmly said, "I will comply with your request; but do not suppose that your conduct will not be judged and punished."

"Silence!" said the voigt; "these are useless words. Nothing will happen to you, that you do not deserve. We have a supreme court of judicature, and we have laws; and to their judgment you must submit. No one, not even the king, can call us to account for a conscientious and just execution of the law."

A fearful truth was contained in this declaration, the importance of which Marstrand fully recognised. He would be destroyed, not by an arbitrary stretch of power, but by legal forms; and if any shadow of proof could be produced against him, he was lost.

"Follow me," said the voigt. He preceded him, and on both sides of the prisoner walked two armed men; Paul Petersen endeavored to assume a sad and sympathizing countenance as he looked at him, which Marstrand returned with a glance of contempt.

"How is Helgestad?" he asked the voigt.

"He is out of his senses," responded Paulsen; "you have brought much misery upon him."

"Not I! Oh, not I! Others have done it, who must answer for it."

The voigt made no answer, for the procession, as it passed along, was received with imprecations and insulting shouts. The guards advanced against the most hostile persons, who cried vengeance on the false Dane, and wished to tear him to pieces on the spot. The wild mass of half-drunken men to which he was exposed, with Afraja and his fellow-sufferers, were aroused to such a pitch of fury, that he was in momentary expectation of being stoned to death, or assassinated. He trembled not at the prospect of such an end, and he calmly looked upon the infuriated crowd. A discouraging reflection arose in his mind, when he thought that there was more than one among them who had received benefits at his hands, and yet not a voice nor an arm was raised in his behalf. It seemed to him as if many of the traders and proprietors would have been gratified to see him delivered to these half-savage Quanes and Islanders.

Paul stepped before him, as the voigt was powerless to repel the crowd, and laying his hand upon the shoulder of the prisoner, in a stern and commanding voice, he exclaimed, "Obey, and desist from violence, or you will rue it! This man has fallen into the hands of the law, which will judge him. He will not escape the punishment he may have merited. Judgment will be pronounced upon him in open court in

Tromsöe, before the judges. But do you be gone, unless you wish to be arrested and severely punished."

These words produced more effect than all that the voigt had said. They feared the secretary, because they knew him. The crowd fell back, leaving an open space, and Paul said, with a sympathising expression, "I have this time saved your life, and may God help me, as your judge, to pronounce your acquittal."

He nodded to his companion, who hurried Marstrand down the steps and into the government cutter, the sail of which being immediately raised, she bore out to sea.

An hour later, Helgestad was carried down the same way to his boat, and laid upon its cushions, to return to Orenaes. He was restored to his reason, but he could not speak. Hannah held his trembling head, and his eyes roved wildly around in all directions.

"This has been a sad market," sighed Paul, as he pressed the hand of Ilda. "Take care of your father! I will return as soon as I can."

"The will of God be done!" she answered in her customary calm, self-possessed manner.

CHAPTER XXIV.

A WEEK had elapsed, and the preparations were all made in Tromsöe for the holding of the court. The proceedings were of too simple a nature to require a long delay. The criminals for whose trial it was called were in close custody; a sufficient number of witnesses were on the ground, the six associate judges were soon found, and the public feeling was as sound as could have been desired. The court day, which, after the ancient custom, was holden on Friday, was eagerly looked forward to. The bitterness of feeling and lust of vengeance had rather increased than diminished, and a knowledge of the events at Lyngen market, had been diffused over the whole country, with comments that were admirably adapted to stimulate the Norman population to the utmost animosity.

The Lapps, as the report ran, appeared in a numerous body to murder all the traders. The long-studied schemes of the mischievous brain of Afraja were to have been brought into execution on this occasion.

The hearing of the prisoners had rendered all clear and certain that was desired. Trembling with anxiety and fear, they confessed whatever the secretary wished. Afraja had held gatherings, had spread hatred and contempt against the foreign intruders, had encouraged the Lapps to resistance, and the great conspiracy was finally devised which was to have exploded at the Lyngen market.

Mortuno had been an active coöperator in all these plans, the success of which was frustrated by his death. Paul Petersen, who, to his own imminent danger, had discovered the conspiracy, and captured the dangerous Lapp, appeared in the light of a bold and resolute man, who had rendered his fellow-countrymen a signal service. All were indebted to him for the sagacity with which he had delivered them from danger, for his intrepid patriotism, and for the arrest of the Dane, who had made common cause with the conspirators.

A peculiar incredulity was indeed manifested on the last head. It seemed impossible that a nobleman, and an officer of the guard, should have joined with the degraded race of Lapps in an undertaking which every man of sense would pronounce both impracticable and foolish. But the Dane, during all his residence in the country, had been the advocate of the Lapps, and was their constant friend and protector. He had fallen in love with a Lapland maiden, and, as would be clearly proven from the evidence on the trial, he was with Afraja in the Kilpisjaure, when the courageous sorenskriver made his appearance there.

The most fearful tales were told of his relations with Helgestad, and his proceedings at the Balsfiord. He was accused of the most shameful ingratitude, and the greatest folly. He had basely repaid with treachery the friendship which had been bestowed upon him. He endeavored to inveigle Helgestad's daughter into his net, to prevent the marriage of Björnarne, and to induce the maiden, who secretly clung to him, to enter into a scandalous intrigue. Strong as was the effort to cover the reproach which had fallen upon Helgestad's house, it could not be entirely denied that the unfortunate and only son of the rich proprietor had cherished a culpable passion for Gula.

Helgestad's misfortunes gave occasion to other complaints, which, for the most part, were directed against Marstrand. However numerous and bitter were the enemies of Helgestad on account of his pride and craftiness of dealing, yet his afflictions and mortified feelings excited universal sympathy.

Towards the end of the following week, the documents were ready, the judges were summoned, and on the ensuing day the court was to be held. Paul Petersen was engaged late in the evening in his office in the preparation of the proceedings. From time to time he paused in his labors, listened to the wind, and fell back in his arm-chair with a slight moan; but he repressed his feelings, and continued to work, even when the noise of voices and steps was heard close at hand.

At length, he opened the door, and, as he looked up, his uncle stood before him. The voigt yet had on his travelling cap and cloak.

"Peace and happiness be with you, Paul," he said. "They are all here. I have just arrived from Lyngenfiord with Helgestad, Ilda, and Hannah. But how you look!" he continued, in an anxious manner, with a shake of the head; "you seem ill, Paul; your hands are burning hot, and your face is sadly changed. What is the matter?"

"Nothing," responded Petersen, smiling. "I have worked hard, and been much vexed by the scoundrels. How is Helgestad?"

"Tolerably well," said the voigt. "He speaks with composure of Björnarne's death. They found the body in Kaagsund, but so firmly locked in embrace with the Lapland maiden, that the two could not be separated. They buried them both in the same grave."

"So they are united for ever," said Paul, jestingly. "How is Ilda?"

"All well. She, you know, never weeps nor complains."

"Why should she weep?" exclaimed the secretary. "If Björnarne had not been drowned, he would have caused her trouble enough, for he would never have given up the black-eyed witch. Now he is gone, and she is left sole heir."

"And when next week comes?" nodded the voigt.

"The pastor," said Paul, "has already announced the wedding. How admirably well all goes on, uncle!"

The uncle and nephew regarded each other smilingly. "Preserve your courage," whispered the voigt. "I think that Helgestad can no longer be driven. He is greatly changed from what he was. He sits and ruminates, and speaks but little. He has received a blow from which he will never recover. He cannot last much longer, and then he will leave you all."

Paul listened with indifference. "How does Afraja conduct himself?" asked the uncle.

"Not a word can be extracted from him," said Paul. "But what did you find at the Balsfiord?"

"Nothing. No kind of writing that could serve our purposes. Only some deeds of possession, and a couple of bags containing money."

"These may also be brought in evidence," muttered the secretary. "The proud Dane refused to answer. Give me the deeds, uncle — So——" He took them in his hands, and regarded them with a scornful and exulting expression. "By heavens! the fool shall never get them back again."

"I hope not," said the voigt; "but what will you do with him?"

After some moments' reflection, Paul replied, "It would have been better if I had not protected him against the drawn knives of the fishermen and Quanes. And now who knows what will become of him?"

"And the sorcerer?" whispered the voigt.

"Hush!" said the secretary. "I hear talking. Go down to our guests, uncle; I will follow you."

When the voigt had left the room, Paul arose, took the light, and placed himself before the looking-glass. His face was sunken, and although redder than usual, it looked wasted and sickly. "My beauty does not increase," he exclaimed jestingly to himself, "but I shall please her so much the more." He threw off his coat and exposed his side, where he had been wounded. It was not healed, but was swollen and discolored, and had an offensive appearance.

"Damnation!" he muttered; "I must do something. I suffer from pain, and cannot confide my affairs to any one." He rubbed it with ointment, bound it up, and dressed it with the greatest care.

When he entered the guest-chamber, Helgestad was sitting in the great chair by the fire, the two maidens at a table, and the voigt between them. Helgestad held a glass in his hand, but he was not as jovial as formerly in emptying it, under all sorts of calculations. He gazed at the smoking drink with a vacant stare, slowly raised his head as he heard the secretary's voice, and extended his lean, sinewy hand. His whole body and face seemed to be wasting away. The huge bones everywhere protruded, and the yellow skin stretched over them like parchment.

"Heartily welcome," said Paul, "and to you, beloved Ilda, my especial greeting."

Ilda spoke a few words, and the conversation then turned on Helgestad's indisposition and health and the voyage, but it was of a monotonous and broken character, and soon came to a pause.

Ilda also seemed changed. The tall, stout maiden had not indeed fallen off, but the deep earnestness of her character had increased. She occasionally smiled in past times with some cordiality of feeling, but her countenance was now fixed and immovable; her complexion had become transparent, and the expression of her eyes was so stern, that Paul could not endure it. He exerted himself to be merry, and to amuse the company, but it was a painful and unsuccessful effort. He clearly perceived the light in which he was regarded by all; and Helgestad shook his head, and, with a deep-drawn sigh, said, "It was different when Björnarne was alive. Bring him back; it will do you good."

"Would to God I could do it," responded the secretary; "but I can only punish those who are the authors of all this mischief. I would not have disturbed your repose, but it may be necessary for you to testify before the court. Strengthen yourself for to-morrow, and collect your thoughts."

"I will," said Helgestad; "but it were better if Björnarne were here."

"Does he always talk so?" asked Paul, turning to Hannah, with whom he spoke for the most part.

"His memory sometimes seems to fail him," she replied; "but all is often clear and distinct, and he sees farther than he formerly did."

Paul reflected upon what she said, and looked at her with an inquiring glance. "After what has happened here, I suppose you will desire to return to Bergen as soon as possible," said Paul.

"I shall remain until my father comes to some decision on the subject," was her answer.

"My sweet Ilda cannot have a more beautiful bridesmaid."

"How?" she said; "do you think of marrying in the midst of all this trouble?"

"I must. Ilda needs a protector, and the old man there desires a substitute for his lost son. Ask Ilda herself; she is too intelligent not to confess that in such a sad state of things, she has need of me as her husband."

"Courage!" exclaimed the voigt. "Of what use is it to grieve over what is past and beyond remedy? Drain your glass, Helgestad; I will give you another good son, and take in exchange your dear daughter. Look to the table, Paul; you are the lord of the house. Heads up, Niels! you have been a proud man all your life—be so now."

He clapped Helgestad on the shoulder with such force as to startle him. "All will yet turn out well, friend," he resumed; we will live in the happiness of our children, and forget our grief. When the court is over, we will all go to Lyngenfiord, and quietly celebrate Paul and Ilda's union."

"Right," said Helgestad; "the court must be over first. Have you secured Afraja, so that he cannot escape?"

"Dismiss all fears; he is closely confined in a secure cellar. Sorcerer as he is, he cannot get out from thence until the officers fetch him."

"And where is John Marstrand?" asked Hannah.

"In a clean chamber under the roof. A baron must always be alone. We have a small pair of chambers there above, for persons of rank."

"Horror above and below, and we in the midst of the turmoil," said Hannah, laughing. "What will be done with the two sinners?"

"The Lapp will cost us a good quantity of charcoal," said the voigt. "*Lovman* Errickson has already looked to that and the tar. Should the Dane also be condemned, we can easily provide for his execution."

At these fearful words, Ilda started up from her seat. She had turned deadly pale; but Paul, opening the side-door, in a friendly tone, said, "Come, dearest Ilda. Take a seat, for the first time, at the table in my house; and let us be as happy as we can."

But how could there be joy at this repast? Helgestad had become somewhat more animated, from the copious draught he had imbibed; though he was but a faint resemblance of his former self. The events of the morrow, and the many curious incidents connected with it, formed the principal subject of conversation.

Intelligence had been received at Lyngenfiord, that Klaus Hornemann lay sick at Alten; and the voigt inferred that this was the work of heaven, as, otherwise, the pastor would have intermeddled in the late proceedings.

"I regret, on the contrary," said Paul, "that he is not here, to satisfy himself of the perfect legality of our actions. He has also written me a letter, in which he makes a report to the governor, and requests a delay of proceedings. I am sorry that I cannot agree with him."

"And why not?" asked Ilda.

"Ask my uncle," he said. "The whole country demands justice, and every one understands the subject. Finnmark has its supreme court; and an appeal to the governor would be universally condemned. The excitement is so great, that we should be regarded as traitors to the rights and interests of the land."

"But how can a righteous judgment be pronounced," said Hannah, "where, as you say, the excitement and bitterness of feeling is so great?"

Paul shrugged his shoulders. "I would sincerely regret the delivery of an unjust decision. Afraja's crimes are, however, so clear, that there can be but little fear of a mistake."

"Treason, rebellion, homicides, and heathen witchcraft!" exclaimed the voigt.

Helgestad opened his eyes, and smiled as he was wont to do in times past. "Nuh!" said he, "you must remember to make the scoundrel confess where his treasures are. We must extort from him what we wish, and I shall thus be compensated for all the evil the villain has done me."

The secretary was not pleased with this revelation. He winked to Helgestad to be silent, and, at the same time, said, "If he really possesses treasures, he must confess their place of concealment, as his property must compensate the injuries he has inflicted. Nothing is to be expected from his companions."

Helgestad eyed him with a long and malicious look. "You are a wise fellow, and will hold firmly to your own. You would like to have had Loppen, and now you take Balsfiord. But keep a sharp look-out, Paul. You have brought the Dane to what he is — but many are of the opinion that you act unjustly with him. The birds, around, sing curious songs. One sang me a ditty — nuh!" he muttered, "you have my word, it can never happen again."

"I hope we understand each other," said Petersen. "No bird's song can sow distrust between us."

"Tell me one thing," said Helgestad, as he opened his large eyes. "Did Björnarne never speak with you of her — of the maiden — of the accursed witch?"

"Of Gula — never! Upon my honor."

"The pastor will assert it. There are those who believe" — his wild eye flashed upon the secretary, and then he laughed, and struck the table. "It is an infernal lie! They have branded me before all the people. The false Dane has proclaimed it. I hope you have him secure, Paul Petersen, and that you will not let him go."

His vindictive passion at last gave way to drowsiness. In the midst of his remarks, he appeared to lose the thread of his discourse; and as he fell back in his chair, he muttered to himself, "I wish, however, Björnarne were here, that he might hear what is said."

Paul hastened to bring this scene to an end. He spoke in a soft and conciliatory tone — hoped that a good, quiet sleep would refresh and invigorate him — and he, at last, consigned Helgestad to the care of his uncle and the maidens.

When he was alone in his chamber, he walked up and down, threw himself in his arm-chair, and as quickly started up again. Then he stood still, as he heard Helgestad's heavy tread above his head: looked up, and laughing, said, "You are right, old fool. I hold fast to what I have, and I will keep a good account with you. All that you have saved and treasured up is now mine — Loppen, Balsfiord, and your miracle of beauty and wisdom—Ilda. What have they insinuated to the old man? What has the cursed pastor written? Before he can bestir himself, all will be over.

"And all is over," said he, as he took a light, and went into his office.

He opened a great, dark closet, black with age, and lighted the interior. All kinds of terrible instruments lay upon the shelves — screws and iron wedges, rusty chains, and dusty cords. He took out one of them, a broad iron band, which could be tightened by means of a screw.

"How ingenious is the mind of man," he murmured, "when it exerts itself to serve God, and the cause of truth!"

He heard a noise, and as he looked around, he shrunk back with fear. Ilda was standing a few paces before him.

"What have you there?" she asked, before he could speak.

"An approved means against falsehood and treason."

"Do you make use of such things?"

"To-morrow they may be employed," he said.

She clasped her hands, as in great anguish, and looked at him steadily. "I must speak with you," she said, softly.

"Come, then," said the secretary, shutting up the closet "How gladly, my sweet-heart, will I chat with you!"

"Stay," she said, "you must hear me on this spot. I have a request to make of you?"

"What can it be, that I will not comply with?"

Ilda drew a deep breath; her head seemed, for a moment, to sink under its weight; and then she drew herself up, looking like some supernatural being, in her black dress.

"Save him," she said, with difficulty uttering the words; "save John Marstrand from the ignominy which threatens him, and I will bless you."

"How can I save him, dear Ilda?"

"You know that he is innocent," she continued. "Oh! by God's eternal mercy, dismiss that false smile; you know, also, that Afraja is not guilty of the crime that you charge him with."

"I will rejoice at the acquittal of your friend," said Paul.

"You lie, you dissemble!" exclaimed Ilda, and her hands .embled with emotion. "There is an eye which penetrates every heart, and an ear which hears every thought. Look at me, Paul, and judge yourself."

"That," he answered, "I leave to you, and, as I fear, your judgment will be cruelly severe."

"No," she said, taking his hand, "I will stand by you, whatever may happen. I will serve you as your maid; you shall hear no complaint. Take all that I have; take me, myself, when you please; I am your property. But, save the innocent man; save him! Upon my knees I will swear to obey you."

As she kneeled before him, his eyes glowed with rage and scorn. "You kneel before me," he said, in a measured tone, as if he wished to prolong her torments; "why do you kneel? Speak the truth; I will listen to you. How can you intercede, on your bended knees, for this wretched Dane?"

She bowed down her head, and, after a moment, calmly raised herself up, and in a firm tone said in reply—"Because I love him."

"Do you love him yet?"

"Now and forever!" she said.

He bit his lips. "Oh you noble soul," he exclaimed, "how candid you can be! You will love him forever! And wher you lie by my side, you will imagine that his arms embrace you."

"No!" she said, "my misery will always be with me."

"How sorry I am that I must increase it," he interrupted; "and how lamentable it would be, if I should to-morrow send your tenderly-beloved friend in flames to heaven, with the sorcerer, his associate."

Ilda lifted up her arms in an imploring attitude; but another voice behind her at the door, exclaimed, "That will he not; but, it may be, that the devil is nearer to yourself than you think."

"Charming!" cried Paul. "I thought that the comedy had yet another act. You are never wanting, Hannah Fandrem, with your jests and insults upon me."

"I hope soon to see all your hypocrisy defeated," said Hannah, as she approached Ilda. "I am here for your protection, and will speak a word with you in my own way, as I best understand how to reach your heart.

"This cruel, infatuated people, will have its victim. Kill the old man, if you dare; vengeance will not fail to overtake you. Many Lapps will cross over to Sweden or to the Frozen Ocean, to deliver themselves from your cruelty; trade will diminish, the markets will decline, and the government will also put a stop to your hangman's work. Do as you please, you must indeed be short-sighted, if, blinded by hatred, you cannot see what will happen, if you make a victim of Marstrand. The government will never pass over in silence the death of a nobleman. You will be called to account for it, and the sword will be suspended over your own head."

"Let it be," said Paul, "until you cut the threads."

"Do not interrupt me," she continued, "and jest not. "If Helgestad were not my cousin, and Ilda not my friend, I would have raised my hand against you to-day; but it needs not my aid. Beware, false man; I hope your days are numbered. Witnesses will rise up against you, who will prove that you are the cause of all this trouble. No devices, however ingenious can save you from condign punishment. You, who believe in nothing, who daily revile the Supreme Being, you seek to destroy an old man because he is not a Christian, and on a charge of practising witchcraft! But Klaus Hornemann will come and stand up against you; and if no one does, I will. Set John Marstrand free, or you shall hear from me to-morrow. I will enter the court, and cry aloud, 'This man murdered Björnarne, and stimulated his passion for Gula to madness, that he might be cursed, disinherited, and disowned.' This you well know, avaricious man; and you will be obliged to pay me the thirty thousand dollars which Helgestad promised as indemnity money if Björnarne refused me; and by your crafty tricks he has done so. Give Herr Marstrand his liberty; restore him to the possession of Balsfiord, of which you wish to rob him, and thus you may escape, until you fall into the hands of God. Exert yourself for the innocent man, serve him, and perhaps he will be silent for Ilda's sake and her family, touching your crimes; and he may leave the infliction of retributive vengeance to heaven. And now I am done with you. Let us go, Ilda. Let him show if he has sagacity enough to save himself from his own snares."

With folded arms, and a sneer on his lips, Paul had listened in silence to her remarks; and some time after she had withdrawn, he returned to his chamber.

"It is not you whom I fear," he said. "Appear when you please, a thousand voices will force you to be silent. Whatever is to happen will happen." He took a light and some keys from a shelf, and proceeded to a side-room where an officer of the court sat by a table, with his head buried in his hands. Upon the entrance of the severe judge, he jumped up.

"Open the door," said Petersen. The man slid the bolt back, and introduced him to a passage-way, which led down some half-dozen steps. The building was a log structure, as all the others, but it rested upon massive blocks of stone, forming an arched vault. Upon either side were partitions of thick plank, one of which was secured by a great lock, which, on being opened, Paul entered into a narrow chamber or cell, and so low that he could not stand upright in it. He held up the lamp, and threw its light upon the shapeless and motionless mass in the corner. A chain, firmly secured to the wall, was attached to an iron ring, which enclosed the neck of the unhappy prisoner, whose head and face, concealed beneath his disordered hemp-like hair, were buried in his hands, as he sat upon a stone seat, with his elbows on his knees.

The sorenskiver seated himself near the door, set the light down before him on the ground, and then said, in a mild tone, "This is a sad abode, Afraja, for a man who has grown old in the fresh air of a gamme. To-morrow is court-day, and God have mercy upon you! You have, thus far, refused to answer; you have obstinately despised all admonition; and I am now come, for the last time, to ask you if you repent, and are of a more humble frame of mind.

"See," he continued, as he received no reply, "it may be that I can render you a service. It is a fearful death to be burned alive; and now is the autumn, the season when your animals long for the mountains, when the wind blows cold, and the seven stars glitter over the Kilpis."

A deep-drawn sigh was heard from the dark corner, at the sound of which Paul laughed. "It is better to live," he resumed, "than to be burnt to ashes; better to beg for mercy, than to await your fate like a dumb beast. You are a reflecting man. You cannot be foolish enough to dream that your foot will ever freely tread again the fjelds, or that your eyes will ever again see the brown herds."—He paused, and then continued in a gentle whisper, "I can save you; I alone am able to restore you to liberty; and I will do it, if you are wise."

"Will you do it?" asked Afraja, as he lifted up his head for the first time, and stroked back his long yellow hair from his shrunken face.

"Poor old fellow," said Petersen, "you have grown pale;

but the damp air has done your eyes good—they look as bright and large as ever. Yes, I repeat, I will do it. You shall be liberated; you shall again have your gamme and animals; you shall lie down in the fresh snow, instead of in the flames; but you must be wise and open your ears.

"That I can accomplish what I attempt," he continued in response to Afraja's fixed stare, "all admit. I give you my word, that you shall not be committed to the flames, if you penitentially fall on your knees to-morrow, declare your witchcraft a fraud and superstition, curse your Jubinal with all his tribe of gods, beg for the holy baptism, and solicit mercy for all your past wickedness. You will be condemned to imprisonment and to be whipped, but I will open this door myself, and save your back."

"And you?" asked the old man.

"I—I come to myself last. I have only one thing to ask of you. You are old and childless. Mortuno, the gallant fellow, is dead, and Gula lies in her grave — out of gratitude, you must make me your heir. This is all I ask of you, and it is, certainly, but little. You have money; where is it? Open your heart, Afraja, and trust me. By heavens! you will not repent it. Be frank, old scoundrel. I know that you have precious secrets in your keeping — that you know where are hidden mines, and caves of silver, where the pure ore glitters. Lie not, for I have proofs!"

"Yes, Herr," said Afraja, "you are right. There is more silver there than all the reindeer in Finnmark could carry away. There, hang long, shining clusters from the roof—there, it springs from all the walls, and projects from all the seams of the rock. The palace of Jubinal is not more brilliant, and the water-trolls which, you say, lie in their grottoes of dazzling stones in the bottom of the sea, do not possess such treasures as I."

The secretary listened with intense interest—his eyes expanded wide with a greedy expression—he stretched his head forward, his hands trembled, and his breast swelled with a consuming desire.

"Do you know of more than one of such caves," he inquired, as he timidly looked around, through fear that some one might overhear him.

"Many! Many!" responded Afraja. "So great, that no foot can measure them; a garden of silver-flowers and plants, such as no eye ever saw."

"Good!" muttered Petersen hastily; "you will guide me to this silver-cave. Swear by your Jubinal, that you will lead me there, and I will stand by you."

"Will you, indeed?" whispered the prisoner.

"Rely upon me. You cannot have a better friend."

"You my friend?"

"I tell you, that I will protect you to your end. Look, here is a bottle of nectar for you. To-morrow, you shall leave this hole; it will go well with you. You shall daily receive meat and drink; and before two weeks shall have elapsed, you will be on your mountains."

Afraja had risen to his feet; the chain rattled about his iron collar, and his slender body tottered, but he held his head proudly erect, and his eyes glowed with a strange fire.

"Take it, and make yourself glad," said Petersen, "but swear first, by Jubinal, that you observe such an oath."

"Sorenskriver," said the old man, extending his arm, "I know of silver — mountains of silver; no other person is acquainted with them; but if I could live until Jubinal's kingdom comes, and were I to burn until Jekel destroys the world, you should know nothing of the treasure!"

"Remember, you fool," answered Paul, with a sinister smile, "remember, fire does harm."

"Wolf as you are, your bloody, vindictive threats do not frighten me. Fire is in your eyes — burning fire in your veins. You will howl like a wild beast, and I will laugh at you!" He laughed like one possessed.

After endeavoring for some moments to conquer his rage, the secretary said, "Wait till to-morrow, and then we will see if you will laugh, miserable creature."

"A curse upon you!" cried Afraja, and such a long, fearful curse echoed back again from the rock-bound walls, that Paul, unable to restrain his fury, kicked the Lapp with such violence as to throw him down.

"Until morning!" he exclaimed, shaking his fist, "when all will be over with you." As he shut the door, Afraja's yelling laugh of scorn resounded after him.

Paul Petersen was alone in an upper room of the building. His face glowed with a fever-heat, and his brain was swollen to bursting. In his heart burned an insatiable desire to know and to possess the coveted treasure, which overcame the consciousness that he was unwell.

He mounted up the steps, and listened to a closely-guarded chamber. He noiselessly drew back the bolt, opened the lock, and entered. It was also a prison, but a better one than that which he had just left. A small cross-barred window let in light and air, and on the bed, in the corner, Marstrand lay breathing.

"There he sleeps!" muttered Paul. "He can sleep, and soundly, too!"

He advanced to the bed, and, as the light fell upon Marstrand's face, Paul perceived that he was smiling in his sleep, and he heard him murmur, in an audible tone, "It is you, Ilda — you are coming to me."

"Wake up! Wake up!" cried Petersen, shaking the sleeper by the arm. "I have something to say to you."

Marstrand awoke. "Why do you disturb me, in the middle of the night?" he said, ill-humoredly.

"When we will extricate a man from a falling house, before the rafters fall in, we do not think of the time and the hour," responded the secretary.

"You would be the last to assist in such a case," said Marstrand.

"I think," said Paul, "we have both but little time to waste in disputes. Answer me a question, for much depends upon it. Afraja, in order to win you over to his criminal projects, discovered to you the hiding-place of the silver treasures?"

Marstrand made no reply.

"Herr Marstrand," resumed Petersen, "can effect great changes, if he will. I pity your fate, and I would gladly do something for you. I have promised a certain person to assist you."

"I have no need of your protection," exclaimed the prisoner, jumping up.

Petersen paid no attention to the movement. "We could come to an understanding," he said, in a friendly manner; "even the Balsfiord could belong to you again."

"It is mine, and such it shall remain."

"If you do not prefer to select a better residence. God knows how far my sympathy might carry me! It is not pleasant to be arraigned before an open court, and surrounded by a fanatical people; it would be better, perhaps, to withdraw to a distance, and to wait in a quiet house until the storm has blown over."

"I would not go, if all the doors stood wide open," responded Marstrand.

"Good; remain, then. I hope you may succeed in obtaining an honorable acquittal, through a skilful defence."

"I hope that lies and malice will be confounded."

"Take my advice, and I will help you, to the best of my ability. Had we understood each other better, it would be different with us now."

"Away with all pretence," said Marstrand. "I think we understand each other well enough. To the point, Herr Petersen. What do you want?"

"To repeat my question," replied Paul; "where is the sil ver cave, to which Afraja conducted you?"

"I know nothing of your silver cave."

"You know nothing of it?" asked Paul, as he thrust his hand into his pocket. Look, this piece of silver was found in your coat. It was torn off the rock, to which it was attached; and it resembles those silver flowers which, sometimes, grow in rich caves. Has your memory been refreshed?"

The prisoner pondered a moment, and then said, "No, I know nothing of it! What I know, could not help you; and if I knew of what you wish for, I would never yield to your request."

"No?"

"No, never!"

"Think what you do."

"Deceit, and nothing but deceit," said Marstrand. "You will learn nothing from me."

"Will you not accept my hand? Shall Ilda have implored me in vain, upon her bended knees, for your salvation?"

"Miserable man!" cried Marstrand; "upon her knees before you? You lie! I could beat your brains out, if I did not know that you were the greatest villain on the earth."

He repelled him from him; and the secretary hurriedly drew back.

"Now it is over!" he muttered, as he ascended the steps. "He shall die, even if the king were his cousin!"

CHAPTER XXV.

The morning of the court-day broke, and it was a bright, clear day. Tromsöe is situated upon an island, which is separated from the main land by an arm of the sea. It lies close to a flat shore, behind which rises a naked height, which was then much more bare than now, as some structures have been erected upon it. Three to four hundred people dwelt in this chief settlement of Finnmark — mostly fishermen, some mechanics, and the serving-people of the traders; but the population had increased tenfold, on this day — for multitudes had gathered there, from all parts, far and near. On the preceding day there was, already, a concourse from the land; during the night, many a boat steered into Trommensund; and when the sun arose, the water was alive with large and small craft. From the islands and the fiords, they repaired thither — undervoigts, clerks of court, pastors, and traders, with their wives and children, as to a festival; besides a large number of the half-savage people, from the three or four races of people who had settled here.

They established themselves upon the open square, in the huts and shops, and along the shore, where they feasted and drank, and cursed the obstinate heathen who lay in the dungeon, without uttering a word; and they observed, with joy, the heaps of billets of wood that were piled up in the court-yard. The noise, laughter, and greetings of the new-comers increased, the later it grew; the throng gradually pressed towards the court-house, and formed a circle around the square, in the midst of which a somewhat elevated stage had been erected. A table stood upon it, covered with red cloth, surrounded by chairs; behind the seat of the judges were several long benches; before the table were two rude wooden seats; and in the corner was another table, upon which lay a red cover.

The aristocracy had found accommodations in the surrounding houses, and in the court-house. All the windows were filled with maidens and women, in their finest attire; head pressed upon head around the court-square, in glazed hats, and caps of skin and fur; and the multitude of hard, weather-beaten faces of the men, and the women in long curls, and various-colored garments, with children upon their shoulders, and sucklings at the breast, formed a curious and motley spectacle.

A bell was suddenly heard, and the procession issued from the court-house, in the van of which was the voigt, in embroidered coat, with undervoigts and officers of the court, followed by his aids, and the secretary, bearing the records and documents; in the rear were the six associate judges, and the chief traders, in their long, dark coats.

The voigt took the middle seat, the secretary sat on his left, and the associate judges on both sides. The other officers, Lovmen, Lensmen, and favored persons, took places on the benches.

There was an universal and profound silence, and all eyes were fastened upon the voigt, who rose up, and striking the table with a white staff, said, in a loud voice, "The court is opened! May God Almighty be with us, and assist us to a righteous judgment! Bring the prisoners before the court."

After some minutes' delay, they were brought forward, and a sullen murmur, rising and falling like the distant roar of the sea, accompanied the procession. The women leaned forward from the windows, the men pressed over their heads, and the whole multitude violently swayed about in their eagerness to catch a glimpse of the chief actors of the drama. It would be difficult to decide which of them excited most interest among the spectators. The old, deformed, and bent Afraja could hardly sustain himself on his feet. His chains had been removed, and he had been presented with a clean Lappish blouse. His grey head was unbared to the air; his long hair fell over his shoulders; and his countenance, despite his sufferings and emaciation, was dignified and impressive. His eyes roved over the faces of the hostile and infuriated mass around him, with a clear and unshrinking gaze.

When he ascended the low stage, his companion in misfortune gave him his arm; for no one else would assist him. Even this compassionate action seemed to increase the prevailing animosity.

"Shame upon you!" cried a woman, who stood before him. "See how he presses him to himself," exclaimed many. "He has a fine appearance," said a stalwart fisherman, "and one can hardly believe he is a Dane. He is all false."

Marstrand wore his plain blue coat, as a Gaard proprietor; but there are figures which, even in the rags of a beggar, lose nothing of their native grace. His tall, slender figure, proudly towered up; his beautiful brown hair was bound with a riband. When he reached the top of the stage, he seemed to be inclined to speak; but he sat down, and waited until the poor Lapp prisoner had taken his seat.

The secretary now stood up and began his discourse. After a general introduction, in which he mentioned that, for a long time, there had been no trial for a capital offence, and that the high court of Finnmark was assembled for the execution of the law and the maintenance of order, he described the wicked actions of the Lapps for a considerable period, and then he spoke of Afraja as one of the worst plagues of all honorable, well-disposed people; of his intrigues and cunning malice; and after he had given a long description of the various attempts to convert him to Christianity, he arraigned him for his obdurate paganism, his sorcery, and criminal schemes to spread murder and fire throughout Finnmark.

"For all this," he continued, "witnesses are present who have made affidavit of its truth, whom you shall hear, worthy men of the court. As to the second person accused, John Marstrand, baron of the Danish nobility, and formerly officer and chamberlain of His Majesty Christian VI., there exists the strongest suspicion that he was cognisant of all the evil purposes of Afraja, and had leagued with him for their execution."

When the secretary pronounced his name, and almost before the sentence was finished, in a firm and loud voice Marstrand said, "Every word that you have spoken of me is a lie, and he who has devised this accusation is a calumniator!"

"Silence!" said Paul Petersen, "until it is time to speak."

"Now is the time," rejoined Marstrand. "I will speak; I will declare before this court, that I am an innocent, slandered man, and that my life and property are wickedly assailed. I hurl back the accusation upon him from whom it has proceeded. You, Paul Petersen, you have spun the threads of this web of lies, and you hold it in hand. I accuse you as the first and worst criminal in the country!"

The surprise at this bold conduct and declaration caused a general silence. The spectators looked in dumb amazement on the two men. The tall and stately figure of the Dane, with his expressive face, and his bold resolution, made a much different impression from that of the secretary, who, for some moments, appeared to be greatly embarrassed, and at a loss what course to take. But he soon recovered his self-possession. His dark blood-shot eyes tempered their ferocity of expression; hate and anger retreated from his countenance; and, as he extended his arm, the fearful cry which had arisen among the people, after the momentary silence, was immediately hushed.

"You cannot injure me, Herr Marstrand," he said; "for you are a fallen man in the eye of the law. I saved your life at the Lyngen market, and would do it now, if a popular indignation should be excited by your disgraceful conduct. Be quiet, you men! and you, Herr, do not make your cause worse, for you have enough already to bear."

An universal grunt of approbation followed this remark. Marstrand saw around him nothing but dark, infuriated, and menacing faces. "I speak for the last time," he exclaimed, to protest against these proceedings! I was not only a Danish nobleman, an officer, a chamberlain of the king, but I am such now. No court can pronounce a judgment upon the accusation preferred against me, but that at the head of which stands the king. Do what you please against me, but rest assured that it will not go unavenged. I appeal to the grace of his Majesty, to the high Council of State, and to the Governor of Norway!"

These exclamations did not fail to make an impression. The multitude responded, indeed, with an outcry, and with objurgations, of all kinds, against the privy council and the governor; but there were reflecting persons, who, on hearing the name and threatened vengeance of the king, remembered the odious light in which the privileges of Finnmark had, for a long time, been regarded. It was often attempted, but not entirely accomplished, to increase the crown officers, and, of a consequence, the taxes, and to more completely subject the country to the will of the king and the governor. Advantage could be taken of this occasion to annihilate the privileges of the province, and to reduce it into complete subjection.

The sorenskriver was not, however, moved by such considerations. "These objections cannot be admitted," he said. "Here is our law, here are our rights! Will you not answer?"

"No!"

"And you, Afraja — do you persist in your silence?"

"Let me hear what I should answer," replied the Lapp.

"Do you deny that you yet adhere to your pagan gods?"

"No," replied the old man, in a loud tone "All my forefathers worshipped Jubinal, and so do I."

"You are a contemner of Christian instruction. You make a jest of the Most High, and the church; and you pray and offer sacrifice in the Saitas."

"I worship and sacrifice in the holy enclosure of stone, which is consecrated to the universal Father."

"And you have also encouraged your people to the same practices."

"I have neither persuaded nor threatened any one," said the old man. "Jubinal's white dove sits upon the shoulders of those who hear the flap of its wings. Jubinal is not a God who procures children by force and cruel punishment."

His clear eye looked upon the pastor, who was sitting with Heinrick Sture, upon the bench; and a smile overspread his face, as he heard their fanatical threats.

"So you do not deny your horrible heathenism," resumed the secretary; "but do you deny that you are a sorcerer?"

"No!" replied Afraja.

"How! do you confess it?"

"I am a *Seidmann*. I am acquainted with magic spells. The gods listen to me!" said Afraja, in a grave and deliberate manner.

The whole multitude was astounded. Amid a noiseless silence, Paul Petersen inquired, "Do you also confess that you have practised witchcraft and sorcery?"

"Many of your Christians came to me," said the Lapp, "to purchase the assistance of my gods. They wanted their cattle, their grass, and their oats to thrive, or they wished luck for their nets, and a good wind for their sails. Your God could not give them all this."

"Will you blaspheme, you wretch!" exclaimed Heinrick Sture.

The people kept silent, for there were many among them who had bought all sorts of fortune of Afraja.

"Do you know this picture?" asked the secretary, as he took

from his pocket a rudely-formed picture of metal, which the unfortunate Olaf had once received.

"I know it."

"What is it?"

"I gave it to your companion," said Afraja, "when you said to me, he must have a good wind."

"Can you also make a good wind?"

"I can."

"But you lied. There came wild weather, and Olaf was drowned; and with him, Björnarne, Helgestad's only son, and your own child."

Afraja's head trembled with emotion; but as he raised himself up, his eyes gleamed, and with increased strength, he replied, "I knew what would happen. I saw signs in heaven, which none else saw; and I heard Pekel's roaring voice."

"So you sold this witch-charm to destroy those persons?"

"I wished to destroy you, for you are more cruel than the wolf and the bear!" exclaimed Afraja.

"You thus committed wilful murder," continued Petersen, with unshaken composure. "Hate me as much as you please, but tell me why you wished to cause the death of innocent people?"

"Who is innocent among you?" asked Afraja. "Are you not all robbers, who have taken our property from us? Do you not hate us? Do you not torment us? Do you not despise us, as if we were venomous reptiles? Are not all your actions violent and unjust; and did you not, blood-thirsty, false-hearted man, break into my gamme? and has your uncle there, your grandfather, and your whole race, not acted as infamously?"

"And for this reason, it was your intention to drive us from the country? For this reason, you would have made a beginning at Lyngen market, had not your nephew, Mortuno, been wanting?"

Afraja dropped his head on his breast, and his hands clasped together. "Jubinal's arms have received my children," he said; "they live with him in ever-blooming gardens. I shall soon be with him, and I fear you not. You will perish in torment and shame. Woe to your race! May it end like you!"

"Do you confess that you intended to fall upon the Norwegian people with fire and sword?" asked the secretary.

"As the wolf is driven off who falls upon our herds, so would I chase you away," answered the old man.

"And now confess, as you are so bold," exclaimed Petersen, "confess aloud; "What intercourse had you with John Marstrand, of Balsfiord?"

Afraja turned to the Dane, and as he lifted up his hands, he said, "Blessings upon you; blessings and joy! Because you were good and just, was I your friend and servant."

"Did you not give him money, to pay his debts?'

"I did so, because you and Helgestad sought to ruin him."

"And what did he give you in exchange?"

"I asked nothing — I was grateful."

"Lie not, traitor?" exclaimed the secretary, with wild, rolling eyes. "He made a compact with you; you promised him your daughter, with whom he had long had an intrigue. He knew of your crime, and sold you kegs full of powder, which I, myself, found in your hut, and destroyed. Out with the truth, for it is clear as the light of day. Confess, or I will force you to an avowal!"

"You will force me to confess?" asked the old man. "You see, I conceal nothing. What can you do with me?"

An officer, at a sign from the secretary, removed the top of the neighboring table; and rough and cruel as the people, for the most part, were, a cold shudder ran through the whole mass. There lay exposed to view the old screws, iron vices, the sharp wedges, and pincers, which had been preserved in the old closet, in the court-house.

"By authority of law, we are permitted, and it is our duty to proceed to apply the pains of the Question, when an obstinate culprit will not confess. I warn you, Afraja, and I ask you once again, if John Marstrand, of Balsfiord, did not know what you were doing; and if he was not in combination with you, for the execution of plots, for which he provided you with powder and lead?"

"On my honor! On my conscience! Before the presence of the eternal God, I knew nothing of it!" exclaimed Marstrand. "Who could believe such an unheard-of and dishonorable thing of me?"

"Seize him, officers!" shouted the secretary. "Away with him! Take the screw!"

"Hold!" cried a voice from out the circle of spectators. "Hold, in the name of God!"

Paul Petersen clinched his hands, his eyes glared fiercely, and his countenance wore an expression of pain, which seemed to torture him to the quick. He recognised the voice and the man, to whom the throng gave place, and whom he had least expected to see; at the sight, he was seized with an indescribable rage and fear.

"Klaus Hornemann!" he said, to the voigt. "What does the fanatic want? I will make him repent it, if he officiously meddles in this affair."

The voigt leaned towards him, and they both spoke in secret with the associate judges, pastors, and government officers, while the old missionary pressed forward to the steps. In his black dress, over which fell his long, white locks—his venerable face upraised — and his large, blue eyes, full of noble enthusiasm — he commenced, with great impressiveness, to appeal for pity.

"Voigt of Tromsöe!" he said, "I beg you to adjourn this court. I have been lying sick, otherwise I would have come here sooner. When I heard of the day of this trial, I got up from bed — and I hope I have not arrived too late."

"Why should I adjourn the court?" asked the voigt, in a severe and excited tone.

"Because there is much investigation yet to be made in this affair."

"There is but one point yet to be inquired into," interrupted the secretary; "and that is, whether John Marstrand knew of the crime of the Lapp. Afraja himself has acknowledged that he is a heathen, a contemner of the church, and a sorcerer. He has also confessed, that with a view to do him harm, he sold an idolatrous charm to Olaf Veigand, and that he had formed a plan to murder all the Normans and their dependants, or to drive them from the country. Did he not make this confession?"

"Yes, yes," shouted numerous voices, and the associate judges nodded assent.

"My God!" exclaimed the old pastor, "do not enter with him into judgment. Yes, he is a heathen; but can the eyes of the blind be opened with a sword? Foolish, presumptuous man! how can you call yourself a sorcerer? Were you such—did you possess superhuman power, and did you hold communion with spirits and gods, you would not be sitting abandoned here; you would be able to set yourself at liberty."

"The devil deceives his own children!" exclaimed Heinrick Sture.

"Judges and gentlemen," said Hornemann, "listen not to such accusations. Woe to those who walk in darkness, for they will have no part in the light. But our God is a God of love, who pities the weak and erring. Leave it to Him to reform and punish."

"They must be judged," exclaimed another spiritual personage.

"Yes," said Klaus, "by him, the high and righteous Judge, who pities the weak."

"The law is here to punish criminals," said the voigt; "we are here to perform our duties, and cannot suffer any one to deride our authority."

"Herr Voigt," responded the pastor, "I honor and esteem

the power which is assembled in the king's name; but I come from a higher Master, who commands me to speak without fear. There is no law in existence which can be applied to pagan worship and to sorcery."

"You are wrong!" interrupted Petersen. "We have the code of King Christian the Fourth, and his decrees concerning paganism and witchcraft, which are all in full activity with us at the present day."

"And these cruel edicts and punishments, which originated in a dark and barbarous age, would you apply them now? You cannot, and you dare not!"

"Here are worthy, honorable men enough; here are pastors, servants of God, as you yourself; here are judges and gentlemen from all parts of the country, and here are assembled Gaard proprietors and the people. I ask whether we cannot try and punish, according to the law, this Lapp, who confesses his crime?"

"Right! Sorenskriver, right!" cried many voices. A part sprang from their seats with uplifted arms; others fell into a fury; Heinrick Sture pressed towards the old pastor, and several attempted to seize him, and drag him from the stage.

"In the name of God! In the name of our Saviour!" exclaimed the old man, "you shall not prevent me. Hear me, all! Hear me! You know me, my course of life."

"We are acquainted with your course of life among the Lapps, and how you always protected them," cried Sture.

"Commit no injustice—shed not blood!" continued Klaus. "If any one must judge, it must be the representative of the King in Norway. Discontinue this court, inform him of what has occurred, and leave it to him to decide."

"Do you think," said Petersen maliciously, "you could succeed in this manner? For years you have made reports in praise of the virtue of the Lapps, and in condemnation of our cruelty. We, however, commit no injustice. We, the authorities of this country, esteem and honor the law."

The secretary had struck a chord, which moved every heart. The defence of the rights of the country against the governor, the maintenance of its freedom and privileges, and a resolution not to be overruled by the decrees and commands from Copenhagen and Trondheim, was the construction put upon this declaration of the secretary.

A furious outcry arose. "Hear me! Hear me!" vainly implored Klaus Hornemann.

"Priest of Baal, who has forsaken his God!" shouted Heinrick Sture.

"Breach of the peace! Insult to the court!" exclaimed the signiors on the benches.

"Lead him away, officers!" commanded the voigt.

The old man, in his humiliation, wept bitterly. In the anguish of his heart, he raised his hands to heaven, exclaiming, "My God! protect the innocent!"

A profound silence ensued, in which his voice could be heard. "If I cannot save the sinful Lapp," he said, "I will testify on behalf of John Marstrand. Pile not crime on crime. The governor alone can judge him. Do not invite the vengeance of God and man upon you! I will produce proofs that he is innocent."

"Out with him! Take him in custody," cried Paul Petersen, "his testimony is of evil import."

The officers of the court surrounded him. "I myself—I myself," he exclaimed, as he was dragged out of the court, "will complain of these atrocities before the throne of the king."

The consultation was held in the midst of the tumult and outcry. The secretary, for some time, lay back exhausted in his seat. He was red from pain and anxiety, but he at length jumped up, and spoke in a violent manner. The associate judges, however, did not appear to share his opinion. He sat down again, and endeavored to compose himself, and to reflect, and then stood up, listened, and took the vote.

When quiet was restored, the table upon which the fearful instruments of torture lay was covered; he then turned to Afraja.

The old man had sat as quiet as if he had not observed the noise; and when he heard his sentence, his face was directed upon the judge with a firm and friendly expression. He laughed to himself, and never before seemed so much at ease.

"As you have confessed," said Paul Petersen, "that you are a pagan and a sorcerer, and that you devised an infamous plot to expel with fire and sword all the Normans from this country, you shall be led to the judgment place at Tromsöe, where your impious body shall be burned to ashes, and scattered to the winds. This shall be done to-day, as long as the sun is in the heavens. As to you, John Marstrand of Balsfiord, you shall witness the execution of this sentence, and then be banished forever from the land; and as a further punishment, you are to be carried to Trondheim in chains, where the governor of Norway will deal with you as he may see fit. Such is the judgment of the high court of Tromsöe, in the name of the king, and according to the laws of the land, well-grounded evidence, and our strict duty to man and God!"

CHAPTER XXVI.

Evening was approaching. The sun looked red upon the high mountain peaks, which rose around the Tromsöesund. A blue mist hung over the ravines, and the city was mysteriously silent; the houses seemed deserted; not a human being was to be seen; no cowering, smoking Quane on the shore-steps; no fisherman on the water, and no women at the doors. Nothing but empty boats, rocking on the swelling water, and closed windows around the still square.

Suddenly a long wild cry of a thousand voices broke from the hill-side, resounded over the land and sea, and was echoed back and back again from the dark mountains, until it grew weaker and weaker, and died away in the distance. A column of smoke rose up, as if issuing from an immense chimney. Heavy and black, it whirled around, illuminated occasionally by jets of flame, which, shooting up from the earth, flashed across it, and disappeared again. The earth was covered by the smoke which enveloped the multitude of people, as if it would conceal their deeds; but above the black veil was the pure light of the sun. Great white birds flew athwart the blue sky; they bore Afraja's soul to the gardens of Jubinal.

There were only three persons in the court-house, who fell upon their knees on hearing the shouts, and wept. The old pastor, Klaus Hornemann, was there, who had been ordered by the voigt, under severe threats, not to leave the house, until permission was given him; and Ilda and Hannah kneeled by his side.

"All-merciful Father!" prayed the venerable man, "graciously receive into thy hands all that is immortal of him. Oh!

my God, be with thy creature in his extremity. Cool the flames, call him to thee, alleviate his pains, as thou didst those of the crucified Redeemer."

"The wretched murderers!" cried Hannah, starting to her feet. "Why am I not a man! Why have I no power! Wherefore can God permit such unheard-of cruelty to be practised!"

"Who can fathom the ways of God!" said Klaus, sighing.

"God, if thou art God," exclaimed Hannah Fandrem, with intense passion; "if thou art just, and a being with eyes to see wickedness and crime, send down thy avenging angel!"

"Pray not for vengeance, dear daughter," mildly replied the missionary; "pray for humility, faith, and light. Oh!" he continued, "unless man in his rude imperfection were instructed and improved through fearful examples! Perhaps it was to happen so, and these cruelties were necessary, in order to put an end to them forever. The news of them will everywhere produce a feeling of horror and consternation, and the terrible laws will at length be condemned and repealed. Oh, my poor children! Is not human nature like a wild field full of thorns? Does not the history of humanity show us, that every step in the path of improvement must be paid for with blood and sorrow? We dare not question or find fault with the views of the eternal wisdom of the Creator. He has ordered that such events shall take place. No one lives and dies in vain; the Lord has decreed his fate, and his end was as it ought to be."

"That may be a consolation in faith," replied Hannah, "but I cannot admit it where injustice is done. John Marstrand lives; they wish to carry him in chains to Trondheim; and God knows if he will ever reach there. I will accompany him, and will never leave his side; though another should do this," she continued in a low tone, and with a glance at Ilda.

"That is also a work which I have to accomplish," said Klaus. "Yes, my child, let us unite to take care of our friend, and ease his lot. I am certain his sufferings will end in Trondheim; the governor will be a just judge."

"And you, Ilda, will you yet think of nothing but submission and obedience?" asked Hannah.

"I obey the will of God," was the gentle answer.

"Oh!" exclaimed Hannah, "obey also the voice in your eart, which tells what you ought to do."

"Has he not shown you his power?" continued Ilda. "Has not his almighty hand been suddenly felt in your dark ways, and has he not lighted up your path?"

"No, Ilda. He has visited your father with retribution; he has set me free from him, to whom I was a plague, and in his torment, I forgot my despair; but he has not restored to me — what was mine.

"And Helgestad," she continued, as Ilda did not speak, "is he not gone to witness with pleasure the death of the victim, whose wealth he would divide with the murderer? Has he not here, in your own hearing, agreed with the fearful bridegroom as to how they both should possess the Balsfiord; and how Marstrand's property should at last be yours? Did you not see how Helgestad's avarice revived, in his half-dead face? Has he not already almost forgotten Björnarne in this insatiable passion for riches, and will you live with this insane, criminal man, subject yourself to his will, and yet think it is the will of God?"

"My place is by my father," said Ilda. "Oh, my noble, beloved friend, strengthen me, that I may be able to bear the burden which has been laid upon me."

At this moment, a cannon-shot thundered through the air, and its powerful echo was answered by the shouts of the multitude, who thronged the streets on the edge of the harbor, on their return from the bloody scene on the hill.

Two vessels were coming up the sound under full sail. One was a brig-of-war, and the other a sloop. Both carried the government flag. The Danish cross fluttered in the evening light, and the decks were covered with armed men, soldiers and sailors.

The people looked at the ships with intense curiosity, indulging in all sorts of conjectures as to their unexpected appearance. Some voices bade them welcome; a disorderly mass of people began to shout, and waved their hats. Others said it was a pity that the spruce soldiers had not been present at the court, and had not witnessed the burning of the sorcerer; and more reflecting persons whispered it was well that all was over.

In the meantime, the voigt approached the shore with a suite of pastors and the principal families. Broad-shouldered men, with their wives and children, in close array, followed. They were in part occupied by the remembrance of the fearful tragedy and its incidents; and were curious to know the meaning of the cannon-shot. The pastor of Lyngenfiord spoke to all that would give him a hearing, of the blasphemous impenitence of the old heathen, who had insultingly repelled his proffered assistance, and derided his admonition. "You all heard his dreadful laughter in the midst of the flames," he said; "those who stood near me, saw how the devil took the sorcerer in his arms, and carried him off to the eternal lake of brimstone. In a moment, he had disappeared in a cloud of smoke and flame that burst up from hell."

There were credulous persons enough who listened with a shudder, and were comforted by Heinrick Sture's animadversions; in the rear of this company, however, followed the sorenskriver, Petersen, who was slowly and with difficulty led along by Helgestad. But he overcame all his illness and suffering, and they who saw his feverish, flushed face, and heard him laugh, had no idea of his internal pain.

"Now," said he, "we have settled matters. On Thursday, dear father-in-law, the marriage must take place. I can wait no longer."

"And you must bring the affair at Balsfiord to a close. I must have the Balsfiord."

"Well, insatiable man," exclaimed Petersen, "you shall have it. I give you my hand and word, that it shall be yours in two weeks."

Helgestad burst into a fierce laugh, came to a stand, and looked around him. At that moment, Marstrand was led by. Officers of justice surrounded him, but his step was firm, and his countenance calm and fearless. When he came opposite to the two men, he fixed his eyes with such contempt and scorn upon them, that Helgestad ceased laughing, and the secretary bit his lips in rage.

"He is as insolent a cock as ever," said Niels; and with his former shrewdness, he added, "I hope you know of some means of preventing his return to Trondheim. It would be a pity for you and for me. I hate him! I must surely have the Balsfiord."

"You shall be secure, and you may sleep quietly," responded Paul. "You hate him, but I love him so dearly, that I will not separate from him so easily. When my marriage takes place, he shall be there; and when I live here with my sweet Ilda, I will have him in the house as a witness of my happiness. Behind lock and key, indeed, but yet as a witness. At present, it is too late in the year, and the voigt cannot send him to the south before the spring, by which time much good may happen to him."

Niels' eyes sparkled with delight. He perfectly comprehended the calculations of Paul, and with his best grunt and grin of former days, he said, "Nuh! you have no superior in the country. Do what you will, you swim on the surface; but I will have the Balsfiord; I must have it, and then, then"—He suddenly grasped his forehead, as if he had lost the thread of his thoughts, and murmured to himself, "I wish, however, that Björnarne were here, and that he would come soon!"

At this moment, another cannon was discharged, and Petersen laughingly exclaimed, "What fool of a coast-guard is shooting away his powder there? Let him wait till Thursday, when we will invite him to the wedding."

They had reached the houses, when they met the voigt returning to them with a grave face. "Come quickly," said he, "we have strange guests. Two vessels have come to anchor, close at hand, both of them royal men-of-war! They have put out boats, and swarm with red-coats."

"They are also coming to my wedding," said Paul, smiling. "What the deuce, uncle! do you, yourself a soldier, fear soldiers?"

"They bode us no good," muttered the dignitary.

"Let it be evil, then, and let us retaliate it. Have we not arms enough? Are not the people of Finnmark with us, and are there not enough upon the ground? Come, uncle, keep your head erect; I will teach these red-coats manners."

A loud roll of the drum interrupted their conversation; and, when they reached the landing, they met a company of soldiers that had just landed. Several officers were engaged in drawing them up in order, and a large circle of spectators surrounded them. The curiosity was intense and universal. Even the officers of justice, with their prisoner, stood still, and looked on from a distance, as the voigt, secretary, pastors, and the chief people, approached the commanding officer.

The voigt took off his gold-laced hat, made a low bow with a wide swing of his three-cornered *chapeau*, and, in an ostentatious manner, addressed the officers as follows:

"My dear sirs, officers of our most gracious Majesty, I bid you welcome to Tromsöe. As, however, I have received no intelligence of your unexpected visit, permit me to ask whence you come, and what is your purpose?"

The grim old captain did not appear to be particularly inclined to enter into conversation. He gave a side-glance at the voigt, and carelessly said, "All that I know is, that we sailed from Tromsöe; all else is the affair of the commander."

"And who is the commander?"

"There he comes," responded another officer.

A boat, bearing a pendant, put off from the brig, in the stern of which stood a slender young naval officer, wearing a plumed hat with broad borders. Another person in citizen's dress was alongside of him. No one knew these strangers, but as the voigt, with his companions, arrived at the landing, the soldiers presented arms, and a blast was blown on the trumpet, by way of salute. The officer quickly ascended the steps, and with a sharp and frowning countenance he looked upon the greeting dignitary.

"Are you the voigt of Tromsöe?" he inquired.

"Yes, sir."

"And are you the secretary, his nephew?"

"I am," replied Paul. "But who are you?"

The officer proudly smiled, "The adjutant of the Governor of Norway, who has sent me hither to look after your proceedings in this country."

"Dahlen!" cried a voice from the crowd. A tumult arose, and chains clanked. Marstrand had driven back the officers and set himself free.

"What does this mean?" exclaimed the commissioner. "An officer, a chamberlain of the king, and a nobleman, in chains? Who has dared to commit this outrage?"

"I!" replied Paul; "I recommend you to respect the law and the sentence! This man, John Marstrand of Balsfiord, has been condemned to be sent to Trondheim in chains, because he is an arch-traitor."

"Arch-traitor!" said Dahlen. "Have you, my poor friend, sunk to such a depth of degradation?"

"You know that I am incapable of committing such a crime," replied Marstrand.

"Off with the chains!" exclaimed the commissioner. "Alas! I have arrived too late to save the old man whom you have murdered; but tremble for the examination, the wrath of the king, and the punishment. Voigt of Tromsöe, and you, Herr Secretary, I arrest you in the name of his Majesty!"

"You, me — You arrest me!" cried Petersen. His eyes gleamed with rage, and his limbs trembled. "Countrymen! Friends!" he exclaimed, "will you suffer your rights to be outraged and trodden under foot by soldiers?"

At a sign from Dahlen, a dozen grenadiers sprang upon the voigt and secretary. The remainder of the company advanced with fixed bayonets to the right and left; the people rushed back on one another; and the same scenes occurred among them as they had practised upon the Lapps. Panic-struck, they fled before this armed demonstration. The threatened vengeance of the king resounded in their ears, and no voice dared to oppose it. Those who had raved the loudest were the first to draw back, wished themselves far away, and threw all the blame upon the accursed Paul Petersen, his uncle, and his hangers-on. The door of the court-house was now free, and Hannah came out of it on the arm of the person who had accompanied Dahlen, followed by Ilda and old Klaus.

Hannah flew with a scream, and with open arms, to meet her lover. She gazed upon him as upon an image of a dream, as a dazzling meteor, that shoots athwart the open heaven and disappears. Her delighted eyes were fastened upon him, and it seemed as if she dared not remove them.

"It is I," he said, pressing her to his bosom; "I am flesh and blood, and not a shadow, dear Hannah."

"And here is my brother Christi," she exclaimed. "He and you, and all is true!"

"It is a lie! Lie and damnation!" groaned Paul Petersen. "This way. Set me free — let me — I will!"

He endeavored to shake off the guard who held him fast. There stood Ilda alongside of the pastor, and Marstrand publicly kneeled to her before all the people. The long-closed heart burst its fetters, and a stream of passionate love gushed forth. The cold, reserved, discreet Ilda, embraced his head with both her hands; her tears fell upon his brow, and her lips bent towards his.

"My dear Ilda," he exultingly exclaimed, "I am free; I am at your side!"

"The blessing of God rest upon you!" she said. "God's richest blessings, dearly beloved man. I will never leave you!"

Paul Petersen uttered a brute-like howl, and fell down in a senseless state.

CHAPTER XXVI.

A MONTH afterwards, the investigation was completed at Tromsöe, at the conclusion of which, Voigt Paulsen was sent off in a government vessel to Trondheim, where, after being imprisoned for some time upon the rocks of Murkholm, he was one morning found hanged. His nephew had been called from the world sooner than himself. On the second day after the arrival of the commission of inquiry, he died, a raving maniac. The wound, which had been inflicted upon him by Mortuno, hastened his death; and his dying hours were marked by intense suffering of mind and body.

When he was dead, every one endeavored to throw the whole burden of his own share of guilt upon him; and even the voigt vainly attempted the same perfidy.

Niels Helgestad had now become perfectly stupid. He was carried back to Lyngenfiord, where he was tortured by a dreadful anxiety whenever he beheld Dahlen, although the latter endeavored to tranquillize him by the assurance that all should be forgiven and forgotten; while he repeatedly related to him the circumstances of his escape in that fearful night.

He had clung to a fragment of the shattered boat, until he

succeeded in scaling the steep precipice of the fiord. He received assistance in the morning, but he lay sick for a long time; and when he at length came to Trondheim, and made a confidant of his protector the governor, the latter refused him any further aid in his follies. Hannah's brother Christi, however, suddenly made his appearance in the northern capital, in search of him. From him he learned Hannah's condition, and at the same time that Fandrem, under the influence of his son, had become an entirely changed and repentant man. He was even willing to pay the forfeit-money, if he could get his child back again; at the same time, pressing letters of complaint and requests arrived from Klaus Hornemann to the governor, beseeching him to send a commissioner to Finnmark, and also charging the voigt and secretary in Tromsöe with the worst crimes. In a long private letter to his friend the governor, Klaus had also discussed the relations of Hannah and Marstrand, had given a description of Helgestad, and expressed the fear that the noble-minded and credulous Marstrand would fall a victim to the secret intrigues of the voigt and secretary, and the avaricious trader who aimed at acquiring possession of the Balsfiord. In this letter, Afraja's history was also unfolded, as well as the passion of Björnarne for Gula; so that the old general, when he had read it through, sent for his adjutant, and gave it to him to read. "Forward," said he, "my young friend, obtain your bride, tear your friend from the claws of the villains, and see what good can be done for him. Above all, however, secure for me the base secretary; bring the fish-trader to reason, and procure the reindeer shepherds a humane treatment. In two days the expedition will be ready."

Dahlen's warmest wishes were thus suddenly fulfilled, and he came at the proper time, at least to set his friend at liberty. The two legal officers who accompanied him, were provisionally placed at the head of the government, and they issued severe decrees and sent reports to Trondheim, from whence their propositions were despatched to Copenhagen. In the following year, a decree was issued from the capital, abolishing all the old laws concerning idolatry and witchcraft, and abrogating all authority for the discovery of truth by means of the rack, or any other instrument of torture. On the 29th of March, 1743, a royal proclamation was published, forbidding, under severe penalties, the casting of reproach upon the Lapps, on account of their religious belief and their occupation, as they were thenceforth placed on a footing of perfect equality with the other subjects of his majesty.

But of what avail are royal proclamations, when contempt has implanted itself in the human heart! No one can enforce esteem; happy, if he is powerful enough to secure forbearance and tolerance. Finnmark received another organization — its privileges were changed and restricted — new divisions were made — new judges and voigts appointed, taxes were increased, and the stubborn malcontents were punished. Many Lapps, however, migrated deep into the interior of Sweden with their herds, and nothing more was to be seen of Afraja's great property, his animals, and his *gammes*.

Long before, however, this happened, on a beautiful autumn day, when the sun was beaming upon the black brow of the Kilpis, a boat crossed over the Lyngenfiord, and Klaus Hornemann, in the old church, united Ilda and Marstrand, and Hannah and Dahlen, in the holy bonds of matrimony. Her brother was present, with some officers and friends, and Niels Helgestad sat in his chair, smiling and nodding like a child.

And thus he sat for some years upon the bench before the Gaard, looking over the fiord, and occasionally muttering to himself, "Would that Björnarne were here, and that he would come soon!"

Marstrand's descendants were numerous; and he built a great house at Strommen. His name was widely known and respected. Honor, consideration, and happiness, he enjoyed in abundance. But he could not realize the wealth which Helgestad had promised him out of the Balself. He could extract but little profit from the wood speculation; so he finally gave it up, and cultivated the little valleys of the fiord with greater zeal and advantage.

No one ever found Afraja's treasures. Many things are told of the wonders of the silver-caves in Enare Traesk; and many persons have endeavored to discover them, but always in vain.

When the pious old pastor returned from his wanderings among the *gammes*, he rested in Lyngenfiord, and left the letter which Hannah Dahlen had written from Trondheim. Her father was reconciled; he had verified the boast of her husband, for he had led her on his arm into his house, and had even gone to the baptism of his first grandson.

They have all, a long time ago, laid down in eternal rest; the grave has swallowed up both hate and love. When, however, as you sail through the labyrinthine sounds and water-passes, you may chance to meet a yacht, whose huge sail is surrounded by a black border, and you ask the meaning of this sign of mourning, the sad story will again spring to life.

More than an hundred years ago, the pilot will tell you that here lived a pious old pastor, who did so much good, that all people, rich and poor, adore his memory, and will ever hold him in affectionate remembrance. When he died, in their grief and woe, they surrounded their sails with a black stripe, and their vessels always carry it to this day; and for hundreds and hundreds of years will their descendants speak of the venerable and good Klaus, and of the deep gloom that settled upon the dwellers on the coast, and the roving tribes of the icy deserts, when his earthly mission closed, and he was summoned on high, to meet a just reward for his good deeds on earth.

THE END.

www.ingramcontent.com/pod-product-compliance
Lightning Source LLC
LaVergne TN
LVHW021233110826
845150LV00002B/326

* 9 7 8 1 4 2 5 5 6 2 0 9 0 *